D0429363

E A R T H

EARTH

DAVID BRIN

BANTAM BOOKS
NEW YORK · TORONTO · LONDON · SYDNEY · AUCKLAND

E A R T H
A Bantam Spectra Book/June 1990

Library of Congress Cataloging-in-Publication Data

Brin, David.
   Earth / David Brin.
     p. cm.
   I. Title.
PS3552.R4825E27   1990
813'.54—dc20   90-4
               CIP

ISBN 0-553-05778-2

Published simultaneously in the United States and Canada

Bantam Books are published by Bantam Books, a division of
Bantam Doubleday Dell Publishing Group, Inc. Its trademark,
consisting of the words "Bantam Books" and the portrayal of
a rooster, is Registered in U.S. Patent and Trademark Office
and in other countries. Marca Registrada. Bantam Books,
666 Fifth Avenue, New York, New York 10103.

PRINTED IN THE UNITED STATES OF AMERICA

TO OUR COMMON MOTHER

AUTHOR'S PREFACE

As writers go, I suppose I'm known as a bit of an optimist, so it seems only natural that this novel projects a future where there's a little more wisdom than folly . . . maybe a bit more hope than despair.

In fact, it's about the most encouraging tomorrow I can imagine right now.

What a sobering thought.

PART I

PLANET

First came a supernova, dazzling the universe in brief, spendthrift
glory before ebbing into twisty, multispectral clouds of new-forged
atoms. Swirling eddies spiraled until one of them ignited—a
newborn star.

The virgin sun wore whirling skirts of dust and electricity.
Gas and rocks and bits of this and that fell into those pleats,
gathering in dim lumps . . . planets . . .

One tiny worldlet circled at a middle distance. It had a
modest set of properties:

mass—*barely enough to draw in a passing asteroid or two;*

moons—*one, the remnant of a savage collision, but big
enough to tug deep tides;*

spin—*to set winds churning through a fuming atmosphere;*

density—*a brew that mixed and separated, producing an
unpromising surface slag;*

temperature—*heat was the planet's only voice, a weak one,
swamped by the blaring sun. Anyway, what can a planet tell the
universe, in a reedy cry of infrared?*

"This exists," it repeated, over and over. "This is a condensed
stone, radiating at about three hundred degrees, insignificant on
the scale of stars.

"This speck, a mote, exists."

A simple statement to an indifferent cosmos—the signature of
a rocky world, tainted by salty, smoke-blown puddles.

But then something new stirred in those puddles. It was a

triviality—a mere discoloration here and there. But from that moment the voice changed. Subtly, shifting in timbre, still faint and indistinct, it nevertheless seemed now to say,

"I . . . am . . ."

C
O
R
E

An angry deity glowered at Alex. Slanting sunshine cast shadows across the incised cheeks and outthrust tongue of Great Tu, Maori god of war.

A dyspeptic idol, Alex thought, contemplating the carved figure. *I'd feel the same if I were stuck up there, decorating a billionaire's office wall.*

It occurred to Alex that Great Tu's wooden nose resembled the gnomon of a sundial. Its shadow kept time, creeping to the measured ticking of a twentieth century grandfather clock in the corner. The silhouette stretched slowly, amorously, toward a sparkling amethyst geode—yet another of George Hutton's many geological treasures. Alex made a wager with himself, that the shadow wouldn't reach its goal before the sinking sun was cut off by the western hills.

And at this rate, neither would George Hutton. *Where the devil is the man? Why did he agree to this meeting, if he didn't plan on bloody showing up?*

Alex checked his watch again, even though he knew the time. He caught himself nervously tapping one shoe against the nearby table leg, and stopped doing it.

What have Jen and Stan always told you? "Try to learn patience, Alex."

It wasn't his best-known virtue. But then, he'd learned a lot the last few months. Remarkable how it focused your mind, when you guarded a secret that might mean the end of the world.

He glanced toward his friend and former mentor, Stan Goldman, who had set up this appointment with the chairman of Tangoparu Ltd. Apparently unperturbed by his employer's tardiness, the slender, aging theoretician was immersed in the latest issue of *Physical Review.*

No hope for distraction there. Alex sighed and let his eyes rove George Hutton's office one more time, hoping to get a measure of the man.

Of course the conference table was equipped with the best and latest plaques, for accessing the World Data Net. One entire wall was taken up by an active-events screen, a montage of real-time views from random locations across the Earth—zeppelins cruising above Wuhan . . . sunrise in a North African village . . . the urban lights of any city in the world.

Original holographic sculptures of mythical beasts shimmered by the entrance to the suite, but nearest the desk were Hutton's dearest treasures, minerals and ores collected over a lifetime grubbing through the planet's crust—including a huge blood zircon, glittering on a pedestal just below the Maori war mask. It struck Alex that both objects were products of fiery crucibles—one mineral, the other social. Each denoted resilience under pressure. Perhaps this said something about George Hutton's personality, as well.

But then, perhaps it meant nothing at all. Alex had never been a great judge of people. Witness the events of the last year.

With a sudden click and hum, the hallway doors parted and a tall, brown man appeared, breathing hard and coated with perspiration.

"Ah! You made yourselves at home. Good. Sorry to keep you waiting, Stan. Dr. Lustig. Excuse me, will you? I'll only be a moment." He peeled a sweaty jersey off broad shoulders, striding past a window overlooking the sailboats of Auckland harbor.

George Hutton, I presume, Alex thought as he lowered his outstretched hand and sat back down. *Not much for formality. That's just as well, I suppose.*

From the open door to the lavatory, Hutton shouted. "Our game had delay after delay for injuries! Minor stuff, fortunately. But I'm sure you understand, I couldn't let the Tangoparu team down when I was needed. Not during the finals against Nippon Electric!"

Normally, it might seem odd for a businessman in his fifties to neglect appointments for a rugby game. But the dusky giant toweling himself off in the loo seemed completely unselfconscious, aglow with victory. Alex glanced at his former teacher, who now worked for Hutton here in New Zealand. Stan only shrugged, as if to say billionaires made their own rules.

Hutton emerged wearing a dressing gown and drying his hair with a terry-cloth towel. "Can I offer you anything, Dr. Lustig? How about you, Stan?"

"Nothing, thank you," Alex said. Less reticent, Stan accepted a Glenfiddich and spring water. Then Hutton settled into a plush swivel chair, stretching his long legs beside the kauri-wood table.

Whatever happens, Alex knew, *this is where the trail ends. This is my last hope.*

The Maori engineer-businessman regarded him with piercing brown eyes. "I'm told you want to discuss the Iquitos incident, Dr. Lustig. And the miniature black hole you let slip out of your hands there. Frankly, I thought you'd be sick of that embarrassment by now. What did some press hacks call it then? A possible *China Syndrome*?"

Stan cut in. "A few sensationalists set off a five-minute panic on the World Net, until the scientific community showed everybody that tiny singularities like Alex's dissipate harmlessly. They're too small to last long by themselves."

Hutton raised one dark eyebrow. "Is that so, Dr. Lustig?"

Alex had faced that question so many times since Iquitos. By now he had countless stock answers—from five-second sound bites for the vid cameras to ten-minute lullabies for Senate investigators . . . all the way to hours of abstruse mathematics to soothe his fellow physicists. He really ought to be used to it by now. Still the question burned, as it had the first time.

"Talk to me, Lustig," the reporter, Pedro Manella, had demanded on that ashen afternoon in Peru, as they watched rioting students set Alex's work site ablaze. *"Tell me that thing you made isn't about to eat its way to China."*

Lying had become so reflexive since then, it took some effort to break the habit today. "Um, what did Stan tell you?" he asked George Hutton, whose broad features still glistened under a thin gloss of perspiration.

"Only that you claim to have a secret. Something you've kept from reporters, tribunals . . . even the security agencies of a dozen nations. In this day and age, that's impressive by itself.

"But we Maori people of New Zealand have a saying," he went on. "A man who can fool chiefs, and even gods, must still face the monsters he himself created.

"Have *you* created a monster, Dr. Lustig?"

The question direct. Alex realized why Hutton reminded him of Pedro Manella on that humid evening in Peru, as tear gas wafted down those debris-strewn streets and canals. Both big men had voices like Hollywood deities. Both were used to getting answers.

Manella had pursued Alex onto the creaking hotel balcony to get a good view of the burning power plant. The reporter panned his camera as the main containment building collapsed amid clouds of powdery cement. Cheering students provided a vivid scene for Manella to feed live to his viewers on the Net.

"When the mob cut the power cables, Lustig," the persistent journalist asked while shooting, *"that let your black hole out of its magnetic cage. It fell into the Earth then, no? So what happens now? Will it emerge again, blazing and incinerating some hapless place halfway around the world?*

"What did you make here, Lustig? A beast that will devour us all?"

Even then, Alex recognized the hidden message between the

words. The renowned investigator hadn't been seeking truth; he wanted reassurance.

"No, of course I didn't," Alex remembered telling Manella on that day, and everyone else since then. Now he let go of the lie with relief.

"Yes, Mr. Hutton. I think I made the very Devil itself."

Stan Goldman's head jerked up. Until this moment, Alex hadn't even confided in his old mentor. *Sorry, Stan,* he thought.

Silence stretched as Hutton stared at him. "You're saying . . . the singularity didn't dissipate like the experts said? That it might still be down there, absorbing matter from the Earth's core?"

Alex understood the man's incredulity. Human minds weren't meant to picture something that was smaller than an atom, and yet weighed megatons. Something narrow enough to fall through the densest rock, yet bound to circle the planet's center in a spiraling pavane of gravity. Something ineffably but insatiably *hungry*, and which grew ever hungrier the more it ate . . .

Just thinking about it put in sudden doubt the very notions of *up* and *down.* It challenged faith in the ground below your feet. Alex tried to explain.

"The generals showed me their power plant . . . offered me a blank check to construct its core. So I took their word they'd be getting permission soon. *Any day now,* they kept telling me." Alex shrugged at his former gullibility. An old story, if a bitter one.

"Like everybody else, I was sure the Standard Physical Model was correct—that no black hole lighter than the Earth itself could possibly be stable. Especially one as tiny as we made at Iquitos. It was *supposed* to evaporate at a controlled rate, after all. Its heat would power three provinces. Most of my colleagues think such facilities will be cleared for use within a decade.

"But the generals wanted to jump the moratorium—"

"Idiots," Hutton interrupted, shaking his head. "They actually imagined they could keep a thing like that secret? These days?"

For the first time since Alex's bombshell, Stan Goldman put in a comment. "Well, George, they must have thought the plant well isolated in the Amazon."

Hutton snorted dubiously, and in retrospect Alex agreed. The idea was harebrained. He'd been naïve to accept the generals' assurances of a calm working environment, which proved as untrustworthy as the standard models of physics.

"In fact," Goldman went on. "It took a leak from a secrets registration service to set that Manella character on Alex's trail. If not for that, Alex might still be tending the singularity, safe inside its containment field. Isn't that right, Alex?"

Good old Stan, Alex thought affectionately. *Still making excuses for his favorite student, just as he used to back in Cambridge.*

"No, it's not. You see, before the riot, I was already preparing to sabotage the plant myself."

While this seemed to surprise Goldman, George Hutton only tilted his head slightly. "You had discovered something unusual about your black hole."

Alex nodded. "Before 2020, nobody imagined such things could be made in the laboratory at all. When it was found you could actually fold space inside a box and make a singularity . . . that shock should have taught us humility. But success made us smug, instead. Soon we thought we understood the damned things. But there are . . . subtleties we never imagined."

He spread his hands. "I first grew suspicious because things were going too bloody well! The power plant was extremely efficient, you see. We didn't have to feed in much matter to keep it from dissipating. The generals were delighted of course. But I started thinking . . . might I have accidentally created a new *type* of hole in space? One that's stable? Able to grow by devouring mere rock?"

Stan gaped. Alex, too, had been numbed by that first realization, then agonized for weeks before deciding to take matters into his own hands, to defy his employers and defang the tiny, voracious beast he'd helped create.

But Pedro Manella arrived first, amid a flurry of accusations, and suddenly it was too late. Alex's world collapsed around him before he could act, or even find out for certain what he'd made.

"So it is a monster . . . a *taniwha*," George Hutton breathed. The Maori word sounded fearsome. The big man drummed his fingers on the table. "Let's see if I've got this right. We have a purported *stable* black hole, that you think may orbit thousands of miles below our feet, possibly growing unstoppably even as we speak. Correct? I suppose you want my help finding what you so carelessly misplaced?"

Alex was nearly as impressed with Hutton's quickness as he was irked by his attitude. He suppressed a hot response. "I guess you could put it that way," he answered, levelly.

"So. Would it be too much to ask how you'd go about looking for such an elusive fiend? It's a little hard to go digging around down there in the Earth's core."

Hutton obviously thought he was being ironic. But Alex gave him a straightforward answer. "Your company already makes most of the equipment I'd need . . . like those superconducting gravity scanners you use for mineral surveys." Alex started reaching for his valise. "I've written down modifications—"

Hutton raised a hand. All trace of sardonicism was gone from his eyes. "I'll take your word for now. It will be expensive, of course? No matter. If we find nothing, I'll take the cost out of your *pakeha* hide. I'll skin you and sell the pale thing in a tourist shop. Agreed?"

Alex swallowed, unable to believe it could be so simple. "Agreed. And if we do find it?"

Lines furrowed Hutton's brow. "Why . . . then I'd be honor bound to take your pelt anyway, tohunga. For creating such a devil to consume our Earth, I should . . ."

The big man stopped suddenly. He stood up, shaking his head. At the window, Hutton stared down at the city of Auckland, its evening lights beginning to spread like powdered gemstones across the hills. Beyond the metropolis lay forested slopes slanting to Manukau Bay. Twilight-stained clouds were moving in from the Tasman Sea, heavy with fresh rain.

The scene reminded Alex of a time in childhood, when his grandmother had taken him to Wales to watch the turning of the autumn leaves. Then, as now, it had struck him just how temporary everything seemed . . . the foliage, the drifting clouds, the patient mountains . . . the world.

"You know," George Hutton said slowly, still contemplating the peaceful view outside, "back when the American and Russian empires used to face each other at the brink of nuclear war, this was where people in the Northern Hemisphere dreamed about fleeing to. Were you aware of that, Lustig? Every time there was a crisis, airlines suddenly overbooked with "vacation" trips to New Zealand. People must have thought this the ideal spot to ride out a holocaust.

"And that didn't change with the Rio Treaties, did it? Big War went away, but then came the cancer plague, greenhouse heat, spreading deserts . . . and lots of little wars of course, over an oasis here, a river there.

"All the time though, we Kiwis still felt lucky. *Our* rains didn't abandon us. Our fisheries didn't die.

"Now all those illusions are gone. There's no safe place any longer."

The big man turned to look at Alex, and despite his words there was no loathing in the tycoon-engineer's eyes. Nor even bleakness. Only what Alex took to be a heavy resignation.

"I wish I could hate you, Lustig, but you've obviously subcontracted that job quite ably yourself. And so you deprive me even of revenge."

"I'm sorry," Alex apologized sincerely.

Hutton nodded. He closed his eyes and took a deep breath.

"All right then, let's get to work. If Tane, father of the Maori, could go into the bowels of the Earth to battle monsters, who are we then to refuse?"

☐ For more than two decades, we at **The Mother** have maintained our famed list of Natural Tranquility Reserves—rare places on Earth where one might sit for hours and hear no sounds but those of wilderness.

Our thirty million worldwide subscribers have led in vigilantly protecting these reserves. All it takes is a single thoughtless act, by air traffic planners for instance, to convert a precious sanctuary into yet another noisy, noisome place, ruined by the raucous clamor of humanity.

Unfortunately, even so-called "conservation-oriented" officials still seem obsessed by archaic, TwenCen views of preservation. They think it's enough to save a few patches of forest here and there from development, from chemical leaks or acid rain. Even when they succeed, however, they celebrate by opening hiking trails and encouraging ever higher quotas of sightseers, who predictably leave litter, trample root systems, cause erosion, and worst of all jabber at the top of their lungs in gushing excitement over "being one with nature."

It's surprising the few animals left can find each other amid the bedlam, to breed.

Excluding Greenland and Antarctica, seventy-nine Tranquility Reserves were reported in our last roundup. We're now sad to report that two failed this year's test. At this rate, soon there will be no terrestrial silence zones left at all.

And our Oceania correspondents report matters growing worse there, as well. Too many landlubbers seem to be heading off the standard shipping lanes—vacationers who seek out nature's serenity, but in so doing bring to silent places the plague of their own voices.

(And then there is that catastrophe the Sea State, perhaps better left unmentioned here, lest we despair entirely!)

Even the southern Indian Ocean, Earth's last frontier of solitude, trembles under the cacophony of our cursed ten billions and their machines. Frankly, it wouldn't surprise this writer if Gaia eventually had enough, if she awoke from her fitful slumber and answered our noise with a shaking such as this tired planet has never known.

—From the March 2038 edition of **The Mother.** [☐ Net access PI-63-AA-1-888-66-7767.]

● There are many ways to propagate. (Such a lovely word!) This late
H in her long life, Jen Wolling figured she knew just about all of
O them.
L   Especially where the term applied to biology—to all the
O varied means Life used to foil its great enemy, Time. So many were
S those ways, Jen sometimes puzzled why everyone fussed so over
P the traditional one, sex.
H   True, sex had its points. It helped ensure variability in a
E species—a gambler's game, mixing one's own genes with
R another's, betting that beneficial serendipities will outweigh the
E inevitable errors. In fact, sex had served most higher life forms
well enough and long enough, to become reinforced with many
pleasurable neural and hormonal responses.

In other days Jen had plumbed those pathways in vivo and with
gusto. She had also mapped those same roads more precisely, in charts
of pristine yet still passionate mathematics. Hers had been the earliest
computer models to show theoretical bases for feeling, logical
rationales for ecstasy, even theorems for the mysterious art of
motherhood.

Two husbands, three children, eight grandchildren, and one
Nobel Prize later, Jen knew motherhood from every angle, even
though its fierce hormonal flows were now only memories. Ah, well.
There were other types of propagation. Other ways even an old
woman might leave an imprint upon history.

"No, Baby!" she chided, pulling a bright red apple away from the
bars dividing the spacious lab in two. A gray tentacle waved between
the steel rods, snatching at the fruit.

"No! Not till you ask for it politely."

From her desk nearby, a young black woman sighed. "Jen, will
you stop teasing the poor creature?" Pauline Cockerel shook her head.
"You know Baby won't understand unless you accompany words with
signs."

"Nonsense. She comprehends perfectly. Observe."

The animal let out a squeaky trumpet of frustration. Acquiescing,
it rolled back its trunk to wind the tip round a mat of shaggy fur,
hanging low over its eyes.

"That's a good girl," Jen said, tossing the apple. Baby caught it
deftly and crunched happily.

"Pure operant conditioning," the younger woman sniffed.
"Hasn't anything to do with intelligence or cognition."

"Cognition isn't everything," Jen replied. "Politeness, for

instance, needs to be ingrained at deeper levels. It's a good thing I came down here. She's getting spoiled rotten."

"Hmph. If you ask me, you're just rationalizing another bout of PNS."

"PNS?"

"Post-Nobel syndrome," Pauline explained.

"Still?" Jen sniffed. "After all these years?"

"Why not? Who said anyone recovers?"

"You make it sound like a disease."

"It is. Look at the history of science. Most prizewinners turn into either stodgy defenders of the status quo—like Hayes and Kalumba— or iconoclasts like you, who insist on throwing stones at sacred cows—"

"Mixed metaphor," Jen pointed out.

"—and carping about details, and generally making nuisances of themselves."

"Have I been making a nuisance of myself?" Jen asked innocently.

Pauline cast her eyes heavenward. "You mean besides coming here randomly, unannounced, and meddling in Baby's training?"

"Yeah. Besides that."

With a sigh Pauline plucked one data plaque from a jumble of the wide, wafer-thin reading devices. This one was dialed to the latest issue of *Nature* . . . a page in the letters section.

"Oh, that," Jen observed. She had come here to the hermetic, air-conditioned pyramid of London Ark, in order to escape the flood of telephone and Net calls piling up at her own lab. Inevitably, one would be from the director of St. Thomas's, inviting her to a pleasant lunch overlooking the river, where he'd once again hint that an emeritus professor in her nineties really ought to spend more time in the country, watching ultraviolet rays turn the rhododendrons funny shades of purple, instead of gallivanting around the globe poking her nose into other researchers' business and making statements about issues that were none of her concern.

Had anybody else spoken as she had, at last week's World Ozone Conference in Patagonia, they would have returned home to more than mere letters and phone calls. In today's political climate, the gentlest outcome might have been forced retirement. Good-bye lab in the city. Good-bye generous consultancies and travel allotments.

That little Swedish medal certainly did have its compensations. To become a laureate was a little like being transformed into that famous nine-hundred-pound gorilla—the one who slept anywhere it wanted to. Glimpsing her own tiny, wiry reflection in the laboratory window, Jen found the metaphor delicious.

"I only pointed out what any fool should see," she explained. "That spending billions to blow artificial ozone into the stratosphere isn't going to solve anything. Now that greedy idiots have stopped spewing chlorine compounds into the air, the situation will correct itself soon."

"Soon?" Pauline was incredulous. "*Decades* is soon enough to restore the ozone layer? Tell that to the farmers, who have to fit their livestock with eye covers."

"Shouldn't eat meat anyway," Jen grumbled.

"Then tell all the humans who'll get skin lesions because . . ."

"The U.N. supplies hats and sunglasses to everyone. Besides, a few pence worth of cream clears away precancerous—"

"What about *wild animals* then? Savannah baboons were doing fine, their habitat declared safe just ten years ago. Now so many are going blind, they have to be collected into the arks after all. How do you think we'll cope with that here?" Pauline gestured into the vast atrium of London Ark, with its tier upon tier of enclosed, artificial habitats. The huge edifice of hanging gardens and meticulously regulated environments was a far cry from its origins in the old Regent's Park Zoo. And it was only one out of almost a hundred such structures, scattered all over the world.

"You'll cope the way you have all along," Jen answered. "By stretching facilities, putting in extra hours, making do—"

"For now! But what about tomorrow? The next catastrophe? Jen, I can't believe I'm hearing this. You led the fight for the arks, from the beginning!"

"So? Am I a traitor then, if I say that part of the job has succeeded? Why, in some places we've even made additions to the gene pool, like Baby here." She nodded toward the furry pachyderm inside the big cage. "You should have faith in your own work, Pauline. Habitat restoration will come off the drawing boards someday. Most of these species should be back outside in only a few centuries—"

"Centuries!"

"Yes, surely. What's a few hundred years, compared to the age of this planet?"

Pauline sniffed dubiously. But Jen cut in, putting on a touch of Cockney accent for good measure. "Cor, why d'ye take it all so bloody personally, dearie-o? Step back a minute. What's the worst that can happen?"

"We could lose every unprotected terrestrial species massing over ten kilos!" the young woman replied fiercely.

"Yes? For good measure, let's throw in the contents of these arks —the protected species—and every human being. All ten billion of us. That'd be some holocaust, to be sure.

"But how much difference would it make to the *Earth*, Pauline? Say, ten million years from now? Not much, I'll wager. The old girl will wait us out. She's done it before."

Pauline's mouth was slack, her expression stunned. For a moment Jen wondered if she'd really gone over the top, this time.

Her young friend blinked. Then a suspicious smile spread. "You are awful! For a minute there I actually started taking you seriously."

Jen grinned. "Now . . . you know me better than that."

"I know you're an unrepentant curmudgeon! You live to get a rise out of people, and someday ,your contrary habits will be your undoing."

"Hmph. Just how do you think I've remained interested in life *this* long? Finding ways to keep amused . . . that's my secret of longevity."

Pauline tossed the reading plaque back onto the cluttered desk. "Is that why you're going to South Africa next month? Because it'll outrage everybody on both sides?"

"The Ndebele want me to look over their arks from a macrobiological perspective. Whatever their politics and race problems, they are still vital members of the Salvation Project."

"But—"

Jen clapped her hands. "Enough of that. It has nothing to do with our little project in stirpiculture, right here. *Mammut americanum.* Let's have a look at Baby's file, shall we? I may be retired, but I'll bet I can still recommend a better neural factor gradient than the one you're using."

"You're on! It's in the next room. I'll be right back."

With a youthful grace that Jen watched lovingly, Pauline hurried out of the lab, leaving Jen to ponder alone the mysterious ways of ambiguity in language.

It was, indeed, a bad habit, this toying with people. But as the years flickered by it grew easier. They all *forgave* so, almost as if they expected it . . . demanded it of her. And because she tested everybody, taking contrary positions without prejudice, fewer and fewer people seemed to believe she meant anything she said at all!

Perhaps, Jen admitted honestly, that would be the world's long-term revenge on her. To attribute everything she said to jest. That would be some fate for the so-called "mother of the modern Gaian paradigm."

Jen stroked Baby's trunk, scratching the bulging forehead where induced neoteny had given the elephant-mammoth hybrid an enlarged cortex. Baby's brow-fur was long and oily, and gave off a pungent, tangy, yet somehow pleasant odor. The worldwide network of genetic arks had a surfeit of pachyderms, even this new breed— ''Mammontelephas''—with half its genes salvaged from a 20,000-year-old cadaver exposed by the retreating Canadian tundra. So many of them bred true, in fact, that there were some to spare for experiments in extended childhood in mammals. Under strict supervision by the science tribunals and animal rights committees, of course.

Certainly the creature *seemed* happy enough. "How about it, Baby?" Jen murmured. "Are you glad to be smarter than the average elephant? Or would you rather be out on the plains, rolling in mud, uprooting trees, complaining about ticks, and getting pregnant before you're ten?"

The pink-tipped trunk curled around her hand. She stroked it, tenderly. "You're awfully important to yourself, aren't you? And you *are* part of the whole.

"But do you really matter, Baby? Do I?"

Actually, she had meant every word she said to Pauline—about how even mass extinctions would be essentially meaningless in the long run. A lifetime spent building the theoretical foundations of biology had convinced her of that. The homeostasis of the planet—of *Gaia*—was powerful enough to survive even great cataclysms.

Many times, sudden waves of death had wiped out species, genuses, even entire orders. Dinosaurs were only the most glamorous victims of one episode. And yet, across each murderous chasm, plants kept removing carbon dioxide from the air. Animals and volcanoes continued putting it back again, give or take a few percentage points.

Even the so-called greenhouse effect that had everyone worried— melting icecaps, spreading deserts, and driving millions before the rising seas—even that catastrophic outcome of human excess would never rival the great inundations following the Permian age.

Jen very much approved of the way everyone marched and spoke out and wrote letters these days, passing laws and designing technologies to "save the Earth" from twentieth-century errors. After all, only silly creatures fouled their own nests, and humanity couldn't afford much more silliness. Still, she took her own, admittedly eccentric view, based on a personal, quirky, never-spoken identification with the living world.

Out in the atrium, a low rumble echoed off the walls of the glass cavern. She recognized the deep, purring growl of a tiger, her totem animal according to a shaman she'd spent one summer with, before the last century ended. He had said hers was "the spirit of a great mother cat . . ."

What nonsense. But oh, what a handsome fellow he had been! She recalled his aroma of herbs and wood smoke and male musk, even though it was hard right now to pin down his name.

No matter. He was gone. Someday, despite all the efforts of people like Pauline, tigers might be gone, too.

But some things endured. Jen smiled as she stroked Baby's trunk.

If we humans annihilate ourselves, mammalian genes are rich enough to replace us with another, maybe wiser race within a few million years. Perhaps descendants of coyotes or raccoons, creatures too adaptable ever to need refuge in arks. Too tough to be wiped out by any calamity the likes of us create.

Oh, Baby's delicate species might not outlast us, but Norway rats surely will. I wonder what kind of planetary custodians their descendants would make.

Baby whimpered softly. The elephant-mammoth hybrid watched her with soft eyes that seemed troubled, as if the creature somehow sensed Jen's disturbing train of thought. Jen laughed and patted the rough gray flesh. "Oh, Baby. Grandma doesn't mean half the things she says . . . or thinks! I just do it to amuse myself.

"Don't worry. I won't let bad things happen. I'll always be watching over you.

"I'll be here. Always."

☐ *World Net News: Channel 265/General Interest/Level 9+* (transcript)

"Three million citizens of the Republic of Bangladesh watched their farms and villages wash away as early monsoons burst their hand-built levees, turning remnants of the crippled state into a realm of swampy shoals covered by the rising Bay of Bengal. . . ."

[Image of tear-streaked brown faces staring in numb dismay at the bloated bodies of animals and canted, drowned ruins of farmhouses.]

[☐ Viewer option: For details on cited storm, voice-link STORM 23 now.]

"These are the die-hards, who have refused all prior offers of resettlement. Now, though, they face bitter a choice. If they accept full refugee status, joining their brethren in Siberian or Australian New Lands, it will also mean taking all the conditions attached, particularly that they must swear population restriction oaths. . . ."

[Image of a pregnant woman with four crying children, pushing her frightened husband toward fair-skinned medics. Zoom on one doctor's hammer and sickle shoulder patch . . . a nurse's Canadian maple leaf. Members of the screening team wear kindly smiles. Too nervous to show resentment, the young Bengali signs a clipboard and passes under the tent flap.]

[☐ To read out specific oaths, voice-link REFUGE 43.]
[☐ For specific medical procedures, voice-link VASECT 7.]

"Having reached the limits of their endurance, many have agreed to the host nations' terms. Still, it's expected some will refuse even this last chance and elect instead the harsh but unregulated life as citizens of Sea State, whose crude rafts already sail the fens and shallows where formerly stretched great, jute estates. . . ."

[View of barges, rafts, salvaged ships of all shapes and sizes, clustered under pelting rain. Crude dredges probe skeletons of a former village, hauling up lumber, furniture, odds and ends to use or sell for scrap. Other, quicker boats are seen pursuing schools of silvery anchovies through newly inundated shoals.]

[☐ Real-time image 2376539.365x-2370.398, DISPAR XVII satellite. $1.45/minute.]

[☐ For general background, link SEASTATE 1.]
[☐ For data on specific flotilla, link SEA BANGLA 5.]

"Already, spokesmen for Sea State are asserting sovereignty over the new fishing grounds, by right of reclamation. . . ."

[□ Ref. UN document 43589.5768/ UNORRS 87623ba.]

[Diplomats in marble halls, filing papers.]
[Surveyors mapping ocean expanses.]

[□ Time-delayed images APW72150/09, Associated Press 2038.6683]

"As expected, the Republic of Bangladesh has issued a protest through its U.N. delegation. Though, with their capital now underwater, the remonstrations begin to sound like those of a tragic ghost. . . ."

[View of a brown-skinned youth in a greasy bandanna, grasping a rusty railing, staring toward an uncertain future.]

● To Stan Goldman it was a revelation, watching Alex Lustig hurry
from work site to work site under the vaulted, rocky ceiling. *You
never can tell about someone till you see him in a crisis*, he
mused.

Take Alex's familiar gangling stoop. It no longer appeared
lazy or lethargic down here, half a kilometer underground. Rather,
the lad seemed to lean forward for leverage as he moved, pushing a
slow-moving tractor here, a recalcitrant drill bit there, or simply
urging the workers on. Air resistance might have been the only
thing slowing him down.

Stan wasn't the only one watching his former student, now
transformed into a lanky, brown-haired storm of catalysis. Sometimes
the other men and women laboring in this deep gallery glanced after
him, eyes drawn by such intensity. One group had trouble connecting
data lines for the big analyzer. Lustig was there instantly, kneeling on
the caked, ancient guano floor, improvising a solution. Another team,
delayed by a burned-out power supply, got a new part from Alex in
minutes—he simply ripped it out of the elevator.

"I guess Mr. Hutton will notice when no one comes up for
dinner," Stan overheard one tech say with a shrug. "Maybe he'll use a
rope to lower us a replacement part."

"Naw," another replied. "George will lower dinner itself. Unless
Dr. Lustig plugs us all with intravenous drips so we don't even have to
stop to eat."

The remarks were made in good humor. *They can tell this isn't
just another rush job, but something truly urgent.* Still, Stan was
glad necessity forced him to stay by his computer. Or else—age and
former status notwithstanding—Alex would have drafted him by now
to help string cables across the limestone walls.

Moment by moment, a laboratory was taking shape below the
mountainous spine of New Zealand's North Island.

It was still only the three of them—Stan, George, and Alex—who
knew about the lost singularity, the Iquitos black hole that might now
be devouring the planet's interior. The techs had been told they were
seeking a "gravitational anomaly" far deeper than any prior scan for
trace ores or hidden methane had ever looked. But most of them knew
a cover story when they heard one. The leading rumor—exchanged
with fleeting smiles—was that the boss had found a map to the
subterranean Lost World of Verne and Burroughs and TwenCen
B-movies.

They'll have to be told soon, Stan thought. *Alex and I can't handle the scans all by ourselves.* Probing for an object smaller than a molecule, through millions of cubic kilometers of stressed minerals and liquid metal, would be like chasing a hurtling needle through countless fields of haystacks.

As if they'd be able to do anything about it if they did find the *taniwha* down there. Even Stan, who understood most of Alex's new equations, could bring himself to believe the terrifying results for only a few seconds at a time.

I have four grandchildren, a garden, bright students with all their creative lives ahead of them, a woman who has made me whole by sharing my life for decades. . . . There are books I've saved for reading "later." Sunsets. My paintings. Tenure . . .

Such wealth, modest in monetary terms, nonetheless made George Hutton's billions seem like no big difference in comparison. It was hard, yet poignant, to be forced at this late date to take inventory and realize that.

I am a rich man. I don't want to lose the Earth.

Stan's satchel computer chimed, interrupting his morbid turn of thought. In a small volume above the open briefcase, an image took shape—of a gleaming cylinder whose surface sheen wasn't quite metallic, nor plastic, nor ceramic. Rather, it glistened slickly, like a liquid held fast in some tubular constraint of force.

That took long enough, he thought irritably, checking the figures. *Good. The main antenna can be built using today's technology. Nothing complicated, just simple microconstructors. Programming the little buggers, though . . . that's going to be a headache. Can't afford any lattice faults, or the gravity waves it radiates will scatter all over the place.*

For longer than he could remember, Stan had heard excited predictions about how nanomachines would transform the world, create wealth out of garbage, build new cities, and save civilization from the dire prospect of ever-dwindling resources. They would also scour your arteries, restore brain tissue to youthful vigor, and mayhaps even cure bad breath. In reality, their uses were limited. The microscopic robots were energy gluttons, and they required utterly well-ordered environments to work in. Even to lay down a uniform crystalline antenna, molecule by molecule in a nutrient-chemical bath, would require attention in advance to every detail.

Carefully, he used Alex's equations to adjust the design, teasing the cylinder into just the right shape to send delicate probes of radiation downward through those fiery circles of hell below, in search of an elusive monster. It was blissfully distracting work.

When the explosion struck, the initial wall of sound almost

knocked Stan off his stool. Booming echoes reverberated down the rocky galleries. A scream followed, and a hissing roar.

Men and women dropped tools, rushing to a bend in the cave where they stared in apparent horror. Alex Lustig plowed past the throng toward the commotion. Stan stood up, blinking. "What . . . ?" But none of the running techs stopped to answer his question.

"Get a ladder!" someone cried.

"There's no time!" another shouted.

Negotiating a maze of pipes and wires cluttering the floor, Stan finally managed to nudge past a rank of gawkers and see what had happened. It looked at first as if a steam line had broken, jetting hot vapor across a wall festooned with gridlike latticework. But the wind that suddenly hit him wasn't searing. It knocked him back with a blast of bitter cold.

Is it just the liquid nitrogen? Stan worried, bending into the frigid gale. *Or did the helium line break as well?* The first would be a setback. The latter might mean catastrophe.

He managed to join a crowd of techs sheltering behind one of the chemosynthesis vats. Clutching flapping work coats, the others stared toward the tangle of scaffolding, where a broken pipe now spewed cutting cold. Meters beyond that impassable barrier, two figures huddled on a teetering catwalk. The shivering workers were isolated, with no visible way to escape or to reach the cutoff valve atop the towering cryogenics tanks.

Someone pointed higher, near the arched ceiling, and Stan gasped. There, dangling from a cluster of stalactites, hung Alex! He had one arm draped through a gap between two of the hanging rock-forms, just above where they fused. It looked like an awfully precarious perch.

"How'd he get up *there*?"

Stan had to repeat the question over the roar of frigid, pressurized gas. A woman in a brown smock pointed to where a metal ladder lay crystallized and shattered amid the jetting frost. "He was trying to get past the jet to the cutoff valve . . . but the ladder buckled! Now he's trapped!"

From his perilous position, the young physicist gestured and shouted. One of the techs, a full-blooded Maori from George Hutton's own *iwi*, started scrambling for pieces of hardware. Soon he was whirling a heavy object at the end of a cable, sending it flying on an upward arc. Alex missed the tool itself, but caught the cable round his left arm. Bits of crumbling limestone rained from his shaky roost as he used his teeth and one hand to reel in a drill with a rock-bolt bit already in place.

How can he find the leverage to . . .

Amazed, Stan watched Alex throw his legs around the half-column. Hugging the stalactite, he applied the drill to the strongest section, just above his head. The hanging rock shuddered. Cracks appeared, crisscrossing the pillar at Alex's midriff. If he fell, he would carom off some toppled scaffolding straight into the supercold jet.

Stan withheld breathing as Alex drove the bit, tested it, and quickly passed a loop of cable through the grommet, giving it his weight just as the greater part of the stalactite gave way, falling to strike the debris below with a crashing noise. The crowd shouted. Dangling in midair, Alex struggled for a better grip while everyone below saw what the tumbling stone had done to his inner thighs. Bleeding runnels dripped through the remnants of his tattered trousers, joining rivulets of sweat as he strained to tie a loop knot. Encountering the roaring gas, the bloody droplets exploded into sprays of reddish snow.

Stan breathed again when Alex slipped his shoulders through the loop and let the cable take his weight. Still gasping, the young man turned and shouted over the noise. "Slack! . . . Pump!"

Two of the techs holding the cable looked puzzled. Stan almost rushed over to explain, but the Maori engineer caught on. Gesturing to the others, he began letting out more cord and then pulled most of it back just before Alex's feet neared the icy jet. The process repeated, letting out rope, pulling it back. It was a simple exercise in harmonic resonance, as with a child's swing, only here the plumb was a man. And he wouldn't be landing in any sandbox.

Alex's arc grew as the tether lengthened. With each pass he came nearer the supercold shroud of liquefied air, a blizzard of sparkling snowflakes whirling in his wake. He called down to those manning the straining cable. "Fourth swing . . . release!"

Then on the next pass—"Three!"

Then—*"Two!"*

Each time his voice sounded more hoarse. Stan nearly cried out as he saw the arc develop. They were going to release too soon! Before he could do anything though, the men let go with a shout. Alex sailed just over the jet, past the two stranded survivors, to collide with the tangled gridwork atop the centermost cryo tank. Immediately he scrambled for purchase on the iced surface. The woman next to Stan grabbed his arm and hissed sharply as Alex began a fatal slide . . .

. . . and stopped just in time, with one arm thrown around a groaning pipe.

A sharp crackling noise made Stan jump back as one of the nearby chem-synthesis tanks crinkled, folding inward from the cold. Fiber-thin control lines flailed like wounded snakes until they met the helium jet, at which point they instantly shattered into glassy shards.

"They've cut the flow topside," someone reported.

Stan wondered, was the helium partial pressure already high enough to affect sound transmission? Or was the fellow's voice squeaky out of fear?

"But there's too much already in those tanks," another said. "If he can't stop it, we'll lose half the hardware in the cavern. It'll set us back weeks!"

There are three lives at stake, too, Stan thought. But then, people had their own priorities. Hands took his sleeve again . . . this time several senior engineers were organizing an orderly evacuation. Stan shook his head, refusing to go, and no one insisted. He kept vigil as Alex worked his way toward the cutoff valve, hauling himself hand over hand. The pipes were left discolored. Patches of frozen skin, mixed with blood, Stan realized with a queasy feeling.

Centimeter by centimeter Alex neared the collapsed catwalk. One wall staple remained in place, imbedded in limestone. Barely able to see, Alex had to hunt for it, his foot repeatedly missing the perch.

"Left, Alex!" Stan screamed. "Now *up!*"

His mouth open wide, exhaling a dragon's spume of crystallized fog, Alex found the ledge and swung his weight onto it. Without pausing, he used it to hurl himself at the valve.

After all his struggles getting there, turning the handle was anticlimactically easy. At least that part of the cryo system was built well. The wailing shriek tapered off, along with the icy pressure. Stan staggered forward.

Past him sped rescue teams with ladders and stretchers. It took moments to pull down the two injured workers and hustle them away. But Alex would not be carried. He came down on his own, gingerly. Huddled in blankets, arms locked by those guiding him, he looked to Stan like some legendary Yeti, his bloodless face pale and sparkling under a crystal frosting. He made his escorts stop near Stan, and managed a few words through chattering teeth.

"M-my fault. Rushing things-s . . ." The words drowned in shivering.

Stan took his young friend's shoulder. "Don't be an ass; you were grand. Don't worry, Alex. George and I will have everything fixed by the time you get back."

The young physicist gave a jerky nod. Stan watched the medics bear him away.

Well, he thought, wondering at what the span of a few minutes had revealed. Had this side of Alex Lustig been there all along, hidden within? Or would it come to any man called upon by destiny, as that poor boy obviously was, to wrestle demons over the fate of the world?

☐ Long ago, even before animals appeared on dry land, plants developed a chemical, lignin, that enabled them to grow long stems, to tower tall above their competitors. It was one of those breakthroughs that changed things forever.

But what happens after a tree dies? Its proteins, cellulose, and carbohydrates can be recycled, but only if the lignin is first dealt with. Only then can the forest reclaim the stuff of life from death.

One answer to this dilemma was discovered and exploited by ants. One hundred trillion ants, secreting formic acid, help prevent a buildup which might otherwise choke the world beneath a layer of impervious, unrotting wood. They do this for their own benefit of course, without thought of what good it does the Whole. And yet, the Whole is groomed, cleaned, renewed.

Was it accidental that ants evolved this way, to find this niche and save the world?

Of course it was. As were the countless other accidental miracles which together make this wonder work. I tell you, some accidents are stronger, wiser than any design. And if saying that makes me a heretic, let it be so.

—Jen Wolling, from **The Earth Mother Blues**, Globe Books, 2032. [☐ hyper access code 7-tEAT-687-56-1237-65p.]

● *Pleiades* dipped its nose, and Teresa Tikhana welcomed back the
E stars. *Hello, Orion. Hello, Seven Sisters,* she silently greeted her
X friends. *Did you miss me?*
O As yet, few constellations graced the shuttle's forward
S windows, and those glittered wanly next to the dazzling Earth,
P with its white, pinwheel storms and brilliant vistas of brown and
H blue. Sinuous rivers and fractal, corrugated mountain ranges—
E even the smokestack trails of freighters crossing sunburned seas—
R all added up to an ever-changing panorama as *Pleiades* rotated out
E of launch orientation.
Of course it was beautiful—only down there could humans live

without utter dependence on temperamental machinery. Earth was home, the oasis; that went without saying.

Still, Teresa found the planet's nearby glare irksome. Here in low orbit, its dayside brilliance covered half the sky, drowning all but the brightest stars.

Vernier rockets throbbed, adjusting the ship's rotation. Valves and circuits closed with twitters and low chuckles, a music of smooth operation. Still, she scanned—checking, always checking.

One plasma screen showed their ground track, a few hundred kilometers from Labrador, heading east by southeast. NASA press flacks loved ground path indicators, but the things were next to useless for serious navigation. Instead, Teresa watched the horizon's tapered scimitar move aside to show more stars.

And hello, Mama Bear, she thought. *Good to see your tail pointing where I expected.*

"There's ol' Polaris," Mark Randall drawled to her right. "Calculating P and Q fix now." Teresa's copilot compared two sets of figures. "Star tracker fix matches global positioning system to five digits, in all nine degrees of freedom. Satisfied, Terry?"

"Sarcasm suits you, Mark." She scanned the figures for herself. "Just don't get into the habit of calling me Terry. Ask Simon Bailie, sometime, why he came home from that peeper-run wearing a sling."

Mark smiled thoughtfully. "He claims it was 'cause he got fresh with you on the Carter Station elevator."

"Wishful thinking," she laughed. "Simon's got delusions of adequacy."

For good measure, Teresa compared satellite and star tracker data against the ship's inertial guidance system. Three independent means of verifying location, momentum, and orientation. Of course they all agreed. Her compulsive checking had become notorious, a sort of trademark among her peers. But even as a little girl she had felt this need—one more reason to become a pilot, then astronaut—to learn more ways to know exactly where she was.

"Boys can tell where north is," other children used to tell her with the assurance of passed-down wisdom. "What girls understand is people!"

To most sexist traditions, Teresa had been impervious. But that one seemed to promise explanations—for instance, for her persistent creepy feeling that all maps were somehow wrong. Then, in training, they surprised her with the news that her orientation sense was far *above* average. "Hyperkinesthetic acuity," the doctors diagnosed, which translated into measurable grace in everything she did.

Only that wasn't how it felt. If this was superiority, Teresa wondered how other people made it from bedroom to bath without getting lost! In dreams she still sometimes felt as if the world was on the verge of shifting capriciously, without warning. There had been times when those feelings made her wonder about her sanity.

But then everyone has quirks, even—especially—astronauts. Hers must be harmless, or else would the NASA psych people have ever let her fly left seat on an American spacecraft?

Thinking of childhood lessons, Teresa wished at least the other part of the old myth were true. If only being female automatically lent you insight into people. But if it were so, how could things ever have gone so sour in her marriage?

The event sequencer beeped. "Okay," she sighed. "We're on schedule, oriented for rendezvous burn. Prime the OMS."

"Aye aye, Mem Bwana." Mark Randall flicked switches. "Orbital maneuvering system primed. Pressures nominal. Burn in one hundred ninety seconds. I'll tell the passengers."

A year ago the drivers' union had won a concession. Nonmembers would henceforth ride below, on middeck. Since this trip carried no NASA mission specialists, only military intelligence officers, she and Mark were alone up here on the flight deck, undistracted by nursemaid chores.

Still, there were minimal courtesies. Over the intercom, Mark's low drawl conveyed the blithe confidence of a stereotypical airline pilot.

"Gentlemen, by the fact that your eyeballs have stopped shiftin' in their sockets, you'll realize we've finished rotating. Now we're preparin' for rendezvous burn, which will occur in just under two and a half minutes. . . ."

While Mark rambled, Teresa scanned overhead, checking that fuel cell number two wasn't about to act up again. Station rendezvous always made her nervous. All the more so when she was flying a model-one shuttle. The noises *Pleiades* made—its creaking aluminum bones, the swish of coolant in old-style heat-transfer lines, the squidgy sound of hydraulic fluid swiveling pitted thrusters—these were like the sighs of a one-time champion who still competed, but only because the powers-that-be found that less expensive than replacing her.

Newer shuttles were simpler, designed for narrower purposes. Teresa figured *Pleiades* was perhaps the most complex machine ever made. And the way things were going, nothing like it would ever be built again.

A glitter over near Sagittarius caught her eye. Teresa identified it without having to check: the old international Mars mission—

scavenged for components, and the remnants parked in high orbit when that last bold venture had been canceled, back when she was still in grade school. The new rule for harder times was simple—space had to pay for itself with near-term rewards. No pie in the sky. No investment in maybes. Not when starvation remained an all too likely prospect for such a large portion of humanity.

". . . checked our trajectory three different ways, folks, and Captain Tikhana has declared that all's well. Physics has not broken down . . ."

Overlaid across the constellations were multicolored graphics displaying the vessel's orbital parameters. Also in the forward window, Teresa saw her own reflection. A smudge had taken residence on her cheek, near where a curl of dark brown hair escaped her launch cap . . . probably a grease speck from adjusting a passenger's seat before launch. Rubbing just smeared it out, however, overaccentuating her strong cheekbones.

Great. Just the thing to make Jason think I'm losing sleep over him. Teresa didn't need any more aggravation, not when she was about to see her husband for the first time in two months.

In contrast, Mark Randall's reflection looked boyish, carefree. His pale face—demarcated from the white of his spacesuit by the anodized helmet ring—showed none of the radiation stigmata that now scarred Jason's cheeks . . . the so-called "Rio tan," acquired working outside through the sleeting hell of the South Atlantic magnetic anomaly. That escapade, a year ago, had won Jason both a promotion and a month's hospitalization for anticancer treatments. It was also about when troubles in their marriage had surfaced.

Teresa resented Mark's smooth complexion. It should have been a confirmed bachelor like him who volunteered to go out and save the peepers' beloved spy-eye, instead of Jason I'm-married-but-what-the-heck Stempell.

It also should have been some bachelor who signed up to work cheek by jowl with that blonde temptress June Morgan. But once again, guess who raised his hand?

Easy, girl. Don't get your blood up. The objective is reconciliation, not confrontation.

Mark was still regaling the Air Force men below. ". . . remind me to tell you how one time she an' her old man smuggled a homemade sextant on a mission. Now any other married couple might've chosen something more useful, such as . . . ."

With her right hand, Teresa made a gesture whose meaning had changed little since the days of Crazy Horse. Spacer sign-talk for *cut the crap.*

"Um, but I guess we'll save that story for another day. Please remain strapped in as we make our last burn before station rendezvous." Randall switched off the intercom. "Sorry, boss. Got a little carried away there."

Teresa knew he was unrepentant. Anyway, that episode with the sextant wasn't much compared to the tall tales told about some astronauts. None of that mattered. What was important was that you lived, the ship lived, the mission got done, and you were asked to fly again.

"Burn in five seconds," she said, counting down. ". . . three, two, one . . ."

A deep-throated growl filled the cabin as hypergolic motors ignited, adding to their forward velocity. Since they were at orbital apogee, this meant *Pleiades'* perigee would rise. Ironically, that in turn would slow them down, allowing their destination, the space station, to catch up from behind them.

The station's beacons showed on radar as a neat row of blips strung along a slender string, pointing Earthward. The lowermost dot was their target, Nearpoint, where they'd offload cargo and passengers.

Next came the cluster of pinpoints standing for the Central Complex, twenty kilometers farther out, where scientific and development work took place in free-fall conditions. The final, topmost blip represented a cluster of facilities tethered even higher— the Farpoint research lab, where Jason worked. They had agreed to meet at the halfway lounge, if offloading went well at her end and if his experiments let him get away.

They had a lot to talk about.

All motors shut off as a sequencer by her knee shone zero. The faint pressure on her backrest departed again. What replaced it wasn't "zero-g." After all, there was plenty of gravity, pervading space all around them. Teresa preferred the classic term "free fall." An orbit, after all, is just a plummet that keeps *missing*.

Unfortunately, even benign falling isn't always fun. Teresa had never suffered spacesickness, but by now half the passengers were probably feeling queasy. Hell, even peepers were people.

"Commence yaw and roll maneuver," she said, as a formality. The computers were managing fine so far. Thrusters in the shuttle's nose and tail—smaller than the OMS brutes—gave pulsing kicks to set the horizon turning in a complex, two-axis rotation. They fired again to stabilize on a new direction.

"That's my baby," Mark said softly to the ship. "You may be gettin' on in years, but you're still my favorite."

Many astronauts romanticized the last *Columbia*-class shuttle.

Before boarding they would pat the seven stars painted by the shuttle's entry hatch. And, while it went unspoken, some clearly thought beneficent ghosts rode *Pleiades*, protecting her every flight.

Maybe they were right. *Pleiades* had so far escaped the scrapyard fate of *Discovery* and *Endeavor*, or the embarrassing end that had befallen old *Atlantis*.

Privately, though, Teresa thought it a pity the old crate hadn't been replaced long ago—not by another prissy model-three job, either, but by something newer, better. *Pleiades* wasn't a true spaceship, after all. Only a bus. A local, at that.

And despite all the so-called romance of her profession, Teresa knew she was little more than a bus driver.

"Maneuver completed. Switching to hook-rendezvous program."

"Yo," Teresa acknowledged. She toggled the Ku band downlink. "MCC Colorado Springs, this is *Pleiades*. We've finished siphoning external tank residuals to recovery cells and jettisoned the ET. Circularization completed. Request update for approach to Ere—" Teresa stopped, recalling she was talking to Air Force. "—for approach to Reagan Station."

The controller's tinny voice filled her earphones.

"Roger, *Pleiades*. Target range check, ninety-one kilometers . . . mark."

"Yes?" Randall interrupted with a weak smirk. It was a stale joke, which, fortunately, control didn't hear.

"Doppler twenty-one meters per second . . . mark. Tangential v, five point two mps . . . mark."

Teresa did a quick scan. "Verified, control. We agree."

"An' thar she blows," said Mark, peering through the overhead window. "Erehwon, right on schedule."

"Ixnay, Mark. Open mike."

Randall hand signed so-what indifference.

"Roger, *Pleiades*," said the voice from Colorado Springs. "Switching you over to Reagan Station control. MCC out."

"Reagan, shmeagan," Mark muttered when the line was clear. "Call it peeper heaven."

Teresa pretended not to hear. On the panel by her right knee she punched the PROG button, then tapped 319 EXEC. "Rendezvous and retrieval program activated," she said.

Between their consoles there appeared a holographic image of *Pleiades* itself—a squat dart, black on the bottom and white on top, her gaping cargo bay radiators exposed to the cooling darkness of space. Filling the greater part of the bay was a closed canister of powder blue. The peepers' precious spy-stuff. Colonel Glenn Spivey's treasure. And heaven help anyone who laid even a smudge on its wrapper.

Behind the cargo several white spheres held tons of supercold propellants, recovered from the towering external tank after it had fueled the shuttle through liftoff. Dumping the two-million-liter tank into the Indian Ocean had been their preoccupation early in orbital insertion—a routine waste that used to outrage Teresa, but that she no longer even thought about anymore. At least they were rescuing the residuals these days. All that leftover hydrogen and oxygen had countless uses in space.

While Mark talked to Erehwon control, Teresa caused the snare mechanism to rise from the rim of the cargo bay. The stubby arm— sturdier than the remote manipulator used for deploying cargos— extended a telescoping tip ending in an open hook.

"Erehwon confirms telemetry," Mark told her. "Approach nominal."

"We've got a few minutes then. I'll go look in on the passengers."

"Yeah, do that." Of course Mark knew she had another reason for getting up. But this time he judiciously kept silent.

Unbuckling, then swiveling to use the seat back as a springboard, Teresa cast off toward the rear of the flight deck. Before automation, a mission specialist used to watch over the cargo from there. Now only a window remained. Through it she surveyed the peepers' package, and beyond, the cryocanisters. If the coming hook-snatch maneuver worked, they'd save half the hydrazine and dinitrogen tetroxide back there, as well—another valuable bonus to offload. Otherwise, most of the reserve would be used up matching orbits.

She brought her head near the chill window to peer at the snare arm, rising from the starboard platform. It was locked, just as the computer said. *Just checking,* Teresa thought, unrepentant of her need to verify in person.

She twisted and dove through a circular opening in the "floor." Five Air Force officers in blue launch suits looked up as she swam into the spacious cabin known as middeck. Two of the passengers looked sick, averting their eyes as Teresa floated by. At least there were no windows here, so they were spared the added misery of horizon disorientation. A third of all first-timers had to adapt several days before their fluttering stomachs allowed them to appreciate scenery, anyway.

"That was a smooth launch, Captain," the elder sickly one enunciated carefully. He wore two drug-release patches behind one

ear, but still looked pretty shaky. Teresa knew the man from other
flights, and he'd been ill on those too.

*Must be pretty damned irreplaceable if they keep sending him
up.* As Mark Randall colorfully put it, guys like this never had to
prove they had guts.

"Thank you," she replied. "We aim to please. I just wanted to see
how you all were doing and to say we'll be meeting the Nearpoint
snare in about twenty minutes. Station personnel will need an hour to
offload cargo and salvaged residuals. Then it'll be your turn to ride the
elevator to Central."

"That's if you manage to hook the snare, Ms. Tikhana. What if
you miss?"

This time it was the man seated forward on the left, a stocky
fellow with eyes shaded by heavy brows, and bright colonel's eagles on
one shoulder. White sideburns offset his roughened skin—a patchy
complexion that came from repeated treatments to slough off
precancerous layers. Unlike Ra Boys or other groundside fetishists,
Glenn Spivey hadn't acquired his blotchy pigmentation on a beach.
He had won the dubious badge of honor the same way Jason had—
high over Uruguay, protected by just the fabric of his suit as he fought
to save a top-secret experiment. But then, what were a dozen or so rads
to a patriot?

They obviously hadn't mattered to Jason. Or so her husband had
implied from his recovery bed after his own encounter with the South
Atlantic radiation zone.

*"Hey look, hon. This doesn't change our plans. There are sperm banks.
Or when you're ready, we can make some other arrangement. Some of our
friends must have some damn high quality . . . Hey, babe, now what's the
matter?"*

The infuriating density of the man! As if that had been foremost
on her mind while he lay in a hospital with tubes in his arms! Later,
the subject of children did contribute to the widening gulf between
them. But at the time her only thought was, *"Idiot, you might have
died!"*

With professional coolness, Teresa answered Colonel Spivey.
"What if the station can't hook *Pleiades* midpass? In that case we'll do
another burn to match orbits the old-fashioned way. That'll take time
though. And there'll be no residual propellant to offload after
docking."

"Time and hydrazine." Spivey pursed his lips. "Valuable
commodities, Ms. Tikhana. Good luck."

Twice since she had come down here, the colonel had glanced at
his watch—as if nature's laws could be hurried like junior officers,

with a severe look. Teresa tried to be understanding, since it did take all kinds. If it weren't for vigilant, paranoid spy-types like Spivey, always poking and peeping to see to it the provisions of the Rio Treaties were kept, would peace have lasted as long as it had? Ever since the Helvetian War?

"Safety first, Colonel. You wouldn't want to see us wrapped in twenty kilometers of spectra-fiber tether material, would you?"

One of the younger peepers shivered. But Spivey met her eyes in shared understanding. They each had priorities. It was far more important they respect than like each other.

Back at her console, she watched the bottom portion of the station come into view—a cluster of bulbous tanks and plumbing hanging from a silvery line. Far above, other station components glittered like jewels strung far apart on a very long necklace. Most distant, and invisible except by radar, lay Farpoint Cluster, where Jason worked on things she still knew next to nothing about.

They were passing over the Alps now, a battered, crumpled range, whose bomb craters were only now emerging from winter's coating of snow. It was an awesome juxtaposition, showing what both natural and man-made forces could do, when angry.

But Teresa had no time for sightseeing. Her attention focused on Nearpoint—hanging like a pendulum bob, closest to the Earth.

Just below the fluid-pumping station hung a boom that flexed and stretched as its operator played out line like a fisherman, casting for the big one.

Teresa's eyes roamed over her instruments, the station, the stars, absorbing them all. Moments like this made all the hard work worthwhile. Every part of her felt unified, from the hands lightly flexing *Pleiades'* vernier controls to the twin hemispheres of her brain. Engineer and dancer were one.

For the present all anxieties, all worries, vanished. Of the countless jobs one could have, on or off the world, this one gave her what she needed most.

"We're coming in," she whispered.

Teresa knew exactly where she was.

□

"Once upon a time, the great hero Rangi-rua lost his beautiful Hine-marama. She died, and her spirit went to Rarohenga, the land of the dead.

"Rangi-rua was beset with grief. Inconsolable, he declared that he would follow his wife into the underworld and fetch her back again to Ao-mārama, the world of light.

"With Kaeo, his ever-faithful companion, Rangi-rua came to the swirling waters guarding the entrance to Rarohenga. There, he and Kaeo dove into the mouth of hell, down where the heartbeat of Manata sends shivers through the earth. Against this power they swam and swam until, at last, they reached the other bank, where the spirit of Rangi-rua's lovely wife awaited him.

"Now, to be fair it must be said that Rangi-rua and Kaeo may not have been the only mortals to accomplish this feat. For the *pakeha* tell a similar story of one called Orpheus, who did the very same thing for the sake of his lover—and it is said he even managed the crossing on his own.

"But Rangi-rua outdid Orpheus in the most important thing. For when Rangi-rua emerged again into the light of father sun, both his friend and his lover were at his side.

"But Orpheus failed because, like all *pakeha*, he just couldn't keep his mind on one thing at a time."

● C O R E Sitting in front of his holographic display—sole illumination in the deserted lab—Alex recalled George Hutton's performance at the celebration, earlier in the evening, reciting Maori legends to the tired but happy engineers by firelight. Especially appropriate had been the tale of Rangi-rua's, speaking as it did of fresh hope, snatched from the very gates of hell.

Later, though, Alex found himself drawn back to the underground laboratory. All the machinery, so busy earlier in the day, now lay dark and dormant save under this pool of light, which spilled long shadows onto the nearby limestone walls.

Rangi's legend had touched Alex, all right. It might apply to his present state of mind.

Don't look back. Pay attention to what's in front of you.

Right now what lay before him was a depiction of the planet, in cutaway view. A globe sliced like an apple, revealing peel and pulp, stem and core.

And seeds, Alex thought, completing the metaphor.

The eye couldn't make out Earth's slight deviations from a sphere. Mountain ranges and ocean trenches—exaggerated on commercial globes—were mere dewy ripples on this true-scale representation. So thin was the film of water and air compared to the vast interior.

Inside that membrane, concentric shells of brown and red and pink denoted countless subterranean temperatures and compositions. With a word, or by touching the holo's controls, Alex could zoom through mantle and core, following rocky striations and myriad charted rivers of magma.

Okay, George, he thought. *Here's a* pakeha *allegory for you. We'll start by cutting a hole straight through the Earth.*

From the surface of the globe, he caused a narrow line to stab inward, through the colored layers. *Drill a tunnel, straight as a laser, with mirror-smooth walls. Cover both ends and drop a ball inside.*

It was an exercise known to generations of physics students, illustrating certain points about gravity and momentum. But Alex played the scenario in earnest.

Assuming that inertial and gravitational mass balance, as they tend to do, anything dropped at Earth's surface accelerates nine point eight meters per second, each second.

His fingers stroked knobs, releasing a blue dot from the outer rim. It fell slowly at first, even with the time rate magnified. A millimeter here stood for an awful lot of territory in the real world.

But after the ball falls a good distance, acceleration has changed.

In 1687, Isaac Newton took several score pages to prove what smug sophomores now demonstrated on a single sheet—ah, but Newton did it first!—that only the spherical portion "below" a falling object continues to apply net gravity, until acceleration stops altogether as the ball hurtles through the center at a whizzing ten kilometers per second.

It can't fall any farther than that. Now it's streaking upward.

(Answer a riddle—where is it you can continue in a straight line, yet change directions at the same time?)

Now more and more mass accumulates "below" the rising ball. Gravity clings, draining kinetic energy. Speed slackens till at last— neglecting friction, coriolis effects, and a thousand other things— our ball lightly bumps the door at the other end.

Then it falls again, hurtling once more past sluggish, plasti- crystal mantle layers, past the molten dynamo of the core, plummeting then climbing till finally it arrives "home" once more, where it began.

Numbers and charts floated near the giant globe, telling Alex the round trip would take a little over eighty minutes. Not quite the schoolboy perfect answer, but then schoolboys don't have to compensate for a real planet's varying density.

Next came the neat trick. The same would be true of a tunnel cut through the Earth at any angle! Say, forty-five degrees. Or one drilled from Los Angeles to New York, barely skimming the magma. Each

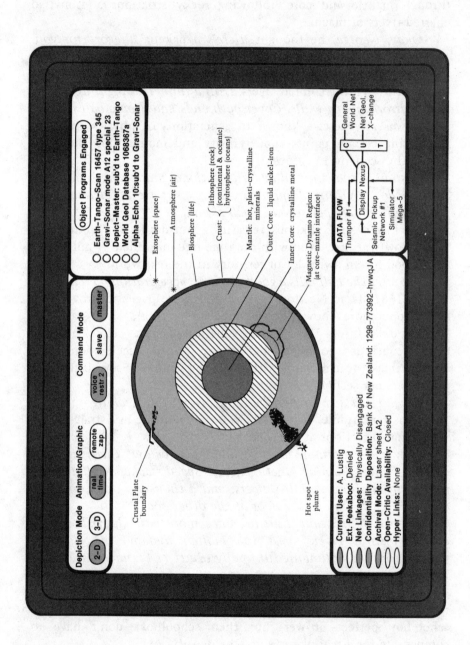

Depiction Mode | Animation/Graphic | Command Mode

2-D | 3-D | real time | remote zap | voice restr 2 | slave | master

Object Programs Engaged

○ Earth-Tango-Scan 16457 type 345
○ Gravi-Sonar mode A12 special 23
○ Depict-Master: sub'd to Earth-Tango
○ World Geol Database 1068367z
○ Alpha-Echo 10:sub'd to Gravi-Sonar

Exosphere (space)

Atmosphere (air)

Biosphere (life)

Crust: { lithosphere (rock) (continental & oceanic) hydrosphere (oceans)

Mantle: hot, plasti-crystalline minerals

Outer Core: liquid nickel-iron

Inner Core: crystalline metal

Magnetic Dynamo Region: (at core-mantle interface)

Crustal Plate boundary

Hot spot plume

DATA FLOW

C — General World Net
U — Net Geol.
T — X-change

Display Nexus

Thumper #1

Seismic Pickup Network #1

Simulator Mega-5

Current User: A. Lustig
Ext. Peekaboo: Denied
Net Linkages: Physically Disengaged
Confidentiality Deposition: Bank of New Zealand: 1298–773992–hvwqJA
Archival Mode: Laser sheet A2
Open-Critic Availability: Closed
Hyper Links: None

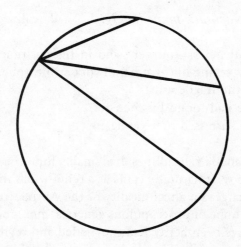

round trip took about eighty minutes—the period of a pendulum with
the same span as the Earth.

*It's also the period of a circular orbit, skimming just above the
clouds.*

Alex soon had the cutaway pulsing with blue dots, each falling at
a different angle, swiftly along the longer paths, slowly along shorter
ones. Besides straight lines there were also ellipses, and many-petaled
flower trajectories. Still, to a regular rhythm, they all recombined at
the same point on the surface, labeled PERU.

*Of course, things change when you include Earth's rotation
. . . and the pseudo-friction of a hot object pushing against material
around it . . .*

Alex was procrastinating. These simulations were from his first
days in New Zealand. There were better ones.

His hands hesitated. The palms were still blotchy from skin grafts
after that helium explosion debacle. Ironically, they hadn't trembled
half as much, then, as after today's astonishing news.

Alex wiped away all the whirling dots and called another orbit
from memory cache. This figure—traced in bright purple—was smaller
than the others—a truncated ellipse subtly twisted from Euclidean
perfection by irregularities in the densely-packed core. It didn't
approach Peru anymore.

This was no theoretical simulation. When their first gravity scans had shown the thing's awful shadow, horror had mixed with terrible pride.

It didn't evaporate immediately, he had realized. *I was right about that.*

It was awful news. And yet, who in his position wouldn't feel heady emotions, seeing his own handiwork still throbbing, thousands of miles below the fragile crust?

It lived. He had found his monster.

But then it surprised him yet again.

After Pedro Manella's headlines had made him the world's latest celebrated bad-boy, it naturally came as a relief when the World Court dismissed all charges on a technicality of the Anti-Secrecy Laws. Alex was seen as the dupe of unscrupulous generals, more fool than villain.

It might have been better had they jailed and reviled him. Then, at least, people in authority might have listened to him. As it was, his peers dismissed his topological arguments as "bizarre, overly complex inventions." Worse, special interest groups on the World Data Net made him a gossip centerpiece overnight.

". . . classic symptoms of guilt abstraction, used by the subject to disguise early childhood traumas . . ." one correspondent from Peking had written. Another in Djakarta commented, "Lustig's absurd hints that Hawking's dissipation model might be wrong mesh perfectly with the shame and humiliation he must have felt after Iquitos . . ."

Alex wished his Net clipping service were less efficient, sparing him all the amateur psychoanalyses. Still, he had made himself read them because of something his grandmother once told him.

A hallmark of sanity, Alex, is the courage to face even unpleasant points of view.

How ironic then. Here he was, vindicated in a way he could never have imagined. He now had proof positive that the standard model of micro black holes was flawed . . . that he had been on the right path with his own theories.

Right *and* wrong, in the best combination of ways.

Then why can't I leave this cave? he wondered. *Why do I feel it isn't over yet?*

"Hey, you stupid *pakeha* bastard!" A booming voice ricocheted off the limestone walls. "Lustig! You promised to get drunk with us tonight! *Tama meamea,* is this any way to celebrate?"

Alex had the misfortune to be looking up when George Hutton switched on the lights. His world, formerly confined to the dim pool of the holo tank, suddenly expanded to fill the cavern-lab Hutton's wealth had carved under the ancient rock.

Alex's blinking eyes focused first on the thumper, a shining rod two meters in diameter and more than ten long, caged to a universal bearing in a bowl excavation larger than some lunar craters. It resembled the work of some mad telescope maker who had neglected to make his instrument hollow, crafting it, instead, of perfect, superconducting crystal.

The gleaming cylinder pointed a few degrees off vertical, just as they had left it after that final bracketing run. Banks of instruments surrounded the gravity antenna, along with ankle-deep layers of paper, shredded by the ecstatic technicians when the good news had finally been confirmed.

Beyond the thumper, a flight of steps led upward to where George Hutton stood, waving a bottle and grinning. "You disappoint me, fellow," the broad-shouldered billionaire said, sauntering downstairs unevenly. "I planned getting you so pissed you'd spend the night with my cousin's *poaka* of a daughter."

Alex smiled. If that was what George wanted him to do, he was bound to comply. Without Hutton's influence he'd never have been able to sneak into New Zealand incognito. There'd have been no long hard search through the awesome complexity of the Earth's interior, improvising and inventing new technologies to hunt a minuscule monster. Worst of all, Alex might have gone to his grave never knowing what his creation was up to down below—if it was quietly dissipating or, perhaps, proceeding at a leisurely pace to devour the world.

At first, sighting it several days ago on a graviscan display had seemed to confirm their worst fears. The nightmare, reified.

Then, to everyone's relief and astonishment, hard data seemed to point another way. Apparently the thing *was* dying . . . evaporating more mass and energy into the Earth's interior than it sucked in through its narrow event horizon. True, it was thinning much more slowly than the obsolete standard models predicted. But in a few months, nevertheless, it would be no more!

I really should celebrate with the others, Alex thought. *I should put aside my last suspicions, crawl into any bottle George offers me, and find out what a* poaka *is.*

Alex tried to stand, but found he couldn't move. His eyes were drawn back to the purple dot, circling the innermost colored layer.

He felt a large presence nearby. George.

"What is it, friend? You haven't found an error, have you? It is . . ."

Alex caught Hutton's sudden concern, "Oh, it's dissipating all right. And now . . ." He paused. "Now I think I know why. Here, take a look."

With a word he banished the model of the Earth, replacing it with a schematic drawn in lambent blue. Reddish sparkles flashed at the rim of the object now centered in the tank. They swept toward a central point like beads caught in water, swirling down a drain.

"This is what I thought I was making, back when His Excellency persuaded me to build a singularity for the Iquitos plant. A standard Kerr-Prestwich black hole."

Hutton took a stool next to Alex and watched with those deceptive brown eyes. One might guess he was a simple laborer, not one of Australasia's wealthiest men.

The image in the tank looked like a rubber sheet that had been stretched taut and heated, and then had a small, heavy weight dropped onto it. The resulting funnel had finite width and depth in the display, but both men knew that the real thing—the hole in space it represented—had no bottom at all. The reddish dots represented bits of matter drawn in by gravitational tides, caught in a swirling disk. The disk brightened as more matter fell, until a ring of fierce brightness burned near the funnel's lip. Below this came a sudden cutoff within which only pitch blackness reigned.

Nothing escapes from inside a black hole's event horizon. At least, there's no direct escape.

Alex glanced at George. "Cosmologists say many singularities like this must have been created when the universe began. If so, only the biggest survive today. Smaller ones evaporated long ago, as predicted in the 1970s by Stephen Hawking. A simple singularity—even with charge and rotation—has to be extremely heavy to be stable . . . to pull in matter faster than it's lost by vacuum emission."

He pointed to the outskirts of the depression, where bright white pinpoints flashed independently of the hot ring of accreting material.

"Some distance out, the tight stress-energy of infolding gravity causes spontaneous pair production . . . ripping particle-antiparticle twins—an electron and a positron, for instance—out of the vacuum itself. It isn't exactly getting something from nothing, since each little genesis costs the singularity some field energy. And that's debited to its mass."

The sparkles formed a halo of brilliance—creation in the raw.

"Generally, one newborn particle falls inward and the other escapes, resulting in a steady weight loss. A tiny hole like this one can't pull in new matter fast enough to make up the difference. To prevent dissipation you have to feed it."

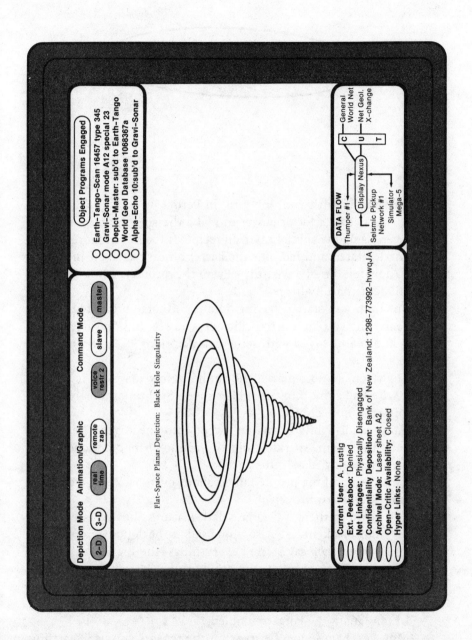

Depiction Mode **Animation/Graphic** **Command Mode**

2-D 3-D   real time remote zap   voice restr 2 slave master

Flat-Space Planar Depiction: Black Hole Singularity

Object Programs Engaged

○ Earth-Tango-Scan 16457 type 345
○ Gravi-Sonar mode A12 special 23
○ Depict-Master: sub'd to Earth-Tango
○ World Geol Database 1068367a
○ Alpha-Echo 10:sub'd to Gravi-Sonar

DATA FLOW

Thumper #1

Display Nexus

Seismic Pickup
Network #1
Simulator
Mega-5

C — General World Net
U — Net Geol. X-change
T

Current User: A. Lustig
Ext. Peekaboo: Denied
Net Linkages: Physically Disengaged
Confidentiality Deposition: Bank of New Zealand: 1298–773992–hvwqJA
Archival Mode: Laser sheet A2
Open-Critic Availability: Closed
Hyper Links: None

"As you did with your ion gun, in Peru."

"Right. It cost a lot of power to make the singularity in the first place, even using my special cavitron recipe. It took even more to keep the thing levitated and fed. But the accretion disk gave off incredible heat." Alex felt briefly wistful. "Even the prototype was cheaper, more efficient than hydro power."

"But then you started having doubts," George prompted.

"Yeah. The system was *too* efficient, you see. It didn't need much feeding at all. So I toyed with some crazy notions . . . and came up with this."

A new schematic replaced the funnel. Now it was as if a heavy *loop* of wire had sunk into the rubber sheet. Still unfathomably deep, the depression now circled on itself.

Again, reddish bits of matter swept into the cavity, heating as they fell. And again, sparkles told of vacuum pair production—the singularity repaying mass into space.

"This is something people talked about even back in TwenCen," Alex said. "It's a *cosmic string.*"

"I've heard of them." George's dark features showed fascination. "They're like black holes. Also supposed to be left over from that explosion you *pakeha* say started everything—the Big Bang."

"Uh-huh. They aren't truly funnel-things drawn in circles, of course. There's a limit to how well you can represent . . ." Alex sighed. "It's hard to describe this without math."

"I know math," George grumbled.

"Mm, yes. Excuse me, George, but the tensors you use, searching for deep methane, wouldn't help a lot with this."

"Maybe I understand more'n you think, white boy." Hutton's dialect seemed to thicken for a moment. "Like I can see what your cosmic string's got that black holes don't. Holes got no dimensions deep inside. But strings have length."

George Hutton kept doing this—play-acting the "distracted businessman," or "ignorant native boy," then coming back at you when your guard was down. Alex accepted the rebuke.

"Good enough. Only strings, just like black holes, are unstable. They dissipate too, in a colorful way."

At a spoken word, a new display formed.

The rubber sheet was gone. Now they watched a loop in space, glowing red from infalling matter, and white from a halo-fringe of new particles, showering into space. Inflow and outgo.

"Now I'll set the simulation in motion, stretching time a hundred-million-fold."

The loop began undulating, turning, whirling.

"One early prediction was that strings would vibrate incredibly fast, influenced by gravitational or magnetic . . ."

Two sides collided in a flash, and suddenly a pair of smaller loops replaced the single large one. They throbbed even faster than before.

"Some astronomers claim to see signs of gigantic cosmic strings in deep space. Perhaps strings even triggered the formation of galaxies, long ago. If so, the giant ones survived because their loops cross only every few billion years. Smaller, quicker strings cut themselves to bits . . ."

As he spoke, both little loops made lopsided figure eights and broke into four tinier ones, vibrating madly. Each of these soon divided again. And so on. As they multiplied, their size diminished and brightness grew—bound for annihilation.

"So," George surmised. "Small ones still aren't dangerous."

Alex nodded. "A simple, chaotic string like this couldn't explain the power curves at Iquitos. So I went back to the original cavitron equations, fiddled around with Jones-Witten theory a bit, and came up with something new.

"This is what I thought I'd made, just before Pedro Manella set off his damned riot."

The tiny loops had disappeared in a blare of brilliance. Alex uttered a brief command, and a new object appeared. "I call this a *tuned* string."

Again, a lambent loop pulsed in space, surrounded by white sparks of particle creation. Only this time the string didn't twist and gyre chaotically. Regular patterns rippled round its rim. Each time an indentation seemed about to touch another portion, the rhythm yanked it back again. The loop hung on, safe from self-destruction. Meanwhile, matter continued flowing in from all sides.

Visibly, it grew.

"Your monster. I remember from when you first arrived. I may be drunk, Lustig, but not so I'd forget this terrible *taniwha.*"

Watching the undulations, Alex felt the same mixed rapture and loathing as when he'd first realized such things were possible . . . when he first suspected he had made something this biblically terrible, and beautiful.

"It creates its own self-repulsion," he said softly, "exploiting second- and third-order gravities. We should have suspected, since cosmic strings are superconducting—"

George Hutton interrupted, slapping a meaty hand onto Alex's shoulder. "That's fine. But today we proved you *didn't* make such a thing. We sent waves into the Earth, and echoes show the thing's dissipating. It's dying. Your string was out of tune!"

Alex said nothing. George looked at him. "I don't like your silence. Reassure me again. The damned thing is for sure dying, right?"

Alex spread his hands. "Bloody hell, George. After all my mistakes, I'd only trust experimental evidence, and you saw the results today." He gestured toward the mighty thumper. "It's your equipment. You tell me."

"It's dying." George said, flat out. Confident.

"Yes, it's dying. Thank heaven."

For another minute the two men sat silently.

"Then what's your problem?" Hutton finally asked. "What's eating you?"

Alex frowned. He thumbed a control, and once again a cutaway view of the Earth took shape. Again, the dot representing his Iquitos singularity traced lazy precessions among veins of superheated metal and viscous, molten rock.

"It's the damn thing's orbit." Equations filed by. Complex graphs loomed and receded.

"What about its orbit?" George seemed transfixed, still holding the bottle in one hand, swaying slightly as the dot rose and fell, rose and fell.

Alex shook his head. "I've allowed for every density variation on your seismic maps. I've accounted for every field source that could influence its trajectory. And still there's this deviation."

"Deviation?" Alex sensed Hutton turn to look at him again.

"Another influence is diverting it. I think I've got a rough idea of the mass involved. . . ."

The bigger man swung Alex around bodily. The Maori's right

hand gripped his shoulder. All signs of intoxication were gone from Hutton's face as he bent to meet Alex's eyes.

"What are you telling me? Explain!"

"I think . . ." Alex couldn't help it. As if drawn physically, he turned to look back at the image in the tank.

"I think something else is down there."

In the ensuing silence, they could hear the drip-drip of mineral-rich water, somewhere deeper in the cave. The rhythm seemed much steadier than Alex's heartbeat. George Hutton looked at the whiskey bottle. With a sigh, he put it down. "I'll get my men."

As his footsteps receded, Alex felt the weight of the mountain around him once more, all alone.

☐ In ages past, men and women kept foretelling the end of the world. Calamity seemed never farther than the next earthquake or failed harvest. And each dire happening, from tempest to barbarian invasion, was explained as wrathful punishment from heaven.

Eventually, humanity began accepting more of the credit, or blame, for impending Armageddon. Between the world wars, for instance, novelists prophesied annihilation by poison gas. Later it was assumed we'd blow ourselves to hell with nuclear weapons. Horrible new diseases and other biological scourges terrified populations during the Helvetian struggle. And of course, our burgeoning human population fostered countless dread specters of mass starvation.

Apocalypses, apparently, are subject to fashion like everything else. What terrifies one generation can seem obsolete and trivial to the next. Take our modern attitude toward war. Most anthropologists now think this activity was based originally on *theft* and *rape*—perhaps rewarding enterprises for some caveman or Viking, but no longer either sexy or profitable in the context of nuclear holocaust! Today, we look back on large-scale warfare as an essentially silly enterprise.

As for starvation, we surely have seen some appalling local episodes. Half the world's cropland has been lost, and more is threatened. Still, the "great die-back" everyone talks about always seems to lie a decade or so in the future, perpetually deferred. Innovations like self-fertilizing rice and super-mantises help us scrape by each near-catastrophe just in the nick of time. Likewise, due to changing life-styles, few today can bear the thought of eating the flesh of a fellow mammal. Putting moral or health reasons aside, this shift in habits has freed millions of tons of grain, which once went into inefficient production of red meat.

Has the Apocalypse vanished, then? Certainly not. It's no longer the hoary Four Horsemen of our ancestors that threaten us, but new dangers, far worse in the long run. The by-products of human shortsightedness and greed.

Other generations perceived a plethora of swords hanging over their heads. But generally what they feared were shadows, for neither they nor their gods could actually end the world. Fate might reap an individual, or a family, or even a whole nation, but not the entire world. Not then.

We, in the mid-twenty-first century, are the first to look up at a sword we ourselves have forged, and *know*, with absolute certainty, it is real. . . .

—From **The Transparent Hand**, Doubleday Books, edition 4.7 (2035). [☐ hyper access code 1-tTRAN-777-97-9945-29A.]

E
X
O
S
P
H
E
R
E

"All right, babe. The first elevator heading down will be crammed with cargo, but Glenn Spivey put in a word, so I should be able to hitch a ride on the next one. I may even be in Central before you."

Teresa shook her head, amazed. "Spivey arranged it? Are we talking about the same Colonel Spivey?"

Her husband's face beamed from the telecom screen. "Maybe you don't know Glenn as I do. Underneath that beryllium exterior, there's a heart of pure—"

"—of pure titanium. Yeah, I know that one." Teresa laughed, glad to share even a weak, tension-melting joke.

So far, so good, she thought. Right now it felt great just looking at him, knowing he was a mere forty kilometers away, and soon would be much closer. Jason, too, sounded eager to give this a try.

Someone had once told Teresa it was too bad about her husband's smile, which sometimes transformed his intelligent features into those of an awkward puppy dog. But Teresa found his grin endearing. Jason might be insensitive at times—even a jerk—but she was sure he never lied to her. Some faces just weren't built to carry off a lie.

"By the way, I watched you snag that hook, first pass. Did you take over from the computer again? No machine pilots that smoothly."

Teresa knew she was blushing. "It looked like the program was stuttering, so I . . ."

"Thought so! Now I'll have to brag insufferably at mess. It'll be your fault if I lose all my friends up here."

The capture maneuver was actually simpler than it looked. *Pleiades* now hung suspended below the space station, from a cable stretched taut by gravitational tides. When it was time to go, they'd simply release the hook and the shuttle would resume its original ellipse, returning to mother Earth having saved many tons of precious fuel.

"Well, I reckon it's cause I'm paht Texan," she drawled, though she was the first in all her lineage ever to see the Lone Star State. "Ergo mah facility with the lasso."

"It also explains why her eyes are brown," Mark Randall inserted from nearby.

Jason's image glanced toward Teresa's copilot. "I don't dare comment on that, so I'll pretend I didn't hear it." Then, back to Teresa, "See you soon, Rip. I'll reserve a room for us at the Hilton."

"I'll settle for a broom closet," she answered, and hang it if Randall took the wrong meaning. Some people just couldn't imagine that a husband and wife, meeting for the first time in months, might want above all else to make contact, to talk quietly and preserve something neither of them wanted to lose.

"I'll see what I can arrange. Stempell out."

After securing the hook, their first task had been to offload tons of liquid hydrogen and oxygen. Likewise the extra orbital maneuvering propellants Teresa's careful piloting had saved. Every kilo of raw material in orbit was valuable, and the station offloading crew went through the procedures with meticulous care.

The holo display showed *Pleiades* suspended, nose upward, just below the bottom portion of the station—Nearpoint—the section closest to Earth. It was a maze of pipes and industrial gear hanging by slender, silvery threads many miles into the planet's gravity well. Teresa watched nervously as three station operators in spacesuits finished draining the aft tanks. Only when the hoses were detached at last did she release a knot of tension. Explosive, corrosive liquids, flowing only meters from her heat shielding, always made her edgy.

"Crew chief requests permission to commence cargo offloading," Mark told Teresa.

"Granted."

From the maze above, a giant, articulated manipulator arm approached *Pleiades'* cargo bay. A spacesuited figure waved from the bay, guiding the arm gingerly toward the mysterious Air Force package.

Colonel Glenn Spivey observed from the window overlooking the bay. "Easy does it. Come on, you bastards, it's not made of rubber! If you ding it—"

Fortunately, the crew outside couldn't hear his backseat driving. And Teresa didn't mind. After all, he was charged with equipment worth several hundred million dollars. Some anxious muttering at this point was understandable.

So why do I detest the man so much? she wondered.

For months Spivey had been working closely with her husband on some unspoken project. Perhaps it was her dislike of being excluded, or that nasty word "secrecy." Or perhaps the resentment came simply from seeing the colonel take up so much of Jason's attention, at a time when she was already jealous of others.

"Others" . . . meaning that June Morgan woman, of course. Teresa allowed herself a brief remise of resentment. *Just don't let it cause an argument,* she reminded herself. *Not this time. Not up here.*

She turned away from Spivey and scanned the status boards again —attitude, tether strain, gravity gradient—all appeared nominal.

In addition to the hook-snatch docking trick, tethered complexes like this one offered many other advantages over old-style "Tinkertoy" space stations. Long, metalized tethers could draw power directly from the Earth's magnetic field, or let you torque against those fields to maneuver without fuel. Also, by yet another quirk of Kepler's laws, both tips of the bola-like structure experienced faint artificial gravity—about a hundredth of a g—helpful for living quarters and handling liquids.

Teresa appreciated anything that helped make space work. Still, she used remote instruments to examine the braided cables. Superstrong in tension, they were vulnerable to being worn away by microscopic space debris, even meteoroids. Statistical reassurances were less calming than simply checking for herself, so she scanned until she was sure the fibers weren't on the verge of unraveling.

Overhearing Spivey, clucking like a nervous hen as his cargo cleared the bay, Teresa smiled. *I guess maybe we're not that different in some ways.*

The Russians and Chinese had similar facilities in orbit, as did Nihon and the Euros. But the other dozen or so space-capable nations had abandoned their military outposts as costs rose and the skies came increasingly under civil control. Rumor had it Spivey's folk were trying to cram in as much clandestine work as possible before "secrecy" became as outmoded up here as below.

The crane operator loaded the Colonel's cargo into an old shuttle tank—now the station freight elevator—and sent it climbing toward the weight-free complex, twenty klicks above.

"Request permission to prepare the airlock for transit, Captain." Spivey was already halfway down the companionway to middeck, impatient to join his mysterious machine.

"Mark will help just as soon as the tunnel is pressurized, Colonel."

One spacesuited astronaut examined the transparent transitway connecting *Pleiades'* airlock to Nearpoint. He waved through the rear window, signing "all secure."

"I'll see to Spivey," Mark said, and started to unstrap.

"Fine." But Teresa found herself watching the spaceman outside. He had remained in the bay after finishing, and she was curious why.

Climbing atop one of the tanks at the aft end, the station crewman secured his line to the uppermost insulated sphere . . . then went completely motionless, arms half outstretched before him in the limp, relaxed posture known as the "spacer's crouch."

Teresa quashed her momentary concern. *Of course. I get it.*

A little ahead of schedule for once, the fellow was seizing a chance that came all too rarely. He was watching the Earth roll by.

The planet filled half the sky, stretching toward distant, hazy horizons. Directly below paraded a vastly bright panorama that never repeated itself, highlighted topographies that were ever-familiar and yet always startling. At the moment, their orbital track was approaching Spain from the west. Teresa knew because, as always, she had checked their location and heading only moments before. Sure enough, soon the nubby Rock of Gibraltar hove into view.

Great pressure waves strained against the Pillars of Hercules, as they had ever since that day, tens of thousands of years ago, when the Atlantic Ocean had broken through the neck of land connecting Europe and Africa, pouring into the grassy basin that was to become the Mediterranean. Eventually, a new balance had been struck between sea and ocean, but ever since then it had remained an equilibrium of tension.

Where the great waterfall once surged, now diurnal tides interacted in complex patterns of cancelation and reinforcement, focused and reflected by the funnel between Iberia and Morocco. From on high, standing waves seemed to thread the waters for hundreds of kilometers, yet those watery peaks and troughs were actually quite shallow and had been discovered only after cameras took to space.

To Teresa, the patterns proved beautifully, once again, nature's love affair with mathematics. And not only the sea displayed wave motion. She also liked looking down on towering stratocumulus and wind-shredded cirrus clouds. From space the atmosphere seemed so thin—too slender a film to rely all their lives upon. And yet, from here one also sensed that layer's great power.

Others knew it too. Teresa's sharp eyes picked out sparkling glints which were aircraft—jets and the more common, whalelike zeppelins.

Forewarned by weather reports on the Net, they were turning to escape a storm brewing west of Lisbon.

Mark Randall called from the middeck tunnel. "The impatient so-and-so's already got the inner door open! I better take over before he causes a union grievance."

"You do that," she answered quietly. Mark could handle the passengers. She agreed with the cargo handler, out in the bay. For a rare instant no duties clamored. Teresa let herself share the epiphanic moment, feeling her breath, her heartbeat, and the turning of the world.

My God, it's beautiful. . . .

So it was that she was watching directly, not through *Pleiades'* myriad instrumentalities, when the color of the sea changed—subtly, swiftly. Pulsations throbbed those very storm clouds as she blinked in amazement.

Then the Earth seemed suddenly to bow out at her. It was a queer sensation. Teresa felt no acceleration. Yet somehow she knew they were *moving*, rapidly and non-inertially, in defiance of natural law.

It did occur to her this might be some form of spacesickness—or maybe she was having a stroke. But neither consideration slowed the reflex that sent her hand stabbing down upon the emergency alarm. With the same fluid motion, Teresa seized her space helmet. In that time-stretched second, as she spun around to take command of her ship again, Teresa caught one indelible glimpse of the crewman in the cargo bay, who had turned, mouth open in a startled, silent cry of warning.

Back in training, other candidates used to complain about the emergency drills, which seemed designed to wear down, even break the hothouse types who had made it that far. Whenever trainees felt they had procedures down pat, or that they knew the drill for any contingency, some smartaleck in a white coat inevitably thought up ways to make the next practice run even nastier. The chief of simulations hired engineers with sadistic imaginations.

But Teresa never cursed the tiger teams, not even when they threw their worst at her. She used to see the drills as a never-ending exercise in *skill*. Perhaps that was why she didn't quail or flinch now, as a storm of noise assailed her.

The master alarm barely preceded the first peal from the shuttle's backup gyroscope. As she was shutting that down, the characteristic buzzer of the number one hydraulics line started chattering. Station Control wasn't far behind.

"Gotcha *Pleiades*, we're onto it. . . . It looks like . . . no . . ."

Voices shouted in the background. Meanwhile, *Pleiades'* accelerometers began singing their unique, groaning melody.

Teresa protested—*We can't be accelerating!* But her inner sense said differently. Logic would have her shut off the sensors—which were obviously giving false readings. Instead she switched on the shuttle's main recorder.

Amber lights blazed. She acted quickly to close a critical OMS pressurization line. Then, as if she didn't already have enough troubles, Teresa's peripheral vision started blurring! She could still see down a tunnel. But the zone narrowed even as she shouted—"No. Dumpit, *no!*"

Colors rippled across the cabin, turning the cockpit's planned intricacy into a schizophrenic's fingerpainting. Teresa shook her head sharply, hoping to drive out the new affliction. "Control, *Pleiades*. Am experiencing—"

"Terry!" A shout from behind her. "I'm coming. Hold on . . ."

"*Pleiades*, Control. We're . . . having trouble—"

A shrill squeal interrupted over the open link from Erehwon; it made her wince in dread recognition.

"Mark, check the boom!" Teresa cried over her shoulder as she peered through a narrowing isthmus at the computer panel by her right knee. The thing was so obsolete it couldn't even take voice commands reliably. So more by rote than sight she flipped a toggle over to MANUAL OVERRIDE.

"*Pleiades*, we're going blind—"

"Same here!" she snapped. "I've got acceleration too, just like you. Tell me something I don't know!"

The voice fought through gathering static. "We're also getting anomalous increase in tether tension . . ."

Teresa felt a chill. "Mark! I said check the boom!"

"I'm trying!" He shouted from the ceiling port. "It . . . looks fine, Terry. The boom's okay—"

". . . extremely high anomalous electric currents in the tether . . ."

Two amber blurs switched over to red. "Put your helmet on and get ready to jettison the transitway," Teresa told her copilot as more alarms whistled melodies she had never before heard outside a simulator. Teresa felt rather than saw Mark slip into his seat as she pushed aside a switch guard and punched the red button beneath. Instantly they heard a distant crump as explosive charges tore away the plastic tunnel recently attached to their airlock.

"Transitway jettisoned," Mark confirmed. "Terry, what the hell's going—"

"Get ready to blow the boom itself," she told him. By touch,

Teresa punched buttons on the digital autopilot, engaging the shuttle's smaller reaction-control motors. "DAP on manual. RCS engaged. When we break off, we'll hang for a minute before dropping. But I think—"

Teresa paused suddenly as one of the red smudges turned amber. "—I think—"

Another switched from crimson to yellow-gold. And another. Then an amber light went green.

As quickly as it had arrived, the frightening rainbow began melting away! She blinked twice, three times. Starting in the middle, the visual blurriness evaporated. Acuity returned as warning lights and musical alarms subsided one by one.

"*Pleiades* . . ." Station Control sounded breathless. Buzzers were shutting down over there, as well. "*Pleiades*, we seem to be returning—"

"Same here," she interrupted. "But what about the tether tension!"

"*Pleiades*, tether tension . . . is slackening." Control's tone was relieved. "Must have been transient, whatever the hell it was. There may be some backlash though . . ."

Mark and Teresa looked at each other. She felt stretched, pummeled, abused. Was it really over? As more amber lights winked out, they inventoried damage. Miraculously, *Pleiades* seemed unharmed.

Except, of course, for the million-dollar transit tube she'd just jettisoned. The passengers weren't going to appreciate being ferried like so many beachballs, in personal survival enclosures. But their resentment couldn't match that of the bean-counters in Washington, if no justification were at hand.

"Jeez. What if we'd gone ahead and blown the boom?" Mark muttered. "Better put that squib on safety, Terry." He nodded toward the primed trigger, flashing dangerously between their seats.

"Hold on a sec." Teresa's eyes roved the cockpit, seeking . . . anything. Any clue to the mysterious episode. She tapped her throat mike. "Control, *Pleiades*. Confirm your estimate that backlash will be minimal. We don't want to face—"

That was when her gaze lighted on the inertial guidance display, showing where in space their ring laser gyroscope thought they were. She read it like a newspaper headline. The numbers were bizarre and rapidly changing in ways Teresa didn't like at all!

Eye flicks took in the corresponding readouts of the star tracker and satellite navigation systems. They were in total conflict, and *none* of them agreed with what the seat of her pants was telling her.

"Control! I'm disengaging, under emergency protocols."

"Wait *Pleiades*! There's no need. You may increase our backlash!"

"I'll take that chance. Meanwhile, better check your own inertial units. Have you got a gravitometer?"

"Affirmative. But what . . . ?"

"Check it! *Pleiades* out."

Then, to Mark, "You blow the boom, I'll handle the DAP. Jettison on count of three. One!"

Randall had his hands on the panel, still he remonstrated. "You sure? We'll catch hell . . ."

"Two!" She gripped the control stick.

"Terry—"

Intuition tickled. She felt it—whatever it was—returning with a vengeance.

"Blow it, Mark!"

Before she even felt the vibration of the charges, Teresa activated her vernier jets in translational mode, doing as any good pilot would in a crisis—guiding her ship away from anything more substantial than a thought or a cloud.

"What the *hell* is going on up here? Have you both lost your minds?"

A sharp voice from behind them. Without turning she snapped, "Colonel Spivey, strap in and shut up!"

Her harried, professional tone worked better than any curse or threat. Spivey might be obnoxious, but he was no fool. She sensed his quick departure and swept him from her mind as reaction jets wrestled the orbiter's reluctant mass slowly away from the station's tangle of cranes and storage tanks. On the back of Teresa's neck all the tiny hairs shivered.

"*Pleiades*, you're right. The phenomenon is periodic. Anomalous tension is returning. Gravitometer's gone crazy . . . tides of unprecedented—"

A second voice interrupted, cutting off the controller. "*Pleiades*, this is Station Commander Perez. Prepare to receive emergency telemetry."

"Affirmative." Teresa swallowed, knowing what this meant. She felt Mark lean past her to make sure the ship's datasuck boxes were operating at top speed. In that mode they recorded every nuance for one purpose only, so endangered spacers could obey rule number one of their trade . . .

Let the next guy know what killed you.

The station commander was dumping his operational status into *Pleiades* in real time—a dire measure for the chief of a secret military station. That made Teresa all the more anxious to get away fast.

She ignored navigational aids, checking orientation by instinct and estimate. Teresa groaned on realizing that two main thrusters were aimed at Nearpoint's cryo tanks, risking a titanic explosion if she fired them. That left only tiny verniers to nudge the heavy shuttle. She switched to a roll maneuver, cursing the slowness of the turn.

"Oh, shit! Mark, is that guy still in the cargo bay?"

The creepy nausea was returning, she could tell as she fought the sluggish spacecraft. Nearby, Mark laughed suddenly and a bit shrilly. "He's still there. Helmet pressed to the window. Guy's mad, Terry."

"Stop calling me Terry!" she snapped, turning to get a fix on Nearpoint again. If the tanks were clear now . . .

Teresa stared. They weren't there anymore!

Nothing was there. Tanks, habitats, cranes . . . everything was gone!

Alarms resumed their blared warnings. With her instruments turning amber and red again, Teresa decided Erehwon was none of her business now. She punched buttons labeled X-TRANSLATIONAL and HIGH, then squeezed the stick to trigger a full-throated hypergolic roar, sending *Pleiades* where she figured the station and tether *weren't*.

Mark called out pressures and flow rates. Teresa counted seconds as the blurriness encroached again. "Move, you dumpit bitch. Move!" She cursed the massive, awkward orbiter.

"I found the station." Mark announced. "Jesus. Look at that."

Through a narrowing tunnel Teresa glanced at the radar screen. She gasped. The bottom assembly was more than five kilometers below them and receding fast. The tether had stretched suddenly, like a child's rubber toy. "Damn!" she heard Mark Randall cry. Then Teresa had difficulty hearing or seeing anything at all.

This time the squidgy feeling went from her eyes straight back through her central sinus. The blaring of new alarms mixed with strange noises originating within her own skull. One alert crooned the dour song of a cooling system gone berserk. Unable to see which portion, Teresa flicked switches by touch, disabling all the exchange loops. She had Mark close down the fuel cells as well. If the situation didn't improve before they ran out of battery juice, it wouldn't matter anyway.

"All three APUs are inoperable!" Mark shouted through a roar of crazy noise.

"Forget 'em. Leave 'em turned off."

"*All* of them?"

"I said all! The bug's in the hydraulic lines, not the APUs. All long fluid lines are affected."

"How do we close the cargo bay doors without hydraulics?" he protested through rising static that nearly drowned his words. "We won't . . . able to . . . during reentry!"

"Leave that to me," she shouted back. "Close all lines except rear hypergolics, and pray they hold!"

Teresa thought she heard his acknowledgment, and a clicking that might have been those switches being closed. Or it could have been just another weird sensory distortion.

Without hydraulics they couldn't gimbal the main maneuvering rockets. She'd have to make do with RCS jets, flying blind in a chiarascuro of distortion and shadow. By touch Teresa disengaged the autopilot completely. She fired the small jets in matched pairs, relying on vibration alone to verify a response. It was true seat-of-the-pants flying, with no way to confirm she was moving *Pleiades* farther from that dangerously overstretched tether, or perhaps right toward it. . . .

Sound became smell. Roiling images scratched her skin. Amid cacophonous static Teresa thought she actually heard *Jason*, calling her name. But the voice blew away in the noisome gale before she could tell whether it was real or phantom—one of countless chimeras clamoring from all sides.

For all she knew, she was permanently blind. But that didn't matter. Nothing mattered except the battle to save her ship.

Vision finally did clear, at last, with the same astonishing speed as it had been lost. A narrow tunnel snapped into focus, expanding rapidly till only the periphery sparkled with those eerie shades. Screaming alarms began shutting down.

The transition left her stunned, staring unbelievingly at the once-familiar cabin. The chronometer said less than ten minutes had passed. It felt like hours.

"Um," she commented with a dry throat. Once again, *Pleiades* had the nerve to start acting as if nothing had happened. Red lights turned amber; amber became green. Teresa herself wasn't about to recover so quickly, for sure.

Mark sneezed with terrific force. "Where—where's Erehwon? Where's the tether?" A few minutes thrust couldn't have taken them far. But the approach and rendezvous display showed nothing at all. Teresa switched to a higher scale.

Nothing. The station was nowhere.

Mark whispered. "What happened to it?"

Teresa changed radar settings, expanding scale again and ordering a full-spectrum doppler scan. This time, at last, a scattering of blips appeared. Her mouth suddenly tasted ashen.

"There's . . . . pieces of it."

A cluster of large objects had entered much higher orbit, rising rapidly as *Pleiades* receded in her own ellipse. One transmitted an emergency beacon, identifying it as part of the station's central complex.

"We better do a circularization burn," Mark said, "to have a chance of rescuing anybody."

Teresa blinked once more. *I should've thought of that.*

"Check . . . check all the tank and line pressures first," she said, still staring at the mess that had been the core of Reagan Station. Something had rent the tethers . . . and all the spars connecting the modules, for good measure. That force might return anytime, but they owed it to their fellow spacers to try to save those left alive.

"Pressures look fine," Mark reported. "Give me a minute to compute a burn. It'll be messy."

"That's okay. We'll use up our reserves. Kennedy and Kourou are probably already scrambling launchers—" She stopped, ears perked to a strange tapping sound. Another symptom? But no, it came from behind her. She swiveled angrily. If that damned Spivey had come back . . .

A *face* in the rear window made Teresa gasp, then she sighed. It was only their inadvertent hitchhiker, the spacesuited crewman, his helmet still pressed against the perspex screen.

"Hmph," she commented. "Our guest doesn't look as pissed off as before." In fact, the expression behind the steamed-up faceplate beamed unalloyed gratitude. "He must have seen Nearpoint come apart. By now it may already be in the atmos . . ."

She stopped suddenly. "Jason!"

"What?" Mark looked up from the computer.

"Where's the upper tip? Where's Farpoint!"

Teresa scrabbled at the radar display, readjusting to its highest scale on autofrequency scan—taking in the blackness far from Earth just in time to catch a large blip that streaked past the outer edge of the screen.

"Sweet Gaia . . . look at the doppler!" Randall stared. "It's moving at . . . at . . ." He didn't finish. Teresa could read the screen as well as he.

The glowing letters lingered, even after the fleeting blip departed. They burned in the display and in their hearts.

Jason, Teresa thought, unable to comprehend or cope with what she'd seen. Her voice caught, and when she finally spoke, it was simply to say, "Six . . . thousand kilometers . . . per second."

It was impossible of course. Teresa shook her head in numb,

unreasoning disbelief that Jason would have, could have, done this to her!

"*Kakashkiya,*" she sighed.

"He's leaving me . . . at two percent of the goddamn speed of light . . ."

☐ It was Atē, first-born daughter of Zeus, who used the golden apple to tempt three vain goddesses, setting the stage for tragedy. Moreover, it was Atē who made Paris fall for Helen, and Agamemnon for Breises. Atē filled the Trojans' hearts with a love of horses, whose streaming manes laid grace upon the plains of Ilium. To Ulysses she gave a passion for new things.

For these and other innovations, Atē became known as Mother of Infatuation. For these she was also called Sower of Discord.

Did she realize her invention would eventually lead to Hecuba's anguish atop the broken walls of Troy? Some say she spread dissension only at her father's bidding . . . that Zeus himself connived to bring about that dreadful war ". . . so its load of death might free the groaning land from the weight of so many men."

Still, when he saw the bloody outcome, Zeus mourned. Gods who had supported Troy joined those backing Hellas, and all agreed to lay the blame on Atē.

Banished to Earth, she brought along her invention, and its effects would prove as far-reaching as that earlier boon—the gift of Prometheus. Indeed, what could Reason ever accomplish for mankind by itself, without Passion to drive it on?

Infatuation spread, for well and ill. Life, once simple, became vivid, challenging, confusing. Hearts raced. Veins sang with recklessness. Wild gambles paid off fantastically, or tumbled into memorable fiascos.

There came to Earth a thing called "love."

Infatuation forever changed the world. That is why some came to call it the "Meadow of Atē."

● The last tremors had ended, but it still took several minutes for
C the technicians to crawl out from under their desks. Through
O cascading hazes of limestone dust they peered about, making sure
R the quake was really over. Some cast awed glances toward the
E nexus console, where Alex Lustig had remained throughout the
unexpected temblors.

One unspoken thought circulated among them—that any bloke who could make the Earth rattle was surely one to reckon with.

Inside, Alex wasn't quite as calm as he seemed. In truth, exhaustion and sheer astonishment were what had kept him at his station while others dove for cover, far more than bravado or showy courage. This sudden power to cause earthquakes was a completely unexpected side effect of their project, and of trivial importance next to the news he now saw before him.

Unfortunately, they had found exactly what they were looking for.

The cutaway hologram told the story. Where only one purple dot had been depicted before—looping a deeply buried orbit about the planet's center—now a second object could be seen circling even lower still. What had been only dire suspicion was now reified and horrible.

"It's down there, all right," George Hutton's chief physicist reported, lifting his hard hat to smooth back sparse white hair. Stan Goldman's hands trembled. "We'll need data from other listening posts to pin it down precisely."

"Can you estimate its mass?" Hutton asked. The Maori tycoon sat on the other side of the console, wearing a scowl that would have made the warriors of Te Heuheu proud. During the quakes he, too, had spurned shelter. But the techs only expected that of him.

Goldman pored over his screen. "Looks like just under a trillion tons. That's several orders heavier than Alex's . . . than the first one. Than Alpha."

"And its other dimensions?"

"Too small to measure on linear scales. It's another singularity, all right."

George turned to Alex. "Why didn't we detect this other thing before?"

"It seems there are more ways to modulate gravity waves than anyone imagined." Alex motioned with his hands. "To pick any one object out of the chaos below, we have to calculate and match narrow bandwidths and impedances. Our earlier searches were tuned to find Alpha, and picked up Beta only by inference."

"You mean—" George gestured at the tank— "there may be *more* of the things down there?"

Alex blinked. He hadn't thought that far ahead. "Give me a minute."

Speaking softly into a microphone, he pulled subroutines from his utility library, creating charts and simulations near the hologram. "No," he said at last. "If there were more they'd affect the others' orbits. It's just those two. And my . . . and singularity Alpha is decaying rapidly."

George grunted. "What about the big one? I take it *that* damn thing is growing?"

Alex nodded, reluctant to speak. As a physicist he was supposed to accept the primacy of objective reality. Yet there remained a superstitious suspicion in his heart, that dark potentialities become real only after you have spoken them aloud.

"Seems to be," he said, with difficulty.

"I agree," added Stan.

Hutton paced through the still-drifting dust, in front of the gleaming gravity-wave generator. "If it's growing, we know several things." He held up one finger. "First, Beta can't be terribly old, or it would have consumed the Earth long ago, neh?"

"It could be a natural singularity left over from the Big Bang, which hit Earth only recently," Stan suggested.

"Weak, very weak. Wouldn't an interstellar object be moving at hyperbolic speeds?" Hutton shook his head. "It might pass through a planet on a fluke, but then it'd just fly off into space again, barely slowed at all."

Alex nodded, accepting the point.

"Also," Hutton went on, "it stretches credulity that such an object would happen to arrive just now, when we have the technology to detect it. Besides, you yourself said small singularities are unstable —be they holes or strings or whatever—unless they're specially *tuned* to sustain themselves!"

"You're saying someone else has . . . ?"

"Obviously! Come on, Lustig. Do you think you're the only bright guy on the planet? Face it, you've been scooped. Preceded! Someone beat you to it, by inventing a better cavitron perhaps, or using something different.

"Probably something different, more sophisticated, since this *taniwha* is worse than your pathetic thing, your Alpha!" George spread a grin absent of mirth. "Accept it, Alex boy. Someone out there whipped you at your own game . . . somebody better at playing mad scientist."

Alex didn't know what to say. He watched the big man's expression turn thoughtful.

"Or maybe it's not just a lone madman this time. I wonder. . . . Governments and ruling cliques are good at coming up with ways to destroy the world. Maybe one was developing some sort of doomsday device? An ultimate deterrent? Maybe, like you, they released it by mistake."

"Then why keep it secret?"

"To prevent retribution, of course. Or to gain time while they plot an escape to Mars?"

Alex shook his head. "I can't speculate about any of that. All I can do is—"

"No." George stabbed a finger at him. "Let me tell you what you can do. First off, you can get busy confirming this data. And then, after that . . ."

The fire seemed to drain out of Hutton's eyes. His shoulders slumped. "After that you can tell me how much time I have left with my children, before that thing down there swallows up the ground beneath our feet."

The frightened techs shifted nervously. Stan Goldman watched his own hands. Alex, however, felt a different sense of loss. He wished he too could react in such a way—with anger, defiance, despair.

Why do I feel so little? Why am I so numb?

Was it because he'd been living with this possibility so much longer than George?

Or is George right? Am I miffed that someone else obviously did a bigger, better job of monster making than I ever could?

Whoever it had been, they were certainly no more competent at keeping monsters caged. Small satisfaction there.

"Before we do more gravity probes," Stan Goldman said. "Hadn't we better find out why that last scan set off seismic tremors? I've never heard of anything like it before."

George laughed. "Tremors? You want quakes? Just wait till Beta's grown to critical size and starts swallowing up the Earth's core. Chunks of mantle will collapse inward . . . then you'll see earthquakes!"

Swiveling in disgust, Hutton strode off toward the stairs to climb back to Ao-mārama—to the world of light. For some time after he departed, nobody did or said much. The staff desultorily cleaned up. Once, Stan Goldman seemed about to speak, then closed his mouth and shook his head.

A nervous engineer approached Alex, holding a message plaque. "Um, speaking of earthquakes, I thought you'd better see this." He slid the sheet onto the console between Stan and Alex. On its face rippled the bold letters of a standard World Net tech-level press release:

TEMBLORS, LEVEL 3 THROUGH 5.2, HAVE HIT SPAIN, MOROCCO, BALAERICS. CASUALTIES LOW. SWARM FOLLOWED UNUSUAL PATTERN IN SPACE, TIME, AND PHASE DOMAINS. INITIAL ONSET—

"Hm, what does this have to do with . . . ?" Then Alex noticed—the Spanish quakes had struck at exactly the same time as the jolts here in New Zealand! Turning to the whole-Earth cutaway, he made some comparisons, and whistled. As nearly as the eyeball had it, the two swarms had taken place one hundred and eighty degrees apart—on exactly opposite sides of the globe.

In other words, a straight line, connecting New Zealand and Spain, passed almost exactly through the planet's core.

He watched the new singularity, the one called Beta, follow a low, lazy trajectory, never climbing far from the inmost zone where density and pressure were highest, where its nourishment was richest.

It does more than grow, Alex realized, amazed the universe could awe him yet again. *It does one hell of a lot more than grow.*

"Stan—" he began.

"You've noticed too? Puzzling, isn't it?"

"Mm. Let's find out what it means."

So they were immersed in arcane mathematics, barely even aware of the world outside, when someone turned a dial to amplify the breathless voices of news reporters, describing a disaster in space.

PART II

PLANET

A modest fire burns longer. So it is, also, with stars.

The brightest rush through lives of spendthrift extravagance to finally explode in terminal fits of self-expression, briefly outshining whole galaxies. Meanwhile, humbler, quieter suns patiently tend their business, aging slowly, gracefully.

Ironically, it takes both types to make a proper potion. For without the grand immoderation of supernovas there would be no ingredients—no oxygen, carbon, silicon, or iron. And yet the steady yellow suns are also needed—to bake the concoction slowly, gently, or the recipe will spoil.

Take a solar mix of elements. Condense small lumps and accrete them to a midsized globe. Set it just the right distance from the flame and rotate gently. The crust should bubble and then simmer for the first few million years.

Rinse out excess hydrogen under a wash of sunlight.

Pound with comets for one eon, or until a film of liquid forms.

Keep rotating under an even heat for several billion years.

Then wait. . . .

☐ For consideration by the 112 million members of the Worldwide Long Range Solutions Special Interest Discussion Group [☐ SIG AeR,WLRS 253787890.546], we the steering committee commend this little gem one of our members [☐ Jane P. Gloumer QrT JN 233-54-2203 aa] found in a late TwenCen novel. She calls it the "Offut-Lyon Plan." Here's Ms. Gloumer to describe the notion:

"Our problem isn't too many people, per se. It's that we have too many *right now.* We're using up resources at a furious rate, just when the last of Earth's surplus might be used to create true, permanent wellsprings of prosperity. Projects such as reforestation, or orbital solar power, or [☐ list of other suggestions hyper-appendixed, with appropriate references] aren't making any progress because our slender margin must be spent just feeding and housing so many people.

"Oh, surely, the rate of population growth has slackened. In a century, total numbers may actually taper off. But too late to save us, I'm afraid.

"Now some insensitive members of this very SIG have suggested this could be solved by letting half the people die. A grim Malthusian solution, and damn stupid in my opinion. Those five billions wouldn't just go quietly for the common good! They'd go down kicking, taking everybody else with them!

"Anyway, do billions really need to die, in order to save the world? What if those billions could be persuaded to leave *temporarily*?

"Recent work at the University of Beijing shows we're only a decade away from perfecting cryosuspension . . . the safe freezing of human be-ings, like those with terminal diseases, for reliable resuscitation at a later time. Now at first that sounds like just another techno-calamity—plugging another of the drain holes and letting the tub fill still higher with people. But that's just small thinking. There's a way this breakthrough could actually prove to be our salvation.

"Here's the deal. Let anyone who wants to sign up be suspended until the twenty-fourth century. The U.N. guarantees their savings will accumu-late at 1% above inflation or the best government bond rate, whichever is higher. Volunteers are assured wealth when they come out the other end.

"In return, they agree to get out of the way, giving the rest of us the elbow room we need. With only half the population to feed, we problem solvers could roll up our sleeves and use the remaining surplus to fix things up.

"Of course, there are a few bugs to work out, such as the logistics of safely freezing five billion people, but that's what SIG discussion groups like this one are for—coming up with ideas and solving problems!''

Indeed. Jane's provocative suggestion left us breathless. We expect more than a million responses to this one, so please, try to be original, or wait until the second wave to see if your point has already been stated by someone else. For conciseness, the first round will be limited to simple eight-gig voice-text, with just one subreference layer. No animation or holography, please. Now let's start with our senior members in China . . .

●   It was truly "mad dogs and Englishmen" weather. Claire wore her
L   goggles, of course, and was slathered with skin cream. Neverthe-
I   less, Logan Eng wondered if he really oughtn't get his daughter out
T   of this blistering sunshine.
H   Not that, to all appearances, anything could possibly harm
O   that creature up ahead, with the form of a girl but moving along
S   the striated rock face like a mountain goat. It never occurred to
P   Logan that Claire might fall, for instance, here on a mere class-four
H   slope. His red-headed offspring strode ahead as if she were crossing
E   a lawn, rather than a forty-degree grade, and disappeared around
R   the next bend in the canyon wall with a final flash of bronzed legs.
E   Logan puffed, reluctantly admitting to himself why he'd been
about to call her back. *I can't keep up with her anymore. It was inevitable, I guess.*

Realizing this, he smiled. Envy is an unworthy emotion to feel toward your own child.

Anyway, right now he was occupied with greater spans of time than a mere generation. Logan teetered on the edge of the period called "Carboniferous." Like some ambitious phylum, aspiring to evolve, he sought a path to rise just a few more meters, into the Permian.

That landmark, which had seemed so stark from far away—a distinct border between two horizontal stripes of pale stone—became deceptive and indistinct up this close. Reality was like that. Never textbook crisp, but gritty, rough-edged. It took physical contact, breathing chalky sediments or tracing with your fingertips the outline of some paleozoic brachiopod, to truly feel the eons imbedded in a place like this.

Logan knew by touch the nature of this rock. He could estimate its strength and permeability to seeping water—a skill learned over years perfecting his craft. Also, as an amateur, he had studied its origins in prehistoric days.

The Carboniferous period actually came rather late in the planet's history. Part of the "age of amphibians," it spanned a hundred million years before the giants known as dinosaurs arrived. Wonderful beasts used to thrive near where he now trod. But it was mostly upon ocean bottoms that life's epic was written, by countless microorganisms raining down as gentle sediment year after year, eon after eon, a process already three billion years old when these clay chapters were lain.

Of course Logan knew volcanic mountains, too. Only last week he'd been scrambling over vast igneous flows in eastern Washington state, charting some of the new underground streams awakened by the shifting rains. Still, mere pumice and tuff were never as fascinating as where the land had once quite literally been alive. In his work he'd walked across ages—from the Precambrian, when Earth's highest denizens were mats of algae, to the nearly recent Pliocene, where Logan always watched out for traces of more immediate forebears, who might by then already have been walking on two legs and starting to wonder what the hell was going on. He regularly returned from such expeditions with boxes of fossils rescued from the bulldozers, to give away to local schools. Though of course Claire always got first choice for her collection.

"Daddy!"

He was negotiating a particularly tricky bend when his daughter's call tore him from his drifting thoughts. A misstep cost him his footing, and Logan felt a sudden, teetering vertigo. He gasped, throwing himself against the sloping wall, spreading his weight over the largest possible area. The sudden pounding of his heart matched the sound of pebbles raining into the ravine below.

It was an instinctive reaction. An overreaction, as there were plenty of footholds and ledges. But he'd let his mind wander, and that was stupid. Now he'd pay with bruises, and dust from head to toe.

"What—" He spat grit and raised his voice. "What is it, Claire?"

From above and somewhere ahead he heard her voice. "I think I found it!"

Logan reset his footing and pushed away. Standing upright required that his ankles bend sharply as his climbing shoes pressed for traction. But beginning scramblers learned to do that on their first outing. Now that he was paying attention again, Logan felt steady and controlled.

Just so long as you do *pay attention*, he reminded himself.

"Found what?" he called in her general direction.

"Daddy!" came exasperated tones, echoing faintly down narrow sidechannels. "I think I found the boundary!"

Logan smiled. As a child, Claire *never* used to call him "Daddy." It had been an affront to her dignity. But now that the state of Oregon had issued her a self-reliance card, she seemed to like using the word —as if a small degree of residual, calculated childishness was her privilege as an emerging adult.

"I'm coming, Geode!" He patted his clothes, waving away drifts of dust. "I'll be right there!"

The badlands stretched all around Logan. Sculpted by wind and rain and flash floods, they no doubt looked much as they had when first seen by whites, or by any people at all. Humans had lived in North America for only ten or twenty thousand years, tops. And though the weather had changed during that time—mostly growing dryer and hotter—it had been even longer since any appreciable greenery found a purchase on these sere slopes.

Still, there was beauty here: beige and cream and cinnamon beauty, textured like hard layers of some great, petrified pastry that had been kneaded hard below and then exposed by rough scourings of wind and rain. Logan loved these rocky deserts. Elsewhere, Earth wore its carpet of life as a softening mask. But here one could touch the planet's tactile reality—mother Gaia without her makeup on.

His job often took him to places like this . . . to map out schemes for managing precious water. It was a role much like the "wildcatters" of twentieth-century lore, who used to scramble far and wide in search of petroleum, until each of the six hundred major sedimentary basins had been probed, palpated, steamed, and sucked dry.

Logan liked to think his goals were more mature, his task more benign and well thought out than that. Still he sometimes wondered. Might future generations look back on him and his world-spanning fraternity the way teledramas now depicted oilmen? As shortsighted fools, even rapists?

His ex-wife, Claire's mother, had decided about that long ago. After his involvement in the project to cover over the lower Colorado River—saving millions of acre-feet of water from evaporation and creating the world's longest greenhouse—she had rewarded him by throwing him out of the house.

Logan understood Daisy's feelings . . . her obsessions, actually. *But what was I to do? We can't save the world without food. Only people with full stomachs become environmentalists.*

All over the planet there were problems crying out for solutions, not tomorrow, but right now. Nations and cities wanted water shifted, pumped and diked. As the seas rose and rains migrated unpredictably, so did his labors, as governments strove desperately to adapt. Great changes were at work, in the air and land and oceans. They were the sort of global transformations one read of in the very rocks themselves . . . such as when one long epoch of geological stability would come suddenly and violently to an end, leaving everything forever recast.

And yet . . . Logan inhaled the scent of sage and juniper.

Nothing had altered this country within man's memory. Not even the greenhouse effect. He rejoiced in places like this, where no one would ever ask for his services. Places *invulnerable* to any works he could imagine.

A red-tailed hawk patrolled the next mesa, cruising a thermal air current that made the intervening gullied slope swim before his eyes. He touched a control near the left strap of his goggles and the bird steadied in view, smart optics enabling him to share its hunt, vicariously. There was a gleam in the raptor's yellow iris as it scanned the sparse cover, seeking prey that might be sheltered there.

The bird passed out of sight. Logan readjusted the goggles and resumed climbing.

Soon he encountered tricky territory. Shards of stone had broken from an undermined outcrop, leaving a treacherous scree in his path. Logan's nostrils flared as he stepped off carefully, arms outstretched for balance. Then he hopped again, a little quicker.

This kind of ground was ideal, of course. Not particularly dangerous—he and Claire carried tracking beepers anyway, and Forest Service 'copters were less than thirty minutes away—but enough so to be thrilling. Logan leaped from boulder to tottering boulder. It lent an added spice of adrenaline to the exhilaration of just being out here in the open, far from the teeming cities or his growling bulldozers, without a care in the world beyond the crucial decision of where he was going to plant his feet next.

At last he landed, surefooted and elated, on another patch of easy slant—no more vertical than horizontal. Logan paused again to catch his breath.

He and Claire had seen many other hikers on their way here, of course. You needed reservations years in advance to get a camping permit. Ironically though, right now the two of them were completely alone in this particular area. While tourists thronged the easy nature trails and aficionados went for hard ascents, intermediate terrain like this often went unvisited for days at a stretch.

Squinting to blur vision a bit, Logan could almost smear out signs of recent human passage . . . those eroded spots where footprints had worn the stone in ways wind or water never could, or bits of paper or foil too small to qualify for antilitter fines. It was so quiet—no drone of aircraft engines at the moment, no voices—that one might even imagine one was treading ground no other person had explored in all of time.

It was a pleasant fantasy.

Logan scanned for his daughter, his goggles adapting to the changing glare. *Now where has she gotten to?*

A giggle made him start. "I'm right above you, dummy!"

Sure enough, there she was. Not five meters uphill, perched on a fifty-degree slope. She must have lain in wait, quiet and unmoving, for at least ten minutes as he approached.

"I never should have let Kala M'Lenko teach you stalking," he muttered.

She tossed her hair, red tinged from the sun. Her skin was copper colored too, saying to hell with the palefaced fashion of the day. Where a normal sixteen-year-old would have worn the latest style in sun hats, she sported a sweatband visor and streaks of white onc-ex cream.

"But you said a girl today oughta have survival skills."

"Thems, you have in plenty. Too plenty, maybe," Logan answered in pidgin Simglish. But he grinned. "Let's see what you found."

Actually, he was pleased with her attitude. As she led him up a path too narrow for footprints, Logan found himself recalling a time some years ago when he had challenged her to "find a rock" in Kansas.

They had been visiting his parents, before the divorce, but long after the Big Drought had forced plains farmers to switch from their beloved corn to sorghum and amaranth. Claire loved the Eng spread, even though the agricooperative it was a part of scarcely resembled the Ma and Pa farms still vivid in story books. At least it was more real than the lavish estate where Daisy had grown up, where Claire hated visiting because her aristo cousins so often cast her in the role of their amusing hick relation, who didn't even know enough to care that she was poor.

"If you can find a rock, I'll give you ten dollars," he had told his daughter on that day, thinking it a simple way to keep her amused during the sluggish stretch until dinnertime. And while the inducement had been mere pocket change, she nevertheless scampered off into the harvested fields, searching through stubble while he lazed in a hammock, catching up on his journals.

It didn't take Claire long to realize plowed fields weren't good places to find stones. So she moved to the verges, where windbreak trees swayed in a bone-dry sirocco. During all that lazy afternoon she kept running back to her father with bits of treasure to show him . . . bottle caps and machine parts, for instance. Or ancient aluminum soft-drink pull-rings, still shiny after seventy years. And all sorts of other detritus from two and a half centuries' ceaseless cultivation. They had fun puzzling over these trophies, and Logan would have been happy with just that. But, typically, Claire never forgot the original challenge.

She brought him hard clumps that proved, under a magnifying glass, to be only hardened dirt. She retrieved agglomerates of clay and chunks of broken cement. Every sample turned into a revelation, a glimpse into the past. Each time she would hurry off again, only to return a few minutes later, breathless with the next sample to be dissected.

Finally, when Logan's mother called them in for supper, he broke the news to Claire. *"There are no stones in Kansas,"* he had said. *"Or at least not in this part of the state. Even after all the terrible erosion, there's still hardly anywhere you can find bedrock. It's all a great plain built up over thousands of years, out of dust and tiny bits blown down from the Rockies.*

"There's just no natural way for a stone to get here, honey."

For an instant he had wondered if he'd taken a father's license too far, teasing the child that way. But his daughter only looked at him and then pronounced, "Well, it was fun anyway. I guess I learned a lot."

At the time Logan wondered at how easily she had accepted defeat. It was only three days later, as they prepared to depart for home, that she said to him, *"Hold out your hand,"* and placed in his palm a heavy, oblong shape, crusty, with a blackened, seared quality to it. Logan remembered blinking in surprise, hefting the stone. He took out his magnifier and then borrowed his father's hammer to chip a corner.

No doubt about it. Claire had found a meteorite.

"There is *a way for a stone to get here, isn't there?"* she had said. Silently, Logan pulled out coins and paid up.

Now, on this Wyoming slope, a much bigger Claire patted the slanting cliff where a sudden change in color could be seen, from mocha to a sort of toffee cream. She pointed to faint outlines, naming fossil creatures whose skeletons were set in stone when this had been the bottom of a great sea, millions of centuries ago. Logan's own trip into memory was relatively minor in comparison, a mere eight years. But eight years which had changed that precocious little girl.

She won't have to be picky to choose a man, he thought. *She'll scare off all but the few who can keep up with her.*

". . . and none of them appear above this line. They all died out right here!'' She stroked the line again. ''This has to be the Permian-Triassic boundary.''

He nodded. ''Fair enough. Shall I take your picture next to it?''

Claire protested. ''But we have to take a scraping! I want to take home—''

''Scraping second. Photo first. Humor Papa.''

Claire let out an exasperated sigh. *But then*, he thought, *It's a dad's job to make light of things. To be hard to impress.*

He touched the controls at the rims of his goggles. ''Now smile,'' he said.

''Oh all right. But wait a minute!''

She grabbed a flat electrobrush from her back pocket, flicked the switch to charge it, and began swiping at her tangled locks. Finally, she swept off her own goggles and ignored the ferocious sun to smile for the camera.

Logan grinned. In many ways, Claire was still quite sixteen.

It had been a good day. But returning to camp, dusty and with the grit of ages between his teeth, Logan looked forward to a quiet evening meal and collapsing in his sleeping bag. His pack, containing the full five kilos of rock samples allowed by Claire's collector's permit, he dropped with relief by the licensed fire ring.

Studiously, Logan pretended not to see the flashing light atop his tiny camp-transceiver. Until he touched the PLAY button, he could still plead ignorance—claim he'd been out of reach somewhere on the mountain. Dammit. The others in his consulting firm had been told, forcefully. He wasn't to be disturbed except in an emergency!

Washing his face with a cloth dipped in a crevice streamlet, Logan tried to be cynical. *They probably want me back ''urgently'' to clear somebody's drain spout.* Returning to the tent, he tossed the wash cloth over the little red beacon.

But he couldn't dismiss it that easily. His imagination betrayed him. While Claire rattled the cooking pot Logan kept envisioning scenes of moving water. As they ate quietly in the gathering dusk, he found himself—like some character out of a Joseph Conrad tale—picturing inundations, deluges, liquid calamities breaking through man's flimsy barriers, setting all works, great and small, in peril.

It was incongruous, here in a parched land where one's very pores gasped, where moisture was assessed in precious droplets. But he had little control over the train of images thrown up by his forboding unconscious. He pictured levees bursting, rivers shifting . . . the Mississippi finally spilling over the worn out dikes confining it, tearing through unprotected bayous to the sea.

Surrendering at last, he flung aside the tent flap and entered to read the damned message. He remained inside for some time.

Emerging at last, Logan saw that Claire had already packed away the utensils and was dismantling her own small shelter under the early stars. He blinked, wondering how she knew.

"Where's the trouble?" she asked, as she rolled the soft fabric tent into a tight ball.

"Uh . . . Spain. There were some strange earthquakes. A couple of dams may be in danger."

She looked up, excitement in her eyes. "Can I come? It won't interrupt my schoolwork. I can study by hyper."

Once again, Logan wondered what fine thing he must have done to deserve a kid like this. "Maybe next time. This'll be just a quick dash. Probably they just want reassurance, so I'll hold their hands a while and then hurry back."

"But Daddy . . ."

"Meanwhile, you've got to spend a lot of time on the Net, catching up, or that college in Oregon could revoke your remote status. Do you want to have to go back to high school? At home in Louisiana? In person?"

Claire shivered. "High school. Ugh. All right. Next time, then. So get your gear; I'll take care of your tent. If we hurry we can make it to Drop Point by eight and catch the last zep into Butte."

She grinned. "Hey. It'll be fun. I've never done a three point five traverse in the dark before. Maybe it'll even be scary."

□

A dust wafts through the hills and valleys of Iceland.

The people of the island nation sweep it from their porches. They wipe it from their windows. And they try not to scowl when tourists exclaim, pointing in delight at the red and orange twilight glow cast by suspended topsoil, scattering the setting sun.

Stalwart Northmen originally settled the land, whose rough democracy lasted longer than any other. For most of twelve centuries their descendants disproved the lie that says liberty must always be lost to aristocrats or demagogues.

It was a noble and distinguished heritage. And yet, the founders' principal legacy to their descendants was not that freedom, but the dust.

Whose fault was it? Would it be fair to blame ninth century settlers, who knew nothing of science or ecological management? In the press of daily life, with a family to feed, what man of such times could have foreseen that his beloved sheep were gradually destroying the very land he planned leaving to his children? Deterioration was so gradual that it went unnoticed, except in the inevitable tales of oldsters, who could be counted on to claim the hillsides had been much greener in *their* day.

Was there ever a time when grandparents didn't speak so?

It took a breakthrough . . . a new *way* of thinking . . . for a much later generation to step back at last and see what had happened year after year, century after century, to the denuded land . . . a slow but steady rape by degrees.

But by then it appeared already too late.

A dust drifts through the hills and valleys of Iceland. The people of the island nation do more than simply sweep it from their porches. They show it to their children and tell them it is *life* floating in ghostlike hazes down the mountain slopes. It is their land.

Families adopt an acre here, a hectare there. Some have been tending the same patch since early in the twentieth century, devoting weekends to watering and shoring up some stretch of heath or gorse or scrub pine.

Pilots on commuter flights routinely open their windows and toss grass seeds over the rocky landscape, in hopes a few will find purchase.

Towns and cities reclaim the produce of their toilets, collecting sewage as if it were a precious resource. As it is. For after treatment, the soil of the night goes straight to the barren slopes, to succor surviving trees against the bitter wind.

A dust colors the clouds above the seas of Iceland.

At the island's southern fringe, a cluster of new volcanoes spills fresh lava into the sea, sending steam spirals curling upward. Tourists gawp at the spectacle and speak in envy of the Icelanders' "growing" land. But when natives look to the sky, they see a haze of diminishment that could not be replaced by anything as simple or vulgar as mere magma.

A dusty wind blows away the hills of Iceland. At sea, a few plankton benefit, temporarily, from the unexpected nurturance. Then, as they are wont to do, they die and their carcasses rain as sediment upon the patient ocean bottom. In time the layers will creep underground, to melt and glow and eventually burst forth again, to bring another island to life.

Short-term calamities are nothing to the master recycling system. In the end, it reuses even dust.

**B
I
O
S
P
H
E
R
E**

• Nelson Grayson had arrived in the Ndebele canton of Kuwenezi with two changes of clothes, a satchel of stolen Whatifs, and an inflated sense of his own importance. All were gone by the time, nine months later, he gathered his tools by the Level Fourteen Ape-iary and stepped through the hissing airlock into a bitter-bright, air-conditioned savannah. By then, of course, it was far too late to regret the reckless way he'd spent the profits from his smuggled software. Too late to seek another career path.

By then, Nelson felt irrevocably committed to shoveling baboon shit for a living.

It was not a highly regarded occupation. In fact, the keepers would have assigned robots the job, if not for the monkeys' annoying habit of nibbling plastic. As yet, robots lacked the kind of survival instincts Nelson had been born with—courtesy of a million years of frightened ancestors.

At least, each of those ancestors had survived long enough to beget another in the chain leading to him. In his former life Nelson had never given much thought to that. But of late he'd grown to appreciate the accomplishment, especially as his employers reassigned him from habitat to habitat—catering to one wild and unpredictable species after another.

Most of his first months had been spent in the sprawling main ark —Kuwenezi Canton's chief contribution to the World Salvation Project, where scientists and volunteers recreated entire ecosystems under multi-tiered, vaulting domes, where gazelles and wildebeest ran across miniature ranges that looked and felt almost real. Nelson's first task had been to carry fodder to the ungulates and report when any looked sick. To his surprise, it wasn't all that hard. In fact, boredom made him ask for a more demanding job. And so they named him dung inspector.

Great. I had to open my mouth. If I ever make it home to Canada, you can bet I'll tell them what kind of hospitality you can expect in South Africa, these days.

It was apparently no different here in ark four—a tapered wedge of steel and reinforced glass two miles from Kuwenezi's main tower, sitting atop the canton's long-abandoned gold mine. Ark four was the gene-crafters' lab, where new types were sought that might endure the sleeting ultraviolet outside or adapt to the creeping deserts and shifting rains.

Nelson had nursed a fantasy that his reassignment here was a

promotion. But then the director had handed him the familiar electroprod and sampler, and sent him to face more baboons.

I hate baboons! I can feel *them lookin' at me. It's like I can tell
what they're thinking.*

Nelson did not like what he imagined going on in the minds of
baboons.

These monkeys were different at least. He could tell soon after
pushing into sight of a copse of grey-green acacia trees, their leaves
drooping in the dusty heat. Clustered beneath those gnarled limbs
were about forty creatures, darker than the tawny beasts he had
known in the main ark, and noticeably larger, too. They moved lazily,
as sensible creatures would under the noon sun—even moderated by
the expanse of reinforced glass overhead. Only idiotic humans like Dr.
B'Keli insisted on work in conditions like these.

Procrastinating, Nelson looked the troop over. Perhaps they
weren't completely natural baboons at all. Nelson had heard rumors
about some experiments . . .

His nostrils flared as fickle air currents wafted his way. They sure
smelled like baboons. And when he shuffled through the sharp savannah grass toward them, Nelson soon knew that any genetic differences
had to be minor. They still moved about on four feet, tails flicking,
stopping to pry open nuts or groom each other or snarl and cuff their
neighbors, jockeying for status and dominance within the stepped hierarchy of the troop.

Oh, they're baboons, all right.

As soon as he came in sight, the troop rearranged itself, with
strong young males taking posts at the periphery. Grizzled, powerful
elders rose up on haunches to watch him nonchalantly.

Nelson knew these creatures lived mostly as vegetarians. He also
knew they ate meat whenever they could. Until the collapse of the
planetary ozone layer and the accompanying weather changes, baboons had been among the most formidable wild species in Africa. It
had amazed Nelson when he first overheard, a month ago, one scientist commenting that mankind had evolved alongside such adversar-
ies.

I'll never call a caveman stupid again, he vowed as one of the
creatures lazily bared impressive fangs at him. *Paranoid, yes. Cavemen
must've been real paranoid. But paranoia ain't so dumb.*

At least the troop appeared calm and well fed. But that was deceptive. Back in the main ark Nelson had come to compare life in a
baboon troop with an ongoing—often violent—soap opera without
words.

He saw one senior male rock on his haunches, watching a pregnant female seek tasty grubs under nearby rocks. Rhythmically smacking his lips, the patriarch pulled in his chin and flattened his ears, exposing white eyelid patches. The female responded by ambling over to sit by him, facing away. Methodically, he began picking through her fur, removing dirt, bits of dead skin, and the occasional parasite.

Another female approached and began nudging the expectant mother to move over and share the male's attention. The screeching fit that ensued was brief and inconsequential as such things went. In a minute the two had been cuffed into silence and all three monkeys turned away, minding their own business again.

Nelson's job was to sample monkey droppings for a routine microflora survey—whatever that was. As he approached, he recalled what Dr. B'Keli had told him after his first, unpleasant encounter with baboons.

"Don't *ever* look them in the eye. That was exactly the wrong thing to do! The dominant males will take it as a direct challenge."

"Fine," Nelson had answered, wincing as the nurse sutured two narrow bites on his posterior. "*Now* you tell me!"

But of course, it really had all been in the introductory tapes he was supposed to have watched, back when his funds first ran out and he found himself willing to take a job, any job. Those painful bites reinforced the then startling revelation that tape learning might actually have practical value, after all.

Tutored by experience, he now kept the electroprod ready, but pointed away in a nonthreatening manner. With his other hand, Nelson pushed the sticklike dung sampler into a brown mass half hidden in the grass. Buzzing flies rose indignantly.

I don't like Dr. B'Keli. For one thing, despite his "authentic" sounding name, the biologist's caramel features were suspiciously pale. He even had light-colored eyes.

Of course whites *could* legally work in all but two of the Federation's cantons. And nobody else, from the director on down, seemed to care that a *blanke* held high position among the Ndebele. Still, Nelson nursed resentment over the subtle discrimination his settler parents used to suffer from whites, back in the Yukon new town of his birth, and had imagined the tables would be turned here, where blacks ruled and even U.N. rights inspectors were held at bay.

Now he knew how naive he'd been, expecting these people to welcome him like a long-lost brother. In fact, Kuwenezi was a lot like those boom town suburbs of White Horse. Both seethed with ambition and indolence, with rising and falling hopes . . . and with authority figures insisting on hard work if you wanted to eat.

Hard work had turned his parents' filthy refugee camp into bus-

tling, prosperous Little Nigeria—commercial center for the new farming districts scattered across the thawing tundra. Little Nigeria's
immigrant merchants and shopkeepers turned their backs on Africa.
They sang "Oh, Canada" and cheered the Voyageurs on the teli. His
folks worked dawn to dusk, sent money to his sister at that Vancouver
college, and politely pretended not to hear when some drunkard pa-
tronizingly "welcomed" them to a frontier that belonged as much to
them as to any beer-swilling Canuck land speculator.

Well, I didn't forget. And I won't.

The sampler finished digesting its bit of dung and signaled. Nelson shook loose the brown remnant. After the initial sensation of his
arrival the baboons had settled down again. Calm prevailed. Momentarily, at least.

Strange, how over the last few weeks he had grown so much more
confident in his ability to "read" the moods of his animal charges.
Behaviors that had been opaque to him before were now clear, such as
their never-ending struggle over *hierarchy*. The word was used repeatedly in those dreary indoctrination tapes, but it had taken personal
contact to start seeing all the ladders of power running through
baboon society.

The males' struggles for dominance were noisy, garish affairs.
Their bushy manes inflated to make them seem twice their size. That,
plus snarling displays of teeth, usually caused one or the other to back
down. Still, over in the main ark Nelson had witnessed one male
savannah baboon spilling a rival's entrails across the gray earth. The
red-muzzled victor screamed elation across the waving grasses.

It had taken a bit longer to realize that females, too, battled over
hierarchy . . . seldom as extravagantly as the males, and involving
not so much simple breeding rights as food and status. Still, their
rancor could be longer lasting, more resolute.

The troop's dominant male stared at him, a huge brute massing at
least thirty-five kilos. Scars along the creature's grizzled flanks
sketched testimony of former battles. Wherever he moved, others
quickly got out of his way. The patriarch's expression was serene.

Now there's a bloke who gets respect.

Nelson couldn't help thinking of his own triumphs and more
frequent failures back in White Horse, where the flash of a knife
sometimes decided a boy's claim to the "tribal pinnacle"—or even his
life. Girls, too, had their ways of cutting each other down. Then there
were all the power pyramids of school and town, of work and society.
Hierarchies. They all had that in common.

Moreover, not one of those hierarchies had appeared to want or value *him*. It was an uncomfortable insight, and Nelson hated the baboons all the more for making it so clear.

Nelson's sweaty grip on the electroprod tightened as a pair of young adults, maybe twenty kilos each, settled down a few meters away to pick through each others' fur. One adolescent turned and yawned at him, gaping wide enough to swallow Nelson's leg up to his calf. Nelson edged away some distance before resuming with another pile of turds.

"I think I might like to work with animals," he had told them when he first arrived at Kuwenezi, his one-way air ticket used up and his supply of bootlegged Whatifs spread across the placement officer's desk.

Shortly before making the fateful decision to come here, Nelson had seen a documentary about the canton's scientists—Africans fighting to save Africa. It was a romantic image. So when asked what work he'd like to do as a new citizen, the first thing to come to mind had been the Ark Project. *"Of course I'll want to invest my money first. I may prefer to work part-time, y'know."*

The placement officer had glanced down at the software capsules Nelson had pirated from the White Horse office of the CBC. *"Your contribution suffices for provisional admission,"* he had said. *"And I think we can find you suitable work."*

Nelson grimaced at the recollection. "Right. Shoveling monkey shit. That's real suitable." But his money was gone now, lavished on instant new friends who proved stylishly fickle when the juice ran out. And back in Canada the CBC had sworn out a local warrant for his arrest.

The sampler beeped. Nelson wiped its tip and glanced back at the two young males. They had been joined by a small female carrying a baby. As he moved on in search of more dung, they followed him.

Nelson kept them in sight while he probed the next pile. The young female looked fidgety. She kept glancing back at the troop. After a couple of minutes, she approached one of the males and held out her baby to him.

After six months in the arks, Nelson had a pretty good idea what the young mother was trying to do. Adult baboons were often fascinated by babies. Top-rank females, *tough mamas* Nelson called them, used this to their advantage, letting others help care for their infants, as if granting their inferiors a special favor.

Other females *feared* uninvited attention to their offspring. Sometimes the one taking the baby never gave it back again. So a low-status mother sometimes tried to recruit protectors.

Still, this was the first time Nelson had ever seen the attempt so direct. The infant cooed appealingly at the big male, and its mother made grooming gestures. But the male only inspected the baby idly and then turned away to scratch after insects in the soil.

Nelson blinked, suddenly experiencing one of those unexpected, unwanted moments of vivid recollection. It was a memory of one Saturday night two years ago, and a girl he had met at the New Lagos Club.

The first part of that encounter had been perfection. She seemed to dial in on him from across the room, and when they danced her moves were as smooth as a rapitrans rail and just as electric. Then there were her eyes. In them he was so sure he read a promise of enthusiasm for whoever won her. They left early. Escorting her home to her tiny coldwater flat, Nelson had felt alive with anticipation.

Meeting her elderly aunt in the kitchen hadn't been promising, but the girl simply sent the old woman off to bed. He remembered reaching for her then. But she held him off and said, *"I'll be right back."*

While waiting, he heard soft noises from the next room. The rustle of fabric heightened his sense of expectation. But when she emerged again, she was still fully dressed, and in her arms she held a two-year-old child.

"Isn't he cute?" she said, as the infant rubbed his eyes and looked up from Nelson's lap. *"Everyone says he's the best-behaved little boy in White Horse."*

Nelson had shelved his sexual hopes at once. His memory was vague about what followed, but he recalled a long, embarrassed silence, punctuated by fumbling words as he maneuvered the child off his lap and worked his way toward the door. But one image he recalled later with utter clarity—it was that last, unnerving, *patient* expression on the young woman's face before he turned and fled.

Nelson realized later she'd been worse than crazy. She'd had a *plan.* And for some reason he came away from that episode feeling he was the one who had failed.

The little mother baboon turned to look directly at him and Nelson shivered at a strange moment of déjà vu. Summoning B'Keli's injunction against direct eye contact, he found much to do, searching for more piles to check.

The expanse of superhard glass overhead might keep out the ultraviolet, but it hardly eased the savannah heat. Artificial mimicry of the greenhouse effect made it stifling, in spite of the blowing fans. As he had been doing for a few weeks now, Nelson took humidity and temperature readings from his belt monitor and noted the direction of the desultory breeze. Slowly, he was coming to recognize the way even a man-made environment had its "seasons," its "natural" responses to unnatural controls.

His sampling path soon took him toward the edge of the habitat where slanted panes met the rim wall. Trays of cables circuited the habitat two meters high. Through the transparent barrier he could see the dun hillsides and sunburnt wheat fields of a land once called Rhodesia, then Zimbabwe, and several other names before finally becoming Ndebele Canton of the Federation of Southern Africa.

It wasn't like any "Africa" Nelson had seen while growing up, lying prone in front of the B-movie channel. No elephants. No rhinos. Certainly no Tarzan here. At least he'd had enough sense not to flee Canada for his parents' lamented homeland. Everyone knew what had become of Nigeria. The rains that had abandoned this land now drenched the Bight of Africa, engulfing abandoned cities there.

Deserts or drowning. Africa just could not get a break.

Closer in view were the sealed chambers below this one, a series of glistening ziggurat terraces leading step by step toward the dusty ground, each sheltering a different habitat, a different midget ecosphere rescued from the ruined continent.

The coterie of curious baboons in his trail had grown by the time Nelson came closest to the glassy wall. They went about their business—eating, grooming, scuffling—but all the time watching him with a nonchalant fascination that drew them in his wake. Each time he finished sampling a pile of feces, several monkeys would poke at the disturbed mass, perhaps curious what he found so attractive about ordinary turds.

Why are they following me? he wondered, perplexed by the monkeys' behavior, so unlike that of their cousins in the main ark. Once, the alpha male stared directly at Nelson, who was careful not to accept the implied challenge. Nervously, he realized the entire troop now lay between him and the corridor airlock.

The little mother and her baby remained his closest adherents. Nelson noticed her anxiety grow as five larger females approached, several of them clearly high-status matriarchs, whose sleek infants rode their backs like lords. One of the newcomers handed her baby to a helper and then began sidling toward the solitary mother.

The young one screeched defiance, clutching her infant close and backing away. Her eyes darted left and right, but none of the creatures nearby seemed more than vaguely interested in her plight. Certainly none of the big, lazy males offered any succor.

Nelson felt a twinge of sympathy. But what could he do? Rather than watch, he turned and hurried several meters to another set of droppings. He wiped his brow on his shirtsleeve and put his back to the blazing sun. In the muggy heat daydreams transported him back to his own room in the cool northlands, with his own bed, his own teli, his own little fridge stuffed with icy Labatts, and his mother's pungent Yoruba cooking wafting upstairs from the kitchen. The reverie was pleasant beyond all expectation, but it shattered in an instant when he felt a sudden sharp tug on his pants leg.

Nelson swiveled, holding the stun-prod in both shaking hands. Then he exhaled an oath. It was only the little female again—now wide-eyed and sweat-damp, wearing a grimace of fear. Still, she did not back away when he shook the rod at her. Rather, she edged forward, trembling and awkward on two feet, clasping her infant with one paw while in the other she held forth something small and brown.

Nelson broke into nervous laughter. "Great! That's all I need. She's offering me shit!"

Flies buzzed as she shuffled another step, extending her piquant gift.

"G'wan, beat it, eh? I got enough to sample. And it's supposed t'be *undisturbed* shit, get it?"

She seemed to understand at least part of it. The rejection part. With some retained dignity she spilled the feces onto the dry earth and wiped her paw on grass stems, all the time watching him.

The other monkeys had backed away when he shouted. Now they returned to their affairs as if nothing had happened. At first glance, one might guess they were content, foraging and lazing in the warm afternoon. But Nelson could sense undercurrents of tension. The patriarch's nostrils flared as he sniffed, then resumed grooming one of his underlings.

This is one troop of insane monkeys, all right. Nelson wondered if there were still openings hauling hay to giraffes. With a resigned sigh he moved on, calculating how many more piles of crap he had to cover before at last he could get out of here, shower, and go nurse a beer or two—or four.

Screams suddenly erupted behind him, shrill peals of panic and fury. Nelson turned, his nerves finally tipped over into anger. "Now I've had *enough* . . ."

The words choked off as a small maelstrom of dark brown landed in his arms. Flailing for balance, he nearly fell over as a screeching creature clawed at his dungarees, scratching his shoulders and arms. Nelson staggered backward swearing, trying to protect his face and throw the baboon off. But the creature only scrambled around behind his shoulders, enclosing his neck in a fierce constriction.

Nelson wheezed. "Damn stupid crazy . . ." Then, just as sud-

denly, he forgot all about the small monkey on his back. He gaped at
the entire troop, now arrayed in a half circle around him.

Moments ticked by, punctuated by the pounding of his heart.
Most of the dark animals merely watched, as if this were great entertainment. The lead male licked himself lazily.

But facing Nelson directly now were five large, grimacing beasts
who appeared to have something much more active in mind. They
paced back and forth, turning and barking at him, tails flicking expres-
sively.

The troop's dominant females, he knew quickly. But why were
they angry with him? The matriarchs' band moved forward. Nelson
did not like the gleam he saw in their eyes.

"Stay . . . stay back," he gasped, and brandished the stunner-
prod. At least he thought it was the prod, until a second glance
showed it to be the *sampler*. Where had the damned prod gone!

He saw it at last several meters away. The biggest male was pressing his broad, multicolored snout against the white plastic, sniffing it.
Cursing, he realized he must have dropped his only weapon in that
initial moment of panic.

Nelson had more immediate problems than recovering Kuwenezi
Ark property. Less savagely intimidating than adult males, the females
nonetheless growled impressively. Their teeth shone saliva-bright, and
he knew why even leopards and hyenas did not dare attack baboons in
a group.

It wasn't hard to figure who it was cowering on his back, pressing
her infant between them. In desperation, the little mother had apparently decided to enlist his "protection" whether he offered it or not.
He stepped sideways, in the direction of the exit, speaking soothingly
to the angry females. "Now . . . take it easy, eh? Peace an' love . . .
uh, nature is harmony, right?"

They didn't seem particularly interested in reason, nor in slogans
borrowed from the Earth Mother movement. They spread to cut him
off.

*I heard they can be pretty mean in their fights between females
. . . I even saw one kill the baby of another. But this is ridiculous!
Don't they care I'm a man? We feed them. We made this place, to
save them!*

He realized with a sinking sensation that only one of these monkeys had any respect for him. And that shivering creature had turned
to him only because nobody more important gave a damn.

Nelson looked around. One of the outer airlocks was just thirty
meters away, opening onto the roof of the habitat below. He had no
sun hat or goggles, but could easily stand the harsh daylight long

enough to dash to another entrance. He began sidestepping that way slowly, maintaining a soothing monologue. "That's right . . . I'll just be goin', then . . . no need for trouble, eh?"

He was halfway to his destination when the following monkeys seemed to grasp his intent. In a blur, two of them moved quickly to cut off that escape. Together, the pair of irate females blocking his path didn't even equal his mass, but their tough hides looked all but impervious while Nelson's own skin, already throbbing and bleeding from his little passenger's unintended damage, seemed tender and useless against those savage, glistening canines.

Both airlocks were out, then. A utilities tray circuited the wall at about man height—the only conceivable refuge in sight. Nelson dropped the sampler and ran for it.

Their angry screeches amplified off the reflecting glass. His pursuers' rapid footfalls paced the pounding of his heart as Nelson poured everything he had into reaching the wall. The sound of snapping jaws triggered a jolt of adrenaline. He took two final strides and leaped for the conduit tray, his fingers tearing for a hold on the slippery metal mesh. Fangs snagged his pants and laid a bloody runnel along his right calf as he swung his legs up at the last moment.

As soon as he was wrapped around the tray, his little passenger scrambled over him to clamber onto the cluster of pipes and cables. One foot squashed his nose as she hoisted her infant onto a nearby stanchion, but Nelson was too exhausted to do more than just hang there while the creatures below leaped and snapped at him some more, missing his rear end by inches. Inside, he had left only enough energy to curse himself for an idiot.

They gave me a chance! he realized. The matriarchs had waited after the young female leaped on him, to see what he'd do. He could have rejected her then—could have pried her loose and put her down.

Hell, all I'd have had to do was sit down . . . *she'd have had to run for it.*

Of course, the conclusion was inevitable anyway. The little monkey didn't have a chance. But at least it wouldn't have involved him. Now Nelson understood the other baboons' anger. He'd violated his own neutrality. He had taken sides.

When he finally caught his breath, he wriggled and puffed his way atop the narrow platform. Seated a meter away, his unwelcome charge licked her baby and watched him. When he moved to sit up, she backed off a bit to give him room.

"You," he panted, pointing at her, "are a lot of trouble."

To his surprise she turned her back on him in a motion he recognized. She was asking him to groom her!

"Fat chance o' that," he muttered.

Morosely, he looked around. The troop seemed content simply to observe for a while. The big male examining Nelson's stunner hadn't found the trigger—worse luck—but he *had* dragged it halfway to the acacia grove before losing interest and abandoning it. Now the nearest exit was much closer than his weapon.

The cabal of high-status females sat calmly on their haunches, looking up at him. One by one they left briefly to check on their own infants—in "day care" with lower-status monkeys—then quickly rejoined the impromptu posse–lynch mob.

Nelson turned and pounded the thick pane of barrier glass behind him in frustration. A low hum was the only response . . . that and bruised knuckles. The Bangkok crystal sheeting was incredibly tough. He didn't even contemplate trying to break it.

Beyond lay lower terraces of the ark tower, each sheltered beneath still more tightly-sealed glass. Nelson could make out forest growth within the ecosystem just below this one. In addition to preserving a patch of jungle, it provided part of the passive atmosphere regeneration that made ark four all but self-sufficient.

Movement caught his eye. Along the treetops below he saw *people* walking through the forest canopy, along a catwalk skyway. Nelson squinted, and recognized both the dark face of the ark director and the coffee features of Dr. B'Keli. They were showing off the new artificial ecosphere to a white woman, small and frail and quite elderly. From their expressions, they seemed eager to make a good impression. She nodded, and at one point reached out to pluck a leaf and rub it between her hands.

"Hey! Up here! Look up here!" Nelson beat the glass—an effort that seemed required given his circumstances, though he had no real hope of being heard.

Sure enough, the group strolled on, oblivious to the drama unfolding over their heads.

Damn them! Damn the arks. Damn the Salvation Project . . . and damn me for ever getting myself into this mess!

At that moment Nelson loathed everybody he could think of—from twentieth-century humanity, who had wrecked Earth's delicate balance, to the voters and bureaucrats of the twenty-first, who spent fortunes trying to save what was left, to his caveman ancestors, who had been stupid enough to grow big, useless brains that everybody was always trying to cram with book learning, when what a guy *really* needed were claws, and big teeth, and skin as tough as old leather!

He remembered the leader of the Bantus, a "youth club" he had tried to join back in White Horse. It wasn't supposed to be run like an old-style urban gang, but that was how it turned out anyway. For months Nelson had come home from an endless series of "initiations," each time more bruised than the last—until it finally dawned on him that he *just wasn't wanted . . .* that his only use to them was as an outlet for their "organized group activity"—the tribe strengthening its internal bonding by beating up on someone else.

He glanced across the prairie at the top male baboon, so serene and in charge, yawning complacently and ferociously. Nelson hated the patriarch and envied him.

If I had a hide like that . . . If I had fangs . . .

His attention was drawn back by the shaking of his unsteady platform. Nelson turned to see that the little female was hopping up and down, grimacing, tugging at his sleeve. "Stop that!" he cried. "This thing isn't built to take that kind of . . ." Then he looked beyond and saw what had her so upset.

Her foes must have found one of the access ladders. Or maybe they had boosted each other, forming a multimonkey pyramid. However they managed it, three of the largest were now picking their way along the cable tray, heading in this direction.

"Oh hell," he sighed. The young mother backed against him. Her infant's dark eyes were wide with fear.

Nelson glanced down at the ground, and saw with surprise that the way was clear below! As he watched, the head male and his followers cleared a path, cuffing other baboons aside. The alpha male looked up at Nelson then, and tilted his head.

With uncanny insight, Nelson suddenly understood. He had only to jump, and he could run all the way to the airlock unmolested before the crazy females caught up with him!

Perhaps. But he'd never make it encumbered. He exchanged a look with the bull. That, it seemed, was part of the bargain. He was not to interfere in the natural working out of their social order. Nelson nodded, comprehending. He waited till the small female next to him was fully engaged, all her attention given to answering the threatening grimaces of her stalkers. At that moment Nelson slipped over the edge.

It was a bad landing. He came to his feet gasping at a sharp twinge in his ankle. Hurriedly, though, he hopped away several meters before pausing to glance back.

Nobody was following him. In fact, the troop mostly faced the other way, watching the drama reach its climax on the ledge overhead. The bull appeared to have dismissed him completely now that he was leaving the scene.

Burdened by her infant, though, the small mother could not fol-

low him. She stared after him instead, blinking with a mute disappointment he could read only too well. Then she had no time for
anything but immediate concerns; with her infant on her back, she
turned to bare her teeth at her assailants.

Nelson backed away another two steps toward the safety of the
exit, now beckoning only twenty or so meters away. Still, he couldn't
tear his eyes away. He was captivated by the small baboon's stand,
grimacing final defiance at her foes, holding them back with brave
lunges. It was an effort she could not keep up for long.

From experience, he knew the other females did not seek *her*
death, only the baby's. It was a bit of savagery he had not questioned
until today. Now though, for the very first time, Nelson wondered
. . . why.

It was so cruel. So awful. It reminded him of *human* nastiness.
And yet, in all the time he had been here, he had never asked the
experts about this or any other matter. It had been as if . . . as if to
do so would be to admit too openly the ignorance he had nurtured for
so long. His frail, rigid facade of cynicism could not bear curiosity.
Once he started asking questions, where would it stop?

Nelson felt a pressure building in his head. It couldn't be restrained. . . .

"Why?" he demanded aloud and felt his voice catch at the
sound.

Protecting her child, the mother backed away awkwardly, shriek-
ing at her enemies.

"Why's it *like* this!" he asked, to no one present save himself.

Barely aware of what he was doing, Nelson found himself limping
forward. He felt eyes track him as he held up his arms.

"Hey, you!" he called. "I'm back. Come on down . . ."

He had no need to repeat himself. The mother monkey grabbed
her baby and launched herself from the doomed redoubt, landing in
his arms as a taut bundle of scrawny brown fur, clawing for purchase
on his already bleeding shoulders. Nelson hurriedly stepped away,
fully resigned that now there was no way he'd reach the airlock in
time. Sure enough, when he glanced back a crowd of angry baboons
were catching up fast. The original pursuers had now been joined by
several more irate monkeys, at least two of them large, pink-faced
males, all dashing his way, screaming.

Nelson did not bother trying to run any further. He turned and
scanned the ground for anything—anything at all—until his gaze fell
upon a white rod.

His dung sampler.

Sighing that it wasn't even the inadequate shock-prod, Nelson snatched it up, carrying the motion through just in time to catch a leaping baboon in the snout. The creature screamed and tumbled whimpering away.

The females scattered, dispersing on all sides. Dark eyes peered at him through the tall grass.

Panting, blinking in surprise, Nelson wondered. *Was that it? Hey, maybe all it takes is the right bluff!*

Then he saw why the females had given up so easily. They were moving aside to make room for a new force.

Rumbling with a low rage, the patriarch and his entourage arrived. Nine big males, their manes fully inflated, ambled with patient assuredness toward him and his frightened, weary charge. Their pace might be confident, but flecks of saliva dripped from their curled lips. Nelson read their eyes, and knew them for killers.

And yet, in that same suspended moment, Nelson had time to feel something he had never before imagined . . . a strange, crystal *calm*. As if this was all somehow familiar. As if he had been in this place, in this very predicament, many times before.

We were all like this, once, he realized, feeling the weight of his makeshift cudgel. *White, black, yellow . . . men, women . . . our ancestors all shared this, long ago . . .*

Back when Africa was new . . .

Human beings had changed the world, for well and ill. Would their efforts now save what was left? Nelson couldn't begin to guess.

All he knew for sure was that for the first time he *cared*.

Nelson and the little mother shared communion in a moment's eye contact. Leaving her baby clinging to his shoulder, she slipped down to stand beside his left knee, guarding his flank.

The pack slowed and circled. The bull shook his head, as if reading something different in Nelson's stance, in his eyes. But Nelson suddenly knew the creature saw only part of it.

We humans almost wrecked the whole world. Humans may yet save it . . .

You don't mess with guys who can do shit like that.

"Okay, it's nine against two," he said, hefting his rude club, smacking its reassuring weight in the palm of his left hand.

"That sounds about right."

When at last they charged, Nelson was ready for them.

☐ **Running Census: Net datum request** [☐ ArBQ-P 9782534782]
U.S. Population Over Age 65

Year	Percent
1900	4.0%
1980	11.3%
2038	20.4%

Voting Clout of U.S. Citizen Age Groups

Citizen Age Group	Percent Who Vote	Political "Clout Factor"
18–25	19%	5
26–35	43%	23
36–52	62%	39
53–65	78%	44
66–99	93%	71

National Comparisons

Nation	Citizenry Over 65	Seniors' Voting Clout
Japan	26.1%	87
U.S.A.	20.4%	71
Han China	20.2%	79
Russian S.F.S.R.	19.1%	81
Yakutsk S.S.R.	12.1%*	37
Yukon Province, Canada	11.7%*	31
Sea State	10.0%	19
Republic of Patagonia	6.2%*	12**

*Biased by effects of immigration.
**Interactive and remote voting outlawed; polling allowed in person only, at voting stations.

The rattling truck stank to high heaven.

It wasn't just the fumes from its gasoline engine—Logan Eng was used to riding high-priority construction equipment. Fragrant, high-octane aromatics were as familiar as the grit of countless deserts or the metal tang of grease and drilling mud. Even the sweat fetor pervading the cracked upholstery spoke pungently of honorable work.

But in addition to all that, Logan's driver was a tobacco addict. Worse, he didn't take his nicotine in pills or spray. No, Enrique Vasquez actually *smoked* paper-wrapped bundles of shredded weed, inhaling the sooty vapors with deep sighs of satisfaction.

Logan eyed in unwilling fascination the glowing ember that seemed ever about to fall off the tip of Enrique's cigarette. So far in this lurching ride across rugged Basque countryside, that mesmerizing bit of ash hadn't yet set off flaming catastrophe. But he could not help picturing it landing amid the floorboards, there igniting a great ball of exploding petrol fumes.

Of course Logan knew better. (With his forebrain!) Only a generation ago, over a billion cigarettes had been consumed each year. And back in TwenCen, the rate had reached staggering *trillions*. If the things were as unsafe as they looked, not a forest or city would be left standing.

"You will want to stay for our National Day celebrations!" Enrique bellowed to be heard over the engine and rattling springs. The hand holding the cigarette draped the open window casing, leaving the other to handle both steering and shifting. The complaining gearbox set Logan's teeth on edge in sympathy.

"I wish I could!" he shouted back. "But my job in Iberia's finished tomorrow. I'm due back in Louisiana—"

"Too bad! It would you make happy. Glorious fireworks we'll see! Everyone drunk gets. Then the young men, fun with the bulls have!"

The Basque were the oldest people in Europe, and proud of their heritage. Some said their language came from the Neolithic hunters who first claimed this land from the retreating ice. In a Bilbao museum, Logan had seen replicas of tiny boats Basque sailors used long ago, to hunt whales out on the rude Atlantic. *They must be very brave or suicidal*, he thought, then and now.

Logan gasped as his guide swerved, sending plumes of dust and gravel billowing toward an onrushing lumber hauler. The drivers exchanged obscene gestures with a vehemence that seemed quite sociable, in its macho way. Enrique shouted parting insults as the pickup roared along the rocky verge of a hundred-meter drop. Logan swallowed hard.

They sped past tumbled stones that must once have been some ancient wall or boundary. Conifer forests blurred where hardscrabble farms and pastures once covered these slopes. Here and there, commercial quick-pine gave way to newer stands of cedar and oak, planted in grudging compliance with the Balanced Reforestation Treaty, though their slower growth would profit only future generations.

Enrique grinned at him, all traces of indignation already forgotten. "So. Have they, the dams' safety, determined yet?"

Logan managed to parse the strange version of Simglish they taught here. He nodded.

"I spent a week in Badajoz, going over every datum within two hundred klicks of the quake epicenter. Those dams will last a long while yet."

Enrique grunted. "In Castile they are good engineers. Not like down in Granada, where the land they are letting go to hell." He spat out the window.

Logan refrained comment. *Never get involved in interregional prejudices* was a principal rule. Anyway, nobody could stop the climate from changing, since the Sahara had vaulted the Straits to begin southern Europe's desertification.

Blame it on the greenhouse effect, Logan thought. *Or the shifting Gulf Stream. Hell, blame it on gnomes. Let the scientists figure out causes. What matters to me is how much we can save.*

Logan closed his eyes and tried to sleep. After all, if Enrique sent the truck over a cliff, watching it happen wouldn't change it. Anyway, if he'd had ambitions to live forever he'd never have become a field engineer. He hardly noticed the rhythmic jouncing of his skull against the metal door frame—a relatively trivial irritant. Dozing, he found himself recalling how Daisy—his former wife and Claire's mother— used to approve of his professional plans.

You'll fight the system from within, she had told him when they were students and in love. *Meanwhile, I'll battle it from the outside.*

The plan had sounded bold and perfect then. Neither of them had figured on the way people change . . . he by learning compromise, she by growing more adamant with each passing year.

Maybe she only married me to get at her family. It wasn't the first time the thought had occurred to Logan. At Tulane, she had said he was the only boy who seemed completely unimpressed with her money and name—which was true enough. After all, financiers just own things, while a skilled person with a job he loves has much, much more.

How strange then, years later, for Daisy to accuse him of being a "tool of rich-pig land rapists." All that time it had been in his head that he was keeping his side of their bargain, forsaking lucrative deals in favor of confronting incompetence in the field, compelling governments and egotistic planners with grandiose schemes to look more than a decade ahead, to work with nature instead of always against her.

Yes, he also had been motivated by a joy of craft and the pleasure of solving real, palpable puzzles. Was that a betrayal? Can't a man have several loves at once—a wife, a child, and the world?

For Daisy, apparently, there could be only one. The world. And on her terms.

The truck passed out of the forest, zooming along dusty headlands. Sunlight reconnoitered the edges of Logan's sunglasses as his thoughts drifted randomly. The zigzag speckles under his eyelids reminded him at one point of waves on a seismograph.

Queer waves, the professor from the University of Córdoba had called them, ecstatically describing the recent surge of bizarre earthquakes. At first Logan's interest had been solely to estimate possible hidden damage to large structures such as dams. But as he looked over the frequency spectrum of the tremors he saw one strangeness more peculiar than all the others.

Sharp peaks at wavelengths of 59, 470, 3,750, and 30,000 meters.

Octaves, Logan realized at the time. *Eightfold harmonics. I wonder what that could possibly mean?*

Then there was the mystery of one drilling tower that had vanished. Water miners, digging an exploratory well when the quakes struck, had run scurrying for shelter, some of them stumbling from vision blurred to the point of blindness. When it was over, and at last they could see again, it was only to stare blankly at the place where the rig had stood. There lay only a hole, as if some giant had come along and uprooted everything!

Including its tower, the entire drill string had just reached a length of 470 meters.

Of course, it could be a coincidence. But even so, what on Earth could convert quake energy into . . .

"Señor." The driver interrupted Logan's lazy musing. Enrique nudged him with an elbow and Logan cracked one eyelid. "Hm?"

"Señor, you can the bay oversee now."

Logan sat up, rubbing his eyes . . . then inhaled sharply. Instantly all thought of quakes and harmonic mysteries vanished. He gripped the door frame, looking across a sea that was the same color as Daisy McClennon's eyes.

For all her craziness, her obsessiveness, the single-mindedness that eventually drove him from their home—his former wife's eyes were still the ideal by which Logan measured all beauties. Amid the noisy student demonstrations where they first met, she had thought it was shared ideological fervor that made him ignore her money and look directly at her instead. But in truth, it had been those eyes.

Transfixed, he didn't even look for the tidal power station that was their destination. He had room right then for just the sea. It was enough to fill his soul.

The poor, tortured transmission screamed as Enrique downshifted and sent the rattling truck careening toward the aquamarine waters of the Bay of Biscay.

☐

Along the banks of the Yenisey River, immigrants lay out their new farms and villages. It is a long, hard process, but they have seen starvation and the ruin of their homelands—covered by rising waters or blowing sands. They look across endless waves of rippling steppe grass and vow to adapt, to do whatever it takes to survive.

Relocation officials tell them—*No, you may not use that valley over there; it is reserved for the reindeer.*

No, you may not tap the river at that spot; flow rates must be maintained for proper oxygenation.

You must choose one of these proven designs for your houses. You'll be glad you did when the arctic winter comes, and you wish the walls were thicker still.

Staring at vast reaches of perspiring tundra, swatting persistent gnats and mosquitoes, the newcomers find it hard to imagine this sweltering place blowing neck-deep in snow. Shivering at the thought, they nod earnestly and try to remember everything they are told. Grateful to be here at all, they thank their Russian and Yakut hosts, and promise to be good citizens.

The tall, well-fed Soviets smile. *That is well*, they say. *Work hard. Be kind to the land. Restrict your birth rate as you have promised. Send your children to school. Before, you were Kurds, Bengalis, Brazilians. Now you are people of the North. Adapt to it, and it will treat you well.*

The refugees nod. And thinking of all those left behind them, waiting to come to the land of opportunity, they vow once more to do well.

"Watching, all the time watching . . . goggle-eye geeks. Soon as I
get out, I'm gonna Patagonia, buy it? That's where the youth
growth is. More ripe fruit like us, Cuzz. And not so many barrel
spoilers . . . rotten old apples that sit an' stink and *stare*
atcha . . ."

Remi agreed with Crat's assessment as the three of them
strode side by side down a gravel path through the park. Roland also
expressed approval, nudging Crat's shoulder. "That's staccato code,
boy-oh."

What brought on Crat's sudden outburst was the sight of yet
another babushka, glaring at them from a bench under one of the
force-grown shade trees as Remi and Roland and Crat scrambled up a
grassy bank from the culvert where they'd been smoking. The very
moment they came into view, the old woman laid her wire-knitting
aside and fixed them with the bug-eyed, opaque gape of her True-Vu
lenses—staring as if they were *freaks* or *aliens* out of some space-fic
vid, instead of three perfectly normal guys, just hanging around, doing
nobody any harm.

"My, my!" Remi whined sarcastically. "Is it my breath? Maybe
she smells . . . *tobacco*!"

"No joke, bloke," Roland replied. "Some of those new goggles've
got sniffer sensors on 'em. I hear the geek lobby in Indianapolis wants
to put even home-grown on the restrict list."

"No shit? Tobacco? Even? Roll over, Raleigh! I just gotta move
outta this state."

"Settlers ho, Remi?"

"Settlers ho."

The stare got worse as they approached. Remi couldn't see the
babushka's eyes, of course. Her True-Vu's burnished lenses didn't really have to be aimed directly at them to get a good record. Still, she
jutted out her chin and faced them square on, aggressively making the
point that their likenesses, every move they made, were being transmitted to her home unit, blocks from here, in real time.

Why do they have to do that? To Remi it felt like a provocation.
Certainly no one could mistake her tight-lipped expression as *friendly.*

Remi and his pals had promised their local tribes supervisor not to
lose their tempers with "senior citizens on self-appointed neighborhood watch." Remi did try, really. *It's just another geek. Ignore her.*

But there were so gor-sucking *many* geeks! According to the Net
census, one in five Americans were over 65 now. And it felt far worse
in Bloomington—as if oldsters were a ruling majority, staking out ev-

ery shady spot with their electronic sun hats and goggle-scanners, watching from porches, watching from benches, watching from lawn chairs . . .

It was Crat whose reserve broke as they approached that baleful inspection. Suddenly he capered. "Hey, granny!" Crat bowed with a courtly flourish. "Why don't you record this!" Roland giggled as Crat swept off his straw cowboy hat to display a garish scalp tattoo.

Merriment redoubled when she actually reacted! A sudden moue of surprise and revulsion replaced that glassy stare. She rocked back and turned away.

"Astonishing!" Roland cried, mimicking their least favorite teen-behaviors teacher at J. D. Quayle High School. He continued in a snooty, midwestern drawl. "It should be noted that this small urban band's totemistic innovation achieved its desired effect . . . which was? Anybody?"

"Shock value!" all three of them shouted in unison, clapping hands, celebrating a minor victory over their natural enemy.

Used to be, you could break a babushka's stare with an obscene gesture or show of muscular bluster—both protected forms of self-expression. But the biddies and codgers were getting harder to shake. Any time nowadays you actually made one of them yank back that awful, silent scrutiny was a triumph worth savoring.

"Freon!" Crat cursed. "Just once I'd like to catch some goggle geek alone, with fritzed sensors and no come-go record. Then I'd teach 'em it's *not polite to stare.*"

Crat emphasized his point with a fist, smacking his palm. Today, since it was cloudy, he had forsaken his normal Stetson for a plaid baseball cap, still acceptable attire for a Settler. His sunglasses, like Remi's, were thin, wire framed, and strictly for eye protection. Nothing electronic about them. They were a statement, repudiating the rudeness of geriatric America.

"Some people just got too much free time," Roland commented as the three of them sauntered near the babushka, barely skimming outside the twenty-centimeter limit that would violate her "personal space." Some oldsters were gearing up with sonar, even radar, to catch the most innocent infraction. They went out of their way to tempt you, creating slow-moving bottlenecks across sidewalks whenever they saw young people hurrying to get somewhere. They hogged escalators, acting as if they *hoped* you'd bump them, giving them any excuse to squeeze that police-band beeper, or raise the hue and cry, or file a long list of nuisance charges.

These days, in Indiana, juries were composed mostly of TwenCen grads anyway. Fellow retirement geeks who seemed to think youth itself a crime. So naturally, a guy *had to* accept the endless dares, skirting the edge whenever challenged.

"Granny could be doin' something useful," Crat paused to snarl, bending to really scrape the zone. "She could be gardening or collectin' litter. But no! *She's* gotta stare!"

Remi worried Crat might spit again. Even a miss would be a four-hundred-dollar fifth offense, and despite Granny's averted gaze those sensors were still active.

Fortunately, Crat let Remi and Roland drag him out of sight into the formal hedge garden. Then he leaped, fist raised, and shouted, "Yow, tomodachis!" pumped by nicotine and a sweet, if minor, victory. "Patagonia, yeah!" Crat gushed. "Would that be dumpit great? Kits like us run it all there."

"Not like here, in the land o' the old and the home of the grave," agreed Remi.

"Huh, say it! Why, I hear it's better'n even Alaska, or Tasmania."

"Better for Settlers!" Roland and Remi chanted in unison.

"And the music? Fuego-fire's the only beat that Yakuti Bongo-Cream *can't* meet."

Remi didn't care much about that. He liked the idea of emigrating for other reasons.

"Naw, cuzz. Patagonia's only the first step. It's a staging area, see? When they open up *Antarctica*, settlers from Patagonia'll have the jump. Just a hop across the water." He sighed. "We'll have new tribes, *real* tribes when the ice melts enough. Set it up our way. Real freedom. Real people."

Roland glanced at him sidelong. Months ago they had qualified as a youth gang, which meant mandatory tribal behaviors classes. That was okay, but Remi's friends sometimes worried he might actually be listening to what the profs were saying. And sometimes he did have to fight that temptation . . . the temptation to be interested.

No matter. It was a good afternoon to be with pals, drooping out in the park. It was well past the sweltering heat of midday—when those without air-conditioning sought shade in the hedge garden for their siestas—so right now people were scarce in this section of the garden. Just a couple of seedy ragman types, slumped and snoring under the fragrant oleanders. Whether they were dozers or dazers, Remi couldn't tell from here. As if the difference mattered.

"Real *privacy*, maybe," Roland agreed. "You just make sure that's in the constitution, Rem, if they nom you to write it."

Remi nodded vigorously. "Dumpit A-okay! Privacy! No gor-suckers watchin' your every move. Why, I hear back in TwenCen . . . aw, shit."

Sure enough, bored with just talking, Crat had gone over the top again. With no one in sight from this hedge-lined gravel path, he started drum-hopping down a line of multicolored trash bins, rattling their plastic sides with a stick, leaping up to dance on their flexing rims.

"*Sweet perspiration . . . Sweat inspiration . . .*" Crat chanted, skipping to the latest jingle by Phere-o-Moan.

"*Sniffin' it stiffens it . . .* " Roland countertimed, catching the excitement. He clapped, keeping time.

Remi winced, expecting one of the bins to collapse at any moment. "Crat!" he called.

"Damn what, damn who?" His friend crooned from on high, dance-walking the green container, shaking its contents of grass cuttings and mulch organics.

"U-break it—U-buy it," Remi reminded.

Crat gave a mock shiver of fear. "Look around, droogie. No civic-minded geepers, boy-chik. And cops need warrants." He hopped across to the blue bin for metals, making cans and other junk rattle.

True, no goggle-faces were in sight. And the police were limited in ways that didn't apply to citizens . . . or else even the aphids on the nearby bushes could be transmitting this misdemeanor to Crat's local youth officer, in real time.

"*An aroma for home-a, and a reek for the street . . .*"

Remi tried to relax. Anyway, what harm was Crat doing? Just having a little fun, was all. Still, he reached his limit when Crat started kicking wrappers and cellu-mags out of the paper-recycle bin. Misdemeanor fines were almost badges of honor, but mandatory-correction *felonies* were another matter!

Remi hurried to pick up the litter. "Get him down, Rollie," he called over his shoulder as he chased a flapping page of newsprint.

"Aw petrol! Lemme 'lone!" Crat bitched as Roland grabbed him around the knees and hauled him out of the last container. "You two aren't sports. You just—"

The complaint cut short suddenly, as if choked off. Picking up the last shred of paper, Remi heard rhythmic clapping from the path ahead. He looked up and saw they were no longer alone.

Bleeding sores, he cursed inwardly. *All we needed were Ra Boys.*

Six of them slouched by the curving hedge, not five meters away, grinning and watching this tableau—Remi clutching his flapping load of paper, and Roland holding Crat high like some really homely ballerina.

Remi groaned. *This could be really bad.*

Each Ra Boy wore from a thick chain round his neck the gleaming

symbol of his cult—a sun-sigil with bright metal rays as sharp as needles. Those overlay open-mesh shirts exposing darkly tanned torsos.
The youths wore no head coverings at all, of course, which would
"insult Ra by blocking the fierce love of his rays." Their rough, patchy
complexions showed where anti-onc creams had sloughed precancerous lesions. Sunglasses were their only allowance for the sleeting ultraviolet, though Remi had heard of fanatics who preferred going
slowly blind to even that concession.

One thing the Ra Boys had in common with Remi and his friends.
Except for wristwatches, they strode stylishly and proudly unencum-
bered by electronic gimcrackery . . . spurning the kilos of tech-
crutches everyone over twenty-five seemed to love carrying around.
What *man*, after all, relied on crap like that?

Alas, Remi didn't need Tribal Studies 1 to tell him that was as far
as teen solidarity went in the year 2038.

"Such a lovely song and dance," the tallest Ra Boy said with a
simper. "Are we rehearsing for a new amateur show to put on the Net?
Do please tell us so we can tune in. Where will it be playing? On Gong
channel four thousand and three?"

Roland dropped Crat so hurriedly, the Ra Boys broke up again. As
for Remi, he was torn between a dread of felonies and the burning
shame of being caught picking up litter like a citizen. To walk just
three steps and put it in the bin would cost him too much in pride, so
he crumpled the mass and stuffed it in his pocket—as if he had plans
for the garbage, later.

Another one joined the leader, sauntering forward. "Naw, what
we have here . . . see . . . are some neo-fem girlie-girls . . .
dressed up as Settlers. Only we caught them being girlie when . . .
when they thought no one was looking!" This Ra Boy seemed short of
breath and a bit droopy eyed. Remi knew he was a dozer when he
lifted an inhaler and took a long hit of pure oxygen from a hip flask.

"Hmm," the tall one nodded, considering the proposition. "Only
problem with that *hypothesis* is, why would anyone want to dress up
like a gor-sucking Settler in the first place?"

Remi saw Roland seize the growling Crat, holding him back.
Clearly the Ra Boys would love to have a little physical humor with
them. And just as clearly, Crat didn't give a damn about the odds.

But even though no geeps were watching now, dozens must have
recorded both parties converging on this spot . . . chronicles they'd
happily zap-fax to police investigating a brawl after the fact.

Not that fighting was strictly illegal. Some gangs with good lawyer programs had found loopholes and tricks. Ra Boys, in particular,
were brutal with sarcasm . . . pushing a guy so hard he'd lose his

temper and accept a nighttime battle rendezvous or some suicidal dare, just to prove he wasn't a sissy.

The tall one swept off his sunglasses and sighed. He minced several delicate steps and simpered. "Perhaps they are *Gaians*, dressing up as Settlers in order to portray yet another *endangered species.* Ooh. I really must watch their show!" His comrades giggled at the foppish act. Remi worried how much longer Roland could restrain Crat.

"Funny," he retaliated in desperation. "I wouldn't figure you could even see a holo show, with eyes like those."

The tall one sniffed. Accepting Remi's weak gambit, he replied in Posh Speech. "And what, sweet child of Mother Dirt, do you imagine is wrong with my eyes?"

"You mean besides mutant ugliness? Well it's obvious you're going blind, oh thou noonday mad dog."

Sarcasm gave way to direct retort. "The Sun's rays are to be appreciated, Earthworm. Momma's pet. Even at risk."

"I wasn't talking about UV damage to your retinas, dear Mr. Squint. I refer to the traditional penalty for self-abuse."

Paydirt! The Ra Boy flushed. Roland and Crat laughed uproariously, perhaps a little hysterically. "Got him, Rem!" Roland whispered. "Go!"

From the scowls on the Ra Boys' patchy faces, Remi wondered if this was wise. Several of them were fingering their chains, with the gleaming, sharp-rayed amulets. If one or more had tempers like *Crat's . . .*

The lead Ra Boy stepped closer. "That a slur on my stamina, oh physical lover of fresh mud?"

Remi shrugged, it was too late to do anything but go with it. "Fresh mud or fecund fem, they're all out of reach to one like you, whose only wet licks come from his own sweaty palm."

More appreciative laughter from Roland and Crat hardly made up for the lead Ra Boy's seething wrath, turning him several shades darker. *I didn't know I'd strike such a nerve with that one*, Remi thought. Apparently this guy had a lousy sex life. *Some victories aren't worth the price.*

"So you're the manly man, Joe Settler?" Ra Boy sneered. "You must be Mister Testo. An Ag-back with a stacked stock, and whoremones for all Indiana."

Here it comes. Remi foresaw no way to avoid exchanging Net codes with this character, which in turn would lead to a meeting in some dark place, with no neighborhood watch busybodies to interfere.

With a small part of his mind, Remi realized the encounter had built up momentum almost exactly along the positive feedback curve described in class by Professor Jameson . . . bluster and dare and counterbluff, reinforced by a desperate need to impress one's own gang . . . all leading step by step to the inevitable showdown. It would be an interesting observation—if that knowledge had let Remi prevent anything, but it hadn't. As it was, he wished he'd never even learned any of that shit.

He shrugged, accepting the Ra worshipper's gambit. "Well, I'm already man-ugly enough, I don't have to pray for more from a great big gasball in the sky. I admit, though, your prayers sure look like they've been—"

Remi realized, mid-insult, that both groups were turning toward a sound—a new set of interlopers had entered the hedge garden. He turned. Along the path at least a dozen figures in cowled white gowns approached, slim and graceful. Their pendants, unlike the Ra Boys', were patterned in the womblike Orb of the Mother.

"NorA ChuGa," one of the Ra Boys said in disgust. Still, Remi noticed the guys in both gangs stood up straighter, taking up masculine poses they must have thought subtle, rather than pretentious. Feminine laughter cut off as the newcomers suddenly noticed the male gathering ahead of them. But their rapid pace along the path scarcely tapered. The North American Church of Gaia hardly ever slowed for anybody.

"Good afternoon, gentlemen," several girls in the front rank said, almost simultaneously. Even shaded by their cowls, Remi recognized several of them from the halls of Quayle High. "Can we interest you in donating to the Trillion Trees Campaign?" one of the dedicants asked, coming face to face with Remi. And he had to blink past a moment's fluster—she was heartbreakingly beautiful.

In her palm she held out brightly colored leaflet chips for any of the boys who would take one. There was an outburst of derisive laughter from the other side of the trail. These were surely young, naive Gaians if they thought to hit up Ra Boys for reforestation money!

Settlers, on the other hand, weren't as ideologically incompatible. More importantly, it struck Remi that this offered a possible out.

"Why yes, sisters!" he effused. "You can interest us. I was just saying to my Settler friends here that tree planting will have to be our very first priority when we get to Patagonia. Soon as it's warmed up down there. Yup, planting trees . . ."

Crat was still exchanging glares with the craziest looking Ra Boy. Grabbing his arm, Remi helped Roland tow him amidst the gliding tide of white-garbed girls. All the way, Remi asked enthusiastic questions about current Gaian projects, ignoring the taunts and jeers that

followed them from the harsh-faced young sun worshippers. The Ra
Boys could say whatever they wanted. On the scale of coups in tribal
warfare, scoring with girls beat winning an insult match, hands down.
Not that actual scoring was likely here. Hardcore Gaian women
tended to be hard to impress. This one, for example.

". . . don't you see that hardwood reforestation in Amazonia is
far more important than planting conifers down in Tierra del Fuego or
Antarctica? Those are new ecologies, still delicate and poorly understood. You Settlers are much too impatient. Why, by the time those
new areas are well understood and ready for humans to move in, the
main battle, to save the *Earth,* could be lost!"

"I see your point," Remi agreed. Anxious to make good their
getaway, he and Roland nodded attentively until the Ra Boys were out
of sight. Then Remi kept on smiling and nodding because of the
speaker's heart-shaped face and beautiful complexion. Also, he liked
what he could make out of her figure under the gown. At one point he
made a show of depositing the trash from his pocket in a brown recycle bin, giving the impression that litter gathering was his routine
habit, and winning a brief approving pause in her lecture.

When they passed a row of hooded cancer plague survivors in
wheelchairs, he slipped some dollar coins into their donation cups,
getting another smile in reward.

Encouraged, he wound up accepting a pile of chip brochures, until at last she began running low on breath as they passed near the
superconducting rails of the cross-park rapitrans line. Then came a
really lucky moment. A newly arriving train spilled youngsters in
school uniforms onto the path, shouting and dashing about. The cascade of children broke apart the tight-knit squadron of Gaians. Remi
and the young woman of his dreams were caught in the whirling
eddies and pushed to one side under one of the rapitrans pillars. They
looked at each other, and shared laughter. Her smile seemed much
warmer when she was off her planet-saving pitch.

But Remi knew it would only be a moment. In seconds, the others would reclaim her. So, as casually as he could, he told her he
would like to see her personally and asked for her net code to arrange
a date.

She, in turn, met his gaze with soulful brown eyes and asked him
sweetly to show his vasectomy certificate.

"Honestly," she said with apparent sincerity. "I just couldn't be
interested in a man so egotistical he insists, in a world of ten billion
people, that *his* genes are desperately needed. If you haven't done the
right thing, can you point to some great accomplishment or virtue, to
justify clinging to . . . ?"

Her words trailed off in perplexity, addressing his back as Remi seized his friends' arms and rapidly departed.

"I'd show her somethin' more important than genes!" Crat snarled when he heard the story. Roland was only slightly more forgiving. "Too damn much theory crammed into that pretty little head. Imagine, invading a guy's privacy like that! Tell you one thing, that's one bird who'd be happier, and a whole lot quieter as a farm wife."

"Right!" Crat agreed. "Farm wife's got what life's about. There's plenty room in Patagonia for lots of kids. Overpop's just propa-crap—"

"Oh, shut up!" Remi snapped. His face still burned with shame, made worse by the fact that the girl obviously hadn't even known what she was doing. "You think I care what a bleeding NorA ChuGa thinks? They only teach 'em how to be—*what?*"

Roland was holding his wristwatch in front of Remi's face, tapping its tiny screen. Lights rippled and the machine sang a warning tone.

Remi blinked. They were being scanned again, and it wasn't just someone's True-Vu this time, but real eavesdropping. "Some tokomak's got a big ear on us," Roland reported irritably.

It was just one thing after another! Remi felt like a caged tiger. Hell, even tigers had more privacy nowadays, in the wildlife survival arks, than a young guy ever got here in Bloomington. *The park used to be a place where you could get away, but not anymore!*

He looked around quickly, searching for the voyeur. Over to the south citizens of many ages were busy tending high-yield vegetables in narrow strip gardens, leased by the city to those without convenient rooftops. Bean pole detectors watched for poachers, but those devices couldn't have set off Roland's alarm.

Nor could the children, running about in visors and sun-goggles, playing tag or beamy. Or the ragged men in their twenties and thirties, over by the reflecting pond, draped in saffron sheets, pretending to be meditating, but fooling no one as they used biofeedback techniques to supply their bottomless, self-stimulated addiction . . . dazing out on endorphin chemicals released by their own brains.

There were other teens around too . . . . though none wore gang colors. The silent, boring majority then, who neither slip-shaded nor dazed—students dressed for fashion or conformity, with little on their minds—some even carrying pathetic banners for tonight's B-ball contest between the Fighting Golfers and the Letterman High Hecklers.

Then he saw the geek—a codger this time—leaning against one of the slender stalks of a sunshade-photocell collector, looking directly at the three of them. And sure enough, amid the bushy gray curls spilling under his white sun hat, Remi saw a thin wire, leading from an earpiece to a vest made of some sonomagnetic fabric.

Wheeling almost in step, the boys reacted to this new provocation by striding straight toward the geezer. As they neared, Remi made out the ribbons of a Helvetian War veteran on his chest, with radiation and pathogen clusters. *Shit*, he thought. *Veterans are the worst.* It would be hard winning any points over this one.

Then Remi realized the coot wasn't even wearing goggles! Of course he could still be transmitting, using smaller sensors, but it broke the expected image, especially when the gremper removed even his sunglasses as they approached, and actually smiled!

"Hello, boys," he said, amiably. "I guess you caught me snooping. Owe you an apology."

Out of habit, Crat squeezed the fellow's personal zone, even swaying over a bit as he flashed his scalp tattoo. But the geek didn't respond in the usual manner, by flourishing his police beeper. Rather, he laughed aloud. "Beautiful! Y'know, I once had a messmate . . . a Russkie commando he was. Died in the drop on Liechtenstein, I think. He had a tattoo like that one, only it was on his butt! Could make it dance, too."

Remi grabbed Crat's arm when the idiot seemed about to spit. "You know using a big ear's illegal without wearing a sign, tellin' people you've got one. We could cite you, man."

The oldster nodded. "Fair enough. I violated your privacy, and will accept *in situ* judgment if you wish."

Remi and his friends looked at each other. Geriatrics—especially those who had suffered in the war—hardly ever used the word "privacy" except as an epithet, when accusing someone of hiding foul schemes. Certainly Remi had never heard of a codger willing to settle a dispute as gang members would, man to man, away from the all-intrusive eye of the Net.

"Shit no, gremper! We *got* you—"

"Crat!" Roland snapped. He glanced at Remi, and Remi nodded back. "All right," he agreed. "Over by that tree. You pitch, we'll swing."

That brought another smile. "I used that expression when I was your age. Haven't heard it since. Did you know slang phrases often come and go in cycles?"

Still chatting amiably about the vagaries of language fashion since his day, the geep led them toward their designated open-air courtroom, leaving a puzzled Remi trailing behind, suddenly struck by the unasked-for exercise of visualizing this wrinkled, ancient remnant as a youth, once as brimming as they were now with hormones and anger.

Logically, Remi supposed it might be possible. Perhaps a few grempers even remembered what it had been like, with some vague nostalgia. But it couldn't have been as bad to be young back then, he thought bitterly. *There was stuff for guys like me to do. Old farts didn't control everything.*

Hell, at least you had a war to fight!

After the Helvetian holocaust, the frightened international community finally acted to prevent any more big ones, putting muscle into the inspection treaties. But that didn't seem like much of a solution to Remi. The world was going straight to hell anyway, no detours. So why not do it in a way that was at least honorable and interesting?

Do not go gentle into that good night . . . Poetry class was just about the only one Remi really liked. *Yeah. Back in TwenCen there were some guys who had it right.*

From a grassy step they could look out over much of downtown Bloomington, a skyline still dominated by preserved TwenCen towers, though several of the more recent, slablike 'topias canted like ski slopes to the north. From somewhere beyond the park boundaries could be heard the ubiquitous sound of jackhammers as the city waged its endless, unwinnable war against decay, renovating crumbling sidewalks and sewer pipes originally designed to last a hundred years . . . back more than a century ago, when a hundred years must have sounded like forever. Bloomington looked and felt seedy, like almost any town, anywhere.

"I like listening to people, watching people," the codger explained as he sat cross-legged before them, displaying a surprising limberness.

"So what?" Roland shrugged. "All you geeks listen and watch. All the time."

The old man shook his head. "No, they stare and record. That's different. They were raised in a narcissistic age, thinking they'd live forever. Now they compensate for their failing bodies by waging a war of intimidation against youth.

"Oh, it started as a way to fight street crime—retired people staking out the streets with video cameras and crude beepers. And the seniors' posse really worked, to the point where perps couldn't steal anything or hurt anybody in public anymore without getting caught on tape.

"But after the crime rate plummeted, did that stop the paranoia?" He shook his gray head. "You see, it's all *relative*. That's how human psych works. Nowadays seniors—you call us geeks—imagine threats where there aren't any anymore. It's become a tradition, see. They're so busy warning off potential trouble, challenging threats before they materialize, they almost *dare* young men like you—"

Roland interrupted. "Hey, gremper. We get all this in Tribes. What's your point?"

The old man shrugged. "Maybe pretending there's still a need for neighborhood watch makes them feel useful. There's a saying I heard . . . *geeks find their own uses for technology.*"

"I wish nobody ever invented all this tech shit," Remi muttered.

The war veteran shook his head. "The world would be dead, dead now, my young friend, if it weren't for tech stuff. Want to go back to the farm? Send ten billion people back to subsistence farming? Feeding the world's a job for trained experts now, boy. You'd only screw things up worse than they already are.

"Tech eventually solved the worst problems of cities, too: violence and boredom. It helps people have a million zillion low-impact hobbies—"

"Yeah, and helps 'em spy on each other, too! That's one of the biggest hobbies, isn't it? Gossip and snooping!"

The old man shrugged. "You might not complain so much if you'd lived through the alternative. Anyway, I wasn't trying to catch you fellows in some infraction. I was just listening. I like listening to people. I like *you* guys."

Crat and Roland laughed out loud at the absurdity of the remark. But Remi felt a queer chill. The geezer really seemed to mean it.

Of course Professor Jameson kept saying it was wrong to overgeneralize. ". . . *because you are gang members, that will color your views of everything. Young males do that when engaged in us-versus-them group bonding. They have to stereotype their enemies, dehumanize them. The problem's really bad here in this part of the city, where the young-old conflict has deteriorated . . .*"

Everybody hated Jameson, all the girlie gangs and dudie gangs— staying in his class only because a pass was required for any hope of earning a self-reliance card . . . as if half the kids were ever going to qualify. Shit.

"I like you because I remember the way it was for me," gremper went on, unperturbed. "I remember when I felt I could bend steel, topple empires, screw harems, burn cities . . ." He closed his wrinkled eyelids for a moment, and when he reopened them, Remi felt a sudden thrill tickle his spine. The old guy seemed to be looking far-away into space and time.

"I did burn cities, y'know," he told them in a low, very distant voice. And Remi somehow knew he had to be remembering things far more vivid than anything to be found in his own paltry store of recollections. Suddenly, he felt awash in envy.

"But then, each generation's got to have a cause, right?" the old-ster continued, shaking free of reminiscence. "Ours was *ending secrecy.* It's why we fought the bankers and the bureaucrats and mobsters, and all the damned socialists to bring everything out into the open, once and for all, to stop all the underhanded dealing and giga-cheating.

"Only now our solution's causing other problems. That's the way things go with revolutions. When I overheard you guys dreaming aloud of privacy—like it was something holy—Jesus, that took me back. Reminded me of my own dad! People used to talk that way back at the end of TwenCen, till my generation saw through the scam—"

"Privacy's no scam!" Roland snapped. "It's simple human dignity!"

"Yeah!" Crat added. "You got no right to follow guys' every move . . ."

But the old man lifted one hand placatingly. "Hey, I agree! At least partly. What I'm trying to say is, I think my generation went too far. We overthrew the evils of secrecy—of numbered bank accounts and insider deals—but now you guys are rejecting *our* excesses, replacing them with some of your own.

"Seriously though, what would you boys do if you had your way? You can't just ban True-Vu and other tech-stuff. You can't rebottle the genie. The world had a choice. Let governments control surveillance tech . . . and therefore give a snooping monopoly to the rich and powerful . . . or let *everybody* have it. Let everyone snoop everyone else, including snooping the government! I mean it, fellows. That was the choice. There just weren't any other options."

"Come on," Roland said.

"All right, tell me. Would you go back to the illusion of so-called privacy laws, which only gave the rich and powerful a monopoly on secrecy?"

Crat glowered. "Maybe. At least when they had a . . . monopoly, they weren't so dumpit rude! People could at least pretend they were being left alone."

Remi nodded, impressed with Crat's brief eloquence. "There's something to that. Who was it said life's just an illusion, anyway?"

The gremper smiled and answered dryly. "Only every transcendental philosopher in history."

Remi lifted his shoulders. "Oh, yeah, him. It was on the tip of my tongue."

The old man burst out laughing and slapped Remi on the knee. In an odd way, Remi felt warmed by the gesture, as if it didn't matter that they disagreed in countless ways or that a gap of half a century yawned between them.

"Damn," the gremper said. "I wish I could take you back to those days. The guys in my outfit . . . the guys would've liked you. We could've shown you some times."

To his amazement, Remi believed him. After a momentary pause, he asked, "Tell us . . . tell us about the guys."

The three of them deliberated later, some distance from the tree, as dusk shadows began stretching across the park. Of course the old man left his big-ear unplugged while they passed judgment. He looked up when they returned to squat before him.

"We decided on a penalty for the way you invaded our privacy," Roland said, speaking for all.

"I'll accept your justice, sirs," he said, inclining his head.

Even Crat grinned as Roland passed sentence. "You gotta come back here again next week, same time, and tell us more about the war."

The old man nodded—in acceptance and obvious pleasure. "My name is Joseph," he said, holding out his hand. "And I'll be here."

Over the next few weeks he kept his promise. Joseph told them tales they had never imagined, even after watching a thousand hypervideos. About climbing the steep flanks of the Pennine Alps, for instance, and then the Bernese Oberland—slogging through gas and bugs and radioactive mud. He described digging out booby traps nearly every meter of the way, and prying out the bankers' mercenaries every ten or so. And he told them of his comrades, dying beside him, choking in their own sputum as they coughed their lungs out, still begging to be allowed to press on though, to help bring the Last War to an end.

He told them about the fall of Berne and the last gasp of the Gnomes, whose threat to "take the world down" with them turned out to be backed by three hundred cobalt-thorium bombs . . . which were defused only when Swiss draftees finally turned their rifles on their own officers and emerged from their shattered warrens, hands high over their heads, into a new day.

As spring headed toward summer, Joseph commiserated over the futility of high school, even under a "new education plan" that forced on students lots of supposedly "practical" information, but never did a guy any good anyway. He held them transfixed talking about the way girls used to be, back before they were taught all that modern crap about psychology and "sexual choice criteria."

"Boy crazy, that's what they were, my young tomodachis. No girlie wanted to be caught for even a minute without a boyfriend. It was where they got their sense of worth, see? Their alpha to omega. They'd do anything for you, believe most anything you said, so long as you promised you loved 'em."

Remi suspected Joseph was exaggerating. But that didn't matter. Even if it was all a load of bull semen, it was *great* bull semen. For the first time in his life, he contemplated the prospect of getting older— actually living beyond twenty-five—with anything but a vague sense of horror. The idea of someday being like Joseph didn't seem so bad . . . as long as it took a long time happening, and providing he got to do as much as Joseph had along the way.

It was the profession of soldiering that fascinated Roland. Its camaraderie and traditions. Crat loved hearing about faraway places and escape from the tight strictures of urban life.

But as for Remi, he felt he was getting something more . . . the beginnings of a trust in *time.*

Joseph was a great source of practical advice, too—subtle verbal put-downs nobody here in Indiana had heard in years, but which would burrow like smart bombs dropped among the gang's foes, only to blow up minutes, even hours, later with devastating effect. One day they met the same group of Ra Boys in the park and left them all scratching their heads in confusion, reluctant even to think of tackling Settlers anytime soon.

Roland talked about joining the Guard, maybe trying for one of the peacekeeping units.

Remi began tapping history texts from the Net.

Even Crat seemed to grow more reflective, as if every time he was about to lose his temper, he'd stop and think what Joseph would say.

No one worried overmuch when Joseph failed to show up one Saturday. On the second unexplained absence though, Remi and the others grew concerned. At home, sitting at his desk comp, Remi wrote a quick ferret program and sent it into the Net.

The ferret returned two seconds later with the old man's obituary.

The mulching ceremony was peaceful. A few detached-looking adult grandchildren showed up, looking eager to be elsewhere. If they had been the sort to cry, Remi, Roland, and Crat would have been the only ones shedding tears.

Still, he had been old. "If any man's led a full life, it was me," Joseph once said. And Remi believed him.

I only hope I do half as well, he thought.

So it came as a shot from the sky when Remi answered the message light on his home comp one evening, and found logged there a terse note from Roland.

OUR NAMES LISTED IN PROGRAM GUIDE FOR A NET SHOW . . .

"Right!" Remi laughed. The law said whenever anyone was depicted, anywhere in the Net, it had to go into the listings. That made each weekly worldwide directory bigger than all the world's libraries before 1910.

"Probably some Quayle High senior's doing a Net version of the yearbook . . ."

But his laughter trailed off as he read the rest.

IT'S ON A REMINISCENCE DATABASE FOR WAR VETS.
AND GUESS WHO'S LISTED AS AUTHOR . . .

Remi read the name and felt cold.

Now, don't jump to conclusions, he told himself. *He might've just mentioned us . . . a nice note about getting to know three young guys before he died.*

But his heart raced as he sought the correct Net address, sifting through layer after layer, from general to specific to superspecified, until at last he arrived at the file, dated less than a month ago.

THE REMEMBRANCES OF JOSEPH MOYERS: EPILOGUE: MY LAST WEEKS—
ENCOUNTERS WITH THREE CONFUSED YOUNG MEN.

This was followed by full sight and sound, plus narration, beginning on that afternoon when they had met and held impromptu court where an elm tree shaded them from the glaring sky.

Perhaps someone neutral would have called the account compassionate, friendly. Someone neutral might even have described Joseph's commentary as warm and loving.

But Remi wasn't neutral. He watched, horrified, as his image, Roland's, and Crat's were depicted in turn, talking about private things, things spoken as if to a confessor, but picked up anyway by some hidden, hi-fidelity camera.

He listened, numbed, as Joseph's editorial voice described the youths who shared his final weeks.

". . . had I the heart to tell them they were never going to Patagonia or Antarctica? That the New Lands are reserved for refugees from catastrophe nations? And even so there isn't enough thawed tundra to go around?

"These poor boys dream of emigrating to some promised land, but Indiana is their destiny, now and tomorrow . . ."

I knew that, Remi thought, bitterly. *But did you have to tell the world I was dumb enough to have a dream? Dumpit, Joseph! Did you have to bare it all to everybody?*

A neutral party might have reassured Remi. The old man hadn't told very many people. It was in the nature of the Net, that vast ocean of information, that most published missives were read by only one or two others besides the author himself. Maybe one percent were accessed by a hundred or more. And fewer than one piece in ten thousand ever had enough viewers, worldwide, to fill even a good size meeting hall.

Perhaps all that had gone through Joseph's mind when he made this last testament . . . that it would be seen by only a few old men like himself and never come to his young friends' attention. Perhaps he never understood how far ferret-tech had come, or that others, who had grown up with the system, might use the directories better than he.

Remi knew it wasn't very likely Joseph's memoirs would work their way up, through good reviews and word of mouth, to best-seller status. But that hardly mattered. It *could* happen. For all the old man knew, Remi's nonchalant ramblings and dreams could be sifted by a million voyeurs or more!

"Why, Joseph?" he asked, hoarsely. "Why?"

Then another face came on screen. Delicate features framed in white. It was a voice Remi had managed to purge from memory, until now.

"I'm sorry, but I just couldn't be interested in a man so egotistical as to insist, in a world of ten billion people, that *his* genes are desperately needed. If you haven't done the right thing, can you point to some great accomplishment or virtue . . . ?"

Remi screamed as he threw the unit through his bedroom window.

Strangely, Roland and Crat didn't seem to grasp what he was so upset about. Perhaps, for all their stylish talk, they didn't really understand privacy. Not really.

They worried, though, over his listlessness and learned not to speak of Joseph when each of them received small royalty checks in their accounts, for their parts in what was fast becoming a small-time social-documentary classic. They spent their shares on their diverging interests, while Remi took his out in cash and gave it to the next NorAChuGa he met . . . for the Trillion Trees.

And so there came a day when he encountered, once again, a small band of Ra Boys in the park, this time without his friends, without any company but his loneliness.

This time the odds mattered not at all. He tore them up, top to bottom, using sarcasm like a slug rifle, assaulting them as he might have taken on Gnome mercenaries, had he been born in a time when there was honorable work for brave men to do and an evil that could be grappled with.

To the Ra Boys' amazement it was he who demanded to exchange net codes. It was he who challenged them to a rendezvous.

By the time Remi actually met them later, in the darkness behind the monorail tracks, however, they'd done their own net research, and understood.

Understanding made their greeting solemn, respectful. Their champion exchanged bows with Remi across the makeshift arena, and even held back for a while, letting his clumsy opponent draw honorable blood before it was time at last to end it. Then, dutifully, one tribesman to another, he gave Remi what he desired most in the world.

For weeks afterward, then, the Ra Boys spoke his name in honor under the Sun.

The Sun, they said, was where at last he had settled.

The Sun was the final home of warriors.

☐

Living species adapt when individuals stumble onto new ways of doing things and pass on those new ways to their descendants. This is generally a slow process. Sometimes, however, a species accidentally opens a door to a whole new mode of existence, and then it flourishes, pushes aside its competition, and brings on many changes.

Sometimes those changes benefit more than just itself.

In the beginning, the Earth's atmosphere contained copious amounts of nitrogen, but not in a form living things could easily turn to protein. Soon however, an early bacterium hit on the right combination of chemical tricks —enabling it to "fix" nitrogen straight from the air. The advantage was profound, and that bacterium's descendants proliferated. But other species profited too. Some plants grew tiny knobs on their roots, to shelter and succor the inventive microbes, and in return they received the boon of natural fertilizer.

In a similar way, once upon a time, the ancestor of all *grasses* fell upon a way to cover soil like a carpet, with tough, fibrous leaves that soak up nearly every ray of sunlight. Other plants were driven back by an onslaught of grasses, some even to extinction. But for certain animals—those making the right counter-adaptations—the advent of grass opened opportunities. Ungulates, with multiple stomachs and the knack of chewing cud, could graze on the tough stems and so spread onto uplands and plains formerly barren of much animal life.

So, too, when *flowering plants* arrived some ferns had to retire, but the victors shared their new prosperity with all the crawling, flying, creeping things that came to feed on nectar and pollinate them. Into newborn niches spread a multitude of novel forms . . . insects, birds, mammals . . .

Of course, sometimes a species' invention only benefited itself. Goats developed an ability to eat almost anything, right down to the roots. Goats proliferated. Deserts spread behind them.

Then another creature appeared, one whose originality was unprecedented. Its numbers grew. And in its wake some other types did flourish. The common cat and dog. The rat. Starlings and pigeons. And the cockroach. Meanwhile, opportunity grew sparse for those less able to share the vast new niches—huge expanses of plowed fields and mowed lawns, streets and parking lots . . .

The coming of the grasses had left its mark indelibly on the history of the world.

So would the Age of Asphalt and Concrete.

● H O L O S P H E R E　Jen Wolling found the Ndebele Rites of Gaia charming. The canton's Kuwenezi Science Collective pulled out all the stops, sparing nothing to put on a show of their piety. To watch the lavish torchlight celebration under a midnight moon, one might imagine they were commemorating Earth Day itself, and not just a going-away party for one old woman they had known barely a fortnight.

Dancers in traditional costumes capered and whirled before the dignitaries' dais, stamping bare feet on the beaten ground to the tempo of pounding drums. Feathered anklets flapped like agitated captive birds. Spears thudded on shields as men in bright loincloths leaped in apparent defiance of gravity. Women in colorful dashikis waved bound sheaves of wheat, specially grown in hothouses for this out-of-season observance.

Jen appreciated the dancers' lithe beauty, taut and powerful as any stallion's. Perspiration flew in droplets or smeared to coat their dark brown bodies in a gleaming, athletic sheen. Their rhythm and power were mighty, exultory, and marvelously sexual, which brought a smile to Jen's lips. Although tonight's purpose was to venerate a gentle metaphoric goddess, the choreography had been co-opted from much older rites having to do with fertility and violence.

"It's far, far better than in the days of neocolonialism," the tall ark director said to her. Sitting cross-legged to her left, he had to lean close to be heard over the percussive cadence. "Back then, the Ndebele and other tribes maintained troupes of professional dancers to pander to tourists. But these young men and women practice in their spare time simply for the love of it. Few outsiders ever get to see this now."

Jen admired the way the torchlight glistened on Director Mugabe's brow, his tight-coiled hair. "I'm honored," she said, crossing her arms over her heart and giving a shallow bow. He grinned and returned the gesture. Side by side, they watched rows of young "warriors" take terrific risks, exchanging whirling spears to the delight of clapping women and children.

Venerable and ancient this dance might be, but there was no correlation here with the primitive. Jen had just spent two weeks consulting with Kuwenezi's experts, learning all about Ndebele Canton's plans for new animal breeds better able to endure the challenging and ever-changing environment of southern Africa. They, in turn, had listened attentively to her own ideas about macroecological management. After all, Jen had virtually invented the field.

By now of course, it had accumulated all the trappings of a maturing technology, with enough details to leave a solitary dreamer-theoretician like her far behind. Specific analyses she left to younger, quicker minds these days.

Still, she occasionally managed to surprise them all. If Jen ever ceased being able to shock people, it would be time to give up this body's brief manifestation and feed her meager store of phosphorus back into the Mother's great mulch pile.

She recalled the expression on that fellow B'Keli's face when, during her third and final lecture, she had begun talking about . . . *specially designed mammalian chimeras . . . incorporating camels' kidneys . . . birds' lungs . . . bear marrow . . . chimps' tendon linkages . . .* Even Director Mugabe, who claimed to have read everything she'd written, was staring glassy-eyed by the end of her talk. Her conclusion about . . . *the rough love of viruses . . .* seemed to have been too much even for him.

When the house lights had come on, she was greeted with stunned silence from the packed crowd of brown faces. There was, at first, only one questioner—a very young man whose northern, Yoruba features stood out amid the crowd of Southern Bantu. The boy's arms and face were bandaged, but he showed no outward sign of pain. All through the talk he had sat quietly in the front row, gently stroking a small baboon and her infant. When Jen called on him, he lowered his hand and spoke with a completely stunning Canadian accent, of all things.

"Doctor . . . are you sayin' that—that people might someday be as strong as chimpanzees? Or be able to sleep through winter, like bears?"

Jen noticed indulgent smiles among the audience when the boy spoke, though Mugabe's expression was one of mixed relief and angst. Anxiety that such an untutored member of their community had been the only one to offer the courtesy of a question. Relief that *someone* had done so in time.

"Yes. Exactly," she had replied. "We have the entire human genome fully catalogued. And many other higher mammals. Why not use that knowledge to improve ourselves?

"Now I want to make clear I'm talking about *genetic* improvement here, and there are limits to how far one can go in that direction. We're already by far the most plastic of animals, the most adaptable to environmental influences. The real core of any self-improvement campaign must remain in the areas of education and child-rearing and the new psychology, to bring up a generation of saner, more decent people.

"But there really are constraints on that process, laid down by the capabilities and limitations of our bodies and brains. And where did those capabilities and limitations come from? Our past, of course. A haphazard sequence of genetic experiments by trial and error, slowly accumulating favorable mutations generation by generation. *Death* was the means of our advancement . . . the deaths of millions of our ancestors. Or, to be more precise, those who failed to become our ancestors.

"Those who did survive to breed passed on new traits, which gradually accumulated into the suite of attributes now at our disposal—our upright stance, our better-than-average vision, our wonderfully dexterous hands. Our bloated brains.

"As for what the latter has done to our skull size, ask any woman who's given birth . . ."

At that point the audience had laughed. Jen noticed some of the tension seeping away.

"Other species have meanwhile collected their own, similar catalogues of adaptations. Many of them at least as wonderful as those we're so arrogantly proud of. But here's the sad part. With one exception—the inefficient interspecies gene transfer performed by viruses—*no animal species can ever profit from another's hard-won lessons.* Until now, each has been in it alone, fending for itself, hoarding what it's acquired, learning from no one else.

"What I am proposing is to change all that, once and for all. Hell, we're already *doing* it! Look at the century-old effort to blend characteristics among plants, to transfer, say, pest resistance from one hardy wild species into another that is a food crop. Take just one such product—legu-corn, which fixes its own nitrogen. How many productive farmlands and aquifers has it saved by eliminating the need for artificial fertilizer? How many people has it saved from starvation?

"Or take another program—to save those species of birds who cannot bear excess ultraviolet by inserting eagle codons, so their descendants' eyes will be as impervious as those of hawks or falcons. The happy accidental discovery of one family can now be shared with others.

"Or take our experiments at London Ark, where we're remaking a vanished species by slowly building a woolly mammoth genome within an elephant matrix. Someday, a species which has been extinct for thousands of years will walk again."

A woman in the third row raised her hand. "But isn't that exactly what the radical Gaians object to? They call it *bastardization* of species . . ."

Jen remembered laughing at that point. "I am not a favorite of the radicals."

Quite a few in the audience had smiled then. The Ndebele shared her contempt for the taunts, even threats, of those who proclaimed themselves guardians of modern morality.

No doubt the original idea behind her invitation to come here had been prestige. Southern Africa suffered partial isolation from the world's ever-tightening web of commerce and communication, largely because the commonwealth still practiced racial and economic policies long abandoned elsewhere. No doubt they were surprised when a Nobel laureate actually accepted. This visit would cause Jen problems when she returned home.

It was worth it though. She'd seen promise here. Cut off as they were, these archaic racialist-socialists were looking at familiar problems in unique ways. Often cockeyed *wrong* ways, but intriguing nonetheless. They had a great advantage in not caring what the rest of the world thought. In that way, they were much like Jen herself.

"What matters to me is the whole," she had replied. "And the whole depends upon diversity. The radicals are right about that. Diversity is the key.

"But it need not be the *same* diversity as existed before mankind. Indeed, it cannot be the same. We are in a time of changes. Species will pass away and others take their place, as has happened before. An ecosystem frozen in stone can only become a fossil.

"We must become smart enough to minimize the damage, and then foster a new diversity, one able to endure in a strange new world."

Of all those in the audience, some had looked confused or resentful. Others nodded in agreement. But one, the boy in the front row, had stared at her as if struck dumb. At the time she had wondered what she'd said that had affected him so.

Jen was jerked back to the present as Director Mugabe spoke her name over the rhythm of the beating drums. She blinked, momentarily disoriented, while hands gently took both her elbows, helping her to stand. Smiling women in bright costumes urged her forward. Their white, perfect teeth shone in the flickering torchlight.

Jen sighed, realizing. As the oldest woman present, and guest of honor, she couldn't refuse officiating at the sacrifice . . . not without insulting her hosts. So she went through the motions—bowing to the Orb of the Mother, accepting the bound wheat, pouring the pure water.

So many people had taken to this sect, movement, *zeitgeist* . . . call it what you will. It was an amorphous thing, without center or official dogma. Only a few of those paying homage to the Mother did so thinking it a religion per se.

Indeed many older faiths had taken the simple, effective measure of co-opting Gaian rituals into their own. Catholics altered celebrations of the Virgin, so that Mary now took a much more vigorous personal interest in planetary welfare than she had in the days of Chartres or Nantes.

And yet, Jen knew many for whom this was more than a mere statement or movement. More than just a way of expressing reverence for a danger-stricken world. There were radicals for whom Gaia worship was a church militant. They saw a return of the old goddess of prehistory, at last ready to end her banishment by brutal male deities —by Zeus and Shiva and Jehovah and the warlike spirits once idolized by the Ndebele. To Gaian radicals there were no "moderate" approaches to saving Earth. Technology and the "evil male principle" were foes to be cast down.

Evil male principle, my shriveled ass. Males have their uses.

For some reason Jen thought of her grandson, whose obsessions in the twin worlds of abstraction and engineering were stereotypical of what radicals called "penis science." It was some time since she had last heard from the boy. She wondered what Alex was up to.

Probably something terribly silly, and utterly earth-shaking if I know him.

Soon came the final act of the evening. The Cleansing. Jen smiled and touched one by one the offerings brought before her by adults and children, each presenting a wicker basket containing broken bits of mundane archaeology.

Scraps of tin . . . broken spark plugs . . . shreds of adamant, insoluble plastic. . . . One basket was nearly filled with ancient aluminum beer cans, still shiny thirty years after they had been outlawed everywhere on Earth. Each collection was the work of one member of this community, performed in his or her spare time over many months. Each basket contained the yield given up by one square meter of soil, painstakingly and lovingly sifted till no trace of human manufacture was detectible, as deep as the individual's time, strength, and piety allowed. In this way, each person incrementally returned a small bit of the planet to its natural state.

Only what was natural? Certainly not the land's contours, which had been eroded and moved wholesale by human enterprise.

Not the aquifers, whose percolating waters would never be quite the same, even where antidumping was enforced and where inspectors granted the precious label "pure and untainted." That only meant the content of heavy metals and complex petro-organics was too sparse to affect one human's health over a normal lifespan. It certainly didn't mean "natural."

Especially, the word didn't apply to that complicated living thing known as topsoil! Winnowed of countless native species, filled with invaders brought inadvertently or on purpose from other continents— from earthworms to rotifers to tiny fungi and bacteria—the loam in some places thrived and elsewhere it died, giving up its dusty substance to the winds. Microscopic victories and defeats and stalemates were being waged in every hectare all over the globe, and nowhere could a purist say the result was "natural" at all.

Jen glanced over her left shoulder to see Kuwenezi's lambent towers. The main ark was dim, but its great glass-crystal face reflected a rippling sister to the moon. Within those artificial habitats dozed plants and animals rescued from a hundred spoiled ecosystems. To the radicals, such arks were glorified prisons—mere sops to humanity's troubled conscience, so that nature's slaughter could go on.

To Jen, though, the great arcologies weren't jails, but nurseries.

Change can't be prevented, only guided.

The radicals were right about one thing, of course. What finally emerged from those glass towers, someday, wouldn't be the same as what had gone in. Jen's public statements—that she did not find that in itself tragic—ensured continued hate mail, even death threats, from followers of a sect she herself had helped found.

So be it.

Death is just another change. And when the Mother needs my phosphorus, I'll give it up gladly.

The local denomination, of course, held that Gaia's true complexion must be that of pure, fecund earth, and yet they seemed not to care about the paleness of her skin. As Jen lifted her arms, they carried their offerings to outsized recycling bins, waiting under the stars. When the last contribution tumbled inside, a shout of celebration rose, commemorating the salvation of several thousand square meters.

This ceremony had delightful idiosyncrasies, but it was essentially similar to others she'd officiated at, from Australia to Smolensk. In all those places, people had taken it for granted that she was an appropriate surrogate—a stand-in for Gaia herself.

Only a surrogate . . . Jen smiled, offering her benediction and forgiving their error. The drums resumed, and dancers rejoined their exertions. But for a moment Jen watched the torchlight play across the faces and the glass towers beyond.

Modern folk, you pay homage to the Mother as a "parable." And I am but a stand-in, tonight, for an abstract idea.

Well, we shall see about that, my children. We shall see.

She had planted seeds during her visit. Some would germinate, perhaps even flower into action.

The young man in the bandages appeared again. She saw him seated across the arena, his baboon companions resting against his knees. He nodded back as she smiled at him, and Jen had a sudden, clear recollection of his final question, yesterday afternoon in the lecture hall.

"You talk about a lot of possibilities Doctor Wolling . . ." he had said. "Maybe we could do some of those things . . . or even all o' them, eh?

"But won't we also have to give up somethin' in return? They say there ain't no such thing as a free lunch. So what'll it cost us, Doctor?"

Jen remembered thinking, What a bright boy. He understood that nothing was ever easy, which her own grandson never seemed to grasp, no matter how often the world smacked poor Alex in the head.

No, Jen thought. *Humanity may have to give up more than a little, if the Earth is to be saved. We may, in the end, find the old gods were right after all. That nothing worthwhile comes without a sacrifice.*

Jen smiled at the boy, at all of them. She opened her arms, blessing the dancers, the audience, the animals in the arks, and the ravaged countryside.

That sacrifice, my children, may turn out to be ourselves.

PART III

PLANET

The newborn world liquefied under pummeling asteroid impacts. Heavy elements sank, generating still more heat, and a dowry of radioactive atoms kept the planet's interior warm even after the surface cooled and hardened.

Eventually, the inmost core crystallized under intense pressure, but the next layer remained a swirling metal fluid, a vast electric dynamo. Higher still congealed a mantle of semisolid minerals—superdense pyroxenes and olivines and lighter melts that squeezed up crustal cracks to spill forth from blazing volcanoes.

Heat drove the circulating convection cells, jostled the plates, drove the fields. Heat built continents and made the Earth throb.

Heat also kept some water molten at the surface. Preorganic vapors sloshed in solution, under lightning and fierce sunbeams. . . .

The process started taking on a life of its own.

□

A range of minor mountains divides the city of Los Angeles. During the city's carefree youth, great battalions of trucks streamed toward the little valleys between those hills, brimming with kilotons of urban garbage.

Coffee grounds and melon rinds, cereal boxes and disposable trays . . .

In those profligate times every purchased commodity seemed to come inside its own weight of packing material. The average family generated enough waste each year to fill home and garage combined.

Newspapers, magazines, and throwaway advertisements . . .

Even earlier, during the fight against Germany and Japan, Los Angeles mandated limited recycling to help the war effort. Citizens separated metals for curbside pickup. Bound paper was returned to pulp mills; even cooking grease was saved for munitions. Those few who weren't glad to help still complied, to avoid stiff fines.

Milk cartons and paper towels . . . and never-used, slightly dented goods, discarded at the factory . . .

After the war, people found themselves released from decades of privation into a sudden age of plenty. With the crisis over, recycling seemed irksome. A mayoral candidate ran on a one-issue promise, to revoke the inconvenient law. He won by a landslide.

Peanut hulls, fast-food bags, and takeaway pizza boxes . . .

The hills dividing L.A. had been formed as the Earth's Pacific Plate ground alongside the North American Plate. As the two huge, rocky masses pressed and scraped, a coastal range squeezed out at the interface, like toothpaste from a tube. The Santa Monica Mountains and Hollywood Hills were mere offshoots from that steady accumulation, but they helped shape the great city that eventually surrounded them.

Boxes from frozen dinners, boxes from new stereos and computers, boxes from supermarket produce sections, boxes, boxes, boxes . . .

Between the hills once lay little valleys of oak and meadow, where mule deer grazed and condors soared—ideal out-of-view spots for landfills. The regiments of trucks came and went, day in and day out. Hardly anyone noticed until quite late that all suitable and legal crevices would be topped off within a single generation. By century's end flat plains stretched between onetime peaks, eerily lit at night by tiki torches burning methane gas—generated underground by the decaying garbage.

Beer and soft-drink cans, ketchup bottles and disposable diapers . . . engine oil, transmission fluid, and electroplating residue . . . chipped ceramic knickknacks and worn-out furniture . . .

Harder times came. New generations arrived with new sensibilities and less carefree attitudes. Pickup fees were enacted and expensive processes found to stanch the flow . . . to cut the flood of trash in half, then to a tenth, then still more.

And yet that left the question of what was to be done with the plateaus between the hills. Plateaus of waste?

Plastic bottles and plastic bags, plastic spoons and plastic forks . . .

Some suggested building there to help relieve the stifling overcrowding—though of course there would be the occasional explosion, and a house or two could be expected to disappear into a sudden mire from time to time.

The family pet, sealed in a bag . . . hospital waste . . . construction debris . . .

Some suggested leaving the sites exactly as they were, so future archaeologists could find a wealth of detail from the prodigal middens of TwenCen California. With an even longer view, paleontologists speculated what the deposits might look like in a few million years, after grinding plates compressed them into layers of sedimentary stone.

Tires and cars, broken stereos and obsolete computers, missing rent money and misplaced diamond rings . . .

It might have been predictable, and yet few saw the answer coming. In a later day of harder times, of short resources and mandatory recycling, it was inevitable that those landfills should draw the eyes of innovators, looking for ways to get rich.

Iron, aluminum, silica . . . nickel, copper, zinc . . . methane, ammonia, phosphates . . . silver, gold, platinum . . .

Claims were filed, mining plans presented and analyzed. Refining methods were perfected and approved. Excavation began between the ancient hills.

Into a past generation's waste, their desperate grandchildren dug for treasure.

The garbage rush was on.

● So now Teresa was a hero, and a recent widow. No combination
E was more appealing to the masses . . . or to NASA press flacks,
X whose attentions she welcomed like an invasion of nibbling ro-
O dents. Fame was a pile of dumpit she could live without.
S   Fortunately, operational people had her for several weeks af-
P ter the Erehwon disaster. Teams of engineers spent from dawn to
H dusk coaxing every bit of useful description from her memory,
E until each night she would fall into bed and a deep, exhausted,
R dreamless slumber. Some outsiders got wind of the intense de-
E briefing and railed for her sake against "gestapo grilling tactics"—

until Teresa herself emerged one day to tell all the well-meaning do-gooders to go fuck off.

Not in so many words, of course. Their intentions were fine. Under normal circumstances it *would* be cruel to scrutinize a recent survivor so. But Teresa wasn't normal. She was an astronaut. A pilot astronaut. And if some all-knowing physician prescribed for her right now, the slip might say—"Surround her with competent people. Keep her busy, useful. That will do more good than a thousand floral gifts or ten million sympathy-grams."

Certainly she'd been traumatized. That was why she also cooperated with the NASA psychers, letting them guide her through all the stages of catharsis and healing. She wept. She railed against fate and wept again. Though each step in grieving was accomplished efficiently, that didn't mean she felt it any less than a normal person. She just felt it all faster. Teresa didn't have time to be normal.

Finally, the technical types had finished sifting her story to the last detail. Other questioners took over then—center chiefs, agency directors, congressional committees. Masters of policy.

Sitting next to Mark at hearing after hearing, Teresa felt waves of ennui as she listened to the same praise, the same lofty sentiments. Oh, not every public servant was posing. Most were intelligent, hard-working people, after their own fashion. But theirs was a realm as alien to her as the bottom of the sea. She was sworn to protect this system, but that didn't make sitting through it any easier.

"They talk and talk . . . but they never ask any of the real questions!" she muttered to Mark, sotto voce.

"Just keep smiling," he whispered back. "It's what we're paid for, now."

Teresa sighed. Anyone in NASA who refused her turn in the public relations barrel was a slacker who did real harm. But why did your smile-burden multiply whenever you did something particularly well? Was that any way to repay initiative? If there were justice, it'd be Colonel Glenn Spivey and the other peepers forced to sit through this, and she'd get the reward she wanted most.

To get back to work.

To help find out what had killed forty people. Including her husband.

Instead, Spivey was probably in the thick of things, helping design a new station, while she had to endure media attention any Hollywood star would swoon for.

As weeks passed, she began suspecting there was more to this than just an awkward overlap of two cultures. They kept urging her to do chat shows and go on lecture circuits. Or, if either she or Mark wanted to take off on a two-month vacation on St. Croix, that would be all right, too.

Tempted by a chance to graduate from astronaut to superstar, Mark succumbed. But not Teresa. She was adamant. And finally she asserted her right to go home.

A domestic service had come by regularly to water the plants. Still, the Clear Lake condo felt cryptlike when she walked through the front door. She went from window to window, letting in the listless, heavy-sweet smells of Texas springtime. Even traffic noise was preferable to the silence.

NASA had forwarded her important messages, providing secretaries to handle fan mail and bills. So she was denied even the solace of busywork during those awkward first hours. Her autosec flashed the queue of her clipping program . . . a backlog of fifteen thousand headlines culled from news services and Net-zines in every time zone. She flushed everything having to do with the accident, and the tally dropped below a hundred. Those she might scan later, to catch up with what was happening in the world.

Teresa wandered room to room, not exactly avoiding thoughts of Jason, but neither did she go straight to the photo album, shelved between the bound-paper encyclopedia and her husband's collection of rare comic books. She didn't need photographs or holo-pages in order to replay moments from her marriage. They were all in her head —the good and not so good—available on ready recall.

All too ready . . .

She slipped two hours of Vivaldi into the sheet-reader and went out to the patio with a glass of orange juice. (Someone had read her file and left two liters of the real thing in her cooler, fresh squeezed from Oregon oranges.)

Beyond the polarized UV screen, Teresa looked out on the swaying elms sheltering several blocks of low apartment buildings, ending abruptly at the white dikes NASA had erected against the rising Gulf of Mexico. The tracks of a new rapitrans line ran atop the levee. Trains swept past on faintly humming superconducting rails.

A bluebird landed on the balcony and chirped at her, drawing a brief smile. When she was little, bluebirds had been threatened all over North America by competition from starlings and other invaders brought to the continent by prior, careless generations of humans. Worried devotees of native fauna built thousands of shelters to help them survive, but still it seemed touch and go for the longest time.

Now, like the elms, bluebirds were resurgent. Just as no one could have predicted which plants or animals would suffer most from the depleted ozone and dryer climate, nobody seemed to have imagined some might actually benefit. But apparently, in a few cases, it was so.

On the downside, Teresa remembered one awful autumn when she and Jason came home almost daily to find pathetic creatures dying on the lawn. Or worse, hopping about in panic because they could no longer see.

Blind robins. Some threshold had been reached, and within weeks they were all dead. Since then Teresa sometimes wondered—had the extinction been universal? Or was the die-off just a local "adjustment," restricted to south Texas? A few words to her autosecretary would send a ferret program forth to fetch the truth in milliseconds. But then, what good would knowing do? The Net was such a vast sea of information, sipping from it sometimes felt like trying to slake your thirst from a fire hose.

Besides, she often found the Net tedious. So many people saw it as a great soapbox from which to preach recipes for planetary salvation.

Solutions. Everybody's got solutions.

One group wanted to draft the entire space program into an effort to suspend ozone generators in the stratosphere. A preposterous idea, but at least it was bold and assertive, unlike the panacea offered by those calling for the abandonment of technology altogether, and a return to "simpler ways." As if simpler ways could feed ten billion people.

As if simpler ways hadn't also done harm. Astronauts suffered few illusions about the so-called "benign pastoral life-style," having seen from space the deserts spread by earlier civilizations—Sumerians, Chinese, Berbers, Amerinds—armed with little more than sheep, fire, and primitive agriculture.

Teresa had her own ideas about solutions. There were more riches on the moon and asteroids than all the bean counters in all the capitals of the world could add up in their combined lifetimes. Lots of astronauts shared the dream of using space to cure Earth's ills.

She and Jason had. They had met in training, and at first it had seemed some magical dating service must have intervened on their behalf. It went beyond obvious things, like their shared profession.

No. I just never met anyone who could make me laugh so.

Their consensus had extended to shopping among the pattern-marriage styles currently in vogue. After long discussion, they finally selected a motif drawn up by a consultant recommended by some other couples they knew. And it seemed to work. Jealousy never loomed as a question between them.

Until late last year, that is.

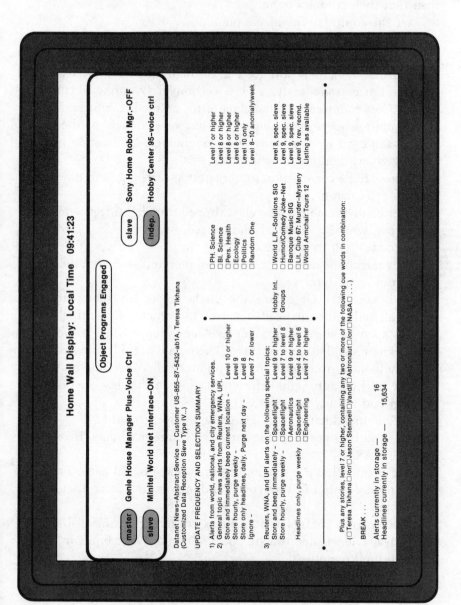

Home Wall Display: Local Time 09:41:23

Object Programs Engaged

master **Genie House Manager Plus–Voice Ctrl**
slave **Minitel World Net Interface–ON**

slave **Sony Home Robot Mgr.–OFF**
indep. **Hobby Center 95–voice ctrl**

Datanet News–Abstract Service — Customer US–855–87–5432–ab1A, Teresa Tikhana
(Customized Data Reception Sieve Type IV...)

UPDATE FREQUENCY AND SELECTION SUMMARY

1) Alerts from world, national, and city emergency services.
2) General topic news alerts from Reuters, WNA, UPI.

Store and immediately beep current location –	Level 10 or higher
Store hourly, purge weekly –	Level 9
Store only headlines, daily. Purge next day –	Level 8
Ignore –	Level 7 or lower

3) Reuters, WNA, and UPI alerts on the following special topics:

Store and beep immediately –	Spaceflight	Level 9 or higher
Store hourly, purge weekly –	Spaceflight	Level 7 to level 8
	Aeronautics	Level 9 or higher
Headlines only, purge weekly	Spaceflight	Level 4 to level 6
	Engineering	Level 7 or higher

□ PH. Science	Level 7 or higher
□ Bl. Science	Level 8 or higher
□ Pers. Health	Level 8 or higher
□ Ecology	Level 8 or higher
□ Politics	Level 10 only
□ Random One	Level 8–10 anomaly/week

Hobby Int. Groups

□ World L.R.–Solutions SIG	Level 8, spec. sieve
□ Humor/Comedy Joke–Net	Level 9, spec. sieve
□ Baroque Music SIG	Level 9, spec. sieve
□ Lit. Club 67: Murder–Mystery	Level 9, rev. recmd.
□ World Armchair Tours 12	Listing as available

Plus any stories, level 7 or higher, containing any two or more of the following cue words in combination:
(□ Teresa Tikhana □/or/□ Jason Stempell □)and(□ Astronaut □/or/□ NASA □ . . .)

BREAK. . . .

Alerts currently in storage —	16
Headlines currently in storage —	15,634

Until that Morgan woman appeared.

Teresa knew she was being unfair. She might as well blame Glenn Spivey. It was also about when Jason started working for that awful man that their troubles began.

Or she could lay the blame on . . .

"Dumpit!" She cursed. All this introspection brought a tightness to her jaw. She'd hoped absolute openness—giving the shrinks everything inside of her—would get her through all these "grief phases" quickly. But personal matters were so completely unlike the physical world. They followed no reliable patterns, no predictabilities. Despite recent optimistic pronouncements about new models of the mind, there hadn't yet been a Newton of psychology, an Einstein of emotions. Perhaps there never would be.

Teresa felt a constriction in her chest as tears began to flow again. "Damn . . . damn . . ."

Her hands trembled. The glass slipped from her fingers and fell to the carpet, where it bounced undamaged, but juice sprayed over her white pants. "Oh, cryo-bilge . . ."

The telephone rang. Teresa shouted on impulse, before the NASA secretaries could intervene.

"I'll take it!" Of course she ought to let her temporary staff screen all calls. But she needed action, movement, something!

As soon as she'd wiped her eyes and stepped inside, however, Teresa knew she'd made a mistake. The broad, florid features of Pedro Manella loomed over her from the phone-wall. Worse, she must have left the unit on auto-send before departing on that last mission. The reporter had already seen her.

"Captain Tikhana . . ." He smiled, larger than life.

"I'm sorry. I'm not giving interviews from my home. If you contact the NASA—"

He cut in. "I'm not seeking an interview, Ms. Tikhana. This concerns another matter I think you'll find important. I can't discuss it by telephone—"

Teresa knew Manella from press conferences. She disliked his aggressive style. His moustache, too. "Why not?" she broke in. "Why can't you tell me now?"

Manella obviously expected the question. "Well, you see, it has to do with matters conjoining onto your own concerns, where they overlap my own . . ."

He went on that way, sentence after sentence. Teresa blinked. At first she thought he was speaking one of those low-efficiency dialects civilians often used, *bureaucratese,* or *social science babble* . . . as impoverished of content as they were rich in syllables. But then she realized the man was jabbering the real thing—bona fide gibberish—phrases and sentences that were semantic nonsense!

She was about to utter an abrupt disconnect when she noticed him fiddling with his tie in a certain way. Then Manella scratched an ear, wiped his sweaty lip on a sleeve, wrung his hands *just so* . . .

The uninitiated would probably attribute it all to his Latin background—expressiveness in gestures as well as words—but what Teresa saw instead were crude but clear approximations of spacer hand talk.

. . . OPEN MIKE, she read. WATCH YOUR WORDS . . . CLASS RED URGENCY . . . CURIOSITY . . .

It was all so incongruous, Teresa nearly laughed out loud. What stopped her was the look in his eyes. They weren't the eyes of a babbler.

He knows something, she realized. Then—*He knows something about Erehwon!*

Manella was implying her phone line might be tapped. Furthermore, he was clearly making assumptions about the *level* of observation. Trained surveillance agents would find his sign language ruse ludicrously transparent. But the charade would probably fool most context-sensitive monitoring devices or agency flacks drafted to listen to the predictably boring conversations of a bus driver like herself. It would also get by any random eavesdropping hacker from the Net.

"All right." She waved a hand to stop him in midsentence. "I've heard enough, Mr. Manella, and I'm not interested. You'll have to go through channels like everybody else. Now, good-bye."

The display went blank just as he seemed about to remonstrate. He was a good actor, too. For it was only in those brown eyes that she saw confirmation of her own hand signs. Signs by which she had answered: MAYBE . . . I'LL RESPOND SOON . . .

She would think about it. *But why does Manella imagine I'd be monitored in the first place? And what is it he wants to tell me?*

It had to be about Erehwon . . . about the calamity. Her heart rate climbed.

At which point she'd had quite enough of this emotional rebellion by her body. She sat cross-legged on the carpet, closed her eyes, and sought the calm-triggers taught to her in high school—laying cooling blankets over her thoughts, using biofeedback to drain away the tension. Whatever was happening, whatever Manella had to say, no good would come of letting ancient fight-flight reactions sweep her away. Cavemen might not have had much use for patience, but it was a pure survival trait in the world of their descendants.

Inhaling deeply, she turned away from the travails of consciousness. Vivaldi joined the chirping bluebirds in an unnoticed background as she sought the center, wherein she always knew when and where she was.

This time though, she couldn't quite be sure that it—the center—was still there anymore at all.

☐

After he succeeded in separating Sky-Father from Earth-Mother, giving their offspring room at last to stand and breathe, the forest god, Tane, looked about and saw that something else was lacking. Only creatures of *ira atua*—the spirit way—moved upon the land. But what could spirit entities ever be without *ira tangata*, mortal beings, to know them? Nothing.

So Tane attempted to bring mortal life to the world. But of all the female spirits with whom he mated, only one possessed *ira tangata*. She was Hine-titama, Dawn Maid. Daughter and wife of Tane, she became mother of all mortal beings.

Later, after the world had been given life, Hine-titama turned away from the surface, journeying deep into the realms below. There she became Hine-nui-te-po, Great Lady of Darkness, who waits to tend and comfort the dead after their journey down Whanui a Tane, the broad road.

There she waits for you, and for you too. Our first mortal ancestor, she sleeps below waiting for us all.

● On his way back to Auckland after two days at the Tarawera Geo-
C thermal Works, Alex found himself ensnared in tourist traffic at
O Rotorua. Buses and minivans threaded the resort's narrow ways,
R hauling Australian families on holiday, gushing Sinhalese newly-
E weds, serene-looking Inuit investors, and Han—the inevitable swell of black-haired Han—nudging and whispering in close-packed mobs that overflowed the pavements and lawns, thronging and enveloping anything that might by any stretch be quaint or "native."

Most shops bore signs in International Ideogramatic Chinese, as well as English, Maori, and Simglish. And why not? The Han were only the latest wave of nouveau moyen to suddenly discover tourism. And if they engulfed all the beaches and scenic spots within four thousand kilometers of Beijing, they also paid well for their hard-earned leisure.

Yet more Chinese piled off flywheel buses just ahead of Alex's little car, wearing garish sunhats and True-Vu goggles that simultaneously protected the eyes and recorded for posterity every kitsch purchase from friendly concessionaires touting "genuine" New Zealand native woodcraft.

Well, it's their turn, Alex thought, nursing patience. *And it surely does beat war.*

Kiwi autumn was still warm and breezy, so he had the side window down. The smell of hydrogen sulfide from the geysers was pungent, but not too noticeable after all his time working underground with George Hutton's people. Waiting for traffic to clear, Alex watched another silvery cruise zeppelin broach a tree-lined pass and settle toward the busy aerodrome at the edge of town. Even from here he made out the crowds crammed into steerage, faces pressed against windows to peer down at Rotorua's steamy volcanic pools.

A decade or two hence it might be the new bourgeois of Burma or Morocco who packed the great junket liners, taking advantage of cheap zep travel to swarm abroad in search of armloads of cheap souvenirs and canned memories. By then of course, the Han would have grown used to it all. They'd be sophisticated individual travelers, like the Japanese and Malays and Turks, who avoided frantic mobs and snickered at the gaucheries of first-generation tourists.

That was the curious nature of the "mixed miracle." For as the world's nations scrimped and bickered over dwindling resources, sometimes scrapping violently over river rights and shifting rains, its masses meanwhile enjoyed a rising tide of onetime luxuries—made necessary by that demon Expectation.

—Pure water cost nearly as much as your monthly rent. At the same time, for pocket change you could buy disks containing a thousand reference books or a hundred hours of music.

—Petrol was rationed on a need-only basis and bicycles choked the world's cities. Yet resorts within one day's zep flight were in reach to even humble wage earners.

—Literacy rates climbed every year, and those with full-reliance cards could self-prescribe any known drug. But in most states you could go to jail for throwing away a soda bottle.

To Alex the irony was that nobody seemed to find any of it amazing. Change had this way of sneaking up on you, one day at a time.

"Anyone who tries to predict the future is inevitably a fool. Present company included. A prophet without a sense of humor is just stupid."

That was how his grandmother had put it, once. And she ought to know. Everyone praised Jen Wolling for her brilliant foresight. But one day she had shown him her scorecard from the World Predictions Registry. After twenty-five years of filing prognostications with the group, her success rating was a mere sixteen percent! And that was better than three times the WPR average.

*"People tend to get dramatic when they talk about the future. When I
was young, there were optimists who foresaw personal spacecraft and immortality in the twenty-first century . . . while pessimists looked at the
same trends and foretold collapse into worldwide famine and war.*

"Both forecasts are still *being made, Alex, with the deadlines always
pushed back one decade, then another and another. Meanwhile, people
muddle through. Some things get better, some a lot worse. Strangely
enough, 'the future' never does seem to arrive."*

Of course Jen didn't know everything. She had never suspected,
for instance, that tomorrow could come abruptly, decisively, in the
shape of a microscopic, titanically heavy fold of twisted space. . . .

Alex maneuvered slowly past a crowd that had spilled into the
street, watching dancers perform a *haka* on the marae platform of an
imposing Maori meeting house. Sloping beams of extravagantly carved
red wood overhung the courtyard where bare-chested men stuck out
their tongues and shouted, stamping in unison and flexing tattooed
thighs and arms to intimidate the delighted tourists.

George Hutton had taken Alex to see the real thing a while back,
at the wedding of his niece. It was quite a show, the *haka*. Evidence of
a rich cultural heritage that lived on.

For a while, at least . . .

Alex shook his head. *It's not my fault there won't be any more*
hakas—*or* Maori—*in a few years' time. I'm not responsible for the
thing swallowing the Earth from within.*

Alex hadn't made that monster—the singularity they called Beta.
He'd only discovered it.

Still, in ancient Egypt they used to kill the messenger.

He would have no such easy out. He might not have been the one
to set Beta on its course, but he *had* made the evaporating Iquitos
singularity, Alpha. To George Hutton and the others, that made him
responsible by proxy—no matter how much they liked him personally
—until Beta's real makers were found.

Alex recalled the image that had begun unblurring in the holo
tank as they probed the monster's involute topology. It was horrible,
voracious, and beautiful to behold. Undeniably there was a genius
somewhere . . . someone a whole lot better than Alex at his own
game. The realization was humbling, and a bit frightening.

Immersed in his own thoughts, he had been driving the little
Tangoparu company car on mental autopilot, threading past one bot-
tleneck after another. Just when it seemed traffic would open up again,
red brake lights forced him to stop hard. Shouts and horns blared
somewhere up ahead.

Alex leaned out the window to get a better look. Emergency

strobes flashed. A bobbing magnus-effect ambulance hovered near one of the massive, blocky tourist hotels, where budget-conscious travelers rented tiny, slotlike units by the cubic meter. The vehicle's spherical gas bag rotated slowly around a horizontal pivot, using small momentum shifts to maneuver delicately near white-suited emergency workers. Alex had no view of the injured, but stains on the clothes of shocked bystanders told of some bloody episode that must have gone down only moments ago.

The crowds suddenly parted and more police hove into view, wrestling along a figure swaddled in restraint netting, who howled and writhed, wild-eyed, with face and clothes flecked in blood and spittle. A green gas cannister at his belt showed him to be a dozer—one of those unfortunates more affected by excess carbon dioxide than other people. In most, such borderline susceptibilities caused little more than sleepiness or headaches. But sometimes a wild mania resulted, made far worse by the close press of crowding human flesh.

Apparently, supplemental oxygen hadn't helped this fellow . . . or the poor victims of his murderous fit. Alex had never seen a mucker up close like this before, but on occasion he had witnessed the effects from a distance.

"You don't get anything, but what something else gets taken away . . ." He distantly recalled Jen saying that last time he visited her office in London, as they stood together at the window watching the daily bicycle jam turn into a riot on Westminster Bridge. *"True-Vu tech put a stop to purposeful street crime,"* she had said. *"So today most killings are outrages of pure environmental overload. Promise me, Alex, you'll never be one of those down there . . . the honestly employed."*

Horribly fascinated, they had observed in silence as the commuter brawl spread onto Brunner Quay, then eastward toward the Arts Center. Recalling that episode, Alex suddenly saw this one take an unexpected turn. The officers hauling the wild-eyed mucker, distracted by frantic relatives at their sleeves, let their grip loosen for just a moment. Even then, a normal man might not have been able to tear free. But in a burst of hysterical strength the maniac yanked loose and ran. Ululating incoherently, he knocked down bystanders and then hurtled through the traffic jam—directly toward Alex's car!

The mucker's arms were pinned. *He can't get far,* Alex thought. *Somebody will stop him.*

Only no one did. Nobody sensible messed with a mucker, bound or unbound.

Deciding at the last moment, Alex kicked his door open. The madman's eyes seemed to clarify in that brief instant, replacing rage with an almost lucid, plaintive expression—as if to ask Alex, *What did I ever do to you?* Then he collided with the door, caroming a few meters before tumbling to the street. Somehow Alex felt guilty—as if he'd just beaten up a helpless bloke instead of possibly saving lives. That didn't stop him, though, from leaping out and throwing himself atop the kicking, squalling man—now suddenly awash with incongruous tears as he cursed in some inland dialect of Han. With no better way to restrain him, Alex simply sat on him till help arrived.

The whole episode—from breakaway to the moment officers applied the spray sedatives they should have used in the first place—took little more than a minute. When the trussed-up mucker looked back at him through a crowd of snapping True-Vu lenses, Alex had a momentary feeling that he understood the fellow . . . far better, perhaps, than he did the gawking tourists around him. There was something desperately fearful and yet longing in those eyes. A look reminding Alex of what he sometimes saw in a mirror's momentary, sidelong glance.

It was a queer, disturbing instant of recognition. *We all create monsters in our minds. The only important difference may be which of us let our monsters become real.*

After wading through congratulatory backpats to his car, Alex looked down and saw for the first time that his clothes were smeared with blood. He sighed. *Why does everything happen to me? I thought academics were supposed to lead boring lives.*

Oh, what I wouldn't give for some good old-fashioned British boredom about now. . . .

No sooner was he seated than the driver behind him blew his horn. So much for the rewards of heroism. Edging around a final tourist bus he saw open lanes ahead at last. Carefully Alex fed the engine hydrogen, spun up the little car's flywheel, and gradually built up speed. Soon the northern reaches of the Mamaku range sped by as he left Rotorua behind and set off across the central plateau.

This highway shared the chief attribute of Kiwi roads—a stubborn resistance to straight lines. Driving entailed carefully swooping round hairpin bends and steep crags, intermittently staring over precipices into gaping, cottony nothingness.

It was easy to see how New Zealand had got its Maori name—Ao Tearoa—Land of the Long White Cloud. Mist-shrouded peaks resembled recumbent giants swathed in fog. The slumbering volcanoes' green slopes supported rich forests, meadows, and over twenty million sheep. The latter were kept mostly for their wool nowadays, though he knew George Hutton and many other natives ate red meat from time to time and saw nothing wrong with it.

In this land of steam geysers and rumbling mountains, one never drove far without encountering another of Hutton's little geothermal power stations, each squatting on a taproot drilled near a vein of magma. Mapping such underground sources had made George wealthy. The network of sensors left over from that effort now helped Alex's team define what was happening in the Earth's core.

Not that anyone expected the scans to offer hope. *How, after all, do you get rid of an unwanted guest weighing a million million tons? A monster ensconced safely in a lair four thousand kilometers deep? You surely don't do it the way the Maori used to placate* taniwha *. . . demons . . . by plucking a hair and dropping it into dark waters.*

Still, George wanted the work continued, to learn how much time was left, and who was responsible. Alex had wrung one promise from George, in case they ever did find the culprit. He wanted an hour with the fellow . . . one hour to talk physics before George wreaked vengeance on the negligent genius with his own hands.

Thinking about the poor man he had encountered so roughly back in Rotorua—remembering the sad yet bloody look in the mucker's eyes—Alex wondered if any of them really had a right to judge.

He had always liked to think he had a passing education in fields outside his own. Alex had known, for instance, that even the greatest mountains and canyons were mere ripples and pores on the planet's huge bulk. Earth's crust—its basalts and granites and sedimentary rocks—made up only a hundredth of its volume and half a percent of its total mass. But he used to picture a vast interior of superdense, superhot melt, and left it at that. So much for geology.

Only when you truly study a subject do you find out how little you knew all along.

Why, just two months ago Alex had never heard of Andrija Mohorovičić!

In 1909 the Yugoslav scientist had used instruments to analyze vibration waves from a Croatian earthquake. Comparing results from several stations, Mohorovičić discovered he could, like bats or whales, detect objects by their reflected sound alone. On another occasion he found a thin layer that would later bear his name. But in 1909 what he heard were echoes of the Earth's very core.

As instruments improved, seismic echolocation showed other abrupt boundaries, along with fault lines, oil fields, and mineral deposits. By century's end, millions were being spent on high-tech listening as desperate multinationals sought ever-deeper veins, to keep the glory days going just a little longer.

A picture took shape, of a dynamic world in ceaseless change. And while most geologists went on studying the outer crust, some curious men and women cast their nets much deeper, beyond and below any conceivable economic reward.

Such "useless" knowledge often makes men rich—witness George Hutton's billions. Whereas Alex's own "practical" project, financed by money-hungry generals, had turned unprofitable to a rare and spectacular degree.

It just goes to show . . . he thought. *You never can tell what surprises life has in store for you.*

Even as Alex admitted his ignorance of geophysics, it was his own expertise that Hutton's techs called upon as they struggled to improve their tools. The gravity antennas employed superconducting wave generators like those in a cavitron—the still-unlicensed machine he'd used in Iquitos. So he was able to suggest shortcuts saving months of development.

It was fun exchanging ideas with others . . . building something new and exciting, out of sight of the suspicious bureaucrats of the scientific tribunals. Unfortunately, each time they laughed together, or they celebrated overcoming some obstacle, someone inevitably stopped short and turned away, remembering what it was all about and how futile their work was likely to be in the long run. Alex doubted that even his great-grandparents' generation, during the awful nuclear brinksmanship of the cold war, had ever felt so helpless or hopeless.

But we have to keep trying.

He switched on the radio, looking for some distracting music. But the first station he found carried only news bulletins, in Simplified English.

"We now tell you more news about the tragedy of Reagan Station. Two weeks ago, the American space station exploded. The ambassador to the United Nations, from Russia, accuses that the United States of North America was testing weapons on Reagan Station. The Russian ambassador does say that he has no proof. But he also does say that this is the most likely explanation . . ."

Most likely explanation indeed, Alex thought. *It just goes to show . . . you never can tell.*

☐ In olden times, to be "sane" meant you behaved in ways both sanctioned by and normal to the society you lived in.

In the last century some people—especially creative people—rebelled against this imposition, this having to be "average." Eager to preserve their differences, some even went to the opposite extreme, embracing a romantic notion that creativity and suffering are inseparable, that a thinker or doer must be outrageous, even crazy, in order to be great. Like so many other myths about the human mind, this one lingered for a long time, doing great harm.

At last, however, we have begun to see that true sanity has nothing at all to do with norms or averages. This redefinition emerged only when some got around to asking the simplest of questions.

"What are the most common traits of nearly all forms of mental illness?"

The answer? Nearly all sufferers lack—

flexibility—to be able to change your opinion or course of action, if shown clear evidence you were wrong.

satiability—the ability to feel satisfaction if you actually get what you said you wanted, and to transfer your strivings to other goals.

extrapolation—an ability to realistically assess the possible consequences of your actions and to empathize, or guess how another person might think or feel.

This answer crosses all boundaries of culture, age, and language. When a person is adaptable and satiable, capable of realistic planning and empathizing with his fellow beings, those problems that remain turn out to be mostly physiochemical or behavioral. What is more, this definition allows a broad range of deviations from the norm—the very sorts of eccentricities suppressed under older worldviews.

So far so good. This is, indeed, an improvement.

But where, I must ask, does *ambition* fit under this sweeping categorization? When all is said and done, we remain mammals. Rules can be laid down to keep the game fair. But nothing will ever entirely eliminate that will, within each of us, to win.

—From **The Transparent Hand**, Doubleday Books, edition 4.7 (2035) [□ hyper access code 1-tTRAN-777-97-9945-29A.]

". . . the most likely explanation. Come now, Captain Tikhana. Surely you aren't taken in by that silly cover story they're spreading? That America was conducting secret weapons tests aboard Erehwon?"

Teresa shrugged, wondering again why she had let Pedro Manella set up this luncheon meeting in the first place. "Why not?" she responded. "The space secretary denies it. The President denies it. But you press people keep printing it."

"Exactly!" Manella spread his hands expansively. "The government's charade is working perfectly. It's a venerable tactic. Keep loudly denying something you didn't do, so nobody will look for what you really did!"

Teresa stared as he twirled a forkful of linguini and made a blithe insouciance of taking it under the portal of his moustache. Fighting a nascent headache, she pressed the pressure points above her eyes. The plastic table top rocked under her elbows, setting plates and glasses quivering.

"Exactly–what–are–you–talking–about?" she said irritably, speaking the words individually. "If you don't start making sense soon, I'm going to switch languages. Maybe you can make yourself understood in Simglish."

The reporter gave her a look of distaste. Known to be fluent in nine tongues, he clearly had no love for the experimental bastard son of English and Esperanto.

"All right, Ms. Tikhana. Let me spell it out for you. I think your husband's team on the space station's Farpoint platform was experimenting with captive black holes."

She blinked, then broke out laughing. "I knew it. You *are* crazy."

"Am I?" Manella wiped his moustache and leaned toward her. "Consider. Although cavitronics research is allowed in a few places, in only one location have investigators been licensed to go all the way— to create full-scale singularities. And then only in orbit around the moon."

"So?"

"So imagine some government decided to do an end run around the international team. What if they wanted to experiment on singularities of their own, in secret, to get a technological head start before the moratorium ends?"

"But the risks of getting caught—"

"Are substantial, yes. But those repercussions would be lessened by keeping all experiments at high altitude until everyone is sure microholes are safe and the tribunals start issuing licenses. Look what happened to that poor imbecile Alex Lustig, when he got caught jumping the gun right on the Earth's surface."

Teresa shook her head. "You're implying the United States was engaged in secret, illegal research in space," she said coolly.

Manella's smile was patronizing, infuriating. Teresa steeled herself to ignore everything but content.

"I'm suggesting," he replied. "That your husband might have been involved in such a program, and never bothered telling you about it."

"I've heard enough." Teresa crumpled her napkin and threw it on the table. She stood, but then stopped as she saw the reporter pull out several glossy photographs and lay them between the place settings. Teresa's fingertips traced the outline of Jason's face.

"Where was this taken?"

"At a conference on gravity physics last year, in Snowbird. See? You can read his name tag. Of course he wasn't in uniform at the time . . ."

"Do you carry a secret camera in your bow tie?"

"In my moustache," he said, with such a straight face that Teresa almost believed him. "This was back when I was hunting for clues to Alex Lustig's whereabouts, before I broke the story on his own particular—"

Teresa flipped the last picture aside. "Nobody trusts photographs anymore, as proof of anything at all."

"True enough," Manella conceded. "They could be faked. But it was a public conference. Call the organizers. He used his own name."

Teresa paused. "So? Among other things, Jason was studying anomalies in the Earth's gravitational field. They're important to orbital mechanics and navigation." Because of that aspect, Teresa had done more than a little reading on the subject herself.

Manella commented with his shoulders. "The Earth's field is twenty orders of magnitude less intense than the sort of gravity they talk about at conferences on the theory of black holes."

Teresa slumped into her seat again. "You're crazy," she repeated. But this time her voice didn't carry as much conviction.

"Come now, Captain. You're an adult. Do not sink to abuse. Or at least keep the abuse relevant. Call me overzealous. Or pushy. Or even pudgy. But don't say I'm crazy when you know I might be right."

Teresa wanted to look anywhere but into the man's dark, piercing eyes. "Why can't you just leave it alone! Even if everything you suspect were true, they paid for it with their lives. The only ones they harmed were themselves."

"And the taxpayers, Ms. Tikhana. I'm surprised you forget them. And perhaps your space program. What will happen to it during the lengthy investigations?"

Teresa winced, but said nothing.

"Besides, even if they only harmed themselves, does that excuse their bosses for violating basic principles of international law? True, most physicists agree cavitrons can't make anything truly dangerous. But until that's verified by a science tribunal, the technology is still quarantined. You know the reasons for the New Technologies Treaty as well as I do."

Teresa felt like spitting. "The treaty's a millstone, dragging us back—" But Manella disagreed, interrupting.

"It's our salvation! You, of all people, should know what harm was done before its enactment. Care to try stepping outside right now without protection? Our grandparents could do so safely, even on a day like today."

She glanced through the coated panes of the restaurant. It was bright out, not a cloud in the sky. Many strollers were enjoying an afternoon on the Mall. But everyone, without exception, wore sun hats and protective glasses.

Teresa knew the UV danger was often overstated. Even a few days' sunbathing on a beach wouldn't appreciably shorten the average person's lifespan. The ozone layer wasn't that badly depleted yet. Still, she got Manella's point. Human shortsightedness had shredded that protective veil, just as it accelerated the spreading deserts and rising seas.

"You Americans astonish me," he went on. "You dragged the rest of us, kicking and screaming, into environmental awareness. You and the Scandinavians chivvied and coerced until the treaties were signed . . . possibly in time to save something of this planet.

"But then, once the laws and tribunals were in place, you became the loudest complainers! Hollering like frustrated children about restraints on your right to do whatever you please!"

Teresa didn't say anything, but answered silently. *We never expected all the damned bureaucracy.*

Her personal grudge was the tribunals' slowness in releasing new rocket designs—studying, then restudying whether this propellant or that one would produce noxious or greenhouse gases. Closing the barn door too late on one problem and closing opportunity's door at the same time.

"The world is too small," Manella went on. "Our frail, frugal prosperity teeters on a precipice. Why do you think I devote myself to hunting down little would-be Fausts like Alex Lustig?"

She looked up. "For the headlines?"

Manella lifted his wine glass. "Touché. But my point remains, Captain Tikhana. Something went on aboard that station. Let's put aside illegality and talk about secrecy. Secrecy meant it wasn't subject to scrutiny and criticism. That's how calamities like Chernobyl and Lamberton and Tsushima happen. It's also why—to be horribly blunt —your husband is right now hurtling at relativistic velocities toward Sagittarius."

Teresa felt the blood drain out of her face. She had a sudden memory . . . not of Jason, but of the slippery way Colonel Glenn Spivey had managed to avoid testifying. Spivey had to know more, much more than he was telling.

Oh, Manella was smart all right. Right down to knowing when his point was made . . . when it was best to stop talking while his victim squirmed for some way out of his infernal trap of logic.

Despairingly, Teresa saw no escape. She had to make a choice between two equally unpalatable avenues.

She could go to the inspector general with this. By federal and treaty law she'd be protected from retribution. Her rank and pay and safety would be secure.

But there was no way the IG could protect the most precious thing left to her—her flight status. Any way it went, "they" would find an excuse not to let her back into space again.

The other choice Manella was clearly, implicitly offering. She subvocalized the half obscenity . . . a *conspiracy*.

Something scratched at the window. She looked outside to see a creature scrabbling against the smooth surface of the glass—a large insect, bizarre and startling until she remembered.

A cicada. Yes, the Net had stories about them.

The city had braced for the reemergence of the seventeen-year cicadas, which from time beyond memory had flooded one summer every generation with noisy, ratcheting insect life, swarming through the trees and keeping everybody awake until they at last mated, laid their eggs, and died. A nuisance, but one whose recurrence was so rare and well timed that Washington regularly made an event of it, with special studies in the schools and humorous reports on the zines.

Only this year something had gone wrong.

Perhaps it was the water, or maybe something let into the soil. No one knew why yet . . . only that when a few, straggling cicadas finally did emerge from their seventeen winters underground, they

were warped, sickly things, mutated and dying. It brought back memories of the cancer plague, or the Calthingite babies of twenty years
ago, and led to dire conjectures about when something like it would
next happen to people again.

Teresa watched the pitiful, horrible little insect crawl away amid
the shrubbery . . . a victim, one of so many without names.

"What is it you want of me?" she asked the reporter in a whisper.

Somehow, she had expected him to smile. She was glad, even
grateful, that he was sensitive enough not to exult openly. With a
sincerity that might even be genuine, Pedro Manella touched her
hand.

"You must help me. Help me find out what is going on."

☐ The World Predictions Registry is proud to present our twenty-fifth annual Prognostication Awards, for accomplishments in the fields of trend
analysis, meteorology, economic forecasting, and whistle blowing. In addition this year, for the first time in a decade, there will be a new category.

For some time a debate has raged in our portion of the Net over the
purpose of the registry. Are we here simply to collate the projections of
various experts, so that over time those with the best accuracy scores may
"win" in some way? Or should our objective be something more far-
reaching?

It can be argued that there's nothing more fascinating and attractive to
human beings than the notion of predicting a successful path through the
pitfalls and opportunities that lie ahead. Entertainment Net-zines are filled
with the prophecies of psychics, soothsayers, astrologers, and stock market analysts, all part of a vast market catering to this basic human dream.

Why not—some of our members have asked—expand the registry to
record all *those* visions as well, and score them as we do the more academic models? At the very least we'd provide a service by debunking
charlatans. But also there's the possibility, even if most offer no more than
sensationalism and fancy, that just a few of these would-be seers could be
making bona fide hits.

What if some crank—without knowing how or why—stumbled onto a
rude but promising trick or knack, one offering him or her a narrow window
onto the obstacle course ahead? These days, with the world in the condition it's in, can we afford to ignore any possibility?

For this reason, on our silver anniversary, we're establishing the new
category of "random prophecy." It will require a database store larger
than all other categories combined. Also, as in the department for whistle

blowing, we'll be accepting anonymous predictions under codenames to protect those fearful for their reputations.

So send them in, you would-be Johns and Nostrodami . . . only please, try not to be *quite* as obscure as the originals. As in the other sections, part of your score will be based on the explicitness and testability of your projections.

And now for honorable mentions in the category of trends analysis . . .

—World Predictions Registry. [□ AyR 2437239.726 IntPredReg. 6.21.038:21:01.]

● C O R E　Once, when he was very young, Alex's gran took him out of school to witness a life ark being launched. Nearly thirty years later, the memory of that morning still brought back feelings of childlike wonder.

For one thing, in those days an adult might think nothing of sending a big, black, gasoline-powered taxi to Croydon to pick up a small boy and then take him all the way back to where St. Thomas's Hospital squatly overlooked long queues of cargo barges filing down the Thames past Parliament. After politely thanking the cabbie, young Alex had taken the long way to the hospital entrance, so he could dawdle near the water watching the boats. Set free temporarily from uniforms and schoolyard bullying, he savored a little time alone with the river before turning at last to go inside.

As expected, Jen was still busy, running back and forth from her research lab to the clinic, giving both sets of assistants revised instructions that only served to introduce still more chaos. Alex waited contentedly, perched on a lab stool while patients from all over Greater London were tested and prodded and rayed to find out what was wrong with them. Back then, while still involved in practical medicine, Jen used to complain she was always being sent the cases no one else could diagnose. As if she'd have had it any other way.

Laboratory science interested Alex, but biology seemed so murky, so undisciplined and subjective. Watching them test victims of a dozen different modern urban maladies, brought on by pollution, tension or overcrowding, he wondered how the workers were able to conclude anything at all.

One of the techs fortunately came to his rescue with a pad of paper and soon Alex was immersed, doodling with maths. On that day —he recalled vividly in later years—it had been the marvelous, intricate, and exacting world of matrices that had him enthralled.

At last Jen called to him as she removed her lab coat. Short, but deceptively strong, she took his hand as they left the hospital and rented two cycles from a hire/drop bubble near the elevated bikeway.

Alex had hoped they'd take a cab. He complained about the weather and distance, but Jen insisted a little mist never hurt anyone, and he could use the exercise.

In those days bicycles weren't yet lords of London's streets, and Alex had to endure a harrowing blur of horns and shouting voices. Keeping up with Jen seemed a matter of grim survival until at last the green swards of Regent's Park opened up around them in a welcome haven of calm.

Black banners hung limply as they dropped off the bikes at a canal-side kiosk, below green and blue Earthwatch placards. Demonstrators stood nearby with ash-smeared brows, protesting both the ark program and the recent events that had made it necessary. One damp-haired speaker addressed tourists and visitors with an intensity that blazed in Alex's memory ever afterward.

"Our world, our mother, has many parts. Each—like the organs in our bodies, like our very cells—participates in a synergistic whole. Each is a component in the delicate balance of cycle and recycle which has kept this world for so long an oasis of life in the dead emptiness of space.

"What happens when you or I lose a piece of ourselves? A finger? A lung? Do we expect to function the same afterward? Will the whole ever work as well again? How, then, can we be so blithe at the dismembering of our world? Our mother?

"Gaia's cells, her organs, are the species that share her surface!

"Here, today, hypocrites will tell you they're saving species. But how? By amputating what's left and storing it in a jar? You might as well cut out a drunkard's liver and preserve it in a machine. For what purpose? Who is saved? Certainly not the patient!"

Alex watched the speaker while his grandmother bought tickets. Most of the fellow's words left him perplexed on that day. Still, he recalled being fascinated. The orator's passion was unusual. Those who held forth on Sundays at Speakers' Corner seemed pallid and overwry in comparison.

One passage in particular he recollected with utter clarity. The fellow stretched his hands out at passersby, as if pleading for their souls.

". . . humans brought intelligence, sentience, self-awareness to the world, it cannot be denied. And that, by itself, was good. For how else could Gaia learn to know herself without a brain? That was our purpose—to furnish that organ—to serve that function for our living Earth.

"But what have we done?"

The demonstrator wiped at the ash stains above each eye, runny from the intermittent drizzle. "What kind of brain slays the body of which it is a part? What kind of thinking organ kills the other organs of its whole? Are we Gaia's brain? Or are we a cancer! One she'd be far better off without?"

For a moment, the speaker caught Alex's eye and seemed to be addressing him especially. Staring back, Alex felt his grandmother take his hand and pull him away, past metal detectors and sniffer machines into the relative tranquility of the grounds inside.

On that day nobody seemed much interested in the bears or seals. The African section held few tourists, since that continent had been declared stabilized a few years before. Most people thought the great die-back there was over. For a time, at least.

Passing the Amazona section, Alex wanted to stop and see the golden lion tamarins, their large enclosure outlined in bright blue. There were quite a few other blue-rimmed areas there. Guards, both human and robot, focused on anyone who approached those specially marked exhibits too closely.

The yellow-maned tamarins looked at Alex dispiritedly, meeting his eyes as he passed. To him it seemed they too were aware of what today's activity was about.

Crowds were already dispersing in the newly expanded section of the zoo devoted to creatures from the Indian subcontinent. He and Jen were too late for the official ceremony, naturally. Gran had never been on time for anything as long as he'd known her.

Still, it didn't really matter. The mass of visitors weren't here to listen to speeches but to bear witness and know that history had marked yet another milestone. Jen told him they were "doing penance," which he figured must mean she was a Gaian, too.

It wasn't until many years later that he came to realize millions thought of her as *the* Gaian.

While they queued, the sun came out. Vapor rose from the pavement. Jen gave him a tenner to run off for an ice lollie, and he made it back just in time to join her at the place where the new border was being laid.

Half the exhibits in this section were already lined in blue. Guards now patrolled what had only a month ago been standard zoo enclosures, but which were now reclassified as something else entirely. This was before the hermetically sealed arks of later days, back when the demarcation was still mostly symbolic.

Of course the extra animals, the refugees, hadn't arrived yet.

They were still in quarantine while zoos all over the world debated who would take which of the creatures recently yanked out of the collapsing Indian park system. Over the months ahead, the exiles would arrive singly and in pairs, never again to see their wild homes.

Painters had just finished outlining the blackbuck compound. The deerlike animals flicked their ears, oblivious to their changed status. But in the next arena a tigress seemed to understand. She paced her enlarged quarters, tail swishing, repeatedly scanning the onlookers with fierce yellow eyes before quickly turning away again, making low rumbling sounds. Jen watched the beast, transfixed, a strange, distant expression on her face, as if she were looking far into the past . . . or to a future dimly perceived.

Alex pointed a finger at the great cat. Although he knew he was supposed to feel sorry for it, the tiger seemed so huge and alarming, it gave him a ritual feeling of security to cock his thumb and aim.

"Bang, bang," he mouthed silently.

A new plaque glittered in the sunshine.

> LIFE-ARK REFUGEE NUMBER 5,345
> ROYAL BENGAL TIGER
> NOW EXTINCT IN THE WILD.
>
> MAY WE EARN THEIR FORGIVENESS THROUGH THESE ARKS
> AND SOMEDAY GIVE THEM BACK AGAIN THEIR HOMES.

"I've looked into the gene pool figures," Jen had said, though not to him. She stared at the beautiful, scary, wild thing beyond the moat and spoke to herself. "I'm afraid we're probably going to lose this line."

She shook her head. "Oh, they'll store germ plasm. And maybe someday, long after the last one has died . . ."

Her voice just faded then, and she looked away.

At the time Alex had only a vague notion what it was all about, what the ark program was for, or why the agencies involved had at last given up the fight to save the Indian forests. All he knew was that Jen was sad. He took his grandmother's hand and held it quietly until at last she sighed and turned to go.

Those feelings lingered with him even long after he went away to university and entered physics. *Everyone is either part of the problem or part of the solution,* he had learned from her. Alex grew up determined to make a difference, a big difference.

And so he sought ways to produce cheap energy. Ways that would require no more digging or tearing or poisoning of land. Ways to give billions the electricity and hydrogen they insisted on having, but without cutting any more forests. Without adding poisons to the air.

Well, Alex reminded himself for the latest time. *I may have failed at that. I may have been useless. But at least I'm not the one who killed the Earth. Someone else did that.*

It was a strange, ineffective solace.

No, another part of him agreed. *But the ones who did it—whatever team or government or individual manufactured Beta—they, too, might have begun with the purest of motives.*

Their mistake might just as easily have been my own.

Alex remembered the tigress, her savage, reproachful eyes. The slow, remorseless pacing.

The hunger . . .

Now he pursued a far deadlier monster. But for some reason the image of the great cat would not leave him.

He remembered the blackbucks, gathered in their pen all facing the same way, seeking security and serenity in numbers, in doing everything alike. Tigers weren't like that. They had to be housed separately. Except under rare circumstances, they could not occupy the same space. That made them harder to maintain.

There were analogies in physics . . . the blackbucks were like those particles called bosons, which all sorted together. But fermions were loners like tigers. . . .

Alex shook his head. What a bizarre line of contemplation! Why was he thinking about this right now?

Well, there was that postcard from Jen . . .

Not really a postcard—more a snapshot, sent to one of his secret mail drops in the Net. It showed his grandmother, apparently as spry as ever, posing with several black men and women and what looked like a tame rhinoceros—if such a thing were possible. Transmission marks showed it had been sent from the pariah Confederacy of Southern Africa. So Jen was making waves, still.

It runs in the family, he thought, smiling ironically.

He jerked slightly as someone nudged him on the shoulder. Looking up, he saw George Hutton standing over him.

"All right, Lustig, I'm here. Stan tells me you wanted to show me something before we begin the next test run. He says you've added to your bestiary."

Alex jerked, still remembering the life ark. "I beg your pardon?"

"You know . . . black holes, microscopic cosmic strings, *tuned* strings . . ." George rubbed his hands in mock anticipation. "So, what have you come up with this time?"

"Well, I've been wrong before . . ."

"And you may be again. So? Each time you goof, it's brilliant! Come on, then. Show me the final loop, or lasso, or lariat, or . . ."

He trailed off, eyes widening at what Alex manifested in the holo tank. *"Bozhe moi,"* George sighed. An expression Alex knew was definitely not Maori.

"I call it a *knot singularity,"* he replied. "An apt name, don't you think?"

The blue thing did resemble a knot of sorts—a Gordian monstrosity with the same relationship to a boy scout's clove hitch as a spaceship had to a firecracker. The writhing orb was in ceaseless motion—loops popping out of the surface and quickly receding again—making Alex think of a ball of angry worms. All around the rippling sphere was emitted a shining light.

"I—I suppose that thing is made of . . . strings?" George asked, then swallowed.

Alex nodded. "Good guess. And before you ask, yes, they're touching each other without reconnecting and dissipating. Think of a neutron, George. Neutrons can't exist for long outside an atom. But contained inside, say, a helium nucleus, they can last nearly forever."

George nodded soberly. He pointed. "Look at that!"

The loops popping out of the roiling mass mostly throbbed and flailed quickly before being drawn back in. Now though, a string extended farther out than usual and managed to cross over on itself beyond the knot.

In a flash it burned loose and floated away from the greater body. Released from the whole, the liberated loop soon twisted round itself again. With another flash of reconnection there were two small ones in its place. Then four. Soon, the rebel string had vanished in a rush of division and self-destruction.

As they watched, another loop cut itself off in the same way, drifting off to die. Then another. "I think I see," George said. "This thing, too, is doomed to destroy itself, like the micro black hole and the micro string."

"Correct," Alex said. "Just as a black hole is a gravitational singularity in zero macrodimensions, and a cosmic string is a singularity in one, a knot is a discontinuity in space-time that can twist in three, four . . . I haven't calculated how many directions it can be tied in. I can't even dream what the cosmological effects might be, if any truly big ones were made back at the beginning of the universe.

"What all three singularities have in common is this. It doesn't pay to be small. A small knot is just as unstable as a microstring or a microhole. It dissipates—in this case by emitting little string loops which tear themselves apart in a blaze of energy."

"So," George said. "This is what you now think you made in your cavitron, in Peru?"

"Yes, it is." Alex shook his head, still unable to really believe it himself. And yet no other model so accurately explained the power readings back at Iquitos. None so well predicted the mass and trajectory they had observed during the last week. It still astonished Alex he could have constructed such a thing without knowing it was even theoretically possible. But there it was.

Silence between the two men remained unbroken for moments.

"So now you have a model that works," George said at last. "First you thought you had dropped a black hole into the Earth, then a tuned string. Now you call it a knot . . . and yet it still is harmless, dissipating."

Hutton turned back to look at Alex again. "That still doesn't help you explain Beta, does it? You still have no idea why the other monster is stable, self-contained, able to grow and feed at the Earth's core, do you?"

Alex shook his head. "Oh, it's a knot all right. *Some* kind of knot singularity. But exactly what type . . . that's what we try to start finding out today."

"Hmm," Hutton looked across the underground chamber, past the waiting technicians to the gleaming new thumper, freshly built to specifications Alex and Stan Goldman had developed, now tuned and ready to send probing beams of gravity downward, inward.

"I'm concerned about those earthquakes," George said.

"So am I."

"But there's no way to avoid taking risks, is there, hm? All right, Lustig. Go on, give the order. Let's see what the thing has to say, face to face."

Alex waved to Stan Goldman, stationed by the thumper itself, who rolled his eyes in a swift prayer and then threw the master timing switch. Naturally, nobody in the chamber actually heard the sound of coherent gravitons, fired downward from the superconducting antenna. Still, they could *imagine.*

Alex wondered if the others, too, were listening for an echo, and fearing just what would be heard.

☐ *Worldwide Long Range Solutions Special Interest Group* [☐ SIG AeR,WLRS 253787890.546], random sampling of today's bulletin board queries. [☐ Abstracts only. Speak number or press index symbol for expanded versions.]

(54,891)   "Why, after all these years, haven't they figured out how to separate valuable elements from seawater? It must be a conspiracy by the mining companies! Any comments out there? Or suggested references I can look up?"

(54,892)   "Ever since I was little, back in TwenCen, I kept hearing about *fusion power*—how it'd provide cheap, clean, limitless energy someday. They said it was 'only' twenty years or so from being practical, but that was sixty years ago! Can someone index-ref some teach-vids on the subject, so a lay person like me can find out where they're at today?"

(54,893)   "I hear in Burma and Royal Quebec they're letting convicted killers choose execution by *disassembly*, so their organs can go on living in other people. One fellow's still 87% alive, they recycled him so well! Can anyone help me trace the origins of this concept? Where does execution leave off and a kind of immortality for felons begin?"

(54,894)   "How about fighting the greenhouse effect by sending lots of dust into the atmosphere, to block sunlight like those volcanoes did during the chill snap of '09? I recently found a swarm of references to something called *nuclear winter* they were all worried about back during TwenCen. It might have been scary when there were all those bombs lying around, but right now I think we could use some winter around here! Anyone interested in starting a subforum about this?"

(54,895)   "Why jiltz poor wire-heads whose only tort is self-perving? Sure they're vice lice, but where's the fraction in evolution in action? I say let 'em unbreed themselves, and stop forcing therapy drugs on the pleasure-centered!"

(54,896)   "My company blood test shows a 35% higher than average genetic presensitivity to cell-muting by trace chlorine. The boss says, stop using public swimming pools or lose my supra-insurance. Can she use a company test to tell me what to do on my free time? Any public domain law programs on the subject?"

(54,897)   "Say, does anyone else out there feel he or she's *missing something*? I mean, I can't pin it down exactly, but . . . do *you* feel something's going on, but nobody's telling you what it is? I don't know. I just can't shake this feeling something's happening . . ."

●   The Bay of Biscay glowed with the same radiant, sapphire hues
L   Logan remembered in Daisy McClennon's eyes. He fell for those
I   delicate shades again as he traveled swiftly southward aboard a
T   Tide Power Corporation minizeppelin. The beauty of the waters
H   was chaste, serene, pure, but all that would change once Eric
O   Sauvel's engineers had their way.
S   Sauvel sat next to him, behind the zep's pilot, gesturing to
P   encompass the brilliant seascape. "Our silt stirrers are already scat-
H   tered across eight hundred square kilometers, where bottom sedi-
E   ments are richest," he told Logan, raising his voice slightly above
R   the softly hissing motors.
E   "You'll provide power directly from the Santa Paula barrage?"

"Correct. The tidal generators at Santa Paula will feed the stirrers via superconducting cables. Of course any excess will go to the European grid."

Sauvel was a tall, handsome man in his early thirties, a graduate of École Polytechnique and chief designer of this daring double venture. He hadn't welcomed Logan's first visit a few weeks ago, but changed his mind when the American suggested improvements for the main generator footings. He kept pressing to have Logan back for a follow-up. It would be a lucrative consultancy, and the partners back in New Orleans had insisted Logan accept.

At least this trip was more comfortable than that hair-raising truck ride from Bilbao had been. That first time, Logan had only seen the tidal barrage itself—a chain of unfinished barriers stretching across a notch in the Basque seaboard. Since then he'd learned a lot more about this bold type of hydraulic engineering.

All along this coastline the Atlantic tides reached great intensity, driven by wind and gravity and funneled by the convergence of France and Spain. Other facilities already drew gigawatts of power from water flooding into the Iberian bight twice a day, without adding a single gram of carbon to the atmosphere or spilling an ounce of poison upon the land. The energy came, ultimately, from an all but inexhaustible supply—the orbital momentum of the Earth-Moon system. On paper it was an environmentalist's dream—the ultimate renewable resource.

But try telling that to those demonstrators, back in Bordeaux.

This morning he had toured the facility already in place across the former mudflats of the Bassin d'Arcachon, near where the rivers Garonne and Dordogne flowed past some of the best wine country in the world. The Arcachon Tidal Power Barrage now supplied clean energy to much of southwestern France. It had also been bombed three times in the last year alone, once by a kamikaze pilot pedaling a handmade ornithopter.

Demonstrators paced the facility's entrance as they had for fourteen years, waving banners and the womb-shaped Orb of the Mother. It seemed that even a pollution-free power plant—one drawing energy from the moon's placid orbit—was bound to have its enemies these days. The protestors mourned former wetlands, which some had seen as useless mud flats, but which had also fed and sheltered numberless seabirds before being turned into a dammed-up plain of surging, turbid saltwater.

Then there was the other half of Eric Sauvel's project, about which still more controversy churned. "How much sediment will you raise with your offshore impellers?" Logan asked the project manager.

"Only a few tons per day. Actually, it's amazing how little sea bottom muck has to be lifted, if it's well dissolved. One thousand impellers should turn over enough nutrients to imitate the fertilizing effect of the Humboldt Current, off Chile. And it will be much more reliable of course. We won't be subject to climatic disruptions, such as El Niño.

"Preliminary tests indicate we'll create a phytoplankton bloom covering half the bay. Photosynthesis will . . . is the correct expression *skyrocket*?"

Logan nodded. Sauvel went on. "Zooplankton will eat the phytoplankton. Fish and squid will consume zooplankton. Then, nearer to the shore, we plan to establish a large kelp forest, along with an otter colony to protect it from hungry sea urchins . . ."

It all sounded too good to be true. Soon, yields from the Bay of Biscay might rival the anchovy fisheries of the eastern Pacific. Right now, in comparison, the bright waters below were as barren as the gleaming sands of Oklahoma.

That, certainly, was how Sauvel must see the bay today, as a vast, wet desert, a waste, but one pregnant with potential. Simply by lifting sea floor sediments to nourish the bottom of the food chain—drifting, microscopic algae and diatoms—the rest of life's pyramid would be made to flourish.

Dry deserts can bloom if you provide water. Wet ones need little more than suspended dirt, I suppose.

Only we learned, didn't we, how awful the effects can be on land, if irrigation is mishandled. I wonder what the price will be here, if we've forgotten something this time?

A lover of deserts, and yet their implacable foe, Logan knew stark beauty was often found in emptiness, while life, burgeoning life, could sometimes bring with it a kind of ugly mundanity.

So the tradeoffs—a bird marsh exchanged for a dead but valuable energy source . . . a lifeless but beautiful bay bartered for a fecund sea jungle that could feed millions . . .

He wished there were a better way.

Well, we could institute worldwide compulsory eugenics, as some radicals propose—one child per couple, and any male convicted of any act of violence to be vasectomized. That'd work all right . . . though few effects on population or behavior would be seen for decades.

Or we could ration water even more strictly. Cut energy use to 200 watts per person . . . though that would also stop the worldwide information renaissance in its tracks.

We might ground all the dirigible liners, end the tourism boom, and settle down to regional isolationism again. That would save energy, all right . . . and almost certainly finish the growing internationalism that's staved off war.

Or we could force draconian recycling, down to the last snippet of paper or tin foil. We could reduce caloric intake by 25 percent, protein by 40 percent . . .

Logan thought of his daughter and threw out all brief temptation to side with the radicals. He and Daisy had responsibly stopped at one child, but of late Logan was less sure about even that restriction. A person like Claire would cure many more of the world's ills than she created by living in it.

In the end, it came down to utter basics.

Nobody's cutting my child's protein intake. Not while I'm alive to prevent it. Whatever Daisy says about the futility of "solving" problems, I'm going to keep on trying.

That meant helping Sauvel, even if this pristine ocean-desert had to be overwhelmed by clouds of silt and algae and noisome, teeming fish.

The glare of sunlight off the water must have been stronger than he realized. Logan's eyes felt funny. A spectral, crystal shine seemed to transform the air. He blinked in a sudden daze, staring across a sea made even more mesmerizing than any mere iris shade. It loomed toward him, seizing him like a lover, with a paralyzing captivation of the heart.

Shivers coursed his back. Logan wondered if a microbe might feel this way, looking with sudden awe into a truly giant soul.

All at once he knew that the sensations weren't subjective after all! The minizep shook. Tearing his gaze from the hypnotic sea, Logan saw the pilot rub her eyes and slap her earphones. Eric Sauvel shouted to her in French. When she answered, Sauvel's face grew ashen.

"Someone has sabotaged the site," he told Logan loudly to be heard over the noise. "There's been an explosion."

"What? Was anybody hurt?"

"No major casualties, apparently. But they wrecked one of the anchor pylons."

The weird effects were ebbing even as Sauvel spoke. Logan blinked. "How bad is it?"

The engineer shrugged, an expressive gesture. "I do not know. Everyone appears to have been affected in some way. Even I sensed something just a moment ago—perhaps subsonics from the blast."

Sauvel leaned to his left and peered. "We're coming into sight now."

At first it was hard to see that anything had happened at all. There were no plumes of smoke. No sirens wailed across the sloping shelf overlooking Santa Paula inlet. On both banks the half-finished energy storage facilities looked much as Logan remembered them.

The fjordlike cove began as a wide gap in the coastline that narrowed as it penetrated inland. Crossing it at a chosen point lay rows of monoliths, like gray military bunkers, each linked to the next by a flexible dam. Twice daily, tides would drive up the natural funnel and over those barriers, pushing turbines in the process. Then, as moon and sun drew the water away again, it would pay another toll. Back and forth, ebb and flow, the system needed no steady stream of coal or oil or uranium, nor would it spill forth noxious waste. Spare parts would be the only ongoing cost, and electricity its sole output.

Logan scanned the pylons and generator housings. One or two of his suggestions had already been put into effect, he saw. Apparently, the modifications had worked. But as yet he saw no signs of damage.

"Over there!" Sauvel pointed to one end of the barrage chain. Emergency vehicles flashed strobe lights, while magnus floaters and police helicopters scoured the surrounding hillsides. Their pilot answered repeated demands for identification.

Logan sought telltale signs of violence but spotted no blackened, twisted wreckage, no sooty debris. When Sauvel gasped, he shook his head. "I don't see . . ."

He followed Sauvel's pointing arm and stared. A new tower had been erected on the shore, reaching like a construction crane fifty meters high. Its nose drooped, heavy with some cargo.

Only as they neared did Logan notice that the spire was strewn with green, stringy stuff—*seaweed*, he realized, and from the sagging tip there dangled a man! The "tower" was no tower at all, but an important piece of the tidal barrage . . . the shoreline anchor boom. A *horizontal* structure. At least it was supposed to be horizontal. Designed to withstand fierce Atlantic storms, it had lain flat in the water, until . . .

"The devil's work!" Sauvel cursed. Some force had contrived to stand the boom on end like a child's toy. Watching rescue vehicles close in to save the dangling diver, they verified by radio that there were no other injuries. Emergency crews could be heard complaining, there was no trace to be found of the purported bomb!

Logan felt a growing suspicion they'd never find any.

He didn't laugh. That would be impolite to his hosts, whose work had been set back days, perhaps weeks. But he did allow a grim smile, the sort a cautious man wears on encountering the truly surprising. He felt as he had a few weeks ago, when examining those strange Spanish earthquakes—and the case of the mysterious, disappearing drilling rig. Logan made a mental note to tap the world seismological database as soon as they reached shore. Maybe there was a connection this time, as well.

Something new had entered the world all right. Of that much, he now felt certain.

☐

A great reservoir lay under the North American prairie. The Ogallala aquifer spread beneath a dozen states—a vast hidden lake of pure, sweet water that had trickled into crevices of stone through the coming and going of three ice ages.

To the farmers who had first discovered the Ogallala it must have seemed a gift from Providence. Even in those days, the sun used to parch Oklahoma and Kansas, and the rains were fickle. But wells drilled only a little way down tapped a life source as clear and chaste as crystal. Soon circles of irrigation turned bone-dry grassland into the world's richest granary.

Day by day, year after year, the Ogallala must have seemed as inexhaustible as the forests of the Amazon. Even when it became widely known that it was being drawn down several feet each year, while recharging only inches, the farmers didn't change their plans to drill new wells, or to install faster pumps. In abstract, to be sure, they knew it could not last. But abstractions don't pay the bank. They don't see you through this year's harvest. The Ogallala was a commons without a protector, bound for tragedy.

So the American Midwest was fated to suffer through another of the many little water wars that crackled across the early part of the century. Still, although bitterness ran high, the casualty figures were lower than from the rioting in La Plata, or the Nile catastrophe. That was probably because, by the time the battle over the Ogallala aquifer was fully joined, there remained little but damp pores, here and there, for anyone to fight over.

Dust settled over brown, circular patches where bounty had briefly grown, coating rusting irrigation rigs and the windows of empty homes.

Following close behind the dust, there blew in sand.

● *Twinkle, twinkle, little star . . .*

E   Despite some trepidation, Teresa schooled herself to stay calm
X during her first trip back into space. She checked frequently, but
O her beacons didn't wobble. The continents hadn't shifted percep-
S tibly. Her old friends, the stars, lay arrayed as she remembered
P them. Sprinkled road signs, offering unwinking promises of a con-
H stancy she had always relied upon.
E   *How I wonder what you are . . .*
R   "Liars," she accused them. For their promise had proven false
E once already. Who, after going through what she had, could ever
be certain those constellations might not choose to go liquid again, melting and flowing and becoming one with the chaos within her?

"What was that, Mother? Did you say something?"

Teresa realized she'd spoken aloud to an open mike. She glanced outside, where distant, spacesuit-clad figures crawled over a lattice-work of girders and fibrous pylons. They were too far away to make out individual faces.

"Uh, sorry," she said. "I was just . . ."

A second voice cut in. "She's just cluckin' to make sure her chicks are okay. Right, Mommy?"

That voice she knew. Traditional it might be, for a work party on EVA to call the watch pilot "Papa." Or in her case, "Mother." But only Mark Randall had the nerve to call her "Mommy" over an open channel.

"Can it, Randall." Colonel Glenn Spivey this time, stepping in to curtail idle chatter. "Is anything the matter, Captain Tikhana?"

"Um . . . no, Colonel."

"Very well, then. Thank you for continuing to monitor us, quietly."

Teresa punched her thigh. Damn the man! Spivey's version of politeness would spoil fresh-picked apples. She twisted her cheek-mike away so the next stray word wouldn't draw that awful man's attention.

I'm not myself, she knew. Extraneous talk on open channel just wasn't her style. But then, neither were espionage or treason.

She glanced toward her left knee. The tiny recorder she'd placed there was tucked well out of sight, tapping the shuttle's main computer via a fiber barely thick enough to see. It had been almost too easy. The instruments required were already aboard *Pleiades*. It was just a matter of modifying their settings slightly, so narrow windows of data could be snooped by her little data store.

It helped that this was a construction mission. For hours at a stretch, she would be left alone while Randall and Spivey and the others were outside, supervising the robots that were erecting Erehwon II. Defense wanted the new edifice put in place quickly, which involved using those undamaged portions of Reagan Station, plus parts cobbled from spares and rushed up on heavy boosters.

That was an advantage of "national security" as a priority. The calamity wouldn't be allowed to paralyze all space activity, as happened after the *Challenger* disaster or that horrible Lamberton fiasco. On the other hand, other programs were being stripped for this. Civilian space was going to suffer for a long time to come.

Out in the blackness, Teresa watched figures systematically dismantle a giant cargo lifter—opening the great rocket like an unfolding flower. Space Jacks, like butchers in an oldtime abattoir, bragged they could find a use for "everything but the squeal." It was a far cry from back when NASA had first tried to assemble an entire working space station, unbelievably, out of nothing but tiny capsules and gridwork, every bit hauled to orbit *inside* shuttles.

Unhappy over the hurried pace, this construction squad had unanimously chosen her to be Mother, to watch over them from *Pleiades'* control deck. Management dared not buck the drivers' and spinners' unions when it came to crew safety, so Teresa had escaped the talk-show circuit, after all.

The irony was, for the first time in her career she found herself preoccupied in other ways. She did her job, of course. Because the other 'nauts were counting on her, she meticulously took telemetry readings, making doubly sure her "chicks" were all right. Still, Teresa kept turning around to glance through the rear window at the Earth. It wasn't the planet's beauty that distracted her, but a nervous sense of expectation.

The NASA psychologist had warned there were always difficulties, first time up again after a trouble mission. But that wasn't it. Teresa knew it was important to get back in the saddle. She had confidence in her skills.

No, her gaze kept drifting Earthward because that was where she'd seen the first symptoms. Those weird optical effects the psychers had largely dismissed as stress hallucinations, but which had given her an instant's warning last time.

Stop being so nervous, she told herself. *If Manella's right, it can't happen again. He thinks Erehwon was torn apart when some stupid malf released a micro black hole up at Farpoint lab. Whatever Frankenstein device they were playing with must have blown its energy all at once.*

By that reasoning it was a single exploding singularity that had, by some unknown means, carried the first men—or what was left of them—to the stars.

For the fortieth time, she tried to figure out how they might have done it. How could anybody build and conceal a *black hole*, for heaven's sake—even a micro black hole—in space without word getting out? The smallest hole with a temperature low enough to be contained would need the mass of a midget mountain. You don't go hauling that kind of material into low earth orbit without someone noticing. No, the thing would have been built by *cavitronics*—that new science of quantum absurdities, of forces nobody had even heard of forty years ago, which let foolish men create space-warped sinkholes out of the raw stuff of vacuum itself.

Cavitronics. In spite of reading popular accounts, Teresa knew next to nothing about the field. Who did?

Well, Jason, apparently. She had thought him incapable of ever lying to her. Which showed just how little she knew about people after all.

What amazed Teresa most was that Spivey and his co-conspirators could actually hide such a massive thing up here, in Earth's crowded exosphere. True, Farpoint had been isolated. Getting there required two consecutive twenty-kilometer elevator rides.

Still, how does one hide a gigaton object in Low Earth Orbit? Even compressed to a pinpoint, its presence would have perturbed the trajectory of the whole complex. She'd have been able to tell every time she piloted a mission to Erehwon, from subtle differences in her readings. No. Manella had to be wrong!

Then she remembered how those DOD men in powder blue uniforms had sequestered the recordings, as soon as *Pleiades* returned from that horribly extended mission. Teresa had assumed it was for accident analysis. But somehow the data never were made public.

She mentally catalogued ways a pilot could really tell the mass of the upper tip, assuming all shuttles docked far below. The list was shockingly small.

What if . . . she pondered. *What if, each trip to Erehwon, the shuttle's operating parameters were adjusted, its inertial guidance units altered beforehand?*

It wouldn't take much, she decided. Worse than dishonest, it would be horribly unprincipled to lie to a pilot about her navigation systems, to purposely make them give false readings.

But it could be done. After all, she'd only see what she expected to see.

The thought was appalling. This wasn't the sort of thing one took to the union steward!

Over the next hour Teresa answered calls from the work party, computed some corrections for them, and shepherded one woman and her robot back on course from a five-degree deviation. She double-checked the modification and watched till the astronaut and her cargo were back on station. Meanwhile though, her head churned with arguments both for and against the scenario.

"They simply couldn't have gotten away with it!" she cried out at one point.

"Beg pardon, Mama?"

It was Mark again, calling from the site where he was unreeling great spools of ultra-strong spectra fiber.

"*Pleiades* here. Um, never mind."

"I distinctly heard you say—"

"I'm—practicing for the Space Day talent show. We're doing *Hound of the Baskervilles*."

"Cheery play. Remind me to lose my ticket."

Teresa sighed. At least Spivey hadn't cut in. He must have been preoccupied.

"They couldn't have gotten away with it," she muttered again after turning her mike completely off. "Even if they could have finagled *Pleiades* to give false readings . . ."

She stopped, suddenly too paranoid to continue aloud.

Even if they could fool Pleiades, *and me, into ignoring gigatons of excess mass, they couldn't have disguised it from the real observers . . . the other space powers! They all keep watch on every U.S. satellite, as we watch everyone else up here. They would have spotted any anomaly as big as Manella talks about.*

Teresa felt relieved . . . and silly for not having thought of this sooner. Manella's story was absurd. Spivey couldn't have hidden a singularity on Farpoint. Not unless . . .

Teresa felt a sudden resurgent chill. *Not unless all the space powers were in on it.*

Pieces fell into place. Such as the bland, perfunctory way the Russians had accused America of weapons testing, then let the matter drop. Or the gentlemen's agreement about not making orbital parameters public beyond three significant figures.

"*Everyone* is cheating on the treaty!" she whispered, in awe.

Now she understood why Manella was so insistent on acquiring her help. There might be more of the damned things up here! Half the stations between LEO and the moon might contain singularities, for all she knew! The data in her little recorder might be the key to tracking them down.

The enormity of her situation was dawning on her. Much as she resented the science tribunals for blocking some space technologies, Teresa nevertheless wondered what the world might have been like by now without them. Probably a ruin. Did she then dare help cause a scandal that could bring the entire system crashing down?

After all, she thought, *it's not as if Spivey's people ignored the ban completely. They put their beast out here, where . . .*

Again she slammed her thigh.

. . . where it killed friends, her husband . . . and put the space program back years!

Teresa's eyes filmed. Her balled fist struck over and over until the hurt turned into a dull, throbbing numbness. "Bastards!" she repeated. "You gor-sucking bastards."

So it was with grief-welled eyes that Teresa didn't even notice sudden waves of color sweep the cabin, briefly clothing what had been gray in hues of spectral effervescence, then quickly fading again.

Outside, among the growing girders and tethers, one or two of the workers blinked as those ripples momentarily affected peripheral vision. But they were trained to concentrate on their jobs and so scarcely noticed as the phenomena came and swiftly passed away again.

By Teresa's knee, however, the little box quietly and impartially recorded, taking in everything the shuttle's instruments fed it.

PART IV

PLANET

The planet had orbited its sun only a thousand million times before it acquired several highly unusual traits, far out of equilibrium.

For one thing, none of its sister worlds possessed any free oxygen. But somehow this one had acquired an envelope rich in that searing gas. That alone showed something odd was going on, for without constant replenishment, oxygen must quickly burn away.

And the planet's temperature was unusually stable. Occasionally ice sheets did spread, and then retreated under glaring sunshine. But with each swing something caused heat to build up or leak away again in compensation, leaving the rolling seas intact.

Those seas . . . liquid water covering two thirds of the globe . . . no other world circling the sun shared that peculiar attribute. Then there was the planet's pH balance—offset dramatically from the normal acidic toward a rare alkaline state.

The list went on. So far from equilibrium in so many ways, and yet so stable, so constant. These were strange and unlikely properties.

They were also traits of physiology.

☐ For all you farmers out there scratchin' in the dry heat, tryin' to get your sorghum planted before the soil blows away, here are a few little har-hars from bygone days. After all, if you can't laugh at your troubles, you're just lettin' em get the upper hand.

> *"Yesterday I accidentally dropped my best chain down one of the cracks in my yard. This morning I went to see if I could fish it out, but by golly, I could still hear it rattling on its way down!"*

Found that one in a book of jokes told by sod flippers here in the Midwest a hundred years ago, during the first Dust Bowl. (And yes, there was a first one. Had to be, didn't there?) These gems were collected by the Federal Writers Project back in the 1930s . . . their version of Net Memory, I guess. Here's some more from the same collection:

> *"I had a three-inch rain last week . . . one drop every three inches."*
> *"It was so dry over in Waco County, I saw two trees fighting over a dog."*
> *"It's so dry in my parts, Baptists are sprinkling converts, and Methodists are wipin' 'em with a damp cloth."*

As I sit here in the studio, spinning the old two-way dial, I see some of you have carried your holos out to the fields with you. I'll try to talk loud so you can find your set later under the dust!

Well, okay, maybe that one wasn't so good. Here's two from the book I guess must be even worse.

> *"My hay crop is so bad, I have to buy a bale just to prime the rake."*
> *"This year I plan to throw a hog in the corn trailer and pick directly to him. Figure I shouldn't even have to change hogs till noon."*

Anybody out there understand those last two? I have free tickets to the next Skywriters concert in Chi-town for the first ten of you to shout back good explanations. Meanwhile, let's have some zip-zep from the Skywriters themselves. Here's "Tethered to a Rain Cloud."

● Roland fingered the rifle's plastic stock as his squad leaped off the truck and lined up behind Corporal Wu. He had a serious case of dry mouth, and his ears still rang from the alert bell that had yanked them out of exhausted slumber only an hour before.

Who would've imagined being called out on a real raid? This certainly broke the routine of basic training—running about pointlessly, standing rigid while sergeants shouted abuse at you, screaming back obedient answers, then running some more until you dropped. Of course the pre-induction tapes had explained the purpose of all that.

". . . Recruits must go through intense stress in order to break civilian response sets and prepare behavioral templates for military imprinting. Their rights are not surrendered, only voluntarily suspended in order to foster discipline, coordination, hygeine, and other salutary skills . . ."

Only volunteers who understood and signed waivers were allowed to join the peacekeeping forces, so he'd known what to expect. What *had* surprised Roland was getting accepted in the first place, despite mediocre school grades. Maybe the peacekeepers' aptitude tests weren't infallible after all. Or perhaps they revealed something about Roland that had never emerged back in Indiana.

It can't be intelligence, that's for sure. And I'm no leader. Never wanted to be.

In his spare moments (all three of them since arriving here in Taiwan for training) Roland had pondered the question and finally decided it was none of his damn business after all. So long as the officers knew what they were doing, that was enough for him.

This calling out of raw recruits for a night mission didn't fill him with confidence though.

What use would greenies like us be in a combat operation? Won't we just get in the way?

His squad double-timed alongside a towering, aromatic ornamental hedge, toward the sound of helicopters and the painful brilliance of searchlights. Perspiration loosened his grip on the stock, forcing him to hold his weapon tighter. His heartbeat quickened as they neared the scene of action. And yet, Roland felt certain he wasn't scared to die.

No, he was afraid of *screwing up*.

"Takka says it's eco-nuts!" the recruit running beside him whispered, panting. Roland didn't answer. In the last hour he'd completely had it with scuttlebutt.

Neo-Gaian radicals might have blown up a dam, someone said.

No, it was an unlicensed gene lab or maybe an unregistered national bomb—hidden in violation of the Rio Pact. . . .

Hell, none of the rumored emergencies seemed to justify calling in peach-fuzz recruits. It must be *real* bad trouble. Or else something he didn't understand yet.

Roland watched the jouncing backpack of Corporal Wu. The compact Chinese noncom carried twice the weight any of them did, yet he obviously held himself back for the sluggish recruits. Roland found himself wishing Wu would pass out the ammo *now*. What if they were ambushed? What if . . . ?

You don't know anything yet, box-head. Better pray they don't *pass out ammo. Half those mama's boys runnin' behind you don't know their rifles from their assholes.*

In fairness, Roland figured they probably felt exactly the same way about him.

The squad hustled round the hedge onto a gravel driveway, puffing uphill toward the glaring lanterns. Officers milled about, poring over clipboards and casting long shadows across a close-cropped lawn that had been ripped and scraped by copters and magnus zeps. A grand mansion stood farther upslope, dominating the richly landscaped grounds. Silhouettes hastened past brightly lit windows.

Roland saw no foxholes. No signs of enemy fire. So, maybe ammo wouldn't be needed after all.

Corporal Wu brought the squad to a disorderly halt as the massive, gruff figure of Sergeant Kleinerman appeared out of nowhere.

"Have the weenies stack weapons over by the flower bed," Kleinerman told Wu in flat-toned Standard Military English. "Wipe their noses, then take them around back. UNEPA has work for 'em that's simple enough for infants to handle."

Any recruit who took that kind of talk personally was a fool. Roland just took advantage of the pause to catch his breath. "No weapons," Takka groused as they stacked their rifles amid trampled marigolds. "What we supposed to use, our hands?"

Roland shrugged. The casual postures of the officers told him this was no terrorist site. "Prob'ly," he guessed. "Them and our backs."

"This way, weenies," Wu said, with no malice and only a little carefully tailored contempt. "Come on. It's time to save the world again."

Through the bright windows Roland glimpsed rich men, rich women, dressed in shimmering fabrics. Nearly all looked like Han-Formosans. For the first time since arriving at Camp Pérez de Cuellar, Roland really felt he was in Taiwan, almost China, thousands of miles from Indiana.

Servants still carried trays of refreshments, their darker Bengali or Tamil complexions contrasting with the pale Taiwanese. Unlike the agitated party guests, the attendants seemed undisturbed to have in their midst all these soldiers and green-clad marshals from UNEPA. In fact, Roland saw one waiter smile when she thought no one was looking, and help herself to a glass of champagne.

UNEPA . . . Roland thought on spying the green uniforms. *That means eco-crimes.*

Wu hustled the squad past where some real soldiers stood guard in blurry combat camouflage, their eyes hooded by multisensor goggles which seemed to dart and flash as their pulse-rifles glittered darkly. The guards dismissed the recruits with barely a flicker of attention, which irked Roland far worse than the insults of Wu and Kleinerman.

I'll make them notice me, he vowed. Though he knew better than to expect it soon. You didn't get to be like those guys overnight.

Behind the mansion a ramp dropped steeply into the earth. Smoke rose from a blasted steel door that now lay curled and twisted to one side. A woman marshal met them by the opening. Even darker than her chocolate skin was the cast of her features—as if they were carved from basalt. "This way," she said tersely and led them down the ramp—a trip of more than fifty meters—into a reinforced concrete bunker. When they reached the bottom, however, it wasn't at all what Roland had expected—some squat armored slab. Instead, he found himself in a place straight out of the Arabian Nights.

The recruits gasped. "Shee-it!" Takka commented concisely, showing how well he'd picked up the essentials of Military English. Kanakoa, the Hawaiian, expressed amazement even more eloquently. "Welcome to the elephant's graveyard, Tarzan."

Roland only stared. Tiny, multicolored spotlights illuminated the arched chamber, subtly emphasizing the shine of ivory and fur and crystal. From wall to wall, the spoils of five continents were piled high. More illicit wealth than Roland had ever seen. More than he could ever have imagined.

From racks in all directions hung spotted leopard pelts, shimmering beaver skins, white winter fox stoles. And shoes! Endless stacks of them, made from dead reptiles, obviously, though Roland couldn't begin to conceive which species had given its all for which pair.

"Hey, Senterius." Takka nudged him in the ribs and Roland looked down where the Japanese recruit pointed.

Near his left foot lay a luxurious white carpet . . . the splayed form of a flayed polar bear whose snarling expression looked *really* angry. Roland jerked away from those glittering teeth, backing up until something pointy and hard rammed his spine. He whirled, only to goggle in amazement at a stack of elephant tusks, each bearing a golden tip guard.

"Gaia!" he breathed.

"You said it," Kanakoa commented. "Boy, I'll bet Her Holy Nibs is completely pissed off over this."

Roland wished he hadn't spoken the Earth Mother's name aloud. Hers wasn't a soldierly faith, after all. But Kanakoa and Takka seemed as stunned as he was. "What is all this?" Takka asked, waving at the heaped stacks of animal remains. "Who in the world would want these things?"

Roland shrugged. "Used to be, rich folks liked to wear gnomish crap like this."

Takka sneered. "I knew that. But why now? It is not just illegal. It's . . . it's—"

"Sick? Is that what you were going to say, Private?"

They turned to see the UNEPA marshal standing close by, looking past them at the piled ivory. She couldn't be over forty years old, but right now the tendons in her neck were taut as bowstrings and she looked quite ancient.

"Come with me, I want to show you soldiers something."

They followed her past cases filled with pinned, iridescent butterflies, with gorilla-hand ashtrays and stools made from elephants' feet, with petrified wood and glittering coral no doubt stolen from nature preserves . . . all the way to the back wall of the artificial cave, where two truly immense tusks formed a standing arch. Tiger skins draped a shrine of sorts—a case crafted in dark hardwood and glass, containing dozens of earthenware jars.

Roland saw veins pulse on the backs of her hands. The recruits fell mute, awed by such hatred as she radiated now. Nothing down here impressed them half as much.

Roland found the courage to ask, "What's in the jars, ma'am?"

Watching her face, he realized what an effort it took for her to speak right now, and found himself wondering if he'd ever be able to exert such mastery over his own body.

"Rhinoceros . . . horn," she said hoarsely. "Powdered narwhal tusk . . . whale semen . . ."

Roland nodded. He'd heard of such things. Ancient legends held they could prolong life, or heighten sexual prowess, or drive women into writhing heat. And neither morality nor law nor scientific disproof deterred some men from chasing hope.

"So much. There must be a hundred kilos in there!" Takka commented. But he stepped back when the UNEPA official whirled to glare at him, her expression one of bleak despair.

"You don't understand," she whispered. "I hoped we'd find so much more."

Roland soon discovered just what use recruits were on a mission like this.

Sure enough, he thought, resigned that he had only begun plumbing the depths of exhaustion the peacekeeping forces had in store for him. Hauling sixty-kilo tusks up the steep ramp, he and Private Schmidt knew they were important pieces in a well-tuned, highly efficient, rapid-deployment force whose worldwide duties stretched from pole to pole. Their part was less glamorous than the on-site inspectors prowling Siberia and Sinkiang and Wyoming, enforcing arms-control pacts. Or the brave few keeping angry militias in Brazil and Argentina from each other's throats. Or even the officers tagging and inventorying tonight's booty. But after all, as Corporal Wu told them repeatedly, they also serve who only grunt and sweat.

Roland tried not to show any discomfort working with Schmidt. After all, the tall, skinny alpine boy hadn't even been born yet when the Helvetian War laid waste to much of Central Europe, and anyway you couldn't exactly choose your background. Roland made an effort to accept him as a native of "West Austria" and forget the past.

One thing, Schmidt sure spoke English well. Better, in fact, than most of Roland's old gang back in Bloomington. "Where are they hauling this stuff?" his partner asked the pilot of one of the minizeps as they took a two-minute breather outside.

"They've got warehouses all over the world," the Swedish noncom said. "If I told you about them, you wouldn't believe me."

"Try us," Roland prompted.

The flier's blue eyes seemed to look far away. "Take what you found in that tomb and multiply it a thousandfold."

"Shee-it," Schmidt sighed. "But . . . ."

"Oh, some of this stuff here won't go into storage. The ivory, for instance. They'll implant label isotopes so each piece is chemically unique, then they'll sell it. The zoo arks harvest elephant tusks nowadays anyway, as do the African parks, so the beasts won't tear up trees or attract poachers. That policy came too late to save this fellow." He patted the tusk beside him. "Alas."

"But what about the other stuff? The furs. The shoes. All that powdered horn shit?"

The pilot shrugged. "Can't sell it. That'd just legitimize wearing or using the stuff. Create demand, you see.

"Can't destroy it, either. Could *you* burn billions worth of beautiful things? Sometimes they take school groups through the warehouses, to show kids what real evil is. But mostly it all just sits there, piling up higher and higher."

The pilot looked left and right. "I do have a theory, though. I think I know the real reason for the warehouses."

"Yes?" Roland and Schmidt leaned forward, ready to accept his confidence.

The pilot spoke behind a shielding hand. "*Aliens.* They're going to sell it all to aliens from outer space."

Roland groaned. Schmidt spat on the ground in disgust. Of course real soldiers were going to treat them this way. But it was embarrassing to have been sucked in so openly.

"You think I'm kidding?" the pilot asked.

"No, we think you're crazy."

That brought a wry grin. "Likely enough, boy. But think about it! It's only a matter of time till we're contacted, no? They've been searching the sky for a hundred years now. And we've been filling space with our radio and TV and Data Net noise all that time. Sooner or later a starship *has* to stop by. It only makes sense, no?"

Roland decided the only safe reply was a silent stare. He watched the noncom warily.

"So I figure it's like this. That starship is very likely to be a *trading vessel* . . . out on a long, long cruise, like those clipper ships of olden times. They'll stop here and want to buy stuff, but not just any stuff. It will have to be light, portable, beautiful, and totally unique to Earth. Otherwise, why bother?"

"But this stuff's dumpit contraband!" Roland said, pointing to the goods stacked in the cargo bay.

"Hey! You two! Break's over!" It was Corporal Wu, calling from the ramp. He jerked his thumb then swiveled and strode back into the catacomb. Roland and his partner stood up.

"But that's the beauty of it!" the pilot continued, as if he hadn't heard. "You see, the CITES rules make all these things illegal so there won't be any economic *market* for killing endangered species.

"But fobbing it all off on alien traders won't create a market! It's a one-stop deal, you see? They come once, then they are gone again, forever. We empty the warehouses and spend the profits buying up land for new game preserves." He spread his hands as if to ask what could be more reasonable.

Schmidt spat again, muttering a curse in Schweitzer-Deutsch.

"Come on Senterius, let's go." Roland followed quickly, glancing only once over his shoulder at the grinning pilot, wondering if the guy was crazy, brilliant, or simply a terrific sculptor of bullshit.

Probably all three, he figured at last, and double-timed the rest of the way. After all, fairy tales were fairy tales, while Corporal Wu was palpable reality.

As he worked, Roland recalled the days not so long ago when he and his pals Remi and Crat used to sit in the park listening to old Joseph tell them about the awful battles of the Helvetian War. The war that finally did end war.

Each of them had reacted differently to Joseph's eventual betrayal —Remi by turning tragically cynical, and Crat by declaring void anything spoken by anyone over thirty. To Roland, however, what lasted were the veteran's tales of combat—of comrades fighting shoulder to shoulder, hauling each other through mountain passes clogged with germ-laden, radioactive mud, struggling together to overcome a wily, desperate foe. . . .

Of course he didn't actually wish for a real war to fight. Not a big one on the vast, impersonal scale the old vet described. He knew battle sounded a lot more attractive far away, in stories, than it would seem in person.

Still, was this to be the way of it from now on? Hauling off contraband seized from CITES violators? Manning tedious observer posts separating surly, bickering nations too poor and tired to fight anyway? Checking the bilges of rusting freighters for hidden caches of flight capital?

Oh, there were real warriors in the peacekeeping forces. Takka and some of the others might get to join the elite units quelling fierce little water wars like the one going on now in Ghana. But as an American he'd have little chance of joining any of the active units. The Guarantor Powers were still too big, too powerful. No little country would stand for Russian or American or Chinese troops stationed on their soil.

Well, at least I can learn how *to be a warrior. I'll be trained, ready, in case the world ever needs me.*

So he worked doggedly, doing as he was told. Hauling and lifting, lifting and hauling, Roland also tried to listen to the UNEPA officials, especially the dark woman. Had she really wished they had found more of the grisly contraband?

". . . thought we'd traced the Pretoria poaching ring all the way here," she said at one point as he passed by laden with aromatic lion skins. "I thought we'd finally tracked down the main depot. But there's so little white rhino powder, or—"

"Could Chang have already sold the rest?" one of the others asked.

She shook her head. "Chang's a hoarder. He sells only to maintain operating capital."

"Well, we'll find out when we finally catch him, the slippery eel."

Roland was still awed by the UNEPA woman, and a bit jealous. What was it like, he wondered, to care about something so passionately? He suspected it made her somehow more alive than he was.

According to the recruitment tapes, training was supposed to give him strong feelings of his own. Over months of exhaustion and discipline, he'd come to see his squadmates as family. Closer than that. They would learn almost to read each other's thoughts, to depend on each other utterly. If necessary, to die for one another.

That was how it was supposed to work. Glancing at Takka and Schmidt and the other strangers in his squad, Roland wondered how the sergeants and instructors could accomplish such a thing. Frankly, it sounded awfully unlikely.

But hell, guys like Kleinerman and Wu have been soldiering for five thousand years or so. I guess they know what they're doing.

How ironic, then, that they finally made a science of it at the very end, just as the profession was trying to phase itself out of existence forever. From the looks given them by the UNEPA marshals, that day could come none too soon. Necessity allied the two groups in the cause of saving the planet. But clearly the eco-officers would rather do without the military altogether.

Just be patient, Roland thought as he worked. *We're doing the best we can as fast as we can.*

He and another recruit disassembled the shrine at the back of the cavernous treasure room, carefully unwinding snakeskin ropes binding the two huge archway tusks. They were lowering one of the ivory trophies to the floor when Roland's nostrils flared at a familiar smell. He stopped and sniffed.

"Come on," the Russian private groused in thickly accented Standard. "Now other one."

"Do you smell something?" Roland asked.

The other youth laughed. "I smell dead animals! What you think? It stink worse here than Tashkent brothels!"

But Roland shook his head. "That's not it." He turned left, following the scent.

Naturally, soldiers weren't allowed tobacco, which would sap their wind and stamina. But he'd been quite a smoker back in Indiana, puffing homegrown with Remi and Crat—as many as eight or ten hand-rolled cigs a week. Could a noncom or UNEPA be sneaking weed behind a corner? It had better not be a *recruit*, or there'd be latrine duty for the entire squad!

But no, there weren't any hiding places nearby. So where was it coming from?

Corporal Wu's whistle blew, signaling another short break. "Hey, Yank," the Russian said. "Don't be a *pizdyuk*. Come on."

Roland waved him to silence. He pushed aside one of the tiger skins, still sniffing, and then crouched where he had first picked up the scent. It was strongest near the floor beside the glass case—now emptied of its brown jars of macabre powder. His fingers touched a warm breeze.

"Hey, give me a hand," he asked, bracing a shoulder against the wood. But the other recruit flipped two fingers as he walked away, muttering. *"Amerikanskee kakanee zassixa . . ."*

Roland checked his footing and strained. The heavy case rocked a bit before settling again.

This can't be right. The guy who owned this place wouldn't want to sweat. He'd never sweat.

Roland felt along the carved basework, working his way around to the back before finding what he sought—a spring-loaded catch. "Aha!" he said. With a click the entire case slid forward to jam against one of the huge, toppled tusks. Roland peered down steep stairs with a hint of light at the bottom.

He had to squeeze through the narrow opening. The tobacco smell grew stronger as he descended quietly, carefully. Stooping under a low stone lintel, he entered a chamber hewn from naked rock. Roland straightened and pursed his lips in a silent whistle.

While this hiding place lacked the first one's air of elegant decadence, it did conceal the devil's own treasure . . . shelves stacked high with jars and small, bulging, plastic bags. "Hot damn," he said, fingering one of the bags. Gritty white powder sifted under a gilt-numbered label adorned with images of unicorns and dragons, though Roland knew the real donor must have been some poor, dumb, mostly blind rhino in southern Africa, or another equally unprepossessing beast.

"The freaking jackpot," he said to himself. It was definitely time to report this. But as he turned to head back upstairs, a voice suddenly stopped him.

"Do not move, soldier-fellow. Hands up or I will shoot you dead."

Roland rotated slowly and saw what he'd missed in his first, cursory scan of the room. At about waist level, near a smoldering ashtray in the corner of the left wall, some of the shelving had swung aside to reveal a narrow tunnel. From this opening a middle-aged man with Chinese features aimed a machine pistol at him.

"Do you doubt I can hit you from here?" the man asked levelly. "Is that why you don't raise your hands as I command? I assure you, I'm an expert shooter. I've killed lions, tigers, at close range. Do you doubt it?"

"No. I believe you."

"Then comply! Or I will shoot!"

Roland felt sure the fellow meant it. But it seemed this was time for one of those inconvenient waves of obstinacy his friends used to chide him for, which used to get him into such trouble back home.

"You shoot, and they'll hear you upstairs."

The man in the tunnel considered this. "Perhaps. On the other hand, if you were to attack me, or flee or call for help, the threat would be immediate and I would have to kill you at once."

Roland shrugged. "I ain't goin' nowhere."

"So. A standoff, then. All right, soldier. You may keep your hands down, as I see you're unarmed. But step back to that wall, or I will consider you dangerous and act accordingly!"

Roland did as he was told, watching for an opportunity. But the man crawled out of the tunnel and stood up without wavering his aim once. "My name is Chang," he said as he wiped his brow with a silk handkerchief.

"So I heard. You been a busy guy, Mr. Chang."

Brown eyes squinted in amusement. "That I have, soldier boy. What I've done and seen, you could not imagine. Even in these days of snoops and busybodies, I've kept secrets. Secrets deeper than even the Helvetian Gnomes had."

No doubt this was meant to impress Roland. It did. But he'd be damned if he'd give the bastard any satisfaction. "So what do we do now?"

Chang seemed to inspect him. "*Now* it's customary for me to bribe you. You must know I can offer you wealth and power. This tunnel bears a floater trolley on silent rails. If you help me take away my treasure, it could begin a long, profitable relationship."

Roland felt the piercing intensity of the man's scrutiny. After a moment's thought, he shrugged. "Sure, why not?"

Now it was Chang's turn to pause. Then he giggled. "Ah! I do enjoy encountering wit. Obviously you know I am lying, that I'd kill you once we reached the other end. And I, in turn, can tell you have more urgent goals than money. Is it honor you seek, perhaps?''

Again, Roland shrugged. He wouldn't have put it quite that way.

"So, again we have a standoff. Hence my second proposition. You help me load my trolley, at gunpoint. I will then depart and let you live.''

This time Roland's pause was calculated only to delay. "How do I know . . .''

"No questions! Obviously I can't turn my back on you. Agree or die now. Begin with the bags on the shelf by your shoulder, or I'll shoot and be gone before others can come!''

Roland slowly turned and picked up two of the bags, one in each hand.

The "trolley" did indeed float a few millimeters above a pair of gleaming rails, stretching off into interminable darkness. Roland had no doubt it was meant for swift escape, or that Chang would be long gone by the time UNEPA traced the other end. The guy seemed to have thought of everything.

He tried to carry as little as he could each trip. Chang lit a cigarette and fumed, watching him like a cat as Roland leaned over the tiny passenger's pallet to lay his loads in the trolley's capacious cargo hamper.

Roland's experience with babushkas and grempers back in Indiana helped, for he seemed to know by instinct how to just brush the inside edge of provocation. Once, he fumbled one of the clay jars. It hit hard and trickled powder onto the tunnel floor, crackling where bits struck the silvery rails. Chang hissed and the knuckles of his hand whitened on the pistol grip. Still, Roland figured the geep wouldn't shoot him just yet. He'd do it at the last moment, probably when the trolley was ready to go.

"Hurry up!" the Han millionaire spat. "You move like an American!''

That gave Roland an excuse to turn and grin at the man. "How'd you guess?" he asked, slowing things another few seconds, stretching Chang's patience before grabbing two more jars and resuming work.

Chang kept glancing up the stairs, obviously listening . . . but never letting his attention waver long enough to give Roland any foolish notions. *You should've reported the secret passage the minute you found it,* Roland thought, cursing inwardly. Unfortunately, the opening was behind the display case, and who knew when it would be discovered? Too late for Private Roland Senterius, probably.

The look in Chang's calculating eyes made Roland reconsider the scenario. *He knows that I know I'll have to jump him, just before the end.*

What's more, he knows that I know that he knows.

That meant Chang would shoot him *before* the last moment, to prevent that desperate lunge. But how soon before?

Not too soon, or the smuggler would have to depart with a half-empty trolley, abandoning the rest of his hoard forever. Clearly, Chang's profound greed was the one thing keeping Roland alive. Still, he'd have to do it before the cargo hamper was topped off . . . before Roland's adrenaline was pumping for the maximum, all-or-nothing effort.

Five loads to go, Roland thought while fitting more jars snugly into place under Chang's watchful eye. *Will he do it at three? Or two?*

He was delivering the next load, beginning to screw up his courage, when a noise echoed down the steep stair shaft, preempting all plans.

"Senterius! It's Kanakoa. And Schmidt. What the hell you doing down here?"

Roland froze. Chang edged against the wall near the steps, watching him. There came the scrape of footsteps on stone.

Dumpit, Roland cursed. He was bent over the trolley in an awkward position, much too far away to attack Chang with any chance of success. In addition, his hands were laden with bags. If only he were carrying jars, that could be thrown . . .

"Senterius? What are you doing, asshole? Smoking? Kleinerman'll roast all of us if they catch you!"

Roland suddenly realized why Chang was watching him so intently. *Chang's following my eyes!*

Roland's gaze could not help widening when one booted foot appeared on the topmost visible step. Chang was using him to gauge where the other recruits were, to tell when the moment was just right for killing all three of them! In holding onto seconds of life, Roland knew suddenly, horribly, he was murdering Kanakoa and Schmidt.

Still, even knowing that, he remained statuelike. In Chang's eyes he saw understanding and the glitter of contemptuous victory. *How did he know?* Roland railed inside. *How did he know I was a coward?*

The admission belied every one of his dreams. It betrayed what Roland had thought were his reasons for living. The realization seared so hot it tore through his rigor and burst forth in a sudden scream.

"*Cover!*" he cried, and threw himself onto the pallet, slamming home the trolley's single lever. Almost simultaneously a series of rapid bangs rattled the narrow chamber and Roland's leg erupted in sudden agony. Then there was blackness and the swift whistle of wind as the little car sped into a gloom darker than any he had ever known.

Seconds ticked while he battled fiery pain. Clenching his jaw to keep from moaning, Roland desperately hauled back on the lever, bringing the trolley to a jerky halt in the middle of the arrow-straight shaft. Waves of dizziness almost overwhelmed him as he rolled over onto his back and clutched his thigh, feeling a sickening, sticky wetness there.

One thing for certain, he couldn't afford the luxury of fainting here. Funny—he'd been taught all that biofeedback stuff in school, and drilled in it again here in training. But right now he just couldn't spare the time to use any of those techniques, not even to stop the pain!

"There are two types of simple thigh wounds," memorized words droned as he wrestled the belt from his waist. *"One, a straight puncture of muscle fiber, is quite manageable. Treat it quickly and move on. Your comrade should be able to offer covering fire, even if he can no longer move.*

"The other kind is much more dangerous . . ."

Roland fought shivers as he looped the belt above the wound. He had no idea which type it was. If Chang had hit the femoral artery, this makeshift tourniquet wasn't going to do much good.

He grunted and yanked hard, cinching the belt as tight as he could, and then slumped back in reaction and exhaustion.

You did it! He told himself. *You beat the bastard!*

Roland tried to feel elated. Even if he was now bleeding to death, he'd certainly won more minutes than Chang had intended giving him. More important still, Chang was brought down! In stealing the smuggling lord's only means of escape, Roland had ensured his capture!

Then why do I feel so rotten?

In fantasy Roland had often visualized being wounded, even dying in battle. Always though, he had imagined there'd be some solace, if only a soldier's final condolence of victory.

So why did he feel so dirty now? So ashamed?

He was alive now because he'd done the unexpected. Chang had been looking for heroism or cowardice—a berserk attack or animal rigor. But in that moment of impulse Roland had remembered the words of the old vet in Bloomington. "A fool who wants to live will do anything his captor tells him. He'll stand perfectly still just to win a few more heartbeats. Or he may burst into a useless charge.

"That's when, sometimes, it takes the most guts to retreat in good order, to fight another day."

Yeah, Joseph, sure. Roland thought. *Tell me about it.*

As his heart rate eased and the panting subsided, he now heard what sounded like moans coming down the tunnel. Kanakoa or Schmidt, or both. Wounded. Perhaps dying.

What good would I have done by staying? Instead of a leg wound, he'd have gone down with several bullets in the heart or face, and Chang would have gotten away.

True enough, but that didn't seem to help. Nor did reminding himself that neither of those guys back there were really his friends, anyway.

"Soldier boy!" The shout echoed down the narrow passage. "Bring the trolley back or I'll shoot you now!"

"Fat chance," Roland muttered. And even Chang's voice carried little conviction. Straight as the tunnel was, and even allowing for ricochets, the odds of hitting him were low even for an expert. Anyway, what good was a threat, when to comply meant certain death?

It wasn't repeated. For all the millionaire knew Roland was already at the other end.

"Why *did* I stop?" Roland asked aloud, softly. At the terminus he might find a telephone to call an ambulance, instead of lying here possibly bleeding to death.

A wave of agony throbbed up his leg. "And I thought I was so smart, not becomin' a dazer."

If he'd ever slipped over that line—using biofeedback to trip-off on self-stimulated endorphins—he'd certainly have a skill appropriate for here and now! What would have been self-abuse in Indiana would be right-on first aid at a time like this.

But then again, if he'd ever been a dazer, he wouldn't even be here right now. The corps didn't accept addicts.

Suddenly the cavern erupted in thunder, shaking the very walls. Roland covered his ears, recognizing pulse-rifle fire. No doubt about it, the real soldiers had arrived at last.

The gunshots ended almost immediately. *Could it be over already?* he wondered.

But no. As the ringing echoes subsided, he heard voices. One of them Chang's.

". . . if you throw down grenades. So if you want your wounded soldiers to live, negotiate with me!"

So Chang claimed two captives. Roland realized gloomily that both Schmidt and Kanakoa must have been caught, despite his shouted warning.

Or maybe not! After all, would Chang admit to having let one recruit escape down the tunnel? Perhaps he only had one of the others and used the plural form as a ploy. Roland clung to that hope.

It took a while for someone in authority to begin negotiations. The officer's voice was too muffled for Roland to make out, but he could hear Chang's side of the exchange.

"Not good enough! Prison would be the same as death for me! I accept nothing more rigorous than house arrest on my Pingtung estate. . . .

"Yes, naturally I will turn state's evidence. I owe my associates nothing. But I must have the deal sealed by a magistrate, at once!"

Again, the officials' words were indistinct. Roland caught tones of prevarication.

"Stop delaying! The alternative is death for these young soldiers!" Chang shouted back.

"Yes, yes, of course they can have medical attention . . . after I get my plea bargain! Properly sealed! Meanwhile, any sign of a stun or concussion grenade and I shoot them in the head, then myself!"

Roland could tell the marshals were weakening, probably under pressure from the peacekeeper CO. *Dammit!* he thought. The good guys' victory would be compromised. Worse, Chang surely had means at his estate for another escape, even from state detention.

Don't give in, he mentally urged the officers, though he felt pangs thinking of Kanakoa, or even Schmidt, lying there dying. *If you plea bargain, the bastard'll just start all over again.*

But Chang's next shout carried tones of satisfaction. "That's better! I can accept that. You better hurry with the document though. These men do not look well."

Roland cursed. "No!"

He rolled over and reached into the cargo hamper, tossing bags and jars onto the tracks ahead. They split and shattered. Narwhal tusks and rhino horns coated the tracks in powdered form, obstructing further travel in that direction. Then Roland fought fresh waves of nausea to writhe around on the narrow trolley, facing the direction he had come.

He'd worried he might have to manipulate the lever with his feet. But there was a duplicate at the other end. A red tag prevented the switch from being pushed passed a certain point. This Roland tore out, ripping one of his fingers in the process.

"Yes, I am willing to have my house arrest fully monitored by cameras at all times . . ."

"I'm sure you are, carni-man," Roland muttered. "But you don't fool *me*."

He slammed the lever home and the trolley glided forward. What began as a gentle breeze soon was a hurricane as power flowed from the humming rails.

You forget, Chang, that your estate is still on Mother Earth. And my guess is that Mom's had just about enough of you by now . . .

The light ahead ballooned in a rapidly expanding circle of brilliance. Roland felt solenoids try to throw the lever back, but he strained, holding it in place. In an instant of telescoped time, he saw a figure turn in the light, stare down the shaft, raise his weapon . . .

"Gaia!" Roland screamed, a battle cry chosen at the last second from some unknown recess of faith as he hurtled like a missile into space.

It was a mess the UNEPA team came down to inspect, after peacekeeping personnel pronounced it safe, and once the wounded boy had been rushed off to hospital. They were still taking pictures of the two remaining bodies when the green-clad Ecology Department officials came down the steep stairs at last to see what had happened.

"Well, here's your missing cache, Elena," one of them said, picking carefully through the white and gray powders scattered across the floor. Three walls of shelves were intact, but a fourth had collapsed over two quiet forms, sprawled atop each other in the corner. There, the snowdrifts had been stained crimson.

"Damn," the UNEPA man continued, shaking his head. "A lot of poor beasts died for one geek's fetish."

Elena looked down at her enemy of all these years. Chang's mouth gaped open—crammed full of powder that trailed off to the limp hand of the young recruit she had spoken to early in the evening. Even dying, riddled with bullets, this soldier apparently had a sense of symmetry, of poetry.

A peacekeeping forces noncom sat near the boy, smoothing a lock of ruffled hair. The corporal looked up at Elena. "Senterius was a lousy shot. Never showed any promise at all with weapons. I guess he improvised though. He graduated."

Elena turned away, disgusted by the maudlin, adolescent sentiment. *Warriors,* she thought. *The world is finally growing up though. Someday soon we'll be rid of them at last.*

Still, why was it she all of a sudden felt as if she had walked into a temple? Or that the spirits of all the martyred creatures were holding silent, reverent watch right now, along with the mourning corporal?

It was another woman's low voice Elena seemed to hear then, so briefly it was all too easy to dismiss as an echo or a momentary figment of exhaustion. Still, she briefly closed her eyes and swayed.

"There will be an end to war," the voice seemed to say, with gentle patience.

"But there will always be a need for heroes."

□

After the breakup of the supercontinent Pangaea, millions of years passed while the Indian landmass wandered northward away from Africa, creeping across the primordial ocean in solitary splendor. Then, once upon an eon, India collided head on, into the belly of Asia.

Great crustal blocks buckled from the slow-motion force of that impact, gradually, inexorably piling mountains higher and higher until a huge plateau towered through the atmosphere, creating a vast wall that diverted air to the north and trapped the southern winds in a pocket.

During each winter the land beneath this pocket cooled, lowering air pressure, drawing moisture-laden clouds onto the foothills to pour down monsoon rains. Each summer the countryside warmed again, raising pressures, driving the clouds back to sea.

This regular cycle of wet and dry seasons made routine the bounty of the great alluvial plains below the mountains, fertilized by the plateau's silty runoff. When human beings arrived to clear the forests and plant crops, they found a land of untold fecundity, where they could build, and create culture, and have babies, and make war, and have more babies, and make love, and have more babies still . . .

Came then a time—only an eyeblink as the ages mark it—when the pattern changed. Gone were the great forests that had cooled the valleys with the transpired breath of ten billion trees. Instead, the soot of cook fires and industry rose into the sky like a hundred million daily sacrifices to individual, shortsighted gods.

Not only in India, but all around the world, temperatures steadily climbed.

As always with such changes, the sea resisted, and so the first grand effects were seen onshore. The chill of winter vanished like a memory, and summer's ridge of high pressure remained in place year-round over a hardpan that had once welcomed fertile farms.

In fact, it rained now more than ever. Only now the monsoons stayed where they were born . . . at sea.

● The trick to reading, Nelson Grayson decided, was slipping into
B the rhythm of the words, but not letting that get in the way of
I *listening*. Nelson concentrated on the sentences zigzagging across
O the page.
S
P Although many struggled to keep their faith in a static,
H unchanging universe, it was already apparent to the
E best minds preceding Darwin that Earth's creatures had
R changed over time. . . .
E

The worst thing about studying, Nelson had decided, was *books*. Especially this old-fashioned kind, with motionless letters the color of squashed ants splayed across musty paper. Still, this dusty volume contained Kuwenezi's sole copy of this essay. So he had to stick with it.

> Evolutionists themselves argued over *how* species changed. Darwin's and Wallace's "natural selection"—in which diversity within a species provides grist for the grinding mill of nature—had to pass ten thousand tests before it triumphed conclusively over Lamarck's competing theory of "inheritance of acquired traits."
> But even then arguments raged over essential details. For instance, what was the basic unit of evolution?
> For years many thought it was *species* that adapted. But evidence later supported the "selfish gene" model—that *individuals* act in ways that promote success for their descendants, caring little for the species as a whole. Examples of individual success prevailing over species viability include peacocks' tails and moose antlers . . .

Nelson thought he understood the basic issue here. A good example was how people often did what was good for themselves, even if it hurt their family, friends, or society.

But what do peacocks' tails have to do with it?

Nelson sat beneath overhanging bougainvillaeas. Nearby, the gentle flow of water was punctuated by the sound of splashing fish. The air carried thick aromas, but Nelson tried to ignore all those deceptively natural sensoria for the archaic paper reading device in his hands.

If only it were a modern document, with a smart index and hyper links stretching all through the world data net. It was terribly frustrating having to flip back and forth between the pages and crude, flat illustrations that never even moved! Nor were there animated arrows or zoom-ins. It completely lacked a tap for sound.

Most baffling of all was the problem of new words. Yes, it was his own damn fault he had neglected his education until so late in life. But still, in a normal text you'd only have to touch an unfamiliar word and the definition would pop up just below. Not here though. The paper simply lay there, inert and uncooperative.

When he'd complained about this, earlier, Dr. B'Keli only handed him another of these flat books, something called a "dictionary," whose arcane use eluded him entirely.

How did students back in TwenCen ever learn anything at all? he wondered.

Darwin spoke of two types of "struggle" in the wild—conflict *between* individuals for reproductive success, and the struggle of each individual against the implacable forces of nature, such as cold, thirst, darkness, and exposure.

Good, Nelson thought. *This is what I was looking for.*

Influenced by the dour logic of Malthus, Darwin believed the first of these struggles was dominant. Much of the "generosity" we see in nature is actually quid pro quo—or "you scratch my back and I'll scratch yours." Altruism is generally tied to the success of one's genes.

Still, even Darwin admitted that sometimes cooperation seems to transcend immediate needs. Examples do exist where working together for the common good appears to outweigh any zero-sum game of "I win, you lose."

The book suddenly jolted as a brown paw slapped it. A long snout, filled with gleaming teeth, thrust into view. Feral brown eyes glittered into his.

"Oh, not now, Shig," Nelson complained. "Can't you see I'm studyin'?"

But the infant baboon craved attention. It reached out and squeaked appealingly. Nelson sighed and gave in, though his arms were still tender with freshly healed scar tissue.

"What do you have there, eh?" He pried open the little monkey's paw. Something reddish and half gnawed rolled out—a piece of fruit purloined from a forbidden source. "Aw, come on, Shig. Don't I feed you more'n enough?"

Of course this was night shift and no one else was around to witness the minor theft. He dug a small depression in the soft loam and buried the evidence. With all recycling factors above par, one pilfered fruit probably wouldn't trigger catastrophe.

A broad expanse of tinted crystal panes separated this portion of the biosphere from the star-sprinkled night. More than mere practicality had gone into creating this enclosed miracle of biological management. The tracks and runners, the sprinklers and sprayers, were so tastefully hidden one might think this an arboretum or greenhouse rather than a high-tech sewage plant.

Settling Shig in his left arm, Nelson tried to resume where he'd left off.

> This latter view of evolution—that it includes a place for kindness and cooperation—certainly is an attractive one. Don't all our moral codes stress that helping one another is the ultimate good? We're taught as babes that virtue goes beyond mere self-interest. . . .

Affronted at being ignored, Shig dealt with the insult by turning and *sitting* on the open book, then looking about innocently.

"Oh, yeah?" Nelson said, and retaliated by tickling the infant, whose jaws gaped in a silent laughter as he writhed and finally escaped by toppling onto the soft grass.

Then, switching states quickly, the little baboon suddenly crouched warily, sniffing the brookside foliage and listening. Shig's gaze swept the pebbly banks of the nearby stream and the maze of dripping vines crisscrossing overhead. Then, suddenly, a larger baboon emerged from the rustling plantain beds and Shig let out a squeak of pleasure.

Nell sniffed left and right before climbing down and sauntering toward her offspring, tail high. Sleek and well fed, she hardly resembled the scraggly outcast Nelson had rescued from ark four's savannah biosphere. Nelson couldn't help comparing her transformation to his own. *We've come a long way from sampling shit for a living,* he thought.

While in the hospital he at first had worried what the scientists would do to him for leaving six male baboons battered and whimpering beneath the dusty acacia trees. Self-defense or no, Nelson had visions of dismissal, deportation, and a year's corrective therapy back in a Yukon rehab camp.

But apparently the Ndebele regarded his exploit in ways he hadn't imagined. Director Mugabe, especially, spoke of the episode having "a salutary effect on the baboons' relationship with their caretakers . . ."

If by that he meant the troop would henceforth treat humans more respectfully, Nelson supposed the director had a point. Beyond that though, the people of Kuwenezi claimed to appreciate the "warrior's virtues" he'd displayed. Hence the battery of placement exams that followed his release from care, and his astonishing assignment here, with the prestigious title of Waste Management Specialist/2.

"Of course the pay's still shitty," he reminded himself. Nevertheless, the skills he learned here were in high demand and would guarantee his prospects if he did well.

Modern cities dealt with sewage biologically these days, imitating nature's own methods. The flow from tens of millions of toilets coursed through settling and aerating paddies the size of large farms. One stretch might be a riot of bulrushes and aloe, bred to remove heavy metals. Next, a scum of specially designed algae would convert ammonia and methane into animal fodder. Finally, most urban treatment plants ended in snail ponds, with fish to eat the snails, and both harvested to sell on the open market.

The water that emerged was generally as pure as any mountain stream. Purer, given the state of most streams these days. It was to this craft at recycling water that most now credited the survival of modern cities. Without it, the least consequence nearly everywhere would have been war.

The problem with bio-treatment, though, was that it took acres and acres. A life ark had no room for that. The refuge ecospheres had to be self-contained, and self-*supporting*, or weary taxpayers might someday forget their pledge to fund these living time capsules, preserving genetic treasures for another, more fortunate age.

So Director Mugabe had decreed that this system must be "folded." What might have covered hectares now fit into the area of a large auditorium.

Diluted sewage first seeped between the sandwiched glassy layers overhead, encountering special algae and sunlight. After aeration, the green slurry then sprayed over suspended trays of vegetation. Dripping slowly down the hanging roots, filtered water at last fell to the streamlet below, where duckweed completed the process, helped by several species of fish that thrived here, even though they were now extinct in the wild.

Shig climbed onto his mother's back and Nell carried her infant over to the miniature river to splash at the shallows playfully. Naturally the recycling plant was deserted at this hour. At first nervous about handling a shift all by himself, Nelson soon found the task strangely easy, as if the complex interplay of details—adjusting flows and checking growth rates—seemed natural, even obvious somehow. Mugabe and B'Keli said he possessed a "knack," whatever that meant. The whole thing had Nelson terribly puzzled, if also pleased.

Back in school he hadn't given much thought to what the teachers said—about how vegetation took in carbon dioxide, nitrates, and water, and used sunlight to turn those ingredients into oxygen, carbohydrates, and protein. In essence, plants converted animals' waste products into the very things animals needed for living, and vice versa. Those lessons had been part of his curriculum since preschool, including all the ways man's industry had thrown the system out of balance.

Still, he was pretty sure nobody had ever told him about benzene or hydrogen cyanide or ammonia, or all the other bizarre chemicals given off in trace amounts by creatures like himself. Chemicals which —if it not for all sorts of hardworking bacteria—would have choked the atmosphere and killed everybody off long before humans ever fooled around with fire.

"Were you aware of the importance of wool moths and hair beetles?" Dr. B'Keli had asked when Nelson first started showing an interest. "If it weren't for those specialized eaters of fur and hair, we mammals would have covered the land with a layer of sheddings more than two meters thick by now. Think of that, next time you spread mothballs to save your favorite sweater!"

Nelson shook his head, certain he was being had. *I might be a changed person, but I still don't like Dr. B'Keli.*

Still, it had gotten him thinking. What made the system of cycle and recycle work so well for millions of years? For every waste product it seemed there was some species out there willing to consume it. Every plant or animal depended on others and was depended on by others still.

Even more amazing, the interdependence was usually a matter of *eating* one other! As individuals, each creature tried hard to avoid becoming anyone else's meal. And yet, it was all this eating and being eaten, this preying and being preyed upon, that made the great balancing act work!

Months ago, he would never have allowed himself the presumed weakness of curiosity. Now it consumed him. The pattern of symmetry had been going on for three billion years, and he wanted to know everything about it.

How? How did it all come about?

That visiting professor some weeks back, the old woman from

England, had called the process "homeostasis" . . . the tendency of some special systems to stay in balance for a long time, even if they're rocked by temporary setbacks.

Nelson mouthed the word.

"Homeostasis . . ."

It had a sensual sound to it. He picked up the book again and found his place.

Nearly every culture has laws to shelter family, tribe, and nation from the impulses of individuals. In recent times we've extended these codes of protection to include those without family, the weak, even the alien, and agonize that we don't live up to these standards perfectly. A kind of cultural quasi-citizenship has even been granted some of our former food animals—whales, dolphins, and many other creatures with whom it's possible now to feel a sense of kinship.

Arguing endlessly over ways and means, most of us still agree on a basic premise, an ideal. If asked to envision paradise, we would indeed have the lion lie down with the lamb, and all people, great and small, would treat each other with kindness.

But it's important to remember these are *our* morals, based on *our* background as particularly social mammals. Creatures who need a nurturing tribe—who are helpless and lost without a clan.

What if intelligence and technology had been discovered by some other species, say crocodiles? Or otters? Would they share our ideas of fundamental morality? Even among humans, despite our *talk* about caring for others, all too often it's "look out for number one."

Still, I'd like to suggest here that the drift from egotism toward cooperation is an inevitable one. It derives from basic patterns that have guided the evolution of life on Earth for three and a half billion years and continue to shape and transform our world.

Yes, Nelson thought. *She's the only one I've found who talks about the real stuff. I don't understand half of what she says, but it's here. This is where I start.*

He stroked the scratchy paper pages, and for the first time thought he understood why some oldtimers still preferred such volumes to modern books. The words were here, now and always, not whispering ghosts of electronic wisdom, sage but fleeting like moon-beams. What the volume lacked in subtlety, it made up for in solidity.

Like me, maybe?

Nelson laughed.

"Right! Dream on, eh?"

He returned to the text. When the monkeys returned from their bath, they found him deeply immersed in an adventure they could not begin to follow. This time, however, they merely sat and watched, letting him do this strange human thing in peace.

□

For half a century the city of West Berlin was something of an ecological island.

Its isolation wasn't total of course. Water seeping underground ignored political boundaries, as did the rain and pollution from Communist factories just beyond the wall. Except for one frightening episode, just after the Second World War, food and consumer goods flowed from the Federal Republic by rail and road and air.

Still, in many ways the city was an oasis less than ten miles by twenty, whose several million shut-ins interacted hardly at all with the territory surrounding them.

With no place to send their waste, Berliners of those days had to pioneer recycling. Refuse was strictly separated for curbside pickup. Even sidewalks were made of stone tiles so they could be stacked during street repairs and then reused.

Despite the city's flashy night life and reputation for irreverence, West Berlin had more park area per capita than New York or Paris. Gardeners grew more of their own food than other urbanites. One proud mayor proclaimed that, should humanity ever send a generation ship to the stars, it ought to be crewed by West Berliners.

A mayor of Bonn promptly suggested that would be a very good idea.

Berliners dismissed his sarcasm as churlish, and went on living.

● "You did not make Pele as angry this time, you well-endowed
C *pakeha tohunga.*"
O   The old priestess reached over to pat Alex's knee. With a
R reedy voice she went on complimenting him. "You must be learn-
E ing better foreplay! Keep it up. That, surely, is the way to win
Pele's favor."

Alex's face reddened. He looked to George Hutton, sitting on a woven mat nearby. "*Now* what's she talking about?"

The big Maori glanced across the fire pit at Meriana Kapur, who grinned as she stirred the coals with an iron poker. Quiescent flames licked higher and the tattoos on her lips and chin seemed to flicker and dance. The crone appeared ageless.

"Auntie's referring to the fact that there were fewer and milder quakes after the recent scans. That must mean the Earth goddess found your, er, probings . . . more acceptable this time."

George said it with a straight face. Or *almost* straight. The ambiguity was just enough to make Alex suppress an impulse to laugh out loud.

"I thought Pele was a Hawaiian spirit, not Maori."

George shrugged. "The Pacific's cosmopolitan today. Hawaiian priests consult ours in matters of body magic, while we defer when it comes to volcanoes and planetary animism."

"Is that where you studied geophysics, then?" Alex smirked. "In a shaman's hut, beside a lava flow?"

He was surprised when George nodded earnestly, without taking offense. "There, and MIT, yes." Hutton went on to explain. "Naturally, Western science is paramount. It's the central body of knowledge, and the old gods long ago admitted that. Nevertheless, my ventures wouldn't have got backing from my family and *iwi* and clan, had I not also apprenticed for a time with Pele's priests, at the feet of Kilauea."

Alex sighed. He shouldn't be surprised. Like California fifty years ago, contemporary New Zealand had gradually transformed its longstanding tradition of tolerance into a positive fetish for eccentricity. Of course George's people saw nothing inconsistent in mixing old and new ideas to suit their eclectic style. And if that occasionally made staid outsiders blink in wonder, so much the better.

Alex refused to give George the satisfaction. He shrugged and turned to regard the priestess once again.

Here under the hand-carved beams of the centuries-old meeting house, he had only to squint to imagine himself transported in time. Even her tattoos looked genuine . . . unlike those the entertainers at Rotorua put on and took off as easily as hair or skin color. Still, it was doubtful many ancient Maori women, even priestesses, reached Auntie's age with all their own teeth still in place, as hers were, gleaming straight and white from a life of hygiene and regular professional care.

Alex realized she was waiting for a reply, and so he nodded slightly. "Thank you, Auntie. I'm glad the goddess found my attentions . . . pleasing."

George planted a hand on his shoulder. "Of course Pele liked them. Didn't the Earth move for *you?*"

Alex shrugged the hand aside. George had insisted they come here tonight, implying it was important. Meanwhile Alex chafed for the lab and his computer. One more simulation might break the logjam. Maybe if he kept at it, kept trying . . .

"You pursue a great *taniwha* that has burrowed into Our Mother," the priestess said. "You seek to grasp its nature. You fear it will devour Our Mother and ourselves."

He nodded. A colorful appraisal, but it summed things up rather well. Their most recent gravitational tomography scans had lit up Earth's interior with a startling clarity that struck George's technicians dumb, sketching the planet's deep layers in fine, prickled, searing complexity that defied all previous geophysical models.

The search had revealed both "*taniwha*s," the two singularities slowly orbiting near the planet's heart. Both the shriveled, evaporating remnant of his own Alpha and the ominous, massive spectre of Beta had shown up as tiny, perfect sparkles within the maelstrom. Everything he'd surmised about the larger beast had been confirmed in those scans. The cosmic knot was growing, all right. And the more closely he examined its convoluted world-sheets, its torturous topology of warped space-time, the more beautiful it grew in its implacable deadliness.

Unfortunately, he was no closer to answering any of the really basic questions, such as when and where the thing had originated. Or how it was that probing for it triggered earthquakes at the surface, thousands of miles away.

Hell, he couldn't even figure out the thing's orbit! Prior to these recent scans he'd been so sure he had Beta's dynamics worked out— the way gravity and pseudo-friction and centrifugal forces balanced in its slow whirl about the inner core. But its trajectory had shifted after the first scan. Some additional factor must have nudged it. But what?

Auntie Kapur tapped a steady beat on a miniature ceremonial drum—which some called a *zzxjoanw*—while making fatidic statements about amorous goddesses and other superstitious nonsense.

". . . You reach deep within Pele's hidden places, touching Her secrets. She would not permit this of just any man. You are honored, nephew."

Gaia worship took many forms, and this Pele-venerating version seemed harmless enough. He'd even heard Jen speak favorably of Auntie's cult, once. Under other circumstances he might have found all this very interesting, instead of a damned nuisance.

"Have no fear," she went on. "You will tame this beast you pursue. You will keep it from harming Our Mother."

She paused, looking at him expectantly. Alex tried to think of something to say.

"I am an unworthy man," he answered, modestly.

But the old woman surprised him with a quick, reproachful glare. "It's not for you to judge your worthiness! You serve, as a man's seed serves the woman who chooses him. Even the *taniwha* serves. You would do well, boy, to consider the lesson of the tiny kiwi bird and her enormous egg."

Alex stared. The suggestion seemed so bizarre—and the tension of the last few weeks had him wound up so tight—that he couldn't contain himself any longer. He guffawed.

Auntie Kapur tilted her head. "You are amused by my metaphors?"

"I . . ." He held up one hand placatingly.

"Would you prefer I used other terms? That I ask you to contemplate the relationship between 'zygotes' and 'gametes'? Would you understand better if I spoke to you of dissipative structures? Or the way, even amid catastrophe, life creates order out of chaos?"

Alex was unable to react except by blinking. While she stirred the coals again, George whispered, "Auntie has a biophysics degree from the University of Otago. Don't make assumptions, Lustig."

Trapped—by a movie cliche! Alex had known this was a modern person sitting across from him. And yet her pose—what Stan Goldman would call her "schtick"—had drawn him in.

"You . . . you're saying the singularity won't harm the Earth? That it might instead trigger some . . ."

Auntie reached over the coals and rapped him sharply on the back of his hand. "I say nothing! It's not my job to tell you, a 'genius,' what to think—you, who have many times my brains and whose prowess impresses even Our Mother. Those are silly endowments but they serve their purposes.

"No, I only pose you *questions*, at a time when you're obviously concentrating much too closely on your problem. You show every sign of being ensnared by those very brains of yours—of being cornered by your postulates! To nudge you off balance then, I offer you the wisdom of sperm and egg.

"Heed my words or not. Do as you will. I have confused you and that is enough. Your unconscious will do the rest."

She concluded rattling the drum, then put it aside and dismissed both men with a brusque wave. "I forbid further work until you've rested and distracted yourselves. You are commanded to get drunk tonight. Now go.''

The priestess watched the fire pit silently as they stood up. Alex grabbed his shoes and followed George out of the meeting house, into a starry night. Ten feet down the path, however, the two men stopped, looked at each other, and simultaneously broke into fits of laughter. Alex nearly doubled over, his sides hurting as he desperately tried to catch his breath. George slapped him roughly on the back. ''Come on,'' the big Maori said. ''Let's get a beer. Or ten.''

Alex grinned, wiping his eyes. ''I . . . I'll join you in an hour or so, George. Honestly. I only have to check one simulation and . . . what's the matter?''

Suddenly frowning, George shook his head. ''Not tonight. You heard what Auntie said. Rest and distraction.''

For the third time that evening, Alex gaped. ''You can't take that crazy old bat seriously!''

George smiled sheepishly, but also nodded. ''She is a bit of a ham. But where her authority applies, I obey. We get drunk tonight, white fellow. You and I, now. Whether you cooperate or not.''

Alex had a sudden vision of this massive billionaire holding his head under a beer tap, while he sputtered and fought helplessly. The image was startlingly credible. *Another believer*, he sighed inwardly. They were everywhere.

''Well . . . I wouldn't want to flout tradition. . . .''

''Good.'' George slapped Alex on the back once more, almost knocking him over. ''And between rounds I'll tell you how I once substituted for the great Makahuna, back in '20, when the All Blacks smashed Australia.''

Oh, no. Rugby stories. That's all I need.

Still, Alex felt a strange relief. He'd been commanded to seek oblivion, and by no less than a spokeswoman for Gaia herself. On such authority—despite his agnosticism—he supposed he could let himself forget for just one night.

Alex had been in pubs all over the world, from the faded elegance of the White Hart, in Bloomsbury, to rickety, firetrap shanties in Angolan boom towns. There had been that kitschy Russian tourist bistro, near the launch site at Kapustin Yar, where dilute, vitamin-enriched vodka was served in pastel squeeze tubes to background strains of moon muzak . . . very tacky. He'd even been to the bar of the Hotel Imperial, in Shanghai, just before the Great Big War Against Tobacco finally breached that mist-shrouded last bastion of smoking, driving grumbling addicts into back alleys to nurse their dying habit.

In comparison, the Kai-Keri was as homey and familiar as the Washington, his own local back in Belsize Park. The bitter brown ale was much the same. True, the crowd around the dart board stood closer than in a typical British pub, and Alex had gotten lost during his last two trips to the loo. But he attributed that to the coriolis effect. After all, everything was upside down here in kiwi land.

One thing you wouldn't see in Britain was this easy fraternizing of the races. From full-blooded Maoris to palefaced, blond *pakeha*s and every shade in between, nobody seemed to notice differences that still occasionally caused riots back home.

Oh, they had names for every pigmentation and nationality, including postage stamp island states Alex had never even heard of. The *New Zealand Herald* just that morning had run an outraged exposé about promotion discrimination against Fijian guest-workers in an Auckland factory. It had sounded unfair, all right . . . and also incredibly picayune compared with the injustices and bigotries still being perpetrated almost everywhere else, all over the world.

Actually, Alex figured Kiwis fretted over such small-scale imperfections so they wouldn't feel left out. Harmony was all very good in theory, but in practice it sometimes seemed a bit embarrassing.

Soon after arriving in New Zealand, he had asked Stan Goldman just how far the attitude stretched. How would Stan feel, for instance, if his daughter came home one night and said she wanted to marry a Maori boy?

Alex's former mentor had stared back in surprise.

"But Alex, that's exactly what she did!"

Soon he also met George's family, and the wives and husbands and kids of several Tangoparu engineers. They had all made him feel welcome. None seemed to blame him for the deadly thing that was growing in the Earth's core.

And you're not *responsible. It's not your monster.*

Again, the reminder helped, a little.

"Drink, Lustig. You've fallen behind Stan and me."

George Hutton was accustomed to getting his way. Dutifully, Alex took a breath and lifted the tapered glass of warm brew. He closed his eyes, swallowed, and put it down again, empty.

When he reopened them, however, the pint had magically resurrected! Was this divine intervention? Or defiance of entropy? The detached portion of Alex's mind knew someone must have poured another round, presumably from a pitcher that even now existed somewhere outside his diminishing field of vision. Still, it was fun to consider alternatives. A negentropic time-reversal had certain arguments in its favor.

With yet another of his unraveling faculties, Alex listened to Stan Goldman's recollections from dimly remembered days at the end of the last century.

"I was thinkin' about becoming a biologist in the late nineties," his former research advisor said. "That's where all the excitement was then. Biologists think of those days the way we physicists look back on the early nineteen-hundreds, when Planck an' Schrödinger were inventing the quantum, and old Albert himself nailed the speed o' light to the bleeding reference frame . . . when the basis for a whole science was laid down.

"What a time that must have been! A century's engineering came out of what those lucky bastards discovered. But by my time it was all lookin' pretty dumpit boring for physics."

"C'mon, Stan," George Hutton protested. "The late nineties, boring? For physics? Wasn't that when Adler and Hurt completed grand unification? Combinin' all the forces of nature into one big megillah? You can't tell me you weren't excited then!"

Stan brought one spotted hand to his smooth dome, using a paper serviette to dab away spots of perspiration. "Oh, surely. The unification equations were brilliant, elegant. They called it a "theory of everything" . . . TOE for short.

"But by then field theory was mostly a spectator sport. It took almost mutant brilliance to participate . . . like you have to be eight feet tall to play pro basketball these days. What's more, you started hearing talk about closing the books on physics. There were profs who said 'all the important questions have been answered.' "

"That's why you thought about leaving the field?" George inquired.

Stan shook his head. "Naw. What really had me depressed was that we'd run out of *modalities*."

Alex had been pinching his numb cheeks, in search of any feeling. He turned to peer at Stan. "Modalities?"

"Basic ways and means. Chinks in nature's wall. The lever and the fulcrum. The wheel an' the wedge. Fire an' nuclear fission.

"Those weren't just intellectual curiosities, Alex. They started out as useless abstractions, sure. But, well, do you remember how Michael Faraday answered, when a member of Parliament asked him what *use* would ever come of his crazy 'electricity' thing?"

George Hutton nodded. "I heard about that! Didn't Faraday ask, um . . . what *use* was a newborn baby?"

"That's one version," Alex agreed, commanding his head to mimic the approximate trajectory of a nod. "Another story has him answering—'I don't know, sir. But I'll wagell, er . . . *wager* someday you'll tax it!'" Alex laughed. "Always liked that story."

"Yeah," Stan agreed. "And Faraday was right, wasn't he? Look at the difference electricity made! Physics became the leading science, not just because it dealt in fundamentals but also 'cause it *opened doors*—modalities—offering us powers we once reckoned belonged to gods!"

Alex closed his eyes. Momentarily it seemed he was back in the meeting house, with Auntie Kapur slyly referring to the ways of heavenly beings.

"Grand unification depressed you because it wasn't *practical*?" George asked unbelievingly.

"Exactly!" Stan stabbed a finger toward the big geophysicist. "So Hurt described how the electroweak force unifies with chromodynamics and gravitation. So what? To ever *do* anything with the knowledge, we'd need the temperatures and pressures of the Big Bang!"

Stan made a sour look. "Pfeh! Can you see why I almost switched to quantum biology? *That* was where new theories might make a difference, lead to new products, and change people's lives."

Hutton regarded his old friend with clear disappointment. "And I always thought you math types were in it for the beauty. Turns out you're as much a gadget junky as I am." He waved to a passing barmaid, ordering another round.

Goldman shrugged. "Beauty and practicality aren't always inconsistent. Look at Einstein's formulas for absorption and emission of radiation. What elegance! Such simplicity! He had no idea he was predicting *lasers*. But the potential's right there in the equations. . . ."

Alex felt the words wash over him. They were like swarming creatures. He had a strange fantasy the things were seeking places within him to lay their young. Normally, he had little use for the popular multimind models of consciousness. But right now the normal, comforting illusion of personal unity seemed to have been dissolved by the solvent, alcohol. He felt he wasn't singular, but many.

One self watched in bemusement while a dark pint reappeared before him, again, as if by magic. Another subpersona struggled to follow the thread of Stan's rambling reminiscence.

But then, behind his tightening brow, yet more selves wrestled over something still submerged. Benumbed by fatigue and alcohol, logic had been squelched and other, more chaotic forces seemed to romp unfettered. Ninety-nine to one the results would be just the sort that sounded great during a party and like gibberish the morning after.

". . . when, out of nowhere, the cavitron appeared! Imagine my delight," Stan went on, spreading his gnarled hands. "All of a sudden we found there was, after all, a way to gain access to the heart of the new physics!"

The elderly theoretician made a fist, as if grasping tightly some long-sought quarry. "One year the field seemed sterile, sexless, doomed to mathematical masturbation or worse—perpetual, pristine theoretical splendor. The next moment—boom! We had in our hands the power to make singularities! To move and shape space itself!"

Stan appeared to have temporarily forgotten the tragic consequences of that discovery. Even so, Alex took sustenance from his friend's enthusiasm. He recalled his own feelings on hearing the news —that the team at Livermore had actually converted raw vacuum into concentrated space-time. The possibilities seemed endless. What he himself had envisioned was cheap, endless energy for a shaky, impoverished world.

"Oh, there remained limitations," Stan went on. "But the chink was there. The new lever and fulcrum. Perhaps a new wheel! I felt as Charles Townes must have, the day he bounced light back and forth through the lattice in that pumped-up ruby crystal, causing it to . . ."

Alex's chair teetered backward as he stood suddenly. He steadied himself with his fingertips against the tabletop. Then, staring straight ahead, he stumbled awkwardly through the crowd, weaving toward the door.

"Alex?" George called after him. "Alex!"

A stand of Norfolk pine, twenty meters from the rural pub, drew him like flotsam from a roaring stream. In that eddy the air was fresh and the chatty hubbub no longer sought to overwhelm him. Here Alex had only the rustle of boughs to contend with, a gentle answer to the wind.

"What is it?" George Hutton asked when he caught up a minute later. "Lustig, what's the matter?"

Alex's mind spun. He swiveled precariously, torn between trying to follow all the threads at once and grabbing tightly onto just a few before they all blew away.

He blurted, "A laser, George. It's a laser!"

Hutton bent to meet Alex's eye. It wasn't easy, both men wavered so.

"What are you talking about? *What's* a laser?"

Alex made a broad motion with his hands. "Stan mentioned Einstein's abs—absorption and emission parameters. But remember?

There were *two* 'B' parameters—one for spontaneous emission and one for *stimulated* emission from an excited state."

"Speaking of an excited state," George commented. But Alex hurried on.

"George, George!" He spread his arms to keep balance. "In a laser, you first create an—an inverted energy state in an excited medium . . . get all the outer electrons in a crystal hopping, right? The other thing you do is you place the crystal inside a *resonator*. A resonator tuned so only one particular wave can pass back and forth across the crystal . . ."

"Yeah. You use two mirrors, facing each other at opposite ends. But—"

"Right. Position the mirrors just so, and only one wave will reach a standing state, bouncing to and fro a thousand, million, jillion times. Only one frequency makes it, one polarization, one orientation. That one wave goes back and forth, back and forth at the speed of light—causing *stimulated emission* from all the excited atoms it passes, sucking their excited energy into one single—"

"Alex—"

"—into a single coherent beam . . . all the component waves reinforcing . . . all propagating in parallel like marching soldiers. The sum is far greater than the individual parts."

"But—"

Alex grabbed George's lapels. "Don't you see? We fed a single waveform into such a medium a few weeks back, and again two days ago. Each time, something *emerged*. Waves of energy far greater than what we put in!

"Think about it! The Earth's interior is a hot soup of excited states, like the plasma in a neon tube or a flashed ruby crystal. Given the right conditions, it took what we fed it and magnified the output. It acted as an amplifier!"

"The Earth itself?" George frowned, now seriously puzzled. "An *amplifier*? In what way?"

Then he read something in Alex's face. "Earthquakes. You mean the earthquakes! But . . . but we never saw any such thing in our old resource scans. Echoes, yes. We got echoes and used them for mapping. But never any amplification effect."

Alex nodded. "Because you never had a resonator before! Think of the mirrors in a laser, George. They're what create the conditions for amplification of one waveform, one orientation, into a coherent beam.

"Only, we're dealing in *gravity* waves. And not just any gravity waves, but waves specifically tuned to reflect from—"

"From a singularity," George whispered. "Beta!"

He stepped back, wide-eyed. "Are you saying the *taniwha* . . ."

"Yes! It acted as part of a gravity wave resonator. With the amplifying medium consisting of the Earth's core itself!"

"Alex." George waved a hand in front of his face. "This is getting crazy."

"Of course the effect ought to be muddy with only one mirror, and we had only Beta to bounce off of. The second series of tests conformed to that sort of a model."

Alex stopped and pondered. "But what about that first scan, weeks ago? That time our probe set off *narrow*, powerfully defined quake swarms. That output beam was so intense! Focused enough to rip apart a space station . . ."

"A space station?" George sounded aghast. "You don't mean *we* caused the American station to . . ."

Alex nodded. "Didn't I tell you that? Tragic thing. Awful luck it just happened through a beam so narrow."

"Alex . . ." George shook his head. But the flow of words was too intense.

"I understand why the amplification was muddy the second time —just what you'd expect from a one-mirror resonator. But that first time . . ." Alex slammed his fist into his palm. "There *must* have been two reflectors."

"Maybe your Alpha, the Iquitos black hole . . ."

"No. Wrong placement and frequency. I . . ." Alex blinked. "Of course. I have it."

He turned to face George.

"The other singularity must have been aboard the space station itself. It's the only possible explanation. Their being directly in line with the beam wasn't coincidental. The station hole resonated with Beta and *caused* the alignment. It fits."

"Alex . . ."

"Let's see, that would mean the outer assembly of the station would be carried off at a pseudo-acceleration of . . ."

He paused and looked up through a gap in the branches at the stars overhead. His voice hushed in awe. "Those poor bastards. What a way to go."

George Hutton blinked, trying to keep up. "Are you saying the Americans had an unlicensed . . ."

Again, however, Alex's momentum carried him. "We'll need a name, of course. How about 'gravity amplification by stimulated emission of radiation'? Might as well stay with traditional nomenclature."

He turned to look at George. "Well? Do you like it? Shall we call it a graser'? Or would 'gazer' sound better. Yes, 'gazer,' I think."

Alex's eyes glittered. Pain dwelled there, mixed equally with a startled joy of discovery. "How does it feel, George, to have helped unleash the most powerful 'modality' ever known?"

The two men looked at each other for a stretched moment of time, as if each were suddenly acutely aware of the pregnant relevance of sound. The silence was broken only when Stan Goldman called from the door of the pub.

"Alex? George? Where are you fellows? You're taking a long time relieving yourselves. Are you too drunk to find your zippers? Or have you found something else out there that's interesting?"

"We're over here!" George Hutton called, and then looked back at Alex, who was staring at the stars again, talking to himself. In a somewhat lower voice, George added, "And yes, Stan, it appears we've found something interesting after all."

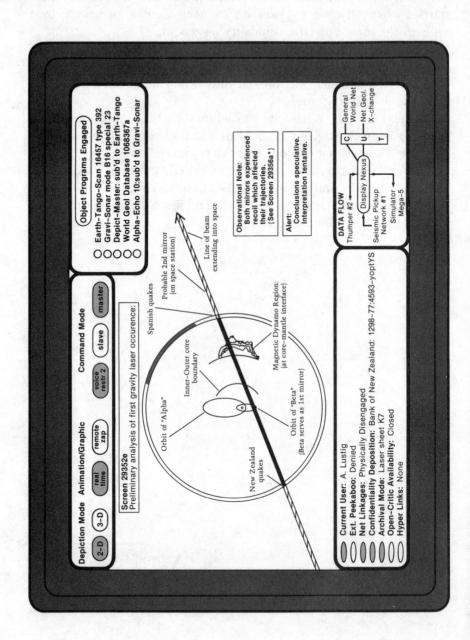

PART V

PLANET

In the new world's earliest days, there was no one to speak ill of carbon dioxide, or methane, or even hydrogen cyanide. Under lightning and harsh sunlight those chemicals merged to stain the young ocean with amino acids, purines, adenylates . . . a "primeval soup" which then reacted still further, building complex, twisting polymers.

Mere random fusings would have taken a trillion years to come up with anything as complex as a bacterium. But something else was involved beyond just haphazard chemistry. Selection. Some molecules were stable, while others broke apart easily. The sturdy ones accumulated, filling the seas. These became letters in a new alphabet.

They, too, reacted to form still larger clusters, a few of which survived and accrued . . . the first genetic words. And so on. What would otherwise have taken a trillion years was accomplished in a relative instant. Sentences bounced against each other, mostly forming nonsense paragraphs. But a few had staying power.

Before the last meteorite storm was over or the final roaring supervolcano finally subsided, there appeared within the ocean a chemical tour de force, surrounded by a lipid-protein coat. An entity that consumed and excreted, that made true copies of itself. One whose daughters wrought victories, suffered defeats, and multiplied.

Out of alphabet soup there suddenly was told a story.

A simple tale as yet. Primitive and predictable. But still, a raw talent could be read there.

The author began to improvise.

☐ **Worldwide Long Range Solutions Special Interest Group** [☐ SIG AeR,WLRS 253787890.546] **Steering Committee Report.**

For weeks now there's been a marathon debate going on over in subgroup six (techno-cures), category nine, forum five, concerning the relative merits of nano-constructors versus Von Neumann machines as possible sources of wealth to replace our tired planet's exhausted mines and wells.

The word "exhausted" applies as well to the weary moderators of this tag-team endurance round. Finally the forum chair said, "Enough already! Don't any of you people have jobs? Families?"

We agree. It's all very well to talk about how these two technologies might someday "generate enough wealth to make even TwenCen America look like a Cro-Magnon tribe." But one of the purposes of this SIG is to take ideas beyond mere speculation and offer the world feasible plans!

So let's call a pause on this one, people. Get some sleep. Say hello to your children. Come back when you can show a workable design for a truly sophisticated machine that can make copies of itself—whether grazing on lunar soils or swimming in a nutrient bath. Then the rest of us will happily supply the carping criticism you'll need to make it work.

In sharp contrast, the soc-sci freaks in group two have had some very witty forums about the current fad of applying tribal psychology to urban populations. At one point over half a million Net users were tapping in, taking our SIG, once more, all the way up to commercial-grade use levels! Digest-summaries of those forums are already available, and we commend group two's organizers for running such a lively, productive debate.

● They were still pumping out Houston from last week's hurricane
E when she got into town. Teresa found it marvelous how the city
X had been transformed by the calamity.
O   Avenues of inundated shops rippled mysteriously just below
S floodline, their engulfed wares glimmering like sunken treasure.
P The towering glass office blocks were startling vistas of blue and
H white and aquamarine, reflecting the summer sky above and
E bright-flecked waters below.
R   Limp in the humidity, rows of canted trees marked the
E drowned borderlines of street and sidewalk. Their stained trunks
testified to even higher inundations in the past. Under fluffy clouds

pushed by a torpid breeze, Houston struck Teresa like some hypermodernist's depiction of Venice, before that lamented city's final submergence. A wonderful assortment of boats, canoes, kayaks, and even gondolas negotiated side streets, while makeshift water taxis plowed the boulevards, ferrying commuters from their residential arcologies to the shimmering office towers. With typical Texan obstinacy, nearly half the population had refused evacuation this time. In fact, Teresa reckoned some actually reveled living among the craggy cliffs of this manmade archipelago.

From the upper deck of the bus she saw the sun escape a cloud, setting the surrounding glazed monoliths ablaze. Most of the other passengers instantly and unconsciously turned away, adjusting broad-brimmed hats and polarized glasses to hide from the harsh rays. The only exceptions were a trio of Ra Boys in sleeveless mesh shirts and gaudy earrings, who faced the bright heat with relish, soaking in it worshipfully.

Teresa took a middle path when the sun emerged. She didn't react at all. It was, after all, only a stable class G star, well-behaved and a safe distance removed. Certainly, it was less dangerous down here than up in orbit.

Oh, she took all the proper precautions—she wore a hat and mild yellow glasses. But thereafter she simply dismissed the threat from her mind. The danger of skin cancer was small if you stayed alert and caught it early. Certainly the odds compared favorably with those of dying in a helizep accident.

That wasn't why she'd avoided taking a heli today, skipping that direct route from Clear Lake, where the NASA dikes had withstood Hurricane Abdul's fury. Teresa had used a roundabout route today mostly to make sure she wasn't being followed. It also provided an opportunity to collect her thoughts before stepping from frying pan to fire.

Anyway, how many more chances would she have to experience this wonder of American conceit, this spectacle that was Houston Defiant? Either the city moguls would eventually succeed in their grand, expensive plan—to secure the dikes, divert the water table, and stabilize everything on massive pylons—or the entire metropolis would soon join Galveston under the Gulf of Mexico, along with large patches of Louisiana and poor Florida. Either way, this scene would be one to tell her grandchildren about—assuming grandchildren, of course.

Teresa cut off a regretful twinge as thoughts of Jason almost surfaced. She concentrated on the sights instead as they passed a perseverant shopkeeper peddling his soaked fashions from pontoons under a sign that read, "PRESHRUNK, GUARANTEED SALT RESISTANT." Nearby, a cafe owner had set up tables, chairs, and umbrellas atop the roof of one of their bus's stranded, wheeled cousins and was doing a brisk business. Their driver delicately maneuvered past this enterprise and the cluster of parked kayaks and dinghies surrounding it, then negotiated one of the shallow reefs of abandoned bicycles before regaining momentum on Lyndon Johnson Avenue.

"They ought to keep it this way," Teresa commented softly, to no one in particular. "It's charming."

"Amen to that, sister."

With a momentary jerk of surprise, Teresa glanced toward the Ra Boys and saw what she had not noticed before, that one of them wore a quasi-legal big ear amplifier. He returned her evaluation speculatively, touching the rims of his sunglasses, making them briefly go transparent so she could catch his leer.

"Water makes the old town sexy," he said, sauntering closer. "Don'tcha think? I love the way the sunlight bounces off of everything."

Teresa decided not to point out the minor irregularity, that he wore no sign advertising his eavesdropping device. Only in her innermost thoughts . . . and her lumpy left pocket . . . did she have anything to hide.

"You'd like that, wouldn't you?" she answered, giving him a measured look he could take as neither insult nor invitation. It didn't work. He sauntered forward, planted one foot on the seat next to her, leaned forward, and rubbed the close-cropped fuzz covering his cranium.

"Water serves the sun, don't ya know? We're *supposed* to let it come on come on come. It's just one of His ways o' lovin', see? Coverin' Earth like a strong man covers a woman, gently, irresistibly . . . wetly."

Fresh patches of pink skin showed where over-the-counter creams had recently cleared away precancerous areas. In fact, Ra Boys weren't many more times as likely to develop the really deep, untreatable melanoma tumors than other people. But their blotchy complexions heightened the image they desired—of dangerous fellows without respect for life. Young studs with nothing to lose.

Teresa felt the other passengers tense. Several made a point of turning toward the young toughs, aiming their True-Vus at them like vigilant, crime-fighting heroes of an earlier era. To these the boys offered desultory, almost obligatory gestures of self-expression. Most of the riders just turned away, withdrawing behind shadow and opaque lenses.

Teresa thought both reactions a bit sad. *I hear it's even worse in some cities up north. They're nothing but teenagers, for heaven's sake. Why can't people just relax?*

She herself found the Ra Boys less frightening than pathetic. She'd heard of the fad, of course, and seen young men dressed this way at a few parties Jason had taken her to before his last mission. But this was her first encounter with sun worshippers in daylight, which separated nighttime poseurs from the real thing.

"Nice metaphors," she commented. "Are you *sure* you didn't go to school?"

Already flushed from the heat, the bare-shouldered youth actually darkened several shades as his two friends laughed aloud. Teresa had no wish to make him angry. Dismembering a citizen—even in self defense—wouldn't help her now-precarious position with the agency. Placatingly, she held up one hand.

"Let's go over them, shall we? Now you seem to be implying the rise in sea level was caused by your sun deity. But everyone knows the Antarctic and Greenland ice sheets are melting because of the Greenhouse Effect—"

"Yeah, yeah," the Ra Boy interrupted. "But the greenhouse gases keep in heat that *originates* with the sun."

"Those gases were man-made, were they not?"

He smiled smugly. "Carbon dioxide and nitrous oxides from cars and TwenCen factories, sure. But where'd it all come from originally? Oil! Gas! Coal! All buried and hoarded by Her Nibs long ago, cached away under her skin like blubber. But all the energy in the oil an' coal —the reason our grempers dug and drilled into Old Gaia in the first place—*that* came from the sun!"

He bent closer. "Now, though, we're no longer enslaved to Her precious hoard of stolen fossil fat-fuel. It's all gone up in smoke, wonderful smoke. Bye-bye." He aimed a kiss at the clouds. "And there's nowhere else to turn anymore but to the source itself!"

Ra worshippers were backers of solar energy, of course, while the more numerous Gaians pushed wind power and conservation instead. As a spacer, Teresa ironically found her sympathies coinciding with the group whose appearance and style were the more repulsive. Probably all she had to do was let these fellows know she was an astronaut and all threat and bluster would evaporate. Honestly, though, she liked them better this way—loud, boisterous, reeking of testosterone and overcompensation—than she would as fawning admirers.

"This city ain't gonna last long anyway," the Ra Boy continued, waving at the great towers, up to their steel ankles in Gulf waters.

"They can build their levees, drive piles, try to patch the holes. But sooner or later, it's all goin' the way of Miami."

"Fecund jungle's gonna spread—" one of the others crooned through a gauzy, full-backup mouth synthesizer. Presumably it was a line from a popular song, though she didn't recognize it.

The growling motors changed pitch as the bus approached another stop. Meanwhile, the leader leaned even closer to Teresa. "Yessiree, blistery! The Old Lady's gonna brim with life again. There'll be lions roaming Saskatchewan. Flamingoes flocking Greenland! And all 'cause of Ra's rough lovin'."

Poor fellow, Teresa thought. She saw through his pose of macho heliolatry. Probably he was a pussycat, and the only danger he presented came from his desperate anxiety not to let that show.

The Ra Boy frowned as he seemed to detect something in her smile. Trying harder to set her aback, he bared his teeth in a raffish grin. "Rough, wet loving. It's what women like. No less Big Mama Gaia. No?"

Across the aisle, a woman wearing an Orb of the Mother pendant glared sourly at the Ra Boy. He noticed, turned, and lolled his tongue at her, causing her fashionably fair skin to flush. Not wearing True-Vus, she quickly looked away.

He stood up, turning to sweep in the other passengers. "Ra melts the glaciers! He woos her with his heat. He melts her frigid infundibulum with warm waters. He . . ."

The Ra Boy stammered to a halt. Blinking, he swept aside his dark glasses and looked left and right, seeking Teresa.

He spotted her at last, standing on the jerry-rigged third-floor landing of the Gibraltar Building. As the waterbus pulled away again, raising salty spumes in its wake, she blew a kiss toward the sun worshipper and his comrades. They were still staring back at her, with their masked eyes and patchy pink skins, as the boat driver accelerated to catch a yellow at First Street, barely making it across before the light changed.

"So long, harmless," she said after the dwindling Ra Boy. Then she nodded to the doorman as he bowed and ushered her inside.

She had one stop to make before her meeting. A walk-in branch of a reputable bank offered an opportunity to unload her burden.

Usually a cash transaction would cause raised eyebrows, but in this case it was customary. The smiling attendant took her crisp fifties and led her to an anonymity booth, where Teresa promptly sealed herself in. She took a slim sensor from one pocket and plugged it into a jack in the side of her wallet, which then served as a portable console while she scanned every corner of the booth for leaks. Of course there were none. Satisfied, she sat down and disconnected the sensor. As she was doing that, however, her hand accidentally stroked the worn nub of the wallet's personal holo dial, causing a familiar image to project into space above the countertop.

Her father's eyes crinkled with smile lines and he looked so proud of her as he silently mouthed words she had long ago memorized. Words of support. Words that had meant so much to her so often since he first spoke them . . . on every occasion since when she found herself bucking the odds.

Only none of those other crises was ever nearly as dire as the business she'd gotten herself into now. For that reason she held her hand back from touching the sound control or even replaying his well-remembered encouragement in her mind.

She was too afraid to test it. What if the words wouldn't work this time? Might such a failure ruin the talisman forever, then? Uncertainty seemed preferable to finding out that this last touchstone in her life had lost its potency, that even her father's calm confidence could offer no security against a world that could melt away any time it chose.

"I'm sorry, Papa," she said quietly, poignantly. Teresa wanted to reach out and touch his gray-flecked beard. But instead she turned off his image and firmly turned her attention to the task at hand. From her pocket she drew one of two data spools, inserting it into a slot in the counter. Picking a code word from the name of a college roommate's pet cat, she created a personal cache and fed in the contents of the spool. When the cylinder was empty and erased, she breathed a little easier.

She was still embarked on a dangerous enterprise that might cost her her job, or even lead to jail. But at least now she wouldn't become a pariah for the modern sin of keeping secrets. She'd just registered her story—from the Erehwon disaster to her recent, surreptitious orbital data collection for Pedro Manella. If any of it ever did come to trial, now she'd be able to show with this dated cache that she had acted in good faith. The Rio Treaties did allow one to withhold information temporarily—or try to—so long as careful records were maintained. That exception had been left in order to satisfy the needs of private commerce. The treaties' drafters—radical veterans of the Helvetian War—probably never imagined that "temporary" might be interpreted to be as long as twenty years or that the registering of diaries like hers would become an industry in itself.

Teresa sealed the file, swallowing the key in her mind. Such was her faith in the system that she simply left the empty spool lying there on the countertop.

"I wish you hadn't done that."

"Done what, Pedro?"

"You know what I mean. What you did when you got back to Earth."

Manella regarded her like a disapproving father. Fortunately, Teresa's own dad had been patient and understanding—and thin. In other words, nothing like Pedro Manella.

"All I did was refuse to shake hands with Colonel Spivey. You'd think I'd have slapped him across the face or shot him."

Looking down at the blue lagoons of Houston, the portly newsman shook his head. "In front of net-zine cameras? You might as well have done exactly that. What's the public to think when a shuttle pilot steps out of her spacecraft, accepts the thanks of all the other astronauts, but then pointedly turns away and spits when the mission supervisor steps up for his turn?"

"I did not spit!" she protested.

"Well it sure looked that way."

Teresa felt warm under the collar. "What do you want from me? I'd just verified—at least to my satisfaction—that the bastard must have had a *black hole* on Erehwon. He recruited my husband into an illegal conspiracy that caused his death! Did you expect me to kiss him?"

Manella sighed. "It would have been preferable. As it is, you may have jeopardized our operation."

Teresa folded her arms and looked away. "I wasn't followed here. And I got you your data. You asked nothing else of me." She felt put-upon and resentful. As soon as she had arrived, and Manella's assistants scurried off with her second spool, Pedro had launched into this Dutch uncle lecture.

"Hmph," he commented. "You didn't actually say anything to Spivey, did you?"

"Nothing printable or relevant. Unless you count commentary on his ancestry."

Manella's scowl lifted slightly. Much as he disapproved of her actions, he clearly would have liked to have been there. "Then I suggest you let people assume the obvious—that you and Spivey had been having an affair—"

"*What?*" Teresa gasped.

"—and that your anger was the result of a lovers'—"

"Dumpit!"

"—of a lovers' tiff. Spivey may suspect you're on to his activities, but he'll not be able to prove anything."

Teresa's jaw clenched. The unpalatability of Manella's suggestion was matched only by its inherent logic. "I'm swearing off men forever," she said, biting out the words.

Infuriatingly, Manella answered only with a raised eyebrow, economically conveying his certainty she was lying. "Come on," he replied. "The others are waiting."

A chart projection hung over the far end of the conference room. It wasn't holographic, merely a high-definition, two-dimensional schematic of the multilayered Earth. A nest of simple, concentric circles.

Innermost, extending from the center about a fifth of the way outward, was a brown zone labeled SOLID INNER CORE—CRYSTALLINE IRON + NICKEL . . . 0–1227 KILOMETERS.

Next came a reddish shell, about twice as thick. LIQUID OUTER CORE —IRON + OXYGEN + SULFUR . . . 1227–3486 KILOMETERS, the caption read.

The beige stratum beyond that took up nearly the rest of the planet. MANTLE, the legend stated. OXIDES OF SILICON, ALUMINUM, AND MAGNESIUM (ECLOGITES AND PERIDOTITES IN PEROVSKITE FORM) . . . 3486– 6350 KILOMETERS.

All three great zones featured subdivisions marked by dashed lines, tentative and vague lower down, with captions terminating in question marks. At the outermost fringe Teresa discerned a set of thin tiers labeled, ASTHENOSPHERE, LITHOSPHERE, OCEANIC CRUST, CONTINENTAL CRUST, HYDROSPHERE (OCEAN), ATMOSPHERE, MAGNETOSPHERE. Outlining that final zone, curving arrows rose from near the south pole, to reenter in Earth's far northern regions.

The speaker at the front of the room was a trim blonde woman who pointed to those arching field lines.

"We were especially interested in the intense high-energy region astronauts call the 'South Atlantic devil,' a magnetic dip that drifts westward about a third of a degree per year. These days it hovers over the Andes . . ."

Using a laser pointer, she traced the high, diffuse fields that were her specialty. The woman obviously knew a thing or two about spaceborne instrumentation.

She ought to, Teresa thought.

As a consultant transferred to Houston two years ago, June Morgan had become friends with several members of the astronaut corps, including Teresa and her husband. In fact, Teresa had been glad, at first, when June was assigned to work with Jason on a recent Project

Earthwatch survey. Now, of course, Teresa knew her husband had
been using that assignment to cover other work for Colonel Spivey.
That hadn't kept him from getting to know June better, though. A
whole lot better.

When Manella had brought Teresa in to introduce to everybody,
June barely met her eyes. Officially, there was no grudge between
them. But they both knew things had gone farther than any modern
marriage contract could excuse. The one Teresa had signed with Jason
made allowances for long separations and the planetbound spouse's
inevitable need for company. Their arrangement was no "open marriage" stupidity, of course. It set strict limits on the duration and style
of any outside liaison and specified a long list of precautions to be
taken.

The agreement had sounded fine four years ago. In theory. But
dammit, Jason's affair with this woman had violated the spirit, if not
the letter, of their pact!

Perhaps it had been Teresa's fault for following her curiosity, for
checking who Jason had seen while she was away on a long-duration
test flight. She had been shocked to learn that it was a NASA person
. . . a scientist no less! A groupie, even a bimbo, would have been
okay. No threat there. But an *intelligent* woman? A woman so very
much like herself?

She recalled the feeling of menace that had flooded her then,
creating a horrible tightness in her chest and a blindness in her eyes.
For hours she had walked familiar neighborhoods completely lost, in a
cold panic because she had absolutely no idea where she was or in
what direction she was heading.

"You want me to give her up?" Jason had asked when she finally
confronted him. "Well, of course I'll give her up, if you want me to."

His infuriating shrug had driven her crazy. He'd managed to
make it sound as if *she* were the one being irrational, choosing this
particular case to get jealous about all of a sudden. Perhaps illogically,
she didn't find his blithe willingness to go along with her wishes calming, for underneath his acquiescence she fantasized a regret she could
not verify in any way.

His sojourns aloft were generally longer than hers. She had spent
many more long days alone on Earth between missions, surrounded all
the time by overtures. She'd seldom availed herself of those dubious
comforts, whatever the freedoms allowed by their contract. That he'd
been less reticent when *he* was home alone hadn't bothered her till
then. Men were, after all, inherently weasels.

She'd tried to remain civilized about it, but in the end Teresa let him go to space that last time with barely an acknowledgment of his farewell. For weeks their telemetered messages were terse and formal.

Then came that fatal day. As she was docking her shuttle, unloading her cargo and preparing to send Spivey's peepers across the transitway, Teresa had been emotionally girding herself to make peace with Jason. To begin anew.

If only—

Teresa pushed away memory. It probably wouldn't have worked out. What marriage lasted these days, anyway? All men are pigs. She missed him terribly.

One glance told Teresa she wasn't alone in mourning. Meeting June Morgan's eyes in that brief moment, she knew the other woman's pain was akin to her own. *Damn him. He wasn't ever supposed to fling with anyone he liked. Especially someone like me! Someone who might compete for his love.*

That instant's communication seemed to cause the blonde scientist to stumble briefly in her address. But she quickly recovered.

". . . so for . . . for most of the twentieth century, Earth's total magnetic field weakened at an . . . average rate of four hundredths of a percent per year. And the decline has steepened recently. That, combined with a greater than expected drop in the Earth's ozone layer, leads to a growing suspicion we may be about to experience a rare event—a complete geomagnetic reversal."

The man across from Teresa raised his hand. "I'm sorry, Dr. Morgan. I'm just a poor mineralogist. Could you explain what you mean by that?"

June caused the display to zoom in upon a long, jagged, S-shaped range of undersea mountains, threading the middle of the sinuous Atlantic Ocean. "This is one of the great oceanic spreading centers, where older crust is pushed aside to make room for new basalt welling up from the mantle. As each fresh intrusion cools and hardens, the rock embeds a frozen record of Earth's magnetism at the time. By studying samples along these ridges, we find the field has a habit of suddenly flipping its state . . . from northward to southward, or vice versa. The change can be quite rapid. Then, after a long period of stability, it flips back the other way again.

"Way back during the Cretaceous, one stable period lasted almost forty million years. But in recent times these flip-flops have taken to occurring much more rapidly—every three hundred thousand years or so." June put up a slide showing a history of peaks and valleys crowding ever closer together, ending with a slightly wider patch near the righthand edge. "Our latest stable interval has exceeded the recent average."

"In other words," Pedro Manella suggested, "we're overdue for another flip."

She nodded. "We still lack a good explanation of how geomagnetism is generated, down where the core meets the mantle. Some even think sea level has something to do with it, though according to the Parker model . . ." June stopped and smiled. "The short answer? Yes, we do seem overdue."

"What might be the consequences, if it flipped today?" Another woman at the table asked.

"Again, we're not sure. It would certainly impair many navigational instruments—"

Teresa's nostrils flared. She'd known this. Yet hearing it said aloud felt like a direct challenge.

"—and it might eliminate some protection from solar proton storms. Space facilities would need shielding or have to be abandoned altogether."

"And?" Manella prompted.

Isn't that enough? Teresa thought, horrified.

The speaker sighed. "And it might wreck what's left of the ozone layer."

A murmur of consternation spread among those assembled. Pedro Manella loudly cleared his throat to get their attention. "Ladies, gentlemen! This is serious of course. Still, it's only background to our purpose here today." He turned to regard June. "Doctor Morgan, let's get to the point. How might your geomagnetic data help us track down any illegal black hole singularities on or near the Earth?"

"Mmm, yes. Well it's occurred to me there've been some recent anomalies, such as this new drift in the South Pacific . . ."

Teresa listened attentively. Still, she couldn't help wondering. *Why did Manella insist I come here today? I could have sent my data by courier.*

Not that she had anything better to do. Perhaps Pedro wanted her to tell the others about the subjective sensations she'd experienced during the catastrophe, or to recite the story of Erehwon's destruction one more time.

No matter. Teresa was used to being a team player. Even in a quasi-illegal band like this one, most of whose members she didn't even know.

Damn it, she thought. *I just want to know what's going on.*

For now that meant cooperating with Manella, and even June Morgan, putting aside personal feelings and helping any way she could.

□ Like most other religious special interest groups on the Net, we in the Friends of St. Francis Assembly [□ SIG.Rel.disc. 12-RsyPD 634399889.058] have been discussing the Pope's latest encyclical, *Et in Terra pax et sapientia,* which sanctions veneration of the Holy Mother as special protector of the Earth and its species. Some say this stands alongside his predecessor's acceptance of the population oath as a breakthrough concession to common sense and the new worldview.

Not all take this attitude, however. Consider the manifesto published yesterday on the Return to the Robe Channel [□ SIG.Rel.disc. 12-RsyPD 987623089.098] criticizing His Holiness for ''. . . succumbing to both creeping Gaianism and secular humanism, both incompatible with Judeo-Christian hermeneutics . . .''

I just had a voice-text exchange with the Monsignor Nassan Bruhuni [□ pers.addr. WaQ 237.69.6272-36 aadw], leading author of the manifesto, during an open question session. Here's a replay of that exchange.

Query by T.M.: ''Monsignor, according to the Bible, what was the very first injunction laid by the Lord upon our first ancestor?''
Reply by Msgr. Bruhuni: ''By first ancestor I assume you mean Adam. Do you refer to the charge to be fruitful and multiply?''
T.M.: ''That's the first command *mentioned*, in Genesis 1. But Genesis 1 is clearly just a summary of the more detailed story in Genesis 2. Anyway, to 'multiply' can't have been first *chronologically*. That could only happen after Eve appeared, after sex was discovered through sin, and after mankind lost immortality of the flesh!''
Msgr. B.: ''I see your point. In that case, I'd say the command not to eat of the Tree of Knowledge. It was by breaking that injunction that Adam fell.''
T.M.: ''But that's still only a *negative* commandment . . . 'Don't do that.' Wasn't there something else? Something Adam was asked actively *to* do?

''Consider. Every heavenly intervention mentioned in the Bible, from Genesis onward, can be seen as a *palliative* measure, to help mend a fallen race of obdurate sinners. But what of the original mission for which we were made? Have we no clue what our purpose was to have been if we hadn't sinned at all? Why we were created in the first place?''
Msgr. B.: ''Our purpose was to glorify the Lord.''
T.M.: ''As a good Catholic, I agree. But *how* was Adam to glorify? By singing praises? The heavenly hosts were already doing that, and even a parrot can make unctuous noises. No, the evidence is right there in Genesis. Adam was told to do something very specific, something *before* the fall, before Eve, before even being told not to eat the fruit!''

Msgr. B.: "Let me scan and refresh my . . . Ah. I think I see what you refer to. The paragraph in which the Lord has Adam *name all the beasts*. Is that it? But that's a minor thing. Nobody considers it important."

T.M.: "Not important? The very first request by the Creator of His creation? The only request that has nothing to do with the repair work of mortality or rescue from sin? Would such a thing have been mentioned so prominently if the Lord were merely *idly curious*?"

Msgr. B.: "Please, I see others queued for questions. Your point is?"

T.M.: "Only this—our original purpose clearly was to glorify God by going forth, comprehending, and *naming* the Creator's works. Therefore, aren't zoologists, crawling through the jungle, struggling to name endangered species before they go extinct, doing holy labor?

"Or take even those camera-bearing probes we have sent to other planets. . . . What is the first thing we do when awe-inspiring vistas of some faraway moon are transmitted back by our little robot envoys? Why, we reverently name the craters, valleys, and other strange beasts discovered out there.

"So you see it's impossible for the end of days to come, as your group predicts, till we succeed in our mission or utterly fail. Either we'll complete the preservation and description of this Earth and go forth to name everything else in God's universe, or we'll prove ourselves unworthy by spoiling what we started with—this, our first garden. Either way, the verdict's not in yet!"

Msgr. B.: "I . . . really don't know how to answer this. Not in real time. At minimum you've drawn an intriguing sophistry to delight your fellow Franciscans. And those neo-Gaian Jesuits, if they haven't thought of it already.

"Perhaps you'll allow me time to send out my own ferrets and contemplate? I'll get back to you next week, same time, same access code."

So that's where we left it. Meanwhile, any of you on this SIG are welcome to comment. I'll answer any useful remarks or suggestions. After all, if there's anything I seem to have on my hands these days, it's free time.

—Brother Takuei Minamoto [□ UsD 623.56.2343 -alf,e.]

● *It was a laser.*
C He still couldn't get used to the idea. A gravity laser. Imagine
O that.
R *I wonder where the power comes from.*
E "Mr. Sullivan? May I freshen your drink, sir?"

The flight attendant's smile was professional. Her features and coloration clearly Malay. "Yes, thank you," he replied as she bent to pour, her delicate aroma causing him to inhale deeply. "That's a lovely scent. Is it Lhasa Spring?"

"Why . . . yes sir. You are perceptive."

She met his eyes, and for an instant her smile seemed just *that* much more than perfunctory. It was a well-measured look that fell short of provocative, but also seemed to promise a litle more than mere professionalism during the long flight ahead.

Alex felt content as she moved on to serve the next passenger. It was nice flirting amiably with an exotic beauty, without the slightest temptation to ruin it by trying for too much. The last few months had left his libido in a state of suspension, which had the pleasant side effect of allowing him the freedom to appreciate a young woman's smile, the fine, well-trained grace of her movements, without flashing hormones or unwarranted hopes getting in the way.

It had been different during his first year of graduate school, when he temporarily forsook physics to explore instead the realm of the senses. Applying logic to the late-blooming quandaries of maturity, he had parsed the elements of encounter, banter, negotiation, and consummation, separating and solving the variables one by one until the problem—if not generally solved—did appear to have tractable special solutions.

The mapping wasn't exact, of course. According to Jen, biological systems never translated exactly onto mathematical models, anyway. Still, at the time he acquired certain practical skills, which garnered him a reputation among his classmates and friends.

Then, curiosity sated, his interests changed trajectory. Companionship and compatibility became desiderata more important than sex, and he even aspired for joy. But these proved more elusive. Seduction, it seemed, contained fewer variables and relied less on fate than did true love.

Disappointment never banished hope exactly, but he was persuaded to shelve aspiration for a while and return to science. Only at

Iquitos did hope suffer truly mortal wounds. Compared to that loss, sex was a mere incidental casualty.

I know what Jen would tell me, he thought. *We moderns think sex can be unlinked from reproduction. But the two are connected, deep down.*

Alex knew most of the time he was in denial about the coming end of the world. He had to be, in order to do his work. In such a state he could even enjoy studying Beta, the elegant, deadly monster in the Earth's core.

But denial can only rearrange pain, like a child re-sorting unloved vegetables on his plate, hoping a less noticeable pattern will deceive parental authority. Alex knew where he'd quarantined his bitter outrage. It still affected the part of him most intimately tied to life and the propagation of life.

Alex imagined how his grandmother might comment on all this.

"Self-awareness is fine, Alex. It helps make us interesting beasts, instead of just another band of crazy apes.

"But when you get right down to it, self-awareness is probably overrated. A complex, self-regulating system doesn't need it in order to be successful, or even smart."

Thinking about Jen made Alex smile. Perhaps, after the hard work of the months ahead was done, there'd be time to go home and visit her before the world ended.

Stan Goldman had been left in charge in New Zealand, continuing to track Beta while Alex went to California on a mission to beg, wheedle, and cajole ten years' raw data from the biggest observatory in the world. This was a mission he had to take on himself, for it required calling in many old favors.

From a small building on the UC Berkeley campus, his old friend Heinz Reichle ran three thousand neutrino detectors dispersed all over the globe. The planet was almost transparent to those ghostly particles, which penetrated rock like X rays streaming through soft cheese, so Reichle could use the entire worldwide instrument round the clock to track nuclear reactions in the sun and stars. For his part though, Alex hoped the disks full of data in his luggage would show a thing or two about the Earth's interior as well, perhaps helping the Tangoparu team track the awful Beta singularity to its source.

Alex still wanted to meet the person or persons responsible—almost as badly as George Hutton did.

I'd like to know how they were able to create such a complex, twisted knot of space. They can't have used anything as simple as a Witten mapping. Why, even renormalization would have taken—

The airplane's public address system came to life, interrupting his thoughts. From the seat back in front of him projected the smiling, confident visage of their captain, informing everyone that the Hawaiian Islands were coming into view.

Alex shaded his window against internal reflections and gazed down past layers of stratospheric clouds to a necklace of dark jewels standing out from the glittering sea. Back in the days of turbojets, this would have been a refueling stop. But modern hypersonic aircraft— even restricted by the ozone laws—just streaked on by.

He had seen Hawaii much closer than this anyway, so it wasn't the chain itself but the surrounding waters that suddenly interested him. From this height he saw patterns of tide and color—resonant standing waves and subtly shaded shoals of plankton luminance— outlining each bead in the nearly linear necklace of islands. Polarized sunglasses, especially, brought out a richness of detail.

Once, Alex would have looked on this phenomenon with pleasure but little understanding. Time spent with George Hutton's geologists had corrected that. The islands weren't static entities anymore, but epic, rocky testimonials to change. From the big island westward, beyond the thousand-meter cliffs of Molokai, all the way past lowly Midway, a chain of extinct volcanoes continued arrow straight for thousands of miles before zigging abruptly north toward the Aleutians. That bent path to the arctic circle was also a trip back in time, from the towering, ten thousand cubic mile basalt heap of Mauna Loa, past weathered, craggy elder isles like Kauai, to ancient coral atolls and eventually prehistoric, truncated seamounts long conquered by the persistent waves.

On the big island, two memorable volcanoes still spumed. But most activity had already shifted still further east, where the newest sibling was being born—an embryonic, as yet unemerged isle already named Loihi.

Most of the planet's volcanoes smoldered where the edges of great crustal plates met gratingly, or rode up over each other—as along this great ocean's famous Ring of Fire. But Hawaii's trail of ancient calderas lay smack in the middle of one of the biggest plates, not at its rim. The Hawaiian Islands had their origins in a completely different process. They were the dashed scars left as the Central Pacific Plate cruised slowly above the geological equivalent of a blowtorch, a fierce, narrow tube of magma melting through anything passing over it.

George Hutton had likened it to pushing thick aluminum foil slowly over an intermittent arc welder. Part of George's wealth had come from tapping power from such hot spots in the mantle.

Oh, yes. Hawaii certainly testified that there was energy down there.

But you can't generate a laser . . . or a gazer . . . from just any lump of hot matter. You need excited material in an inverted state. . . .

There it was again—his thoughts kept drawing back to the problem, just as the *taniwha* kept pulling in atoms as it orbited round and round the Earth's core.

At first he'd been certain the amplified gravity waves originated from Beta itself. After all, what bizarre energy levels might lay within the roiling, folded world-sheets of a cosmic knot? In fact, on that night in New Zealand when Alex experienced his moment of drunken inspiration, he had also felt a wave of desperate hope. What if the knot *itself* was being stimulated to emit gravity radiation? Could Beta be forced somehow to give up energy faster than it could suck atoms from the core?

Alas, scans showed the beast hadn't lost any weight at all, despite the titanic, Earth-rattling power released in the gazer beam. The only apparent effect on Beta had been to shift its orbit slightly, making it harder than ever to trace its history.

And so Alex still had no idea where the energy came from. Add another gnawing, frustrating mystery to the list. It was one thing to know he and everyone else were doomed to be destroyed. But to die ignorant? Not even having looked on the face of his destroyer? It was not acceptable.

"Mr. Sullivan? Pardon me, sir."

Alex blinked. By now Hawaii was long gone from sight. He turned away from the blue Pacific to meet the almond eyes of the beautiful ASEAN Air flight attendant.

"Yes? What is it?"

"Sir, you've received a message."

From her palm he took a gleaming data sliver. Alex thanked her. Unfolding his comp-screen, he slipped the chip inside and keyed access. Instantly, a holo of George Hutton frowned at him, sternly, under bushy eyebrows. A short row of block letters appeared.

THIS JUST ARRIVED ON A NET RECEPTION BOARD IN AUCKLAND, UNDER YOUR *REAL NAME*, MARKED URGENT. THOUGHT YOU'D BETTER SEE IT RIGHT QUICK—GEORGE.

Alex blinked. Only a few people on the planet knew he'd gone to New Zealand, and those obligingly used his cover name. Hesitantly, he touched the screen and instantly a flat-image photograph appeared in front of him, rather smudgy and amateurish looking. It showed a crowd of people—tourists, apparently—looking admiringly at a disheveled, youngish man, lanky and a little underweight. The center of attention was holding another man to the ground—a wild-eyed fellow with flecks of froth at the corners of his mouth.

I should have expected this, Alex thought with a sigh. Tourists loved using their True-Vu goggles. There must have been many records of his minor "heroics" in Rotorua. Apparently a few had made it onto the net.

He looked at his own image and saw a fellow who didn't really want to be where he was, or doing what he was doing.

I should not have interfered. Now look what's happened.

He touched the screen again to see the rest of the message, and suddenly a new visage loomed out at him—one he knew all too well.

Talk about looking on the face of your destroyer . . .

It was Pedro Manella, dressed in a brown suit that matched his pantry-brush mustache. The portly reporter grinned a frozen, knowing grin. Alex read the text below and groaned.

ALEX LUSTIG, I KNOW YOU'RE IN NEW ZEALAND SOMEWHERE. FROM THERE GENERAL DELIVERY WILL GET THIS TO YOU.

ARRANGE A MEETING WITHIN TWO DAYS, OR THE ENTIRE WORLD WILL BE HUNTING FOR YOU, NOT I ALONE.

—MANELLA

That man was as tenacious as a remora, as persistent as any *taniwha*. Alex sighed.

Still, he wondered if it really mattered anymore. In a way, he looked forward to watching Pedro Manella's face when he told the man the news.

It was an unworthy anticipation. A grown man shouldn't covet revenge.

Ah, he thought, *but we are legion. I contain multitudes. And some of the people making up "me" aren't grown-ups at all.*

☐ Each of the allies had its own reasons for entering the bloody conflict now variously known as the "Helvetian War," the "Secrecy War," and the "Last-We-Hope"—perhaps the most bizarre and furious armed struggle of all time.

A leading factor in the industrial north was the laundering of profits for drug merchants and tax cheaters. Overburdened with TwenCen debt, citizens of America and Pan-Europe demanded those groups at least pay their fair share, and resented the banking gnomes for sheltering criminals' ill-gotten gains.

International banking secrecy was even more hated in the developing world. Those nations' awesome debts were aggravated by "capital flight," whereby leading citizens had for generations smuggled mountains of cash to safe havens overseas. Whether honestly earned or looted from national treasuries, this lost capital undermined frail economies, making it even harder for those left behind to pay their bills. Nations like Venezuela, Zaire and the Philippines tried to recover billions removed by former ruling elites, to no avail. Eventually, a consortium of restored democracies stopped railing at their ex-dictators and instead turned their ire on the banking havens themselves.

Still, neither taxpayer outrage up north nor cash starvation in the south would have been enough to drive the world to such a desperate, unlikely confrontation were it not for two added factors—a change in morality and the burgeoning Information Age.

Those were the days of the great arms talks, when mutual, on-site inspection was seen as the only possible way to ensure de-escalation. As each round of weapons reductions raised the verification ante, the international corps of inspectors became sacrosanct. Words like "secrecy" and "concealment" began taking on their modern, obscene connotations.

To increasing numbers of "blackjacks"—or children of century twenty-one—the mere idea of secrecy implied scheming dishonesty. "What're *you* hiding, zygote?" went the now corny phrase. But in those days it conveyed the angry, revolutionary spirit of the times.

That wrath soon turned against the one remaining power center in whom secrecy was paramount and unrepentant. By the time the members of the Brazzaville Consortium gathered to write their final ultimatum, they were no longer in a mood for compromise. Belated conciliatory words, broadcast from Berne and Nassau and Vaduz, were too little and far too late to stifle the new battle cry: . . . *Open the books. All of them. Now!*

Would the allies have gone ahead, suspecting what death and horror awaited them?

Knowing what we do now, about what lay buried under the Glarus Alps, most agree their only mistake was not declaring war sooner. In any event, by the second year of fighting, mercy was hardly on anybody's agenda anymore. Only vengeful modern Catos could be heard, crying from the rooftops of the world—

Helvetia delenda est!

By then it was to the death.

—From **The Transparent Hand**, Doubleday Books, edition 4.7 (2035). [☐ hyper access code 1-tTRAN-777-97-9945-29A.]

Pedro insisted they change vehicles three times during their roundabout journey from the Auckland aerodrome. At one point he bought them both new clothes, straight off the rack in a tourist clip joint in Rotorua. Changing at the store, they abandoned their former attire on the off chance someone might have planted a tracking device on them.

Teresa went along with these measures stoically, absurd and melodramatic as they seemed. Without appropriate experience or instincts to guide her, she could only hope Manella knew what he was doing.

Strangely, the Aztlan reporter appeared to grow calmer, the closer they neared the arranged rendezvous. He drove the final kilometers of winding forest highway with a peaceful smile, humming atonal compositions of dubious lineage.

Teresa's contribution was to work away silently at her cuticles and rub a hole in the thin carpet with her right foot each time Pedro tortured the little rental car's transmission or took a curve too fast. It didn't help that they still drove on the left in this country, putting the passenger in a position she normally associated with having control. She had never found it easy letting someone else drive—even Jason. She was close to snatching the wheel out of Pedro's hands by the time bright signs began appearing along the side of the road.

WAITOMO CAVES. JUST AHEAD.
COME SEE THE WONDER OF THE WAIKATO.

One of the billboards depicted a family of happy spelunkers, helmet lamps glowing as they pointed at astonishing sights just offstage.

"We've entered their security perimeter, by now," Manella said. To seem more relaxed, he'd have to close his eyes and go to sleep.

"You think so?" Teresa knew he didn't mean the tourist concessionaires. She frowned at the blur of conifers rushing past her window. Manella glanced at her and smiled. "Don't fret. Lustig isn't a violent type."

"How do you explain what happened in Iquitos then?"

"Well, I admit he is . . . highly accident prone." When Teresa laughed bitterly, Pedro shrugged. "That doesn't release him from responsibility. *Au contraire.* Unlucky people should exercise special caution, lest their bad luck come to harm others. In Lustig's case—"

"His message hinted he knew something about the destruction of

Erehwon. Maybe he caused it! He might be working with Spivey, for
all we know."

Manella sighed. "A chance we'll have to take. And now we're
here."

Signs pointed left to public parking. Pedro swooped down,
around, and into a slot with a display of panache Teresa could have
lived without. She emerged to a syncopation of crackling vertebrae,
feeling more respect than ever for the pioneers of Vostok, Mercury,
and Gemini, who first ventured into space crammed into canisters
approximately the same size of the tiny car.

She and her companion crossed the highway to the ticket booth,
paid for two admissions, and joined other tourists passing under one of
the ubiquitous carved archways that seemed a New Zealand trademark. Teresa glanced at those gathering for the two o'clock tour, a
sparse assortment of winter travelers that included hand-holding
Asian newlyweds, retirees with Australian accents, and local children
in quaint woolen school uniforms. For all she knew, any of them
might be agents for the mysterious organization they'd tracked to this
place.

The meeting had been set up with delicacy and circumlocution,
each side taking precautions against a possible double cross. It all
struck Teresa as anachronistic, and hopelessly adolescent.

Unfortunately, adolescents ran the world. Big, irresponsible adolescents like Jason or this Lustig fellow, whose dossier read like the
biography of a high-tech Peter Pan. Even worse were serious, bloody-
minded types like Colonel Spivey, whose games of national security
were played with real multitudes serving as pawns. She recalled how
intensely the man had worked during the recent space mission. Spivey
was driven, all right. Sometimes that could be a good thing.

It could also make some people dangerous.

"You're sure these people will keep their word?" she whispered to
Manella.

He looked back with amusement. "Of course I'm not sure! Lustig
may be nonviolent, but what do we know about his backers?" Again,
he shrugged. "We'll find out soon enough."

Ask a foolish question . . . Teresa thought.

Their tour guide arrived at last, a dark-haired, dark-skinned young
man with broad shoulders and a pleasant smile. The guide cheerfully
beckoned them to follow him along a wooden walk that hugged the
steep hillside, and soon had them traversing along mist-shrouded waterfalls. Teresa kept close to Manella at the end of the queue.

She caught herself glancing backward to see if anyone was sneaking up behind them, and made herself stop doing it.

The vegetation changed as they passed under a rain forest canopy. Exotic birds flitted under moist foliage that looked so healthy you might never imagine how many other places like this were withering elsewhere on the planet. Here even the smells seemed to convey strength, diversity. This jungle felt as if it were a long way from dying. Inhaling felt like taking a tonic. That calmed her a bit. She took deep breaths.

They turned a corner and suddenly the cave entrance yawned ahead of them. The gap in the mountainside was appropriately dark, foreboding. Steps proceeded downward between slippery metal banisters, with bare bulbs spaced at intervals apparently calculated to maximize eerie shadows, to thrill visitors with an illusion of creaking decrepitude and mystery.

Teresa listened idly as the guide recited something having to do with great birds, cousins of the legendary moa, who used to get trapped in caves like these during prehistoric times, leaving their bones to be discovered by astonished explorers many centuries later.

As they descended, he used a beam to point out features of the grottoes, carved over thousands of years by patient underground streams, then embellished with fluted limestone apses by centuries of slow seepage. In places the ceiling gave way to shafts and chimneys that towered out of sight or dropped into total blackness, lined with soda-straw draperies and crystalline, branchlike helicites. Curling galleries curved out of view, hinting at an interminable maze that would surely swallow anyone foolish enough to leave the wooden walkway.

It was, indeed, quite beautiful. Still, Teresa felt little true surprise or awe. It was all too familiar from prior exposure on TV or in netzines. She nodded familiarly at stalactites and stalagmites, acquaintances already encountered in the past by proxy. Rather than eerie or strange, they were neighbors she had learned a lot about over the years, long before ever meeting them in person.

The good side of the world media village was the sense it gave ten billion that each of them had at least some small connection with the whole. The bad side was that no one ever encountered anything, anymore, that was completely new.

Perhaps that was why I became an astronaut, in hopes of someday seeing some special place before the cameras got there.

If so, lots of luck. The vast mountain ranges of the moon were still unclimbed. And at present rate, they probably never would be. Likewise the steep canyons, ice sheets, and red vistas of Mars.

Teresa scanned craggy terraces, shaped over millennia by the slow drip-dripping of carbonate-rich water. No doubt she and Pedro were already being watched by Alex Lustig's mysterious organization. Their instructions had been to keep to the rear. If Pedro knew anything more, he hadn't told her.

"Now we'll be going down another set of stairs," their guide announced. "Hold onto the rail because the lights grow dimmer, to let our eyes adapt for the Grand Cave."

The visitors voices grew hushed as they descended plank steps, put there to protect the limestone floor from the erosive rub of countless feet. Once, Teresa caught a white flash of teeth as Manella turned to grin at her. She ignored him, pretending not to see.

Soon it was hardly pretense. Colliding with Pedro's broad back was her first warning the descent had ended. Whispers diminished to an occasional giggle as people bumped awkwardly. A cough. A faint, familiar hiss as someone in the crowd took oxygen from a hip flask, followed by a mumbled apology.

Listening carefully, Teresa made out rhythmic thumping sounds and a faint splash. The tour leader spoke from somewhere to her left. "We'll divide the group now and continue by water. Each boat will have a guide, standing in the prow, who will pull you along by hauling on ropes arrayed along the ceiling."

As her eyes adapted, Teresa soon made out smudges here and there—the edge of the dock and several small vessels moored alongside, with a man's or woman's silhouette at the bow. She even thought she could trace a webbery of cables draped across the rock overhead.

"Interesting mode of transport," Pedro commented as they watched the first boat depart. More tourists were helped into the next one and the queue moved forward.

"As each boat rounds the bend ahead," the chief guide continued. "You'll leave behind the last illumination. Your pilot will be operating by memory and touch alone. But don't worry, we only lose one or two boatloads a year."

A poor joke, but it touched off nervous titters.

"A few more turns and you'll arrive at the main grotto, where our famous worms will perform their unique show for you—the centerpiece of Waitomo Caves. Then, by another route, you'll be returned here to the landing. We hope you enjoy your visit to the wonder of the Waikato."

Some wonder. So far Teresa hadn't seen anything particularly impressive. Much bigger caves were regularly featured on the National Geographic net-zine.

The tourists just ahead of them boarded a boat. There was room remaining at the back, but their guide held out a hand to stop Manella. "You, sir, look just a bit heavy to add here. I'll take you two in the last one myself."

As Pedro sniffed indignantly, the guide helped them into the final boat. Then he moved to the bow and cast off. The dim remaining light disappeared behind them as he pulled the ceiling-spanning ropes hand over hand and they passed around a bend into pitch darkness.

Teresa tried using biofeedback to speed her adaptation to the dark and found it disconcerting how little training helped. You couldn't amplify what doesn't exist.

By now there were no signs of the other boats. They might have drifted over a cliff, for all Teresa knew. Or perhaps some stealthy monster waited just ahead, plucking each group silently and swiftly from their stygian barges.

The waters were chill to her fingertips when she dragged them alongside. They also seemed to have a faint oily quality. Bringing a few drops to her lips, she tasted minerals. It wasn't unpleasant though. The underground river was slow but clear and fresh. It tasted timeless.

"Some years the water rises too high to let boats pass," the guide told them in a soft voice. "And during droughts they can be stranded."

"Are there eyeless fish, down here?" Teresa asked.

The native's low, disembodied laughter seemed to dance along the sculpted rocks. "Of course! What sort of buried river would this be without such? They live on seeds, pollen, and insect larvae carried down here from *ki waho,* the outside world. Some of those larvae survive to become flies, which in turn feed . . ."

Teresa grabbed the gunnels quickly as she sensed something massive approach from the left—moments before their boat grated against rock, tipping slightly. "Just a second," the voice told them. "I have to step out to guide us around this column. Hold on."

She traced the faint scrape of a boot on a sandy bank. Without any sight at all, not even the dark eclipse of Manella in front of her, she sensed only vague movement as their vessel scoured along a limestone verge and then emerged round a corner into a starry night.

Teresa gasped. Stars? Sudden disorientation left her staring at the brilliant vault overhead, amazed.

But it was early afternoon when we arrived. How . . . ?

Automatically, she sought her friends, the familiar constellations, and recognized *none* of them. Everything had changed! It was as if she'd passed through some science fictional device, to a world in some distant galaxy. The swirl of stellar clusters arced overhead in vast, regal, and totally alien splendor.

Teresa blinked, suffering from acuity of senses. Hearing told her she was underground. Her internal gyroscope said she was less than two kilometers from the car. And yet the clinquant stars screamed of open sky. She shook her head. *Wrong. Wrong. Readjust. Don't make assumptions!*

All this happened in a narrow instant, the time it took for her to notice that every one of these "stars" shone the same exact shade of bright green. In half a second Teresa settled the sensory clash, seeing how this artful hoax was perpetrated.

The boat rocked as a figure occulted the false constellations, stepping back into the bow. The guide's silhouette eclipsed bright pinpoints as he hauled away at a line of blackness overhead. "Our cave worms make their homes along the roof," his voice echoed softly. "They produce a phosphorescence that lures newly hatched flies and other insects whose eggs and larvae were swept here from the outside world. The bright spots lead those insects not outside, not back into Te Ao-mārama, but onto sticky snares."

Something was wrong. Teresa sat forward. She whispered. "Pedro, his voice . . ."

With uncanny accuracy, Manella grabbed her hand and squeezed for silence. Teresa tensed briefly, then forced herself to relax. This must be part of the plan. With effort she sat back and made the best of the situation. There was nothing else to do, anyway.

Now she felt sheepish for even momentarily mistaking the lights overhead for stars. Their slow passage let her estimate parallax . . . ranging from one and a half to three meters above them. She could, in fact, follow the rough contours of the ceiling now. Anyway, there was no twinkle from atmospheric distortion. Some of the "stars" were, in fact, large oblong shapes.

Still . . . She blinked, and suddenly rationalization departed once more. For another thrilling moment Teresa purposely enjoyed the illusion again, looking out on an alien sky, on the fringes of some strange spiral arm with fields of verdant suns—the mysterious night glitter of a faraway frontier.

Their guide's shadow was the black outline of a nebula. The nebula moved. So, she suddenly noticed, did a regular, straight boundary. A rectangular blackness, free of green, passed over them as if demarking a gate. Soon Teresa heard a low rumble of motors and sensed a barrier roll behind them. The emerald starscape vanished.

"Now, if you'll please cover your eyes," the shadow said. She felt Manella move to comply, but only shaded hers. To close them completely would demand too much trust.

A sharp glow suddenly grew ahead of them. Perhaps it was only a dim lamp, but the glare felt intense enough to hurt her dark-adapted retinas. It quickly drove out all remaining trace of the worm phosphors. Teresa bade them farewell regretfully.

The boat bumped once more and stopped. "Come this way please," the voice told them. She felt a touch on her arm and Teresa let herself be led, blinking, out of the swaying craft. Her eyes tearing somewhat from the brightness, she had to squint past rays of diffraction to see who had replaced their original guide. It was a brown-haired man, lightly freckled, who clearly owned no Polynesian ancestry at all. Right now he regarded Pedro with an expression she couldn't read, but obviously carrying strong emotion.

"Hello, Manella," he said, apparently making an effort to be polite.

It was Teresa's first chance to scrutinize Alex Lustig in person. In photographs he had appeared distant, distracted, and some of that quality was present. But now she thought she perceived something else as well, possibly the expression of one who has sought strangeness, and found much more than he had ever bargained for.

Pedro used a kerchief to wipe his eyes. "Hello yourself, Lustig. Thanks for seeing us. Now, I hope you have a good explanation for what you've been up to?"

Here they were deep underground, out of contact with any of their own people or, in fact, any legal authority—and sure enough, old Pedro was slipping right back into the role of paternal authority figure.

"As you wish." Alex Lustig nodded, apparently unfazed. "If you two will follow me, I'll tell you everything. But I warn you, it will be hard to believe."

Of course Pedro wouldn't let someone else get the last word in, even with a line like that.

"From you, my boy, I expect no less than the completely preposterous and utterly calamitous."

An hour later Teresa wondered why she only felt anesthetized, when she really ought to loathe the man. Even if he hadn't made the monster eating away at the Earth's heart, he was still the one who had brought this thing to her attention.

Then there was his role in triggering the burst of coherent gravity waves that drove Jason and nine others on their one-way journey to the stars. That, too, should be reason enough to despise Alex Lustig. And yet the only emotions she felt capable of right now were more immediate ones . . . such as the wry pleasure of seeing Pedro Manella for the first time at a loss for words.

The big man sat across from Lustig, hands folded on a table of dark wood, his notepad completely forgotten. Pedro's eyes kept flicking to a large holographic cutaway of the Earth, more vivid and detailed than anything their group had been able to construct back in Houston. Delicately traced minutiae cast orange, yellow, and reddish shades across one side of Manella's face, lending false gay overtones to his bleak expression.

There were only the three of them here in a sparsely furnished underground chamber. After providing his guests with refreshments, Lustig had launched into his briefing without assistance, though twice he had lifted a headset to consult someone outside. Naturally, the man had help. Despite his "solitary wizard" reputation, there was no way he could have figured all this out by himself.

The possibility of a hoax occurred to Teresa several times, but she recognized that as wishful thinking. Lustig's calm thoroughness bespoke credibility, however insane or horrible his conclusions.

". . . so it was only this week, by combining gravity scans with neutrino observations, that we were able to pin down at last where the energy is coming from . . . the elevated state powering the gazer effect. It's at the base of the mantle, where the geomagnetic field draws on currents in the outer core . . ."

Technically, the story wasn't hard to follow. While searching for his Iquitos black hole, Lustig and his associates had stumbled across a much more dangerous singularity already present at the center of the Earth. They tried using tuned gravity waves to trace that one's trajectory and history, but that touched off internal reflections, amplifying gravitons much as photons are between the mirrors of a laser. In this case the "gazer mirrors" consisted of the mysterious Beta itself plus the experimental black hole onboard station Erehwon. What blasted forth was a great wave of warped space-time, spearing in the general direction of Spica.

Lustig was a good teacher. He kept his math to low-level matrices and used figures to graphically lay out this tale of catastrophe. It sounded all too plausible—and she wouldn't have believed a single word if she hadn't witnessed so much firsthand. The sudden, horrible stretching and contraction of Erehwon's tether, for instance. Or the relativistic departure of the Farpoint lab. *Or those colors.*

What had Teresa becalmed in an emotional dead zone was the realization that all her concerns were over. What point was there in worrying about internal politics at NASA, or her next flight itinerary, or her failed marriage, if the whole world was coming to an end soon?

The mystery singularity—Lustig's "cosmic knot"—must have started small. But Beta had grown till now it teetered near a critical threshold. She read the accretion rate off a side screen. Clearly the thing was poised for a voracious binge that could have only one conclusion.

One conclusion . . . So far he had spared them an explicit simulation of what would happen when matter began flowing into Beta's maw in megatons per second. Teresa figured it would start with shock waves disrupting the planet's deep, ancient convection patterns. Earthquakes would roll and volcanoes spume as great seams opened in the crust. Then, undermined from within, the outer layers would collapse.

Ironically, little would happen to things in orbit, like the moon or satellites. Earth's total mass below would stay the same, only converted into a far more compact form. If she happened to be on a mission at the time, she'd get to watch the whole show . . . until the singularity revealed its bare glory and seared her spacecraft out of existence in a blast of gamma radiation.

Teresa shook herself. This was no time for a funk. Later, at home, she could climb under the covers, curl in a ball, and hope to die.

". . . that one of our problems was finding the inverted energy distribution that's being tapped by the gazer beam. Where does all the power come from?" The Englishman ran a hand through his hair. "Then it all made sense! The Earth's magnetic dynamo is the source. Specifically, discrete superconducting domains where—"

Teresa started, sitting upright. "What did you say?"

Alex Lustig regarded her with pale blue eyes. "Captain Tikhana? I was referring to current loops, where the lower mantle meets the liquid core—"

She interrupted again. "You spoke of superconductivity. Down there? We still have trouble cooling rapid transit lines on a summer day, but you say there are superconducting areas thousands of miles below, where temperatures reach thousands of degrees?"

The British physicist nodded. "Don't forget, *pressures* at the base of the mantle exceed ten thousand newtons per square centimeter. And then there's a delightful coincidence one of my colleagues noticed only recently. The bottommost mineral state, before mantle gives way to metallic core, seems to consist of various oxides pressed into a perovskite structure—"

"Per . . . ovskite?"

"A particularly dense oxide arrangement that forms readily under pressure."

"I still don't get it," she said, frowning.

He spread his hands. "Relatives of these same perovskites happen to be among the best industrial superconductors! This coincidence led us to consider a weird notion . . . that there are places, thousands of kilometers below us, where electric current flows completely free of resistance."

The very idea made Teresa close her eyes. Once upon a time, superconductivity had been associated only with utter cold, near absolute zero. Only in recent decades had "room temperature" superconductors joined a few other breakthroughs to help salvage the hard-pressed world economy. Now she envisioned loops and titanic circuits, flowing in perfect, resistance-free fire. It was a startling notion. "These superconducting domains . . . they're the excited zones you tap with the gravity resonator?"

"We think so. Energy levels drop each time, but are quickly pumped up again by convection."

Silence held. When Manella spoke again, he shook his head. "So many wonderful discoveries . . . all made under the shadow of an angel of death. Okay, Lustig, you've had your fun. Now tell us what we need to know."

"Know for what?"

Pedro pounded the tabletop. "For revenge! Who released this thing? And when? Where do we find them?"

From the other man's countenance, Teresa guessed this wasn't the first time he had heard that request. "I don't know the answer yet," he replied. "It's hard to trace its trajectory back, taking into account friction and accretion and inhomogeneities in the core . . ."

"You can't even begin to guess?"

The physicist shrugged. "By my calculations the thing shouldn't even exist."

"Of course it shouldn't exist! But somebody made it, obviously. You said you understood the basic principles."

"Oh, I do . . . or thought I did. But I'm having trouble seeing how anyone could make such a large knot with any energy source available on Earth today."

"Wasn't it smaller when it fell?"

"Surely. But remember, practical cavitronics is only about eight years old. When I extrapolate that far back from Beta's present size and growth rate, it's still too bloody heavy. No structure on Earth could have supported it."

Manella glowered. "Obviously you've made some mistake."

Teresa saw something flash briefly in Alex Lustig's eyes—an anger that quenched as quickly as it came. With surprising mildness, he nodded. "Obviously. Perhaps it is eating faster than my theory predicts. This isn't an area anyone has much experience in."

At that moment Teresa felt the weight of the cave around her, as if all the tons overhead were pressing on her chest. Partly to overcome faintness, she spoke the critical question.

"How . . ." She swallowed. "How much time do we have?"

He blew a sigh. "Actually, that part's fairly easy. However rapidly it grew in the past, the asymptotic threshold remains the same. If it continues sucking in matter, faster and faster . . . I'd say we have about two years until major earthquakes begin. Another year before volcanic activity chokes the atmosphere.

"Then of course, things accelerate rapidly as the singularity's growth feeds on itself. Ninety-five percent of the Earth won't be swallowed till the last hour. Ninety percent in the final minute or so."

Teresa and Pedro shared a bleak look. "My God," she said.

"That, of course, is what will happen if it continues along the path now marked out for it." Alex Lustig spread his hands again. "I don't know about you lot. But personally, I'd rather not leave the thing to do its job unmolested."

Teresa turned and stared at the physicist. He glanced back with raised eyebrows.

"Do you mean . . . ?" she began, and was unable to speak.

He answered with a shrug. "Surely you don't imagine I agreed to meet with you two just to satisfy my arch nemesis and his craving for headlines, do you? We'll need your help, if we're to stand a chance of getting rid of the damned thing."

Manella panted. "You . . . have a way?"

"A way, yes, though it doesn't offer very good odds. And it's going to take more resources than I or my friends have at hand."

He looked back and forth between his two stunned visitors.

"Oh now, don't take it like that. Look at it this way, Pedro. If we pull this off, you and my friend George can spend many fine years, forever if necessary, arguing how to find and punish the brainy bastards responsible for this thing."

His expression then turned darker and he looked down. "That is, if this works."

PART VI

PLANET

World Ocean rolled, stroked by driving winds and tugged by barren Sister Moon.

For millions of years, twin tidal humps of churning water swept round and round, meeting little resistance but the sea floor itself. Only here and there did some lone, steaming volcano thrust high enough to reach open sky, daring to split the driving waves.

Eventually more islands sweated out, then more still. As the crust heaved and shifted, many of those mafic barges collided and merged until newborn continents towered over the waters. Onto those sere platforms ceaseless rains fell, nurturing nothing.

Only sheltered below the waves did life wage its continuing struggle to improve or die. One-celled creatures divided prodigiously, without planning or intent, experimenting with new ways of living.

One lucky family line chanced onto the trick of using sunlight to split water and make carbohydrates. That green patrimony took off, filling half the world's niches.

The day's length altered imperceptibly as Earth exchanged momentum with her moon. Eon by eon, the seas grew saltier and then stabilized. The sun brightened, also gradually. Sometimes the rolling waters changed color as some innovative microbe gained a sudden temporary advantage, burgeoned, outstripped its food supply, and died back again.

Then one tiny organism consumed another, but failed to devour its prey. Instead, the two coexisted and a deal was struck. An accidental sharing of responsibilities. A symbiosis.

One from many, and metazoa—multicellular life—was born.

That innovation, cooperation, changed everything.

□ **Worldwide Long Range Solutions Special Interest Group** [□ SIG AeR,WLRS 253787890.546] **special notice to our members.**

See this morning's major news release by the Los Alamos Peace Laboratory [□ Alert K12-AP-9.23.38:11:00 S.pr56765.0] for the latest test results from their solenoidal fusion test reactor. They report achieving a confinement-temperature product more than *five times* better than before, with almost none of those pesky stray neutrons that caused the Princeton disaster of 2021.

This may be it! After so many false leads over so many years. According to LAPL's chief of engineering, ". . . clean, efficient, and virtually limitless fusion power may now be only twenty or twenty-five years away. . . ."

Those wanting technical details or to see the raw data from yesterday's experiment, just press [□ Tech.PD1 236423994234.0975 aq], or voice-link "solenoid-fusion five" now.

● Claire Eng slogged through a pond of mucky water, hauling one
H end of a nylon net, concentrating hard to keep her footing on the
Y plastic pool liner. She couldn't afford to make one wrong move in
D this slimy soup.
R   *Not if I don't want to spend two hours washing gunk out of*
O *my hair,* she thought.
S   Just beyond the net and its row of floating buoys, a throng of
P panicky fish protested being herded into this corner of the pond.
H Their splashing sent ripples lapping too close to the tops of her
E waders. The fish—and the odorous green gunk they lived in—
R were ready for harvest. Unfortunately, both smelled awfully ripe,
E too.

Claire spat greasy, rank droplets. "Come on, Tony!" she complained to the dark-haired boy at the other end of the net. "I still have homework to do, and Daisy's sure to be a gor-suck pain about chores."

Tony finished tying his end to a stainless steel grommet and hauled himself out of the pond. On the concrete bank, under a row of potted, overhanging mulberry trees, he used a hose to rinse off his waders before shucking them. "Be right with you, Claire," he called cheerfully. "Just hold tight another minute!"

Claire tried to be patient, but her hat and sunglasses had come askew while helping drive hordes of hapless fish toward their doom. Now she had to face the relentless Louisiana sun unprotected. The afternoon was muggy, fly smitten, and she almost wished she'd had an excuse not to help her friend harvest this month's tilapia crop. But, of course, she couldn't let Tony down. Not with the Mexican megafarms cutting prices these days, driving small-time fish ranchers to the edge.

Angling her head away from the glare, she looked out across the endless flat expanse of Iberville Parish, dotted with cedar groves, rice paddies, and square dark patches of gene-designed quick-cane. And countless fish ponds—chains of low watery ovals, mulberry rimmed and glistening—the cool, efficient protein factories that let chefs in Baton Rouge and New Orleans maintain a spicy culinary tradition long after the Gulf coast fisheries had gone away.

In the distance, she made out a straight, tree-lined hummock, stretching north to south—the East Atchafalaya Basin Protection Levee, one of so many mammoth earthworks thrown up by the Army Corps of Engineers over more than a century, to forever stave off the meeting of two great waters. Endless miles of dikes and channels and monumental spillways lined the Mississippi River, the Gulf, and nearly every flow path conceived in the corp's computerized contingency plans. Tagging along with her father, and later in her own right, Claire had walked nearly every meter of the vast project. From Logan she had inherited a fascination for hydraulic engineering and an abiding contempt for the sort of techno-arrogance that spoke words like "forever."

"Idiots," she muttered. Now the corps was offering Congress a new plan, one "guaranteed" to keep the Mississippi from doing what it was absolutely bound to do eventually—shift its banks and find a new way to the sea. Logan's private estimates suggested the new levees would keep Old Man River out of the Atchafalaya Valley for another three decades, maximum. Claire considered her father an optimist. "Ten more years, tops," she said in a low voice.

She'd miss this land when it all disappeared . . . its criss-crossing little bayous and streams. The dead-still, humid air, thick with tangy Cajun cooking that bit right back when you put it in your mouth. And the old grempers and gremmers, sitting on benches, telling lies about days when there were still patches of mangrove swamp in these parts, thick with deer and 'gators and even "critters" never catalogued by science.

Claire narrowed her eyes and briefly saw the same flat parish roiling under hectare after kilohectare of foamy brown water, a mighty river hauling a continent's silt down this shortcut to the sea—along with every farm and house and living soul in its path.

But Daisy won't move. Hell, nobody listens to me, and I'm tired of being called "Cassandra" by all my friends.

In a matter of months she'd be gone from here anyway. Maybe people would pay better attention after she won a reputation elsewhere. After making a name for herself . . .

"Here, hand me the end."

She gave a start as Tony tapped her shoulder from the concrete bank. Straining, she dragged the line nearer. It took both of them, hauling together, to pull it taut and tie it off.

"Thanks, Claire," Tony said. "Here, let me help you out."

To her astonishment, he didn't wait for her to slosh over to the ladder. Tony grabbed her shoulder straps and hauled her onto the apron by strength alone. Dripping, she sat there while he hosed off her waders, grinning.

Showoff, she thought. Still, she couldn't help being impressed. At seventeen Tony was in full growth, changing every day and proud of it. She remembered when he had first surged past her in height, only a short time ago, and she had felt a passing, irrational wave of envy toward her childhood friend. Even in a world leveled for women by technology, there were times when sheer size and power still had their advantages.

Testosterone has its drawbacks, too, Claire reminded herself as she hung the rubber overalls to dry. Her remote-school in Oregon included a curriculum about the many reasons why women could count their blessings that they weren't male, after all. Still, lately she'd been surprised to catch Tony gazing at her with looks of bashful admiration. Surprising, that is, till she realized.

Oh. It's sex.

Or something nicer, actually, but closely related. Anyway, whatever it was, Claire wasn't ready to deal with it right now. Since puberty she had avoided girls her own age, because of their precocious, single-minded, one-topic focus. At fourteen and fifteen, boys seemed more interested in doing things—in projects on the World Net or neat stuff in the real world. Now though, inevitably, her male friends were catching up and starting to go goofy too.

"I've got to stay for the harvester truck," Tony told her, looking down. "Want to wait with me? We could head over to White Castle, after. Maybe join Judy and Paul . . ."

Judy and Paul were a long-standing couple. To hang out with them in public would make a statement, turning Claire and Tony into "Tony-and-Claire." She wasn't sure she wanted to become half of such a four-legged creature, quite yet. Far safer the amorphous throngs of teenagers who gathered at the dry-skating rink, or the Holo-Sim Club. . . .

"I'm sorry, Tony. I really have to go. Daisy—"

"Yeah, I know." He cut her off quickly, making a show of nonchalance. "You gotta deal with Daisy, poor kid. Well, good luck. Let me know if you can get away later."

She clambered down slippery steps to the duckboard walkway. "Yeah, I'll buzz. Or maybe tomorrow we'll go out with the team after your lacrosse game."

"Yeah." He brightened, shouting after her. "Just watch. We'll turn those guys into holey swiss cheese, full of rads and rems!"

Claire waved one last time and then turned to hurry home under the shadow of towering canebrakes, across tiny bridges where retirees idled with fishing poles, smiling at her with lazy familiarity, and finally past the long-abandoned refinery, now stripped of everything but crumbling, worthless concrete.

Why does being a teenager make you so impatient? she pondered as she neared Six Oaks, her mother's tiny autarchy on the bayou. Claire knew she couldn't put Tony off much longer without hurting him. *The profiler at school says I'm just a gradual type. No cause for worry if I'm slower than other kids, or more cautious.*

But what if the tests missed something? What if there's something wrong with me?

Abstractly, Claire knew these were typical thoughts for her age. Every adolescent wonders if he or she's the vanguard of the latest wave of mutants, made unhuman by some rare, fundamental flaw. Each quirk or idiosyncrasy gets magnified out of all proportion. A zit is the first stage of leprosy. A rebuff means banishment to the Sahara.

Knowing all that helped a little . . . though only a little.

I just hope that when I'm finally ready, Tony or someone like him will be ready for me.

She turned away from the refinery towers—slowly decomposing into gravelly sediment—without even seeing them, and took one last turn between an aisle of willows to hurry the rest of the way home.

Many houses in the area had columns and porticos more reminiscent of old movies than real history, but the effect was particularly anachronistic at Six Oaks. At first squint you might think you were looking at a miniature version of Tara, but satellite dishes and a forest of bristling antennas quickly dispelled any sense of antebellum charm. And while other families maintained rooftop photocells and supplementary water heaters, few kept enough to dispense entirely with the parish power grid.

After all, though, this was Daisy McClennon's "island," where self-sufficiency meant more than a trendy fad or even good citizenship, but had over the years become a militant faith. And Claire was fast turning into an apostate.

Unlike the neighbors, *chez* McClennon had no account with any of the local food-testing services. Why bother, when you grew amaranth and pejibaye palm fruit and marama beans and lentils in your own little horticultural paradise . . . a glassed-in wonder of nutritional productivity that Claire's mother had designed herself? It had been purchased with inherited money, but of late Daisy seemed to expect Claire to maintain it single-handedly.

Not much longer though, Daisy. Six months more and I'm gone.

Probably, her mother would barely notice when she left. Daisy'd just hire on some oath-pledged refugee, or one of those Han or Nihonese college kids who kept passing through these days, taking a year off working their way around the world from zep passage to zep passage in the latest Asian fad. If so, Daisy was due for a surprise. No modern, self-indulgent Nihonese kid would work as hard as Daisy expected for just room and board and electric.

"Aw, hell," Claire sighed on catching sight of the wind generator. Speaking of electric, those limp vanes meant current would be rationed again. And guess who had top priority around here?

Claire made her rounds with rapid efficiency, starting at the methane pit, where she checked fluid levels in the crap digester. It was supposed to be "zero maintenance," but that guarantee was by now a bitter joke. *I'll bet my rich cousins never have to do chores*, she thought with halfhearted crankiness. Alas, even Logan agreed with her mother on one thing: that "hard work builds character." So even if she had been able to live with her father, it wouldn't have been that much easier. And to be honest, she had met her relatives in the McClennon clan. Horrible, stuck-up creatures, living off wealth neither they nor their parents ever had a hand in creating. None of *them* would be hurt by a little honest labor, for sure.

Still, there's got to be a middle ground. Claire grunted as she fought to clear a drip-irrigator in the main greenhouse, blowing down one nozzle till spots swam before her eyes. *Maybe I just wish Daisy'd do her share around here.*

At least the bee zapper was working. For years their hives had been under seige by Africanized swarms, seeking to take over as they had everywhere else in the area, ruining all the once-profitable apiaries in the parish. Chemicals and spray parasites did no good. But a few weeks ago Claire had found a net reference by a fellow in Egypt, who'd discovered that the African strain beat their wings faster than the tame European variety. Burrowing into archaic TwenCen military technology, he had adapted sensor-scanner designs from an old, defunct project called "Star Wars." Now Claire and a few thousand others were testing his design and reporting weekly results to a network solutions SIG.

Like a glittering scarecrow, the cruciform laser system watched over her squat hives. When she had first turned it on, the surrounding fields had come startlingly alight with hundreds of tiny, flaming embers. The next morning, ash smudges were all that remained of the vicious invaders within line of sight. But her own honeybees were untouched. Now she looked forward to a sweet profit and her first stingless summer.

Perfect timing, she thought ironically. *Just as I'm about to move away.*

Before going inside, there was one last chore to do. Claire clambered down to the little creek behind the house, to check on Sybil and Clyde.

The piebald gloats bleated at her. They had finished eating all the water hyacinths within reach along that stretch of bank, so she readjusted their tethers to bring them near another weed-clogged area. Without such creatures, every waterway in the South would be choked with rank tropical opportunists by now, flourishing unstoppably for lack of natural controls.

Some neighbors made pets of their channel-clearing gloats, or the other type bred specially to eat kudzu vines. Claire liked animals, but she didn't want to feel any ties here, so she kept this relationship strictly businesslike. Anyway, what was the point in trying to maintain every tiny canal, as if canals weren't mortal like everything else?

The Mississippi's coming anyway, she thought, looking out toward the land she both loved and longed to leave behind. *You better get used to the idea, Atchafalaya. You're gonna know greatness, whether you like it or not.*

After adjusting Clyde's protective goggles, Claire brushed at his speckled coat. "What's this? Some sort of mange?" The gloat bleated irritably as puffs of dry fur floated from its patchy side. "All right. All right. I'll look into it." Sighing, Claire took a sample and patted the creatures, who were soon munching exotic weeds again, contentedly.

Echoes of gunfire and rocking explosions rattled the walls as she passed her mother's suite of rooms. Music blared—the strains of some oldtime movie Daisy was condensing for a Net entertainment group.

Though she perpetually proclaimed contempt for the industry, Daisy's expertise at compressing oldtime flicks was legendary. Skillfully, she could pack ninety tedious minutes into a crisp forty or less, speeding the languid pace of classics like *The Terminator* or *Deliverance* to suit the time-devouring appetites of modern viewers.

Or, for others wanting *more* out of a particular film, Daisy McClennon would expand the original . . . adding material from film archives or even computer-generated extrapolations. It brought in a steady income that allowed her to contemptuously spurn the despised family trust fund.

Most of the time.

Besides, a career working on the Net had one more advantage— the occupation lacked any obvious impact on the real environment of the Earth.

"Tread lightly on our world's toes" went the motto of one of Daisy's eco-freak organizations, the sort whose members didn't take off their shoes inside their houses, but instead removed them before going outside. That particular group had as their totem emblem a fierce Chinese dragon, curled and snarling, representing an angry, violated ecosphere fed up with swarming, pestilential humanity. The same reptilian icon stretched above the hearth of the main sitting room, Daisy's favorite part of the villa, but one seldom visited anymore by Claire.

Hell, she was too damn busy maintaining the rest of it! Claire cursed roundly when she saw that Daisy had neglected even to empty the trash, supposedly on her own list of chores. Not content with the normal five recycling bins, her mother insisted this house have twelve. *And* three mulch piles. Then there were the soap maker, the yoghurt maker, the midget brewery . . .

Claire thought of a recent stylish trend among her peers. *Oh, I'd make a swell Settler. I can grow herbal medicines, make my own paper, grind ink from bark and lamp black . . . and fix the water pump's gaskets myself, since mother hates buying parts from Earthraping manufacturers.*

City folk, tending high-yield gardens and a few clip-wing ducks on the roof, loved pretending that made them rough and independent, blithely ignoring all the ways they still counted on society's nurturing web, the tubes and ducts that piped in clean water, power, gas . . . and carried off a steady stream of waste. Ironically, few kids ever grew up better qualified to homestead a new frontier than Claire. And few had so little desire to do so.

After all, who in their right mind would want to live that way?

Oh, reducing your impact was moral and sensible, up to a point. Beyond which there was a lot to be said for labor-saving devices! Claire swore her own place would have a microwave-infrasound cooker. And an *electric* garbage disposal, oh please. And maybe, just for that first year of celebration—a licentious, never-ending gallon of store-bought *ice cream.*

Changing out of her sweaty work clothes in the privacy of her own room, Claire paused by a shelf of mementos brought by her father from trips all over the planet. A ten-million-year-old spider, encased in Dominican amber, lay next to fossils from the Afar desert and a beautiful hardwood dolphin, carved by a Brazilian engineer Logan had met in Belem.

Her mineral collection wasn't exactly world class. But there was a lovely polished slab of bright green smithsonite, alongside its cousins jadeite and entrancing malachite. More yellowish than green, the hypnotic, translucent autainite had come from France, and the purple erythrite from deep in the Atlas Mountains of Morocco.

None of these minerals were particularly rare, not even the disk of glittering "star" quality quartz hanging over her mirror—where she let down her reddish-brown hair and checked for stray droplets from Tony's pond. Picking up the crystal lens, she peered through it at her own image, wishing the highlights it gave her hair might somehow translate into the real world, where she so often envied other girls their shining locks.

As a child, she had thought the bit of quartz magical. But Logan had emphasized that it was a routine miracle. The Earth contained veins and seams and whole flows of beautiful mineral forms that took only a practiced eye to discover and a little skill to prepare. In contrast, Claire had been shocked when an uncle thought to please her one birthday with a "unique" gift—a slice of fossilized tree trunk. It had subsequently taken her weeks to investigate and discover its origins, then anonymously donate it back to the petrified forest it had been stolen from in the first place.

There was a difference, of course. Many common things could be beautiful, even magical. But in a world of ten billion people, true rarities shouldn't be owned. At least on that point she, Logan, and Daisy all agreed.

Claire put the crystal back. Beside the mirror lay her favorite treasures, several beautiful chert arrowheads. Not archaeological relics, but even better. Logan had taught her to chip them herself, during one of their too infrequent camping trips. To be fair, Claire admitted both her parents had taught her useful things. Only Logan's lessons always seemed much more fun.

Under the window, nesting in her neglected model of the Bonnet Carré Spillway, her pet mouse, Isador, twitched his nose as Claire stopped to pet him and feed him seeds.

The wall screens of her Net unit flickered on idle, showing new assignments from the remote-school in Oregon. But Claire first checked for personal messages. And sure enough, there was a blip from her father winking on her priority screen! At a spoken command, it lit up with a bright picture of Logan Eng standing atop a bluff overlooking a bay of brilliant blue water. To save power, she took the message in written form. Rows of letters shone.

HI MICRO-BIOTA. SAW AMAZING THINGS HERE IN SPAIN. SPELL THAT *"UH-MAZING*!"(□ SEE ATTACHED PIX.)

HAVE CRAZY THEORY TO EXPLAIN THESE EVENTS. WROTE A PAPER ABOUT IT FOR A SPEC-FACT SIG. IF I'M RIGHT, SOMETHING MIGHTY FISHY IS GOING ON!

ATTACHED A DRAFT (□) FOR YOU TO LOOK AT, IF YOU LIKE. A LITTLE TECHNICAL. NOTION'S PRO'BLY NONSENSE. BUT YOU MAY FIND THE ABSTRACT AMUSING.

MY BEST TO DAISY. SAY I'LL COME TO DINNER AFTER CLEARING PAPERWORK JAM AT OFFICE.

LOVE YOU, HONEY.—DADDY □

Claire smiled. He wasn't supposed to call himself "Daddy." That was *her* affectation.

She touched the DATA APPENDED tag and called up Logan's speculative paper. Claire recognized the net-zine he was submitting it to . . . one where scientists could let their hair down without risking their reputations. She had a hunch Logan was really going to set off a ripe one this time.

Then she frowned. Suddenly suspicious, Claire queried her security program.

"Dumpit!" she cursed, stamping her feet in annoyance. Logan's blip had been snooped since reception. And it didn't take a genius to know who the snooper was. *"Dumpit, Daisy!"*

The older generation as a whole seemed to have no respect for privacy, but this was downright insulting. As a brilliant hacker, Daisy could have brushed aside her daughter's simple security system and read Claire's mail without leaving traces. That she hadn't even bothered to cover her tracks showed either blithe indifference or straight contempt.

"Only half a year and I'm gone from here," Claire told herself, repeating it like a mantra to calm down. "Only half a year."

She wished, oh *how* she wished, that at sixteen, almost seventeen, that didn't feel like eternity.

Meanwhile, in another room not far away, all four walls flickered with light and sound. And every glimmer found its own reflection in Daisy McClennon's eyes.

To the left, a full-sized Davy Crockett—soot smeared and bloodied, but undaunted—defended the Alamo in color far more brilliant than ever imagined by the original director. Soon, sophisticated equipment under Daisy's subtle guidance would add a third dimension and more. For the right price, she'd even intensify the experience with smell and the floor-rattling concussion of Mexican cannonballs.

Her best, most pricey enhancements were so good, in fact, they had to carry a truth-in-reality warning . . . a little pink diamond flashing in one corner, signifying "this isn't real" to those with weak hearts or soft minds. While many called her an artist, Daisy did holo-augmentations for cash income, period. The other walls of her laboratory were devoted to her really important work.

Columns of data flowed like spume over a waterfall. Torrents— and yet mere samplings from the river, the *ocean* of information that was the Net. Daisy's blue eyes skimmed scores of readouts at once.

Here a UNEPA survey assayed remaining rain-forest resources. Next to it rippled a project proposal by a major mining company. And over to the right, one of her subroutines patiently worked its way through a purloined list of antisabotage security procedures for the West Havana Nuclear Power Station . . . still apparently impregnable, but Daisy had hopes.

The visible portion of the flow was only a sliver, a fragment distilled and sent back to this nexus by her electronic servants—her *ferrets* and *foxes*, her *badgers* and *hounds*—data-retrieval programs euphemistically named after beasts, some now extinct but known in earlier times for their tenacity, hunger, and unwillingness to take "no" for an answer. All over the world, Daisy's electronic emissaries searched and probed at her bidding, prying loose secrets, correlating, combining, devouring.

Daisy's cover business helped explain her prodigious computing needs, her means. But actually, she lived and worked for ends. Into the universe of data she sent forth guerrillas, her personal contingents in the war against planet rapists.

Such as Chang. It was she who had tipped UNEPA off to the

whereabouts of that awful man's grisly cache near Taipei. News of Chang's death had come as a welcome surprise. She'd been so sure he'd escape or at worst get a wrist slap. Perhaps those wimps at UNEPA were getting some guts, after all.

But now, on to other things. Daisy sat padmasama on a silk cushion amidst a cyclone of pictures and data. Her eyes quickly sifted what her creatures brought her . . . industrial "development" plans . . . laxity by weak, compromise-ridden public agencies . . . betrayal by bribed, gor-sucked officials. And worse.

Within the movement, her name was spoken in hushed tones, with respect, awe, and a little fell dread. In another era, Daisy might have heard the voices of angels in church bells. Today, though, her talents truly flowered as she plucked the schemes of builders as well as the prevarications of moderates, even half a world away.

"So Logan thinks his idea's just *amusing* . . . probably nonsense . . ." she whispered as she wove her ex-husband's recent paper into a special database. Of course she couldn't follow his more arcane mathematical derivations, but that didn't matter. She had programs for that. Or human consultants just a net call away.

". . . the station's anchor boom couldn't have been lifted by any known explosive. For lack of other explanations, I'm led to imagine incredibly focused seismic waves . . ."

Daisy's nostrils flared as she watched a panned view of the hated tidal power project. Yet another example of Logan's selling out. Of his futile, foredoomed effort to "solve" the world's problems. In bargaining with evil, of course, he had bartered away his soul.

Still, she knew him. She knew her former love better than he knew himself. Logan's poorest hunches were often better than other engineers' best analyses.

"It'd be just like him to latch onto something big and not even trust his own instincts," she sighed.

Daisy stared at the broken tidal barrage. Anything that could disrupt a big project like that interested her. There were people she knew . . . others who also despised the slow, reformist methods of the North American Church of Gaia. A loose network of men and women who knew how to take action. This news of Logan's might mean some new threat. Or perhaps an opportunity.

Daisy's eyes stroked the data flow pouring endlessly from the Net sea. The blue eyes of a hunter, they flashed and sought. Their patience was that of mission, and in them dwelled the perseverance of dragons.

□

Sleep little children, you be good,
Do your chores just like you should.
Eat your food now, clean your plate,
Poor kids dream of getting what you ate.

Play square always, don't tell lies,
'Cause secret-keepers always die,
Grumbling and all alone,
Underground just like a Gnome.

Do you like money? Just you know,
Some types help while others glow.
Earth-Bonds serve us, all our days,
But Swiss gold gives off gamma rays.

● "Whatever we do," Teresa Tikhana had said earlier, before the
C meeting broke up. "We can't let any of the space powers in on
O this. I'm sure now they were all in cahoots with Spivey's illegal
R research on Erehwon. Heaven only knows what they'd do if they
E got their hands on *gravity lasers* and *cosmic knots.*"

So they decided not to publicly announce the impending end of
the world, or their bold, if unlikely, plan to fight it. Big governments
were already the prime suspects for having created Beta, losing it, and
then hiding the story to escape responsibility. If so, the powers that be
wouldn't think twice about wiping out George Hutton's little band to
keep the foul secret a little longer.

Perhaps he and the others were leaping to wrong conclusions. All
in all, Alex did find the scenario garish and a bit too weird. But it fit
the facts as they knew them. Besides, they simply couldn't afford to
take chances.

"We'll deal with the *taniwha* ourselves, then," George Hutton
had summarized at the end of the meeting.

"It'll be hard to set up the resonators without anyone noticing,"
Alex reminded everybody. But Pedro Manella had agreed with George.
"Leave that part to Hutton and me. We'll provide everything you
need."

The portly Aztlan reporter had seemed so relaxed, so confident.
No sign remained of the emotion he'd shown on first hearing of the

monster at the planet's heart. Even a slim hope, it seemed, was enough
to fill him with energy.

Alex felt uncomfortable putting such trust in a man who—by his
own recent reckoning—had ruined his life. Of course it was actually
thanks to those riots in Iquitos, triggered by Manella, that his own
crude Alpha singularity had fallen and he'd been forced to go looking
for it. If not for the fellow's meddling in Peru, Alex would probably
have paid no more attention to the center of the Earth than . . .

He leaned back in his swivel chair and realized he had no adequate simile for comparison. The center of the Earth *was* essentially
the last place one thought of. *And yet, without it where would any
of us be?*

In front of Alex, the planet's many layers glowed fulgent in the
final schematic presented at the now-adjourned meeting. This ghostly,
near-spherical Earth circumscribed a geometric figure—a tetrahedral
pyramid whose tips pierced the surface at four evenly spaced locations.

EASTER ISLAND (RAPA NUI):	27° 6' 20" S,	109° 24' 30" W
SOUTH AFRICA (NEAR REIVILO):	27° 30' 36" S,	24° 6' E
IRIAN JAYA (NEW GUINEA):	2° 6' 36" S,	137° 23' 24" E
WEST GREENLAND (NEAR GODHAVN):	70° 38' 24" N,	55° 41' 12" W

Four sites. I'd rather have had twelve. Or twenty.

He'd said as much to Stan and George and the other geophysi-
cists. *There's no telling what will happen when we start pushing at
Beta in earnest. It's certain to drift and tumble. That array of resonators should be a dodecahedron or icosahedron for full coverage, not a
pyramid.*

But a pyramid was all they could manage.

It wasn't a matter of money. That George had in plenty, and he
was willing to spend every farthing. His political contacts in the Polynesian Federation meant two sites would be readily available, no questions asked. But to set up beyond the Pacific basin, their tiny cabal
would need help. Especially if word wasn't to leak out.

Back in the last century, undercover, *secret* maneuverings were
more the rule than the exception. Nations, corporations, drug cartels,
and even private individuals habitually concealed monumental
schemes. But arms inspections were followed by tourism, as jetliners
and then zeps began nosing through swathes of sky once reserved for
warcraft. Data-links laced metropoleis to donkey-cart villages. Of the
three great centers of TwenCen secrecy, state socialism had collapsed

before Alex was even born, and finance capitalism met its ruin soon after that, amidst the melted Alps.

In hindsight, the Helvetian tragedy probably hadn't even been necessary, for not even the fabled gnomes could have kept their records private much longer in a world filled with amateur snoops— data hackers with as much free time and computing power as ingenuity.

That left the third relict, and the strongest. The great nation states still maintained "confidential" services—permitted the victors by the same treaty that had ended such things for everyone else. Those agencies could have helped the Tangoparu team set up their gravity-wave array in total secrecy. But then, those same agencies were almost certainly the enemy, as well.

George thinks they made Beta and are hiding their mistake to save their own hides, even if it means eventually dooming everyone.

Alex couldn't imagine that kind of thinking. It made him ashamed to be a member of the same species. To hear Teresa Tikhana describe her Colonel Spivey, though, she might as well be talking about a creature from another planet.

Were Spivey and his collaborators even now struggling to find a solution as well? Perhaps that's what Teresa's husband had been working on, out in space. If so, the government boys never seemed to have stumbled on the gravity laser effect. And at this point, Alex would be damned if he'd give it to them.

Of course if we succeed the secret will come out near the end anyway. It'll be hard to ignore a sunlike fireball rising out of the Earth, accelerating toward deep space at relativistic speeds.

By then, he and the others had better have prepared to go into hiding. In addition, Alex himself would feel compelled to take memory destroyers as soon as Beta was safely on its way, to prevent spilling what he had learned by coincidence and accident and mental fluke. In principle, it was only what he deserved, of course, for the sin of hubris. Still, he'd regret losing his mental image of the knot singularity, its intricate ten-space foldings, its awful, ignescent beauty. That loss would haunt him, he knew. Almost, he would rather die.

As if I'll get a choice. It's a long shot this will work at all.

They were taking a terrible chance. Using gravity-wave recoil to move Beta sounded fine in theory. But some of their initial test gazer beams for unknown reasons had interacted with matter at the planet's *surface*—coupling with an earthquake fault in one case, with man-made objects in another. It was still a mystery why this happened or what the consequences might be once they really got started.

But what choice do we have?

Alex looked at the glowing points where the tetrahedron met Earth's surface. Four sites where they must build mammoth superconducting antennas without anyone finding out. And they had so little time.

The resonators had to be evenly spaced and on dry land—not easy to arrange on a world two thirds covered in water. It had taken his computer two whole seconds to search and finally find the best arrangement.

"We only have a few months," Teresa Tikhana said, interrupting Alex in his brooding. The American astronaut sat across the table from him in the darkened room, watching the same display. They had both fallen silent after the others left, each thinking alone.

In response, he nodded. "After that, Beta will be too massive to budge, even with the gazer. We'd only excite resonant states Stan thinks could make it even worse."

Teresa shivered. When she sat up, she looked around in a way Alex had noticed before—as if she were checking her surroundings in some manner he couldn't fathom. "You'll be setting up the resonator on Rapa Nui, won't you?" she asked, suddenly.

"Yes. That's the anchor point, so—"

"It's a special place, you know." Her voice was hushed. "That's where *Atlantis* is."

"Um . . . Atlantis?" Perplexed, at first he thought she must be referring to the island's eerie Neolithic history, or the haunting monoliths to be found there. Then he remembered. "Oh. The space shuttle that crashed long ago. Is it still there?"

Teresa Tikhana's jaw tightened briefly. "It didn't crash. Captain Iwasumi made a perfect emergency landing under impossible conditions. It was the fools in charge of bringing *Atlantis* home . . . they *dropped* her."

It must have happened when she was only a child, yet the woman covered her eyes in pain. "She's still down there, stripped, a shell. A monument on a pedestal. You should visit her if you get the chance."

"I'll do that. I promise."

She looked up. Their eyes met briefly, then Teresa sighed. "I'd better pack. Dr. Goldman and I have a plane to catch."

"Of course." He stood up. "I . . . I'm glad you're with us, Captain Tikhana. Your help is going to be vital." Alex paused. "Also . . . as I said. I'm so very sorry about your husband—"

She raised a hand, cutting off another embarrassing apology. "It was an accident. If anyone's to blame for blindness—for not picking up on what was happening . . ." She trailed off, shaking her head.

"We'll drop you a coded message when we get to Godhavn, Dr. Lustig."

"Have a safe trip, Captain." Hesitantly, he offered his hand. After
a moment, she took it. Her slim, calloused grip betrayed a single faint
tremor before she quickly let go again. Then she turned away, departing for her quarters in another part of the cave.

"And good luck," Alex added softly after she had gone. "We're
all going to need more than a little of that, too."

□ *World Net News: Channel 265/General Interest/Level 9+* *(surface transcription)*

"Central Amazonia. This is Nigel Landsbury reporting in real time for the BBC. I've come here to this desolate land to cover a scene both tragic and historic, as Brazilian national forces pursue Tupo rebels to their last redoubts.

[Image of desert. Scrub bush and cracked clay. Heat waves rise from the hardpan all the way to a blurry horizon. A reporter's voice carries over the sound of crackling burning.]

[□ For raw footage voice-link "AMAZONIA One" now.]

"Here an armed detachment of FLS fighters was caught an hour ago, just short of the edge of the Chico Mendes National Salvation Park . . ."

[□ For background reports, link "FLS REBELS" or "CHICO MENDES PARK."]

[Camera pans, and viewer suddenly sees smoke rising from burning vehicles surrounded by strewn bodies. Military helicopters shred the plumes as uniformed soldiers hustle past, prodding prisoners with hands . on their heads.]

"The campesinos who died or were captured here today could not have hidden for long in their rain-forest refuge. The sensor technology [□ link "SENSOR-TEK"] *that cuts short so many would-be guerrilla movements nowadays would be no less effective under the canopy. Their cause was lost as soon as it turned violent, with the massacre of the last Quich'hara Indian village, two weeks ago."*

[Still panning, camera takes in the reporter himself, tan clothes whipped by a relentless dry wind. Just to his left, startlingly, there appears the sharp edge of a towering forest . . . a sudden transformation from caked clay to tight-packed, slender, swaying trees.]

"But there is a further, ultimate irony . . . that this forest the rebels wanted to claim for their impoverished families . . . their paradise for escape from the strict regimen of the crowded urban poor . . . is doomed anyway. Yes-

[Closeup on the reporter's face, awash with memory of tragedy.]

[□ Report: Braz. Nat. WeRe 6309467/q/ 3509.]
[□ Rebuttal: NorAChuGa 2038-421/Pres. Isl.]

terday, the Brazilian government admitted the failure of the "preservation islands" approach to saving Amazonia, recognizing at last that you cannot save a patch, here and there, of a whole ecosystem."

"Contracts have already been signed to harvest the dying hardwoods of Chico Mendes Park, removal of the large animals to life arks, and cryosuspension of as many insect and plant seed types as can be catalogued in time. This systematic approach, tested last year with some small success in Manaus Province, has never before been tried on such a vast scale. Experts doubt more than five percent of the remaining species can be registered before harvesters must complete their work."

[Closeup of the forest edge . . . yellowed leaves crumble to dust in a human hand.]

[☐ Contract: Braz. Nat. PaRe 9867984/i/ 567.]
[☐ Contract: Life Ark 62 LeSs 2393808/k/ 78.]

"Still, what is to be done? How can you keep alive a rain forest where there is no rain?"

[☐ Link WEATHERNET ALPHA-YEAR SUMMARY 2037—2956a*.]

[Cut back to the resigned features of the reporter.]

"Transpiration, evaporation, humidity renewal . . . science can give names to all the reasons why the preservation islands plan failed. Some blame the worldwide warming. Whatever the reason, however, it is we who must live with what remains. And it is the poor who in the end are caught in the middle."

[Camera returns to the scene of burning. One dusty corpse, arms outstretched toward the supposed refuge of the forest, can be seen clutching a single green leaf.]

[☐ Real-time image NorSat 12. $1.12/minute.]

"This is Nigel Landsbury . . . re-
porting from Amazonia."

[□ Reporter   bio: N.LANDSBURY–BBC3.
Credibility ratings: AaAb-2 Viewer's Union
(2038).   AaBb-4,   World   Watchers   Ltd.
(2038).]

[Reporter looks upward, and the camera follows his gaze to a sky dun with
floating dust.]

●   Stan Goldman watched Auntie Kapur stir the fire with a crooked
M   stick. A mist of ash lifted in its wake, and the coals brightened
E   briefly to compete with the old woman's blue-flickering computer
S   display. Beyond those twin pools of light, the ocher columns of
O   the meeting house melted into moist shadows of a New Zealand
S   mountain forest. Auntie preferred this setting for their final meet-
P   ing before everyone dispersed to Earth's four corners. Beginning
H   such a covert enterprise in darkness seemed appropriate to their
E   dim chances.
R   "Rapa Nui will be easiest," the priestess told Stan and
E   George. The glinting sparks set her chin tattoo designs in eerie
motion. "My sisters there will provide every facility, and the Chilean
authorities will be no problem."

"That's good," Stan said. He rubbed his eyes, blaming exhaustion
and bits of drifting ash for the stinging. It was long past his normal
bedtime—as if anything were "normal" anymore. But at least Ellen
would be waiting up for him, and he hoped to salvage something of
their last night together.

"That island's the anchor point," he went on. "Site one has to be
there, with no allowance for error."

"Then it's agreed, that's where Alex must go," George Hutton
said.

Stan nodded. "Of course. Alex should get the safest site, and the
one where the most delicate control is needed, since only he truly
understands that thing down there."

"Do not count on Rapa Nui being safe." Meriana Kapur regarded
Stan severely. "It is an island of awful power. A place of death and
horrible old gods. I agree Lustig must be the one to go there, to that
focal point. But not because it is *safe*."

Auntie had a way of making statements one could not answer.
Stan glanced at George and saw his friend nod reverently. As a *pakeha*

kiwi—a white New Zealander, and one who hadn't even been born here—Stan felt it wiser simply to defer to the Maori when they spoke of such things.

"Very well. We still have to finalize the teams to go set up the other three resonators."

George Hutton spoke gruffly. "I've decided I'll handle Irian Jaya myself."

Stan turned and blinked at him. "But we need you to coordinate everything. Our equipment . . . ."

The billionaire waved one hand. "All can be accomplished by hyper, using company codes and colloquial Taupo speech. But some things have to be done in person. I must be there to arrange matters with certain friends among the Papuans."

"Do you have a specific site in mind?"

George smiled. "The perfect site. I discovered it during a resource survey ten years ago . . . a series of deep caves even greater than the Mulu caverns, in Borneo."

"But I never heard. How did you keep them secret? And why?"

"How is easy, my friend." George put one finger to his lips. "Besides me, only chief engineer Raini knows about it, and she swore me an oath. It didn't qualify as a "mineral resource," per se, so we simply neglected mentioning it to the Papuan government."

"But it *is* a resource! Caves like the Mulu generate income from tourism . . ."

Stan stopped, suddenly aware of the irony. No more than a kilometer away were the grottoes of Waitomo, wonders of nature now reduced to yet another brief stop in the travel itineraries of millions, its ancient floors trampled, its limestone seeps forever altered by rivulets of vapor condensed from myriad human exhalations, its glowworm constellations demoted from silent, awesome mysteries to a few more frames in the next tourist's automatic camera.

"That's *why* enough for me," George answered. "Another reason I want to take this task is to see the Irian caves once again. If there's time near the end, you too must join me there, my old friend. You've never seen their like. We'll drink a toast to Earth, down where no stone has ever felt the brush of human voices."

The look in George's eye told more than his words. But Stan shook his head. "If it gets that close and we know we've lost, I'll take Ellen to Dunedin to be with the grandkids." He shook his head. This was getting much too morbid. "Anyway, I'll be doing a job of my own up north, at site three. That'll be plenty vivid enough for me, staring at all that ice."

Auntie Kapur was still studying her screen and the map overlay

Alex Lustig had prepared. "According to our Pommie genius, your requirements are less severe. You can set up your small Greenland resonator anywhere within several hundred kilometers of the tip of our mythical pyramid. Do you have any place in mind?"

"I have some friends working on the Hammer Dig, east of Godhavn. Everyone knows I'm interested in the project, so it won't be much of a surprise if I show up with a team to do some local gravity scans. It'll be a perfect cover."

"Hmm." Auntie Kapur was clearly worried. Sites one and two were within the Pacific Rim, in reach of her network of sympathizers and coreligionists. There were Gaians in Greenland too, of course, but of a completely different sect. Stan and Teresa would be pretty much on their own up there.

"You know all this is going to make us subject to the secrecy laws," Stan said dryly. "We could get in trouble."

The others looked at him, then burst out laughing. It was a welcome if momentary break in the tension. Normally a serious thing, breaking the provisions of the Rio Treaties was at this point the least of their worries.

"That leaves Africa," George summarized when they got back to business. And indeed, the final site would be the toughest. Tangoparu Ltd. had never done business in the area where they had to set up the last resonator. Their geological maps were obsolete, and to make matters worse, the region was on the U.N.'s Stability and Human Rights Watch List. Nobody on their team knew anyone there well enough to rely on. Not well enough to help them set up a thumper in absolute privacy.

"I've already started putting out feelers," Auntie Kapur said. "With a nested hyper search I ought to find someone trustworthy who can get us in."

"Just make sure to run your search routine by Pedro Manella. He's in charge of net security," Stan cautioned. "We don't want some bored hacker's ferret program arousing attention—"

He stopped when Auntie gave him an indulgent look, as if he were trying to teach his own mother to tie her shoes.

She's not much older than me, he thought. *I'm a grandfather and a full professor. So how does she always manage to make me feel like a little boy, caught with a frog in his pocket?*

Maybe it's something she learned in priestess school, while I was studying inconsequential stuff like the workings of stars and the shape of space.

"I'll be careful," she promised, remaining vague. But in her eyes

Stan read something that seemed to say she knew exactly what she was doing.

□

Back in the year 1990, the people of the United States of America paid three billion dollars for eighteen thousand million disposable diapers. Into these snug, absorbent, well-engineered products went one hundred million kilograms of plastic, eight hundred million kilograms of wood pulp, and approximately five million babies. The babies weren't disposable, but all the rest went straight into the trash stream.

Early designs for "disposable" diapers had included degradable inner liners, meant to be flushed down the toilet while the outer portion was reused. But that method was soon abandoned as inconvenient and unpleasant. Modern parents preferred just balling up the whole offensive mess and tossing it into the garbage. Tons of feces and urine thus bypassed urban sewage systems and went instead by flyblown truck through city streets to landfills, incinerators, and the new, experimental recycling plants. Along with them went hepatitis A, the Norwalk and Rota viruses, and a hundred other air- and water- and insect-borne threats.

As the price of landfill dumping rose above $100 a ton, by 1990 it was costing Americans $350 million a year just to get rid of single-use diapers, so for every dollar spent by parents on disposables, other taxpayers contributed more than ten cents in hidden subsidy.

That didn't include, of course, the untold cost of the 1996 New Jersey Rota epidemic. Or the nationwide hepatitis outbreaks of '99.

But what could be done? To busy young families, needing two wage earners just to make ends meet, *convenience* was a treasure beyond almost any price. It could make the difference between choosing to have a child or giving up the idea altogether.

Packaging and disposal fees might have let old-fashioned diaper services compete on even terms. But that, and other bullet-biting measures, voters succeeded in putting off for another generation . . . for another, harder century.

These, after all, were the waning years of high-flying TwenCen. And nothing was too good for baby.

Anyway, if the bill wouldn't come due for another twenty years or so, all the better. Baby would be a superkid, raised on tofu and computers and quality time. So baby could pay for it all.

● Jen Wolling missed her postman.

H   Who would have imagined it, back when she was a blonde
O fireball tearing up turn-of-the-century biology? Even then she'd
L known the future would offer surprises, but the changes that
O amazed her most turned out not to be the grand ones—those mile-
S stones noted breathlessly by media pundits—but *little* things, the
P gradual shifts people overlooked simply because they crept up on
H you bit by bit, day by day.
E   Such as the steady disappearance of postmen. Amid the grow-
R ing worldwide data culture few had foreseen that consequence—
E an end to those punctual footsteps on the walk, to the creak of the
letter box, to the friendly "hello" rustle of paper envelopes. . . .

Without fanfare, Britain's twice-a-day deliveries went every other
day, then once weekly. Letter carrying was "deregulated"—turned
over to private services, which then charged by the minute and made a
production number of signing over a single envelope.

What Jen missed most was the routine *mundanity* of mail time. It
used to come as a welcome break, an excuse to tear herself away from
the flat, cramped, eye-wearying computer screens of those days,
stretching her crackling back as she hobbled over to pick up the daily
offering of multicolored envelopes.

Most of it had been junk of course. What was Sturgeon's first law?
Ninety percent of anything is crap.

But ah, that remaining ten percent!

There were letters from dear friends (which, amidst a month-long
wrestling bout of abstract theory, often served to remind her she *had*
friends). And there were technical journals to leaf through, scribble
on the margins, and leave in the corner to pile up like geologic sediments. . . .

And beautiful, real-paper magazines—*Natural History* and *National Geographic* and *Country Life*—their glossy pages conveying
what modern hyper versions could not, despite high-fidelity sound
and stereo projection.

Trees regularly died for human literacy in those days. But that
was one sacrifice even Jen didn't begrudge. Not then, nor even today
as she opened the curtains to spill morning light onto library shelves
stacked high with books printed on rag paper, some even bound in
burnished leather that had once adorned the backs of proud animals.

This library could bring a small fortune from collectors . . . and
the sharp opprobrium of vegetarians. But one of the advantages of the

electronic age was that you could maintain a universe of contacts while keeping all prying eyes out of your own home, your castle.

It also has disadvantages, she thought as she scanned the list of bulletins awaiting her this morning. Her autosecretary displayed a column of daunting figures. Back when communication had still been a chore, half these correspondents would have been too lazy or thrifty to spend the time or a stamp. But now, message blips were as easy and cheap as talk itself. Easier, for copies could be made and transmitted ad infinitum.

Yes, indeed. Sometimes Jen longed for her postman.

You don't miss water or air, either—not till the well runs dry, or the oxygen partial pressure drops to twenty percent.

She took a subvocal input device from its rack and placed the attached sensors on her throat, jaw, and temples. A faint glitter in the display screens meant the machine was already tracking her eyes, noting by curvature of lens and angle of pupil the exact spot on which she focused at any moment.

She didn't have to speak aloud, only *intend* to. The subvocal read nerve signals, letting her enter words by just beginning to will them. It was much faster than any normal speech input device . . . and more cantankerous as well. Jen adjusted the sensitivity level so it wouldn't pick up each tiny tremor—a growing problem as her once athletic body turned wiry and inexact with age. Still, she vowed to hold onto this rare skill as long as possible.

Tapping certain teeth made colors shift in the tanks and screens. A yawn sent cyclones spinning within a blue expanse. Sometimes, under a talented operator, a subvocal could seem almost magical, like those "direct" brain-to-computer links science fiction writers were always jabbering about, but which, for simple neurological reasons, had never become real. This was as close as anyone had come, and still ninety percent of existing subvocals were used at most to make pretty 3-D pictures.

How ironic then, that Jen had been taught to use hers at age sixty-two. So much for adages about old dogs and new tricks!

"Hypersecretary, Sri Ramanujan," she said.

Mists cleared and a face formed, darkly handsome, with noble Hindu features. For her computer's "shell" persona Jen could have chosen anything from cartoon alien to movie star. But she had picked this system's unique designer as a model. In those eyes she recognized something of the young consultant from Nehruabad, his life-spark peering out from the cage of his useless body.

"Good morning, Professor Wolling. During the last twenty-four hours there have been three priority-nine world news items, two regional alerts for

Britain, and four on general topics from Reuters, your chosen neutral-bias news agency. None of the alerts were in categories listed by you as critical."

Citizens had to subscribe to a minimum news-input or lose the vote. Still, Jen was anything but a public events junky, so her nine-or-greater threshold was set as high as allowed. She'd scan the headlines later.

"You have received six letters and thirty five-message blips from individuals on your auto-accept list. Sixty-five more letters and one hundred and twelve blips entered your general delivery box on the Net.

"In addition, there were four hundred and thirteen references to you, in yesterday's scientific journals. Finally, in popular media and open discussion boards, your name was brought up with level seven or greater relevance fourteen hundred and eleven times."

It was clearly another case of human profligacy—this typical turning of a good thing into yet another excuse for overindulgence. Like the way nations suffering from greenhouse heat still spilled more than five billion tons of carbon into the atmosphere each year. A prodigious yield that was nevertheless nothing compared to the species' greatest harvest—*words*.

And to think, some idiots predicted that we'd someday found our economy on information. That we'd base money on it!

On information? The problem isn't scarcity. There's too damned much of it!

The problem usually wasn't getting access to information. It was to stave off drowning in it. People bought personalized filter programs to skim a few droplets from that sea and keep the rest out. For some, subjective reality became the selected entertainments and special-interest zines passed through by those tailored shells.

Here a man watches nothing but detective films from the days of cops and robbers—a limitless supply of formula fiction. Next door a woman hears and reads only opinions that match her own, because other points of view are culled by her loyal guardian software.

To avoid such staleness, Jen had hired a famous rogue hacker, Sri Ramanujan, to design her own filter. "Let's see what happens to that list," she said aloud, "when we use threshold seven, categories one through twenty."

"And the surprise factor, Professor Wolling?"

Jen felt in a good mood. "Let's go with twenty percent."

That meant one in five files would pop up randomly, in defiance of her own parameters. This way she *asked* Ramanujan to unleash purposely on her a little of the chaos his devilish virus-symbiont had once wreaked on thirteen million Net subscribers in South Asia—

jiggling their complacent cyberworlds to show them glimpses of different realities, different points of view.

After he was caught, being sent to that hospital-jail in Bombay hardly mattered to Sri Ramanujan, whose own body had been a prison since infancy. But cutting off his net privileges had been an added punishment far worse than any death sentence.

"As you wish, Jen Wolling."

The simulated visage seemed pleased. He bowed and disappeared, making way for unreeling sheaves of data. Colors demarked significant passages, enhanced by her semantic-content filter.

Her eyes focused on text which glowed with reddish highlights. *Ah, the little devil*, she thought, for the program had slipped in a cluster of hate mail.

". . . Wolling has become a loose cannon. Her recent trip to Southern Africa proves she's lost all sense of propriety.

"But what irks most is her recent cavalier reassessment of the essential Gaian paradigm—a scientific model she herself helped develop so many years ago! She is becoming a senile embarrassment to biological science . . ."

Jen found the style familiar, and sure enough, the signature was that of an old colleague, now a bitter opponent. She sighed. It was strange to find herself regularly assaulted as unscientific whenever she deviated an iota from "accepted" principles . . . principles based upon her own earlier theories.

Well, she admitted to herself. *Maybe sometimes I deviate more than an iota. And I do enjoy causing a stir.*

She flicked her tongue. Electromagnetic sensors read her intent and swept the diatribe away without comment. Another glowed redly in its place.

". . . Wolling is an embarrassment to our cause to save Our Mother. Isn't it enough she pays homage to the reductionist values of patriarchal western science, giving that discredited realm the devotion she properly owes Gaia?

"In giving ammunition to Earth-rapists—to Zeus-Jehovah-Shiva worshippers—she betrays Our Mother . . ."

Strange how one word could mean so many things to so many different people. To biologists, "Gaia" described a theory of planetary ecological balance and regulated feedback loops. But to devoted mystics it named a living goddess.

Another tongue flick, and a third tirade slid into place.

". . . Evolution has always been driven by the death of species. Take the so-called catastrophes of the Permian and Triassic and Cretaceous, when countless living types were annihilated by environmental shocks. Now, according to Wolling and Harding, these were dangerous times for the Earth, when the so-called "Gaia homeostasis" almost collapsed. But that simply isn't true! Today's so-called ecological crisis is just another in a long series of natural . . ."

Smiling made the display shimmer. Here were representatives of three different, unasinous points of view, each deeply opposed to the others, and yet all attacking her! She leafed through other crimson diatribes. Some Madrid Catholics poured calumny on her for assisting the gene-resurrection of mastodons. A white antisegregation society fired fusillades at her for visiting Kuwenezi. One of the "ladybug combines" accused her of undermining the trillion-dollar organic pest-control industry, and so on. In most cases the writer clearly didn't even understand her real position. Should a rare piece of vituperation actually show cleverness, it would go into a clipping file. But none of today's hate-grams offered anything illuminating, alas.

The technical citations were hardly any more interesting. Most were doctoral theses referring to her old papers . . . the "classics" that had led to that damned Nobel prize. She selected five promising ones for later study, and dumped the rest.

Among the personal messages was one bona fide letter from Pauline Cockerel, asking Jen to come visit London Ark.

"Baby misses you."

The young geneticist added an animated montage of the young demi-mastodon in action. Jen laughed as Baby lifted her trunk in a grinning trumpet of victory, while chewing a stolen apple.

There were a few other friendly notes, from loyal colleagues and former students. And a data packet from Jacques, her third husband—containing a folio of his latest paintings and an invitation to his next showing.

All of these merited replies. Jen tagged and dictated first-draft answers, letting the syntax-checker convert her clipped short-speech into clear paragraphs. In fact, sometimes thoughts streamed faster than judgment. So Jen never "mailed" letters till Tuesdays or Fridays, when she scrupulously went over everything carefully a second time.

She glanced at the clock. Good, the chore would be done well before morning tea. Only two letters to go.

". . . I'm real sorry to bother you. You probably don't remember me. I sat in the front row during your talk . . ."

This writer wasn't adroit at short-speech. Or he lacked a conciseness program to help him get to the point. Jen was about to call up one of her standard fan mail replies when one highlighted line broke through.

". . . at Kuwenezi. I was the guy with the little baboons . . ."

Indeed, Jen remembered! The boy's name had been . . . Nelson something-or-other. Uneducated, but bright and earnest, he had asked the right questions when his more sophisticated elders were still trapped in a morass of details.

". . . I've been studying hard, but I still don't understand some things about the Gayan Paradime . . ."

Jen nodded sympathetically. The word "Gaian" had become nearly as meaningless as "socialist" or "liberal" or "conservative" were half a century ago . . . a basket full of contradictions. She sometimes wondered what James Lovelock and Lynn Margulis would have thought of where their original, slim monographs had led. Or the Russian mystic, Vernadsky, who even earlier had proposed looking at the Earth as a living organism.

Perhaps these times were ripe for a new church militant, as in the waning days of the Roman Empire. Maybe great movements liked having living prophets to both idealize and later crucify. Veneration followed by varicide seemed the traditional pattern.

With Lovelock and Margulis and Vernadsky long gone, the new faithful had to settle for Jen Wolling—founding saint and heretic. At times it got so she even wished she'd never had that epiphany, so long ago on the frosty shoulders of Mount Snowdon, when the turning leaves had suddenly revealed to her the jewellike mathematical clarity of the Gaia metaphor.

No regrets. Jen shook her head. *I cannot regret those equations. For they are true.*

Once, when young Alex had come to her complaining of the awful burden, being a Nobelist's grandson, she had told him, "Some fools think I'm smart because I found a few tricks, to make math serve biology. But you and I know a secret . . . that someday you'll go places where I can't. Prize or no damned prize."

She missed her grandson and wondered what mischief he was up to.

Jen shook herself out of a mental random walk. Bearing down, she returned to the letter from the black teenager in Kuwenezi.

". . . the part that confuses me most is how animals and plants fight each other for survival. Like hunting and being hunted? Nobody 'wins' those wars, cause every soldier dies anyway, eventually? Most of the time, what looks to them like fighting isn't really fighting at all! Cause each of them *depends* on the others.

"Like, a herd of deer depends on wolfs to keep deer numbers down, or else they'd overgrase and then all starve to death . . . And the *wolfs'* numbers are controlled by how many deer there are to eat.

"This is what they mean by homeostasis, isn't it? One kind of animal *regulates* another, and it's regulated back . . ."

Jen skimmed ahead to a highlighted area.

"But what about Man? Who or what regulates *us?*"

She nodded appreciatively. There were scores of good books she could refer the young man to. But he must have already accessed the standard answers and found them unsatisfying.

We are an unregulated cancer, proclaimed many eco-radicals. *Man must cut his numbers and standard of living by a factor of ten, or even a hundred, to save the world.*

Some even suggested it would be better if the destroyer species— *Homo sapiens*—died out altogether, and good riddance.

Those pursuing the "organic" metaphor suggested the problem would be solved once humanity adjusted to its proper role as "brain" of the planetary organism. *We can learn to regulate ourselves,* pronounced the moderators of the North American Church of Gaia, as they pushed "soft" technologies and birth control. *We must learn to be smart planetary managers.*

There were still other opinions.

Everything would be fine on Earth if humans just left! That was the message of the space colonization movement, as they promoted plans for cities and factories in the sky. *Out in space, resources are endless. We'll move out and turn the little blue planet into a park!*

To Madrid Catholics and some other old-line religious groups, *The world was made for our use. The end of days will come soon. So why "regulate," when it's all temporary anyway? One unborn human fetus is worth all the whales in the sea.*

A group based in California offered a unique proposal. "Sheckleyans" they called themselves, and they agitated—tongue in cheek, Jen imagined—for the genetic engineering of new *predators* smart and agile enough to prey on human beings. These new hunters would cull the population in a "natural" manner, allowing the rest of the race to thrive in smaller numbers. Vampires were a favorite candidate predator—certainly canny and capable enough, if they could be made—but another Sheckleyan subsect held out for *werewolves,* a less snooty, less aristocratically conceited sort of monster. Either way, romance and adventure would return, and mankind, too, would at last be "regulated." Jen sent the Sheckleyans an anonymous donation every year. After all, you never could tell.

These were just some of the suggestions, both serious and whimsical. But Jen realized the young man deserved more than stock answers. She put his letter on the high-priority heap—the pile of items she would go over carefully later, in the hours before bed.

One letter to go then. The last one had arrived on auto-accept, so the sender knew her private code. Jen scanned with rising irritation.

Someone seemed to be advertising vacation homes on the Sea of Okhotsk!

That's all I need.

But then she suddenly remembered. *Vacation homes . . .*

It was a mnemonic cue. "Sri Ramanujan," she said aloud. "I think this message may be in cipher. Please see if we own a key to break it."

The face of the young Hindustani appeared briefly.

"Yes, Jen Wolling. It uses a private code given you years ago by the Pacific Society of Hine-marama. I'll have it translated in a minute."

Ah, Jen thought. This had to be from the New Zealand priestess, Meriana Kapur. It was ages since she'd seen the Maori woman, whose cult took the Gaia concept rather literally. But then, so had Jen during one phase.

"Here it is, Professor."

Ramanujan vanished again, leaving a totally transformed message in his place.

A totally *innocuous* message, as well. What she read now consisted of a rambling series of disconnected reminiscences . . . some the two women had experienced together, long ago, and some clearly made up. Jen noticed that none of the sentences were even highlighted. Her semantic-content program couldn't find a single explicit statement to set in bold!

But then, gradually, she smiled. *Of course. This isn't senility, it's diamond blade sharpness! There are ciphers within ciphers. Codes within codes.*

Apparently, Auntie Kapur wanted to be sure only Jen understood this message. Certainly no busybody hacker's automatic snooping program would sort meaning out of this, not without the shared context of two women who had lived a very long time.

Vagueness can be an art in itself.

Jen's smile faded when it began dawning on her how seriously the Maori priestess took this. The precautions began to make sense as glimmerings of meaning penetrated.

". . . I'm afraid Mama's unexpected ulcer has only one possible cure. Repairing the hole requires drastic measures . . . but the regular doctors would only interfere if they knew. (We think they originally caused the problem.) . . ."

There were more passages like that. Hints and allusions. Was Meriana saying the world itself was in danger? A danger worse than the big power nuclear standoff of long ago?

A passing reference was missed until her third reading. Then Jen realized Kapur was referring to her grandson.

Alex? But what could he be involved in that could pose such a threat to . . .

Jen gasped. *Oh, that bloody boy. This time he must really have done it!*

Nobody with any sense kept confidential notes on a computer. So from a desk drawer she took out an expensive pad of real paper and a pencil. Carefully this time, Jen went through her friend's letter line by line, jotting references and probable meanings. It wasn't any form of code-breaking a machine could perform, more like the ancient Freudian art of analyzing free associations, a sleuthing through the subjective world of impressions and wild guesses. A very human sort of puzzle, thousands of years older than the discrete patternings of cybernetics.

Exactly what is it they want of me? Jen wondered what she, an old woman, could do to help Auntie and Alex in a situation as dire as this. Finally, though, it became clear. *Africa. Ndebele Canton . . . Meriana heard of my visit there. She thinks I can help get them in. Secretly.*

Jen sat back, amazed. *Secretly? These days?*

The idea was absurd.

She chewed her lip.

Well . . . it would be a challenge, at least.

By Pauling and Orgell . . . I'll bet I can do it.

One thing for certain, Auntie's letter demanded an immediate response. No waiting till Friday for this one.

And that lad in Kuwenezi—Nelson Grayson. It looked as if the young man with the pet baboons might be getting his answers in person after all.

□ **Net Vol. A8230-761, 04.01.38: 11:24:12 UT; User M12-44-6557-Bac990 STATISTICAL REQUEST [Level: generic/colloquial]**

Earth Land Surface Area (In millions of square kilometers)

	1988	2038
Total	149	142
In desert, mountain, tundra	101	111
In arable land	40	29
In cultivated land	13	11
In fish farms	0.002	0.12

Census Counts (in billions of individuals)

	1988	2038
Human beings	5.2	10.6
Domestic cattle	1.2	0.2
Domestic sheep	1.0	0.5
Domestic hogs	0.5	0.5
Domestic dogs and cats	0.4	0.02

● On a different continent, but only milliseconds away by light-cable, another woman also sailed the data sea. Only while Jen Wolling carefully navigated a dinghy, Daisy McClennon sailed a privateer's sloop, in search of prey.

On her work wall, a science fiction space epic stepped frame by frame through a flashy battle sequence—her video processor inserting new special effects, making already grand starships even more magnificent. Matted stars and planets grew three dimensional, and explosions more titanic than ever. With such magic Daisy breathed new life into old classics, though for a diminishing, specialized audience.

Again, however, Daisy's attention swerved from her cash crop of embellished movies to other scenes and truer obsessions. The news services told of recent raids by Bedouin rebels, attacking the International Petroleum Reservation. She checked the reports' accuracy by other means and discovered that U.N. peacekeepers were understating the amount of oil spilled from pipelines severed by the nationalists, but not by enough to cause a scandal, unfortunately. Daisy had learned from hard experience never to cry "coverup!" unless the payoff was worthwhile.

Now *here* was a likely target. Blue symbols off Luzon showed one of the floating barge-towns of the Sea State, heading northward toward Japan. UNEPA was supposed to make sure the nation of refugees obeyed its rules. But sure enough, only two inspector boats showed in the vicinity. Nowhere near enough.

I wonder what Sea State is up to, she asked herself.

Keying an oceanographic database, Daisy noted that a large migration of spinner porpoises would intersect the path of the flotilla in a few weeks' time. UNEPA had recently downgraded spinners from "threatened" to "watch" status, which meant those with proven need were allowed to harvest limited numbers. Sea State could always establish proven need.

"Gotcha!" Daisy said, and sent a coded alert to an activist group in Nagasaki. When that Sea State flotilla reached its destination, there'd be a party waiting to pounce on the slightest infraction.

What next?

For a while she thought she had managed to trace a twisty money trail, proving that an official in Queensland had gor-sucked to local hotel interests. But the carni-man was smarter than usual. Computer taps on his accounts failed to report any unusual purchases in real estate or minerals futures.

For this case, her background as a McClennon helped. Before becoming a family black sheep, she had witnessed many of the ways her cousins and uncles sheltered and moved money without letting it show up on the net. So she called in a few favors from fellow radicals in Australia, who could arrange to snoop the Queensland official in person. Sooner or later, she was going to get the guy.

A timer beeped. She was supposed to get up and do some chores around the compound, or else Claire would raise a fit. This work in the Net was important for world survival, but her daughter didn't seem to care about that . . . probably wished she lived more like her spoiled cousins.

Well, there's no getting out of it, I suppose, Daisy sighed. It probably was past time she took a turn of her own at the cess pit. Or was it greenhouse maintenance Claire had been after her about?

But as she rose, Daisy caught a sudden change in one of her alert boxes, highlighting a name from her special watch list. For years she had maintained a tiny lamprey program attached to the home unit of the infamous Jennifer Wolling. All that time, her little spy had sampled and assessed what the apostate biologist was up to. Now, from London, it reported Wolling's ciphered message.

"Hmm," Daisy pondered, sitting down again. "The witch hardly ever tries to hide anything. What's she up to now?"

With trivial ease, Daisy traced the memorandum to its source. Of course. The Pacific Gaians were just the sort to conspire with Wolling. Compromisers, they worshipped an anemic goddess who seemed willing to settle for a world only *half* destroyed by man, with most of its species preserved in glass bottles, relying on technological "solutions" thrown together by bright idiots like Logan Eng. . . .

The cipher code was a good one. It took an hour to crack it. And when Daisy finally read the decrypted letter, she found a second layer filled with personal references and context-laden hints—the hardest kind of puzzle for an outsider to untangle.

That only made it more tempting, of course. Daisy knew about some new language programs, almost intelligent in their own right, that might apply here. And there were human consultants who owed her favors, too. Some of them might pick up connections she missed.

If all else failed, she also had certain contacts among *enemy* groups, as well . . . big corporations and government agencies with fantastic resources at their command. Among those, too, were also men and women indebted to her for past services. Daisy had dealt with devils before, when it suited her purposes. Sometimes honest rapists were preferable to mealy-mouthed compromisers.

She transferred the partially deciphered letter into her "possible clues" file, along with other anomalies like her ex-husband's paper on the mysterious Spanish quakes.

Ignored to her left, small screens monitored all twenty hectares of Six Oaks, the realm she and Logan had built here on the bayou, where she practiced self-reliance and "zero impact" far more faithfully than the pallid versions preached by the NorAChuGas. Not just "good faith efforts," but *independence* from the mines and factories and polluting power plants of industrial society . . . and from her own damned, smug, aristocratic family.

One of those displays showed her daughter standing on a stepladder next to the greenhouse, her hair tied back in a kerchief and arms covered with putty as she scraped the labels off newly bought sheets of glass and fitted them one by one to replace those cracked in a recent storm.

But Daisy did not see, nor did she recall her promise. Drawn once more to the holo screens, her blue eyes roved the electronic sea, the data ocean, seeking the blood foes of her world. Practicing the art of vendetta. Pursuing prey.

☐ No animal is as likeable as an individual, and yet so loathsome in large groups. Voracious, implacable, using up everything in sight, this creature has been a bane to the Earth. Within a few millennia it has stripped vast portions of the planet, turning them into barren desert.

The animal isn't Man, though humankind helped it multiply in vast numbers. It is the *goat*. A boon to smalltime nomads, the goat is an immeasurable calamity to the planet's biosphere. Even today, it shares as much blame for the advancing sands as global warming or ill-planned irrigation.

That is why we, the Preservation Alliance of North Africa, have reluctantly taken action to sacrifice one species for the good of all. It is why we come onto the Net today, via this untraceable routing, to announce what we have done.

Some say the preferred target of a winnowing should be humanity itself, which has perpetrated even worse harm. That may be so, but we admit to squeamishness about murdering the billions of people it would take to make a difference.

Besides, the Helvetian War proved *Homo sapiens* to be biologically adept, highly resistant to engineered diseases. The major powers' biocrisis teams would make matters moot within a few weeks anyway. Only a few million would die before cures were found, resulting in no long-term ecological change, just our own pursuit as criminals.

None of these drawbacks apply to our other target species, however.

We are certain the world will retrain the remaining pastoral shepherds once their destructive herds are eliminated. And we emphasize that our virus has been carefully tested. The disease is quite specific to goats. It should have no other effect than to correct a horrible mistake of man and nature.

One purpose of this announcement is to appeal to workers in biolabs. Think carefully when you're asked to seek a cure. By your minor sabotage you may save a forest or a million hectares of Sahel! *Drop* that test tube into an autoclave, and you may save a hundred species otherwise doomed to perish before this rapacious menace! Remember, civil disobedience is your right under the Charter of Rio.

Another purpose is, of course, to seek public discussion. Criticism and data on the effects of our peremptory measure may be sent to the general and open display board [□ OpDBaq1.779.-66-8258-BaB 689.] We will read your comments regularly, and we welcome your suggestions.

Sincerely,

The Preservation Alliance of North Africa

● This time of year, Davis Strait thronged with traffic. Great freight-
M ers plowed the choppy waters, following strobing marker buoys all
E the way to Lancaster Sound and the shortcut to Asia. Solar arrays
S and rigid wing-sails lent the sleek vessels a family resemblance to
O the clipper ships of yore, on which men once upon a time had
S risked their lives seeking this selfsame Northwest Passage. Now
P and then, the shadows of dirigibles, like passing clouds, darkened
H the sea nearby. The zeppelin crews, bound for Europe or Canada,
E leaned out to wave at the high-tech sailors below.
R   It was a far cry from when Roald Amundsen had come this
E way, to spend three hard years battling toward Alaska. Today the
voyage took two weeks, and all looked peaceful here in the realm of
the midnight sun.

Of course, Stan Goldman knew, *appearances can be deceiving.*

From this height he could make out a place along Greenland's western verge where a vast, growling glacier met the open sea. Beacons detoured commerce round a chain of lumbering behemoths wrapped in reflective foil. The insulated bergs resembled great, silvery, alien mother ships, as mammoth engines pushed them south toward thirsty lands.

Eventually, the giant island would run out of white treasure, unbelievable as it might seem up here, where a snowy plateau still spanned one entire horizon. In fact, it had already retreated a long way, leaving stark, sheer fjords cut into a serrated coast. Lichens and mosses spread like velvet across new plains and valleys, just below this hired zeppelin. After close to a million years, spring had come at last to Greenland.

And yet, there is a cost. There's always a cost.

Stan had just finished reading dire news about these northern seas. Species counts were down again. No one had seen a bowhead whale in years. And migratory birds, the litmus of ecological health, were laying fewer eggs.

Many blamed the old nemesis, pollution. Down below, UNEPA and Kingdom of Denmark launches sniffed among the great freighters . . . as if any captain would dare drop even a paper cup into this heavily policed waterway. Actually though, climatic changes, rather than dumping, might be at fault. Temperate-zone creatures could flee the spreading deserts by moving north. But where could polar bears go when their dens turned to slush?

Of course, palm trees wouldn't be growing up here any time soon. A man immersed in those bright waters would still be unconscious in minutes and dead from hypothermia inside an hour. And six months from now, the sun would vanish for another winter.

There are limits, Stan reassured himself. *Mankind may be able to mess with the climate, but we can't change the seasons or shift Earth's axial tilt.*

Almost at once, however, he reconsidered. *Is even that beyond our reach now?* He pondered some implications of Alex Lustig's equations and found himself weighing notions unimaginable only weeks ago. *I wonder if it might be possible to . . .*

Stan shook his head firmly. Such meddling had already brought about nothing but calamity.

"Kalâtdlit-Nunât."

Stan turned to his traveling companion. "I beg your pardon?"

Teresa Tikhana lifted a small reading plaque. "Kalâtdlit-Nunât. It's what the Inuit people—the Eskimos—call Greenland."

"The Inuit? I thought their second language was Danish."

Teresa shrugged. "Who says two languages are enough? How does the saying go? 'A man with only one ethnicity stands on just one leg.' . . . Come on, Stan. How many languages do *you* speak?"

He shrugged. "You mean besides International English and Physics? . . . And the Maori and Simglish and Han they taught us in school?" He paused. "Well, I can get along in General Nihon and French, but . . ."

He laughed, seeing her point. "All right. Let's hear it again."

Teresa coached him till he could pronounce a few indigenous politenesses. Not that there'd be much time for idle chitchat where they were going—a rough outpost in the middle of a wasteland. He'd always wanted to see this tremendous frozen island, but this mission wasn't for tourism.

Stan glanced across the aisle. The other members of their expedition had gathered near a forward window, whispering and pointing as the cargo ships and vacuum-packed icebergs fell behind. Stan listened now and then, to make sure the technicians kept their voices low and stayed away from taboo subjects.

"You're sure we can't use the old NATO base at Godhavn?" Teresa asked. "It's got every facility. And the science commune using it now is pretty free and open, I hear."

"They're mostly atmosphere researchers, right?" Stan asked.

"Yeah. First set up to monitor radioactive fallout from the Alps. Now they're part of the Ozone Restoration Project, such as it is."

"Reason enough to avoid the place, then. You'd surely be recognized."

The woman astronaut blinked. "Oh, yeah." Self-consciously Teresa brushed back strands of newly blonde hair, dyed just for this journey. "I—guess I'm just not used to this way of thinking, Stan."

In other words, she hadn't the advantage of growing up as he had, during the paranoid twentieth, when people routinely maintained poses for the sake of anything from ideology to profit to love—sometimes for whole lifetimes.

"Try to remember," he urged, dropping his voice. "We're breaking Danish territorial law, bringing you in under a false passport. You're supposed to be on vacation in Australia, right? Not halfway around the world, smuggling undocumented gear into . . . Kalâtdlit-Nunât."

She tried to look serious, but couldn't suppress a smile. "All right, Stan. I'll remember."

He sighed. If their conspiracy hadn't been critically shorthanded, he'd never have agreed to bringing Teresa along. Her competence, charm and fascinating mind would be welcome of course. But the risk was awfully great.

"Come on," she said, nudging his elbow. "Now you're starting to look like Alex Lustig."

Nervously, he laughed. "That bad?"

She nodded. "I thought we 'nauts were a sober-pussed bunch. But Lustig makes Glenn Spivey look like a yuk artist. Even when he smiles, I feel like I'm attending a wake."

Maybe, Stan thought. *But how would you look if you had that poor boy's burdens on your back?*

Stan withheld comment though. He knew Teresa, too, was suffering from a coping reaction. Her way of dealing with this awful crisis was to go into denial. Certainly she'd never let it interfere with her work, but Stan imagined she simply let the reason for their desperate venture slip her mind, any chance she got.

"It's poor Alex's upbringing at fault," Stan answered in his best Old Boy accent. "English public schools do that to a lad, don't'cha know."

Teresa laughed, and Stan was glad to hear the pure, untroubled sound. *She has enough reason for denial.* Of all the members of their cabal, she had been the first struck personally by the lashing tail of the *taniwha*—the monster in the Earth's core.

More of them would share that honor before long. Stan thought of Ellen and the grandkids and his daughter back in England. Faces of students and friends kept popping up at odd moments, especially during sleep. Sometimes it felt like going through a photo album of treasures already lost.

Stop. It's useless to maunder this way.

He sought distraction outside. The Northwest Passage lay behind them, now. To the left, fleets of smaller boats could be seen threading craggy offshore islets, bound for a bustling seaport just ahead.

"Godhavn," Teresa said, reading her guidebook again. She gestured at the piers and factories lining the bay. "And what does the Net say is this city's principal industry?" She inhaled deeply through her nose. "I'll give you three guesses."

Stan didn't have to sniff the cannery aroma. Those trawlers were returning from the rich banks offshore—where arctic upwellings nourished clouds of silvery fish. So far UNEPA safeguards had managed to save that vital resource for mankind's ravenous billions, so all wasn't lost up here. Not yet at least.

The canneries had created a boomtown, and no lack of eager immigrants seeking their fortunes on a new frontier. Others came simply for elbow room, to escape the close press of neighbors back home.

It probably wasn't all that different a thousand years ago, Stan figured. *Back then, too, men chased wealth and breathing space. And Red Erik knew just how to lure them to this faraway shore. Even its name—Greenland—was an early, inspired example of sneaky advertising.*

Viking settlements had sprouted along the rocky coast. And the Scandinavians were lucky at first, arriving during a warm spell brought on by sunspots and Earth's subtly variable orbit.

But what astronomy gave, astronomy could take away. By the fifteenth century, cycles had turned again. The "little ice age"—a time of scanty summers and scarcer sunspots—froze the rivers Seine and Thames at Christmastime, and icebergs were seen off Spain. Ironically, Irish sailors reported news from the struggling Greenland colony only decades before another dawning—when Christopher Columbus and John Cabot drew the world's attention back to strange lands rimming the ocean sea. But by the time voyagers next set foot on the great island, all sign of living Europeans had vanished.

Stan found it hard to imagine history repeating itself here. The wharves and factories all shared a thick-walled look of determined permanence, as if defying nature to do her worst.

And yet, Stan pondered. *Other eras had their certainties, and look at them now.*

Soon the cannery town fell away as their pilot steered up one of the broad valleys, carved over ages by endless tons of ancient, compressed snow. Now the vales below flowed with newborn streams. Reindeer clattered over algae-stained rocks, spooked by the airship's shadow into skittish flight.

Up ahead lay the grand glacier itself. Here, and in Antarctica, the ice ranges grew three kilometers thick, storing half the fresh water on Earth. Only the fringes of that stockpile had melted so far, but when it thawed in earnest, the world's coastlines would really start to rise.

The removal of so much weighty ice couldn't help but affect the crust underneath. Rebound-reverberations were already being felt far away. In Iceland, two fierce new volcanoes sputtered. There would be more as time went on.

Especially if we don't solve the problem of gazer beams coupling with surface matter, Stan thought. It still puzzled him that resonant gravity waves sometimes set off tremors in the outer crust. He hoped there'd be an answer soon, or just trying to get rid of the *taniwha* might cause massive harm.

Two days to get set up . . . another three to grow our thumper and test Manella's data-links to the other stations . . . got to figure ways to work in tandem with Alex's group—and George's and Kenda's . . .

He'd gone over it all so many times, and still it seemed a wild-eyed plan—trying to shove a superheavy, microscopic bit of folded space into a higher orbit by poking at it repeatedly with invisible rays . . . yep, it sounded pretty farfetched, all right.

Stan caught a metallic glint up ahead, just short of the fast-approaching ice sheet. That must be their goal, where the glacier's retreat had recently revealed clues to an enigma. Where some believed an awful killing had taken place a long time ago.

They say every spot on Earth has a story, a library *of stories to tell, If that is so, then this island specializes in mysteries.*

With rising impatience Stan watched Greenland's second coast, its inner shore, where a new, encroaching fringe of land lapped against a continent of ancient whiteness.

The tiny scientific outpost perched beside an icy rivulet, near enough towering cliffs to wear their shadow each long arctic morning. A greeting party waited by the mooring towers as automatic snaring devices seized the zep and gently drew it down.

Every other dirigible landing in Teresa's experience had been at commercial aerodromes, so she found this rough-and-ready process fascinating, and oddly similar to the no-frills approach used in space.

The pilot certainly would have let her sit in the cockpit, if only she identified herself. But of course that wasn't possible. So she made do instead by leaning out the window like a gawking tourist, bursting with questions she wasn't allowed to ask and suggestions she dared not offer. After the gondola settled with a bump and scrape, Teresa was the last to get off, lingering by the control cabin listening to the crew go through their shutdown checklist.

The Tangoparu techs had already begun offloading their supplies when she finally debarked. Teresa started over to lend a hand, but Stan Goldman called her to meet some people wearing knit caps and Pendleton shirts. It was hard to pay attention to introductions, though. She felt distracted by the ice plateau, towering so near it set her senses quivering.

Then there was the *smell*—cool, invigorating, and inexplicably drawing. She helped her colleagues haul the gear and inflate their solitary dome. But all the while Teresa kept glancing toward the glacier, feeling its presence. At last, when all the heavy labor was done, she could bear it no longer. "Stan, I've got to go to the ice."

He nodded. "I understand. We'll erect the toilet next. I'm sorry . . ."

Teresa laughed. "No, I mean really. I'll be back in a couple of hours. It's just something I have to do."

The elderly physicist blinked twice and then smiled. "Of course. You worked hard studying gravitonics all the way out here. Go ahead. We'll just be setting up the vats anyway. You won't be needed until tomorrow morning."

She touched his sleeve. "Thanks, Stan." Then, impulsively, Teresa leaned over and kissed his grizzled cheek.

The Tangoparu team had set up some distance from the rest of the settlement, so she shunned the main path and set off cross-country, over the gravelly moraine. Having never approached a primary glacier before, she had no way of judging distances. There were no trees or familiar objects for comparison; by eye alone, it might be anywhere from one to ten kilometers away. But her inner sensoria told Teresa she could make it there and back before supper. Anyway, nothing out here could harm her even if she miscalculated. In her thermal suit she could even wait out the brief summer night if she had to.

No, this wasn't a dangerous place—certainly not compared to space.

Nevertheless, her heart leaped in her chest when a shadow swept the pebbly surface, looming from behind her with startling speed. Teresa felt its sudden presence and whirled in a crouch, squinting at a blurry form like a huge ball cupped in an open fist.

She sighed, straightening and trying to pretend the abrupt appearance hadn't scared the wits out of her. Even against the afternoon sun, she recognized one of those Magnus effect minicranes, used all over the world for utility lifting and hauling. They were to helicopters what a zep was to a stratojet. In other words, cheap, durable, and easy to run on minimal fuel. Like zeps, minicranes maintained buoyancy with inflated hydrogen. But this smaller machine moved by rotating the bag itself between vertical prongs. A queer, counterintuitive effect of physics let it maneuver agilely.

Shading her eyes, Teresa watched the operator lean out of his tiny cabin. He shouted something in Danish. She called back. *"Jeg tale ikke dansk! Vil De tale engelsk?"*

"Ah," he answered quickly. "Sorry! You must be one of Stanley Goldman's people. I'm on my way to the dig now and could use some ballast. Do you want a ride?"

Actually, she didn't. But Teresa found it hard to say no. After all, it would be selfish to stay away from camp any longer than she had to.

"How do I board?"

As the machine drew close, the whir of the spinning bag was no longer swept away by the wind. The small control assembly hung suspended beneath by two forks from the central axis, and its engine gave off a hissing whine. In answer to her question, the pilot simply leaned down and offered his hand.

Well, she who hesitates is lost . . .

Teresa ran to meet the little airship. At the last moment, she leaped, his grip seized her wrist and she was hauled, gently but swiftly, inside.

"Lars Stürup," he said as the bouncing settled down. There was a hiss of released gas and they began rising.

"I'm Ter . . ."

She stopped and covered her gaffe by coughing, as if from exertion. ". . . terribly glad to meet you, Lars. I'm . . . Emma Neale." It was the name on her borrowed passport, lent by a Tangoparu scientist whose skills were less needed here than Teresa's.

Blond and fair, Lars looked more Swedish than Danish. He wore his sleeves rolled up, displaying well-developed forearms. "Pleased to meet you, Emma, I'm sure. We don't get many new people up here. What's your line? Paleontology? Paleogeochemistry?"

"None of the above. I'm just here to help Stan do some seismic scans."

"Ah." Lars nodded. "Those will be useful. Or so Dr. Rasmussen says. She hopes they'll help us find remnants of the meteorite."

Looking across the crushed moraine, Teresa thought that rather optimistic. "How can anything be left, after what this land has been through since then?"

The pilot grinned. "The thing hit pretty dumpit hard. Buried lots of stuff good. Of course the ice scraped off hundreds of meters. But by using radar from space you can find plenty of buried features that are invisible up close."

Tell me about it. Teresa had assisted in many such orbital surveys, using microwaves to trace lost tombs in Egypt, Mayan ruins in Mexico, and the tracks of ancient watercourses that had last flowed back when the Sahara bloomed and prehistoric humans hunted hippos in the lush fens of Libya.

She was tempted to demonstrate her own knowledge, but then, what would Emma Neale know of such things? "That's very interesting," she said. "Please go on."

"Ah! Where to begin? To start off, it's on Greenland we find some of the oldest rocks ever discovered—formed less than half a billion years after the planet itself!"

Lars gestured broadly as he spoke, frequently taking his hands from the controls to point out features of the terrain below. Teresa found his cavalier piloting both disturbing and somehow exciting. Of course, one could take liberties with a slow, forgiving vehicle like this. Still, the young man's proud confidence permeated the tiny cabin. A streak of oil stained the calloused edge of his right hand, where in hurried washing he mightn't notice it among the curling hairs. He probably did all his own maintenance, something Teresa envied since guild rules only let astronauts watch and kibitz when their craft were serviced.

". . . so underneath we find remnants of a huge crater. One of several that asteroids made when they struck the Earth about sixty-five million years ago . . ."

He kept glancing sideways at her, pointing here and there across the tumbled terrain. Teresa suddenly realized, *He's preening for me!* Naturally, she was used to men trying to impress her. But this time, her reaction came out more pleased than irritated. It was a dormant, unaccustomed feeling that made her suddenly nervous and oddly exhilarated. *I should consider remaining a blonde,* she thought idly.

The glacier loomed now—a chill mass that set her internal compass quivering. She could sense it stretching on and on toward the deep heart of this minicontinent, where it lay in layers so dense the rocky crust sagged beneath it. Layers that had been put down, snowflake by snowflake, over inconceivable time.

Now coming into view below the white cliff was the site where machines could be seen biting into the frozen ground, scientifically sifting a deep excavation for ancient clues. Still talking and pointing things out like a tour guide, Lars steered his craft toward the activity.

"Um . . . could I ask a favor?" Teresa interrupted the young pilot's monologue.

"Of course. What may I do for you?"

Teresa pointed nearby. "Could you drop me off there? Near the ice?

Lars clearly wasn't one to let schedules interfere with gallantry. "Anything you wish, Emma." With a sure hand on the controls he turned his machine into the wind spilling off the glacier, increasing spin and plowing through the stiff, cold current. As the buffeting grew, Teresa began regretting her request. After all, she could have walked. It would be silly to survive so many orbital missions only to meet her end in a wrecked utility craft, just because a young man wanted to impress her.

"Lars . . . ," she began, then stopped herself, recalling how bravely and silently Jason had used to watch whenever she let him sit behind her pilot's seat during a launch.

Jason . . . A flux of images and feelings rose like steamy bubbles. Diverting them, Teresa inexplicably found herself instead picturing Alex Lustig! And especially the gray worry forever coloring that strange man's eyes. Almost, she let herself recall the terrible thing he hunted.

"Get ready to jump!" Lars shouted over wind as he jockeyed the minicrane toward a sandy bank. Teresa slid the door open and watched the ground rise. Glancing back, she caught a look of shared adventure from the young Greenlander. "Thanks!" she said, and leaped. Recoil sent the lifter soaring as she braced for a hard landing.

The impact knocked the breath out of her, but it wasn't as bad as some training exercises. She rolled to her feet only slightly bruised and waved to show all was well. The pilot banked his craft nimbly and gave her thumbs up. He called, but all she could make out was, ". . . see you soon, maybe!" Then he was gone, blown downwind by the icy freshet.

Shivering suddenly, Teresa closed her collar zip and stepped into that breeze. Soon she was scrambling over rocky debris that must have been freshly exposed only this very spring.

Ice. So much ice, she thought.

Ice like this was a spacer's dream—to make water for life-support or fuels for transport. There were a thousand ways spaceflight could be made cheaper and safer and better, if only enough ice were available out there. Earth had her oceans. There was water in the Martian permafrost, in comets, and in the moons of Jupiter. But all those sources were too far away, or too deep inside a gravity well, to offer hope to a parched space program.

If only orbital surveys had found deposits at the moon's poles, as if wishing ever made things so.

But this . . . this continent of ice.

She reached out to touch the glacier's flank. Under a rough crust, Teresa found a thin layer much softer than expected. Deep within, though, she knew it had to be almost diamond hard.

At the very point where the ice stopped, she bent and picked up a polished pebble.

Among the oldest rocks known, he said. And I'm probably the first to touch this one. The first sentient being to stand at this particular spot.

That was why she had been drawn here, she now realized. *There are no unclimbed mountains left on Earth . . . and no plans to let anyone scale the peaks of Aristarchus or the shield volcanoes of Tharsus.*

Jungles crash to make way for houses. The world sweats in every pore the breath and touch of humanity. There's not a single place left where you can go and say to a new part of the universe—"Hello, we've never met. Let me introduce myself. I am Man."

A new thought occurred to her.

If I were this planet, I guess I'd be feeling pretty damn sick of us by now.

Teresa inhaled the bracing air flowing off the ice. In evaporating, it gave off odors trapped inside crystal lattices ages ago—back when there were no living beings around with minds or speech . . . nor any concept that it can be worth half a lifetime just to reach such a place . . . to stand where no one ever has before.

She closed her eyes. And while her intellect wouldn't let her realize her deepest fear, that all this might soon be gone forever, nevertheless she stood there for a time and worshipped the only way a person like her could worship—in silence and solitude, under the temple of the sky.

☐ **Net Commercial Data Comparison request**
Uit 152383568.2763: Price contrasts in standard
1980 international dollars.

Skilled Services (typical in each category)	Average 2038 Price	Annual Trend
Cosmetic surgery (complete face-lift)	$202.00	−1.0%
Custom-designed ferret program	$113.00	−2.0%
Full genetic susceptibilities workup	$176.00	−2.5%
One-hour lawyer consultation	$ 21.00	−3.5%
One-hour home visit, microtoxin surveyor	$ 76.00	+1.0%

Standard Material Products	Average 2038 Price	Annual Trend
One liter gasoline	$ 93.00	+2.5%
One ream bleached bond paper	$ 52.00	+5.5%
D-cell nonrechargeable battery	$ 47.00	+4.0%
One pair true-vu sensu-record goggles, with net access	$ 8.50	−2.0%

Commentary: The effects of rising education continue devastating prices of once prestigious services, while resource exhaustion keeps pushing up the cost of material goods, except photonics and electronics, which have escaped upward spirals because of competitive innovation. One ironic consequence is that profit margins in those fields are narrow, and the industries now flourish principally due to the sustained inventiveness of amateurs.

MANTLE

● The *pakeha* had a saying . . . "It's only a little white lie."

George Hutton enjoyed collecting inanities like that. To whites, there seemed to be as many shades of untruth as Eskimos had words for snow. Some lies were evil, of course. But then there were "half-truths" and "metaphors" and the sort your parents told you, "for your own good."

As he crawled through a narrow, twisty stone passageway, George remembered one fine, lazy evening at the Quark and Swan, bearding poor Stan Goldman about such western hypocrisies. Because it would gall his friend, who loved novels, George particularly disparaged that mendacity called "fiction," in which one person, a "reader," actually pays an "author" to *lie* about events that never happened to people who never even existed.

"So all your Maori fairy tales are true?" Stan had asked in hot response.

"In their own way, yes. We non-western peoples never made this artificial distinction between real and imagined . . . between 'objective' and 'subjective.' We don't have to suspend disbelief in order to hear and accept our legends . . ."

"Or to adopt six impossible worldviews before breakfast! That's how you Maori get away with claiming your ancestors never lied. How can anyone lie when they're able to believe two contradictory things at the same time?"

"Are you accusing me of inconsistency, white fellow?"

"You? A man with fifty technical patents in geophysics, who still makes sacrifices to Pele? Never!"

Inevitably, the argument ended with them shouting, noses half a meter apart . . . then breaking up in waves of laughter until someone recovered enough to order the next round.

All right, George admitted to himself as he felt for a narrow ledge along the polished stone of an underground streamway. *It's easy to be sanctimonious about the lies of others. But it's quite another thing when you find yourself trapped, having to deceive or face losing all you love.*

Pulling back from the rock face, he sent his helmet beam ahead and saw that the worst was over. A few more teetering steps and he'd be able to jump to something vaguely like a walking path, with enough headroom to stand instead of hunching like a gnome in a maze.

He took the traverse quickly and landed agilely, hands spread wide for balance. Adjusting the lamp, George peered up a narrow, scending tube of water-smoothed limestone to where a sharp wedge divided the twisting channel. One passage scattered his beam among tapered, glittering columns, where mineral-rich seeps had formed arches reminiscent of the Caliph's Palace in Córdoba. He hadn't noticed that gallery on his outward journey. Now he paused to sketch the opening in his pocket plaque.

The accepted thing to do would be to publish the map, of course. There would be money, prestige. But the Net wasn't ever getting this datum, he had vowed.

How do you justify a lie? George asked himself as he carefully retraced his steps, heading back the way he'd come.

A decade ago, on first discovering these immense caverns beneath the mountains of New Guinea, he had chosen to refrain from telling his clients about them. Was that theft, to keep this marvel for himself? Perhaps. Worse than theft though, was the lie itself.

To believe six impossible or contradictory things before breakfast . . . Yes, Stan. And one impossible thing I believed was that I could save this place.

He had to squeeze headfirst through the next opening, sliding down a chute into a sparkling, miniature chapel. Knobby calcite growths covered not only the walls but the floor as well, catching the lamplight in dazzling crystalline reflections. "Cave coral," it was called . . . a common enough phenomenon till humans invented spelunking, penetrating the depths to seek Earth's hidden treasures. Now the coral was gone from nearly every known cave on Earth, scavenged bit by bit by souvenir hunters—each rationalizing that just one more fragment wouldn't be missed.

Passing again through the minute cathedral, George sought the exact footprints he had made on the trip out—tiny breaks and smudges among the glassy shards. These he tried to step in, but there was no way to avoid adding some slight, incremental harm this time, as well.

"The world is made of compromises," he seemed to hear Stan Goldman say, though his friend was far away at the moment, doing his own part amid the icy wastes of Greenland. "You must make trade-offs, George, and live with the consequences."

"A *pakeha* way of looking at things . . . ," George muttered half aloud as he exited the coral suite, wriggling sideways through a narrow crack into another streamway. Whispering echoes skittered around him like tiny creatures. Among the soft reverberations he imagined Stan's reply.

"Hypocrisy, Hutton! Who do you think you're talking to, some California tourist? Using *'pakeha'* science made you a bloody billionaire! It gave you power to do good in the world. So use it!"

One of life's joys was to have friends who gave you reality checks . . . who would call you on your crap before it rose so high you drowned in it. Stan Goldman was such a friend. Together, in Wellington, their wives still had each other for company. But now George, alas, would have to make do imagining what Stan might say.

As he panted, squeezing his massive bulk through a cramped stricture between sodastraw draperies, the echoes of his breathing came back to him as a voice that wasn't there.

"Dump the sanctimony about wishing you were really a noble savage, Hutton . . . Admit you're as Western as I am."

"Never!" George grunted as he popped free, into the final stretch of open passageway. Gasping, with hands on his knees, he seemed to hear his friend's voice converging like a conscience from every wall.

"What, never . . . ?"

George stood up straight at last, and grinned.

"Well . . . hardly ever." The ringing in his ears sounded musically like laughter until it faded away. Setting out again, he thought, *There are no non-Western peoples anymore.*

Indeed, there wasn't a Maori alive whose blood didn't flow with multicolored blends of English, Scots, Samoan, and scores of other flavors. Nor had any living Maori grown up without color video or the omnipresent, all-pervading influence of the Net.

Still, I am more than just another homogenized gray man of bland gray times! And if I'm forced by circumstances to lie, then at least I can look on my lies as a Maori should, as appalling things!

And to that, at last, Stan Goldman's surrogate voice remained silent. His friend, George knew, would not disagree.

Turning a bend in the passage, he stopped and turned off his lamp. At first the sudden blackness was so utter, his hand was lost in front of his face. At last, however, he made out an incredibly faint glimmer, reflecting off a rupicoline wall ahead. That could only mean one thing, that he was nearly back to the site.

Dialed to its lowest level, the lamp still made him blink when it came back on. He set out again, first scrambling over a ledge and then ducking under a hanging rock drapery to emerge at last on a balcony overlooking the grotto where he and the others had come to battle demons.

Unlike their comfortable, furnished caverns back in New Zealand, only a few stark floodlights cast intimidating shadows across this great gallery. Sleeping bags lay strewn on piles of hay purchased from a Papuan farmer who plowed the hillsides overhead, not suspecting what vast counties lay beneath his hissing tractor. A portable recycling unit stood in one corner, taking in the team's wastes and returning a necessary if unpalatable fraction of their needs.

None of these discomforts mattered to George's veterans, of course. So it had to be the virgin nature of these secret caves that had everyone talking in whispers, softly, respectfully, as if to spare the place any more violation than necessary. George wasn't the only one to go off on solitary reverent explorations. During the brief rest periods their medic demanded between long stints of labor, most of the crew now and then took off just to get away for a little while.

There were other, larger caverns in this network—one even bigger than Good Luck Cave, in Sarawak, dwarfing forty sports stadia. But this one served their needs and so had been sacrificed for the project. Several meters of sediment had been cleared away, exposing hard rock where a large hemispherical basin had been dug.

Nearby lay the metal frame that would hold their new thumper, and beyond that stood the tank where the crystal cylinder itself was slowly growing, atom by atom, under the direction of a myriad of simple, tireless nanomachines. In two days the perfect lattice would be a finely tuned superconducting antenna, and their real work would begin.

George climbed down a series of gour pools over which small waterfalls had once cascaded. He'd been away only half an hour, yet his crew had already resumed work.

No need to play foreman here. It's amazing what a strong motivator it can be, when you have a slim chance to save the world.

A slight, dark-featured man looked up at George from inside the bowl-like excavation, standing on a wooden scaffold.

"So my friend, did you find your river?"

George's Papuan friend, Sepak Takraw, had enlisted to help their shorthanded team. Enlisted under false pretenses, for George had told him they were probing for deep methane—a recurring grail ever sought by countries that had once been rich in oil, but now grew used to paucity again and hated it. Sepak's vow of confidentiality was titanium clad, of course. Still, George couldn't justify letting any more people know the true nature of their mission. Perhaps later he'd get to tell Sepak. After they succeeded. Or when they knew for sure they'd failed.

"Ah." George lifted his shoulders. "The river is no more."

"Too bad." Sepak sighed. "Maybe the farmers took it away."

"It's a thirsty world." George nodded. "So. How does the foundation look?"

Sepak gestured into the bowl, where two of George's engineers were scrutinizing the smooth wall with instruments. "As you see, we're all but finished. Only bloody-damn Kiwi perfectionism keeps them at it. Since Helvetians went extinct, you lot are the worst nit-pickers around.''

George smiled at the mixed compliment. However much they bickered, both Maori and *pakeha* New Zealanders agreed that any job worth doing was worth doing well. Tangoparu Ltd. had built its reputation on that fetish for accuracy.

And all the more so this time. The parameters Alex Lustig gave us will be difficult enough to meet without human error.

''They finally tired of my impatience and chased me away. Such impertinence. Here, help me out of this pit, will you?''

George hoisted his small friend. Once on his feet, Sepak laid down his tool bag and took out a small flask. It was a mild local brew, but one notorious for playing hell with anyone not used to it. So naturally, he offered George a swig. George shook his head. He had taken a vow.

When next I drink, it will be to our world's salvation . . . or standing over the bloody ruin of the bastards who wrecked her.

''Suit yourself.'' Sepak knocked back a swallow and then slipped the flask into a pouch embroidered with beaded butterfly designs. He was a full-blooded member of the Gimi tribe, which took pride in a very special distinction. Of all nations, clans, and peoples on Earth, only among native Papuans were there still a few left alive who remembered when the planet had not been a single place.

This year was the centennial of the 1938 Australian expedition which discovered the Great Valley of central New Guinea, isolated until then from any contact with the outside world. The last ''unknown'' tribes of any size had been found there, living as they had for countless generations—tending crops, waging war, worshipping their gods, thinking their long notch between the mountains the sum totality of existence.

Until the Australians arrived, that is. From that moment, the Age of Stone was extinct. The universal Era of the Electron soon enveloped everyone—one world, one culture, one shared vocabulary. One shared Net.

Overhead, Sepak's great-great-uncle was among the celebrities being interviewed for global news channels—one of just a few who remembered when the tall white outsiders arrived. ''The last first contact,'' was how media referred to the event.

Or at least, Stan Goldman might insist optimistically, *the last first contact to occur on Earth.*

Sepak would talk about it at the least excuse. Clearly, he saw no distinction between Maori and *pakeha,* dismissing all non-Papuans as "whites," in the generic sense. In the odd, reverse pecking order of modern ethnicity-chic, there was no higher status than to have a great-grandfather who had once chipped his own tools from native stone. Who, in pure, primitive innocence used to reverently and with relish consume the flesh of his neighbors.

Sepak looked along one of the galleries, where polished stone ripples fell away toward shrouded mysteries. "So. No more river. Too bad. What good is a glorious cave without a stream to make it laugh and sing? What's become of the thing that carved this mighty place? Such a mundane end, to be sucked away to irrigation wells."

"There are signs the river flowed only a few decades ago." From his pocket, George unfolded a handkerchief. Sepak peered at a few glinting slivers. "What are they?"

"Fish bones."

The Papuan sighed. Whatever sightless species had once lived atop this tiny ecosphere's food chain, a few wan skeletons were its only legacy.

George knew that millions above ground would share his sense of loss if they were told. These days, it might even lead to calls for action. Although the uniqueness of this particular line was forever gone, perhaps some other species, locked away in some preserve or life ark, might prosper here if only the water returned. But George would keep his secret, only wondering what these parched channels might have been like when a chuckling, lightless miracle coursed their hidden beds.

Again, he thought he knew what Stan Goldman might say.

"Hey, all right. We make mistakes. But who told us, back when we started digging and mining and irrigating, that it would come to this? No one. We had to find out for ourselves, the hard way.

"So where were those damned UFOs and charioted gods and prophets when we really needed them? No one gave us a guidebook for managing a planet. We're writing it ourselves now, from hard experience."

Concealing a sad smile, George also knew how he'd reply.

I mourn the moa, whom my own ancestors drove into extinction. I mourn the herons and whales, slaughtered by the pakeha. *I mourn you too, little fishes.*

When all of this was done, he would fill glasses for his friends, and drink to each lost species. And then, if there was enough beer left in the world, he'd also toast those yet to die.

"Come on, Sepak," George said, folding away his handkerchief. "You can help me adjust the crane assembly. It has to be perfect when we lift the cylinder out of its bath."

"Precision, precision." Sepak sighed. Notwithstanding his engineering degree from the University of Port Moresby—and skin no darker than George's—he muttered, "You honkies put too much faith in your precious machines. They'll steal your souls, trust me. We Gimi know about this. Why just the other day my grandfather was telling me . . ."

Content to receive a healthy dose of his own medicine, George listened politely while they worked together—suffering in ironic role reversal the very same sort of guilt trip he'd inflicted on countless others since he first learned how.

Stan would just love this, George thought, and listened humbly while Sepak turned the tables on him, milking the everflowing teat of Western shame for all it was worth.

□

. . . And so She stopped first at the planet Venus to see if that might be the place. But when She sipped the atmosphere, She exclaimed, "Oh no! This is much too hot!"

Then She went to Mars, and once more cried out. "Here it's much too thin and cold!"

At last, however, She came to Earth, and when She tasted the sweet air She sang in delight. "Ah, now this one is just right!"

● It wasn't much, as sculptures go. Especially on an island renowned
C for its monuments. A small pyramid of stone, that was all—jutting
O from a sandy slope, where sparse grasses swayed to restless ocean
R breezes. A black-winged Chilean kestrel took off with a screeching
E cry as Alex climbed the low hill to get a better look at a three-sided nub of polished granite. At first sight, it was something of a disappointment.

Come on, Lustig. Get with the spirit. It's only the tip of something much, much bigger. Imagine it doesn't end just below ground, but keeps slanting down, down, ever downward . . .

He knew how those edges were aimed, probably far better than the original artist who had put the sculpture here, seven decades ago.

Imagine the Earth surrounds a solid pyramid, with four faces and four vertices, whose tips just pierce the surface . . .

He pictured a vast, stony tetrahedron—like one of the magic geometric forms Johannes Kepler used to think kept planets well ordered in the sky. Before Alex stood not a modest, unassuming monument, but one apex of the largest sculpture in the world. One *containing* the greater part of the world.

Similar carvings had been placed in Greenland, New Guinea, and South Africa, in one of the only arrangements that let each vertex emerge on dry land. For reasons similar to the artist's, Alex had chosen the same four sites to place his secret resonators. It was more than mere happenstance, therefore, that had brought him here to Rapa Nui.

Standing over the stone pinnacle, Alex turned slowly, hands in his pockets, taking in the treeless, rocky plain. Westward a few kilometers jutted the cliffs of Rano Kao, one of the island's three large, dormant volcanoes, overlooking a sea of frothy whitecaps. Not counting trivial islets, the wind riven by that jagged prominence arrived after crossing eight thousand miles of unimpeded ocean.

How strange to think on such scales, when all my training is to contemplate the infinitely small.

Standing here, he knew with utter precision where the other Tangoparu teams were dispersed around the globe. Probably none of them would encounter their local portions of the Whole Earth Sculpture. Sites two and four were offset from the actual monuments by several hundred kilometers.

But this was the hub. Few islands were so small compared with the vast ocean surrounding them. Alex could not have missed this apex had he tried.

Some say pyramids are symbols of luck, he pondered. *But I'd still prefer a dodecahedron.*

Rapa Nui had been chosen as headquarters for other reasons, not least of which was security. Here the Pacific Society of Hine-marama had more influence than the "national" authorities in faraway Chile. Under the society's umbrella they could bring in a large crew, sparing Alex the need to supervise construction, leaving him time to wrestle the cloud of numbers and images in his head.

Those images followed him everywhere, even walking along the cinder cone of an ancient volcano or contemplating strange monuments on an isle of monuments.

Just north of Rano Kao, for instance, near Rapa Nui's solitary town and landing strip, squatted a white shape that had once been a proud bird of space. Now guano streaked and forlorn, the shuttle *Atlantis* perched permanently on a rusted platform for visitors to gawk at and birds to use in other ways. Keeping his promise to Captain Tikhana, Alex had paid his respects to the stripped hulk, once a multibillion-dollar vessel of aspiration, but now just another Easter Island obelisk. The sensations engendered had been forlorn.

Like the first time he had seen the native statues this place was famous for. There had been that same woebegone feeling.

. . . as if this were a place hopes came to die.

Alex turned southward. There, by the tiny, crashing bay of Vaihu, stood a row of seven towering carvings, called *moai,* pouting under heavy basalt brows. Several bore cylindrical topknots made of reddish scoria. They faced inland, seamed with cement where latter-day restorers had pieced them together from broken fragments. The glowering sentinels did not seem grateful. Rather, they radiated grim, obdurate resentment.

Before departing for the Arctic, Stan Goldman had given Alex a slim book about Easter Island, with old-style paper pages. "You're going to one of the saddest, most fascinating places on Earth," the elderly physicist had told him. "In fact, it has a lot in common with Greenland, where I'm headed."

Alex couldn't imagine two places less alike—one a continent in its own right, covered with ice, the other a flyspeck, broiling and nearly waterless amidst the open ocean. But Stan explained. "Both were experiments in what it might be like to plant a colony on another world—tiny settlements, isolated, without trade or any outside support, forced to live by their wits and meager local resources for generation after generation."

Stan concluded grimly. "In neither case, I'm afraid, did humanity do very well."

Indeed, from what Alex later read, Stan had understated the case. Hollywood images of Polynesian paradises ignored the boom-and-bust cycles of overpopulation that hit every archipelago with desperate regularity—cycles resolved by one means chiefly—the bloody culling of the adult male population. Nor did movies refer to that other holocaust—the slaughter of native species—not just by people, but by the pigs and rats and dogs the colonists brought with them.

The Polynesians weren't particularly blameworthy. Humans had a long history of making messes wherever they went. But Alex recalled his grandmother once explaining the importance of *scale.* The smaller, more isolated the ecosystem, the quicker any damage became fatal. And there were few places on Earth as small, isolated, or fatal as Rapa Nui.

Within a few generations of humanity's arrival, around 800 AD, not a tree was left standing. Without wood for boats, the settlers then had to abandon the sea, along with all possibility of escape or trade. What remained was native rock, from which they cut rude homes . . . and these desolate icons.

Overpopulation and boredom left open only the one option—

endless war. One brief century after the great statues had been raised, nearly every one had been smashed in tribal forays and reprisals. By the time Europeans arrived—to arrogantly rename the place after a Christian holiday—the natives of Rapa Nui had nearly annihilated each other.

As if we moderns do much better. It only takes a bit more power, and greater numbers, to accomplish what the Easter Islanders never could . . . to foul something as big as the ocean itself.

Earlier, he had strolled the island's one narrow beach, up at Anakena, where Hotu Matu'a long ago first landed with his band of hopeful settlers. And what Alex at first thought was white sand turned out to be bits of shredded *styrofoam*, ground from "peanuts" and other packing material spilled thousands of miles away. The stuff had been outlawed when he was still in university. Yet it still washed ashore everywhere. Scraggly sea birds poked through the detritus. They might not be dying, but they certainly didn't look well, either.

Jen, he thought, wishing his grandmother were here to talk to. *I need you to tell me it's not already too late. I need to hear there's enough left to be worth saving.*

The glowering statues stared inland, seeming to share Alex's gloomy premonitions.

Oh, the new gravity resonator worked all right. In its first test runs it had picked out Beta's familiar glitter in brighter detail than ever. Echoes bracketed the massive, complex singularity within *twenty meters* inside Earth's fiery bowels.

So far, so good. But in those reverberations Alex had also seen how fast the *taniwha* was growing.

Damn, we have hardly any time at all.

He looked beyond the dour stone figures, and in his imagination he suddenly pictured Ragnarok. Steam billowed as the sea was rent by sudden gouts of flame, leaving behind a measureless, bottomless hole.

Then, back into the unplugged depths, the despoiled ocean poured.

"Here's the news," June Morgan told him when he returned to the prefab hall the technicians had built not far from Vaihu. It felt like a small sports arena set upon a flat expanse of naked bedrock. Under the opaque roof they had erected their computers and the master resonator . . . a gleaming cylinder newly born from its vat of purified chemicals and now anchored to swiveled bearings. Alex said, "Just give me a summary, will you, June?"

Though she wasn't part of the original cabal, June had proven invaluable, along with several of Pedro Manella's "new people." Her expertise on magnetism came in particularly handy as they traced the fields lacing Earth's core, seeking those weird zones of superconducting current discovered only weeks ago.

Also, June was a demon for organization. As the hurried days passed, Alex came to rely on her more and more.

"Site two reports they'll have full readiness in just a few hours," the blonde woman said, confirming that George Hutton's group in New Guinea was on schedule. "Greenland team says they'll be in operation by tomorrow afternoon."

"Good." Alex had known Goldman and Tikhana would come through. "What about Africa?"

She lifted her eyes. "They were supposed to report in again two hours ago but . . ." She shrugged. With their program so delicately balanced, failure at even one location would be disastrous. And the African team was in territory completely out of their control. Still, it was amazing Jen had managed getting them into Kuwenezi at all.

"Don't worry about it. My grandmother's never been on time for an appointment in her life. Still, she somehow always comes through. We won't need site four for a while yet.

"As for us, however, the time's come," he concluded, raising his voice. "So let's get busy."

He sat at a nearby station, showing the familiar holographic display of a cutaway Earth, with side projections for every factor he could possibly want to follow. Their earlier probes had set off all types of vibrations below—gravitational, sonic, electrical. Likening the planet to a complex, untempered bell seemed more appropriate each time they tapped it. At the world's surface, all this "ringing" sometimes manifested in trembling movements—a resonant coupling Alex was just beginning to sort out. At worst, if they weren't careful they might release pent-up faulting strains, already on the verge of bursting.

"Hmm," he pondered, looking at the latest output. "Looks like the tremors weren't so bad this time, even though we increased power. Maybe we're getting the hang of this."

New maps indicated many zones below where raw power waited to be tapped, as soon as their network was complete. *It's a whole world down there*, Alex thought. *And we've only just begun exploring it.*

Now the border between liquid core and mantle was shown in such detail, it appeared like the surface of an alien planet. There were corrugations which looked startlingly like mountains, and rippling expanses that vaguely resembled seas. *Shadow continents* mimicked thousands of kilometers below the familiar ones. Far under Africa, for instance, an intrusion of nickel-iron bobbed like an echo of the granite frigate floating far above.

There was "weather," too—plumes of plasti-crystalline convection circulating in slow-motion currents. Occasionally, unpredictably, these streamways flickered into that astonishing, newly discovered state, and electricity flowed in perfect strokes of lightning.

It even "rained." Long after most of Earth's iron and nickel had separated from the rocky minerals, settling into the deep core, metal droplets *still* coalesced and migrated downward, pelting the boundary with molten mists, drizzles, even downpours.

I shouldn't be surprised. Convection and change of state would have to operate down there, too. Still, it all seemed eerie and suggested bizarre notions. Might there be "life" on those shadow masses? Life to which the plastic, tortured perovskites of the mantle made up an "atmosphere"? To whom the overhead scum of granite and basalt was as diaphanous and chill as high cirrus clouds were to him?

"Ten minutes." June Morgan gripped her clipboard plaque nervously. And Alex noticed others glancing his way with similar looks. Still, in his own heart he sensed only icy calm. A grim, composed tranquility. They had studied the monster, and now teratology was finished. It was time to go after the thing, in its very lair.

"I'd better get ready then. Thanks, June."

He reached for his subvocal, fitting the multistranded device over his head and neck. As he adjusted the settings, he recalled what Teresa Tikhana had said to him back in the Waitomo Caves, just before they parted.

". . . It's a long way to the next oasis, Dr. Lustig. You know that, don't you? Someday we may find other worlds and perhaps do better with them. But without the Earth behind us, at our backs, we'll never ever get that second chance . . ."

To which Alex mentally added, *If we lose this battle, we won't deserve another chance.*

He showed none of this, however. For the sake of those watching him, he grinned instead and spoke with a soft, affected burr.

"All right, lads, lassies. Shall we invite our wee devil out to dance?"

They laughed nervously.

Swiveling in its gimbaled supports, the resonator turned with accuracy finer than any human eye could follow. It aimed.

And they began.

PART VII

PLANET

A tug of war began, between sea and sky and land.

In the ocean, life was carnivorous and simple, a pyramid founded on the very simplest forms, the phytoplankton, which teemed in great colored tides wherever sunlight met raw materials. Of the elements they needed to grow and flourish, hydrogen and oxygen could be taken from the water, and carbon from the air. But calcium and silicon and phosphorus and nitrates . . . these had to be acquired elsewhere.

Some you got by eating your neighbor. But sooner or later, everything suspended in the sea must drop out of the cycle to join the ever-growing sediments below. Cold upwelling currents replenished part of the loss, dragging nutrients back up from the muddy bottoms. But most of the deficit was made up at the mouths of rivers, draining rain-drenched continents. Silt and minerals, the raw fertilizer of life, dripped into the sea like glucose from an intravenous tap.

On land, it took a long time for life to gain a foothold. And for a very long time there were just frail films of cyanobacteria and fungi, lacing the bare rock surfaces with filaments and tiny fibers. These first soils kept moisture in contact with stone longer, so weathering hastened. The flow of calcium and other elements to the sea increased.

Plankton are efficient when well fed. And so, after the breakup of Gondwanaland, when many great rivers fed shallows teeming with green life, carbon was sucked from the air as never before. The atmosphere grew transparent.

At that time the sun was less warm. And so, deprived of its greenhouse shield, the air also cooled. Ice sheets spread, covering more and more of the Earth until, from north and south, glaciers nearly met at the equator.

This was no mere perturbation. No mere "ice age." Reflecting sunlight into space, the icy surface stayed frozen. Sea levels dropped. Evaporation decreased because of the chill. There was less rain.

But less rain meant less weathering of continental rocks . . . less mineral runoff. The plankton began to suffer and grew less efficient at taking carbon out of the air. Eventually, the removal rate fell below replenishment by volcanoes and respiration. The pendulum began to swing the other way.

In other words, the greenhouse grew back. Naturally. Within a few tens of millions of years the crisis was over. Rivers flowed and warm seas lapped the shorelines again. Life resumed its march —if anything, stimulated by the close call.

A tug of war . . . or a feedback loop . . . either way it succeeded. What matter that each cycle took epochs, saw countless little deaths and untold tragedies? Over the long term, it worked.

But nowhere was it written, in water or in stone, that it absolutely had to next time.

☐ Dear Net-Mail User [☐ EweR-635-78-2267-3 aSp]:

Your mailbox has just been rifled by EmilyPost, an autonomous courtesy-worm chain program released in October 2036 by an anonymous group of net subscribers in western Alaska. [☐ ref: sequestered confession 592864 -2376298.98634, deposited with Bank Leumi 10/23/36:20:34:21. Expiration-disclosure 10 years.] Under the civil disobedience sections of the Charter of Rio, we accept in advance the fines and penalties that will come due when our confession is released in 2046. However we feel that's a small price to pay for the message brought to you by EmilyPost.

In brief, dear friend, you are not a very polite person. EmilyPost's syntax analysis subroutines show that a very high fraction of your net exchanges are heated, vituperative, even obscene.

Of course you enjoy free speech. But EmilyPost has been designed by people who are concerned about the recent trend toward excessive nastiness in some parts of the net. EmilyPost homes in on folks like you and begins by asking them to please consider the advantages of politeness.

For one thing, your credibility ratings would rise. (EmilyPost has checked your favorite bulletin boards, and finds your ratings aren't high at all. Nobody is listening to you, sir!) Moreover, consider that courtesy can foster calm reason, turning shrill antagonism into useful debate and even consensus.

We suggest introducing an automatic delay to your mail system. Communications are so fast these days, people seldom stop and think. Some net users act like mental patients who shout out anything that comes to mind, rather than as functioning citizens with the human gift of tact.

If you wish, you may use one of the public-domain delay programs included in this version of EmilyPost, free of charge.

Of course, should you insist on continuing as before, disseminating nastiness in all directions, we have equipped EmilyPost with other options you'll soon find out about. . . .

● When the tiny settlement had first been established on the salty
L verge of the Gulf of Mexico, tall ships wearing high-top wings of
I white sailcloth had to ride the tidal flow through a measureless,
T reedy delta in order to reach it. Negotiating the shifting channels
H took a good pilot. Still, the new trading post lay within easy reach
O of piping seabirds. Sailors at anchor could hear breakers boom
S against sand bars.
P The port was meant to be a point of contact between three
H worlds—freshwater, saltwater, and the continental ocean of prairie
E rumored to stretch beyond the western hills. The village thrived
R in this role and became a town. The town, a metropolis. Time
E crawled by, as inexorable as the river.

Once a city has grown great and venerable, it takes on its own justification. Centuries passed. Eventually, the original raison d'être for New Orleans hardly mattered anymore. A living thing, it fought to survive.

Logan Eng strolled a levee watching barges glide past sunken abandoned docks. Once, this had been the second-busiest port in North America, but today cargo ships passed on by, toward the big tube-reloading stations at Memphis, for example. This muggy evening, the main redolence was of mint-scented pine oils, added by the city to cover other, less pleasant aromas. Environment Department launches sniffed each barge suspiciously. But according to Logan's ex-wife, it wasn't bilge dumping that gave the river that greasy brown pungency, but the town's own creaking sewers.

Of course, Daisy McClennon never lacked for causes. As student protestors, long ago, they had shared the same battles. Those had been great days to be young and on the side of righteousness.

But time affects relationships, as well as cities. And Daisy, the purist, found it ever harder to accept Logan, who had in his heart something called compromise. Their first big fight came early on, when Alaska, Idaho, and other holdouts finally began taxing household toxics like canned paints and pesticides, to encourage proper disposal. Logan had been elated, but Daisy wrinkled her nose, detecting a sellout. "You don't know string pullers and deal makers like I do," she had declared. "If they gave in so easily, it was to forestall bigger sanctions later. They're experts at testing the wind, then giving you moderates just enough rope. . . ."

Logan came to envy other people, whose marriages might wither or flourish over mundane things like money or sex or children. For their part, he and Daisy had always earned more than they needed, even in these tight times. And their lovemaking used to be so good that even in middle age he still thought her the most desirable woman alive.

How absurd that little differences in *politics* should come between them! Differences he, personally, found inscrutable.

He still vividly recalled that final, bitter evening, wiping biodegradable dish soap from his hands as he tried to catch her eyes. "Hey! I'm on your side!" he had pleaded.

"No you're not!" she had screamed back. A handmade plate shattered on the wall. "You build dams! You help irrigators ruin fertile land!"

"But we have new ways . . ."

"And every one of your new ways will just bring on more catastrophes! I tell you, I can't live anymore with a man who sends *bulldozers* tearing across the countryside . . ."

He recalled her eyes, that evening ten years ago, so icy blue and yet so full of fire. He had wanted to hold her, to inhale her familiar scent and beg her to reconsider. But in the end he went out into the night . . . a humid night like this one . . . carrying suitcases and a feeling ever afterward of exile.

Ironically, Daisy had been as good as her word. She could tolerate him, if not his views, just so long as he didn't live in the same house. Shared custody of Claire was handled so easily, Logan had to wonder. Was it because Daisy knew he was a good father? Or because the issue simply didn't loom as large to her as the latest cause?

"People talk as if the old days of capitalist rapists ended on the beaches of Vanuatu, and with the sack of Vaduz," she had pronounced just last Sunday, over a dinner of neo-Cajun blackened soycake. "But I know better. They're still there, behind the scenes, the profiteers and money men. Anti-secrecy laws just drove them undercover.

"All this talk of using tax policy to 'assess social costs' . . . what a dumb idea. The only way to stop polluters is to put them against walls and shoot them."

This from a vegetarian, who thought it murder to harm a perennial plant! At one point during the meal, Logan's daughter caught his eye. I just have to live with Daisy till college—Claire's look of commiseration seemed to say—You had to be *married* to her!

Actually, a part of Logan perversely enjoyed these monthly exposures to Daisy's fanaticism. Among his engineering peers he so often took the pro-Gaian side in arguments, it was actually refreshing to have the roles reversed occasionally.

Ideologies are too seductive anyway. It does a man good to see things from a different point of view.

Take the scene from this levee. Logan found it hard to get excited over simple sewage. It was only biomatter, after all, headed straight for the gulf. Not something *really* serious, like heavy metals in an aquifer or nitrates in a lake. The brown stuff out there wouldn't make pleasant drinking water. (Who *drank* from the Mississippi anyway?) But the ocean could absorb one hell of a lot of fertilizer. No cities lay downstream, so officials looked away when the Old Dame . . . leaked. New Orleans had special problems anyway.

From atop the splattered dike, Logan spied the massive flood barrier city fathers had built to fight aggressive tidal surges. The price for that impressive edifice lay behind him—a town still elegant and proud, but wracked by neglect.

Logan had toured Alexandria, Rangoon, Bangkok, and other threatened cities, assessing similar panoramas of grandeur and loss. Sometimes his advice had actually helped, like at Salt Lake, where the rising inland sea now surrounded a thriving sunken municipality. More often, though, he came home feeling he'd been battling mud slides with his bare hands. The death of Venice, apparently, hadn't taught anybody anything.

Sometimes you just have to say good-bye.

Here in New Orleans, earnest men and women worked to save their unique town. He'd recently helped the Urban Corporation anchor seventeen downtown blocks against further sinking into the softening ground. Tonight they were rewarding him with a night in the old French Quarter, still gay and full of life—though now the Dixieland strains echoed off these riverside barricades, and barges rolled by even with wrought-iron balconies.

At one point he just had to get away, for his ringing ears to cool off and the fiery cuisine to settle. Excusing himself, he left to stroll the muggy, jacaranda-scented evening, stepping aside for lovers and wandering groups of Ra Boys on the prowl. The Big Easy had class all right. In decline, there remained an air of seedy blaisance, and even the inevitable bandit types believed in courtesy.

He listened to the barge horns and thought of the manatees that had inhabited this area, back when La Salle's men first poled their way through endless marshes, trading ax heads for furs. The manatees were long gone, of course. And soon . . . relatively soon . . . so would New Orleans.

The dying of any city begins at its foundation. The French had faced a huge expanse of bayous and reed beds where the Mississippi deposited silt far into the Gulf. This posed a problem. *You want to* build a town at the mouth of a great river, but which mouth? Natural rivers have many.

They chose the most navigable one, and used a Chippewa word to call it "Mississippi." But nature paid no heed to names. Channels silted up, and the river kept bulling new paths to the sea.

It was natural, but men found it inconvenient. So they started dredging, saying, "This shall be the main channel, always and forever."

Dredged mud piled up along the banks of a trough that pushed ever outward, carrying its load of plains dust and mountain sediment deeper into the gulf. Not a fan but a finger, poking mile by mile, year after year, in the general direction of Cuba.

Meanwhile the rest of the delta began eroding.

Logan had inspected hundreds of kilometers of embankments, thrown up in forlorn efforts to save the doomed shore. More tall levees contained the river, whose gradient flattened over time. Suspended silt began falling out even north of Baton Rouge. Soon the sluggish current no longer held back the sea. Salinity increased.

Upstream, the Mississippi fought like an anaconda, writhing to escape. The contest was one of raw power. And Logan knew where it would be lost.

Can you hear it calling? He asked the captive waters. *Can you hear the Atchafalaya, beckoning you?*

Fortunately, Claire would move away long before the Mississippi burst through the Old River Control Structure or some other weak point, spilling into that peaceful plain of cane fields and fish farms. But Daisy? She'd never budge. Perhaps she didn't believe *because* the warning came from him, and that made Logan feel vaguely guilty.

In effect, he could only pray the Corps' new barriers were as good as they claimed. It was possible. Schools now taught youngsters to think in terms of decades, not mere months or years anymore. Maybe that culture had worked its way even to Washington.

But rivers see decades, even centuries, as mere trifles.

The Mississippi rolled by. And, not for the first time, Logan wondered if Daisy might be right after all. *I try to find solutions that work with Earth's forces. I like to think I've learned from the mistakes of past engineers.*

But didn't they, too, think they built for the ages?

He remembered what Shelley had written, about an ancient pharaoh.

"My name is Ozymandias, king of kings:
Look on my works, ye Mighty, and despair!"

Now the pyramids of Giza, symbols of man's conquest of time, were crumbling under the smoggy breath of fifty million denizens of Cairo. The monuments of Ramses were flaking to dust, blowing away to become thin layers in some future geologist's dissection of the past.

Can we build nothing that lasts? Nothing worth lasting?

Logan sighed. He had been away too long. He turned away from the patient river and took the rusted, creaking iron stairs back into the ancient city.

A man in blue stood near the door of the restaurant, his crewcut and patchy skin exaggerated by the rhodium flicker of the entrance sign. At first, Logan thought the fellow was a Ra Boy in mufti. But a second glance showed him to be too old, and much too formidable to be a Ra Boy.

Normally, Logan would have left out the second glance, but one does look twice when someone steps up and grabs your elbow. Logan blinked. "I beg your pardon?"

"No. It's I who must apologize. You're Logan Eng, may I assume?"

"Uh . . . I won't serve time for keeping it mum." The flip cliché rolled out before he could regret it, but the sallow-faced man appeared not to notice. He let go of Logan's arm only as they moved away from the doorway.

"My name is Glenn Spivey, colonel, United States Aerospace Force."

The stranger held out an ID that projected a holographic sphere ten centimeters across, emblazoned with crusty military emblems.

"Please go ahead and use your wallet plaque to verify my credentials, Mr. Eng."

Logan started to laugh. Partly in relief this wasn't a robbery and partly at the incongruity. As if anyone would *want* to fake such a garish thing!

"I'm sure I believe you . . ."

But the other man insisted. "I really would prefer you check, sir."

"Hey, what's this about? I have people waiting . . ."

"I know that. This shouldn't take long. We can talk soon as you've verified my bona fides. It's for your own protection, sir."

In the stranger's eyes, Logan recognized a tenacity far exceeding his own. Arguing was clearly futile.

"Oh, all right." He took out his wallet and aimed its lens first at Spivey and then at the man's glowing credential. Quickly he dialed the private security service he used for such things and pressed his thumb to the ident-plate. In three seconds the tiny screen flashed a terse confirmation.

All right, the fellow was who he said he was. Logan might have preferred a robber.

"Shall we go for a walk then, Mr. Eng?" Spivey motioned with one arm.

"I just finished walking a piece. Can we sit down? I really only have a moment . . ."

His protest trailed off as the officer showed him to a long black car parked at the curb. One glance told Logan the thing was made of steel throughout, and ran on high-octane gasoline.

Astounding. Work vehicles were one thing. Out in the field, machines needed that kind of power. But what use was it here in a city? This told him more than he'd learned by reading Spivey's ID.

Logan felt like a desecrator, planting his work pants on the plush upholstery. When the door hissed shut, all sound from the blaring, cacophonous street instantly vanished. "This is a secure vehicle," Spivey told him, and Logan quite believed it.

"All right, Colonel. What's all this about?"

Spivey held up one hand. "First I must tell you, Mr. Eng, that what we're about to discuss is highly classified. Top secret."

Logan winced. "I want my lawyer program."

The officer smiled placatingly. "I assure you it's all legal. You must be aware certain government agencies are exempt from the open-access provisions of the Rio Treaties."

Logan knew that. Disarmament hadn't ended all threats to peace or national security. Nations still competed, and in principle he accepted the need for secret services. Still, the idea made him intensely uncomfortable.

Spivey went on. "If you wish, though, we can record our conversation, and you may deposit a copy with a reputable registration service. Which one do you use for business? I'm sure you often sequester proprietary techniques for weeks or months before applying for patents."

Logan relaxed just a bit. *Sequestering* a conversation, to keep it confidential for a short time, was another matter entirely . . . so long as a legal record was kept in a safe place. In that case, he wondered why Spivey used the word "secret" at all.

"I deposit with Palmer Privacy, but—"

Spivey nodded. "Palmer will be satisfactory. Because we'll be discussing matters of national safety, however, and a possible threat to public welfare, I must ask for a ten-year sequestration, at ultimate level."

At that level, only a high court could open the record before expiration. Logan swallowed. He felt as if he had stepped into a bad flat-movie from the twentieth century, one made all too realistic in Daisy McClennon's enhancement lab. He was tempted to look around for the flashing pink star, installed to cue viewers that this wasn't real.

"Naturally, my agency will reimburse the extra cost, if that's a concern," Spivey added.

After a moment's hesitation, Logan nodded. "Okay." His voice felt very dry.

Spivey took out two recording cubes, black, with tamper-proof seals, and set them into a taper. Together, they went through the ritual, establishing names and conditions, time and location. At last, with both cubes winking, the colonel settled back in his seat. "Mr. Eng, we're interested in your theories about the incident at the Biscay tidal barrage."

Logan blinked. He had been imagining things this might be about, from person smuggling, to waste-dumping scams, to insider trading. He traveled widely and met so many colorful types that there was no telling how many might be involved in the ceaseless, sometimes shady jockeying of governments and corporations. But Spivey had surprised him with this!

"Well, Colonel, I'd have to classify that paper more under the heading of science fiction than theory. After all, I published in a database for speculative . . ."

"Yes, Mr. Eng. *The Alternate View*. Actually, you may be surprised to learn our service keeps close tabs on that zine, and similar ones."

"Really? It's just a forum for crackpot ideas . . ." He read the other man's look. "Well, maybe not as crackpot as some. Most subscribers are technical people. Let's say it's where we can publish things that don't belong elsewhere—certainly not the formal journals. Most of the ideas aren't to be taken seriously."

He felt uncomfortably sure Spivey was watching his every move, taking his measure. Logan didn't like it.

"Are you saying you think your hypotheses worthless?" the man asked levelly.

Logan shrugged. "There are lots of notions that seem to work on paper, or in Net simulations, but can't be justified in the real world."

"And your notion was?" Spivey prompted.

Logan thought back to the case of the missing drill rig in southern Spain—and the anchor boom that had been lifted on end at the tidal power station—both without any sign of sabotage.

"All I did was calculate how a special type of Earth movement could have caused the strange things I saw."

"What kind of Earth movement?"

"It's . . ." Logan lifted both hands parallel. "It's like, well, pushing a child on a swing. If you shove at the right frequency, matching the natural pendulum rhythm, you'll build momentum with each stroke—"

"I'm aware of how resonance works, Mr. Eng. You suggested the Spanish anomalies were caused by a special *type* of seismic resonance. Specifically, the sudden arrival of extremely narrowly focused earthquakes and corresponding gravity variations—"

"No! I didn't say that was the cause! I merely showed such waves would be consistent with observed events. It's an amusing idea, that's all. I can't really say why I even bothered with it."

The government man inclined his head slightly. "I'm sorry I misspoke. You sound upset about it."

"A man's reputation is important. Especially in my field. People understand play, of course. So I was careful to make clear that's all I was doing, playing with an idea! It's quite another thing to say, '*this is what happened.*' I didn't do that."

Spivey regarded him for a long interval. Finally, he opened a slim briefcase and pulled out a large-format reading plaque. "I'd appreciate it if you'd leaf through this, Mr. Eng, and consider what you see in light of your . . . *playful* exercise."

Logan thought of protesting. By now his associates in the restaurant might be worried. Or they might be incoherent from alcohol or assume he'd gone off to bed. . . .

He took the plaque. Making certain the recording cubes could read over his shoulder, he put his thumb on the page-turn button and began skimming. Silence stretched in the limo as he read. Finally, he said, "I don't believe it."

"Now you understand why I insisted you check my credentials, Mr. Eng, so you'll know this is no hoax."

"But this episode here . . ."

"You haven't seen the actual recording, yet. It's much more vivid than numbers. Allow me." The man expertly dialed the correct data page. "This was taken by a high-altitude reconnaissance blimp, above our Diego Garcia Naval Station, in the Indian Ocean."

Depicted now in front of Logan was a moonlit seascape. Calm waters glistened under still tropical air.

Suddenly, the ocean surface flattened in eight places. Despite the angle of view and foreshortening, Logan could tell the dimples formed a perfect octagon.

As quick as the dips appeared, they suddenly ballooned *outward*, joined now by an outer ring of smaller bulges, twenty in all. Scale numbers ran down the side of the screen, and Logan whistled.

The hillocks collapsed again, much quicker than normal gravity could have pulled them down. Forty-nine depressions replaced them this time. The center eight were now too deep for the camera to measure.

Then, suddenly, the screen erupted with light. Faster than Logan could follow, a handful of bright streaks speared upward, perpendicular to the ocean. They were gone in an instant, leaving behind a diffracting pattern of circular ripples, spreading and subsiding until at last all was still once more.

"That's the best example," Spivey commented. "It was accompanied by seismic activity bearing some similarity to the Spanish quakes."

"Where . . ." Logan asked hoarsely. "Where did the water go?"

The colonel's smile was distant, enigmatic. "Just missed the moon, by less than three diameters. Of course, by that point it was pretty diffuse. . . . Are you all right, Mr. Eng?" Genuine concern suddenly crossed Colonel Spivey's face as he leaned forward. "Would you like a drink?"

Logan nodded. "Yes . . . thank you. I think I need one very much."

For a little while, despite the car's whispering air-conditioner, he found it rather difficult to breathe.

☐ **Net Vol. A69802-11 04/06/38 14:34:12UT.User G-654-11-7257-Aab12 AP News Alert: 7+: Key-select: "Conservation," "animal rights," "conflict":**

In the ongoing, sometimes violent confrontation between the International Fish and Fowl Association and the animal rights group known as No-Flesh, a surprise development today. To the amazement of many, the Hearth Conclave of the North American Church of Gaia has intervened in favor of the world's largest organization of duck hunters.

According to the Most Reverend Elaine Greenspan, sister-leader of Washington State and this month's spokesper for the conclave:

"We have examined all the evidence and decided that in this case neither hunting nor the consumption of animal tissue harms Our Mother. Rather, the activities of IFFA are clearly beneficial and meritorious."

In light of the church's long-standing abjuration of the slaughter of warm-blooded animals, Greenspan explained:

"Our position against red meat is often misunderstood. It's not a moral stand against carnivorality, per se. There is nothing inherently evil about eating or being eaten, for that is clearly part of Gaia's plan. Human beings evolved with meat as part of their diet.

"Our campaign has been waged because great herds of grazing cattle and sheep were destroying much of the Earth. Vast quantities of needed grain were being wasted as fodder. And finally, modified food animals such as beef steers are abominations, robbed of the ultimate dignity of wild creatures, to have a chance to fight or flee, to struggle to survive.

"After hearing the arguments of IFFA representatives, we find that none of these objections apply to them.

"Similarly, our broad stand against *hunting* was based on the scarcity of wildlife in comparison with the chief predator, humankind. But this does not hold where hunters are few, responsible, and sportsmanly, and where the prey species is renewable.

"Contrary to our initial expectations, we have determined that IFFA duck hunters have been among the most ardent supporters of conservation, spending millions to buy up and preserve wetlands, pursuing polluters and poachers, and regulating their own activities admirably. Any complete ban on hunting would, we estimate, lead to catastrophic loss of remaining migratory routes. The church therefore rules that IFFA is beneficial to society and to Gaia, and grants its blessing."

In fact, there are precedents for this surprising action. Thirty years ago, for instance, the church campaigned against the selling off of many obsolete military bases, which they deemed better preserved in that state than sold to be developed as commercial property.

To today's announcement, however, a spokesper for No-Flesh had only this comment:

"This takes NorA ChuGa hypocrisy to new heights. Killing is killing and murder is murder. All animals have rights, too. Let IFFA and their new allies beware. What they do unto others may yet be visited on them!"

When asked if this was a threat of violence, the spokesper declined elaboration.

Nelson Grayson was having trouble grasping "cooperation" and "competition." The two words were defined as opposites, and yet his teacher claimed they were essentially the same thing.

Moreover, at some deep level Nelson felt he'd secretly suspected it all along.

"I'm still confused, Professor," he admitted at their next meeting, though it cost him to say it. Each time Dr. Wolling granted one of these sessions, he feared she was finally going to give up on his slowness, his need for palpable examples at every point of theory.

She looked pale, sitting across the table from him. That might just be because she spent so much time with those enigmatic strangers, performing mysterious surveys in the abandoned gold mine below ark four. Still, Nelson worried about her health.

Frail she might seem, but her gaze was unwavering. "Why don't you start off where you do understand, Nelson?"

He quashed an urge to consult his note plaque. Once, Dr. Wolling had slapped his hand when he did that too often. *"Respect your own thoughts!"* she had snapped.

"All right," he breathed. "The Gaia theory says Earth stays a good place for life because life itself keeps changing the planet. Otherwise, it would've gone into a permanent ice age, like Mars. Or a runaway, um, greenhouse instability—losing all its water like Venus did."

"More likely Venus than Mars, actually," she agreed. "Earth is rather close to its sun for a water world, near the inner edge of the habitable zone. So how did we avoid a Venus-style trap?"

For this he had a ready answer, the standard one. "Early algae and bacteria helped ocean chemistry take carbon dioxide out of the atmosphere. They bound the carbon into their skeletons, which, uh, sedimented to the sea floor. So the atmosphere got clearer—"

"More transparent to heat radiation."

"Yeah. So heat could escape, and the oceans could stay wet even as the sun got hotter. In fact, the air temperature's stayed roughly the same for four billion years."

"Including ice ages?"

Nelson shrugged. "Trivial fluctuations."

He liked the phrase. Liked the way it rolled off the tongue. He had practiced it last night, hoping there'd be a chance to use it. "Like the heating everybody's so worried about these days. Sure it's making terrible problems, and a big die-back may be coming . . . including maybe us. But that's not so unusual. In a million years or so, the balance will swing back."

Jen Wolling's nod seemed to say he was both right and wrong. Right that the greenhouse effect of the twenty-first century wasn't the first upward jolt in Earth's thermostat. But perhaps wrong that this excursion was like all the others.

Keep to the topic! He reminded himself. That was the problem with intellectual talk. It spun out so many sidetracks, you never got where you were going unless you used discipline. As if "intellectual" and "discipline" were words he had ever imagined applying to himself, only six months ago!

"So," Dr. Wolling said, placing one hand on the other. "Life kept changing Earth's atmosphere in just the right way to maintain a suitable environment for itself. Was this on purpose?"

Nelson felt briefly miffed she'd try to snare him so. Then he realized she was only being a good teacher and giving him an easy one. "That'd be the *strong* Gaia hypothesis," he answered. "It says the homeo . . . um, homeostasis . . . life's balancing act . . . is all part of a plan. The religious Gaian people—" Nelson chose his words carefully out of respect for the Ndebele "—say Earth's history proves there's a god, or goddess, who designed it all to happen this way.

"Then there's the middle Gaia hypothesis . . . where people say the Earth *behaves* like a living organism. That it has all the properties of a living creature. But they don't say it was actually planned. If the organism has any consciousness, it's us."

"Yes, go on," she prompted. "And what's the standard scientific view?"

"That's the weak Gaia theory. It says natural processes just interact in a predictable way with things like oceans and volcanoes . . . calcium runoff from continents and such . . . so carbon dioxide accumulates in the atmosphere when it's cold, but when things get too hot the gas is pulled out, letting heat escape again."

"It's a process, then."

"Yeah, but one with all sorts of built-in stabilities. Not just in temperature. Which is why so many people see a plan."

"Indeed. But I only made you review all that because it bears on your question. How can *competition* be looked at as a close cousin to *cooperation?*

"Think about the Precambrian Era, Nelson, two to three billion years ago, when green algae in the ocean began pulling all that carbon out of the air in earnest. Tell me, what did they pour forth in its place?"

"Oxygen," he answered quickly. "Which is transparent . . ."

She waved one hand. "Forget that for a moment. Think about the biological effects. Remember, oxygen burns. It was—"

"A poison!" Nelson interrupted. "Yeah. The old bacteria were Anna . . ."

"Anaerobic. Yes. They couldn't deal with such a corrosive gas, even though they were the ones putting it there! It was a classic case of learning to live in your own waste products."

Nelson blinked. "Then . . . then there must have been pressure to adapt."

Dr. Wolling's smile transmitted more than just satisfaction. The encouragement both warmed and confused Nelson.

"Exactly," she said. "A crisis loomed for Gaia. Oxygen pollution threatened to end it all. Then some species stumbled onto a correct biochemical solution—how to take advantage of the new high-energy environment. Today, nearly everything you see around you is descended from those adaptable ones. The few surviving anaerobes are exiled to brewery vats and sea bottoms."

Nelson nodded, eager to keep that expression in her eyes. "So Gaia went on changing and getting better—"

"—more subtle. More complicated."

His head hurt from trying so hard. "But . . . it sounds like both at the same time! It was cooperation, because the species making the change had to shift together. Y'know, hunter and hunted. Eater and eaten. None of them could have made it alone.

"But it was competition, too, 'cause each of them was struggling only for itself!"

Dr. Wolling absently waved away a wisp of gray hair. "All right, you see the essential paradox. We've all, at one time or another, wondered about this strange thing—that death *seems* so evil. Our basic nature is to oppose it. And yet, without it there'd be no change, nor any life at all.

"Darwin made the cruel efficiency of the process clear when he showed that every species on Earth tries to have more offspring than it needs in order to replace the prior generation. Every one tries, in other words, to overpopulate the world, and must be regulated by something outside itself.

"What this universal trait means is that the lion not only cannot lie down with the lamb . . . he cannot even be completely comfortable lying down with other lions! At least not without always keeping one eyelid cracked."

Nelson looked at her. "I . . . think I understand."

She tapped the table and sat up. "Tell you what. Let's take an even better example. Do you know anything about the nervous system?"

"You mean the brain and stuff?" Nelson shook his head. How much could a guy learn in a few months? Damn! Even using hypertexts, there was so much knowledge and so little time.

Jen smiled. "This is simple. We'll use a holo."

She must have planned this. One muttered word and the desk projector displayed a cutaway view of a human cranium. Nelson recognized the outlines, of course. As early as third grade, kids were taught about the two hemispheres—how both sides of the brain "thought" in different ways that somehow combined to make a single mind.

Sophistication about such matters increased as you grew older, and sometimes not for the better, as when teenagers put together homemade tomography-scan kits to get real-time activity images of their own brains. Not for greater self-awareness, but so they could learn how to "daze out"—to release the brain's own natural opiates on demand. That honey pot had never tempted Nelson, thank goddess. But he'd seen what it did to friends and almost agreed with those who wanted to outlaw self-scanning devices.

"See the complicated blue mesh?" Dr. Wolling asked. "Those are nerve cells, billions of them, connected so intricately that computer scientists, with all their nanodissectors, still haven't duplicated such complexity. Each synapse—each little nonlinear electric switch—contributes its own tiny syncopated lightning to a whole that's far, far greater than the sum of its parts—the towering standing wave that composes the symphony of thought."

If only I could talk like that, he wished, and instantly chided himself for even dreaming it. He might as well aspire to win his own Nobel prize.

"But look closely, Nelson. The volume taken up by nerve cells is actually small. The rest is water, lymph, and a structure of glial cells and other insulating bodies, which feed and support the nerves and keep them from shorting out.

"Now, consider instead the brain of a fetus."

The image shrank to a smaller, simpler shape. Within the bulging dome, the dazzling blue tracery was now absent.

"Instead of nerves," Jen went on, "we have millions of primitive protocells, pretty much undifferentiated and dividing like mad. So how is it some of these cells know to become nerves, and others humble supporters? Is it all laid down in some plan?"

"Well, sure there's a plan! It's in the DNA . . ." Nelson's voice trailed off as he noticed her watching him. She had to be drawing a parallel, somehow, with the planetary condition. But he couldn't see the connection.

There's a plan, all right. But how? Is there some little guy inside the baby's skull who reads the DNA like a blueprint and says, "You! Become a nerve cell! You there! Become a supporter!"

Or is it done in some simpler . . .

"Uh!" Nelson's head snapped up suddenly and he met her cool gray eyes. "The protocells . . . *compete* with each other . . . ?"

"To become nerve cells, yes. Excellent insight, Nelson. Here, watch closely." Jen touched another control and multicolored lights glowed at pinpoints along the rim of the skull. "These are sites where neural growth factors secrete into the mass of protocells. A different chemical from each control point. Coding in each cell tells it what to do if it encounters such and such a mixture of growth factors. If it gets enough of just the right combination, it gets to be a nerve cell. If not, it becomes a supporter."

Nelson watched, fascinated, as flows of color spread out from each secretion site. Here red and white merged to form a distinct pink blending. Elsewhere a blue stimulant overlapped a green one and formed complex swirls, like stirred paint.

"Also," Dr. Wolling went on, "the cells secrete chemicals of their own, to suppress their neighbors, a lot like the quiet chemical warfare waged by plants . . ."

Nelson grabbed his own set of controls and zoomed in for a closer look. He saw cells writhe and jostle, striving to soak where the colors shone brightest. Different chemical combinations seemed to trigger different behaviors . . . here a frenzy of growth leading to tight bundles of successful nerves. Over there, a sparser network with only a few winners, whose long, spindly appendages resembled spiders' legs.

"It's like . . . as if the different mixes make different environments, eh? Like how different amounts of sunshine and water make a desert here, a jungle there? Like . . . *ecological niches?*"

"Very good. And we know what happens when one niche is damaged or fails. Inevitably it affects the whole, even far away. But go on. How do the cells deal with the different demands of the different environments?"

"They adapt, I guess. So it's . . ." Nelson turned to face his teacher. "It's survival of the fittest, isn't it?"

"Never did like that expression." But she nodded. "You're right again. Only here, the 'food' they compete for isn't really food. It's a brew of substances needed for further development. If a cell gets too little it *dies*, in a manner of speaking. As an astrocyte or other support cell, it lives on. But as a potential nerve cell, it is no more."

"Amazing," Nelson muttered. "Then, the arrangement of nerves in our brain, it comes about because of those scattered little glands, all giving out different chemicals?"

"Not just scattered, Nelson. Well placed. Later I'll show you how just one small difference in the amount of testosterone boys get before birth can make crucial changes. Of course, after birth learning takes over, fully as important as anything that came before. But yes . . . this part really is amazing."

Dr. Wolling shut off the display. Nelson rubbed his eyes.

"Evolution and competition go on *inside* us," he said in awe.

She smiled. "You really are a bright young fellow. I can't tell you how many of my students fail to make that leap. But when you think about it, it makes perfect sense to use inside us the same techniques that helped perfect life on the planet as a whole."

"Then our *bodies* are just like . . ."

She stopped him. "That's enough for now. More than enough. Go feed your pets. Get some exercise. I slipped some readings into your plaque. Go over them by next time. And don't be late."

Still blinking, his mind awhirl, Nelson stood up to go. It wasn't until much later that he seemed to recollect her standing on her toes to kiss his cheek before he left. But by then he was sure he must have imagined it.

As his duties expanded, taking him from the regulated pools and fountains of the recycling dome to the rain forest habitat to the enclosed plain where elands stretched their legs under reinforced crystal panes, the two baboons accompanied Nelson like courtiers escorting a prince. Or more likely, apprentices attending their wizard. For wherever Nelson strode, magical things happened.

I speak a word, and light streams forth, he thought as he made his nightly rounds. *Another, and water rises for animals to drink.*

Voice-sensitive computers made it possible, of course. But even sophisticated systems weren't good enough to manage a place like this. Not without human expertise.

Or where that ain't available, let blind guesswork substitute, eh?

Nelson's reaction to his spate of promotions had been pleasure mixed with irritation.

After all, I don't really know *anything!*

True, he seemed able to tell when certain animals were about to get sick, or when something needed fixing in the air or water. He had a knack for setting overhead filters so the grass grew properly, but guesswork was all it was. He had talents never imagined back in the crowded Yukon, but talent was a poor substitute for knowing what you were doing!

So Nelson went about his duties a troubled wizard, pointing at ducts and commanding them to open, sending squat robots off on errands, rubbing and tasting leaves . . . worrying all along that he hadn't earned this gift. It was like a big joke perpetrated by some capricious fairy godmother. Not knowing where it came from made it seem revokable at any time.

In his reading he encountered another phrase—"idiot savant"— and felt a burning shame, suspecting it referred to him.

A human being knows what he's doin'. Otherwise, what's the point in being human?

So he walked his rounds nodding, listening to the button player in his left ear. Every spare moment, Nelson studied. And the more he learned, the more painfully aware he grew of his ignorance.

Shig and Nell helped. He'd point at a piece of fruit, and they would scurry to bring back the sample. What genetic magic had made them so quick to understand? he wondered.

Or maybe it's just me. Maybe I'm part monkey.

This evening both baboons were subdued as he led them on rounds with unusual intensity. In his head, Nelson's thoughts roiled.

With images of high school . . . the sports teams and the gangs . . . *cooperation and competition.*

Images of his parents, hard at work side by side, striving for long hours to make their business thrive . . . *competition and cooperation.*

Images of cells and bodies, species and planets.

Cooperation and competition. Are they really the same? How can they be?

To some, the conflict seemed inherent. Take economics. The white immigrant, Dr. B'Keli, had given Nelson texts praising enterprise capitalism, in which striving for individual success delivered efficient goods and services. "The invisible hand" was the phrase coined long ago by a Scotsman, Adam Smith.

In contrast, some still promoted the *visible* hand of socialism. In Southern Africa, cosmopolitans like B'Keli were rare. More often, Nelson heard derision of the "soullessness" of money-based economies, and speeches extolling paternalistic equality.

The debate sounded eerily like the one raging in biology, over the supposed sentience of Gaia. "The blind watchmaker" was how some agnostics referred to the putative designer of the world. To them, creation required no conscious intervention. It was a process, with competition the essential element.

Religious Gaians retorted furiously that their goddess was far from blind or indifferent. They spoke of a world in which too many things meshed too well to have come about by any means but teamwork.

Again and again, the same dichotomy. The conflict of opposites. *But what if they're two sides of the same coin?*

He hoped some of Dr. Wolling's references would offer answers. Usually, though, the readings only left him with more questions. Endless questions.

At last he closed the final reinforced airtight door and led Shig and Nell home, leaving behind all the animals he half envied for their lack of complex cares. They didn't know they were locked inside a fragile rescue craft, aground and anchored to the soil of an ailing, perhaps dying, continent. They didn't know of the other arks in this flotilla of salvation, scattered across the Earth like grails, holding in trust what could never be replaced.

They didn't have to try to understand the why of anything, and certainly not the how.

Those worries, Nelson knew, were reserved for the captain and crew. They were the special concerns of those who must stand watch.

☐ . . . Although a body's cells all carry the same inheritance, they aren't identical. Specialists do their separate jobs, each crucial to the whole. If this weren't so, if all cells were the same, you would have just an undifferentiated blob.

On the other hand, whenever a small group of cells strives, unrestricted, for its own supremacy, you get another familiar catastrophe, known as cancer.

What does any of this have to do with social theory?

Nations are often likened to living bodies. And so, oldtime state socialism may be said to have turned many a body politic into lazy, unproductive blobs. Likewise, inherited wealth and aristocracy were egoistic cancers that ate the hearts out of countless other great nations.

To carry the analogy further—what these two pervasive and ruinous social diseases had in common was that each could flourish only when a commonwealth's immune system was weakened. In this case we refer to the free flow of information. Light is the scourge of error, and so both aristocracy and blob-socialism thrived on secrecy. Each fought to maintain it at all costs.

But the ideal living structure, whether creature or ecosystem, is self-regulating. It must breathe. Blood and accurate data must course through all corners, or it can never thrive.

So it is, especially, in the complex interactions among human beings.

—From **The Transparent Hand**, Doubleday Books, edition 4.7 (2035). [☐ hyper access code 1-tTRAN-777-97-9945-29A.]

● H O L O S P H E R E E

Jen watched the glistening pyramid of ark four rise to meet the stars. Or at least that was the effect as the open-cage elevator dropped below the dry ground and began its rickety descent.

Illuminated by the car's bare bulb, the walls of the lift shaft were fascinating to watch. Layer after layer of nitid, lustrous rock drifted past—probably sediments from ancient seas or lake beds or whatever. Stories of the fall and rise of species and orders and entire phyla ought to be revealed in this trip backward through time. But Jen was selectively myopic, unable to read any of the writings on this wall.

Of course, the days were long gone when any scientist, even a theoretician, could do it all alone. Jen had a reputation as an iconoclast. As a shit disturber. But every one of her papers, every analysis, had been based on mountains of data carefully collected and refined by hundreds, thousands of field workers, long before she ever got her hands on it.

I have always relied on the competence of strangers.

She, who had built a theoretical framework for understanding Earth's history, had to depend on others, first, to find and lay out the details. Only then could she find patterns in the raw data.

It was ironic, then. Here she was, the one some called the living founder of modern Gaianism—a movement that had already gone through countless phases of heresy, reformation and counter-reformation. And yet she was illiterate with the Mother's own diary right in front of her, written in palpable stone.

Ironic, yes. Jen appreciated paradoxes. Like taking on a new student when everything might prove futile and pointless within a few short months, anyway.

As pointless as my life . . . as pointless as everybody's life, if some way isn't found to get rid of Alex's monster.

Of course it was unfair to name it so. In a sense, her grandson was humanity's champion, leading their small fellowship to battle the demon. Still, a part of Jen seethed at the boy. It was an irrational corner which couldn't help associating him with that awful thing down there, eating away at the Earth's heart.

Each of us is many, she recalled. *Within every human, a cacophony of voices rages. Despite all the new techniques of cerebrochemical balancing and sanity seeding, those inner selves will persist in thinking unfair thoughts from time to time, and make us utter things we later regret. It may not be nice, but it's human.*

What was it Emerson had said? "A foolish consistency is the hobgoblin of little minds." One might say she had lived by that adage. Watching the rock wall glide past, Jen determined she really must send Alex a note of encouragement. Even a few words could mean a lot to him in this time of struggle. It irritated her that she only seemed to think of it when she was away from her computer, plaque, or telephone.

Then there's security, she thought, knowing full well she was rationalizing.

Dr. Kenda, head of the Tangoparu team here in Kuwenezi, really was fanatical about preventing leaks. Jen had been asked not even to hint to the Ndebele about their true mission here. She could only tell their hosts that the task was vitally important to the Mother. Fortunately, that had been enough so far.

But will it suffice later, when the Earth starts shaking?

Kenda had demanded maps of the entire mine complex. There was disturbing talk of emergency plans and escape scenarios, of dike barriers and aquifer pressures. Jen felt uneasy, hating to think Ndebele hospitality might be repaid with betrayal.

One thing at a time, she told herself. What mattered now was that they were on line, adding their machine's throbbing power to whatever skein of forces Alex had devised to snare the beast below, the *singularity.*

Lost in her thoughts, she hardly noticed as the air grew warmer. Dank, fetid odors rose from deeper down, where decades of seepage had filled the unpumped mine's lower sections. The lift stopped short of those realms, fortunately. Jen pushed open the rattling gate and set off down a tunnel lit by a string of tiny bulbs.

Here and in other similar mines, the old white oligarchy had skimmed the wealth from one of the richest countries in the world. Properly invested, the veins of gold and coal and diamonds might have provided for future generations, white and nonwhite, long after the minerals ran out. Most of the present black cantons did not blame the old oligarchs for racism, per se. After all, they practiced tribal separation themselves. What made them seethe was something much simpler. Theft. And the frittering away of a vast treasure by those too blind to see.

Today, the thieves' blameless descendants were bitter refugees in faraway lands, and the victims' equally blameless progeny had inherited a terrible anger.

Condensation glistened. Jen's footsteps echoed down the side corridors like lifeless, skittering hauntings. At last the light ahead brightened as she neared the open cavern chosen by Kenda's team. There, under a vaulted ceiling, lay the equipment they had brought from New Zealand. And in the center loomed a gleaming cylinder, anchored in bedrock.

The dour Japanese physicist glared sourly as she arrived. Clearly, he chafed at the condition she had imposed, in return for her help in acquiring this site . . . that she be notified before every run and be present as a witness.

"What was the damage, last scan?" she asked.

Kenda shrugged. "A few tremors southeast of the Hawaiian Islands. Nothing to speak of. Hardly any comments on the Net."

Of course she had no way to check after him. Not without sending out her own search programs, which would inevitably leave a trail. So she relied on open news channels, which seemed to have hardly noticed the chain of minor disturbances circuiting the globe. Eventually, someone was sure to spy a pattern, of course. Hawaii, for instance, was at the antipodes from this site. All one had to do was draw a line from there, roughly through the Earth's center . . .

. . . through the devil thing down there . . .

Jen shivered. She was no invalid at mathematical modeling. But just two pages into one of Alex's papers she'd gotten utterly lost in a maze of gauzy unrealities that left her head spinning. She still couldn't bring up an *image* of their enemy. Vanishingly small, titanically heavy, infinitely involute—it was the essence of deadliness. And from childhood, Jen had always feared most those dangers without faces.

"Five minutes, Dr. Wolling," one of the technicians said, looking up from his station. "Can I get you a cup of coffee?" His friendly smile was a marked contrast to Kenda's sour attitude.

"Thank you, Jimmy. No, I think I'd better go get ready now." He shrugged and rejoined the others, staring into video and holo displays, their hands gripping controller knobs or slipped into waldo gloves. Jen walked past them all to the corner unit she'd been assigned, where she was grudgingly allowed to tap in her subvocal. She donned the device and let holographic displays surround her.

She coughed, yawned, cleared her throat, swallowed—setting off waves of color as the unit tried to compensate for all the involuntary motions. With her own computer back home, the clearing process was quick and automatic. Here, deprived of all the custom design that made her terminal a virtual alter ego, she had to do it fresh each time.

Mists dissolved into blankness. Jen dialed the unit's sensitivity upward . . .

. . . and a Tiger flashed out at her, **roared,** and then quickly receded into the background . . .

. . . **sparkles** dashed and hopped . . .

. . . **coruscating words with images . . .**

Even the tiniest signal to her jaw or larynx might be interpreted as a command. Keeping one hand on the sensitivity knob, she concentrated to erase mistakes the machine kept interpreting as nascent words.

Few people used subvocals, for the same reason few ever became street jugglers. Not many could operate the delicate systems without tipping into chaos. Any normal mind kept intruding with apparent irrelevancies, many ascending to the level of muttered or almost-spoken words the outer consciousness hardly noticed, but which the device manifested visibly and in sound.

Tunes that pop into your head . . . stray associations you generally ignore . . . memories that wink in and out . . . impulses to action . . . often rising to tickle the larynx, the tongue, stopping just short of sound . . .

As she thought each of those words, lines of text appeared on the right, as if a stenographer were taking dictation from her subvocalized thoughts. Meanwhile, at the left-hand periphery, an extrapolation subroutine crafted little simulations. A tiny man with a violin. A face that smiled and closed one eye . . . It was well this device only read the outermost, superficial nervous activity, associated with the speech centers.

When invented, the subvocal had been hailed as a boon to pilots —until high-performance jets began plowing into the ground. *We experience ten thousand impulses for every one we allow to become action. Accelerating the choice and decision process did more than speed reaction time. It also shortcut judgment.*

Even as a computer input device, it was too sensitive for most people. Few wanted extra speed if it also meant the slightest subsurface reaction could become embarrassingly real, in amplified speech or writing.

If they ever really developed a true brain-to-computer interface, the chaos would be even worse.

Jen had two advantages over normal people, though. One was a lower-than-average fear of embarrassment. And second was her internal image of her own mind.

Modern evidence notwithstanding, most people didn't *really* believe their personalities comprised many subselves. Dealing with stray thoughts was to them a matter of control, and not, as Jen saw it, negotiation.

I also have the advantage of age. Fewer rash impulses. Imagine giving a machine like this to young, libidinous, hormone-drenched male pilots! Of all the silly things to do.

Having thought that, she had a sudden memory of Thomas, on that summer day when he took her aloft in his experimental midget-zeppelin, back when such things were rare and so romantic. Her golden hair had whipped in his eyes as he held her close, high over Yorkshire. He had been so young, and so very male . . .

The unit couldn't interpret any detail in her vivid recollection, thank heavens! But the sensitivity was set so high, multicolored flashes filled the display, in rhythm to her emotions. Again, a candy-striped feline poked its nose around a corner and mewed.

Back into your lair, tiger, she commanded her totem beast. The creature snarled and slunk back out of sight. The colors also cleared away as Jen consciously acknowledged all the extraneous impulses, quelling their irrelevant clamor.

A clock ticked down. At the one-minute mark there appeared in front of her an image of the Earth's interior—a complex, many-layered globe.

This wasn't one of her own, ideogenous constructs, but a direct feed from Kenda's panel. Deep inside the core, a stylized purple curve showed the orbit of their enemy, Beta. Already that trajectory showed marginal deviations, disturbed by earlier proddings from the four Tangoparu resonators.

Outside that envelope lay a region of blue strands where channels of softened mantle flickered with sudden, superconducting electricity —the temporary concentrations of extra energy Kenda's team needed for the coming push. She listened as the techs maintained a running commentary. They would wait till Beta's orbit brought it behind a likely looking thread, then set off the "gazer"—Alex's bizarre, incredible invention—releasing coherent gravitational waves and giving their foe another tiny nudge.

Jen felt a surge of adrenaline. Whatever the outcome, this was memorable. She hoped she'd live long enough to be proud of all this someday.

Hell, there's a part of me that doesn't care about the pride. It just wants to live longer, period.

There is, within me, a bit that wants to live forever.

It was a conceit that demanded a reply. And so, from some recess of imagination, something caused the subvocal to display a string of gilt words, right in front of her.

. . . If that is what you want, my daughter, that is what you shall have. For did I not promise you exactly that, long, long ago?

Jen laughed. In a low voice she answered. "Yes you did, Mother. You promised. I remember it well." She shook her head, marveling at the texture of her own imagination, even after all these years. "Oh, I am a pip. I am."

Concentrating carefully, Jen ignored further input from her goddess or any other extraneous corner of her mind. She focused instead upon the planned procedure and paid attention to the Earth.

□

To the Efé people, the advancing jungle was just another invader to adapt to. Legends told of many others, even long before the Tall People came and went away again.

To Kau, leader of his small band of pygmies, the forest was more real, more immediate, than that other world had been—back when he used to wear shirts woven in faraway factories and carried a carbine as a "scout" for something called "the Army of Zaire." One thing for certain, the Tall People had been easier to please than any jungle. You could play to their greed or superstition or vanity, and get all sorts of things the jungle provided grudgingly, if at all.

The women, like his wife, Ulokbi, used to work in the gardens of the Lessé people for a share of the crop. In those days, Kau and his brothers hunted as they pleased, taking paper money for many of their kills, flattering themselves they were woodsmen as skilled as their grandfathers had been, before the hills were laced with wires and pipelines and logging roads.

Now the Lessé were gone. Gone too were the gardens, roads, carbines, and armies. In their place had come rain and more rain . . . and jungle such as even Kau's father's grandfather had never seen. Now

Kau tried to remember and teach his grandsons skills he himself once thought quaint.

It was all very strange. Without the old district clinic, many children now died. And yet, Efé numbers were on the rise. Kau could not account for it. But then, one did not try as hard anymore, to account for things.

Now a new invader was seen clambering through the trees. Chimpanzees, spreading from what had been their last redoubts, were also increasing, returning to reclaim their ancient range.

"Are they good to eat, grandfather?" His eldest grandson asked one day, when their path crossed under that of a small ape band, foraging in the canopy overhead. Kau thought back, remembering meat he'd tasted in his youth. It hadn't been all that bad.

But then he recalled, also, when the Efé used to squat at the back of a Lessé village clearing while movies were shown against a tattered screen. One had been a disturbing tale, all about apes that had talked and yet were misunderstood and abused in one of the Tall People's crazy cities. He remembered being sad—thinking of them as his brothers.

"No," Kau told his grandson, improvising as he went along. "They have almost-people spirits. We'll eat them only if we're starving. Never before."

One day, not long after, he awoke to find a mound of fruit piled high beside his hut. Kau contemplated no connection between the two events. He did not have to.

● Teresa rose toward consciousness and for a fey moment felt as if
E she were in two places at once.
X   With the deceitful certainty of dreams, she lay lazily,
O contentedly, beside Jason's warmth. She heard her husband's
S breath and felt his man-sized bulk nearby—its weight and
P strength—which only a little while ago she had welcomed upon
H her, creating a continuum of he, she, and the world.
E   At the same time, another part of her knew that Jason's
R nearness was ersatz, based on a close but oh so different reality.
E   *There's no urgency,* a third voice urged, pleading compromise.
No duty calls. Hold onto the illusion a little longer.

So she tried to go on pretending. After all, can't believing sometimes make dreams come true?

No, it can't. Besides, you're awake now.

And anyway, she went on, just to be mean. *Jason's on a one-way trip to some far star.*

Without opening her eyes, she remembered where she was now. The ice told her. Even kilometers away, the Greenland glacier made her senses dip, tugged at her equilibrium, set her teetering. Just as the sloping mattress seemed to draw her toward the weight beside her.

He doesn't twitch much, she thought about the man sleeping only a foot away, his mass pushing a well into the foam rubber pad. *Jason used to give those sudden, tiny jerks . . . like a dog dreaming he's chasing rabbits.*

A woman has to get used to a lot when she marries, and so Jason's nighttime movements had caused some sleeplessness back at the beginning. But that wasn't half as bad as when he would suddenly, for no apparent reason, stop breathing! The rhythm of his soft snores would cease and she'd snap wide awake in alarm.

It took the base surgeon and a dozen scholarly references to convince her that mild, intermittent apnea in adult males was nothing by itself to worry about. In time she grew accustomed to all of it. To the twitches, the snores, the sudden pauses. In fact, what had been irritating became familiar, comforting, normal.

But just when you get used to someone. Just when you've reached the point where there's nowhere else in the world you feel safer. When you feel all is well. That's when it all gets ripped away from you again. Damned world.

Tears offered one benefit. They washed away the scratchy, "rusty drawer" effect of opening your eyes from sleep. The liquid blur blinked away and the cabin swam into focus—an insulated prefab with ribs of cured, undressed pine. The furniture was spare and economical—a small bureau, chairs, and a table bearing two used candles, two glasses, and an empty wine bottle. An open closet held exactly six changes of clothes, including an impressive arctic suit that wouldn't need much alteration to work on Mars.

If anyone ever got to Mars.

Pervading the room were odors, from the candles, from machinery . . . and others Teresa admitted feeling ambivalent about. Powerful ambivalence.

Hers for instance. Her own sweat. Her shampoo. All mingled with the overpowering aroma of a man.

"Good morning, Emma."

She turned her head on the pillow and saw his pale blue eyes looking into hers. *He's been watching me,* she realized. *He was so still. I thought he was asleep.*

"Mmmp," she said, rubbing her eyes to wipe away any trace of tears. "G'mornin'. What time is it?"

Lars glanced over her head. "Plenty early, yes. Did you sleep well?"

"Fine. Fine." She pushed her pillow back against the headboard and sat up, keeping the sheet above her breasts. They still throbbed pleasantly from his attentive study hours earlier. So intent had he been, so assiduous, one might have thought he intended memorizing them and every other contour of her body.

It had felt good. Had *been* good. A woman needs appreciation, worship, from time to time. There had been a dozen good reasons to say yes to this. He was a nice man. Their quick-scan blood tests had checked out okay. It had been far too long. And Teresa knew she didn't talk in her sleep.

Teresa lived by checklists. They were modern mantras to peace of mind. By any *logical* checklist, she should feel okay about this. Still, there remained an unreasoning part of her which adamantly sought excuses to feel guilty.

"I . . . have packing to do," she said.

"It's only six. I wish you'd stay a while. I will cook breakfast. I melted glacier ice already for coffee." In Japan, they paid fifty thousand yen a kilo for the best ten-thousand-year-old blue ice. Here, of course, one didn't have to pay freight or refrigeration charges or even a resource-depletion tax. Ancient ice lay right outside the front door, in gigatons.

"I have one more survey scan to help with this morning . . . and the zep picks me up at fifteen hundred . . ."

"Emma, I almost have the feeling you want to get away from me."

She'd been avoiding his eyes. Now she looked up again quickly. *Ah,* she thought. *No fair smiling at me like that!*

Lars was everything the teenager inside her could hope to swoon for. Built for power and endurance, he nevertheless was gentle and tactile with those calloused hands. His face was a regular delight: rugged and yet retaining a touch of innocence about the eyes. It pleased Teresa such a young, handsome fellow showed so much enthusiasm for her. It was good for the morale. Good for her self-esteem.

Hell, last night was much better than good. If ever one night's solitary consummation can be called "good." And clearly one night was all this could ever be.

She reached up and caressed his cheek, thrilling to the prickly touch of his morning stubble. For the moment, reality was nice enough. When his hand stroked gently up her side, settling eventually over one breast, she exhaled a sigh that was ninety-five percent pleasure. The rest could go to hell.

"No, Lars. I don't feel I have to get away from you."

As he bent to whisper in her ear, Teresa knew yet another way to feel good about this. "Emma," he murmured, speaking the name on her passport, the woman she was during this brief interlude.

As *Emma* then, she clung to him and again sighed.

Stan Goldman escorted her to the aerodrome when it was time for her to leave. The small cargo zeppelin was already moored, its transparent flanks turned toward the sun to focus every available watt onto its internal photocells.

Together they walked the long way across the open moraine, he immersed in his own thoughts and she in hers. "Here, take a look at this," Stan said at one point, leading her a few meters to the left. "Do you see that?"

"See what?" He was pointing at a jumble of stones.

"Yesterday those were in a stack. I put them there. Today it's toppled."

Teresa nodded. "Quakes." In her valise she carried data on the recent increase in local, low-level Earth tremors, gathered with the finest instruments. "Why the poor man's seismograph, Stan?"

The elderly physicist smiled. "Never put all your confidence in sophisticated gadgets, my dear. It's as bad as trusting faith alone, or math, or your own senses."

Actually, Teresa's nickname in the Bus Driver's Guild was "Show Me" Tikhana. She nodded in agreement. "I'll try to remember that."

"Good. The Lord gave us eyes and imagination, faith and reason, enthusiasm and obstinacy. Each has its place." He kicked one of the fallen rocks. "I'm afraid it won't be long before a lot more people suspect something's going on."

So far only a few obscure sources on the Net were commenting on the pickup in worldwide seismic activity. But she knew what incident had Stan particularly worried. "Have they found that plane yet?" she asked. "The one in Antarctica?"

He shook his head. "They're assuming it crashed. But there's not a peep from the flight transponder. And you heard the report of that ozone scientist, who claimed seeing something flash into the sky? The location corresponds with the plane's last known position . . . and the emergence point of one of our recent beams.

"I'm afraid we've probably inflicted our first casualties."

Teresa forgave Stan his oversight. Or maybe he was right to leave out those killed on Erehwon. That debacle had been a true accident, after all. This time though, despite all their precautions, they were directly to blame. Everyone in the cabal knew this venture would cost even more lives before it was over.

For a few minutes they walked in silence. Teresa thought about cracks in the ice, fractures in the ground, peals of thunder in the sky.

She also thought about how good it felt to breathe the crisp air. To feel the breeze off the glacier on her skin. To be alive.

"I wish I could go with you," Stan said as they neared the bobbing zeppelin. "I'd give anything to talk to Alex and George and find out what's going on in the big picture. Our images of the interior are poor with this slave resonator. The master must be giving Alex such a view of the beast."

Teresa realized he must envy Lustig the chance to map their enemy's anatomy, too small to measure except in units familiar to atoms, denser than a neutron star. "I'll have him send you a portrait with the next courier. You can keep it by your bedside, along with Ellen and the grandkids."

Her gentle teasing made him grin. "You do that."

Standing near the gangway, he offered his hand. She threw her arms around him instead. *I'll also tell Ellen she's a lucky old girl.*

Lifting her eyes over his shoulder, she saw a much taller man at the edge of the field, standing near a big, round lifter-crane. *His hands are probably already stained with oil,* she thought, recalling how, even after Lars had washed, his skin had given off the piquant, exciting tang of engines. They had said their good-byes . . . she with a promise of a future message or visit he probably knew to be a lie. And so he simply lifted his hand and shared with her a soft smile of no regrets.

NASA thought she was still at a seclusion resort in Australia. It wouldn't do to have a random Net inventory show her flitting about on the other side of the globe. But at any moment there were millions drifting across the sky in everything from cruise liners to economy "cattle cars" to tramp freighters like this one. That was why the trip back to New Zealand would include several lighter-than-air legs, linking points where she could sneak long passages on Tangoparu Ltd. turboprops. Settling near a window to observe the crew cast off, Teresa resigned herself to a long time alone with her thoughts.

Two men watched her go. One waving from the docking site and the other farther off, standing next to an open cowling. But as the airship leaped in a rush of released buoyancy, Teresa's gaze lifted beyond the airstrip, beyond the dome where Stan's crew conspired to chivvy a monster, beyond the stony pit where sleuths sought clues to ancient cataclysms. She skimmed breathlessly over the great ice sheet, but even its mass could not hold her. Teresa felt a lifting in her heart. The soft, happy thrumming of the little zep's engines seemed to resonate with the tempo of her pulse.

It was no unaccustomed thing, this affair she had with flight. And yet each time felt as if she'd fallen in love again. It was a romance separate from all earthly ardors, more steadfast, yet unjealous of any other passion.

It's not speed that matters, she thought. *It's the act. It's breaking the bonds.*

Far beyond the unsetting sun, she felt the pull of faraway planets and longed to follow even there.

It's flying . . . , she thought.

So Teresa crossed her arms and settled in to make the best of a long voyage round the world.

□

Elvis roams the open interstates in a big white cadillac.

It has to be him. How else to explain what so many flywheel-bus and commuter-zep riders claim to have seen . . . that plume of dust trailing like rocket exhaust behind something too fast and glittery to be tracked with the naked eye?

Squint and you might glimpse him behind the wheel, steering with one wrist while fiddling the radio dial, then reaching for that never-ending, always frosty can of beer. "Thank you, honey," he tells the blonde next to him as he steps on the accelerator.

The roar of V-8 power, the gasoline smell of freedom, the rush of clean wind blowing back his hair . . . Elvis hoots and lifts one arm to wave at all true Americans who still believe in him.

Certain chatty Net-zines are rife with blurry pictures of him. Snooty tech types claim the photos are fakes, but that doesn't bother the faithful who collect grand old TwenCen automobiles and polish them, saving up for that once-a-year spin down the highway, meeting at the nearest Graceland Shrine for a day of chrome and music and speed and glory.

Along the way, they stop at ghostly abandoned gas stations and check for signs that he's been by. Some claim to have found pumps freshly used, reading empty but still somehow reeking of high octane. Others point to black, bold, fresh tire tracks, or claim his music can be heard in the coyotes' midnight serenade.

Elvis roams the open interstates in a big white cadillac. How else to explain the traces some have found, sparkling like fairy dust across the fading yellow lines?

A pollen of happier days . . . the glitter of rhinestones.

C
O
R
E

● Across eight thousand miles of open ocean, the autumn gale had plenty of time to accelerate, to pick up power and momentum. So did the waves and tides. Over that great stretch, each grew accustomed to mastery. When they met the island's stiff resistance, therefore, they protested in fists of spume that climbed the steep shelf then clenched and shook in rage.

Alex stood at the window of his hut, listening to the storm. Even indoors, he felt each boom with his fingertips. Each breaker set the glass panes vibrating. Rain bursts assaulted the roof in sudden, pelting furies, rattling it like a war drum before receding just as quickly again, driven by the wind to drench some other place.

Out beyond the bluffs, over the sea, luminous backlit clouds advanced on parade, parting now and then to let the moon spread a brief, pearly sheen across the turbid waters.

A lonely color, he thought. *No wonder they say moonlight is for lovers. It makes you want someone to cling to.*

Alex was remembering. Remembering when weather like this had been his friend.

As a student he used to walk the fens and dikes of Norfolk, traveling all the way from Cambridge at the rumor of a squall. They were seldom as powerful as this gale, of course. Easter Island lay unsheltered in the middle of a vast ocean, after all. Still the North Sea used to put on some impressive shows.

The locals must have thought him daft to go out in his wellies and slicker, striding into stiff gusts and cloudbursts. But that hardly mattered. Nothing in the world felt as vivid or as potent as a tempest. That year, facing the torture of exams, he had felt a real need for vividness, for potency. Others craved sunny days, punting on the Cam, but to Alex the sky's power seemed to offer something even better—an anodyne to the ethereal ghostliness of his mathematics and to those uncertain adolescent qualms.

Once, while walking in keraunophilic splendor through a thunderstorm, he had actually experienced a sudden insight into mysteries of transactional quantum mechanics, an intuition that had led to his first important paper. Another time he shouted into the rain, demanding it explain to him why Ingrid . . . yes, that had been her name . . . why Ingrid had dropped him for another boy.

Generally, the thunder answered only irrelevancies. But perhaps it had been the shouting itself that provided a cleansing generally unavailable to Englishmen indoors. Whatever. He usually came away drenched, drained, restored.

Now, though, the fens and farms of Norfolk were drowned. The dikes had surrendered to the sea at last and those problems that once had vexed Alex now seemed trivial in retrospect. What wouldn't he give to have them back, in exchange for today's?

From the darkness behind him there came a rustle. "Alex? Can't you sleep?"

Momentary moonlight filled a trapezoid-shaped portion of the small room as he turned around. June Morgan lay half within that canted illumination, propped on one elbow, watching him from bed. "Sorry," he said. "I didn't mean to wake you."

Her smile was warm, if tired. June's blonde hair was tousled and flattened on one side. "I reached out," she said. "You weren't there."

Alex inhaled deeply. "I'm going to the lab for a little while. I'll be back soon."

"Oh, Alex," she sighed and got out of bed, wrapping the sheet around herself. She crossed the narrow floor and reached up to brush at his wild hair. "If you keep this up you'll kill yourself. You've got to get more rest."

She had a pleasant smell—a feature more important to Alex than it was to most men. *Still, there are some women whose aroma hits me like . . . ah, never mind.*

It was no reflection on June, whom he liked a lot. Probably, it was just a matter of mysterious complementarity—of the right interlocking pheromones. Lucy and Ingrid had smelled like goddesses to him, he recalled . . . similarities between two otherwise completely different lovers, known more than a decade apart. *If only one complementarity carried with it all the others,* he thought wistfully. *Then all we'd have to do is go around sniffing each other behind the ear, to find the perfect mate.*

"I'm all right, really. Much more relaxed." He threw his shoulders back, stretching. "You'd do professionally, as a masseuse."

Her eyes seemed to twinkle. "I have. Someday I'll show you my license."

"I quite believe you. And . . . thanks for being so patient."

She looked up at him. Since it seemed expected of him, and because he knew he really ought to want to, Alex took her into his arms and kissed her. All the while though, he chided himself.

She deserves better. Much better than you can give her now.

Of course she had her own memories and pain. As he held her, Alex wondered if maybe she felt the same way toward him as he did toward her. More grateful than in love.

Sometimes it was enough just to have someone to hold.

Alex said hello to the techs on duty when he arrived. They, in turn, waved and greeted their *tohunga,* their *pakeha*-pommie expert on weird monsters and cthonic exorcism. Several of them crawled over scaffolding surrounding the gleaming gravity wave resonator, giving it required servicing. Their unit's next run wouldn't be for several hours yet, so nearly everyone else was taking advantage of the lull to catch up on sleep.

Those of us who can.

He sat down at his own station, touching panels and bringing displays to light. The subvocal he left on its stand. Lately he'd been having trouble controlling the hypersensitive device. It picked up too many random, useless surface thoughts which insistently manifested in his clenching jaw muscles and a recurring tightness in his throat.

All right, he thought, grimly. *What's the latest death toll?*

Alex dialed the special database he'd set up to track their guilt. Instantly, the far left display unrolled a list of "accidents" reported in the media, whose time and location coincided with one of their emergent beams . . . a ripped zeppelin . . . a minor tidal wave . . . a missing aircraft . . . a mile-long freshwater tanker with its rear end shorn off.

Surely some of these would have happened without our intervention.

Yes, surely. Mishaps occurred all the time, especially at sea. This epoch's ocean sediment consisted of a rain of manmade junk, sunken vessels, and myriad other debris.

But looking at the list, Alex knew some would never join the growing layer on the sea bottom. Some, in all probability, were no longer on Earth at all.

He thought of Teresa Tikhana, the first person he knew who had lost someone to this strange war. She had forgiven him, even now helped carry the burden. After all, what were a few lives against ten billion?

But what if we fail? Those men and women will have been robbed of precious months. Months to spend with their families, with lovers, with summer skies or rain. Robbed of their good-byes.

It was about to get worse, too, because the project had been going exceptionally well. Until yesterday, each of the four resonators had acted independently. Almost every gazer beam had emerged along a line nearly straight through the Earth's core. And opposite each of their four sites lay only open ocean.

But now they had the right parameters. Beta, their *taniwha*, had pulsed and throbbed with every scan. Each time it mirrored amplified gravitons, it also experienced a kick. Those kicks were starting to add up. Soon, if luck held, the trough of its orbit would rise out of Earth's crystalline inner core.

And so the tricky part began—coordinated scans from two or more stations at once. That would be arduous to arrange in secrecy, but Alex wasn't daunted by that, only by the inevitability of doing even more harm. From now on, the beam would emerge in a different location every time, and he'd face hard choices.

Should he scrub one run because a beam might graze a suburb? There were so *many* vast suburbs. What if it happened at a crucial stage, when a beam deferred might mean losing control of their monster for an orbit, or ten . . . or perhaps forever?

Anyway, only a fraction of the beams interacted with the surface world at all. Most passed through silently, invisibly. Alex was only starting to piece together clues as to why some did so while others coupled so dramatically with seismic faults, seawater, or even man-made objects. Unfortunately, they couldn't delay to figure it all out before continuing. They had to go on.

The holo showed Earth's inmost regions. The pink core still enclosed two pinpoints, but his Iquitos singularity had nearly evaporated. Another day and it would be invisible.

The other object, though, was heavier than ever. Ponderously, Beta rose, hovered, and fell again. To Alex it appeared to throb angrily.

Each day, seemingly, he got coded queries from George Hutton asking about the monster singularity's origin. Pedro Manella, running interference for the project in Washington—routing their communications through the most secure channels he could find— added his own insistent questions. Who had created the thing? When and where did the idiots let it fall? Was there evidence that could be shown to the World Court?

Next week Alex would have to answer in person. It was frustrating to have learned so much and still be unable to give a conclusion. But something was queer about Beta's life history, that was certain.

It's got to be fundamental. The thing can't be less than ten years old. And yet it has to be, or no one could have made it!

Above the liquid outer core, the lower mantle glowed many shades of green, tracing ten thousand details of hot, slowly convecting, plasti-crystalline minerals. Some currents looked patient and smooth, like trade winds, while others were spiked cyclones, spearing toward the distant surface.

Dotted lines tracked intense magnetic and electric fields—June Morgan's contribution to the model. Most currents flowed slow and uniform, like heat eddies. But there were also faint traceries of lambent blue—slender, snaking threads that flickered even as he watched in real time—the superconducting domains they had only just discovered. Fragile and ephemeral, they were the energy source used to drive the gazer.

Have they changed? Alex wondered. Every time he looked, the pattern of interlaced strands seemed different, captivating.

A tone startled him, but the watch officer only glanced over from his own console, reassuringly. "New Guinea's about to fire in tandem with Africa, *tohunga.* Don't worry. We're off line ourselves for another four hours."

Alex nodded. "Uh, good." Internally he sighed. *June is right. I'm running myself straight into the ground.*

He was grateful she stayed with him, despite his moodiness and hesitant libido. Theirs was a wartime comradeship of course, to be lived moment by moment, without playing "push me, pull you" over intangibles like permanence or commitment. People tend to worry less about such things when the world itself seems a makeshift, temporary place. One was grateful for what one got.

Among other things, June had at least given him back his sexuality.

Or maybe it's the gazer, Alex wondered. For all the machine's potential destructiveness, he still felt a thrill whenever it suddenly cast beams of titanic power. No one had ever created anything so mighty. Those brief rays were powerful enough to be detected a *galaxy* away . . . provided someone looked in the right direction, at the right moment, tuned to an exact frequency.

He touched a key and saw the computer had finished reworking his design for the next-generation resonator—this one a sphere only a little over a meter across. Spiderweb domain traceries laced an otherwise flawless crystalline structure. Even in simulation it was beautiful, though probably they'd never have time to use it.

He entered a few slight modifications and put the file away again. Alex yawned. Perhaps he might sleep now.

Still he lingered a few minutes to watch the next pulse-run. Seconds ticked down. Beta's image passed beneath a channel of pulsing blue. Suddenly, as Alex watched, yellow lines lanced inward —George Hutton's New Guinea resonator casting its triggering beam inward simultaneously with the one in Southern Africa. The lines met deep within the core, right on target.

Beta throbbed. Blue threads pulsed. And from the combination something flickered like a fluorescent tube coming to life. Suddenly a beam, white and brilliant, speared outward at a new angle, through all the layered shells and into space beyond.

Alex read the impulse generated, compared the recoil coefficients with those calculated in advance and saw they matched within twenty percent. Only then did he check for point of exit, and blinked.

North America. Right in the middle of a populated continent. He sighed. *Well, it had to begin sometime, somewhere.*

He wasn't masochistic enough to sit and wait for damage reports. There'd be guilt enough for later. Right now his duty was to rest. At least he wouldn't be alone. And June didn't seem to mind if he occasionally moaned in his sleep.

Halfway back to his hut, however, negotiating a slippery, narrow path through the wet, waving grass, Alex was caught suddenly in a glare of lightning.

The flash didn't startle him entirely, since bursts of rain still rolled like traffic across the plateau and the air tingled with the scent of ions. Nevertheless he jumped, for the sudden light brought *figures* out of the gloom—stark, tall shapes whose shadows seemed to reach like grasping fingers toward him. During that first stroke, and the black seconds that followed, Alex felt abruptly cornered. His heart raced. The next burst only reinforced that impression of encirclement, but cut off too soon to show what or who was really there. Or, indeed, if anything was there at all.

Only with the third stroke did he make out what company of things stalked the dim slope. Alex exhaled through nostrils flared by pumped adrenaline. *Lord. I must be keyed up, to jump half out of my knickers at the sight of those things.*

It was only the statues, of course . . . more of the eerie monoliths constructed long ago by the native folk of Rapa Nui, in their pessimistic, manic isolation.

They saw the end coming, he thought, looking down the file of awful figures. *But they were dead wrong about the reasons why. They assumed only gods had the power to wreak such havoc on their world, but people caused the devastation here.*

Alex felt compassion for the ancient Pasquans—but a superior sort nevertheless. In blaming gods, they had conveniently diverted censure from the real culprit. The designer of weapons. The feller of trees. The destroyer. Man himself.

More rain pelted him, finding entrance under his hat and collar to send chill rivulets down his spine. Still he watched the nearest of the great statues, pursuing a reluctant thought. Lightning flashed again, exposing stark patterns of white and black underneath those brooding brows. The pouting lips pursed in sullen disapproval.

For more than a hundred years we've known better. No outside power can approach human destructiveness. So we managed not to fry ourselves in nuclear war? We only traded in that damoclean sword for others even worse . . .

Something was wrong, here. Alex felt a familiar nagging sensation —like the tension just before a headache—that often warned him when he was on a false trail. He could sense the brooding stares of the ancient basalt figures. Of course it was the night and the storm, encouraging superstitious musings—and yet still, it felt as if they were trying to tell him something.

Our ancestors used to see all disasters originating outside themselves, he thought. *But we know better. Now we know humanity's the culprit. We assume . . .*

Alex grabbed at the idea before it could get away. Lightning struck again, this time so close the pealing thunder shook his body.

. . . we assume . . .

He knew it was only static electricity, crackling and pounding around him. The atmosphere's equilibration of charge, that was all. And yet, for the first time Alex listened . . . really listened as his ancestors must have, when they too used to stand as he did now, under a growling sky.

The next crackling stroke shook the air and bellowed at him.

*. . . **Don't assume!***

Alex gasped, stumbling backward, staggered by a sudden thought more dazzling and frightening than anything he'd ever known. All at once the great statues made horrifying sense to him. And within the thunder, he now heard the angry voices of jealous gods.

□

World areas expected to be submerged when Greenland and Antarctic ice sheets fully melt. [□ Net Vol. A-69802-111, 04/11/38: 14:34:12 UT Stat-projection request.]

Large portions of Estonia, Denmark, eastern Britain, northern Germany, and northern Poland.
The Netherlands.

Western Siberia (the Occidental Plain) east of the Urals, linking the Black Sea to the Caspian and Azov seas, nearly to the Arctic.

Lowlands of Libya, Iraq.

The Hindustan and Indus valleys in India.

Portions of northeastern China.

Southwestern New Guinea and a large bight extending into the Eastern Australian Desert.

The Lower Amazon and La Plata valleys, the Yucatán Peninsula. Large portions of the states of Georgia, North Carolina, and South Carolina.

Florida. Louisiana . . .

● Logan ignored the insistent beeping of his wrist-pager. Whoever
L was calling, they'd have to wait till his hands stopped shaking.
I Besides, it was easy to dismiss one tiny sound in this cacophony of
T disaster.
H　　Sirens blared as emergency vehicles braved the dark, solitary
O road leading down to where catastrophe had struck only a short
S while ago. Behind Logan, the pilot of his commandeered
P helicopter kept its blades spinning as he argued by radio with the
H Sweetwater County Sheriff's Department, urging the SWAT team
E commander to be less trigger happy and a little more cooperative
R with a federal investigating team.
E　　". . . Look! Don't give me all that dumpit load about state and
local jurisdictions having priority. That don't hold canned shit in a gor-sucked case like this! You see any sign of any burfing terrorists? Do *we* look like a bunch of fucking greeners?"

Logan ignored the racket. He stared at the panorama below, lit by the searchlights of sheriff 'copters already on the scene.

What was left of the Flaming Gorge Dam gleamed like jumbled, broken white teeth below the darker sheen of native canyon rock. Part of the glitter came from roaring water, still spilling over the remains. Most of the great reservoir had already departed downstream toward the Green River Valley. Breathless net reporters told of a swath of devastation, stretching from Wyoming through a corner of Utah, into northwestern Colorado and finally back to Utah again.

But then, Flaming Gorge lay near the intersection of three states, so that was a bit misleading. In fact, the only town evacuated was Jensen, several score miles downstream. And by then, most of the flood's force had been spent ravaging the unpopulated canyons of Dinosaur National Monument.

Unpopulated . . . if you don't count scores of missing or panicked campers. Nor a hapless paleontologist or two.

Logan refused to think about the hurt done those exquisite, fossil-yard badlands. One disaster at a time. He stared at the ruined dam, wondering how such total demolition was accomplished.

It could have been done more economically. Why blow a dam into smithereens when a good *crack* would serve as well?

Besides, why would any eco-guerrilla want to smash the Flaming Gorge Dam? No one left alive remembered the arroyo that had been drowned under the man-made lake. Anyway, even Neo-Gaian radicals recalled the debacle when someone had wrecked the huge Glen Canyon Dam. The resulting mess had been a caution to all sides and restored the world's beauty not one, iota.

This didn't feel like a Greener action, anyway. Within an hour's drive there were scores of more likely targets . . . places where Logan's colleagues were busy altering the land for better or worse. Projects hotly debated in the pub-crit media, not a boring, stolid structure like this stodgy old dam.

No, this has to be our demon again.

Footsteps scuffed the loose gravel to Logan's right. It was Joe Redpath, the assistant assigned him only hours ago for this mission. The tall Amerindian wore twin braids . . . a fashion statement recently adopted on many university campuses as chic and declarative. . . though here Logan figured both hairstyle and attitude were genuine.

"Found some eyewitnesses, Eng," Redpath announced tersely. "Be here in a minute."

"Good. Any word when we'll get satellite scans of the explosion itself?"

The other man nodded. "Half an hour, they say."

"That long?" Logan felt a surge of resentment.

Redpath shrugged. "Spivey has lots of teams. You didn't think you and me were his top boys, did you? Hell, we're backups for the backups, man."

Logan looked squarely at the part-time federal agent. A number of retorts crossed his mind—including telling Redpath where Spivey could take his priorities.

But no. Something was happening in the world. And if Logan wasn't privy to secret knowledge at the top, at least his investigator's warrant took him where events were breaking . . . where he might help solve the puzzle and do some good.

"What do you think of that?" he said, pointing toward the shattered dam.

Redpath watched Logan for another second before turning to survey the scene. "Don't see how they did it." He shrugged. "Shape's all wrong."

"What shape?"

Redpath gestured with his hands. "Shape of the explosion. Dams don't break that way. No matter where you plant the charges."

Logan wondered how Redpath knew. By investigating other cases? Or, perhaps, from practical experience on the other side? To some among society's brightest, cooperation with authority was strictly a conditional matter, in each instance judged by sharply individualized standards. He could well imagine Redpath swinging one way on one occasion and quite another when it suited him.

"I agree. There's a big piece missing."

The local agent inhaled deeply, his eyes roving the tumbled remains. He exhaled and shrugged indifferently. "Carried downstream. We'll find the chunks in the morning."

Logan admired the man's veil. His shield of inscrutability. In this situation, however, it didn't work at all. *He knows damn well the missing chunks aren't downstream! He just doesn't want to admit he's as appalled as I am.*

Their pilot finally gave up arguing with the sheriffs and shut down his whining engine, a sudden, welcome lessening of the din. Far better to wait for clearances from Washington, anyway, than be shot down by trigger-happy provincials.

More footsteps approached. A woman in a National Parks uniform, whom Redpath had deputized only an hour ago, entered the light with a middle-aged man in tow. Two teenagers rushed ahead to point at the blasted dam, making awed sounds.

"We . . . were farther up the reservoir," the father explained when asked. He was dressed in fishing gear. Hand-tied flies dangled from his vest, along with a photo-ID camping permit.

"We'd come ashore and were setting up to cook . . . That's when it all happened." He covered his eyes. "Those poor night fishermen. They were caught in the flood."

This fellow wasn't going to be much use. Shock, Logan diagnosed, and wondered why the ranger had even brought him here. "What was the first thing you saw?" he asked, trying to be gentle.

The man blinked. "We lost the boat. You don't think they'll charge us, do you? I mean, we ought to get a refund for the whole trip . . ."

A tug at Logan's elbow made him turn. "It started with a noise, mister."

One of the teenagers, his hair cut short, Ra Boy style, gestured toward the muddy lake bed below. "It was this low hum. Y'know? Like the water sort of *sang?*"

His sister nodded. A little younger but nearly as tall, she wore a Church of Gaia gown at complete odds with her sibling's sun-worshipper attire. Logan could only imagine the ideological climate in their household.

"It was beautiful but awfully sad," she said. "I thought at first maybe it was the fish in the lake, you know, *moaning?* Because *certain people* were killing and eating them?"

The boy groaned, sending her a disgusted look. "The fish were *put* there so people could come and—"

"How long did the sound last?" Logan interrupted.

Both youths shrugged, nearly identically. The boy said, "How could we know? After what happened next, our subjective memory's sure to be screwed up."

The things they're teaching kids, these days, Logan thought. For all the schools' emphasis on practical psychology, kids still seemed to pick and choose what they wanted to absorb, in this case, apparently, a convenient and plausible excuse for imprecision.

"What did happen next?"

The boy started to speak, but his sister jabbed his ribs. "Things got all blurry for a second or two," she said hurriedly. "With funny colors—"

"Like we were going down this laser suspensor tunnel ride, see?" the boy blurted out. "You know, like at—"

"Then there was this *light*. It was so bright we had to turn and look. It was down in the south . . . over here at the dam—"

"We don't *know* it was here at the dam! We just have the evidence of our eyes to go by, and we were still getting over the colors . . ."

The girl ignored her irate sibling. "There were these *lines*, of light? They went *up*, into the sky . . . sort of like this?" She propped her elbow on one hand and gestured at an angle toward the noctilucent clouds.

Logan looked to her brother for confirmation. "Did you see lines also?"

He nodded. "Except they didn't go up like she said. She thinks *everything* comes out of the Earth. Naw. The lines came down! I think—" he edged closer, conspiratorially "—I think it's aliens, mister. Invaders. Using big solar-powered mirrors . . ."

His sister whacked him on the shoulder. "You should talk about the evidence of our own eyes! Of all the stupid . . ."

Logan held up both hands. "Thank you both very much. Right

now, though, I think your dad needs your help more than I do. Why don't you just give the ranger your access codes, and we'll get in touch later if we need any more information."

They nodded earnestly. *Basically good kids,* Logan thought. He also felt more grateful than ever for the undeserved gift of his own sensible daughter. He could hardly remember the last time Claire's voice had taken on that shrill, whining tone, capable of shattering glass or any adult's peace of mind at twenty paces.

"It opened up!"

Logan turned around. The kids' father was pointing with a shaking hand toward a starry gap in the clouds. "The sky opened up like . . . like my folks used to tell me it would on the day."

"On what day, sir?"

The man looked squarely at Logan, a queer shining in his eyes. "The day of . . . reckoning. They used to say the heavens would open up, and terrible judgment would be delivered."

He gestured at his offspring. "I used to scoff, like these two with their their pagan gods. But lately, it's seemed to me as if . . . as if . . . " He trailed off, glassy eyed. The two teenagers stared, their sibling conflicts instantly abandoned. At that moment they looked almost like twins.

"Daddy?" the girl said, and reached for him.

"Stay away from me!" He pushed her aside. Striding to the edge of the bluff, the man shrugged out of his fishing jacket and threw it to the ground. Then he fell to his knees, looking across the ravaged waste.

Tentatively, perhaps fearing another rejection, first the girl and then her brother followed, standing on each side of their father at the brink of the overlook. But this time, instead of pushing them away, he flung his arms around their knees and clasped them tightly. Above the wailing sirens, the growling helicopters and the still noisy crash of ebbing floodwaters, Logan clearly heard the man sob.

Hesitantly at first, the girl stroked her father's thinning hair. Then she looked across and took her brother's hand.

Logan found the breath tight within his chest. And suddenly he realized why.

What if the guy is right?

Perhaps not precisely. Not about the exact cause of the disturbing omen. The boy's "aliens" were as likely as any mumbledy-jumble from the Book of Revelations.

Still, until this moment it hadn't quite occurred to Logan just what might be at stake. Hour by hour, reports poured in through Colonel Spivey's new database, ranging from the picayune to the catastrophic. From towering chimeras glimpsed at sea to strange tremors and dust devils out in empty deserts. To the sudden disappearance of a great dam. Each day it got steadily stranger.

This may be serious, Logan thought, and felt intensely the late northern chill.

☐ Worldwide Long Range Solutions Special Interest Group [☐ SIG AeR,WLRS 253787890.546].

To the astonishment of many, we've so far avoided the great die-back people keep talking about. New crops plus better management and a shift away from many greedy habits have helped us feed our ten billions. Barely. Most of the time.

Solutions often breed other calamities though. So it was that pundits, seeing this trend, predicted a population runaway toward twenty billion or more, until our numbers finally did bring us to the oft-predicted Precipice of Malthus.

But look. The wave is cresting. After fifty years of struggle, birth rates now appear finally under control, and UNPMA now predicts we'll top out at thirteen billion around the year 2060. Then, slowly, it should taper off a bit. That peak may just be low enough to let us squeak by.

Will it have been modern birth control that brought us up just short of the edge? (If, in fact, we don't topple over it yet.) Or was it something else? A new study [☐ Stat.Sur. 2037.582392.286-wELt] indicates human effort may deserve less credit than we smugly believe.

While vast amounts have been spent getting half the world's women to hold their births to one or at most two, nearly as much money now pours into research and medical aid to help the other half carry even one pregnancy to term. Causes have been proposed for this pandemic of infertility . . . such as women deferring child-bearing until late in life or effects inherited from the sex-crazed eighties, the cancer plagues, or drug-happy 2010s. But new research shows that *pollution* may have played a principal role. Chemical mutagens in the air and water, causing early spontaneous abortions, now appear to lead all other forms of contraception in the industrialized world.

To some Gaian sects, of course, this just validates their worldview, that for every immoderation there is an inevitable counter, some negative feedback to restore a balance. In this case, it isn't we the living who are dying, as Malthus predicted. (At least not in vast numbers.) Rather, equilibrium is being restored by the stressed environment itself, culling the unborn.

It's a cruel, unpleasant notion. But then, anyone who's been alive and aware for any part of the last fifty years is by now used to unpleasant notions . . .

● Daisy had been snooping again.

H   "Dumpit!" Claire pounded the arm of her chair. This time,
Y her mother had gone too far. She'd installed a watchdog program
D right outside Claire's own mailbox! "Did she actually think I
R wouldn't notice something like that?"
O   Probably. So many parents were members of the "reality
S disabled" when it came to having a clear mental image of their
P children. Perhaps Daisy still considered Claire a child when it
H came to the demanding, grownup world of the Net.
E   "I'll show you," Claire muttered as she tapped out code of her
R own. Oh, she knew she'd never be able to tackle Daisy one-on-
E one. But it just might be possible to take advantage of her mother's
preconceived notions.

Vivisector was an object program she'd borrowed from Tony just the other day . . . a tasty little routine going the rounds among young hackers that disassembled other programs and put them back together again without leaving a trace—even while those programs were running. Carefully, Claire sicked Vivisector on her mother's watchdog. Soon its guts were laid out across her inspection screen.

"So, just as I thought." Daisy had assigned the little surrogate to pluck anything piped to Claire from Logan Eng.

"He's not your husband anymore, Mother. Can't you leave the poor codder alone?"

Carefully, Claire excised a core gene from the watchdog, to use as a template. Then she dialed her father's Net access code and performed a hybridization test on the protocols controlling access to his private cache. Sure enough, there was a match. Some lines throbbed redly near the heart of Logan's own security system. Claire tsked.

"Very lazy, Mother. Using close genetic cousins to perform similar tasks? In related databases? I'm disappointed in you."

She wasn't, really. Claire actually felt relieved. Comparing codons from two infiltrators was a technique she knew and understood. No doubt Daisy could have made the trick moot had she tried. And although it showed benign contempt, her mother was capable of worse emotions—like wrath. You didn't want to tangle with Daisy when she was in the latter state. Not at all.

The red lines throbbed. Claire considered going ahead and excising the retrocode. Or writing a warning to her father.

But then, what would be the point? At best Daisy would wind up paying a fine. Then she'd just pay attention to doing the job right.

"Why is she suddenly so interested in Logan's work, anyway?" Claire wondered. Of course her mother disapproved of Logan's career. But there were so many engineers out there who were far worse . . . far less sensitive to environmental concerns. Until now Daisy had seemed tacitly amenable to leaving her ex-husband alone and going after bigger game.

Claire bit her lip. There was one way to find out what was going on without triggering Daisy's alarms. That was to have her mother's infiltrator send duplicates of whatever it stole to *her*, as well as to Daisy.

No. She shook her head. *I won't do that. I'll wait till Logan's back in town and tell him in person.*

Unfortunately, her father was hopping across the continent, sending her little blips from all the sites his new employer sent him to. His messages implied something was up, certainly, and Claire's curiosity was piqued.

But I'll respect his privacy, she determined. *I'm not Daisy.*

With that resolve, she carefully worded a simple message to her father, saying she missed him, and adding a final line: "Mirror-mirror, Daddy. Don't take any funny-looking apples."

It was a bit of shared context code, from back when she used to liken her mother to Snow White's wicked queen, complete with all-seeing, all-knowing magic mirror.

I just hope Logan gets the meaning. It's pretty thin.

Carefully, Claire exited that portion of the Net, leaving all her mother's agents in place. That done, she went back to reading her own mail.

"HI, CLAIRE!"

Tony Calvallo's bright, cheerful face popped out of one message blip, less than an hour old. Had she been wearing her wrist-comp while out repairing the mulch bin, she'd have been able to take his call in person.

"THERE'S A PARTY AT PAUL'S TONIGHT. YOU KNOW HE'S BY THE NORTH MAIN LEVEE, SO WE COULD STROLL OVER THERE ALONG THE WAY AND LOOK FOR SUBSIDENCE CRACKS."

He grinned and winked.

Claire had to smile. Tony was getting better at this . . . keeping up a gentle pressure while remaining all the time light and easy, letting her ultimately control the pace. As for tonight's pretext, it *had* been a long time since she'd inspected the levees over in Paul's part of the valley. Tony was showing more imagination and insight all the time.

Claire bit her lip—enjoying the pressure on sensitive nerve endings. A couple of times lately, she had let Tony kiss her and had been surprised both by his eager roughness and by how much she liked it.

Maybe I'm only a little slower than other girls, instead of plain retarded, as I thought.

Her mother's generation, of course, had been precocious and downright crazy, starting sex on average around age eleven—an appalling notion she figured explained a lot about the present state of the world.

Still, there might be such a thing as moving too slowly. . . .

All right, let's see what happens. Anyway, I can always insist on actually looking for cracks in the levee.

With a smile, she punched Tony's number. Predictably, he answered before the second ring.

At the same moment, Daisy McClennon watched rivers of data stream down the walls of her private chamber, each reflecting another view of the world.

One screen panned the recent Wyoming dam collapse . . . pictures laxly stored by her ex-husband where she could easily get at them. Taking into account other case studies in his file, this series of "coincidences" had gone well beyond happenstance into the realm of enemy action.

She'd already tapped her usual sources and come up with, at best, rumors and vague hints. One of the rich expatriate banking co-ops in Ulan Bator seemed to have an intense interest in these events. So did a Canadian old-money clan in Quebec. Then there were the government spook agencies—one of whom Logan was clearly working for. They were hard to crack, and risky, too. For one thing, some of their best hackers were about her equal. Daisy preferred sniffing round the edges till she knew enough to warrant a full assault.

One possible hint turned in a nearby holo tank—a pictorial globe of the Earth, sliced in half, with lines drawn through the cutaway. The anonymous tip had found its way into her box this morning—no doubt from someone in her web of worldwide contacts. At first it made little sense. Then she saw how each line was pinned, at one end, on the location of one of the "anomalies" in Logan's file. Each line then passed through the center of the Earth to arrive inside one of four broad ovals at the antipodes.

What could that mean? So far nothing much had occurred to her. Daisy was about to discard the hint as spurious when she saw one of the ovals centered on Southern Africa.

I wonder. Jen Wolling seemed to be involved in something she thought serious, even dangerous. Then she up and left for Southern Africa again. Could there be a connection?

There was another link, now that she thought about it. Wolling's collaborators were based in New Zealand. Wasn't that where some of the earliest quakes had been centered?

Daisy poked away at the puzzle, sending her electronic servant beasts to seek and fetch new pieces. Brazenly, she rifled the files of several companies owned by a cousin she hadn't seen in years, but who owed her more favors than an aristocratic prig like him would ever want to be reminded of. One of his companies handled data transfers from Australasia. . . .

Slowly, pieces fell into place. *They're using a communication nexus in Washington. A very good one, in fact. Wouldn't have caught on if it weren't for that little glitch there . . . happened just this morning. What luck.*

Meanwhile, ignored for the moment, the last wall of her workroom shone with her latest video-enhancement handiwork . . . a bootleg, colorized, 3-D version of *The Maltese Falcon*, with extra scenes extrapolated for a set of Chicago collectors who were apparently unhappy that some works were protected in primitive form by the National Treasures Act.

Miles Archer smiled, then took two bullets in the belly, as he had so many times for about a hundred years. Only this time his groans were in digital quad, and the blood that seeped three-dimensionally round his fingers was vivid, spectrally certified to be exactly the correct shade of arterial red.

☐ **Net Vol. A69802-554, 04/20/38: 04:14:52 UT User T106-11-7657-Aab Historical Reenactments Special Interest Group. Key: "Authenticity"**

Brussels—Belgian Historical Society authorities called in the police this morning, to help disperse thirty thousand disappointed history buffs dressed in Napoleonic military uniforms. Some of them had traveled from as far as Taipei to participate in this year's reenactment of the Battle of Waterloo, only to be turned away. Many angrily waved valid registration forms, claiming they already had official membership in the annual pageant.

This reporter asked BHS Director Emile Tousand: Why were so many accepted, only to be turned back at the battleground itself?

"Out of three hundred and fifty thousand applicants, only one hundred and ninety-three thousand qualified with authentic, handmade kits—from muskets to uniform buttons. Of this number, we predicted a no-show rate over thirty percent, especially after this year's increase in coach-class zep tickets."

When asked to explain the discrepancy, Tousand explained.

"It appears we are suffering for our success. Except for Gettysburg and Borodino, ours is the best-respected battle recreation. Many a hobbyist is eager to play a simple foot soldier, even if only to have a radio-controlled blood capsule explode on him the first day."

Then why were so many sent away?

"Our passion is accuracy. How, I beg you, could we have that with more ersatz soldiers than were at the main battle itself? The idea's absurd!

"Besides, environmental groups routinely agitate against us. Unless we keep the trampling and noise below a certain level, musket era reenactments may go the way of those ill-fated attempts to recreate Kursk and El Alamein, back in the teens."

Would that be such a bad thing? Can we afford to have thousands of men marching about, playing war, when that scourge nearly destroyed us only a generation ago?

"Is it a coincidence that as more men join clubs to 'play war,' there has been less and less of the real thing? I can tell you that our boys come to have fun. They get fresh air and exercise, unlike so many whose passive hobbies have turned them into mere net junkies, or even dazers. And there are very few injuries or fatalities."

But don't war games encourage a romantic fascination with the real thing?

"Any sane man knows the difference between falling dramatically before the cameras, because his blood cartridge has been set off, and what it must have been like for real soldiers . . . to actually feel musket balls tearing through your guts, shattering your bones. None of our members fails to weep when staring across the terrible finale—the tableau of the Old Guard, lying in bloody heaps upon their last redoubt. No man who has gazed on it in person could ever long to experience the real thing.

"Fascination, yes. There will always be fascination. But that only increases our appreciation of how far we've come. For all our problems today, I doubt anyone who studies what life was like in bygone times would sanely trade places with any ancestor, peasant or soldier, general or king."

The moon shone on the horizon, setting in an unusual direction. Almost due south.

Of course at that moment *all* land headings were approximately southward. Such was the trickery of crossing over the north pole. Or near it.

Drifting alongside the tiny model-three shuttle *Intrepid*, Mark Randall turned from the moon to look down upon the estuary of the arctic River Ob, artery of the new Soviet grainlands. The steppe stretched across a flat expanse below him, an infinity of dun and green. Mark spoke a single word of command.

"Magnify."

In response, a portion of his faceplate instantly displayed an amplified image. The Ob delta leaped toward him in fine, amplified detail.

"Prepare record sheet six," he continued, as a reticle scale overlaid the ribbon of muddy blue, weaving across a vast, thawing tundra plain. Sensors tracked every movement of his pupils, so Mark could roll the scene as fast as he could look. "Zero in on position twelve point two by three point seven. . . . expand eightfold."

Smoothly, the main telescope in *Intrepid*'s observation bay turned microscopically on magnetic gimbals, focusing on the specified coordinates. Or at least the inertial tracker *said* they were the right coordinates. But Mark's experience working with Teresa Tikhana had rubbed off, especially after the Erehwon disaster, so he double-checked by satellite references and two distinct landmarks—the Scharansky Power Station and the Cargil Corporation grain silos, bracketing the river from opposite shores. "Commence recording," he said.

Between those two landmarks, the waters showed severe agitation —surface ripples and stirred-up bottom mud—each symptom detected in another optical or infrared or polarization band. A flotilla of vessels nosed about the disturbed area. Mark wondered what had churned the River Ob so. It must be important for *Intrepid*'s orders to be changed so abruptly, extending this simple peeper run far beyond normal.

I'm going to talk to the guild about this, Mark thought. *Polar assignments pile up too many rads. They shouldn't be prolonged without extra shielding, or bonus pay. Or at least a damn good reason . . .*

It got especially inconvenient when a model-three shuttle was involved. The HOTOL technology was a pilot's dream during takeoff and landing, but a bizarre, unexpected, and uncorrectable vibration mode meant the crew had to step "outside" during high-resolution camera work, in order not to ruin the pictures with their slightest movements. The flaw would be fixed in the next generation of vehicles . . . in maybe twenty years or so.

He spoke again, commanding the telescope to zero in even closer on the activity below. Now he clearly made out machinery on the dredges, and men standing at the gunwales of squat barges, peering into the river. Mark even saw black figures in the water. Probably divers, since as yet the burgeoning Ob was still too chilly to support other life forms so large. Lab-enhanced photos would, of course, make out even manufacturers' labels on the divers' masks.

Green telltales showed the recording was going well. This kind of precision wasn't possible with surveillance satellites, and manned space stations didn't operate this high in latitude, so *Intrepid* was the only platform available. Mark hoped it was worth it.

Anyway, so much for the rewards of fame and good works. After Erehwon and his tour for NASA on the lecture circuit, it had been good to be promoted to left seat on a shuttle. Still, of late he'd begun wondering if maybe Teresa weren't right to be so suspicious, after all. Something smelled funny about the way he'd been glad-handed and diverted from asking questions about what Spivey and his crew had learned about the disaster.

Apparently that was who he was working for now, anyway . . . Glenn Spivey. The peeper had a large and growing group under him. Quite a few of Mark's friends had been swept into the colonel's growing web of subordinates and investigative teams. But what were they investigating? When Mark asked, old comrades looked away embarrassed, muttering phrases like *national security* or even—*it's secret.*

"Bloody hell," Mark muttered. Fortunately, his suit computer was narrow minded, and didn't try to interpret it as an instruction. After hard experience, the astronaut corps went for literal-minded equipment that was difficult to confuse, if less "imaginative" than what civilians used.

Something moved at the corner of Mark's field of view. He shut down the helmet projection and turned. The spacesuited figure approaching wasn't hard to identify, since his copilot was the only other person within at least a hundred kilometers. Drifting alongside, Ben Brigham touched two fingers of his gloved right hand to a point along the inside of his left sleeve. This was followed by two quick chopping motions, a hand turn, and an elbow flick.

The sun was behind Mark, shining into Ben's face, turning his helmet screen opaque and shiny. But Mark didn't need to see Ben's expression to read his meaning.

Big chiefs hope to catch coyote in the act, his partner had said in
sign talk, descended not from the speech of the deaf, but from the
ancient Indian trade language of the American plains.

Mark laughed. He left the comm channel turned off and used his
own hands to reply. *Chiefs will be disappointed . . . Lightning
never strikes twice in same place . . .*

Although space sign talk formally excluded any gesture that
might be hidden by a vacuum suit, Ben answered with a simple shrug.
Clearly they'd been sent to observe the latest site of the
"disturbances" . . . weird phenomena that were growing ever
creepier since Erehwon was blown to kingdom come.

Still, are we really needed here? Mark wondered. By treaty,
NATO and U.N. and USAF officers were probably already prowling
the disaster site below in person, even cruising by in observation zeps.
The only way *Intrepid*'s orbital examination would add appreciably to
what on-site inspectors learned would be for the shuttle's instruments
to catch a gremlin in the very act. So far routine satellite scans had
captured a few bizarre events on film, at extreme angle, but never yet
with a full battery of peeper gear. . . .

Mark's thoughts arrested as he blinked. He shook his head and
then cursed.

"Oh, shit. Intercom on. Ben, do you feel—"

"Right, Mark. Tingling in my toes. Speckles around the edge of my
visual field. Is it like when you and Rip, on *Pleiades*—?"

"Affirmative." He shook his head again, vigorously, though he
knew that wouldn't knock away the gathering cobwebs. "It's different
in some ways, but basically . . . oh hell." Mark couldn't explain,
and besides, there wasn't time for chatter. He spoke another code
word to start their suits transmitting full physiological data to ship
recorders. "Full view, main scope," he ordered then. "Secondary
cameras—independent targeting of transient phenomena."

The picture of the river loomed forth again. Now, though, the
scene was no longer efficient and businesslike. Men scurried about the
barges like angry ants, some of them diving off craft that bobbed and
shook in the suddenly choppy water.

Tiny windows appeared on Mark's faceplate, surrounding the
main scene as *Intrepid*'s secondary telescopes began zooming in under
independent control. Half the scenes were too blurry to make out as
Mark's eyesight grew steadily worse. Bright pinpoints swarmed inward
like irritating insects.

"What do we do?" Ben's voice sounded scared. Mark, who had
been through this before, didn't blame him.

"Make sure of your tether," he told his copilot. "And memorize

the way back to the cabin. We may have to return blind. Otherwise
. . ." He swallowed. "There's nothing we can do but ride it out."

*At least the ship is probably safe. There aren't other structures
around, like Teresa had to deal with. And a model-three shuttle is
too small to worry about tides.*

Mark had himself convinced, almost.

The outer half of his visual field was gone, though it kept
fluctuating moment by moment. Through the remaining tunnel,
Mark watched a drama unfold far below, where the Ob jounced and
writhed as if someone were poking it with invisible rods. Flow
deformed the hills and depressions nearly as quickly as they formed.
Still, the undulations seemed to take clear geometric patterns.

Then, within a circular area, the Ob simply disappeared!

It was only pure luck none of the study vessels were inside the
radius when it happened. As it was, the boats had a rugged ride as the
columnar hole rapidly filled in.

"Where . . . where'd the water go?" Ben asked.

Joining the growing ringing in Mark's ears came the blare of a
camera alert. One of the secondary pictures suddenly ballooned
outward, rimmed in red. For a moment Mark couldn't make out what
had the computer so excited. It looked like another view of the river
valley, but at much lower magnification, or from higher altitude.

But this image appeared warped somehow. Then he realized it
wasn't unfocused. He was looking down at the Ob through a *lens*. The
lens was a glob of water, which had suddenly manifested in midair at
an altitude of . . . he squinted to read the lidar numbers . . .
twenty-six kilometers!

Mark breathed the sweaty incense of his own dread. Something
tiny and black squiggled *inside* the murky liquid blob that paused,
suspended high above the planet. But before he could order the
telescope to magnify, the entire watery mass was gone again! In its
wake lay only a rainbow fringe of vapor, melting into the speckles at
his eyes' periphery.

"What the . . . ?"

"It's back!" Ben cried. "Fifty-two klicks high! Here . . ." and he
rattled off some code. Another scene, from another instrument,
popped into view.

Now the ground looked twice as far below. The Ob was a thin
ribbon. And the portion of stolen river had reappeared at double the
altitude. Mark had time to blink in astonishment. The black object
within looked like . . .

The spherule vanished again. "Mark," Ben gasped. "I just calculated
the doubling rate. It's next appearance could be—Jesus!"

Mark felt his copilot's hand grab the fabric of his suit and shake it. "There!" Ben's voice crackled over the intruding roar of static. An outstretched arm and hand entered Mark's narrow field of view and he followed the trembling gesture out to black space.

There, in the direction of Scorpio, an object had appeared. He didn't have to command amplification. Even as telescopes slewed to aim at the interloper Mark cleared all displays with one whispered word and stared in direct light at the oblate spheroid that had paused nearby, shimmering in the undiminished sunlight.

What strange force might have hurled a portion of the Ob out here—momentarily, magically co-orbital with *Intrepid*—Mark couldn't begin to imagine. It violated every law he knew. Small flickerings told of bits being thrown free of the central mass. But in its center there floated a large object—

—a *woman*. A diver, wearing a black wetsuit and scuba gear, with twin tanks that Mark bemusedly figured ought to last her another couple of hours, depending on how much she'd already used.

Mark had left only a narrow tunnel of vision, but it was enough. Through the diver's face mask he caught the woman's strange expression—one of rapt fulfillment mixed with abject terror. She began to make a sign with her hands.

"We've got to help her!" he heard Ben shout over the roar of static, preparing to launch himself toward the castaway.

Realization came instantly, but too late. "No, Ben!" Mark cried out. "Grab something. Anything!" Mark fumbled and found a stanchion by the cargo bay door. This he now gripped for all his life.

"Hold tight!" he screamed.

At that moment his helmet seemed to fill with a terrible song, and the world exploded with colors he had never known.

When it was all over, quivering from sore muscles and wrenched joints, Mark gingerly reeled in his copilot's frayed, torn tether. He searched for Ben everywhere. Radar, lidar, telemetry . . . but no instrument could find a trace. Of the hapless Russian diver, also, there was no sign.

Perhaps they have each other for company, wherever they're going, he thought at one point. It was a strange solace.

He did detect other things nearby . . . objects that command insisted he pick up for study. These were bits of flotsam . . . a mud-filled vodka bottle . . . a piece of weed . . . a fish or two.

Then, preparing to head home, he went through the retro protocols several times, double-checking until Command accused him of stalling.

"Can it!" he told them sharply. "I'm just making sure I know *exactly* where I am and where I'm going."

As the pyrotechnics of reentry erupted around the cockpit windows, Mark later realized he'd spoken exactly as Teresa Tikhana would have. To the mission controllers, he must have sounded just like her.

"Hell, Rip," he muttered, apologizing to her in absentia. "I never knew how you felt about that, till now. I promise, I won't ever make fun of you again."

Even much later, when he was once more on the steady ground, Mark walked cautiously toward the crowd of anxious, waiting officials with a cautious gait, as if the tarmac weren't quite as certain a platform as the others believed. And even when he began answering their fevered questions, Mark kept glancing at the horizon, at the sun and sky, as if to check and check again his bearings.

☐ Although claiming they have now completely resolved the technical errors that led to the tragedy of 2029, the governments of Korea and Japan nevertheless today delayed reopening the Fukuoka-Pusan Tunnel. No explanation was given, although it's known a recent spate of unusual seismic activity has caused concern. The temblors do not fit the commission's computer models, and no opening will take place until these discrepancies are explained.

In regional social news, 26-year-old Yukiko Saito, heiress to the Taira family fortune, announced her betrothal to Clive Blenheim, Earl of Hampshire, whose noble, if impoverished line stretches back to well before the Norman Conquest.

The most recent planetological survey indicates that the islands of Japan contain approximately ten percent of all the world's volcanoes.

● How much difference could a month make? The last time Teresa
E had sat at this table, deep inside the secret warrens of Waitomo,
X her personal world had only recently crashed in on her. Now her
O grief was stabilized. She could look back at her passionate
S interlude in Greenland as part of a widow's recovery, and begin
P thinking about other things than Jason.
H   Of course, last time she had also been numb from a
E completely different shock—learning about Earth's dire jeopardy.
R That fact hadn't changed.
E   *But at least we're doing something about it now.* Futile or
not, their efforts were good for the spirit.

George Hutton was just finishing his overall status report. Their
limited success so far was visible in the large-scale display where their
foe could now be seen swinging about on an elongated orbit, rising
briefly out of the crystalline inner sphere into the second layer—the
outer core of liquid metal. No longer a complacent eater, squatting
undisturbed amid a banquet of high-density matter, the purple dot
now seemed to throb angrily.

Teresa approved. *We're coming after you, beast. We've begun
defending ourselves.*

That was the good news. Give or take a few panicky moments, all
four resonators had commenced firing sequences of tandem pulses to
convert the planet's own stored energy into beams of coherent gravity,
recoiling against Beta and gradually shoving it outward toward—

*Toward what? We still haven't figured out what to do with the
damned thing. Push until its growing orbit takes it out of the Earth,
I suppose. But then what? Let a decaying singularity, blazing at a
million degrees, keep whizzing round and round, entering and
leaving, entering and leaving till it dissipates at last in a huge burst
of gamma rays?*

Teresa shrugged. *As if by then the choice will still be in our
hands.* That was one reason the mood at the table was somber.

Another cause was visible on the outermost shell of the planetary
model . . . a pattern of lights signifying where gazer beams had
emerged at land or sea.

Actually, most of the beams pulsed at modes and wavelengths
interacting not at all with surface objects. Often, the only effect was a
local wind shift or eddies in an ocean current. Still, from a quarter of
the sites came rumors of strange colors or thunderclaps in a clear blue
sky. Hearsay about water spouts or disappearing clouds. Accounts of

dams destroyed, of circular swirls cut in wheat fields, of aircraft vanishing without a trace.

Teresa glanced over at Alex Lustig. He had already told of his efforts to avoid population centers, and she didn't doubt his sincerity. Still, something had changed in the man since she had seen him last. By now, in all honesty, she had expected to find him a wreck. Tossed by guilt as he had been when they first met, Teresa figured him due for a nervous breakdown when the toll of innocent victims began to rise.

Oddly, he now seemed at peace listening patiently to each speaker as the meeting progressed, exhibiting none of the nervous gestures she recalled. His expression appeared almost serene.

Maybe it isn't so odd at that, Teresa thought. Beyond the pool of light cast by the display, she saw June Morgan move over behind Lustig and start massaging his shoulders. Teresa's nostrils flared. *They deserve each other,* she thought, and then frowned, wondering what she meant by that.

"We've tried to avoid predictable patterns," George Hutton was saying. "So it would be hard to track down our resonators' locations. No doubt several major nations and alliances and multinationals already suspect the disturbances are of human origin. In fact, we're counting on a suspicious reaction. So long as they're blaming each other, they'll not go looking for a private group."

"Isn't that dangerous?" Teresa asked. "What if someone panics? Especially one of the deterrence powers? It doesn't take much effort to break the treaty seals on a squadron of cruise missiles, you know. Just hammers and some simple software."

Pedro Manella leaned into the light. "That's under control, Captain. First, the seismic occurrences are taking place impartially, worldwide. The only organized pattern anyone will notice is that the disturbances statistically avoid major population centers.

"Second—I've taken care to deposit sequestered announcements with a secret registration service, triggered for net release the instant any power goes to yellow alert."

Alex shook his head. "I thought we weren't going to trust any of the services."

Manella shrugged. "After your own unpleasant experience, Lustig, I don't blame you for feeling that way. But there's no chance of premature release this time. Anyway, the announcement only gives enough hints to get some trigger-happy crisis team to slow down and consult their geologists."

George Hutton touched a control, dimming the globe display and bringing up the room lights. Alex squeezed June Morgan's hand and she returned to her seat. Teresa looked away, feeling at once voyeuristic and resentful. *She's a collector,* Teresa thought. *How can a woman who once wanted Jason also be attracted to a man like Lustig?*

She suppressed an urge to turn around and look at him again, this time in frank curiosity.

"Besides," George Hutton added. "There's a limit to how long we can keep this secret anyway. Sooner or later someone's going to track us down."

"Don't be so sure," Pedro countered. "Our weakest link is the Net, but I have some very bright people working for me in Washington. By keeping traffic to a minimum and using tricks like your Maori mountain-iwi dialect, we could mask our short blips for as long as six months, even a year."

"Hmph." George sounded doubtful and Teresa agreed. Manella's optimism seemed farfetched. There were too many bored hackers out there with free time and kilobit parallel correlators, looking for any excuse to stir up a sensation. Frankly, she wasn't at all sure whether she'd be greeted by her tame NASA flunkies when she got back to Houston or by a pack of security boys, wearing total-record goggles and slapping her with inquiry warrants.

Even so, she looked forward to the trip, riding a stratoliner again under her own name. *I've had it with zeps and aliases for a while.*

"Don't you think the secret will come out when Beta finally emerges through the surface?" George asked. "We won't be hiding from just ferrets then. The whole pack of hounds will be baying for blood."

"Conceded. But by then we'll have our report ready to present to the World Court, won't we, Alex?"

Lustig looked up, as if his thoughts had been far away. "Um. Sorry, Pedro?"

Manella leaned toward him. "We've been after you about this for months! Second only to getting rid of Beta is our need to find out who made the cursed thing. It's not just revenge—though making an example of the bastards will be nice. I'm talking about saving our own skins!"

Teresa blinked. "What do you mean?"

Manella groaned as if he were the only one in the room able to see the obvious. "I mean that, after all the havoc we've set off, and are going to set off in the future, do you think people will simply take our word we just *found* the awful thing down there?

"Hell no! Here we are, led by the one man ever caught building an illegal black hole on Earth. Who do you think they'll blame for

Beta? Especially if the real villains are powerful men, eager to divert responsibility."

Teresa swallowed. "Oh."

All the illegal things they had done—including maintaining secrets and harming innocents—all those she was willing to stand to bar for. The salvation of Earth was powerful justification, after all. But it hadn't occurred to her that that very defense might be denied them . . . that their group might actually be blamed for causing Beta in the first place!

"Shit," she said, in a low voice. Now she understood how Alex Lustig must have felt when he seemed so bitter, last time. Which made it even harder to comprehend the man's tranquil expression right now.

"I hadn't thought of that either," June Morgan said, looking at her as if she'd read her mind. Teresa found herself recalling their friendship, back before things started getting so damned messy. The flux of contrary emotions made her quickly turn away to avoid June's eyes.

Manella concluded. "Beyond all thought of revenge, we need the real culprits to hand over to the mob in our stead. So I ask again, Lustig. *Who are they?"*

On the tabletop Alex's hands lay folded. "We've learned a lot lately," he said in a low voice. "Though I do wish Stan Goldman were here to help. Yes, surely he's needed in Greenland. But what I'm trying to say is, despite many handicaps, I think we've made progress.

"For instance, with June's assistance, we've now got a much better idea how matters must have been when the singularity first fell through the most intense regions of magnetism, which must have *trapped* the thing for some time before chaotic interactions finally let its apo-axis decay."

"Chaos? You mean you can't ever tell . . . ?"

"Forgive me. I was imprecise. The word 'chaos' in this sense doesn't mean randomness. The solution isn't perfect, but it can be worked out."

Manella leaned forward again. "So you've traced its orbit back? To the fools who let it go?"

Teresa sat up, feeling chilled. A strange light seemed to shine in Alex Lustig's eyes.

"It's not easy," he began. "Even a tiny, weighty object like Beta must have suffered deflections. Besides magnetic fields, there were inhomogeneities in the crust and mantle—"

Manella would have none of it. "Lustig, I know that look on your face. You've got something. Tell us! Where and when did it fall? How close can you pinpoint it?"

The British physicist shrugged. "Within approximately two thousand kilometers in point of entry—"

Manella moaned, disappointed.

"—and within nine years, plus or minus, for date of initial impact."

"Years!" Pedro stood up. He slapped the tabletop. "Nine years ago, nobody on Earth was capable of building singularities! Cavitronics was still a harmless theory. Lustig, your results are worse than useless. You're saying that while we're still likely to be destroyed, there's no way to track and punish the guilty ones!"

For the first time, Teresa saw Alex smile openly, a look both empathic and feral, as if he had actually been looking forward to this. "You're right on one count, but wrong on two," he told Manella. "Can't blame you, really. I made the same faulty assumptions myself.

"You see I, too, figured Beta had to have entered the Earth sometime since cavitronics became a practical science. Only after tracing Beta's rate of growth and correcting for some hairy internal topologies did I realize it just has to be a lot older than we'd thought. In fact, those error bars I mentioned are pretty damn good.

"The date of entry was probably 1908. The region, Siberia."

Teresa brought a hand to her breast. "Tunguska!"

George Hutton looked at her. "Do you mean . . . ?" he prompted. But Teresa had to swallow before finding her voice again. "It was the greatest airburst explosion in recorded history—even including that electromagnetic pulse thing the Helvetians set off. Barometers picked up pressure waves all the way round the world."

Everyone watched her. Teresa spread her hands. "Trees were flattened for hundreds of kilometers. But nobody ever found a crater, so it wasn't a regular meteorite. Theorists have suggested a fluffy comet, exploding in the atmosphere, or a bit of intergalactic antimatter, or . . ."

"Or a micro black hole." Alex nodded. "Only now we know it wasn't simply a black hole, but a far more complex construct. A singularity so complex and elegant, it couldn't be an accident of nature." He turned to face the others. "You see our problem. Our models say the thing has to come from a time before mankind possessed the ability to build such things . . . if we could do so even now."

This time both Teresa and Pedro were speechless, staring. George Hutton asked, "Are you absolutely certain no natural process could have made it?"

"Ninety-nine percent, George. But even if nature did stumble onto just the right topology, it's absurd to imagine such an object just happening to arrive when it did."

"What do you mean?"

Alex closed his eyes briefly. "Look. Why would something so rare and terrible just happen to strike the planet at the very time we're around to notice? Earth has been here four and one half billion years, but humans only a quarter million or so. And for less than two centuries have we been capable of noticing anything at all but the bitter end. That coincidence stretches all credulity! As my grandmother might say—it's ridiculous to claim an impartial universe is performing a drama solely for our benefit."

He paused.

"The answer, of course, is that the universe isn't impartial at all. The singularity arrived *when* we're here *because* we're here."

Silence stretched. Alex shook his head. "I don't blame you for missing the point. I, too, was trapped by my modern, Western-masochistic conceit. I assumed only humans were clever or vicious enough to destroy on such a scale. It took a reminder from the past to show me what a stupid presumption that is, after all.

"Oh, I can give you the date and point of entry now. I can even tell you something about the thing's makers. But don't ask me how to take vengeance on them, Pedro. I suspect that's far beyond our capabilities at present."

Some of the others looked at each other in confusion. But Teresa felt queasy. She fought the effects, breathing deeply. No physical crisis could affect her as this series of abstract revelations had.

"Somebody wants to destroy us," she surmised. "It's . . . a *weapon.*"

"Oh yes," Alex said, turning to meet her eyes. "It is that, Captain Tikhana. A slow but omnipotent weapon. And the coincidence of timing is easily enough explained. The thing arrived only a decade or two after the first human experiments with radio.

"Actually, the idea's rather old in science fiction, a horror tale of paranoia that's chillingly logical when you work it out. Somebody out there got into space ahead of us and doesn't want company. So it—or they—fashioned an efficient way to eliminate the threat."

"Threat?" Manella shook his head. "What threat? Hertz and Marconi make a few dots and dashes, and that's a threat to beings who can make a thing like this?' He pointed to one of the flat screens, where Alex's latest depiction of the cosmic knot writhed and wriggled in malefic, intricate splendor.

"Oh yes, certainly those dots and dashes represented a threat.

Given that some lot out there doesn't want competition, it would make sense to eliminate potential rivals like us as early and simply as possible, before we develop into something harder to deal with."

He gestured upward, as if the rocky ceiling were invisible and the sky were all around them. "Consider the constraints such paranoid creatures have to work under, poor things. It may have taken years for our first signals to propagate to their nearest listening post. At that point they must fabricate a smart bomb to seek and destroy the source.

"But recall how difficult it is to send anything through interstellar space. If you want to dispatch it anywhere near the speed of light, it had better be small! My guess is they sent a miniature cavitron generator, one just barely adequate to make the smallest, lightest singularity that could do the job.

"Of course, if you start with a small singularity it'll require quite some time absorbing mass inside the target planet before it can really take off. In this case, about a hundred and thirty years. But that should be adequate, usually."

"It almost wasn't, in our case," Teresa said, bitterly. "If we'd invested more in space, we'd have had colonists on Mars by now. Maybe the beginnings of cities on asteroids or the moon. We could have evacuated some of the life arks . . ."

"Oh, you're right," Alex agreed. "My guess is we're unusually bright, as neophyte races go. Probably most others experience longer intervals between discovering radio and inventing spaceflight. After all, the Chinese almost did something with electricity a couple of times, Babylon and the Romans."

Pedro Manella looked down at his hands. "Smart, but not smart enough. So even if we eliminate this horrible thing the nightmare may not be over?"

Alex shrugged. "I suppose not. We and our descendants, should we live to have any, are at best in for a rough time ahead. As a Yank might put it—" and his voice dropped to a drawl "—the galaxy we're livin' in appears t'be a mighty tough neighborhood."

Manella's face reddened. "You're taking this awfully well to be joking about it, Lustig. Has the news driven you over the edge? Or are you saving up for yet another surprise? Maybe another deus ex machina to pull out of your hat, like last time?"

Teresa suddenly realized that was, indeed, what she was holding her breath for! *He's done it before . . . turned despair around with fresh hope. Maybe this time, too?*

Seeing Alex smile, she felt a surge. But then he shook his head and simply said, "No. I have no new tricks."

"Then why are you grinning like an idiot, Lustig!" Manella roared.

Alex stood up. And though he continued smiling, his hands clenched to a slow beat. "Don't you understand? Can't you see what this means?" He turned left and right, staring at each person in turn, getting back only blank looks. In frustration, he shouted. "It means *we're not guilty.* We haven't destroyed ourselves and our world!"

He pressed both hands on the table, leaning forward intensely. "You all saw what shape I was in, before. I was destroyed by this. Oh, sure, we might succeed in ejecting Beta—I give it a one in four chance now, the best odds yet.

"But what would be the point? If we produce the sort of men who'd drop something like that into the world, and not even care enough to go looking for it again? Would we deserve to go on?

"You all kept telling me, 'Don't take it so personally, Alex.' You said, 'It's not your fault, Alex. *Your* singularity was harmless, not an all-devouring monster like Beta. You're our champion against this thing!'

"Champion?" His laughter was acrid. "Couldn't any of you see how that really made me feel?"

Every other person stared. The physicist's reserve had cracked, and underneath now lay exposed someone more human than the Alex Lustig that Teresa had seen before this. A man, she realized, who had stepped deeper into the borderlands of endurance than most ever dream of.

"I had to identify with the makers of that thing!" He went on. "So long as I knew them to be my fellow humans, I had to take responsibility. Couldn't any of you see that?"

He had started out grinning, but now Alex shivered. June Morgan started to rise, but then suppressed the move. Teresa understood and agreed. She, too, felt an urge to do something for him, and knew the only way to help was to listen till he stopped.

Listen humbly, for she knew with sudden conviction that he was right.

"I . . ." Alex had to inhale to catch his breath. "I'm *smiling,* Pedro, because I was ashamed to be human, and now I'm not anymore. Mere death can't take that from me now. Nothing can.

"Isn't . . . isn't that enough for anyone to smile about?"

It was George Hutton who reached him first—who drew his shaking friend into his massive arms. Then, all at once, the rest of them were there as well. And none of their former jealousies or conflicts seemed to matter anymore. They embraced each other and for a time shared the horror of their newly known danger . . . along with the solace of their restored hope.

PART VIII

PLANET KILLER

Space *was the fabric of its existence.*

A skein of superdense yarn—knitted and purled in ten dimensions—it was unravelable. A deep well—sunk into a microscopic point—it was unfathomable. Blacker than blackness, it emitted nothing, yet the tortured space around it blazed hotter than the cores of suns.

It had been born within a machine, one that had traveled far to reach this modest basin, pressed into the rippling universe-sheet by a lesser star. On arrival, the apparatus set to work crafting the assassin's tight weave out of pure nothingness. Then, in its final death throes, the factory slowed its progeny onto a gentle circular path, skating among the star's retinue of tiny planets.

For two revolutions, the assassin lost mass. There were atoms in space to feed its small but hungry maw, but nowhere near enough to make up for its losses . . . loops of superdense brightness that kept popping out to self-destruct in brilliant bursts of gamma rays. If this went on, it would evaporate entirely before doing its job.

But then it entered a shallow dip of gravity—a brief touch of acceleration—and it collided with something solid! The assassin celebrated with a blast of radiation. Thereafter, its orbit kept dipping, again and again, into high-density realms.

Atoms fell athwart its narrow mouth—little wider than an atom itself. There were still very few real collisions, but where at first it dined on picograms, soon it gobbled micrograms, then milligrams. No meal satisfied it.

Grams became kilograms . . .

It had not been programed to know the passage of years, nor that the feast would have to end someday, when the planet was consumed in one last, voracious gobble. Then it would sit alone again in space, and for a time the solar system would have two suns . . . while the essence that had once been Earth blew away in coruscating photons.

Of all this it neither knew nor cared. For the present, atoms kept pouring in. If a complex, fulgent knot in space can be called happy, then that was its condition.

After all, what else was there in the universe, but matter to eat, light to excrete, and vacuum? And what were they? Just subtly different kinds of folded space.

Space was the fabric of its existence.

Without fuss or intent, it grew.

☐ **Worldwide Long Range Solutions Special Interest Group** [☐ SIG AeR,WLRS 253787890.546]. **Space Colonization Subgroup. Open discussion board.**

Okay, so imagine we get past the next few rough decades and finally do what we should have back in TwenCen. Say we mine asteroids for platinum, discover the secrets of true nanotechnology, and set Von Neumann "sheep" grazing on the moon to produce boundless wealth. To listen to some of the rest of you, all our problems would then be over. The next step, star travel, and colonization of the galaxy, would be trivial.

But hold on! Even assuming we solve how to maintain long-lasting ecologies in space and get so wealthy the costs of starflight aren't crippling, you've still got the problem of *time*.

I mean, most hypothetical designs show likely starships creeping along at no more than ten percent of the speed of light, a whole lot slower than those sci-fi cruisers we see zipping on three-vee. At such speeds it may take five, ten generations to reach a good colony site. Meanwhile, passengers will have to maintain villages and farms and cranky, claustrophobic grandkids, all inside their hollowed-out, spinning worldlets.

What kind of social engineering will that take? Do you know how to design a closed society that'd last so long without flying apart? Oh, I think it can be done. But don't pretend it'll be simple!

Nor will be solving the dilemma of gene pool isolation. In the arks and zoos right now, a lot of rescued species are dying off even though the microecologies are right, simply because too few individuals were included in the original mix. For a healthy gene pool you need diversity, variety, *heterozygosity*.

One thing's clear, no starship will make it carrying only one racial group. What'll be needed, frankly, are *mongrels* . . . people who've bred back and forth with just about everybody and seem to enjoy it. You know . . . like Californians.

Besides, it's as if they've been preparing themselves for it all along. Heck, picture if aliens ever landed in California. Instead of running away or even inquiring about the secrets of the universe, *Californians* would probably ask the BEMs if they had any new cuisine!

● Fast approaching the scene of carnage, a detachment of the Swiss
C navy arrived in the nick of time. Sweeping over the ocean's morn-
R ing horizon, the proud flotilla unfurled bright battle ensigns, fired
U warning shots, and sent the raiders into rout at flank speed.
S
T 　　Rescued! The crews of rusty fishing barges cheered as their
saviors hove into sight, the bright sun at their backs. Only mo-
ments before, all had seemed lost. Now disaster had turned to victory!

Nevertheless, Crat barely took notice. Amid the throng of filthy,
sweat-grimed deck hands, climbing the rigging and waving their ban-
dannas, he was too busy vomiting over the side to spend much effort
cheering. Fortunately, there wasn't much left in his stomach to void
into waters already ripe with bloody offal. His fit tapered into a diminishing rhythm of gagging heaves.

"Here, *fils*," someone said nearby. "Take this rag. Clean yourself."

The voice was thickly accented. But then, nearly everyone aboard
this corroded excuse for a barge spoke Standard English gooky, if at
all. Grabbing at a blur, Crat was dimly surprised to find the cloth
relatively clean. Cleaner than anything he'd seen since coming aboard
the *Congo*, some weeks ago. He wiped his chin and then tried to lift
his head, wondering miserably who had bothered taking an interest in
him.

"No. Do not thank me. Here. Let me giff you something for the
nausea."

The speaker was white haired and wrinkled from the sun. And
despite his age, it was clear that his wiry, sun-browned arms were
stronger than Crat's own soft, city-bred pair. The good samaritan
grabbed the back of Crat's head adamantly and lifted a vapor-spritzer.
"Are you ready? Goot! Breathe in, now."

Crat inhaled. Tailored molecules soaked through his mucous
membranes, rushing to receptors in his brain. The overwhelming dizziness evaporated like fog under the subtropical sun.

He wiped his eyes and then handed back the kerchief without a
word.

"You're a silent one, neh? Or is it because you're choked up over
our triumph?" The old man pointed where the green raiders' rear
guard could still be seen, fleeing westward in their ultrafast boats. Of
course nothing owned by Sea State could hope to catch them.

"Triumph," Crat said, repeating the word blankly.

"Yes, of course. Driven off by the one force they fear most. *Helvetia Rediviva.* The fiercest warriors in all the world."

Crat shaded his eyes against the still-early sun, wondering vaguely where his hat had gone to. By the captain's orders, everybody aboard *Congo* had to wear one to protect against the sleeting ultraviolet . . . as if the average life span on a Sea State fishing boat encouraged much worry about latent skin cancers.

The first thing Crat saw as he turned around was the listing hull of *Dacca* . . . the fleet's cannery barge and the green raiders' main target. Deck hands dashed to and fro, washing down gear that had been sprayed with caustic enzymes. Others cast lines to smaller vessels nearby, as pumps fought to empty water from *Dacca*'s flooding bilges.

The greeners hadn't had any intention of sinking her, just rendering her useless. Still, raiders often overestimated the seaworthiness of ships flying the albatross flag. Crat was too inexperienced to guess if *Dacca*'s crew could save the ship. And damned if he'd ask.

Near the factory ship, a UNEPA observer craft loitered, blue and shiny like something from an alien world—which in a sense it was. The dumpit U.N. hadn't done a gor-sucking thing to stop the greeners. But should *Dacca* drown—or spill more than a few quarts of engine oil saving herself—UNEPA would be all over Sea State with eco-fines.

"There," the oldster said helpfully, nudging Crat's shoulder and pointing. "Now you can get a good look at our rescuers. Over toward Japan."

Is that what those islands are? The mountainous forms were low to the northeast, like clouds. Crat wondered how anyone could tell the difference.

He saw a squadron of low-slung vessels approaching swiftly from that direction, so clean and trim, he naturally at first assumed they had nothing to do with Sea State.

Smaller craft spread out, prowling for greener submarines, while in the center a sleek, impressive ship of war drew near. The nozzles of its powerful cannon gleamed like polished silver. Bulging high-pressure tanks held its ammunition—various chemical agents that it began spraying over poor *Dacca* to neutralize the greeners' enzymes. Although neither dousing was supposed to affect flesh, the new bath caused *Dacca*'s crew to laugh and caper, luxuriating as if it were a Fragonard perfume.

"Ah!" the old man said. "Just as I thought. It is *Pikeman*. A proud vessel! They say she never needs to fight, so fearsome is her name."

Crat glanced sideways, suddenly suspicious. This fellow's eyes glittered with more than mere gratitude at being saved from greener sabotage. There was unmistakable pride in his bearing. From that, and the thick but educated accent, Crat guessed he was no mere refugee from poverty, nor a foolish would-be adventurer like himself. No, he must have joined the nation of the dispossessed because his birthplace was still officially under occupation by all the world's powers—a country whose very name had been confiscated.

Crat remembered seeing that look in the eyes of another veteran, back in Bloomington—one of the *victors* in the Helvetian campaign. How strange, then, to spot it next in one who had lost everything.

Shit. That must've been some dumpit war.

The old man confirmed Crat's suspicions. "See how even at this low estate they must treat us with respect?" he asked, then added in a low voice. "By damn, they had better!"

The rescuing flotilla efficiently dispatched units to repair *Dacca,* while *Pikeman* turned into the wind to launch a tethered guard zeppelin. On closer inspection, Crat saw that the vessel wasn't new at all. Its flanks were patched, like every other ship in Sea State's worldwide armada. And yet the refurbishments blended in, somehow looking like intentional improvements on the original design.

Watching the cruiser's flag flapping in the wind, Crat blinked suddenly in surprise. For a brief instant the great bird at the banner's center, instead of flying amid stylized ocean waves, had seemed to soar out of a blocky cloud, set in a bloody field. He squinted. Had it been an illusion, brought on by his constant hunger?

No! There! The colors glittered again! The Sea State emblem must have been modified, he realized. Stitched in amid the blue water and green sky were holographic threads, flashing to the eye only long enough to catch a brief but indelible image.

Once again, for just a second, the albatross flapped sublimely through a square white cross, centered on a background of deep crimson.

Naturally, during the melee the dolphins had escaped. Even before the Helvetian detachment arrived to drive them off, the green raiders had managed to tear the giant fishing web surrounding the school. Crat groaned when he saw the damage. His hands were already cracked from trying to please a slave-driving apprentice net maker, tying simple knots over and over, then retying half of them when his lord and master found some fault undetectable to any *human* eye.

The calamity went beyond damaged nets, of course. It could mean they'd go hungry again tonight, if the raiders' enzymes had reached the catch already in *Dacca's* hold. And yet, in a lingering corner, Crat felt strangely glad the little creatures had got away.

Oh, sure. Back in Indiana he'd been a carni-man, a real meat eater.

Often he'd save up to devour a rare hamburger in public, just to disgust any NorA dumpit ChuGas who happened to pass by. Anyway, today's prey wasn't one of the brainy or rare dolphin types on the protected lists, or else UNEPA would have interfered faster and a lot more lethally than any green raiders.

Still, even dumb little spinner porpoises looked too much like Tuesday Tursiops, the bottle-nosed hero of Sat-vid kiddie shows. They cried so plaintively when they were hauled aboard, thrashing, flailing their tails . . . Crat's gorge was already rising by the time cawing birds arrived to bicker and feed on factory ship offal.

Then, suddenly, had come the greeners—among them probably former countrymen of Crat's. He recalled seeing well-fed pale faces, jaws set in grim determination as they harassed Sea State's harvesters to the very limits of international law and then some. To Crat, the lurching fear and confusion of the brief battle had only been the final straw.

"Are you feeling better now, *fils?*"

Crat looked up from his makeshift seat, one of the coiled foredeck anchor chains. Squinting, he saw it was the geep again—the old Helvetian—come around to check up on him for whatever reason. Crat answered with a silent shrug.

"My name is Schultheiss. Peter Schultheiss," the fellow said as he sat on a jute hawser. "Here you go. I brought you some portable shade."

Crat turned the gift, a straw hat, over in his hands. Weeks ago he would have spurned it as something from a kindergarten class. Now he recognized a good piece of utilitarian craftsmanship. "Mm," he answered with a slight nod and put it on. The shade was welcome.

"No gratitude required," Schultheiss assured. "Sea State cannot afford eye surgery for all its young men. Nor can we count on U.N. dumpit charity."

For the first time, Crat smiled slightly. The one thing he liked about this disappointing adventure was the way both old and young cursed and suffered alike. Only here at sea, a young man's strength counted for as much as any grandpa's store of experience.

Just wait 'n see, he thought. *When I get used to all this, I'll be tougher 'n anybody.*

That wouldn't be anytime soon, though. First week out, he'd foolishly accepted a dare to wrestle a very small Bantu sailor wearing a speckled bandanna. The speed of his humiliation brought home how useless years of judo lessons were in the real world. There were no rubber mats here, no coaches to blow time out. The jeers and pain that followed him to his hammock proved this dream was going to take some time coming true.

Crat remembered Quayle High and that lousy tribal studies class he and Remi and Roland had to take. Hardly anything spoken by the teacher stuck in memory, except one bit—what old fathead Jameson had said one day about *chiefs*.

"These were clansmen who won high status, respect, the best food, wives. Nearly every natural human society has had such a special place for its high achievers . . . even modern tribes like your teen gangs. The major difference between cultures has not been whether, but *how* chiefs were chosen, and by what criteria.

"Today, neither physical power nor even maleness is a principal criterion in Western society. But wit and quickness still make points . . ."

Crat remembered how Remi and Roland had grinned at each other, and for an instant he had hated his friends with a searing passion. Then, surprisingly, the prof also let drop a few words that seemed just for him.

"Of course even today there are some societies in which the old macho virtues hold. Where strength and utter boldness still appear to matter. . . ."

Each of them had taken to the Settler style for different reasons. Remi, for romance and the promise of a new order. Roland, for the honor of comradeship and shared danger in a cause. For Crat, though, the motive had been simpler. He just wanted to be a chief.

And so, a month ago, he had bought a one-way ticket and begun what he was sure would be his great adventure.

Some fuckin' adventure.

"I think maybe the admiral will give up these fishing grounds now," Schultheiss commented as he looked up toward the bridge. *Congo*'s officers could be glimpsed, pacing, arguing with the other captains by the flicker of a holo display.

Soon they heard the bosuns shouting—all hands to the nets in five minutes, for hauling and stowing. Crat sighed for his throbbing muscles. "D'you think we'll be goin' to town?" he asked.

It was his longest speech yet. Schultheiss seemed impressed. "That is likely. I hear one of our floating cities is heading this way, north from Formosa."

"Soon as we dock," Crat said suddenly, "I'm gonna transfer."

Schultheiss raised an eyebrow. "All Sea State fleets are the same, my friend . . . except the Helvetian units, of course. And I doubt you'd—"

Crat interrupted. "I'm through fishin'. I'm thinkin' of goin' to the dredges."

The old man grunted. "Dangerous work, *fils*. Diving into

drowned cities, tying ropes to furniture and jagged bits of rusty metal, dismantling sunken office buildings in Miami—"

"No." Crat shook his head. "*Deep* dredging. You know. The kind that pays! Diving after . . . noodles."

He knew he hadn't pronounced it right. Schultheiss looked puzzled for a moment and then nodded vigorously. "Ah! Do you mean *nodules*? Manganese nodules? My young friend, you are even braver than I thought!"

From that brief look of respect Crat derived some satisfaction. But then the old man smiled indulgently. He patted Crat's shoulder. "And Sea State needs such heroes to take wealth from the deep, so we can take our place among the nations. If you would be such a man, I'm proud to know you."

He doesn't believe me, Crat realized. Once, that would have sent him into a sputtering rage. But he had changed . . . if only because nowadays he was generally too tired for anger. Crat shrugged instead. *Maybe I don't believe it myself.*

The main winch was out again, of course. That meant *Congo*'s section of the great seine net would have to be hauled aboard by hand.

Now Crat remembered where he'd seen the old Helvetian before. Peter Schultheiss was a member of the engineering team that kept the old tub and her sister vessels, *Jutland* and *Hindustan*, sailing despite age and decrepitude. Right now Schultheiss was immersed headfirst in a tangle of black gears, reaching out for tools provided by quick, attentive assistants.

Nearby, the forward wing-sail towered like a tapered chimney. No longer angled into the wind to provide trim, it had been feathered and would remain so unless old Peter succeeded. Apparently it wasn't *just* the winch this time, but the entire foredeck power chain that depended on the fellow's miracle work.

Now that's a skill, Crat admitted, watching Schultheiss during a brief pause in the hauling. *You don't learn that kind of stuff on the gor-sucking Data Net.*

"Again!" the portside bosun shouted. The barrel-chested Afrikaaner had long ago tanned as dark as any man on his watch. "Ready on the count, ver-dumpit! One-and, two-and, three-and . . . heave!"

Crat groaned as he pulled with the others, marching slowly amidships, dragging the sopping line and its string of float buoys over the side. Scampering net makers busied themselves caring for the damaged seine as fast as it came aboard. It was a well-practiced cadence, one with a long tradition on the high seas.

When next they paused to walk forward again—Crat massaging his throbbing left arm—he sniffed left and right, perplexed by a sour, sooty odor. The sharp sweat tang of unbathed men, which had nearly overwhelmed him weeks ago, now was mere background to other smells, drifting in on the breeze.

At last he found the source over on the horizon, a twisted funnel far beyond the Sea State picket boats, rising to stain the shredded, striated clouds. Crat nudged one of his neighbors, an unsmiling refugee from flooded Libya.

"What's that?" he asked.

The wiry fellow readjusted his bandanna as he peered. "Incinerator ship, I think. No allowed go upwind anybody . . . UNEPA rule, y'know? But we not anybody. So upwind *us* jus' fine okay." He spat on the deck for effect, then again onto his hands as the bosun ordered them to take up the hawser for another round.

Glancing at the smokey plume, Crat knew what Remi would have said. "Hey, you got priorities, I got priorities. All the world's got priorities." Getting rid of land-stored toxic wastes rated higher to most than worrying about one more carbon source. Protecting onshore water supplies outweighed a few trace molecules escaping the incinerators' searing flames, especially when those molecules wouldn't waft over populated areas.

Hey, Crat thought as he heaved in time with the others. *Ain't I population?* Soon, however, he hadn't a thought to spare except on doing his job . . . on keeping jibes about *clumsy dumb-ass Yankees* to a minimum, and keeping the others from trampling him.

Because Crat was concentrating so hard, he never noticed the captain come out on deck to test the brush of the wind, his brow furrowed in concern. Poor as it was, Sea State owed its very existence to computers and to other nations' weather satellites. Regular forecasts meant life or death, enabling rusty fleets and floating towns to seek safety well in advance of approaching storms.

Still, weather models could not predict the smaller vagaries . . . mists and pinprick squalls, microbursts and sudden shifts in the wind. While Crat strained on the line, wearily aware they were still only half done, the captain's eyes narrowed, noticing subtle cues. He turned to call his comm officer.

While his back was turned a pocket cyclone of clear air turbulence descended on the little fleet. The micropressure zone gave few warnings. Two hundred meters to the east, it flattened the sea to a brief, glassy perfection. Men's ears popped aboard the *Dacca,* and blond seamen on the *Pikeman*'s starboard quarter briefly had to turn away, blinking from a needle spray of salt foam.

The zone's tangent happened to brush against *Congo* then, sending the wind gauge whining. Gusts struck the feathered wing-sail, catching the vertical airfoil and slewing it sharply. The brakeman, who had been picking his teeth, leapt for his lever too late as the sail swung hard into the gang of straining laborers, knocking several down and cutting the taut cable like a slanting knife.

Tension released in a snapping jolt, hurling sailors over the railing amid a tangle of fibrous webbing. One moment Crat was leaning back, struggling to do his job despite his aching blisters. The next instant, he was flying through the air! His quivering muscles spasmed at the sudden recoil, and yet for a moment it seemed almost pleasant to soar bemusedly above the water like a gull. His forebrain, always the last to know, took some time to fathom why all the other men were screaming. Then he hit the sea.

Abruptly, all the shrill tones were deadened. Low-pitched sounds seemed to resonate from all directions . . . the thrashing of struggling creatures, the glub of air from panicked, convulsing lungs, the pings and moans of *Congo*'s joints as she slowly aged toward oblivion. A destination that loomed much more rapidly for Crat himself, apparently. His legs and arms were caught in the writhing net, and while the float buoys were gradually asserting themselves, that wouldn't help men who were snared like him, only a meter below.

Strange, he pondered. He'd always had dreams about water . . . one reason why, when all other emigration states had spurned his applications, he finally decided to go to sea. Still, until now the possibility of drowning had never occurred to him. Wasn't it supposed to be a good way to go, anyway? So long as you didn't let panic ruin it? Judging from the sounds the others were making, they were going to have the experience thoroughly spoilt for them.

Something about the *quality* of the sound felt terribly familiar. Maybe he was remembering the womb. . . .

Sluggishly, with a glacial slowness, he started working on escape. Not that he had any illusions. It was just something to do. *Guess I'll be seein' you guys soon, after all*, he told Remi and Roland silently.

His left arm was free by the time one of the thrashing forms nearby went limp and still. He didn't spare the time or energy to look then. Nor even when a gray figure flicked by, beyond the other side of the net. But as he worked calmly, methodically, on the complex task of freeing his other arm, a *face* suddenly appeared, right in front of him. A large eye blinked.

No . . . *winked* at him. The eye was set above a long, narrow grin featuring white, pointy teeth. The bottle jaw and high, curved forehead turned to aim at him, and Crat abruptly felt his inner ears go crazy in a crackling of penetrating static. With a start, he realized the thing was *scanning* him . . . inspecting him with its own sophisticated sonar. Checking out this curiosity of a man caught in a net designed to snare creatures of the sea.

This dolphin was much larger than the little spinners the fleet had been killing only hours ago. It must be one of the big, brainy breeds. Certainly it looked amused by this satiric turnabout.

Damn, Crat cursed inwardly as his right arm came free at last. *No dumpit privacy anywhere. Not even when I'm dying.*

Accompanying that resentment came a dissolving of the peaceful, time-stretched resignation. With a crash, his will to live suddenly returned. Panic threatened as his diaphragm clenched, causing a few bubbles to escape. He must have been underwater only a minute or two, but abruptly his lungs were in agony.

Ironically, it was the dolphin—the fact of having an audience—that made Crat hold on. Damn if he'd give it the same show as the others! Now that his mind was working again—such as it was—Crat began recalling important things.

Like the fact that he had a knife! Sheathed at his ankle, it was one of the few items ship rules wouldn't let you hock. Bending, grabbing, unfolding, Crat came up with the gleaming blade and started sawing at the strands clasping his legs.

Funny thing about the way water carried sound—it seemed to amplify his heartbeat, returning multiple echoes from all sides. Counterpoint seemed to come from the spectator, his dolphin voyeur . . . though Crat avoided looking at the creature as he worked.

One leg free! Crat dodged a loop of netting sent his way by the rolling currents—and in the process almost lost the knife. Clutching it convulsively, he also squeezed out more stale, precious air.

His fingers were numb sausages as he resumed sawing. The sea began filling with speckles as each second passed. Infinite schools of blobby purple fishes encroached across his failing vision, heralding unconsciousness. They began to blur and the feeling spread throughout his limbs as his body began quaking. Any second now it would overcome his will with a spasmodic drive to *inhale.*

The last coil parted! Crat tried to launch himself toward the surface, but all his remaining strength had to go into *not* breathing.

An assist from a surprising quarter saved him . . . a push from below that sent him soaring upward, breaching the surface with a shuddering gasp. Somehow, he floundered over a cluster of float buoys, keeping his mouth barely above water as he sucked sweet air. *I'm alive,* he realized in amazement. *I'm alive.*

The roaring in his ears masked the clamor of men watching from the *Congo,* only now beginning to rush to the rescue. Dimly, Crat knew that even those now bravely diving into the water would never be able to cross the jumbled net in time to reach some still-thrashing forms nearby.

As soon as his arms and legs would move again, Crat blearily turned to the nearest struggling survivor, a stricken sailor only a couple of meters away, churning the water feebly, desperately. The fellow was thoroughly trapped, his head bobbing intermittently just at the surface. As Crat neared, he spewed and coughed and managed to catch a thin whistle of breath before being dragged under again.

Belatedly, Crat realized his knife was gone for good, probably even now tumbling down to Davy Jones's lost and found. So he did the only thing he could. Gathering a cluster of float buoys under one arm, he stretched across the intervening tangle to grab the dying man's hair, hauling him up for a sobbing gasp of air. Each following breath came as a shrill whistle then . . . until the poor sod's eyes cleared enough of threatening coma to fill instead with hysteria. Good thing the victim's arms were still caught then, or in panic he'd have clawed Crat into the trap as well.

Crat's own breathing came in shuddering sobs as he kicked in reserves he never knew he had before. Just keeping his own head above the lapping water was hard enough. He also had to tune out the fading splashes of other dying men nearby. *I can't help 'em. Really can't. . . . Got my hands full.*

Nearby, Crat felt another form approach to look at him. That dolphin again. *I wish someone'd shoot the damned . . .*

Then he recalled that shove to the seat of his pants. The push that had saved his life.

His mind was too slow, too blurry to think of anything much beyond that. Certainly he formed no clear idea to thank the one responsible. But that eye seemed to sense something—his realization perhaps. Again it winked at him. Then the dolphin lifted its head, chattered quickly, and vanished.

Crat was still blinking at strange, unexpected thoughts when rescuers arrived at last to relieve him of his burden and haul his exhausted carcass out of the blood-warm sea.

□

A new type of pollution was first noticed way back in the nineteen-seventies. Given the priorities of those times, it didn't get as much attention as, say, tainted rivers or the choking stench over major cities. Nevertheless, a vocal opposition began to rise up in protest.

Trees. In certain places *trees* were decried as the latest symbols of human greed and villainy against nature.

"Oh, certainly trees are good things in general," those voices proclaimed. "Each makes up a miniature ecosystem, sheltering and supporting a myriad of living things. Their roots hold down and aerate topsoil. They draw carbon from the air and give back sweet oxygen. From their breathing leaves transpires moisture, so one patch of forest passes on to the next each rainstorm's bounty."

Food, pulp, beauty, diversity . . . there was no counting the array of treasures lost in those tropical lands where hardwood forests fell daily in the hundreds, thousands of acres. And yet, take North America in 1990, where there actually were *more* trees than had stood a century before—many planted by law to replace ancient "harvested" stands of oak and beech and redwood. Or take Britain, where meadows once cropped close by herds of grazing sheep were now planted—under generous tax incentives—with hectare after hectare of specially bred pine.

Trash forests, they were called by some. Endless stands of uniformity, stretching in geometric lattice rows as far as the eye could see. Absolutely uniform, they had been gene spliced for quick growth. And grow they did.

"But these forests are dead zones," said the complainers. "A floor covered with only pine needles or bitter eucalyptus leaves shelters few deer, feeds few otters, hears the songs of hardly any birds."

Even much later, as the Great Campaign for the Trillion Trees got under way—losing in some places, but elsewhere helping hold fast against the spreading deserts—many new forests were still silent places. An emptiness seemed to whisper, echoing among the still branches.

It's not the same, said this troubled quiet. *Some things, once gone, cannot be easily restored.*

● The most pleasant thing about the new routine was that it finally
M gave Stan Goldman a chance to take some time off and go argue
E with old friends.
S   The next several Gazer runs would be ordinary. The program
O was on schedule, slowly nudging Beta, beat by beat, into its higher
S orbit. At last Stan felt he could leave his assistant in charge of the
P resonator and take an hour or so off to relax.
H   In fact, it was really part of his job—helping maintain their
E cover. After all, wouldn't their hosts get suspicious if he didn't
R stay in character? The paleontologists at the Hammer site would
E find it odd if old Stan Goldman didn't come by on occasion to talk
and kibitz. So it was with a relatively clear conscience that he made

for the nearby encampment to partake of some beer and friendly conversation.

All in the line of duty of course.

"We ought to have an answer in a few years," said Wyn Nielsen, the tall, blond director of the dig and an old friend of many years. "We'll know when the Han finally launch that big interferometer of theirs. Until then talk is pointless."

They had been disputing whether any nearby stellar systems might have Earthlike planets, and the elderly but still athletic Dane kept to his pragmatic, hard-nosed reputation. "If you have the means to experiment, do it! If not, then wait till experiments *are* possible. Theory by itself is only masturbation."

The small club erupted in laughter. Still, Wyn was no spoilsport. And as everyone else seemed to want to speculate, he merely grumbled good-naturedly and went along.

"We'll see about that Han interferometer," said a woman geologist named Gorshkov, whom Stan had met off and on at conferences for decades. "The Chinese have been talking about it forever. Why can't we answer the question with facilities in orbit right now?"

Stan shrugged. "The Euro-Russian and American telescopes are quite old by now, Elena. Yes, they've detected planets around nearby stars, but only giants like Jupiter and Saturn. Little rocky worlds like Earth are harder to find . . . like picking out the reflected glint of a needle next to a burning haystack, I should think."

"But don't most astrophysical models predict that sunlike stars will have planets?"

This time it was a younger Dane, Teresa's husky friend Lars. The fellow might look like an overbuilt mechanic or an American football hero, but he obviously read a lot.

"Yes and no," Stan replied. "G-type stars like our sun must shed angular momentum in their infancy, and since ours gave nearly all its spin momentum to her retinue of planets, most astronomers think other stars that rotate like the sun must have planets too.

"Furthermore, astronomers think early protostars give off fierce particle winds, which drive away volatile elements. That's why there's so much hydrogen in the outer solar system, while Mercury and Venus, sitting close in, have been stripped of theirs."

"But Earth came out just right," Wyn nodded. "In the middle of a zone where water can stay liquid, right?"

"The Goldilocks effect." Stan nodded. "Life could never have started, or kept going for long, without lots of water.

"But as for Earth being 'in the middle' of the solar system's life zone, well, astronomers have argued over that for more than a cen-

tury. Some used to think that if our world was only five percent closer
to the sun we would have fallen into the Venus trap . . . heat death
by runaway greenhouse warming. And if we'd been just five percent
farther, Earth's seas would have frozen forever.''

''So? What's the modern estimate?''

''Currently? The best models show our sun's life zone is probably
very broad indeed, stretching from just under one astronomical unit
all the way out past three or more.''

Someone whistled. Elena Gorshkov closed her eyes momentarily.
''Wait a minute. That extends past Mars! So why isn't Mars a living
world?''

''Good question. There's evidence Mars once did have liquid water, carving great canyons we have yet to visit, alas.'' To that there was
a general murmur of agreement. Several raised their glasses to opportunities lost. ''Perhaps there were even seas there for a while, where
early life-forms made a brave start before all the water froze into the
sands. The problem with old man Mars wasn't that he spun too *far*
from the sun. The real difficulty was that the Romans named their war
god after a pygmy. A midget world, too small to hold onto the necessary greenhouse gases. Too small to keep those famous shield volcanoes smoking. Too small, by half, for life.''

''Hmm,'' Lars commented. ''Too bad for Mars. But if G stars have
broad life zones, there ought to be many other worlds out there where
conditions were right . . . with oceans where lightning could begin
the first steps. Evolution would have worked in those places, too. So
where—?''

''So where the dickens *is* everybody!'' Wyn Nielsen interjected,
slapping the table.

So we return to the age-old question, Stan thought. Enrico Fermi
had also asked it a hundred years ago. *Where is everybody, indeed?*

In a galaxy of half a trillion stars, there ought to be many, many
worlds like Earth. Surely some must have developed life, even civilization, long ago.

*On paper at least, star travel seems possible. So why, during all
the time Earth was ''prime real estate,'' with no indigenous owners
higher than bacteria or fish, was it never colonized by some earlier
spacefaring race?*

The amount of verbiage that had been spent on the subject—even
excluding flying-saucer drivel—only expanded after the establishment
of the World Data Net. And still there was no satisfactory answer.

''There are lots of theories why Earth was never settled by outsiders,'' he replied. ''Some have to do with natural calamities, like you lot
are investigating here. After all, if giant meteorites wiped out the dino-

saurs, similar catastrophes may have trounced other would-be space travelers. We ourselves may be wrecked by some stray encounter before we reach a level sufficient to—''

Stan's voice caught suddenly. It was as if he'd been struck between the eyes, *twice.*

For a blessed time he had managed to banish all thought of the *taniwha.* So the sudden contextual reminder came like a blow. But the thing that really had him stopped in his tracks was a new thought, one that had swarmed into consciousness following the words—*We ourselves may be wrecked by some encounter. . . .*

He coughed to cover his discomfiture, and someone slapped him on the back. While he took a drink of warm beer, waving concerned helpers away, he thought, *Could our monster have come from outside? Could it* not *be man-made?*

He didn't need to make a mental note to look into the idea later. This was one that would stick with him. *If only I'd been able to break free and go to the meeting in Waitomo!* Somehow, he must find a way to transmit this thought to Alex!

But now was not the time to lose his train of thought. There were appearances to maintain. *Where was I . . . ? Oh yes.*

Clearing his throat, he resumed.

''My . . . own favorite explanation for the absence of extraterrestrials—or their apparent absence anyway—has to do with the very thing we were talking about before, the life zones around G stars like our sun. Astronomers now envision a very broad zone *outward* from our position, where a Gaia-type homeostasis could be set up by life. The farther out you go the less sunlight you have, of course. But then, according to the Wolling model, more carbon would remain in the atmosphere to keep a heat balance. Voilà.

''But note, there's very little habitable zone left *inward* from our orbit. Earth revolves very close to the sun for a water planet. In our case, life had to purge nearly every bit of carbon from the atmosphere to let enough heat escape as the sun's temperature rose. And in a couple of hundred million years even that won't suffice. As old Sol gets hotter, the inner boundary will cross our orbit and we'll be cooked, slowly, but quite literally.

''In other words, we only have a hundred million years or so to come up with a plan.''

They laughed, a little nervously.

''So what's your theory?'' Nielsen asked.

Stan was wondering how to get the center of attention away from himself, so he could find an excuse to sneak away. But he'd have to do it smoothly, naturally. He spread his hands. ''It's really simple. You see, I think Earth must be relatively hot and dry, as water worlds go. Oh, it may not seem that way, with seventy percent of the surface covered by ocean. But that just means that normal life-zone planets must be even wetter!

"One consequence would be less continental land area to weather under rain."

"Ah, I see," a Turkish geochemist said. "Less weathering means less fertilizer to feed life in those seas. Which in turn means slower evolution?"

One of the paleontologists spoke from the fringes of the group. "And the life-forms would have less *oxygen* to drive fast metabolisms like ours."

Stan nodded. "And of course, with less land area, there'd be less chance of evolving these." He held up ten wriggling fingers.

"Huh!" Elena Gorshkov commented, shaking her head. Several arguments erupted at the periphery as the scientists disputed amiably. Nielsen was tapping away at the miniplaque on his lap, probably looking for refutations.

Good, Stan thought. These were bright people, and he liked watching them toss ideas about like volleyballs. Too bad he had to keep his most pressing scientific quandaries secret from them. To know such things as he did, and withhold them from his peers . . . it felt shameful to Stan.

"Aha," Nielsen said. "I just found an interesting paper on continental weathering that supports what Stan says. Here. I'll pipe it to the rest of you."

People drew plaques and readers from their pockets and unfolded them to receive the document, drawn from some corner of the net by Nielsen's quick-and-dirty ferret program. Distracted from his recent desire to leave, Stan too began reaching for his wallet display.

At that moment, though, his watch gave a tiny, throbbing jolt to his left wrist, just sharp enough to get his attention—the rhythm urgent.

While the chatter of excited discussion swelled again, Stan excused himself as if heading for the men's room. Along the way he popped a micro-pickup from the watch and put it in his ear.

"Speak," he said to the luminous dial.

"Stan." It was the tinny voice of Mohotunga Bailie, his assistant, and it carried overtones of fear. "Get back. Right quick." That was all. The carrier tone cut off abruptly.

Stan felt a chill, mixed thoroughly with sudden pangs of guilt. *The taniwha—has it gone out of control? Oh Lord, I shouldn't have left them alone!*

But even as he thought it, he knew in his heart that Beta couldn't have gotten away so suddenly. The physics just weren't there for such a happenstance . . . not from the stable configurations of just an hour ago!

Then it must be one of the beams. This time we must have hit a city. How many died? Oh God, can you forgive us? Can anyone?

With pale, shaking hands he plunged outside where the pearly arctic twilight stretched around two thirds of the horizon. The aurora borealis made flickering, ionized curtains above the Greenland ice sheet. Stan half stumbled, half ran to his little four-wheeled scooter and kicked the starter, sending its balloon tires whining across the glittering moraine, spewing gravel behind it.

All the way back to the Tangoparu shelter, his mind was filled with dire imaginings of what could have put those dread tones in his stolid assistant's voice. Then he crossed a hillock and the dome itself came into view, along with the big, olive-drab helicopter, parked just beyond. Stan's heart did another flip-flop.

It wasn't a problem with Beta after all, he realized suddenly. At least not directly. This was quite another type of calamity.

NATO, he realized, recognizing the uniforms of the armed men patrolling the shelter's perimeter. *Lord love a duck . . . I never thought I'd see those colors again. I'd forgotten they were still in business.*

He knew only one reason the big armed aircraft would have come all this way at such a time of night, bringing soldiers to the door of his laboratory. And it surely wasn't a social call.

They've found us, he realized, knowing he had only seconds to decide what to do.

☐ Plano-Forbes: 2.5 billion
  World Watch: 6.0 billion
  Rocks-Runyon: 10.0 billion

These estimates of the Earth's *maximum sustainable human population* were all made before 1990, as the world's attention began shifting from ideologies and nationalism toward matters of ecological survival. The three appraisals at first sight seem utterly at odds. Yet all were based on the same raw data.

In fact, their differences lie primarily in how each defined the word "sustainable."

To Plano and Forbes, it meant a system lasting at least as long as ancient China had—several thousand years—that would provide all human children with education, basic amenities, and per capita energy use equal to half the consumption of circa 1980 Americans. A sustainable human population would use carbon-based fuels only as fast as vegetation recycled them and would set aside enough wilderness to preserve the natural genome.

These criteria proved impossible to maintain for long periods at population levels exceeding 2.5 billion.*

World Watch used looser constraints for their estimate. For instance, while "American" consumption levels were still seen as spendthrift, the authors did not call for rationing fossil fuels. Food was their critical concern, and although they failed to foresee many important negative and positive trends (e.g., greenhouse desertification vs. self-fertilizing maize) their major difference with Plano-Forbes arose from projecting "sustainability" only a hundred years or so at a stretch.

The Rocks-Runyon model has proven the most accurate one, in the simple sense that it correctly predicted we could (with difficulty) feed ten billion by the year 2040. It also clearly asks the least for the human future. Bare survival was its criterion—muddling through, with little worry spared for even a hundred years, let alone thousands of years, down the road.

And indeed, there are those who argue we shouldn't be concerned so far ahead. After all, science progresses. Perhaps those generations will invent new solutions to make the problems we leave them seem academic.

Perhaps our descendants will be able to take care of themselves.

---

*These figures are challenged by groups promoting space colonization, who project that lunar and asteroidal resources, with limitless solar power, would permit Plano-Forbes lifestyles for ten to twenty billion humans, sustainable for all foreseeable time. Their favorite analogy is Columbus's discovery of the New World. The flaw in such schemes, however, is the initial investment needed before wealth from space can bring prosperity down to Earth. Governments and peoples, already living hand to mouth, will hardly put so much into projects whose bounty might profit their grandchildren, but not themselves.

—From **The Transparent Hand**, Doubleday Books, edition 4.7 (2035). [☐ hyper access code 1-tTRAN-777-97-9945-29A.]

● There was only one entrance to the deep cave complex. When
M armed men in blue helmets rained from the sky on jet-assisted
A parafoils, they had to hunt and thrash through the jungle for a
N time before they found that hidden opening. Then, silently, they
T began repelling down the shadowy chimney.
L   Sepak Takraw awakened to the sound of blaring alarms and at
E first thought it was only another Gazer run . . . whatever those
were. The Kiwis working for George Hutton had remained close-
mouthed about the essential purpose of the gravity scans, though
clearly they had to do with the Earth's deepest interior. Whatever the
Tangoparu techs were doing here in New Guinea, they sure took their
work godawfully seriously—as if the world would end if they made
one bleeding mistake!

Sepak had finally moved his sleeping roll up to a cleft in a narrow,
extinct watercourse, because of the noise they made each time their
big resonator thing fired up, sending bells and whoops echoing
through the deep galleries. This time, however, when he stumbled
toward the lighted chamber rubbing his eyes, he suddenly stopped and
stared down at a scene of utter chaos. Had the New Zealanders finally
done it this time, with all their noise? Invoked Tu, the Maori god of
war?

They were dashing about like addled bowerbirds, and the bright
cylindrical resonator swung wildly within its gimbaled cage as armed
men swarmed into the hall. Sepak slipped into the shadows and kept
very still. *George bloody Hutton. What've you got me into! The
government can't be this upset over us keeping a few caves secret for
a while!*

Anyway, these weren't regular police. Half the soldiers clearly
weren't even native Papuans! Sepak mouthed a silent whistle as com-
mandos rushed past the dazed technicians to secure the area. No,
these weren't locals, nor even U.N. peacekeepers. By damn, they were
real troops . . . ASEAN Marines!

Anyone who did the necessary ferreting knew Earth still bristled
with sovereign military might. Perhaps even several percent of what
used to exist in the bad old days. And even more weaponry lay "in
reserve," in treaty-sealed warehouses. Alliances still trained, still
maintained a balance of power that was very real, for all its generations of stability. Only, on a planet aswarm with real-time cameras and
volatile public opinion, those states and blocs generally took pains to
use their martial forces gingerly.

So Sepak knew this wasn't just a raid over some infraction of the secrecy laws. As the marines briskly rounded up the kiwi engineers, he searched in vain for emblems of the U.N. or other international agencies. He peered for the de rigueur Net-zine reporters.

Nothing. No reporters. No U.N. observers.

It really is national, then, he realized. Which meant more was involved here than just the government of Papua–New Guinea. A whole lot more.

And these guys don't want leaks any more than George Hutton did.

Sepak melted even farther back into the darkness.

By all the holy cargo of John Broom . . . George, what have you got me into?

☐ *Archaic or obsolete activities or occupations:*

. . . flint knapping, entrail reading, arrow fletching . . . smithing, barrel making, art appraising . . . clock making, reindeer herding, dentistry, handwriting . . . game-show host, channeler, UFOlogist . . . drug smuggler, golf course manager, confidential banker . . . sunbathing, drinking tapwater . . .

New service professions:

. . . household toxin inspector, prenuptial genetic counselor, meme adjustment specialist . . . indoor microecologist, biotect, prenatal tutor, cerebrochemical balance advisor . . . Net-SIG consultant, voxpop arbitrageur, ferret designer, insurance lifestyle adjustor . . .

World human population figures :

1982: 4.3 billion
1988: 5.1 billion
2030: 10.3 billion

Teresa began her journey home as she had arrived, in the company of Pedro Manella. For probably the last time, she stepped into a little boat to be conveyed through the Cave of Glowing Worms— their living constellations still shimmering in a subterranean mimicry of night. Then she and Pedro took advantage of the darkness to slip behind a flock of whispering tourists, treading well-worn guide paths past phosphorescent signs lettered in a dozen languages. Finally, they emerged on the flanks of a forested mountain, in New Zealand.

It's like we only first entered for the first time an hour ago, Teresa thought, coaxing an illusion. *Nothing in the intervening weeks has been real. I made it all up—Beta, the trip to Greenland, the gravity laser . . .*

As Pedro stepped ahead of her down the tree-lined path, his shadow moved aside at one point to let glaring afternoon brightness fall upon her face. Teresa fumbled for her sunglasses.

Just a fantasy, that's all it's been, she continued wishing, *including all that stuff about interstellar enemies sending monsters to devour our world.*

It was a good effort, but Teresa had to sigh. She lacked enough talent at self-deception to make it work.

While you're at it, might as well go whole hog and pretend you're nineteen again, with all life's adventures still ahead of you— first flight, first love, that illusion of immortality.

Southern autumn was ebbing fast, chilling toward winter. A breeze riffled her hair—now again her own shade of brown, but longer than at any time since she'd been a teenager. It felt at once sensuous, feminine, and startling each time it brushed against her neck.

Distracted, she suddenly collided with Manella's massive back. "Hey!" Teresa complained, rubbing her nose.

Pedro turned, glancing at his watch, an agitated expression on his face. "You go on to the car," he said. "I forgot something. See you in a nano."

"Sure. Just remember I have a plane to catch at fourteen hundred. We—" Her voice trailed off as he hurried uphill, disappearing round a right-hand fork in the path. *Strange,* she thought. *Didn't we come down the left branch?*

Maybe Pedro had to visit the gents' before the long drive. Teresa resumed walking downhill again, one hand lightly on the guide rail overlooking steep forest slopes. Rain-damp ferns brushed in the wind. The tourist group had gone ahead and were probably spilling into the parking lot to seek their buses or rented runabouts. Perhaps the traffic jam would have cleared by the time Pedro caught up.

Teresa's bags were already in the car. In them lay a packet of doctored photos, depicting her at an Australian hermitage-resort for the past month. They should get by any cursory inspection. And she'd gone over her cover story umpteen times. Soon, at the Auckland airport transit lounge, she would change places with the woman who'd been taking that holiday in her name. After the switch, at last, she'd be Teresa Tikhana once again. No reason for NASA ever to think she hadn't done what they'd asked—taken that long-delayed recuperative holiday.

A new swarm of tourists loomed ahead, a big, intimidating group of determined sightseers climbing rapidly, staring about with their total-record goggles, holding tightly onto their shoulder bags. The tour guide shouted, describing the wonders of these mountains—their hidden rivers and secret byways. Teresa stepped aside to let the throng by. Several of the men looked her up and down as they passed, the sort of cursory, appreciative regard she was used to. Still, though the odds of being recognized were infinitesimal, Teresa turned away. Why take chances?

I wonder what's keeping Pedro? She chewed on a fingernail as she looked across the rain forest. *Why do I feel something's wrong?*

If she were in a cockpit right now, there'd be instruments to check, a wealth of information. Here, she had only her senses. Even her data plaque had been packed in the luggage below.

Glancing behind her, she realized something was distinctly odd about the tour group passing by. *They're sure in a hurry to see the caves. Is their bus behind schedule, or what?*

Every one of them carried pastel shoulder bags to match their bright tourist gear. Four out of five were men, and there were no children at all. *Are they with some sort of convention, maybe?*

She almost stopped one to ask, but held back. Something seemed all too familiar about these characters, as she watched them recede upslope. Their movements were too purposeful for people on holiday. Under their goggles, their jaws had been set in a way that made Teresa think of—

She gasped. "Peepers! Oh . . . burf it!"

Helplessly she realized what her inattentiveness might cost. Without her plaque, she had only her slim wallet to use in an attempt to warn those below ground. Teresa took it from her hip pocket and flipped it open—only to find it wouldn't transmit! The tiny transceiver was jammed.

There was a telephone though, in the gift shop by the park en-

trance. Teresa backed downhill till the last "tourist" vanished round a
bend, then she turned to run—

—and crashed into several more men taking up the rear. One of
them seized her wrist in a ninety-kilo grip.

"Well. Captain Tikhana. Hello! But I heard you were in Queensland. My goodness. What brings you to New Zealand so unexpect-
edly?"

The man holding her arm actually sounded anything but surprised to meet her here. Despite Glenn Spivey's scarred complexion,
his smile seemed almost genuine, empty of any malice. Next to
Spivey, making useless any thought of struggle, stood a big black man
and an Asian. Despite the ethnic diversity, they all seemed cast from
the same mold, with the piercing eyes of trained spies.

A fourth man, standing behind the others, seemed out of place in
this tableau. His features, too, were vaguely oriental. But his stance
shouted *civilian*. And not a very happy one, either.

"You!" Teresa told the peeper colonel, cleverly.

"I hope you weren't planning on leaving so soon, Captain?"
Spivey replied, apparently bent on using one old movie cliché after
another. "I wish you'd stay. Things are just about to get interesting."

". . . warn you, George! The place is swarming with soldiers! They've already taken the thumper and my crew. You and Alex and the others better
clear out . . ."

A hand reached past George Hutton to turn off the sound. The
holo unit went on visually depicting an elderly man in a heavy parka,
obviously worried but now speaking only mime into a portable transmitter. Behind Stan Goldman loomed a titanic, icy palisade.

"I'm afraid the warning wouldn't have done much good, even if it
had come earlier," Colonel Spivey told Hutton and the assembled
conspirators. "We snooped all your files, of course, before running this
kind of operation. Can't afford to be sloppy, you know."

Teresa sat in her old chair, across from Alex Lustig and two seats
from the exit, now guarded by Spivey's ANZAC commandoes. This
time, the underground meeting room was packed with everyone, even
the cook. Everyone except Pedro Manella, that is.

How did he know? She wondered. *How does Pedro always seem
to know?*

She was feeling numb of course. Another few hours and she'd
have been on her way to Houston, back to her comfortable apartment
and her loyal NASA publicity flack.

Now though?

Now I'm cooked. Teresa's thoughts were scattered like leaves. It was only natural, of course, when you contemplated a future in federal prison.

She glanced across the table at Alex and felt ashamed. Certainly *he* wasn't worried foremost about saving his own neck. This event would have effects on more than just one life. *All right, then. We're all cooked.* There was little solace in the reminder.

"How long ago?"

"I beg your pardon, Mr. Hutton?" Spivey asked.

George levered his heavy body to sit up at the head of the table. "How long ago did you snoop our records, Colonel?"

Teresa noticed he didn't ask *how* Spivey's team had broken the Tangoparu security screen. Obviously the great power alliances possessed better infotech than even the best Net hackers. With the deep pockets of governments, and many of the old loyalties to call upon, they could stay two, three, even four years ahead of individual users. So Spivey's next admission took her a bit by surprise.

"You know, it's funny about that," the colonel answered openly. "We looked for you guys a long time. Too long. You had someone running awfully good interference for you, Hutton. We pierced your caches just three days ago, and then only thanks to some anonymous tips and help from civilian consultants like Mr. Eng here."

Spivey nodded toward the vaguely oriental-looking man Teresa had seen on the trail, who blinked nervously when his name was mentioned. Obviously he was no peeper.

One of the Tangoparu technicians stood up to loudly protest the illegality of this invasion. Pulling a cube from his jacket, Spivey interrupted. "I have a document here, signed by the chiefs of NATO, ASEAN, and ANZAC, as well as the New Zealand national security authority, declaring this an ultimate emergency under the security sections of all three pacts and the Rio Treaty. What you people have been up to justifies that label, wouldn't you say? If anything in human history does, a black hole eating up the Earth surely qualifies as an 'emergency.'

"And yet you kept it to yourselves! Hiding it from the press, from the net, and from sovereign, elected governments. So please spare me your righteous indignation."

In the holo tank, Stan Goldman's silent image turned away as he saw someone approaching. Sighing in silent resignation, he reached for a switch and the image cut off abruptly. In its place the familiar cutaway globe rotated again—the Earth, depicted as a multilayered ball of Neapolitan ice cream.

Ah, if only it were true. An ice cream planet. What a wonderful world it would be.

Forcing aside giddiness, Teresa mentally added—*Good luck, Stan. God bless you.*

"Until only a little while ago we thought you people were the ones who *made* the damned monster!" June Morgan shouted at Spivey. "You and your secret cavitron laboratories in orbit and your cozy great power agreements. We felt we had to keep our work hidden or you'd interfere to save your own asses!"

"An interesting, perhaps even plausible, defense," Spivey acknowledged. "But now you know it wasn't we nasty government brutes who manufactured the . . ." He paused.

"The Beta singularity," Alex Lustig prompted, his first comment of the afternoon.

"Thank you."

"You're welcome," Alex nodded enigmatically.

"Yes, well. A few days ago you folks seem to have decided the monster was sent this way instead by *angry aliens.*" He shrugged. "I'm not yet convinced by that colorful scenario. But be that as it may, once you believed that, and knew we weren't Beta's makers, wasn't it your duty then to tell us? After all, aren't we supposed to be the experts at dealing with external aggressors? We're the ones with the resources and organizational skills to take your shoestring operation and—"

"We were arguing about just that when you and your men burst in," George said abruptly. "In hindsight, maybe I was wrong to hold out for continued secrecy."

"Because now it will *remain* secret." Spivey nodded. "You're right in your implication, Mr. Hutton. The alliances I represent see great danger in this situation—danger going far beyond the immediate matter of getting rid of Beta. The last century's proven how dangerous new technologies can be when they're misused. But once it's widely known that something's possible, there's never a second chance to stuff the genie back into its bottle. Do you doubt it'll be different when people hear about *gravity lasers*?"

He looked around the room. "Be honest now, would any of you like to see Imperial Han or the East Asia Coprosperity Sphere, learn how to make these knot singularity things? Or *Sea State*, for heavens' sake?"

"There are science tribunals," June Morgan suggested. "And onsite inspection teams. . . ."

"Yes." Spivey nodded. "A combination that'll work fine, so long as manufacturing such things requires large industrial facilities. But hadn't we better make sure of that, first? That these things *can* be controlled by the peacekeeping agencies? After all, Dr. Lustig's already

shown you can use very small cavitrons to make impressive singularities.''

"Not *that* impressive," Alex cut in, showing his first sign of irritation as he gestured toward a whirling representation of Beta.

"No?" Spivey turned to face him. "With all due respect for your
admitted brilliance, Professor, you're also notorious for truly major
screwups. Can you be so sure you're right about that? Can you absolutely guarantee that Joe Private Citizen won't be able to make planet
killers someday, in his basement, any time he's angry at the world?''

Alex frowned, keeping his mouth shut. Suddenly Teresa thought
of her conversations with Stan Goldman, about the mystery of a universe apparently all but empty of intelligent life. Putting aside Lustig's
theory about alien berserkers, there was yet another chilling possibility.

*Maybe it is trivial to make world-wrecking black holes. Maybe
it's inevitable, and the reason we've never seen extraterrestrial civilizations is simple . . . because every one reaches this stage, creates
unstoppable singularities, and gets sucked down the throat of its
own, self-made demon.*

But no. She knew from the look in Alex Lustig's eyes. *He's not
wrong about this. Beta's beyond our ability to duplicate, now and for
a long time to come. Bizarre as it sounds, the thing was sent here.*

"Hmph." George Hutton grunted. The Maori geophysicist clearly
saw little point in arguing over things already beyond his control.
"Mind if I consult my database, Colonel?"

Spivey waved nonchalantly. "By all means."

George picked up a hush-mike and spoke into it, watching
streams of data flow across his desk screen. After a minute he looked
up. "You have our stations in Greenland and New Guinea. But the
other sites—" He paused.

Spivey looked to his left. "Tell them please, Logan."

The civilian consultant shrugged. He spoke with a soft but startlingly incongruous Cajun accent. "My computer model of recent
Earth, um . . . tremors, indicates the third site has to be on Easter
Island. The last one's inside a fifty-kilometer circle in the northern
part of the Federation of Southern Africa."

George shrugged. "Just checking. Anyway, I see here all is normal
at those two. No troops. No cops. You haven't got them, Colonel."

"Nor are we likely to." Spivey folded his arms, looking quite
relaxed. "None of the alliances I represent have any jurisdiction in
those territories.

"Oh, we could sabotage your sites I suppose. But if you people are
right—if you're not all deluded or crazy—then Earth *needs* those reso-

nators. So I imagine zapping them would be a little self-defeating, wouldn't it?''

That actually won a weak chuckle from a few of those gathered at the table. He continued with an ingratiating smile. "Anyway, our objective isn't to slam you all into jail. Indeed, formal gravamens have been prepared against only one person in this room, and even in that case we might find some room to maneuver.''

Teresa felt all eyes turn briefly toward her. Everyone knew who Spivey meant. The list of likely counts against her was depressing to contemplate—*misappropriation of government property, perjurious nondisclosure, dereliction of duty, . . . treason.* She looked down at her hands.

"No," Colonel Spivey continued with a smile. "We're not here to be your enemies, but to negotiate with you. To see if we can agree on a common program. And first on the agenda, by all means, is how to continue the work you've begun, putting every resource into saving the world.''

Everything the man said seemed so-o-o reasonable. Teresa found it infuriating, frustrating . . . all the way down to realizing her own role in Spivey's game. While others dove right into the subsequent freewheeling discussion, she just sat there, resigned to a pawn's mute, helpless role.

Clearly, with the New Zealand authorities committed to their alliance, extradition proceedings would be straightforward. Spivey could lock her up and throw away the key. Worse, she'd never fly again. No leak to the Net, no public outcry, not even legal gambits by the best live or software lawyers would ever get her back into space again.

The others were in jeopardy too, even though their cases weren't quite as clear-cut. Teresa watched George Hutton's mental wheels spin. With canny shrewdness, the Kiwi entrepreneur poked away at Spivey's cage, testing its walls.

Prosecutions would mean disclosure, wouldn't they? No one knew how deeply Spivey's aversion to publicity really went. Did he seek to keep the secret for months? Years even? Or just long enough to give his side a head start?

The Tangoparu cabal had cards to play, as well. Such as their expertise, which no one else could duplicate in time. George emphasized the point, though it was a weak bluff and everyone knew it. Could they go on strike, refusing to use those skills, when the entire world was at stake?

Spivey countered by taking a lofty tone, making a strong case for teamwork. He dropped hints the criminal cases might be dropped. And within hours of an agreement, the times of short supplies and sleepless nights would end. Fresh manpower would arrive, fresh teams of experts to work round the clock, relieving the tired technicians, helping them guide Beta's orbit slowly outward while making sure the worst tectonic shocks missed populated areas.

Teresa realized Hutton and Lustig were trapped. The benefits were too great, the alternatives too hard. All that remained were the details.

Of course, no one was asking her what *she* thought. But in fairness, she probably looked as if she couldn't care less right now.

"We're particularly interested in this coherent gravity amplification effect of yours, Dr. Lustig." The speaker was one of Spivey's aides, a black man dressed for tourism, but with the bearing of a professional soldier and the vocabulary of a physicist. "Surely the implications of the gazer haven't escaped you?" he said.

"Its implications as a weapon? Oh, they occurred to me." Alex nodded suspiciously. "How could they not? Want to destroy your enemies with earthquakes? Blast their cities into marmite . . . ?"

The officer looked pained. "That isn't what I meant, sir. Other means of triggering quakes have been studied before. You'd be surprised how many there are. All were discarded as worthless bludgeons, lacking precision or predictability—useless in the present geopolitical arena."

"And please note," Colonel Spivey interjected. "It's the very fact that we kept those techniques under wraps, completely secret, that *let* us discard those awful weapons and at the same time keep them out of the wrong hands. Secrecy isn't always obscene."

The black officer nodded and went on. "No, Professor Lustig, I'm not talking about liquefying the ground under the Forbidden City or anything like that. I was thinking instead about the gazer beam *itself*, propagating outward through space.

"Consider your claim that Beta must have been built by alien beings . . . aliens who apparently mean us harm . . . have you given no thought to how the gazer might be aimed? At targets coming into the solar system?" He leaned forward. "I can't help but wonder if our extraterrestrial foes haven't badly underestimated us, by inadvertently giving us the very means we need to defend ourselves."

Alex blinked. A faint smile spread as he sat up straighter. "A defensive weapon . . . using the beam against Beta's builders. Yes." He nodded. "I see your point."

"By damn, you're right!" George Hutton slammed the table.

Dawning enthusiasm glinted in his eyes. "Wouldn't that be justice? To turn their own *taniwha* against them?"

"Um. Wouldn't that mean leaving the, uh, Beta singularity down there . . . inside the Earth?" Logan Eng pointed out hesitantly. ". . . to continue serving as a mirror for the gravity laser?" He motioned with two hands. "Otherwise, no coherent beam."

"Oh. Right." George looked crestfallen. "Can't have that."

"Are you certain?" the military physicist asked. "You say Beta's orbit even now carries it briefly up to regions where the rock density's so low it loses mass. All right, then, what if it were set on just the right trajectory . . . remaining inside the Earth, but balanced to neither grow nor shrink?"

George looked at Alex. "Is that possible?"

While Alex pondered the question, consulting mental resources Teresa could not imagine, June Morgan commented, "It would save us all that worry about how to deal with a million-degree flaming ball when it's finally ejected from the Earth. What do you think, Teresa?" the blonde woman turned and asked her, for some reason.

Teresa pushed her chair back. "I'm feeling very tired," she told Glenn Spivey as she stood up. "I think I'll go lie down for a while." The colonel looked at her for a moment and then nodded for a guard to accompany her. Teresa glanced back from the doorway to see Alex Lustig tracing mathematics in a holo tank, surrounded by excited scientists from both camps. She sighed and turned away.

The guard was an ANZAC commando from Perth, a gung-ho Aussie patriot who was nonetheless solicitous and rather sweet. When she asked if it was possible to have some food sent down, he said he would try.

Her bags were in her old room . . . retrieved from the car and no doubt inspected for good measure. She collapsed onto the same cot she'd awakened in that morning and mumbled a command to put the lights out. Curled up in a ball, clutching a blanket to her breast, Teresa did not feel "home" in any way at all.

In fitful slumber she dreamt the death of stars.

Her old friends. Her guideposts. One by one they flickered out, each with a cry of anguish and despair. Every sigh she echoed in her pillow with a moan.

Something was killing them. Killing the stars.

Poor Jason, she thought in the strange, mixed illogic of sleep. *By the time he reaches Spica it'll be gone. Nothing but black, empty holes. And he so enjoys the light.*

Dreams move on. Now she looked out through the bars of a dungeon, across a dark, glassy-smooth sea, barren of reflections. As she watched, the water acquired a faint luminance . . . a pearly glow that suffused not from above but within. The radiance grew as steam rose; then roiling bubbles burst from a mounting bulge.

The sun rose out of the ocean.

Not the horizon—but the ocean itself. Too brilliant to see, it cast fierce light through her outstretched hand, tracing the contours of her bones. The blazing orb speared upward on a column of superheated vapor. In its wake, mammoth waves rolled across the once-placid sea.

Those water mountains were higher than her prison and heading her way. Yet she didn't care. Even half blinded, she could trace the fireball's trajectory and knew with dreadful certainty, *It isn't going away after all. It's coming back. Coming back to stay.*

Perhaps it was that dreaded thought that stirred her from the nightmare. Or maybe the creepy feeling that someone was treading softly toward her, across the floor of her tiny quarters. Teresa's eyes snapped open, though she was still snared by sleep catalepsy and by her mother's reassuring words.

"Shhh . . . you only imagined it. There are no monsters. There's never anybody there."

A foot collided with the dinner tray, left by the kindly commando. Teresa heard a sharp intake of breath. *Momma,* Teresa thought, as her heart raced and her right hand formed a fist, *you had no idea what you were talking about.*

"Shhh," somebody said, not a meter away. "Don't speak."

She stared at two white blobs . . . a pair of eyes, presumably. Teresa swallowed and tried not to let adrenaline rule her. "Wh . . . who is it?"

A hand settled gently, briefly over her mouth, hushing her without force. "It's Alex Lustig. . . . Do you want to get out of here?"

Why is it, she wondered, that your eyes never completely dark-adapt while you sleep? Only now, staring into the dimness, did she begin making out the man's features.

"But . . . how?"

He smiled. A Cheshire Cat smile. "George slipped me a map. He's staying with the others. Going to try cooperating with Spivey. You and I, though . . . we've got to leave."

"Why you?" She asked hoarsely. "You were in pig heaven, last I looked."

He shrugged. "I'll explain later, if we make it. Right now there's a coffee break going on, and we've maybe fifteen minutes till I'm missed. You coming?"

Teresa answered with action, flinging off the covers and reaching for her shoes.

The Australian was no longer on watch by her door. Instead, a tall, powerful Maori, with permanent-looking cheek tattoos and battle ribbons on his uniform, stood with his back against the opposite wall, his mouth half open in a pleasant leer. At first Teresa wondered if the Kiwi soldier had been won over to their side. Then she saw his glassy look, like a dazer, high on a self-induced enkephalin rush. Only, a dazer wouldn't be a commando. Somehow, Lustig must have drugged him.

"Choline inhibitors. He won't remember a thing," Alex explained. He led her down silent, rock-walled corridors. Each time they approached a door, he referred to a small box before giving the okay to proceed. At last they arrived at the secret quay, where two small boats bobbed in the still, cool waters of Waitomo's underground lake.

"Won't the exits be watched?" she asked. It wouldn't require human guards—just tiny drones, about the size of a housefly.

"This area was swept a few minutes ago. Anyway, nobody but George knows the route we'll be taking."

Teresa wasn't sure she liked the sound of that. But there wasn't much choice. She climbed into the lead boat and cast off as Alex began hauling at the network of ropes lacing the ceiling overhead. As they neared the big doors, the dock lights shut off, plunging them into darkness. The gates rolled aside with a low rumble. Alex grunted, feeling his way from one guide cable to the next. She heard him softly counting, perhaps reciting a mnemonic.

"Are you sure you know what you're—"

He cut her off. "If you want to go back, you know the way."

Teresa shut up. Anyway, soon they were under the false constellations again—those parodies of starlight used by phosphorescent worms to lure their hapless prey. Each vista pretended to show unexplored clusters, galaxies . . . a promise of infinity.

Perhaps all our modern astronomy is wrong, she pondered, gazing across the ersatz starfields. *Maybe the "real" constellations are just like those green dots. No more than lures to bait the unwary.*

She shook her head as the ceiling slid slowly past, carrying with it whole implied universes. That was the problem with nightmares, they clung to you, affecting your mood for hours afterwards. Teresa couldn't afford that now. Nor even settling into "passenger" mode. Action was the proper antidote. She whispered. "Can I help?"

The boat glided smoothly through the water. "Not yet . . ." Alex panted as he groped for something up ahead, almost tipping them over in the process. Teresa gripped the rocking sides. "Ah. Here it is. George's special rope. From here we leave the main cave."

Their craft made a sharp turn, scraping by towers of inky blackness and then embarking under new, unfamiliar skyscapes. A little while later Alex spoke again, now short of breath. "All right. If you take my hand, I'll help you stand . . . carefully! Let me guide you to the cable. . . . Got it? Now that there aren't other ropes about to confuse you, I could use some assistance. Put an elbow on my shoulder to feel my rhythm. Keep to an easy pace at first. Let me know the instant you feel any motion sickness."

Teresa forbore telling him her entire life had been a battle with vertigo. "Lay on, Macduff," she whispered with an effort at cheerfulness.

"And damn'd be him that first cries, 'Hold, enough!' " he finished the quotation. "We're off."

Trying to stand in a swaying boat while dragging on a cable overhead in total darkness—it wasn't exactly the easiest thing Teresa had ever attempted. She almost fell over the first few times. But leaning against him made it easier. They could brace each other on four legs. Soon they were breathing in the same cadence, gliding across the smooth pond with hardly a sound and only the green sprinkle overhead to give the cave walls outlines.

Soon those walls were closing in again, she could tell. The darkness and silence seemed to accentuate her other senses, and she was acutely aware of every faint drip of condensation, every aroma rising from her clothes and his.

The boat bumped once, twice, and then went aground on a rocky bank. "Okay," he said. "Carefully, crouch down and help me feel for the bag of supplies."

Letting go of the rope, they came closer than ever to tipping over. Teresa gasped, clutching him. Together they fell in a heap of arms and legs, gasping—and also laughing with released tension. As they tried to untangle, he grunted. "Ow! Your knee is on my . . . ah, thank you." His voice shifted to falsetto. "Thank you very much." They laughed again, in tearful relief.

"Is this what you were looking for?" she asked, as one hand came upon a nylon bag. She pushed it toward him.

"Yeah," he said. "Now where's the zipper? Don't answer that! Here it is."

There was something bizarre and really rather funny about all this fumbling in the dark. It made your hands feel thick and uncoordinated, as if smothered in mittens. Still, altogether, this beat languishing in a tiny room, feeling sorry for yourself.

"Here, take these," he said, apparently trying to hand her something. But in reaching out she wound up jabbing him in the throat. He made exaggerated choking sounds and she giggled nervously. "Oh, stop. Here, let's do it this way," she suggested, and ran her fingers from his neck down to his right shoulder. She felt his left hand move to cover hers. Together they followed his sleeve down to his other hand.

Funny, she thought along the way. *I had this image of him as being soft, mushy. But he's solid. Are all Cambridge dons built like this?*

With both hands he pressed into hers an object—a pair of goggles. But he didn't let go quite yet.

"We had to get you out," he told her in a more serious tone. "We couldn't let Spivey take you off to jail."

Teresa felt a lump, knowing she had underestimated her friends.

"He'd have used your jeopardy as one more threat, to coerce George and the others," Alex finished. "And we decided we just couldn't allow that."

Teresa pulled her hand away. *Of course. That's completely right. Have to stay practical about this.*

"So you're dropping me off now and going back?" she asked as she adjusted the elastic headband.

"Of course not. First off, we haven't got you out yet. And anyway, I'm not staying to be Colonel Spivey's tool!"

"But . . . but without you the gazer . . ."

"Oh, they'll manage without me, I suppose. If all they want to do is *keep* the damn thing down there—" He paused and caught his breath. "But I'm not bowing out completely. There's method to this madness, Captain Tikhana."

"Teresa . . . please."

There was another pause. "All right. Teresa. Um, got yours adjusted yet?"

"Just a sec." She pulled the strap and toggled the switch by one lens. Suddenly it was as if someone had turned the lights on.

Unlike mere passive infrared goggles, which would have detected very little down here, these monitored whichever way her eyes turned and sent a tiny illuminating beam in just that direction, for just as long as she was looking that way. The only exception was where they detected another set of goggles. To prevent blinding another user, the optics were programmed never to shine directly at each other, so when Teresa looked around for the first time, she made out limestone walls, the inky waterline, the boat—but Alex Lustig's face remained hidden inside an oval of darkness.

"Couldn't have used them before because Spivey had spy sensors—"

Teresa waved aside his explanation. It made sense. "Now where?" she asked.

He pointed downward, and she understood why even the peeper colonel's little robot watchers wouldn't be able to follow them. "Okay," she said. And together they sorted equipment from the nylon bag.

Claustrophobia was the least of her worries as they kicked along a deep, twisting tube, carried by the current of an underground stream. Nor did the bitter cold bother her much—though Teresa kept an eye on the tiny clock readout, calculating the time before hypothermia would become a problem.

Alex's flippers churned the water in front of her, creating sparkling flecks in her goggles' beam. Spectrum conversion always made things look eerie, but here the effect was otherworldly, other-dimensional. The taper of his legs seemed to stretch endless meters, *kilometers* ahead of her, like this surging hypogean torrent.

The river held their lives now and they were helpless to turn back if George Hutton's map proved wrong or if they took some fatal wrong turn. She imagined they might, as in some old movie, be swept downward ever deeper into the Earth's twisting bowels, to some Land That Time Forgot. In fact, though, washing ashore on a misty underground dinosaur refuge was less unsettling to contemplate than some likelier possibilities . . . like meeting their end pinned to a porous wall, the freshet plunging past them through crevices too small for human flesh to pass.

Was Alex planning to lead her all the way to the river's outlet, somewhere on the Tasman Sea? If so, the timing would be tight. Their air capsules weren't rated for more than a couple of hours.

Perhaps it was the coolness, but Teresa's thoughts soon calmed. She found herself wondering at the sculpted shapes of the sweeping, curving tube . . . at the way different hardnesses of stone overlapped in smooth relief and how patient eddies had carved cavities into the ancient mountain, laying bare fine patterns, delicate to the eye.

Those eddies were dangerous. Even with gloves and knee pads it was hard to ward off every sudden invisible surge, every buffet and blow. Teresa felt certain there were daredevils among the world's bored, well-fed majority who would pay George Hutton handsomely for this experience, without ever understanding where they were or what they were seeing.

At one point the river opened into a large chamber with an air pocket. They met at the surface, spitting out their mouthpieces as they treaded water.

"Amazing!" she gasped. And the black oval covering his face seemed to nod in agreement. "Yes, it's unbelievable."

"Where to from here?"

"I . . . think we take the way to the left," he answered after a pause.

Teresa churned her legs, rotating. Yes, the river split here, dividing into two unequal paths. Alex was referring to the narrower, swifter-running branch. "You're sure?"

In answer, he held out the miniplaque that hung from a cord around his neck. "Did you see any other large chambers on the way here? Did I miss one?" She peered at the sketch. A computer graphics device could reproduce only what it was given, and George Hutton's drawing had apparently been scrawled in a hurry. "I . . . I'd have to say you're right. Left it is."

They reset their goggles and mouthpieces and kicked off toward the left-hand opening, and an ominous roaring. Teresa was intensely aware of the annotation Hutton had inscribed at this point on the map, in red letters.

Be careful here! the inscription had said.

Only a few meters into the new stretch, Teresa realized just how friendly the last one had been. No time or energy could be spared for sightseeing or philosophizing now. Curves loomed suddenly out of the froth ahead, confusing her smart goggles. Confusing *her*. Even with the help of slipstreaming—the natural tendency to ride the current's center—it took every ounce of effort just to keep the writhing stone intestine from crushing her!

It can't be much farther, she figured, remembering her brief glimpse at the sketch, unsure whether she was calculating or simply praying. *The last pool has to be just ahead.*

No sooner did she think that though, than suddenly she was caught in a tangle with Alex Lustig's legs. With the river plowing into them from behind, the collision was a series of buffets that made her head ring, knocking dazzling spots before her eyes. The goggles only made things worse by dimming suddenly in response to her pupils' shocked dilation.

A sharp scrape on one leg made Teresa aware of jagged stones, too fresh and rugged to have lain in the smoothing flow for long. A rockfall must have partly blocked the stretch of river. She writhed to one side barely in time to avoid being impaled on one jutting monolith, then had to grab Alex's leg as the current swept her toward another jagged jumble just ahead!

Clutching his ankle, Teresa hadn't time to wonder how *he* had stopped so suddenly. She held on tightly with both arms. Her flippered feet bumped the barricade and instinctively she kicked at it.

Miraculously, it gave way! Glancing quickly downstream, Teresa saw the current sweep away what remained of the precarious barrier. All it had taken was one extra nudge and the impediment was gone. What luck!

She almost let go to continue the journey. But then she paused. *How* is he holding on? a voice insisted. *And why doesn't he let go now that the way is clear?*

Something else had to be wrong. Involuntary shivers were coursing down the man's legs. *He's in trouble,* she realized.

Fighting the current, worming her arms forward one at a time, Teresa climbed up his legs inch by awful inch, seizing at last a solid grip on his belt. She lifted her head to see what Alex was doing.

My God! Bubbles escaped Teresa's mouth as she tried not to cry out. The goggles prevented her from looking within the circle of darkness framing the man's face. But she didn't need any look in his eye to know panic and despair. With growing feebleness, Alex clawed at a thong that gouged deeply into his neck, releasing thin trails of blood every time the current let up a bit. That same current almost dragged Teresa's goggles off as she shifted to try to see around the black circle, to whatever had him trapped.

It was the map plaque. Somehow it had jammed into a crevice left by the cave slide! It was what had stopped them both from crashing among the razor-sharp rocks just seconds ago. Now wedged in place by Alex's struggles, it also anchored the noose that was strangling the life out of him.

There was no time for thought. Teresa's knife was at her ankle, while Lustig's was convenient at his thigh. It would have to be his then. But to take it meant she'd have to let go with one arm! And Teresa knew she couldn't hold on . . . unless.

She took three deep breaths, spat out her mouthpiece and bit down hard on his belt, fastening her teeth as hard as she could. Gripping tight with her left arm, she released the right and fought to bring it to the knife. The river buffeted them like flags. But in spite of the pain, her jaw and shoulder remained in their sockets as her right hand fumbled with the sheath snap and at last brought out the gleaming blade.

Teresa squeezed both arms around him again and wriggled the pungent belt out of her mouth. Now came the hard part—holding her breath while worming her way up Alex's body, centimeter by centimeter. His shirt was in tatters of course, and blood streamers stained the chill water as she noted with one dim corner of her mind that the man's chest was even hairier than Jason's. . . . And that, of all things, he had an erection!

Now? Males are so *bizarre.*

Then she recalled the old wives' tale—that men sometimes grow tumescent when they are close to death. Teresa hurried.

Her arms were close to giving out and her lungs were burning by the time she wrapped her legs around his thighs, held tight with one arm, and reached upstream with the knife. She tried not to stab him in the face or throat as the fickle, trickster river tore and twisted at her grip with sudden surges, forcing her hand this way and that.

He had to be alive and conscious still. Or was it just a reflex that caused Alex to run a hand along her outstretched arm, nudging her aim? All at once, through the metal blade, she felt the taut, bowstring tension of the thong, thrumming a bass tone of death.

Now! Bear down, bitch. Do it!

With a force of will Teresa drove strength into her arm. The thong resisted . . . then parted with a sharp twang that reverberated off the narrow walls.

Suddenly they were tumbling downstream, bouncing against the floor and ceiling. Teresa had to choose between protecting her goggles from the tearing slipstream and cramming the breather tube back into her mouth. She chose breath over sight and grabbed the aerator, quenching her agonized lungs even as the high-tech optics were torn off her head, turning everything black.

The wild ride ended just a few chaotic moments later. Abruptly, the bottom seemed to drop out as she flew into what felt like open air! The former low, thrumming growl now crested to a clear, crashing roar. Gravity took her, and the plummet lasted a measureless time . . . ending at last in a splash at the foot of a noisy waterfall.

The pool was deep and cold and utterly black. Teresa struggled toward what she devoutly hoped would be the surface. When her head finally broached again, she treaded water, spat out her mouthpiece, and drank in the sweetness of unbottled air. Up was up again, and down was down. For a moment it didn't matter that nothing—not even the green glimmer of worms—illuminated her existence. Other people, after all, had gone blind and lived. But no one had ever managed very long without air.

"Alex!" she shouted suddenly, before even thinking of him consciously. He might be knocked out somewhere in this inky lake, drifting away silently, unconscious . . . and she without sight to look for him!

She swam away from the falls until the clatter and spume faded enough to let her hear herself think. "Alex!" she called again. Oh God, if she was alone down here. If he died because she passed within inches, just missing him without even knowing it . . . ?

Was that a sound? She whirled. Had someone coughed? It *sounded* like coughing. She kicked a turn, seeking the source.

"Uh . . . over . . ." More coughing interrupted the faint, croaking voice. "Over . . . here!"

She thrashed the water in frustration. "I lost my goggles, dammit."

The current seemed to be drawing them closer, at least. Next time his voice was clearer. "Ah . . . that must be . . ." He coughed one last time. ". . . must be why I can see your face now. You look terrible, by the way."

He sounded nearby. Alex kept talking to guide her. "Go left a bit . . . um . . . and thank you . . . for saving my life. Yes, that's it. Gets shallow about there . . . left a bit more."

Teresa felt sandy bottom beneath her feet and sighed as she dragged her heavy, shivering body out of the clinging black wetness. "Here, this way," she heard him say, and a hand grabbed her arm. She clutched it tightly and sobbed suddenly with emotion she hadn't been aware of till that moment. Now that all the furious action had stopped, a sudden wave of lygophobia washed over her and she shivered at the intimidating darkness.

"It's all right. We're safe for the time being." He guided her to sit down beside him and put his arms around her to share warmth. "You're an impressive individual, Captain . . . um, Teresa."

"My friends . . . ," she said, catching her breath as she clutched him tightly. "Sometimes, my friends call me . . . Rip."

She knew he was smiling, though she couldn't even see the hand that brushed her stringy, sopping hair out of her eyes. "Well," he said from very close. "Thanks again, Rip." And he held her till the shivering stopped.

Some time later, Teresa borrowed his goggles to look around. The Hadean lake stretched farther to the left and right than the tiny beam could reach, and the ceiling might as well have been limitless. Only echoes confirmed they were underground—and her fey sense, which told her countless meters of ancient rock lay between them and any exit from this place.

She gasped when she saw the extent of poor Alex's scrapes and bruises. "Whoosh," she sighed, touching the noose mark around his throat. It was certain to be permanent.

"A Scotsman, one of my ancestors, died this way," he commented, tracing the bloody runnel with his fingertips. "Poor sod was caught in bed with the mistress of a Stuart prince. Not wise, but it makes for good telling centuries later. My famous grandmother says she always expected to wind up on the gallows, too. Finds the idea romantic. Maybe it runs in the family."

"I know a thing or two about ropes and nooses also," she told him as she dressed his worst cuts. "But I've got a feeling that when you go it'll be a lot flashier than any hanging."

He agreed with a sigh. "Oh, I imagine you're right on about that."

Their supplies were meager, since their hip pouches had been packed in a hurry and hers was torn in the struggle. Besides the first-aid kit and one capsule containing a compressed coverall, there were two protein bars, a compass, and a couple of black data cubes. Carefully scanning the pool, Teresa failed to find her lost goggles or anything else of value.

"How well do you remember George's map?" she asked when they were both a bit recovered. Alex shrugged in what was, to him, utter darkness. "Not too well," he answered frankly. "Had I it to do over again, I'd have made a copy for you. Or we ought to have taken the time to memorize it."

"Mmm." Teresa understood after-the-fact regrets. Her entire career had been about avoiding rushed planning—parsing out every conceivable contingency well in advance. And yet she trained for the unexpected, too. She was always ready to improvise.

"You had no time," she replied. "And Glenn Spivey's no fool."

Alex shook his head. "Back in the conference room he spun out a scenario so reasonable, it almost had me convinced."

"You seemed to be going along when I left. What changed your mind?"

He shrugged. "I didn't so much change my mind as decide I didn't want it made for me. We'd all worked so hard. It was starting to look as if we might be able to deal with Beta ourselves. Though how to expel it safely at the very end—that I still hadn't figured out, yet."

Teresa recalled her dream about the fireball, erupting into the sky from a boiling ocean . . . rising, but certain to return.

"So maybe Spivey's plan's a good one . . . keeping it inside the Earth, but up so high it'll lose mass slowly?"

"Maybe . . . *if* it loses mass fast enough while in the mantle to make up for its gains lower down. *If* there aren't instabilities we never calculated. *If* constant pumping on the gazer doesn't crumble too many farms or cities or change the Earth's innards somehow—"

"Could it do that?"

His face took on a perplexed look. "I don't know. Last time I looked over my big model on Rapa Nui . . . " He shook his head. "Anyway, that's where we've got to go now. From there we can answer Spivey's proposition with one of our own."

What an optimist, Teresa realized, and wondered why she ever thought him dour or lethargic. "How are we supposed to get there?"

"Oh, George says that will be surprisingly easy. Auntie Kapur can get us aboard a Hine-marama zep to Fiji, which isn't a part of ANZAC and has an international jetport. From there, we travel under our own names, quite openly. Spivey won't dare try to stop us . . . not without revealing everything, since, naturally, we'll leave complete diary caches with Auntie before we go."

"Naturally," she nodded. "Knowing Spivey, he'll just wait to talk with us when we get there. He still holds a full hand. And we can't deal with anyone else."

Of course Teresa knew what she and Alex were doing. They were talking as if their fates were actually still in their control. As if they would ever meet that clandestine zeppelin to begin a journey across the Pacific to the land of haunting statues. By putting off their predicament, even for a few minutes, they gave themselves time to calm down, to equilibrate. Time to engage in denial that they really were doomed, after all.

Alex recalled George saying something about exiting the Waterfall Cave via a dry channel, cut halfway up a jumble slope about a quarter of the way forward from the falls themselves. Unfortunately, he coulndn't recall whether that was a quarter of the way *clockwise* or *counterclockwise.* They tried the former first—taking turns peering through the goggles for any sign of an exit—before moving on to the latter. Fortunately, they found the opening at last, not too badly hidden behind a jutting limestone wall.

Unfortunately, one of them would always be effectively blind at any given moment. Because Alex was still a bit shaky from his misadventure in the river, Teresa insisted he lead, wearing the goggles. She assured him she could follow so long as he provided some spoken guidance, plus a hand wherever it got complicated.

The experience of climbing over glassy-smooth boulders in pitch blackness was a unique one for Teresa. At times she had the illusion this wasn't a cave at all, but the surface of some ice moon. The sky was occulted not by stone but by a sooty nebula, hundreds of parsecs in breadth. But at any moment, the moon's rotation might reveal bright stars, shining through a gap in the vast space-cloud . . . or perhaps even some alien planet or sun.

Those were moments of fantasy, of course. And always they were cut short, refuted by her other senses . . . by the bouncing echoes of the receding waterfall and the strange feeling of pressure from the rock overhead . . . reminding her she was actually deep inside a world. A dynamic world, with a habit of changing, shifting, *shrugging* in its fitful slumber.

New Zealand, especially, was a land of earthquakes and volcanoes. And though all that activity went on slowly in comparison to human lives, Teresa felt a sense of danger beyond the prospect of getting lost and starving to death.

At any moment the mountain might simply decide to squash them.

Somehow, strangely, that patina added to all their other jeopardies seemed to compensate a bit. It felt thrilling, somehow. *In that respect we're alike . . . Alex Lustig and I. Neither of us was meant to die in a boring way.*

She thought about all this while, with other parts of her mind, she paid close attention to each stone and every tricky footing. Alex helped her squeeze finally through a narrow slot, into a passageway that coursed with a stiff breeze. Her fingertips brushed the wall to her left, tracing dripping moisture. Alex stopped her then and slipped the goggles into her hand.

The interactive optics read her pupils' dilation and damped power accordingly. Nevertheless, the return of sight left her momentarily dazzled. Pyrites and other deceptively gaudy crystalline forms glittered back at her from all sides, their shine accentuated by the gleety dampness, giving the impression of some hermit's deeply buried shrine. It was lovely. For a moment she was reminded of holos she'd viewed of the Lasceaux and Altamira caves, where her Cro-Magnon ancestors had crept by torchlight to paint the walls with haunting images of beasts and spirits, blowing ocher dust around their hands to leave poignant prints upon the cool stone—markers denoting the one thing she and they intimately shared . . . mortality.

Teresa consulted her compass—though such things were notoriously unreliable underground. Then she took Alex's hand to lead him in what seemed the only direction possible, away from the growling river into the heart of the mountain.

So they alternated, stopping frequently to rest, each taking turns being the leader, then the blind, helpless one. She became quite knowledgeable about the contours of his hands, and their footsteps slowly joined in almost the same subconscious rhythm.

Along the way, to pass the time, Alex asked her to talk about herself. So she spoke of her school years and then her life and Jason. Somehow that seemed easier now. She could speak her husband's name in past tense with sadness but no shame. Teresa also learned a few things about Alex Lustig when his turn came. Perhaps one or two that only slipped between the lines as he told her about his life as a bachelor scientist. In fact, Teresa marveled at how much better a story-teller he was. He made his own labors, in front of chalk boards or holo screens, seem so much more romantic than her own profession as a spacebus driver.

Of course their conversation went in fits and starts. Every third phrase was an interruption. ". . . Lift your left foot . . ." or ". . . duck your head half a meter . . ." or ". . . twist sideways now, and feel for a cut to the right . . ." Each of them took turns verbally guiding and often physically controlling the other one. It was a heavy responsibility, demanding mutual trust. That came hard at first. But there was simply no alternative.

It was during one of her turns to be led that Teresa suddenly felt a passing breeze as they crept along a narrow passage. She turned her head. And even though the fleeting zephyr was gone, she sniffed and began to frown.

". . . so that was when Stan told me I'd better shape up my . . ."

She stopped him by planting her feet and tightening her grip on his hand.

"What is it, Teresa?" She heard and felt him turn around. "Are you tired? We can—"

She held up her free hand to ask for quiet, and he shut up.

Had she really sensed something? Was it because she was blind and paying attention to other senses? Would she have walked right on by if she had been sighted and in the lead? "Alex," she began. "On which side of the corridor was the next branching on George's map?"

"Um . . . as I said, I'm not too certain. I think it was on the left, perhaps four klicks past the lake. But surely we haven't gone that far yet. . . . Or have we?" He paused. "Do you think maybe we've gone past?"

Teresa shook her head. It was a gamble, but the breeze had come from the left. . . .

There were *always* breezes though, little gusts that blew down the cavern from who knew where, bound for places impossible to guess. Still, something in her internal guidance system had seemed to cry out that last time.

"Did George write a note next to the turn?"

She heard him inhale deeply and imagined him closing his eyes as he concentrated. "Yes . . . I believe I see some writing . . . do you think it was something like 'watch out for the skull and bones'?"

She punched fairly accurately and struck his shoulder. "Ow!" he grunted, satisfyingly.

"No," Teresa said. "But the turn must have been unobvious. After all, they don't have to be clear forks in the road. Usually they won't be."

"I guess not. Maybe that's what he wrote down . . . how to look for it. Did you—"

She dragged his wrist. "Come on!"

"Wait. Shouldn't I give you the gog—"

He stumbled just to keep up as she led him back through the utter blackness purely by memory, waving one arm in front of her, trying to find that elusive whisper again.

"Alex!" She stopped so suddenly he collided with her. "Look up! Up and to the right. What do you see?"

"I see . . . Yes. There's an opening all right. But how do you figure . . . ?"

She waved aside his objections. It felt right. Her internal compass, her ever-nervous, never-satisfied sense of direction . . . called her that way. She suppressed a voice of doubt, one that said she was grasping at straws. "Let's give it a try, okay? Shall I give you a boost up? Or want I should go first?"

Alex sighed, as if to say, *What have we got to lose?*

"Maybe I'd better go, Teresa. That way, if it looks like a true passage, I can reach down and lift you."

She nodded in agreement and bent over, lacing her fingers to form a step. Gently, he took her waist and turned her around. "There, that's better. Are you ready then?" He planted one foot in her hands.

"Ready? You kidding?" she asked as she braced to take his weight. "I'm ready for anything."

Even after they had traveled quite some distance along the steep, twisty new path, half crawling, half slithering up slanted chimneys and narrow crevices, Teresa kept refusing his offer to share the goggles. He was doing fine as leader, and she used the excuse that they couldn't risk a transfer in all this chaos. To drop them would be a catastrophe; they might slide or tumble out of sight and never be found again.

But in truth, Teresa felt a queer craving for sightlessness right now. It was strange—difficult to explain even to herself. Why should anyone prefer to stumble along, hands waving, groping in the dark, utterly dependent on another for warning about what low overhang might lay only centimeters from her forehead? What precipice yawned beneath her feet?

And yet, twice she stopped Alex from taking a route that must have seemed reasonable by sight—the wider or flatter or easier path— urging him instead to take a lesser route. They were climbing most of the time, and though Teresa knew that was no guarantee against some dead end just around the next corner, at least upward meant they had only a mountain to contend with, not an entire planet, twelve thousand kilometers across.

This can't be George Hutton's route anymore, she knew after a while. There couldn't have been this many diversions, this many narrow, twisty crawlways indicated on the map they'd lost. Alex certainly realized it as well, but said nothing. Both of them knew they'd never remember how to retrace their steps. The easy banter of an hour ago (or was it four hours? six? fourteen?) gave way to clipped, hoarse whispers as they saved their strength and tried not to think about their growing thirst.

They were blazing their own path now . . . going places no caver must have ever seen before. Teresa didn't see them even now of course, but that didn't matter. The textures were new with every turn. Under her fingertips she became familiar with many different types of rock, without associated names or images to spoil the perfect reality. Substance unsullied by metaphor.

Alex made the tactical decisions, step by step, meter by meter, small-scale choices of how to move each foot, each knee and hand. "Watch your head," he told her. "Bend a bit more. Turn left now. Reach up and to the left. Higher. That's it."

Not once was there any implied rebuke in his voice, for her having led them this way . . . a blind woman pointing vaguely heavenward one moment, the other way the next, quite possibly taking them in circles. *I'm supposed to be scientific. A trained engineer. What am I doing then, trusting both our lives to hunches?*

Teresa quashed the misgivings. True enough, logic and reason were paramount. They were wiser ways by far than the old witchcraft and impulsiveness that used to guide human affairs. But reason and logic also had their limits, such as when they had no data at all to work on. Or when the data were the sort no engineer could grapple with.

We have many skills, she thought during one rest period, as Alex shared the last crumbs of protein bar and then let her lick the wrapper with her dry tongue. *Some are skills we hardly ever use.*

If only water-finding were one of hers. Occasionally they heard what could only be the plinking drip of liquid, somewhere beyond the beam of Alex's goggles—often resonating tantalizingly beyond some rocky wall. Pressing your ear against a smooth surface, you could sometimes even pick up the distant roar and gurgle of the river, or perhaps another one that coursed and threaded these hidden countries below ground.

Sometime during their next stretch, she heard Alex gasp, backing up from what he described as a "bottomless pit." Teresa remained calm as he guided her round an unseen trap that would have been their ossuary if he hadn't spotted it in time.

They rested again on the other side. Hunger and thirst had long since become acute, and then begun fading to dull, familiar aches. But these didn't worry Teresa as much as her growing weakness. Perhaps, a few rest stops from now, they would simply not get up again. Would their bodies then dessicate and mummify? Or was the dryness seasonal? Perhaps in a few months a slow seepage, rich in minerals, would return to these passages and gradually glue their bodies to the rocks where they sat, to seal their crypt and lapidify their bones. Or some wayward, springtime torrent might come crashing through this way, crushing and dissolving their remains, then carrying the bits all the way to distant seas.

Perhaps none of those things would have time to happen. It was still quite possible for Spivey and Hutton to lose control over the Beta singularity, in which case, even the mountain-tomb surrounding her now would prove no more solid than a house made of tissue. The distance between Teresa and her friends in the outer world seemed infinite right now, but would become academic once the *taniwha* reached its ravenous, final maturity, when all their atoms would rendezvous in a sudden, intimate, topological union.

Teresa wondered what that might feel like. It almost sounded attractive in a way, as she contemplated the immediate prospect of starvation. Did other lost explorers got this philosophical when they neared the end?

She wondered if Wegener in Greenland or Amundsen in the Arctic pondered the vagaries of human destiny as they, too, plodded on and on beyond all realistic hope. *Perhaps that, more than cleverness, has been our secret power,* Teresa thought as she and Alex got moving again, choosing yet another branching path. *Even when you run out of answers, there are still possibilities to consider.*

After a while though, even that consoling line of thought petered out. Tiredness settled over her like a numbing weight, thankfully dulling the ache of countless bumps and cuts and scratches. Her knee pads might have been lost some while back, or not, for she could hardly feel anything from those quarters anymore as she crawled or crouched or sidled edgewise through cramped or slanted defiles. All that remained to focus her attention was the rhythm. And an obstinacy that would not let her stop.

She had no premonition when Alex stopped suddenly. Through the hand on his arm, she felt a tremor run through his body. "Come here, Rip," he urged in a hoarse whisper, pulling her alongside him and then over to an inclined shelf. When she was seated on the cool stone, she felt him take her head between his hands and turn it to the left, then downward a bit. "I can't tell," he said in a dry voice. "Is there something over there?"

Teresa blinked. By now she had gotten used to the speckles and entopic flashes the retina seems to "see" even in total darkness—the lies your eyes tell in order to pretend they still have something to do. So it took her a moment to recognize that one of those glimmers was maintaining the same vague, half-imagined, blurry outline, keeping position whichever way she tilted. Teresa gingerly bit her cracked upper lip so the pain would rouse her a bit. In a voice parched and scratchy from thirst, she asked, "Um . . . want to go check it out?"

"No, of course not," he answered with wry, affectionate sarcasm, and squeezed her hand before beginning to guide her down the new channel, this one layered deep with some sort of dust that gave off a strong, musty aroma.

Teresa inhaled and finally realized what was so attractive about the smell. It was a rich pungency, and she could only hope her suspicions were true, that the fragrance wafting her way rose from the thickly lain droppings left by endless generations of flying mammals . . . animals who sheltered below ground, but made their living flying and hunting outside, under an open sky.

Round more bends and turns they followed the faint glimmer, until Teresa began making out the dim outlines of walls and rough columns, contrasting at first only in faint shadings of black, but then with hints of gray and sepia creeping in to lend a detail here and there. Soon she found herself no longer needing as much help from Alex, guiding her own footsteps, detecting obstacles miraculously at long range, while they were still meters away.

Sight . . . an amazing sensation.

It took more steep descending after that, taking care not to make some fatal error in their haste, but at last they came to a place where the floor leveled off and was littered with a carpet of small bones which crunched under their feet. Now, overhead, they could make out thousands of brown, folded forms, hanging from every crack and crevice. The denizens of the cave gave them little notice, wrapped within the cocoons of their wings, sleeping through the day.

Day. Teresa blinked at the concept, and had to hold up a hand to cut the glare reflecting directly off one last cave wall—one facing a source of light brighter than anything she had ever imagined. *I'm sorry I doubted you,* she told the sun, remembering how in her dream she'd presumed it could ever have a rival.

Alex removed the grimy goggles and they looked at each other, breaking out in silent grins over how filthy, horrible, battered and positively wonderful each of them looked to be alive.

They were still holding hands, purely out of habit, when they finished scrambling through the brush covering the cave entrance and stepped into a morning filled with clouds and trees and a myriad of other fine things too beautiful ever to be taken for granted again.

☐ ATTENTION! You have been targeted by a very special net search routine. Please don't purge this message! It originates with the World Association of Mahayana Buddhism, one of the great religious orders of history, and your selection to receive it *was not random.* This is an experiment, a melding of modern science and ancient ways in our continuing search for certain very special individuals.

Those we seek are *tolkus* . . . reincarnated beings who in lives past were saintly, enlightened men and women, or bodhisattvas. In the past, searches such as this were restricted to within a few days' journey of our Himalayan monasteries. But of late, tolkus have been found all over the world, reborn into every race, every native culture and creed. It is cause for rejoicing when one is discovered and thereby helped to full awareness of his or her true powers.

Even when tolkus live their lives unannounced, forgetful of their past or even skeptical of our word, they nevertheless often become teachers or healers of great merit. These powers can be amplified though, through training.

We emphatically denounce claims that Eastern meditation traditions are simply glorified biofeedback techniques for inducing natural opiate highs. Chemical comparisons are crude and emphasize only the superficial. They miss the essential power that can be unleashed by the concentrated human mind. A power *you* may have refined in prior lives and that even now may be within your reach.

Our search is of great importance, now more than ever. Recent strange portents, observed all over the globe, appear to indicate a time of great struggle approaching. Like those of many other faiths, we of Mahayana Buddhism are preparing to face the danger ahead. We have sent into the Net these surrogate messengers to seek out those whose lives, courtesy, works of charity, and creditworthiness indicate they may once have been masters of enlightenment. We ask only that you meditate on the following questions.

Do you believe all beings, large and small, suffer?

Do you believe suffering ends, and that one end can come through what some call Enlightenment, a piercing of life's veil of illusion?

Do you sense that compassion is the essence of correct action?

If these questions resonate within you, do not hesitate. Use our toll-free account to arrange an interview in person.

You may be more blessed than you remember. If so, we have faith you'll know what to do.

● B I O S P H E R E

"So tell me. What do you think of Elspeth?" Dr. Wolling asked as she poured and then passed him a cup of tea.

Nelson stirred in a spoonful of sugar, concentrating on the swirling patterns rather than meeting her eyes. "It's . . . an interesting program," he said, choosing words carefully.

She sat across from him, clattering her own cup and spoon cheerfully. Still, Nelson figured this wasn't going to be an easy session—as if any with this teacher ever were.

"I take it you haven't a lot of experience with autopsych programs?"

He shook his head. "Oh, they had 'em, back home. The school counselors kept offerin' different ones to us. But y'know the Yukon is, well . . ."

"A land of immigrants, yes. Tough-minded, self-reliant." She slipped with apparent ease into a North Canuck accent. "De sort who know what dey know, and damn if any wise-guy program's gonna tell dem what dey tinkin', eh?"

Nelson couldn't help but laugh. Their eyes met and she smiled, sipping her tea and looking like anybody's grandmother. "Do you know how far back autopsych programs go, Nelson? The first was introduced back when I was just a little girl, oh, before 1970. Eliza consisted of maybe a hundred lines of code. That's all."

"You're kidding."

"Nope. All it would do is ask questions. If you typed 'I feel depressed,' it would answer either, 'So you feel depressed?' or 'Why do you think you feel depressed?' Good leading questions, actually, that would get you started picking apart your own feelings, even though the program didn't understand the word 'depressed' at all. If you'd typed, 'I feel . . . orange,' it would have answered, 'Why do you think you feel orange?'

"Funny thing about it, though, Eliza was positively addictive! People used to sit for hours in front of those old-fashioned screens, pouring their hearts out to a fictitious listener, one programmed simply to say the rough equivalent of 'Hmm? I see! Oh, do tell!'

"It was the perfect confidant, of course. It couldn't get bored or irritated, or walk away, or gossip about you afterward. Nobody would cast judgment on your deep dark secrets because *nobody* was exactly who you were talking to. At the same time, though, the rhythm of a true conversation was maintained. Eliza seemed to draw you out, insist you keep trying to probe your feelings till you found out what hurt. Some people reported major breakthroughs. Claimed Eliza changed their lives."

Nelson shook his head. "I guess it's the same with Elspeth. But . . ." He shook his head and fell silent.

"But Elspeth seemed real enough, didn't she?"

"Nosy bitch," he muttered into his teacup.

"Who do you mean, Nelson?" Jen asked mildly. "The program? Or me?"

He put the cup down quickly. "Uh, the program! I mean she . . . it . . . kept after me and after me, picking apart my words. Then there was that, um, free-association part. . . ."

He recalled the smiling face in the holo tank. It had seemed so innocuous, asking him to say the first word or phrase to come to mind. Then the next, and the next. It went on for many minutes till Nelson felt caught by the flow, and words spilled forth quicker than he was aware of them. Then, when the session was over, Elspeth showed him those charts—tracing the irrefutable patterns of his subsurface thoughts, depicting a muddle of conflicting emotions and obsessions that nevertheless only began to tell his story.

"It's the second-oldest technique in modern psychology, after hypnosis," Jen told him. "Some say free association was Freud's greatest discovery, almost making up for some of his worst blunders. The technique lets all the little selves within us speak out, see? No matter how thoroughly a bit or corner is outvoted by the rest, free association lets it slip in that occasional word or clue.

"Actually, we free associate in everyday life, as well. Our little subselves speak out in slips of the tongue or pen, or in those sudden, apparently irrelevant fantasies or memories that just seem to pop into mind, as if out of nowhere. Or snatches of songs you haven't heard in years.''

Nelson nodded. He was starting to see what Jen was driving at, and felt intensely relieved. *So all of this has something to do with my studies, after all. I was afraid she wanted me to face that program 'cause she thought I was crazy.*

Not that he felt all that sure of his own mental balance anymore. That one session had exposed so many raw nerves, so many places where it hurt—memories from a childhood he'd thought normal enough, but which still had left him with his own share of wounds.

He shook his head to knock back those gloomy thoughts. *Everybody has shit like that to deal with. She wouldn't be wasting time on me if she thought I was nuts.*

"You're tellin' me this has to do with cooperation and competition," he said, concentrating on the abstract.

"That's right. All the current multimind theories of consciousness agree on one thing, that each of us is both many *and* one, all at the same time. In that sense, we humans are most catholic beings.''

Obviously, she had just made a witticism, which had gone completely over his head. Fortunately, the session was being recorded by his note plaque and he could hunt down her obscure reference later. Nelson chose not to get sidetracked. "So inside of me I've got . . . what? A barbarian and a criminal and a sex maniac . . .''

"And a scholar and a gentleman and a hero," she agreed. "And a future husband and father and leader, maybe. Though few psychologists anymore say metaphors like that are really accurate. The mind's internal landscape doesn't map directly onto the formal roles of the outer world. At least, not as directly as we used to think.

"Nor are the boundaries between our subpersonae usually so crisp or clear. Only in special cases, like divided personality disorder, do they become what you or I would call distinct characters or personalities.

Nelson pondered that—the cacophony within his head. Until coming to Kuwenezi, he had hardly been aware of it. He'd always believed there was just one Nelson Grayson. That core Nelson still existed. In fact, it felt stronger than ever. Still, at the same time, he had grown better at listening to the ferment just below the surface. He leaned forward. "We talked before about how—how the cells in my body compete and cooperate to make a whole person. And I been reading some of those theories 'bout how individual people could be looked at the same way . . . like, y'know, organs or cells cooperating and competing to make up societies? And how the same . . . metaphor—''

"How the same metaphor's been applied to the role *species* play in Earth's ecosphere, yes. Those are useful comparisons, so long as we remember that's *all* they are. Just comparisons, similes, models of a much more complicated reality."

He nodded. "But now you're sayin' even our *minds* are like that?"

"And why not?" Dr. Wolling laughed. "The same processes formed complexity in nature, in our bodies, and in cultures. Why shouldn't they work in our minds as well?"

Put that way, it sounded reasonable enough. "But then, why do we think we're individuals? Why do we hide from ourselves the fact we're so many inside? What's the *me* that's thinkin' this, right now?"

Jen smiled, and sat back. "My boy. My dear boy. Has anyone ever told you that you have a rare and precious gift?"

At first Nelson thought she was referring to his unexpected talent with animals and in managing the ecology of ark four. But she corrected that impression. "You have a knack for asking the right questions, Nelson. Would it surprise you to learn the one you just posed is probably the deepest, most perplexing in psychology? Perhaps in all philosophy?"

Nelson shrugged. The way he felt whenever Jen praised him was proof enough that he had many selves. While one part of him felt embarrassment each time she did this, another basked in the one thing he wanted most, her approval.

"Great minds have been trying to explain consciousness for centuries," she went on. "Julian Jaynes called it the 'analog I.' The power to name some central locus 'me' seems to give intensity and focus to each individual human drama. Is this something totally unique to humanity? Or just a commodity? Something we only have a bit *more* of than, say, dolphins or chimpanzees?

"Is consciousness imbued in what some call the 'soul'? Is it a sort of monarch of the mind? A higher-order creature, set there to rule over all the 'lower' elements?

"Or is it, as some suggest, no more than another illusion? Like a wave at the surface of the ocean, which seems 'real' enough but is never made of the same bits of water from one minute to the next?"

Nelson knew an assignment when he heard one. Sure enough, Jen next reached into her pouch and took out a pair of small objects, which she slid across the table toward him. "Here are some things to study. One contains articles by scholars as far back as Ornstein and Minsky and Bukhorin. I think you'll find them useful as you write up your own speculations for next time."

He reached for the items, perplexed. One was a standard gigabyte infocell. But the other wasn't even a chip. He recognized the disk as an old-style metal coin and read the words UNITED STATES OF AMERICA imprinted around its rim.

"Take a look at the motto," she suggested.

He didn't know what that meant, so he searched for the most incomprehensible thing on it. "E . . . pluribus . . . unum?" he pronounced carefully.

"Mmm," she confirmed, and said nothing more. Nelson sighed. Naturally, he was going to have to look it up for himself.

By all the numbers, it should have happened long ago.

Jen thought about consciousness, a topic once dear to her, but which she'd given little attention to for some time. Until all these new adventures overturned her pleasant, iconoclastic existence and threw her back to contemplating the basics again. Now she couldn't help dwelling on the subject during her walk back to the Tangoparu digs.

It's close to a century since they've been talking about giving machines "intelligence." And still they run up against this barrier of self-awareness. Still they say, "It's sure to come sometime in the next twenty years or so!" As if they really know.

Stars glittered over the dusty path as she made her way from Kuwenezi's compact, squat, storm-proof ark four, past fields of newly sprouted winter wheat, toward the gaping entrance of the old gold mine. The quandary stayed with her as she rode the elevator deep into the Earth.

Simulation programs keep getting better. Now they mimic faces, hold conversations, pass Turing tests. Some may fool you up to an hour if you aren't careful.

And yet you can always tell, if you pay attention. Simulations, that's all they are.

Funny thing. According to theoreticians, big computers should have been able to perform human-level thought at least two decades ago. Something was missing, and as her conversations with Nelson brought her back to basics, Jen thought she knew what it was.

No single entity, all by itself, can ever be whole.

That was the paradox. It was delicious in a way, like the ancient teaser, "This sentence is a lie." And yet, hadn't Kurt Gödel shown, mathematically, that no closed system of logic can ever "prove" all its own implied theorems? Hadn't Donne said, "No man is an island"?

We need feedback from outside ourselves. Life consists of interacting pieces, free to jiggle and rearrange themselves. That's how you make a working system, like an organism, or a culture, or a biosphere.

Or a mind.

Jen entered the well-lit chamber where the Tangoparu team had their resonator. She stopped by the main display to see where Beta was at present. A purple ellipse marked it's current orbit—now rising at its highest point all the way past the outer core to the lower mantle, where quicksilver flashes seemed to spark and flare with every lingering apogee. Now Beta was losing mass at each apex—a true milestone —though it would be a while yet before its balance sheet went into debit full time and they could all draw a sigh of relief.

Jen watched the mantle's flickerings of superconducting electricity, those pent-up energy stores Kenda's people tapped to drive the gazer effect. One brief, titanic burst had taken place while she was visiting Nelson—triggered in tandem by the Greenland and New Guinea resonators. The next run, scheduled in ten minutes, would unite this African device with New Guinea in an effort to shift Beta's orbital line of apsides slightly.

At first she and the others had been fearful of the news from headquarters—that the NATO-ANZAC-ASEAN alliances had seized two of the four resonators. Kenda worried that all their work would be in vain. Then came word from George Hutton. Everything was to go on as before. The only difference, apparently, was that new supplies and technicians would flood in to help the effort. Jen had been cynical; it sounded too good to be true.

Sure enough, George went on to add that there would be limits to cooperation with Colonel Spivey. Easter Island and South Africa were to remain independent. He was adamant about that. No newcomers would be allowed at those two sites. Kenda's team reacted with a mixture of resigned fatigue and relief. They would have loved the help, but understood Hutton's reasons.

"George isn't so sure about this association, yet," Kenda told them all at a meeting several days ago. *"And that's enough for me."*

Jen wondered why there was no word from Alex. Now that they were communicating over secure military bands, completely independent of the World Data Net, shouldn't the boy feel free to talk openly? Something was wrong, she sensed. More was going on than anyone said.

With a sigh she went to her own station to plug in the subvocal. By now it was almost as easy to calibrate as her home unit, though she still had to do most of it "by hand."

Only this time, after that conversation with Nelson, she paid a little more attention to the extraneous blips and images that popped in and out of the peripheral screens.

At the upper left, several bars of musical score wrote themselves

—an advertising jingle she hadn't heard in years. Below that, poking from a corner, came the shy face of a young boy . . . Alex, as she remembered him at age eight or so. No mystery why that image crept in. She was worried about him, and so must have subvocalized unspoken words that the computer picked up. It, in turn, had gone into her personal archive and pulled out some old photo, feeding it then to an off-the-shelf enhancement program to be animated.

To the uninitiated, it might seem as if the computer had read her thoughts. In fact, it was only highlighting the surface bits, those which almost became words. It was like rummaging through your purse and coming up with an envelope of neglected pictures. Only now her "purse" consisted of terabyte sheets of optical memory, extrapolated by a tool kit of powerful subroutines. And you didn't even have to *intend* in order to rummage. The mind "below" was doing it all the time.

Jen adjusted the sensitivity level, giving her associations more space to each side . . . it was a sort of visually amplified form of free association, she realized. Yet another type of feedback. And feedback was the way life-forms learned and avoided error. Gaia used feedback to maintain her delicate balance. Another word for feedback was "criticism."

A pair of cartoon figures drifted toward each other from opposite screens. The first was her familiar tiger totem . . . a mascot that had been omnipresent, for some reason, ever since this adventure had begun. The other symbol looked like an *envelope* . . . the old-fashioned kind you used to send letters in. The two figures circled round each other, the tiger mewling lowly, the envelope snapping its flap at the cat.

Now why had these manifested when she thought the word "criticism"? As she reflected on the question, written words formed in the tank. The envelope said to the tiger, "YOUR ORANGE STRIPES ARE TOO BRIGHT TO CAMOUFLAGE YOU ON THIS SCREEN! I CAN SEE YOU TOO EASILY!"

"THANK YOU," the tiger acknowledged, and switched at once to gray tones Jen found blurry and indistinct. "WHAT DO YOU CONTAIN?" the tiger asked the envelope in turn. "IT REALLY IS WRONG FOR ONE PART TO KEEP SECRETS FROM THE WHOLE." And a slashing paw ripped open a corner, laying bare a bit of something that sparkled underneath. "WHAT DO YOU CONTAIN?" the great cat insisted.

Though amusing in its own way, Jen decided this was accomplishing nothing. "I'll tell you what it contains," she muttered, making the words official by saying them aloud. She wiped the screen with a simple tap of one tooth against another. "Just more bleeding metaphors."

Gathering herself together, Jen concentrated on the matter at hand. Getting ready for the next run of the gravity laser. She'd gotten to quite enjoy each firing, pretending it was she herself who sent beams of exploration deep into the living world.

Meanwhile, though, a ghostlike striped pattern, like a faint smile, lingered faintly in one corner of the screen, purring softly to itself, watching.

☐ The International Space Treaty Authority today released its annual census of known man-made hazards to vehicles and satellites in outer space. Despite the stringent provisions of the Guiana Accords of 2021, the amount of dangerous debris larger than one millimeter has risen by yet another five percent, increasing the volume of low earth orbit unusable by spacecraft classes two through six. If this trend continues, it will force repositioning or replacement of weather, communications, and arms-control satellites, as well as the expensive armoring of manned research stations.

"People don't think of this as pollution," said ISTA director Sanjay Vendrajadan. "But Earth is more than just a ball of rock and air, you know. Its true boundaries extend beyond the moon. Anything happening inside that huge sphere eventually affects everything else. You can bet your life on it."

● The face in the telephone screen seemed to be changing daily.
L Logan felt a pang, seeing how grown-up Claire was becoming.
I   "She doesn't even think it worth hiding from me!" his
T daughter complained. Behind her, Logan saw the familiar cane
H fields and cypresses of Atchafalaya country, with its monumental
O dikes shading fish farms and lazy bayous. Claire looked frustrated
S and angry.
P   "I'm no great programmer, but she must think I'm a total
H *baby* not to be able to snoop through those pathetic screens be-
E tween my unit and hers!"
R   Logan shook his head. "Honey, Daisy could hide data from
E God himself." He smiled. "Heck, she could even fool Santa Claus
if she put her mind to it."

"I know that!" Claire answered with a furled brow, dismissing his attempt at levity. "Between the house and the *outside world*, she's got watchdogs and griffins and the scariest cockatrice programs anyone's ever seen. Which shows just how much contempt she must have for me, leaving it so easy for me to probe her puzzle palace from my little desk comp down the hall!''

Logan realized this was complicated. Part of Claire's agitation had little to do with Daisy's actual sins. "Your mother loves you," he said.

But Claire only shrugged irritably, as if to say his statement was obvious, tendentious, and irrelevant. "I *have* a psycher program, Dad, thanks. I didn't come all the way out here, beyond range of her local pickups, just to whine that my momma doesn't understand me.''

That was sure what it had sounded like. But Logan held up both hands in surrender. "All right. Pipe me what you found. I'll look it over.''

"Promise?''

"Hey," he said, pausing to cross his heart. "Didn't I pay off on the meteorite?''

That, at last, got a smile out of her. Claire brushed aside a lock of dark hair that had fallen over her eyes in her agitation. "Okay. Here it comes. I encrypted it inside a routine weather forecast, in case one of her ferrets happens across it on the way.''

If one of Daisy McClennon's ferrets finds the blip, simple encryption won't matter. But Logan kept the thought to himself. Almost as soon as she pressed a button, a thousand miles away, his own borrowed data plaque lit up.

INCOMING MAIL.

Logan thought he heard the sound of a copter's engines. He looked up to scan the forest from this slight rise, but there was no sign yet of the pickup vehicle. There was still time to finish the conversation.

"I want to know if you thought about what I said last time," he asked his daughter.

Claire frowned. "You mean about dragging Daisy with me on some sort of 'vacation'? Daddy, have you any idea what my counselor in Oregon is like? I already missed one threshold exam this month because of the storm. Two more and I might have to go back to school. You know, *high school*?''

Logan was almost tempted to ask, *What's so bad about high school? I had some great times in high school.*

But then, the mind has ways of locking out memories of pain and ennui, and recalling only the peaks. Prison for the crime of puberty— that was how secondary school had seemed, when he really thought back on it.

So how do I tell her I'm worried? Worried about things far worse than the off chance she might have to finish her diploma in some public warren? What's six months of bored purgatory against saving her life?

One of Daisy's surrogates might or might not at this moment be snooping the plaque he was using. But Logan knew for certain another force, even more powerful than his ex-wife, was listening to his every word. Glenn Spivey's organization was fanatical about security, and its watch programs would parse all but the vaguest warnings he might offer Claire. Still, Logan had to take a chance.

"I . . . do you remember what Daisy snooped, last time? My paper?" He furrowed his forehead until his eyebrows nearly touched.

"You mean the one about—?" Then, miraculously, she seemed to read his expression. Her mouth went round, briefly. "Um, yeah. I remember what it was about."

"Well, just so you do." Logan pretended to lose interest in the topic. "Say, have you been up to Missouri, lately. I hear they're having a pretty good state fair up around New Madrid, these days. You might pick up some nice specimens for your collection there."

Claire's eyes narrowed to slits. "Um, Tony has to handle the fish harvest all alone since his uncle got laid up. So . . . I'm helping even on weekends. I probably won't get to any fairs this year."

He could see the wheels turning behind those blue eyes. *Not even seventeen, and yet she knows how to read between the lines. Are the new schools doing this? Are teenagers really getting smarter? Or am I just lucky?*

Obviously the reference to New Madrid was setting off alarm bells in Claire's head. Now he had to pray Spivey's spy software wouldn't catch the same contextual cues. "Mm. Tony's a good kid. Just remember, though, how we talked about boys, even the nice ones. Be sure you call the shots, kiddo. Don't let anybody turn the ground to jello under you."

With a show of irritation he could tell was calculated, Claire sniffed. "I can take care of my own footing, Dad."

He grunted with fatherly curmudgeonliness. For the moment, that was all he could do. Let Claire evaluate his veiled warning, as he'd consider hers. *What a team we'd make. That is, if we survive the next year.*

From a distance, across the forested slopes, Logan now heard the real growl of the 'copter carrying the rest of his inspection team. He turned back to his daughter's image. "Time to go, honey. I just . . . hope you know how very much I love you."

He hadn't intended getting so uncharacteristically mushy all of a sudden. But it turned out to be exactly the right thing to do. Claire's eyes widened momentarily, and he saw her swallow, realizing perhaps for the first time just how seriously he took all this.

"Take care of yourself, Daddy. Please." She leaned forward and whispered. "I love you too." Then her image vanished from the small display.

Fallen pine needles blew across his ankles. Logan looked up as the hybrid flying machine—half helicopter, half turboprop—rotated its engines to descend vertically toward a clearing a hundred meters away. Leaning out the side door was Joe Redpath, Logan's sardonic Amerind assistant, whose bored, sullen expression was just his version of a friendly greeting. No doubt Redpath brought news of the colonel's next assignment now that their survey here was finished.

Between Logan and the clearing lay the emergence site—an area about equal to a city block. As usual, the gravity beam's coupling with surface matter had been, well, peculiar. This time roughly a quarter of the pines within the exit zone had been *vaporized*, along with their roots. Those remaining—which had all been either taller or shorter than the missing trees—stood apparently unscathed amid the gaping holes.

Fortunately, no people had been in this remote mountain locale, so it hardly seemed a calamity. Logan would reserve judgment though, till the soil and underlying rocks were scanned by follow-up teams.

But of course, Colonel Spivey was less interested in mineralogical consistency than readouts from his instrument packages, which had been scattered across this mountainside just before the gazer beam was scheduled to pass through. Returning minutes after the event, Logan had dropped in to gather the mud-spattered canisters nearest the center while Redpath and the 'copter crew collected others farther out. Of those at ground zero, two were missing, along with the vanished trees.

The predictions made by Hutton's teams grew sharper with each event. *Soon, we won't have to retreat so far for safety. Soon I'll get to witness one happening up close.*

The prospect was both chilling and exciting.

This improved predictability was helping keep collateral damage to a minimum, at least in alliance territories. Where the beam couldn't be diverted to completely uninhabited areas, people could generally be evacuated on some pretext. It was different, of course, when the exit point lay in "unfriendly territory," where a warning might arouse suspicion. In those cases, the resonator crews could only do their best with aiming alone.

Sometimes, that wasn't enough. In China, an entire village had sunk out of sight last week, when the ground beneath it turned to slurry. And had the vibrations in an Azerbaijani earthquake been just a few hertz closer to the normal modes of certain large apartment buildings, the damage would not have been "minor," but horrendous. Logan shuddered to think about that near catastrophe.

Maybe Spivey's arranging for these close shaves, he pondered as he picked his way past the yawning gaps in the forest loam. *After all, when you're testing a weapon, an intentional "near miss" is just as good as a bull's-eye.*

Only, what if some "near miss" happens to trigger something else? Something unexpected?

New Madrid, he had said to Claire. Not many people knew that Missouri town was distinguished as the site of a particularly stiff seismic jolt back in the early nineteenth century—the most powerful quake to hit the territory of the United States in recorded history, which shook the Mississippi out of its banks and rattled the continent as far away as the Eastern Seaboard. Only a few had died on that occasion, because the population was so sparse. But if something like it struck today, it would make two "big ones" in late TwenCen California look like mere amusement park rides.

Spivey and the others think they can "manage" the monster. But Alex Lustig seemed dubious, and he was the only one with any real understanding.

It troubled Logan that they still hadn't found the British physicist. Perhaps Lustig and that woman astronaut had been victims of foul play. But if so, who could have profited?

Redpath caught the recovered instrument packages Logan slung into the aircraft. "So where to now?" Logan asked as he clambered aboard. The federal officer with the beaded headband barely shrugged. "Somewhere in Canada. They're tryin' to pin it down now. Meanwhile, we ride."

Logan nodded. This was the thrilling part, heading off to yet another site, somewhere in North America, flitting from one place to the next to see what new, weird manifestations the gazer would wreak. Most of the time it came down to interviewing some eyewitness who saw "a cloud disappear" or reported "a thousand crazy colors." But then, when the beam coupling coefficients were close, there might be bizarre, twisty columns of fused earth where none had been before, or gaping holes, or disappearances.

We're saving the Earth, Logan reminded himself dozens of times each day. *The gazer is our only hope.*

True enough. But Glenn Spivey was right about something else, too. While "saving" the world, they were also going to change things.

The flyer took off, gained altitude, then rotated its jets and swung to the northeast. Logan settled in as comfortably as he could and began reading his mail.

So, he thought, when he perused what Claire had sent him. It was a document of agreement—between his ex-wife and the United States Department of Defense.

I always knew Daisy suffered from selective morality. But it seems she'll deal with the Devil himself, if it advances one of her causes.

In this case, the rewards were substantial. Military funds would be used to buy up one thousand hectares of wetlands and donate them to the World Nature Conservancy, protecting them forever from encroaching development. Logan had never heard of a whistle blower getting so much for a single tip. But then, Daisy McClennan was a shrewd negotiator. *I wonder what she sold them.*

Logan frowned as he pieced together that part of the deal. *It was me. She sold me!*

Daisy had been the one who told Spivey about his Spanish paper . . . that he was on the trail of the cause of the anomalies. Reading the date, he whistled. His ex-wife had realized the importance of his discovery back when he thought it nothing but another amusing "just-so" story.

Logan read on, in growing astonishment.

Hell, it wasn't Spivey's peepers who finally cracked the Tangoparus' security. It was Daisy! She's the one who tracked them to New Zealand and gave Spivey the time he needed to get his three-alliance deal worked out.

Logan whistled, in awe and not a little admiration. *Of course I always knew where Claire got her brains. Still, Daisy—*

He rescaled what he had believed about his former wife and lover who, it appeared, felt at liberty to dictate terms to governments and spies. Of course it was conceited and foolish of her to think she could manipulate such forces indefinitely. But Daisy had grown up a McClennon—and therefore almost as cut off from reality as ancient Habsburg princes. That couldn't have been healthy for a youngster's coalescing sense of proportion, or learning to know one's limitations. Even after rebelling against all that, Daisy must have retained a residual feeling that *rules are for the masses, and really only optional for special people.* That reflex would only get reinforced in the simulated worlds of the Net, where wishing really made some things so.

Logan recalled the girl she'd been at Tulane. She had seemed perfectly aware of those handicaps, so eager to overcome them.

Ah, well. Some wounds get better, some just fester. So now she had sold him to Glenn Spivey. What next?

Logan erased the screen and put away the plaque. He settled to watch as the aircraft passed beyond moist forests into drier territory and finally dropped out of the Cascade Range. Soon it was reeling its fleeting shadow behind it across a high desert, still visibly contoured and rippled from massive eruptions and floods that took place in ages gone by. To Logan's eyes, the stories of past cataclysms were as easy to read as a newspaper, and just as relevant. The planet breathed and stretched. And yet it had never occurred to him until recently that humankind might also wreak changes on such a scale.

Funny thing is, in all honesty, I can't tell whether Daisy was right or wrong to do what she did.

One thing, though. I'll bet she didn't worry much about choosing between George Hutton and Glenn Spivey. Two devils, she'd call them, and say they deserved each other. She got her thousand hectares—saved some ivory-billed woodpeckers or whatever. All in a good day's work.

Logan had to laugh, finding it deliciously ludicrous and stupid. That irony compensated, somehow, for the inevitable pang he felt, knowing why, ultimately, she had cast him out years ago—not because of any particular sin or failing on his part, but simply because she preferred by far her own obsessions over the distracting nuisance of his love.

☐ **Free-form Key Word Scan: "Ecology"/"Food Chains"/ "Polar"/"Deterioration"**
Technical Sieve Level: Semiprofessional, Open Discussion.

We've been lulled into complacency by recent increases among gray, humpback and sperm whales. Few of you out there recall another smug time, before the century turn, when whale numbers were also rising because commercial hunting had ended.

But then came the great diebacks in Africa and Amazonia, the Indian collapse, and the Helvetian War. Suddenly the world was too busy to worry about a few blubbery sea creatures. Anyway, how do you deter boatloads of ragged refugees with their crude harpoons. Shoot them? It took the creation of their own state to finally bring that chaos under control.

Decades later, it all seems a bad dream. Blues and bowheads are gone forever, but other whale stocks seem to be recovering at last.

Still, take a look at disturbing new research by Paige and Kast-
ing [□ ref:aSp 4923-bE-eEI-4562831]. The Antarctic ozone has deteriorated
again. I plugged the data into a modified Wolling model and foresee bad
news for the euphotic and benthic phytoplankton the whole Antarctic food
chain depends on. World protein harvests will fall. But even worse will be
the effect on those baleen whales that feed on krill.

Our only ray of hope is the mutation rate, which blooms with increased
B-ultraviolet. We may see tougher plankton variants emerge, though to
expect salvation from that front stretches even my optimism.

● Daisy McClennon felt good.

H   For one thing, business was going well. She'd just finished a
Y lucrative 3-D reprocessing of the entire nine-hundred-episode *Star*
D *Trek* saga, and all three *Rambo* movies. Pretty good for a business
R that had started out as piecework enterprise, a part-time occupa-
O tion for a housewife!
S   Daisy admitted she worked as much for pride as cash. It
P meant independence from the family trust fund, so she could af-
H ford to snub her damned cousins more often than not.
E   *You'll come crawling back,* they had told her long ago. But
R nowadays it was they who came to her asking favors, seeking an-
E swers their hired flunkies couldn't give them.

*They thought I'd never make it on my own. But now I'm a
mover and a changer.*

She was spending less time with movies these days, anyway, and
more of it brokering "special" information. That recent bit of private
espionage for the peepers, for instance. In desperation, the feds had
finally agreed to her price. The coup caused quite a stir in certain parts
of the Green underground, adding to her burgeoning reputation.

Of course, some purists said you shouldn't ever deal with nature-
killing pigs. But Daisy had grown up around wheeler-dealers. *The
trick is to take advantage of their short-term mentality,* she answered
her critics. *Their greed can be turned against them if you have what
they need.*

In this case, the peepers wanted data on a rogue techno-conspir-
acy of some sort. Something having to do with those missing drilling
rigs and water spouts Logan Eng had been so uptight about. Her cus-
tomers didn't want to discuss specifics, and that was fine by her. The
details weren't important anyway. Let them play their adolescent-
male, military-penis games. The deal she'd struck had saved more land

than you could walk across in a day of hard marching. All in exchange for a simple map to the conspirators' front door!

What's more, she was already getting feelers from other clients who wanted information on the same subject. There were ways of getting around her oath of confidentiality to the feds. This affair might be milked a lot farther, for more acres set aside, more watersheds put off limits to rapacious man.

All told, it had been a very profitable month. In fact, it seemed such a pleasant spring day, Daisy put on her hat and sunglasses and gloves and left her den to go for a walk.

Of course once she crossed the bridge, leaving behind her wind generators and mulch turbines and acres of restored native foliage, she had to face all the garbage left by four centuries of desecrators . . . including, still visible above the cypress groves, the decaying spires of derelict riverside refineries. Some of them still seeped awful gunk, many decades after their abandonment and so-called cleanup. Only fools drank unfiltered groundwater from Louisiana wells.

That wasn't all. Ancient power cables and sagging telephone poles laced the parish like atherosclerotic veins, as did concrete and asphalt roads, many no longer used but still stretching like taut lines of scar tissue across the fields and meadows. Even near at hand, in her quiet green neighborhood, there were those Kudzu-covered mounds in the nearby yards, which looked like vine-coated hillocks till you peered close and recognized the blurred outlines of long-abandoned, rusted automobiles.

It all reminded Daisy of why, as the years passed, she left her carefully resurrected patch of nature less and less often. *It's a wonder I had the stomach to spend so much time in this countryside when I was young, instead of getting sick whenever I went outdoors.*

Actually, the family estates were a ways north of here. Still, this general part of Louisiana was where her roots had sunk deeply, for better or for worse. Back when her brothers and sisters and cousins had been dashing madly about, taking *juku* lessons, struggling to live up to their parents' expectations and be better horseriders, better at sports, better world cosmopolitans, always *better* than the children of normal folk—Daisy had fiercely and adamantly opted out. Her passion had been exploring the territory in all directions, the living textures of the land.

And exploring the Net too, of course. Even back then, the data web already stretched round the globe, a domain fully as vast as the humid counties she roamed in the "real" world. Only, in the Net you could make things happen like in stories about magic, by incantation, by persuasion, by invoking sprites and spirits and just the right software familiars to do your bidding for you. Why, you could even *buy* those loyal little demons in brightly colored boxes at a store, like a pair of shoes or a new bridle for your horse! No fairy tale wizard ever had it so easy.

And if you made a mistake on the Net . . . you just erased it! Unlike outside, where an error or faux pas left you embarrassed and isolated, or where a single careless act could despoil a habitat forever.

And it was an egalitarian place, where skill counted more than who your parents were. You could be pen pals with a farm girl near Karachi. Or join an animal rights club in Budapest. Or beat *everybody* at Simulation Rangers and have all the top gamesters on the planet arguing for months whether the infamous hacker called "Captain Loveland" was actually a boy or a girl.

Best of all, when you met someone on the Net, people's eyes didn't widen as they asked, "Oh? Are you one of *those* McClennons?"

It was a touchy subject, brought to mind by a recent message she'd received. Family interests were among those inquiring about the peeper matter. And much as she hated to admit it, Daisy was still snared in a web of favors and obligations to the clan. How else, these days, could she afford to turn so much prime agricultural acreage back to native bayou?

Damn them, she cursed silently, kicking a stone into one of the turbid man-made canals carrying drainage from a cluster of giant fish farms.

Maybe I can use this, though . . . find a way to turn things around on them. If they want the data bad enough, this could win me free of them forever.

For the first time she wondered, really wondered, about the conspiracy Logan and the peepers had been so upset over—that everyone in the world seemed to want to know about. *I assumed it was just more physics and spy stuff.*

Corporations and institutes and governments were always getting in a froth over this or that technological "breakthrough," from fusion power and superconductors to nanotech and whatever. Every time it was "the discovery that will turn the tide, make the difference, harken a new era." Always it seemed imperative to be the first to capitalize. But then, inevitably, the bubble burst.

Oh, sometimes the gadgets worked. Some even made life better for the billions, helping forestall the "great die-back" that had been due decades ago. But to what end? What good was putting off the inevitable a little while longer, which was all Logan and his ilk ever managed, after all? Daisy had learned not to pay much heed to techno-fads. To her fell the task of preserving as much as possible, so that when humanity finally did fall, it wouldn't take everything else to the grave with it.

Now, though, she wondered. *If this thing's got everybody so excited, maybe I ought to look into it myself.*

She turned back well before reaching the little town of White Castle. Daisy didn't want the humming power cables from the nuclear plant to ruin what was left of her mood. Anyway, she'd begun thinking about ways to take advantage of the situation.

If the clan wants a favor, they'll have to give one in return. I want access to Light Bearer. It's the last ingredient I need to make my dragon.

On her way back past the cane fields and fish farms, Daisy contemplated the outlines of her superprogram—one that would make her surrogate "hounds" and "ferrets" look as primitive as those ancient "viruses" that had first shown how closely software could mimic life. She pondered the beautiful new structure mentally. *Yes, I do think it would work.*

Turning a bend, Daisy was roused from her thoughts by the sight of two teenagers up ahead, laughing and holding hands as they strolled atop a levee. The boy took the girl's shoulders and she squirmed playfully, giggling as she avoided his attempts to kiss her, until suddenly she leaned up against him with an assertion all her own.

Daisy's smile renewed. There was always something sweet about young lovers, though she hoped they were being careful about . . .

She took off her sunglasses and squinted. The girl—was her daughter! As she watched, Claire pushed at her boyfriend's chest and whirled to stride away, forcing him to hurry after her.

Make a note to call Logan, Daisy filed for future reference. *Have him talk to the girl about sexual responsibility. She won't listen to me anymore.*

The one time they had had a mother-daughter chat on the subject, it had been a disaster. Claire acted horrified when Daisy did no more than *suggest* the simplest, most effective form of birth control.

"I will *not*. And that's final!"

"But every other method is chancy. Even abstinence. I mean, who knows? You could get raped. Or miscalculate your own mood and act on impulse. Girls your age do that sometimes, you know.

"This way you can be free and easy the rest of your life. You can look on sex the way a man does, as something to seek aggressively, without any chance of, well, complications."

Claire's expression had been defiant. Even contemptuous.

"*I'm* a result of 'complications,' as you call them. Do *you* regret the fact that your old-fashioned birth control methods failed, seventeen years ago?"

Daisy saw Claire was taking it all too personally.

"I just want you to be happy—"

"Liar! You want to cut down the human population just a bit more, by having your own daughter's tubes tied. Well get this, Mother. I intend on experiencing those 'complications' you speak of. At least once. Maybe twice. And if my kids look like they're going to be real problem-solvers, and if their father and I can afford it and are worthy, we may even go for a third!"

Only after Daisy had gasped in shock did she realize that was exactly the reaction Claire had wanted. Since that episode, neither of them ever mentioned the subject again.

Still, Daisy wondered. Might it be it worthwhile to send out a ferret to look for, well, chemical means? Something nonintrusive, undetectable . . .

But no. Claire already did all the cooking. And she probably had her gynecologist watching for any signs of tampering. Daisy made a rule of avoiding meddling wherever it might lead to retaliation. And so she decided to let the matter lay.

The girl will be leaving soon, Daisy pondered as she neared home again. Automatically, a list of chores Claire currently took care of scrolled through her mind. *I'll have to hire one of those oath-refugees, I suppose. Some poor sod who'll work a lot harder than my own lazy kid, no matter how I tried not to spoil her. Or maybe I'll get one of those new domestic robots. Have to reprogram it myself, of course.*

On her way to the back door she nearly tripped over two unfamiliar mounds on the slope overlooking the creek. Fresh earth had been tamped over oblong excavations and then lined with stones.

What the hell are these? They look like graves!

Then she remembered. Claire had mentioned something about the gloats. Their two weed eaters had died last week of some damn stupid plague set loose by a bunch of amateur Greeners over in Africa.

That blasted kid. She knows the proper way to mulch bodies. Why did she bury them here?

Daisy made another mental note, to cast through the Net for other means of keeping the stream clear. It was a dumb compromise anyway, using gene-altered creatures to compensate for man's ecological mistakes. Just the sort of "solution" touted by that Jennifer Wolling witch. Rot her.

What is Wolling up to, anyway? I wonder.

Soon Daisy was sitting before her big screen again. On impulse, she pursued her most recent mental thread.

Wolling.

Daisy ran a quick check of her watchdog programs. *Hmm. She hasn't published a thing since leaving her London flat. Is she sick? Maybe dead?*

No. Too tough to get rid of that easily. Besides, her mailbox shows a simple transrouting to Southern Africa. Now why is that familiar?

Of course it would be trivial to create an associator search program to find out, but Daisy thought of something more ambitious.

Let's use this as a test for my new program!

Last week one of her search routines had brought home a research article by an obscure theorist in Finland. It was a brilliant concept—a hypothetical way of folding computer files so that several caches could occupy the same physical space at the same time. The "experts" had ignored the paper on its first release. Apparently it would take the usual weeks, or even months, for its ideas to percolate upward through the Net. Meanwhile, Daisy saw a window of opportunity. Especially if she could also get her hands on Light Bearer!

If this works, I'll be able to track and record anybody, anywhere. Find whoever's hiding. Pry open whatever they're concealing.

And who better to experiment on than Jen Wolling?

Daisy began filling out the details, drawing bits of this and that from her huge cache of tricks. It was happy labor and she hummed as the skeleton of something impressive and rather beautiful took shape.

Once, the door opened and closed. Daisy sensed Claire leave a tray by her elbow and recalled vaguely saying something to her daughter. She went through the motions of eating and drinking as she worked. Sometime later, the tray disappeared the same way.

Yes! Wolling's the perfect subject. Even if she finds out, she won't complain to the law. She's not the type.

Then, after I've tried it out on her, there's all sorts of others. Corporations, government agencies . . . bastards so big they could hire software guns smart enough to keep me out. Until now!

Of course, the program was structured around a hole where the keystone—Light Bearer—would go. If she could coerce it from her cousins in exchange for information.

There! Daisy stretched back and looked over the entity she'd created. It was something new in autonomous software. *I must name it,* she thought, having already considered the possibilities.

Yes. You are definitely a dragon.

She leaned forward to dial in a shape from her vast store of fantasy images. What popped into place, however, amazed even her.

Emerald eyes glinted from a long, scaled face. Lips curled above gleaming white teeth. At the tip of the curled, jeweled tail lay a socket where Light Bearer would go. But even uncompleted, the visage was impressive.

Its tail whipped as the creature met her gaze and then slowly, obediently, bowed.

You will be my most potent surrogate, Daisy thought, savoring the moment. *Together, you and I will save the world.*

□

It is told how the brave Maori hero Matakauri rescued his beautiful Matana, who had been kidnapped by the giant, Matau.

Searching all around Otago, Matakauri finally found his love tied to a very long tether made from the skins of Matau's two-headed dogs. Hacking away with his stone *mere* and hardwood *maipi* did Matakauri no good against the rope, which was filled with Matau's magical *mana*—until Matana herself bent over the thong and her tears softened it so it could be cut.

Yet Matakauri knew his bride would never again be safe until the giant was dead. So he armed himself and set off during the dry season, and found Matau sleeping on a pallet of bracken surrounded by great hills.

Matakauri set fire to the bracken. And although he did not wake, Matau drew his great legs away from the heat. The giant began to stir, but by then it was too late. The flames fed on his running fat. His body melted into the earth, creating a mighty chasm, until all that remained at the bottom was his still-beating heart.

The flames' heat melted snow, and rain filled in the chasm, forming Lake Whakatipua—which today bears the shape of a giant with his knees drawn up. And sometimes people still claim to hear Matau's heartbeat below the nervous waves.

Sometimes, whenever the mountains tremble, folk wonder what may yet awaken down there. And when.

● *". . . so for the third time they untied Cowboy Bob from the*
C *stake and let him speak to Thunder, his wonder horse."*
O June Morgan's eyes seemed to flash as she leaned toward Alex
R and Teresa.
E *"This time, though, Bob didn't whisper in Thunder's left ear. He didn't whisper in the right. This time he held the horse's face, looked him straight in the eye, and said—'Read my lips, dummy. I told you to go get a Posse!' "*

As June sat back with an expectant smile, Alex had to bite his lower lip to contain himself. He watched Teresa sitting across the room, as her initial confusion gave way to sudden understanding. "Oh! Oh, that's awful!" She laughed while waving at the air, as if to fan away a bad odor.

June grinned and picked up her glass. "Don't you get it, Alex? See, the first two times, the horse brought back women . . ."

He held up both hands. "I got it, all right. Please, Teresa's right. It's bloody offensive."

June nodded smugly. So far, she was having by far the best of it. No joke he or Teresa told was delivered half as well or elicited such approving groans of feigned nausea. Probably, her skill came from being Texan. The only nationality Alex knew who were better at this odd ritual were Australians.

As bearer of good tidings, June could hardly be begrudged. This party in Alex's tiny bungalow was to celebrate an end to weeks of tension.

At least one hopes it's over. I still feel twinges of paranoia, looking over my shoulder for men in snap-brim hats and trench coats.

June had arrived on Rapa Nui this morning with word of Colonel Spivey's complete agreement to their terms. In exchange for their cooperation—and especially Alex's expertise—all charges would be dropped against Teresa and Easter Island would be left alone.

Naturally, Spivey will smuggle in a spy or two. But at least Teresa and I are no longer on the run.

It was still an open question whether there was any place to run to. The struggles against Beta weren't over yet. Still, even the most fatalistic of Alex's technicians were starting to act as if they thought there might be a planet under them by this time next year.

Now if only they can convince me.

Things had changed since theirs was a tiny, tight-knit cabal, wrestling subterranean monsters all alone. Now they were part of a large official enterprise, albeit one still veiled under a "temporary" cloak of security. June was here to cement the partnership, conveying the determination of both Glenn Spivey and George Hutton to make it work, for now. In that role as emissary, she would leave again tomorrow with Alex's chief token of cooperation—a box of cubes with fresh data for the other teams. Her courier route ought to bring her back every week or so from now on.

Teresa, for her part, had gone to great pains to make things clear to June—that her new, close friendship with Alex wasn't sexual.

Not that the two of them hadn't thought about it. At least he had. But on reflection he had come to realize that anything intimate between them would demand more intense attention than either could spare right now. For the time being, it was enough that they had a silent understanding—a link that had never been severed since they emerged hand in hand from that odyssey underground, like twins who had gestated together and shared the same act of being reborn.

For her part, June Morgan's outwardly relaxed posture and easy humor surely overlayed anxiety. Alex's relationship with her had been a wartime affair, mutual, uncomplicated. He had no idea where it stood now and didn't mean to push it.

At least the two women appeared to have buried whatever tension once lay between them. Or most of it, at least. Alex was glad. For one thing, it meant he could stand up now and leave them alone together for a little while.

"If you ladies will excuse me," he said, stepping to the door of the little bungalow. "I have to go see someone about an emu."

June nodded briefly at him, but Teresa was already leaning forward in her chair, almost touching the other woman's arm. "All right then," she said. "Here's one for you, while he's out playing fire drill with the bushes."

Moving quickly, Alex made it outside before she started telling the joke. A long one might have snared him and set off a crisis in his kidneys.

It was a balmy night, though winter had lingered a long time, turning this desolate island even more windblown and sere. Apparently spring would be late and blustery. Even the trees at the experimental reforestation zone up at Vaiteia seemed to shiver and cower whenever the gales picked up.

He didn't bother walking downslope to the shower-commode, shared by five of the prefabricated cottages. Instead, he climbed the hill a ways to where the view was better. As he watered the scrub grass, Alex looked westward toward the lights of Hanga Roa town, just north of Rano Kao's towering cliffs. The solitary jet runway glittered palely next to five compact tourist hotels and a moored cargo zeppelin. Nearer at hand lay the *Atlantis* monument, bottom-lit so that at night the ancient, crippled space shuttle actually seemed caught nobly in the act of taking off.

Since their close escape from New Zealand, wincing and limping from their bruises, he and Teresa had perforce taken up different activities. For her part, she spent most of her days with the old model-one shuttle. Presumably she knew a way inside, past the vandalism alarms. Or perhaps she was just scraping off the graffiti and gull droppings that made the broken spacecraft look so pathetic by daylight.

Possibly, she was just sitting in *Atlantis*'s pilot seat, brooding over the slim likelihood she'd ever see space again—even given a pardon from Spivey's masters.

Anyway, he was busy enough for both of them. Rapa Nui station was again the fulcrum for up to several dozen gazer beams a day, pulsating through the Earth's interior in a dizzying variety of modes and leading to countless surface manifestations. Now, at least, Alex had secure consultation links with Stan Goldman in Greenland, and data streamed in from the NATO ground teams, as well, helping him refine his models with each passing day.

(He'd even had a chance to get in touch with his grandmother, over in Africa. Good old Jen. After berating him several minutes for neglecting her, she had immediately dropped the subject and launched into a long, excited explanation of her new research, which Alex vaguely gathered had something to do with schizophrenia.)

Alex spent a good part of each day watching the singularity on the big display, where Beta could be seen spending more of its time in the "sparse" zones of the lower mantle. Already the monster was on an enforced diet, and soon they'd reach break-even—that milestone when the deadly knot began losing mass-energy as fast as it absorbed it. That would be time for real celebration . . . a true miracle, given their odds just a few months ago.

But then what?

Behind him, he heard the women laugh out loud, Teresa's alto blending harmoniously with June's contralto. It was a sound that cheered him. Finished with his business, Alex found himself suddenly shivering in the chill breeze. He zipped up and walked a little further along the slope, crunching the dry grass underfoot.

Apparently, a surprising number of Colonel Spivey's superiors believed Alex's theory, that Beta was a smart bomb sent by alien foes to destroy humanity. If so, then Spivey had a point. The gazer could become the pivot of Earth's only credible defense. In fact, to hear Spivey put it, the world might someday erect statues to Alex Lustig.

Savior of the planet, forger of our shield.

The image would appeal to any man's vanity. And Alex wasn't sure he had the will to resist. *What if it's true?* he thought, tasting the honey sweetness of Spivey's fable.

The colonel's plan had one more advantage. It meant they might soon reduce the number of pulses to just a nudge now and then.

He scuffed the ground. Inhaled the scented air. Shoved his hands into his jacket pockets. *All right. Keeping it down there makes sense. Maybe.* And yet Alex felt edgy.

Everywhere Beta passes, the minerals seem to change . . . *at least momentarily.*

It was hard to tell how, exactly, even with their wonderfully improved sensitivity. Beta was still a tiny, if ferocious object, with an actual physical zone of influence only millimeters across. The affected track of altered perovskites was consequently extremely thin. Still, with each orbit more slender tubes of transformed mineral glittered in the singularity's wake, flickering oddly.

How can we leave the thing down there when we have no idea what the long-term effects will be?

Maybe it was a good thing he hadn't told Hutton or Spivey about his new resonator, the one with the spherical, compact design. Better to wait and be certain what the colonel's actual scheme was . . . what he was going to do when word inevitably leaked out.

For they weren't going to be able to keep the lid on forever, that was clear to everyone. Spivey's bosses had to be preparing for a political powwow soon.

Maybe all they want is to present the world with a fait accompli, Alex thought hopefully. *"Look, see what we in the West have done? We saved the world! Now, of course, we'll let the tribunals have the keys to the gazer. It's far too dangerous for any one group to control."*

Alex smiled. Yes. Quite possibly that was exactly what they had in mind.

Right. Surely.

On his way back to the bungalow, Alex passed before a row of seaside *moai* sculptures, this strange island's contribution to world imagery. Gloomy and almost identical, they nonetheless struck him differently each time he saw them. On this occasion, despite the wind and sparkling stars, they just looked like huge chunks of stone, pathetically chiseled by desperate folk to resemble stern gods. People did bizarre things when they were afraid . . . as most men and women had been for nearly all the time since the species evolved.

We didn't make Beta though, Alex reminded himself. *So we're foolish, fearful, sometimes crazy, but maybe not damned.*

Not yet, at least.

Back at the bungalow, Alex wiped his feet before entering.

". . . know it's logical, and maybe justified," Teresa said, nodding seriously. "But after Jason . . . well. I can't share again. I don't think I could handle it."

"But that was different—" June stopped and looked up quickly as Alex entered.

"Share what?" he asked. "What's so different?"

Teresa looked away, but June stood up, smiling. She took him by the lapels and drew him into the room. "Nothing important. Just girl talk. Anyway, we decided to call it a night. I have a busy day tomorrow, so—"

"So I've got to go," Teresa said, putting her glass aside. For some reason she wouldn't meet Alex's eyes now, which disturbed him. *What's going on?* he wondered.

Teresa picked up the satchel June had brought along especially for her. Alex had assumed it contained tokens from Spivey, to signal all was forgiven. But Teresa acted as if it were something strictly between herself and the other woman, a peace offering of a different sort entirely. "Thanks for the stuff, June," she said, lifting the case.

"No big deal. Just hardware store goods. What're you going to do with all those catalysts and things?"

Teresa smiled enigmatically. "Oh, a just little tidying up, that's all."

"Mm," June commented.

"Yeah. Mm. So." Teresa shifted her feet. "Well. G'night you two."

After a moment's hesitation, the women kissed each other on the cheek. Teresa squeezed Alex's shoulder, still without meeting his eyes, and went out into the night. He stood in the open doorway, watching her go.

From behind him, June's arms slid under his and wrapped across his chest. She squeezed hard and let out a sigh. "Alex. Oh, Alex. What are we going to do with you?"

Puzzled, he turned around, letting the door close behind him. "What do you mean?"

"Oh . . ." She seemed about to say more, but finally shook her head. Taking his hand she said, "Come on, then. To bed. We both have busy days ahead."

PART IX

PLANET

The Earth's most permanent feature was the Pacific Ocean. Its shape might change with the passing eons, islands rising and falling as its plates collided, merged, and broke apart again. But the great basin remained.

Not so the Atlantic, which opened and closed many times. Slow heat built underneath a sequence of huge, granite supercontinents, splitting them asunder along bursting seams. Then, tens of millions of years later, the now cool center would sink again to halt the rivening and begin drawing the sleeves together again.

The cycle continued—breakup followed by remerging followed by breakup again. And this had important effects on the progress of life. Species that had roamed across broad ranges found themselves divided into subpopulations. Separated bands of cousins went their diverging genetic ways, adapting to new challenges, discovering diverse techniques for living. When the dispersed relations finally were reunited eons later by reconverging continents, these descendants of a common ancestor often could no longer interbreed. They met not as cousins, but as competitors.

As it happened, there came a later period when the vagaries of plate tectonics thrust up two huge mountain ranges—the Himalayas and the Rockies—which virtually blocked the flow of low, moist air across the Northern Hemisphere. This had dramatic consequences on the weather, which in turn isolated still more species, driving them to adapt.

Ebbing, flowing. Inhaling, exhaling. The cycle kept driving changes, improvements.

Eventually, dim flickers of light began to glow on the planet's night side, flickers in the dark that weren't forest fires or lightning.

All this heating and cooling, stirring and recombining had finally brought about something completely new.

☐ **Worldwide Long Range Solutions Special Interest Group** [☐ SIG AeR,WLRS 253787890.546], **Special Subforum 562: Crackpot-Iconoclast Social Theories.**

All this panic about how the Han are engaged in "economic conquest of the globe"—such rubbish! True, their huge, surging economy poses a challenge, especially to the PAN and GEACS trade groups. Instead of endlessly debating the University of Winnipeg Neomanagement Model, China has actually instituted many of its revolutionary features. We can all learn a lesson, especially the Sovs and Canucks, who keep finding themselves underpriced in the manufacture of desal equipment and nanocrystals. The Han already have a corner on blazers and lap-ticks, not to mention consumer items like torque zenners. But talk of "economic conquest" [☐ ref: A69802-111, 5/19/38 K-234-09-17826] or the Han ". . . buying up goddam everything . . ." [☐ ref: A69802-111, 5/12/38 M-453-65-5545] completely ignores history.

Consider the 1950s and 1960s. The United States of America, which then included California and Hawaii, but not Luzon or Cuba, was the world's economic powerhouse. A famous Euroleader named Servan-Schreiber wrote a book called *The American Challenge*, predicting America would soon ". . . own everything worth owning . . ."

Of course it didn't happen. Having achieved success, U.S. citizens demanded payoff for all their hard work. Instead of buying the world, they bought things *from* the world. It became the greatest transfer of wealth in history—far surpassing all forms of foreign aid. The American purchasing dynamo lifted Europe and East Asia into the twenty-first century . . . until the bubble finally burst and Yanks had to learn to pay as you go, like normal people.

For a brief time in the nineteen-seventies, the first and second oil crises made it seem that the new planetary kingpins would be Arab sheiks. Then, in the eighties, *Japan* scared the hell out of everybody. (Look it up!) Through hard work (and by adroitly catering to America's adolescent buying frenzy) the Japanese boot-strapped themselves to economic power that held the world in awe. Everyone predicted that soon they "would own everything."

But each of us takes our turn, it seems, driving the world economy. A new generation of Japanese, wanting more from life than endless toil and a tiny apartment, went on a new buying spree. And in the early years of this century, wasn't it *Russia*—with nearly half the world's trained engineers and newly released from two thousand years of stifling czars and commissars—who were suddenly only too glad to work hard, build to order, and sell cheap whatever the Japanese wanted? Many of you probably remember the consequence a while later, when Russian was proposed to replace Simglish as the second lingua franca. But that passed too, didn't it?

Come on, droogs. Learn to step back and take a long view. Time will come (if the planet holds out) when even the Han will get tired of laboring themselves sick, piling money in the bank with nothing to spend it on.

Then care to predict where the *next* group of hard workers will arise? My money's on those puritan secessionists in New England. Now *those* are people who know how to give an employer a good hour's work for an hour's wage . . .

●　No one congratulated Crat for saving his drowning crewmate.
C　Nobody spoke much about the incident at all. *Things happen*,
R　was the philosophy. So there were a few more widows back on one
U　of the floating towns? Too bad. Life was short; what more could
S　you say?
T　　　Still, Crat apparently wasn't a "go-suck Yankee sof-boy" anymore. There were no more sour looks at mess, or strange objects found swimming in his gruel. Silently, they moved his hammock out of the steamy hold and up to the anchor room with the others.

Only one fellow actually commented on the misadventure with the fishing net. "Jeez, Vato," he told Crat. "I never seen no bugger hold breath so long as you!"

To Crat, who had no idea how long he'd been underwater, the remark seemed like a signal from Providence. An experience that might have turned some men away from swimming forever, instead pointed him to an unexpected talent.

The story of his life had been mediocre plainness at best, and all too often less than that. His image of himself was slow and thick as a stone. The thought of having any unusual abilities astonished Crat. And so, at the very moment he had won acceptance aboard the *Congo*, he renewed his vow to leave first chance—to act on his earlier loose talk about going into salvage.

Not that there was much he'd miss about this old tub. Life on a frontier didn't offer many luxuries. Forced to live here for a week, the average American would never again complain about his own restricted water ration, which in some states topped a lavish hundred gallons a week.

Or take another necessity—Data-Net privileges. Here you simply didn't have them.

Crat used to despise old folks back in Indiana for relying on so many electronic crutches . . . globe-spanning access to news on every topic, to every library, to every dumpit research journal even, instantly translated from any obscure language for mere pennies. Then there were the hobby lines, special interest groups, net-zines, three-vee shows.

Until emigrating, Crat never realized how much *he* depended on all that, too. Aboard *Congo*, though, they had this strange, once-a-day ritual—mail call. Each man answered if his name was shouted, and swapped a black cube with the bosun. You were allowed to pipe two message blips, no more than fifty words each, through the ship's single antenna, ruled dictatorially by the comm officer, a one-eyed, one-legged victim of some past oceanic catastrophe, whom everybody, even the captain, treated with utter deference.

Standing in line, waiting humbly for your miserable blips, was almost as humiliating as evening vitamin call, when a bored U.N. nurse doled each man his pressed capsule of "Nutritional Aid"—the sum total of the world's sense of obligation to the pariah state of refugees. No wonder the great powers were even less generous with the world's true lifeblood, information.

Now and then, during mail call, Crat caught himself wondering why Remi and Roland never wrote to him. Then he remembered with a sudden jerk. *They're dead. I'm the last. Last of the Quayle High Settlers.*

Strange. Believing he was destined for a short life, Crat had long ago decided to live one with no compromises. *He'd* always been the one getting into jams, which his friends always reliably, sensibly got him out of.

Now Remi and Roland were gone, while he still lived. Who could figure it?

Roland, for some reason, had willed Crat his bank balance, augmented by a hero's bonus. There was supposed to be a medal, too. It was probably still out there somewhere, following him around the world in the unreliable tangle of real-matter post. As for Roland's money . . . Crat had blown it all in card games and buying rounds of drinks to his friends' memory. But he did want the medal.

After mail call, off-duty crew retired to the aft deck, where three enterprising Annamese sold a pungent home brew from clay pots. While the flotilla sailed southward from the debacle with the green raiders, Crat discovered he could now stomach the foul-smelling beer. It was a milestone that showed he was adapting.

The evening was dark, with a heavy overcast cutting off most of the stars. A pearly opalescence in the west became a blaze whenever the clouds parted briefly to spill moonlight across the smooth water.

At the fantail, two sets of meditators seemed to square off for a silent, contemplative showdown. Sufis on the portside and neo-Zen adepts to starboard. Beginners in both groups were wired to brain-wave monitors the size of thimbles, which led to earplug button speakers. Using identical, inexpensive techno-aids, each side nevertheless claimed it was true tradition, while the other taught mere dazing. Whatever. Like the majority of the crew, Crat preferred more honest, traditional forms of intoxication.

". . . Commodore bloody misreads his charts—" someone said in the darkness beyond the rear hatch. "That El Niño thing . . . It s'pozed drive all them fish over here Wes' Pacific side, every ten-'leven year so. But bloody dammit commodore, he miss them sure."

"It come more often than every ten year now, I hear," someone else replied. Idly, Crat wondered who they were. Their English was better than average for this barge.

"Dey got de eco-loggy all fucked sure," said someone with a Caribbean accent. "Evryt'ing all change. So I say don't listen to UNEPA bastards, not at all. Dey don' know no t'ing better than we do."

Someone else agreed. "Ach, UNEPA. They wants us dead, just like greeners do, 'cause we mess up they stinking planet. Might catch wrong type dumpit fish. Ooh, bad thing! So better we just *die*. Maybe put something in vitamins. Do us cheap an' quiet."

That was the steady gossip of course, even when Sea State chemists—university-trained men and women from lands now drowned under the rising tides—went from boat to boat reassuring crews and urging them to take the pills, rumors nevertheless spread like viruses. Crat himself sometimes wondered. His tiredness no doubt came mostly from hard work. That *probably* also explained the low ebb of his sex drive. But if he ever did find out somebody was slipping something into the food . . .

The old rage flickered momentarily and he tried to nurse it. But it just damped out, ebbing of its own accord. He lifted his head to glance over *Congo*'s prow at the night lights of the floating town, up ahead. The old Crat would have already been pacing—eager to prowl the red-light district or find a good brawl. Now all he could think of were the clean if threadbare sheets of the transients' barracks and then tomorrow's visit to the meat market.

"Ah, I find you at last. Sorry. I was lost."

Crat looked up. It was his new friend, the elderly Zuricher, Peter

Schultheiss. Peter's was the one face Crat would miss when he transferred off this misbegotten tub. He grinned and held out a full jar. "Got you another beer, Peter."

"Goot. Thanks. Took me some time to find my notebook with the name of my comrade at the market. But I found." He held up a heavy black volume. To Crat's surprise, it wasn't a cheap store-and-write plaque, such as even the poorest deckhand owned, but a binder fat with paper pages! Schultheiss murmured as he flipped the scratchy sheets. "Let's see. He's in here somewhere. This fellow should, if you mention my name, be able to get you jobs in salvage . . . maybe training for the deep-sea work you so desire. Ah, here, let me write it down for you."

Crat accepted the slip of paper. Nearing his rendezvous with the recruiters, he had grown a little less sure he really wanted to try nodule mining—diving far below the reach of light encased in a slimy bubble, sifting mud for crusty lumps. Though well paid, such men tended to have short lives. The alternative of shallow dredging in drowned villages was beginning to sound attractive after all.

Schultheiss looked toward the town lights and sighed.

"What'cha thinkin' about?" Crat asked.

"I was just remembering how, when I was a boy, my father took me with him on a business trip to Tokyo. As our plane came in at night, we saw an amazing sight. The ocean, around every island as far as you could see, was alight! So many lights I could not count them. The water seemed to be on fire. White fire.

"Such a spectacle, I asked my father what festival this was. But he said, no, it was no oriental holiday. It was like this every night, he said. Every night at sea around Japan."

The idea of such extravagance made Crat blink. "But, why?"

"Fishing lights," Peter answered plainly. "At night the ships would run big generators and draw in fish by millions. Very effective, I heard. Efficient, too, if you trade energy for food and don't worry about tomorrow."

Schultheiss paused. His voice seemed far away. "My father and his comrades . . . they prided themselves on future-sightedness. Unlike the Yankees of those days—no offense—he thought he *was* thinking about tomorrow. While the Yanks bought toys and spent themselves poor, my father and his compeers saved. He invested prudently other people's funds for them. Took their money with no questions asked and made it grow like vegetables in a garden."

The old Helvetian sighed. "Maybe it only shows there are many kinds of shortsightedness. Did it ever occur to the Japanese, I wonder, that evolution might change the species they called with their great lights? The easy, stupid ones would die in nets, certainly. But meanwhile those who stayed away would breed future generations. Did they ponder this? No, I think not.

"Likewise it never occurred to my father that the world might someday tire of all its bad men having nice safe places to stash their loot. He never dreamed all the nations might drop their bickering, might get together and say enough, we want our money back. We want the names of those bad men, too . . . men who betrayed our trust, who robbed our treasuries, or who sold drugs to our children.

"How could my poor father imagine the world's masses might come pounding on his door someday to take back in anger what he'd invested so carefully, so well?"

The lights of the floating village now glittered in the old man's moist eyes. Stunned by the depth of this confession, Crat wondered. *Why me? Why is he telling me all this?*

Peter turned to look at him, struggling with a smile. "Did you see *Pikeman*, when she came to rescue us from the greeners? How beautiful she was? People used to joke about the Swiss navy. But only fools laugh now! Ton per ton, it gives Sea State—our adopted nation— the best fighting fleet in the world! So we adapt, in that way and so many others. We Helvetians find new roles in the world, performing them with pride in craft."

Crat noticed the old man's English had improved. Perhaps it was the passion of sudden memory. Or maybe he was letting down a mask.

"Oh, we and our allies were arrogant before the war. *Mea culpa*, we admit that now. And history shows the arrogant must always fall.

"But then, to fall can be a gift, no? What is diaspora, after all, except an opportunity, a second chance for a people to learn, to grow out of shallow self-involvement and become righteous, deep, and strong?"

Schultheiss looked at Crat. "Pain is how a people are tempered, prepared for greatness. Don't you think so, *fils*? That wisdom comes through suffering?"

Crat could only blink in reply, moved, but not knowing what to say. In truth, he wasn't sure he understood what Peter was talking about.

"Yes," the old man agreed with himself, nodding firmly, both guilt and stark dignity evident in his voice. "My people have been chosen for some future, unknown task. Of that I'm sure. A task far greater than perching on safe mountaintops, high and aloof, living high off other people's money."

Peter stared into the night, much farther than Crat felt he himself could see.

"The world's folk will need us yet. Mark my words. And when that day comes, we will not leave them wanting."

At night it had been no more than a sprinkle of lights, rocking gently to rhythmic tides. By day, however, the barge-city came alive with noise and commerce. And rumors. It was said that no place, not even the Net, spread gossip as swiftly or erratically.

Crat had no way of picking up most of the hearsay, though. Unlike the working ships, where discipline required a common language, floating towns were a chaos of tongues and dialects, whispered, murmured, bellowed. All the sea towns were the same. Miniature babels, sprawled horizontally across the nervous ocean.

Night-soil collectors called as they rowed the narrow canals between multistoried housing barges, taking slops lowered down by rope in exchange for a few devalued piasters. Competing to deliver odorous fertilizer to the garden boats, they regularly sped down unbraced passages at risk of being crushed between the rocking, bobbing hulls.

Clothing, washed in sea water, hung from cluttered lines alongside banners proclaiming ideologies and gospels and advertisements in a dozen alphabets. Each district was topped with flat arrays of solar cells linked to broad, winglike rainwater collectors, all tended by small boys who climbed the swaying frames like monkeys. Kite strings angled up into the sky toward generators dipped into high stratospheric winds. By this melange of artifice and gadgetry, the barge city managed to stay alive.

Crat hungrily inhaled the smells of cooking over seaweed fires. The aromas changed from one neighborhood to the next. Still, he kept his hands out of his pockets. His dwindling cash might be needed for bribes before the day was out.

Other aromas were even harder to ignore. Women—workers and mothers and daughters and wives—could be glimpsed through windows left open to catch a stray breeze, dressed in costumes native to countries that no longer existed, sometimes smothered in far too much clothing for these humid climes. Crat knew not to stare; many of them had menfolk who were jealous and proud. Still, at one point he stopped to watch a girl's nimble fingers dance across a floor loom, crafting holo-carpets for export. It was a valued profession and one she had apparently mastered. In comparison, Crat knew his own hands to be clumsy things that couldn't even knot a jute rope properly.

The young woman glanced over at him, her scarf framing a lovely oval face. Crat would have given his heart gladly when she smiled. He stumbled back, however, when another visage suddenly intervened, a crone who snarled at him in some strange dialect. Crat spun away to hurry forward again, toward the Governor's Tower and the Admiral's Bridge, twin monoliths that overlooked the center of town.

In a city rife with odors, the shaded bazaar was an especially pungent place where the fish was generally fresh but everything else was second hand, including the whores beckoning from a provocatively carved wooden balcony along the aft quarter.

Likewise the religions that were pitched from the opposite side, where a dozen midget temples, churches and mosques vied for the devotion of passersby. Here at least one was safe from one all-pervading creed, Gaia-worship. The few NorA ChuGa missionaries who tried preaching in Sea State were glad to depart with their lives. The lesson they took home with them was simple; it takes a full belly before a man or woman gives a tinker's damn about anything as large as a planet.

Other types of outside recruiters were tolerated. The Resettlement Fund's kiosk offered a third form of redemption, equidistant from sex and faith. Queued up there were men, women, whole families who had finally had enough . . . who would sign any document, have any surgery, swear any oath just to set foot on land again—in the Yukon, Yakutsk, Patagonia—anywhere there'd be steady meals and a patch of real ground to farm.

For Sea State this wasn't treason. It was a population safety valve, one far less disturbing than another Crat had witnessed one dim twilight during his first stay on this drifting island-city.

He'd been lazing by one of the sidestream canals, picking away at a roast squid purchased from his shrinking purse, when a dark figure appeared slinking behind one of the shabbier apartment barges. It was a woman, he soon saw, wrapped in black from head to toe. The noise of clattering pots and shouting neighbors covered her stealth as she made her way to where the current was strongest.

Crat faded into a nearby shadow, watching her look left and right. There was a momentary flash of string as she tied two articles together, one heavy, the other wrapped in cloth. Crat had no inkling what was going on, though he thought for a moment he heard a faint cry.

The heavier object splashed decisively as it hit the water, instantly dragging the other bundle after it. Still he didn't catch on. Only when he glimpsed the woman's tired, bleak face and heard her sob did the light dawn. As she hurried away he knew what she had done. But he could only sit in stunned silence, his appetite quite gone.

He tried to understand, to grasp what must have driven her to do such a thing. Crat remembered what old prof Jameson used to say about Sea State . . . how most families who fled there came from societies where all decisions were made by men. In principle, Crat saw nothing wrong with that. He hated the arrogant, independent way girls were taught to act in North American schools, always judging and *evaluating*. Crat preferred how a thousand older, wiser cultures used to do it, before Western decadence turned women into not-women-anymore.

Still, for weeks he was haunted by the face of that anguished young mother. She came to him at night, and in his dreams he felt torn between two drives—one to protect her and the other to take her for his own.

Of course no one was asking him to do either. No one was exactly clamoring to make him a chief.

It was in the bazaar's fourth quadrant, beyond the fish stalls and junk stands and traders hawking enzyme paste, that Crat came at last to the "Meat Market."

"There are opportunities in Antarctica!" one recruiter shouted, near a holo depicting mineshafts and open-pit works, gouging high-grade ores out of a bleak terrain. Icy glaciers loomed in the background.

The images looked stark and honest—showing hard work in a harsh environment. Still, Crat could feel the holo's subsonic music cajoling him to see more than that. The men depicted in those scenes grinned cheerfully beside their towering machines. They looked like *bold* men, the sort who tamed a wilderness and got rich doing so.

"The greeners have been given their dumpit *parks* and *preservation areas* now." The speaker cursed, causing the crowd to mutter in agreement. "Half the bloody continent of Antarctica was set aside for 'em, almost! But the good news is, now the *rest* is open! Open wide for brave souls to go and win with their own strong hands!"

The recruiter sounded like he truly envied such gallant heroes. Meanwhile, the holos showed spare but comfortable barracks, hot meals being served, happy miners counting sheaves of credit slips.

Huh! Maybe company men get to live like that. They can recruit for those jobs anywhere.

In fact, Crat had applied for positions like those before finally falling back on Sea State. And if he hadn't been up to the companies' standards in Indiana, why would they accept him here? *You don't fool me. I can just guess what kind of work you'll offer Sea State volunteers. Work a robot would refuse.*

Even the poorest citizens of the poorest nations were protected by the Rio Charter, except those whose leaders had never signed, such as

Southern Africa and Sea State. That gave them a queer freedom—to volunteer to be exploited at jobs animal rights groups would scream about if you assigned them to a pig. But then, every member of the Albatross Republic supposedly had chosen his own fate rather than accept the world's terms. *Rather than give up the last free life on Earth,* Crat thought proudly. He departed that booth with aloof pride, preferring honest crooks to liars.

Over by the Climate Board, passersby scrutinized the fortnight forecast, of life-or-death interest to all floating towns. Two weeks was just long enough to evade bad storms. The Climate Board was also where the gamblers gathered. Whatever other exotic games of chance were fashionable, you could always get a bet on the weather.

Nearby, a small band played the style known as Burma Rag—a catchy mix of South Asian and Caribbean sounds with a growing following on the net, though naturally little profit ever made it back to Sea State. Crat tossed a piaster into the band's cup, for luck.

The booths he sought lay near the gangway of a sleek little ship, obviously new and powerful and rigged for deep running. In front of the submersible a table lay strewn with rocky, egg-shaped objects, glittering with spongelike metallic knobs. Together, the vessel and ore nodules were probably worth half the town itself, but not many citizens loitered near the well-dressed company solicitors standing there. The real crowd clustered just beyond, where men in turbans jabbered into note plaques while bearded doctors poked and prodded would-be volunteers.

No holos proclaimed the virtues of life in the various Sea State salvage cooperatives. But everyone knew what it was about. *It's about dragging a frayed air hose behind you while you walk the sunken streets of Galveston or Dacca or Miami, prying copper wires and aluminum pipes out of tottering ruins.*

It's working in stinking shit-mud to help raise blocks of sunken Venice . . . hoping a chunk will come up whole so it can be sold off like St. Mark's Square was . . . to some rich Russ or Canuck theme resort.

It's hauling dredges up the bloody Ganges, hired by the Delhi government, but shot at by the local militia of some province that doesn't really exist anymore, except on hilltops.

Crat fingered the note Peter Schultheiss had given him. He edged alongside one queue and tapped a turbaned interviewer on the shoulder. "Can . . . can you tell me where . . ." he peered at the writing. ". . . where Johann Freyers is?"

The man looked at Crat as if he were some loathsome type of sea slug. He shouted something incomprehensible. Undeterred, Crat moved to another station. Again those in line watched him suspiciously. This time, though, the gaunt, sunken-chested fellow in charge was friendlier. Clean shaven, his face showed the stigmata of many long hours underwater—permanently bloodshot eyes and scars where breathing masks had rubbed away the skin.

"Freyers . . . over at . . ." He stopped to inhale, a desperate-sounding whistle. ". . . at . . ." With amazing cheerfulness for one who couldn't even finish a sentence, he smiled. Snapping his fingers brought a young boy forth from under the table. "Freyers," he told the boy in a wheeze.

"Uh, thanks," Crat said, and to his surprise found himself being dragged *away* from the recruiting booths, toward the gangway of the sleek submersible. There, two men in fine-looking body suits conversed quietly with folded arms.

"Are you sure . . . ?" Crat started asking the boy.

"Yes, yes, Freyers. I know." He snatched the note out of Crat's hand and tugged the sleeve of one of the men, whose sandy hair and long face made Crat think of a spaniel. The mainlander looked bemused to receive such a token, turning the paper over as if savoring its vintage. He tossed a coin to the little messenger.

"So you were sent by Peter Schultheiss, hmm?" he said to Crat. "Peter's a landsman known to me. He says you've good lungs and presence of mind." Freyers looked at the note again. "A Yank, too. Have you a full reliance card, by any chance?"

Crat flushed. As if anyone with a card would emigrate to this place. "Look, there's some mistake . . ."

"Well, I assume you at least have high school."

Crat lifted his shoulders. "That's no plishie. Only dacks don't finish high school."

The long-faced man looked at him for a moment, then said in a soft voice. "Most of your fellow citizens have never *seen* a high school, my young friend."

"Of course they have—" Then Crat stopped, remembering he wasn't an American anymore. "Oh. Yeah, well."

Both men continued regarding him. "Hm," the shorter one said. "He'd be able to read simple manuals, in both Common and Simglish." He turned to Crat. "Know any written Nihon or Han? Any kanji?"

Crat shrugged. "Just the first hundred signs. They made us learn simple ideo, uh—"

"Ideograms."

"Yeah. The first hundred. An' I picked up some others you guys prob'ly wouldn't care about."

"Hmm. No doubt. And silent speech? Sign language?"

Crat couldn't see the point to this. "I guess, grade school stuff."

"Tech skills? What kind of Net access did you use at home?"

"Hey, you an' I both know any tech stuff I got is just pissant shit. You wanted someone educated, you wouldn't be *here*, for Ra's sake. There must be three fuckin' *billion* college graduates out there, back in the world!"

Freyers smiled. "True. But few of those graduates have proven themselves aboard a Sea State fishing fleet. Few come so well recommended. And I'd also guess only a few approach us with your, shall we say, motivation?"

Meaning he knows I can't say no to a job that pays good. And I won't complain to no union if they give me tanks with rusty valves or an air hose peeling rubber here an' there.

"So, can we interest you in coming aboard and taking some refreshment with us? We have cheese and chocolates. Then we can talk about getting you tested. I cannot promise anything, my boy, but this may be your lucky day."

Crat sighed. He had long ago cast himself to fate's winds. People looked at him, heard him speak, and figured a guy like him couldn't have a worldview—a philosophy of life. But he did. It could be summed up in five simple words.

Oh, well. What the fuck.

In the end, he let hunger lead him up the gangway after the two recruiters. That and a powerful sense that he had little choice, after all.

☐ Given their declining petroleum reserves and the side effects of spewing carbon into the atmosphere, why were twentieth century Americans so suspicious of nuclear power? Essentially, people were deeply concerned about *incompetence*.

Take the case of the Bodega Bay Nuclear Power Plant. The developers knew full well that its foundations straddled the San Andreas fault, yet they kept it quiet until someone blew the whistle. Why?

It wasn't just hunger for short-term gain. Enthusiasts for a particular project often create their own mental versions of reality, minimizing any possibility things might go wrong. They convince themselves any potential critic is a fool or cretin.

Fortunately, society was entering the "era of criticism." Public scrutiny led to an outcry, and the Bodega Bay site was abandoned. So when the great northern quake of '98 struck, half the State of California was saved from annihilation.

The *other* half was preserved four years later during the great southern quake. Only a few thousand were killed in that tragedy, instead of the millions who would have died if the nuclear facilities at Diablo Canyon and San Onofre hadn't been reinforced beforehand, thanks again to the free give and take of criticism. Instead of adding to the calamity, those power plants held fast to assist people in their time of need.

Other "nuclear" examples abound. Just a few small pumps, installed to placate critics, kept Three Mile Island from becoming another Chernobyl —that catastrophe whose radioactive reverberations bridged the interval from Nagasaki to Berne and delay-triggered the first cancer plagues.

Many still seek uranium's banishment from the power grid, despite its present safety record and improved waste-disposal situation. They warn we are complacent, demanding each design and modification be released for comment on the net.

Ironically, it is precisely this army of critics that inspires confidence in the present system. That plus the fact that ten billion people demand compromise. They won't stand for ideological purity. Not when one consequence might be starvation.

—From **The Transparent Hand**, Doubleday Books edition 4.7 (2035). [☐ hyper access code 1-tTRAN-777-97-9945-29A.]

● Sepak Takraw finished his third circuit of the ASEAN perimeter
M that day and verified that there was still no way out of the trap.
A Elite Indonesian and Papuan troops had secured this little plateau
N deep in rain-drenched Irian Jaya. Nothing got in or out without
T sophisticated detectors tracking and identifying it.
L   Actually, Sepak was impressed by the troops' professionalism.
E One hardly ever got to see military craftsmanship up close, except the presidential band on Independence Day. It was fascinating watching the sentries meticulously use pocket computers to randomize their rounds, so what might have become routine remained purposely unpredictable.

The first few days after finding his own rat-hole path to the surface, Sepak had his hands full just keeping out of the soldiers' way. But then, for all their sophistication, they weren't exactly looking for anyone already *inside* their perimeter. That meant George Hutton's techs had kept mum about him, damn them. Their loyalty planted an obligation on him in return.

So once a day he squirmed through his tiny rocky passage to check up on the Kiwis. For the first few days things looked pretty grim. The boys and girls from New Zealand slumped against the limestone walls, staring at their captors, speaking in monosyllables. But then things changed dramatically. Inquisitors were replaced by a swarm of outside experts who descended on the site in a storm of white coats, treating the New Zealanders with utter deference. Suddenly, everything looked awfully chummy.

Too chummy. Sepak didn't want any part of it. He especially took to avoiding the caverns during meal times, when he'd have to peer over a high gallery and smell civilized cooking. He, meanwhile, had to make do with what his grandfather had taught him to take from the forest itself.

By the bank of a trickling stream, Sepak dabbed streaks of soft clay across his brows, renewing the camouflage that kept him invisible to the soldiers . . . so far . . . and just so long as he didn't try to cross those unsleeping beams at the perimeter. He chewed slowly on the last bits of a juvenile tree python he'd caught yesterday. Or the last bits *he* intended to eat. Grandfather had shown him how to prepare the entrails using some obscure herbs. But he'd been too nauseated to pay much attention that time. Reverence for your heritage was fine. Still, some "delicacies" pushed the limits.

The forest hadn't been hunted this way for several generations. Perhaps that explained his luck so far. Or maybe it was because Sepak had left a cluster of bright feathers and butterfly wings at the foot of a tall tree, as sacrifice to a spirit whose name he'd forgotten, but who his grandfather had said was strong and benevolent.

I'm doin' all right, he thought. *But bloody ocker hell . . . I wish I could take a bath!*

Sepak caught his reflection in the shallow water. He was a sight, all right. Kinky hair greased back with marsupial fat. Dark skin streaked with pale, muddy tans and dabs of leaf sap. Only when he grinned was there any semblance to a twenty-first-century man, whose teeth suddenly seemed too white, too well ordered and perfect.

All around he sensed life slither and crawl, from tiny beetles scrabbling through the forest detritus all the way to the high canopy, where he glimpsed quick patches of fur, the glint of scales, the flash of eyes. Branches rustled. Things slowly stalked other things. You had to be patient to see any of it though. It wasn't a skill you learned in school.

For the most part, the main thing you noticed was the quiet.

Suddenly, the calm was interrupted by a mob of foraging birds, which spilled into the tiny clearing in a storm of feathers. They swept in from the right, a chirping, rowdy chaos of colors and types. After that instant of startlement, Sepak kept perfectly still. He'd read about this phenomenon before, but never seen it until now.

Small, blue-feathered birds dove straight into the humus, flinging leaves and twigs as they chased fleeing insects. Above these, a larger, white- and yellow-plumed species hovered, diving to snatch anything stirred into sight by the bold blue ones. Other varieties swarmed the trunks and looping tree roots. It was amazing to witness how the species cooperated, like members of a disciplined jungle cleanup squad.

Then Sepak noticed some of them squabbling, fighting over this or that squirming morsel, and revised his first impression. The white-and-yellow birds were *opportunistic*, he now saw, taking advantage of the smaller ones' industriousness. He watched a black-tailed root hopper swipe a tidbit already wriggling between the jaws of an irate bird in bright orange plumes. Other breeds did the same, warily keeping an eye out for each other while they worked over the trees' lower bark, gobbling parasites and protein-rich bugs before any competitor could get at them.

This wasn't teamwork, then. It was a balance of threat and bluster and force. Each scrounger fought to keep whatever it found while taking advantage of the others.

Funny. Why do they keep together, then?

It seemed to Sepak the white-and-yellows could have harassed the smaller birds more than they did. They missed opportunities because they were distracted, spending half their time scanning the forest canopy overhead.

He found out why. All at once, several yellows squawked in alarm, triggering a flurry of flapping wings. Faster than an eye-blink, all the birds vanished . . . taking cover a bare instant before a large *hawk* flashed through the clearing, talons empty, screeching in frustration.

The yellows' warning saved everybody, not just themselves.

In moments the raptor was gone, and the multispecies mob was back again, resuming its weird, bickering parody of cooperation.

Each plays a role, he realized. *All benefit from one type's guarding skill. All profit from another's talent for pecking. . . .*

Clearly none of them particularly liked each other. There was tension. And that very tension helped make it all work. It united the entity that was the hunting swarm as it moved out of sight through the towering trees.

"Huh," Sepak thought, marveling how much one could learn by just sitting still and observing. It wasn't a skill one learned in the frenetic pace of modern society. Perhaps, he considered, there might be advantages to this adventure, after all.

Then his stomach growled. *All right,* he thought, rising and picking up his crude spears. *I hear you. Be patient.*

Soon he was loping quietly, scanning the branches, but not as a passive watcher anymore. Now he set out through the trees—listening with his ears, seeking with his eyes—hunting clues to where on this little plateau he might find that next meal.

☐ It's now official. Scientists at NASA confirm that their oldest operating spacecraft, *Voyager 2*, has become the first man-made object to pass completely beyond the solar system.

Actually, the boundaries of the sun's family are debatable. Last century, *Voyager*'s distance exceeded that of Pluto, the ninth planet. Another milestone was celebrated when the venerable spacecraft reached the solar shock front, where it met atoms from interstellar space. Most astronomers, however, say Voyager was still within old Sol's influence until it passed through the "heliopause" and left behind the solar wind, which happened in the year 2037, a decade later than predicted.

Data from Voyager's little ten-watt transmitter help scientists refine their models of the Universe. But what most people find astonishing is that the primitive robot—launched sixty-five years ago—still functions at all. It defies every expectation, by its designers *or* modern engineers. Perhaps some preserving property of deep space is responsible. But a more colorful suggestion has been offered by the Friends of St. Francis Assembly [☐ SIG.Rel.disc. 12-RsyPD 634399889.058], a Catholic special interest group that contends Voyager's survival was "miraculous," in the exact sense of the word.

"We now strongly believe the oldest heavenly commandment commissions humanity to go forth, observe God's works, and glorify Him by giving names to all things.

"In that quest, no human venture has dared so much or succeeded as well as Voyager. *It has given us moons and rings and distant planets, great valleys and craters and other marvels. It plumbed Jupiter's storms and Saturn's lightning and sent home pictures of the puzzle that is Miranda. No other modern enterprise has so glorified the Creator, showing us as much of His grand design, as faithful* Voyager, *our first emissary to the stars."*

A colorful and not unpleasant thought to contemplate these days, as the airwaves fill once more with hints of looming crisis. It's a touch of optimism we might all do well to think about.

This is Corrine Fletcher, reporting for Reuters III from the Jet
Propulsion Laboratory, in New Pasadena, California.

[□ reporter-bio: C.FLETCHER–REUT.III. Credibility ratings: CaAd-2, Viewers' Union (2038).
BaAb-1, World Watchers Ltd., 2038.]

● The paleogeologists wanted to know what was going on.

M   "All these strange events, Stan . . . holes in China, pillars of
E smoke at sea. Do you have any idea what it's about?"
S   Even if there hadn't been a *cordon sanitaire* of Danish and
O NATO soldiers around the Tangoparu dome, Dr. Nielsen and the
S others would certainly have suspected something was happening.
P The whole world suspected, and Stan had never been much good
H at poker.
E   "There are rumors, Stan," Nielsen said shortly after the
R military arrived. "Have you seen today's noon edition of the *New*
E *Yorker*? There's a correlated survey linking many of these bizarre
phenomena into a pattern." Stan shrugged, avoiding the blond
scientist's eyes. But that only intensified suspicion, of course. "Do you
know something about all this Stan? Your graviscan program, those
troops, the strange quakes . . . it's all connected, isn't it?"

What could he say? Stan started avoiding his friends, spending his
few free moments out on the moraine instead, walking and worrying.

He'd been in constant touch with George Hutton, of course, ever
since Alex and Teresa made good their escape from New Zealand. And
he had to admit the logic behind the uncomfortable alliance with
Colonel Spivey. What else could they do? It was Trinity site all over
again—Alamogordo in 1945. The genie was out of the bottle. All they
could do now was try to manage it as well as possible.

SOVS, RUSS, EUROPS AND HAN IN N.Y. TALKS.
GEACPS BOYCOTTS. NATO STALLS.

That was the ScaniaPress headline after one more zine exposé. A
whistle blower inside the EUROP mission to the U.N. told how
private negotiations among the great powers had been going on for
over a fortnight. Outrage roiled through the World Data Net. What
were governments doing—actually keeping people in the dark about a
crisis? How *dare* they?

In absence of solid information, a myriad of rumors flew.

. . . It's the melting of the ice caps that's making the Earth shake . . .

. . . It's secret weapon testing. Treaty violations. We've got to call in the tribunals before it's too late . . .

. . . These aren't earthly phenomena at all. We're being softened up by UFOs . . .

. . . It's an alignment of the planets. The Babylonians were right predicting . . .

. . . Overpopulation—ten billion souls can't stand the pressure. The psychic strain alone . . .

. . . Could we have awakened something ancient? Something terrible? I caught sight of a *dragon*, snooping a public memory file. Have others out there seen it too? . . .

. . . *Gaia*, it is our Mother, shivering in her sleep, at the pain we've caused her . . .

. . . I don't have any idea *what* it is! But I'll bet there are people in high places who do. They have a duty to tell us what's going on!

More headlines on ABC, TASS, Associated Press—

GREAT POWERS POWWOW, NIHON STAYS AWAY.

Holos of departing diplomats are analyzed by professionals and amateur hackers, who enhance every face, every pore, and publish speculative analyses of flesh tones, blink rates, nervous ticks—

. . . the Russ ambassador was scared . . .

. . . the EUROP team knew more than they were telling . . .

. . . clearly there's collusion between NATO and ASEAN . . .

Stan was impressed with the creative energy out there. Data traffic soared, straining even the capacious fiber cable channels. Reserve capacity was brought on-line to cope.

A holopop group, Space Colander, produced a new number called "Straining Reality"—an instant hit. Underground poets sent paeans to strangeness migrating from computer node to computer node, circuiting the globe faster than the sun.

Stan did not participate, of course. Except for his rare walks, he spent most of his time conversing over military lines with Alex and with Glenn Spivey's physicists, piecing together the secrets of the gazer. Some were starting to fall into place, such as how the beams coupled with surface matter. It seemed they had discovered a whole new spectrum, completely at right angles to the colors of light. With these discoveries, science would never be the same.

His darkest premonitions were like the ones those physicists in New Mexico must have felt, nearly a century ago. But those men had been wrong in their worst fears, hadn't they? Their bomb, which might have wrought searing Armageddon, instead proved to be a blessing. After scaring everyone away from major war for three generations, it finally convinced the nations to sign covenants of peace. Perhaps the same sort of result would come of this. Humanity didn't always have to be foolish and destructive.

Perhaps we'll show wisdom this time, as well. There's always a chance.

Hours later Stan was still hard at work, predicting beam-exit points so that Spivey's teams could get there in advance to study the effects, when he found himself blinking at his work screen with a weird picture still planted in his brain. It came and went before he could focus clearly, and now the display showed nothing abnormal. Perhaps it was just a figment of fatigue. Nevertheless, he retained a distinct afterimage . . . of a glittering smile set in a lizard's face, and behind that a whipping, barbed and jeweled tail.

□

In 1828 Benjamin Morrell discovered, off Namibia, a treasure island covered with *guano*. A layer more than twenty-five-feet thick had been deposited by generations of cormorants, cape gannets, and penguins. Morrell called it "the richest manure pile in the world." By 1844 up to five hundred ships at a time crowded round Ichaboe Isle. Eight thousand men carted off tons of "white gold" to make the gardens of England grow. A lucrative if messy business.

Then the guano was gone. The ships departed Ichaboe for Chile, the Falklands, anywhere birds nested near rich fishing grounds. Like Nauru, whose king sold half his tiny nation's surface area to fund his people's buying spree, each newfound deposit lasted a little while, made a few men rich, then vanished as if it had never been.

Many other ecological crises came and went. Shoals of fishes vanished. Vast swarms of birds died. Later, some fisheries recovered. And protected nesting grounds pulled some cormorants and gannets back from the verge of extinction.

Then, one day, someone noticed the birds were again doing what birds do . . . right out there on the rocks. Nor did they seem to mind much when men with shovels came—carefully this time, not to disturb the nestlings—and carried off in bags what the birds no longer had any use for.

It was a renewable resource after all. Or it could be, if managed properly.

Let the fish swarm and the currents flow and the sun shine upon the stony coasts. The birds rewarded those with patience.

● Mark Randall could almost feel all the telescopes aimed at him.
I The sense of being watched caused a prickle on his neck as he
O maneuvered *Intrepid*, toward the strobing flash of the instrument
N package.
O   Naturally, the great powers were observing his ship. And the
S ninety-two news agencies and the Big 900 corporations and
P probably thousands of amateur astronomers whose instruments
H were within line of sight.
E   *Some probably have a better idea what I'm chasing than I*
R *do,* he contemplated.
E   "That thing wasn't put there by any rocket," Elaine Castro
told him as she peered over his shoulder at the spinning cylinder caught in the shuttle's spotlight. "This orbit is too weird. And look. The thing doesn't even have standard attachment points!"

"I don't think it was launched . . . normally," Mark answered. Neither of them was saying anything new. "Need any help prepping for EVA?" he asked his new partner. "You've updated your inertial units?"

The stately black woman laid a space-gloved hand on his shoulder and squeezed. "Yes, Mommy. And I promise, I'll call if I need anything."

Mark blinked with a sudden wave of déjà vu, as if someone else were reading his lines in a play. Since when was he the worrywart, the double-checker, the fanatic for detail?

Since his last partner had been taken from him by something unfathomable, of course. "Well, give me a suit integrity readout from the airlock anyway, before pumping down."

"Aye, aye, Cap'n." She saluted, primly and sarcastically. Elaine fastened her helmet and left to fetch the beeping mystery they'd been sent chasing round the world to claim.

How did you get there? he silently asked the spinning object. There were laws of dynamics that had to be bent just to reach this bizarre trajectory. No record showed any rocket launch during the last month that might have sent that thing on such a path.

But there are other records than those released by NORAD and SERA . . . records of inverted tornadoes and columns of vacuum at sea level . . . of vanishing aircraft and rainbows tied in half hitches.

His panels shone green. Happy green also lit where Elaine's suit proclaimed itself in working order. Still, his eyes roved, scanning telemetry, attitude, life support, and especially navigation. Mark whistled softly between his teeth. He sang, half consciously, in a toneless whisper.

"I yam where I yam, and that's all where I yam . . ."

His crewmate emerged into sight, waving cheerfully as she jetted toward the shining cylinder. Mark watched like a mother bear as she lassoed the spinning object and reeled it behind her to *Intrepid's* stowage bay. Even as Elaine cycled back inside, Mark kept alert, watching not only his instruments, but also the *Earth* . . . which had once seemed such a reliable place, but of late had seemed much more twitchy, and prone even to sudden fits of wrath.

□ Worldwide Long Range Solutions Special Interest Group [□ SIG AeR,WLRS 253787890.546], Special Sub-Forum 562: Crackpot-Iconoclast Social Theories.

Do *hidden influences* control human affairs? Forget superstitions like astrology. I mean serious proposals, like Kondratieff waves, which seem to track technology boom-bust cycles, though no one knows why.

Another idea's called "conservation of crises." It contends that during any given century there's *just so much panic to go around.*

Oh, surely there are ups and downs, like the Helvetian disaster and the second cancer plague. Still, from lifetime to lifetime you might say it all balances out so the average person remains just as worried about the future as her grandmother was.

Take the great peace-rush of the nineties. People were astonished how swiftly world statesmen started acting reasonably. Under the Emory Accords, leaders of India and Pakistan smoothed over their fathers' mutual loathing. Russ and Han buried the hatchet, and the superpowers themselves agreed to the first inspection treaties. Earth's people had been bankrupting themselves paying for armaments nobody dared use, so it seemed peace had come just in time.

But what if the timing was no coincidence? Imagine if, by some magic, Stalin and Mao had been replaced in 1949 by leaders just brimming with reason and integrity. Or *all* the paranoid twits had been given sanity pills, back when the world held just two billion humans, when the rain forests still bloomed, when the ozone was intact and Earth's resources were still barely tapped?

It would have been *too easy*, then, to solve every crisis known or imagined! Without the arms race or those wasteful surrogate wars, per capita wealth would have skyrocketed. By now we'd be launching starships.

If you accept the bizarre notion that humanity somehow thrives on crisis, then it's clear we had to have the cold war from 1950 to 1990, to keep tensions high until the surplus ran out. Only then, with ecological collapse looming, was it okay to turn away from missile threats and ideologies. Because by then we all faced *real* problems.

Now some of you may wonder why I devote my weekly column to such a strange idea. It's because of all these rumors we're hearing on the net. It seems there's a new crisis looming . . . something nebulous and frightening which strains the edges of reality.

Want the truth? I'd been expecting something like this. Really.

You see, for all our problems, it was starting to look as if people had finally begun to grow up . . . as if we'd learned some lessons and were starting to work well together at last. Perhaps we had things too well in hand. So, by conservation of crises, here comes something new to frighten us half to death.

It's just an idea, and admittedly a half-baked, unlikely one. Still, picking apart ideas is what the net is all about.

●   Alone inside a locked spaceship, she wasn't expecting anybody.
E   And yet, there came a knock at the door.
X   Teresa had been wriggling through a cramped space, using a
O torque wrench to tighten a new aluminum pipe. She stopped and
S listened. It came again—a rapping at the shuttle's crew access
P hatch.
H   "Just a minute!" Her voice was muffled by the padded tubing
E around her. Teresa writhed backward out of the recess where she'd
R been replacing *Atlantis*'s archaic fuel-cell system with a smaller,
E more efficient one stripped out of a used car. Wiping her hands on
a rag, she stepped across rattling metal planks to peer through the middeck's solitary, circular window.

"Oh, it's you, Alex! Hold on a sec."

She wasn't certain he could hear her through the hatch, but it took only a few moments to crank the release and swing the heavy door aside. Repairing and cleaning the hatch had been her first self-appointed task, soon after arriving on this tiny island of exile.

Alex waited atop the stairs rising from the pediment of the *Atlantis* monument. Or the shuttle's *gibbet*, as Teresa sometimes thought of it. For the crippled machine seemed to hang where it was, trapped, like a bird caught forever in the act of taking off.

"Hi," Alex said, and smiled.

"Hi yourself."

The slight tension elicited by June Morgan's visit was quite over by now. Of course she shouldn't have felt awkward that her friend's lover happened to pass through from time to time. Alex carried heavy burdens, and it was good to know he could relax that way on occasion. Still, Teresa felt momentary twinges of jealousy and suspicion not rooted in anything as straightforward as reason.

"Thought it time I dropped by to see how you're doing." Alex raised a sack with the outlines of a bottle. "Brought a housewarming present. I'm not disturbing, I hope?"

"No, of course not, silly. Watch your step though. I've torn up the deck plating to get at some cooling lines. Have to replace a lot of them, I'm afraid."

"Um," Alex commented as he stepped over one of the yawning openings, staring at the jumble of pipes and tubing. "So the catalysts June brought you helped?"

"Sure did. And those little robots you lent me. They were able to thread cabling behind bulkheads so I didn't even have to remove any big panels. Thanks."

Alex put the sack down near the chaos of new and old jerry-rigging. "You won't mind if I ask you a rather obvious question?"

"Like why? Why am I doing this?" Teresa laughed. "I honestly don't know, really. Something to pass the time, I guess. Certainly I don't fool myself she'll ever fly again. Her spine couldn't take the stress of even the gentlest launch.

"Maybe I'm just a born picture straightener. Can't leave an honest machine just lying around rusting."

Peering into the jumble of wires and pipes, Alex whistled. "Looks complicated."

"You said it. *Columbia*-class shuttles were the most complex machines ever built. Later models streamlined techniques these babies explored.

"That's the sad part, really. These were *developmental* spacecraft. It was dumb, even criminal, to pretend they were 'routine orbital delivery vehicles,' or whatever the damn fools called them at the time. . . . Anyway, come on. Let me give you a tour."

She showed him where NASA scavengers had stripped the ship, back when the decision had been made to abandon *Atlantis* where she lay. "They took anything that could be cannibalized for the two remaining shuttles. Still, there's an amazing amount of junk they left behind. The flight computers, for instance. Totally obsolete, even at the time. Half the homes in America had faster, smarter ones by then. Your wristwatch could cheat all five at poker and then talk them all into voting Republican."

Alex marveled. "Amazing."

Teresa led him up the ladder to the main deck, where South Pacific sunshine streamed in through front windows smudged and stained by perching seagulls. The cockpit was missing half its instruments, ripped out indelicately long ago, leaving wires strewn across dim, dust-filmed displays. She rested her arms on the command seat and sighed. "So much love and attention went into these machines. And so much bureaucratic ineptitude. Sometimes I wonder how we ever got as far as we did."

"Say, Teresa. Is there a way to get into the cargo bay?"

She turned around and saw Alex peering through the narrow windows at the back of the control cabin. It was pitch black in the bay, of course, since it had no ports to the outside. She herself had been back there only once, to discover in dismay that midges and tiny spiders had found homes there, lacing the vast cavity with gauzy webs. Probably they used cracks *Atlantis* had suffered when she fell onto her 747 carry-plane, ruining both ships forever. The Boeing had been scrapped. But *Atlantis* remained where she lay, her cargo hold now home only to insects.

"Sure. Through the airlock on middeck. But—"

He turned. "Rip. . . . There's a favor I have to ask."

She blinked. "Just name it."

"Come outside then. I brought something in the truck."

The crate had to be winched up the pediment steps. From there it was a tight squeeze through the crew-egress hatch.

"We can't leave it here," Teresa said, panting and wiping her brow. "It blocks my work space."

"That's why I asked about the bay. Do you think we can get it through?"

Just left of the toilet cubicle stood the shuttle's airlock, now the only way into the cargo bay. Teresa looked, and shook her head dubiously. "Maybe if we uncrate your whatever-it-is."

"All right. But let's be careful."

She saw why he was so nervous when they peeled away the inner packing. There, resting inside a gimbaled housing, lay the most perfect sphere Teresa had ever seen. It glistened almost liquidly, causing the eye to skip along its flanks. Somehow, vision flowed on past, missing the thing itself.

"We'll have to carry it by the housing," Alex told her. Teresa bent to get a good grip on the rim as he took the other side. It was very heavy. Like a gyroscope, the silvery ball seemed to stay oriented in exactly the same direction, no matter how they shifted and jostled it. But then, that might have been an illusion. For all Teresa knew, it was spinning madly right in front of her. No ripple in the convex reflection gave any clue.

"What . . . is this thing?" she asked as they paused for breath inside the airlock. There was barely room for the globe and its cradle, forcing them to squeeze side by side to reach the opposite hatch. The close press of Alex's shoulder, as they sidled together, felt at once familiar and warm, recalling times not so long ago of shared danger and adventure.

"It's a gravity resonator," he told her, caressing the sphere with his gaze. "A completely new design."

"But it's so small. I thought they had to be big cylinders."

"They do, to generate a broad spectrum of search waves. But this one's a specialist. This one's tuned. For Beta."

"Ah," Teresa commented, impressed.

They resumed wrestling the shimmery globe into the bay, now lit by three small bulbs. "So why . . . do you want to store a tuned gravity resonator . . . inside a broken space shuttle?"

"I . . . thought you'd ask. Actually, I'm not . . . so much setting it up here as hiding it."

As they rested for a moment, Teresa mopped her forehead. "Hiding? Do you mean from Spivey?"

Alex nodded. "Or his ilk. You know those Maori guards Auntie Kapur insisted on sending us? Well they've already caught spies trying to sneak into the compound. One Nihonese, another pair from the Han. And I'm sure Spivey's got people on the island as well. Auntie's sending reinforcements, but even so I'd rather keep my ace in the hole well concealed."

He rubbed his palms on his trousers to dry them and grabbed the housing again. Together they resumed lifting.

"Hidden up . . ." She grunted as they hauled the resonator over a rib longeron into a stable position near one of the payload attachment points. "Hidden up *my* sleeve." Teresa straightened. "No, that's okay, Alex. I approve. It's not just Spivey. I don't trust any of them, not farther than I could spit.

"So," she continued as Alex fastened the machine down. "Was that a bottle I saw in your hand earlier, I hope?"

Still short of breath, Alex grinned back at her, eyes glittering in the spotlights and their reflection off the perfect superconducting sphere. "Yeah. I know you Yanks like your beer cold. But once you've tasted this I'm sure you'll give up that beastly habit."

"Hmph. We'll see about that." Teresa brushed a wisp of cobweb from her eyes. As Alex turned to go, she paused to watched the tiny shred of spider silk flutter, descend to touch the round globe, and instantly disappear.

It was, indeed, a potent, bitter brew, and Teresa rather liked it. Still, for appearances she said the stuff explained a lot about Englishmen. It obviously stunted your emotional growth. He only laughed and leaned over to refresh her glass.

Teresa sat in the shuttle's command chair while Alex perched cross-legged in the copilot's seat. Neither of them felt any particular need to fill the long silences. So it often was, in Teresa's experience, between people who had faced death together.

"You're worried," she surmised at last, after one extended pause. "You don't think the deal can hold."

"It was hopeless from the start." Alex shook his head. "In retrospect, I can't understand why it took so long for Spivey to find us. But at least we were a small conspiracy, operating on a shoestring. Now? Our beams are producing detectable phenomena all over the globe. The alliances can't keep a thing like this under wraps, not with everyone on Earth prying to find out what's going on."

"Then why did Spivey and Hutton agree to try?"

He shrugged. "Oh, it seemed a good idea at the time. Take care of Beta, get the situation stabilized, then present the world with a fait accompli. And of course it's giving us a chance to characterize the singularity, to prove its origin. Our technical report should let the science tribunals extend inspection to the Earth's core, preventing any new arms race over gazers and such. Then, in an open debate, it could be decided whether to keep Beta around, as a possible planetary-defense weapon, or try to expel it forever."

"Sounds reasonable." Teresa nodded, grudgingly.

"The only problem is, that time's already come! Beta's relatively stable, I have data for a full report, and I'm certain the other great powers have already started clandestine graviscan programs of their own. There was a pulse from Nihon, yesterday—" He shook his head. "I wish I knew what Spivey was waiting for."

"Did you hear about the meeting at the U.N.?" Teresa asked. "Everyone, all the delegates, were talking in parables and double-entendres. Moralizing and posturing, and saying nothing any of the reporters could sink their teeth into."

"Hm." Alex frowned. She sensed him begin to say something, stop, and then start again.

"I . . . I've started fighting him, you know."

"Fighting who?" Then she stared. "You're fighting Spivey! But how?"

"I'm tweaking the beams from South Africa and Rapa Nui, the ones I still control. Using them to pump Beta's orbit higher . . . out to where it'll lose mass faster. And also where the damn thing doesn't leave those weird *tracks* in the lower mantle anymore—"

She interrupted. "Has he reacted? Has Spivey noticed?"

Alex laughed. "Oh has he! Got George to send me a telex. Here's a copy." He pulled the flimsy sheet from a breast pocket. "They're both urging me to go along . . . not to let the side down. You know? All hang together or we'll surely hang separately?

"Then, this morning, New Guinea fired three microseconds late on a routine run."

"What did that do?"

He shook his head. "It pulled energy *from* Beta's orbit, Rip, letting it fall a little lower. Seems our colonel isn't about to let his mirror lose mass. Not while there are more experiments to run."

Silence reigned for many heartbeats, their only measure of time's passage. Finally, Teresa asked, "What can Glenn be trying to do? Surely he can't be planning to use it as a weapon? His superiors can't be that mad!"

Alex stared out through the streaked windshield, beyond a stretch of black-topped runway to a bluff of scrub grass growing scraggly out of the thin volcanic soil. Beyond lay the foam-capped waters of the ash-gray Pacific.

"I wish I knew. But whatever he's after, I'm afraid you and I are mere pawns."

☐ How hot is it? You folks really want to know how hot it is? I see farmer Izzy Langhorne sitting under a cottonwood right now, having his lunch while watching the show. Hey, Izzy, how dumpit hot would *you* spec it?

Aw, no, Izzy, gimme euthanasia! Not with your mouth full! We'll go back to Izzy after he's cleaned up. Lessee now, gettin' a shout-back from Jase Kramer, over by Sioux Falls. Looks like you're having some trouble with your tractor, Jase.

"No, Larry. It's just you . . . have to climb under the suspension of

these Chulalongkorn Sixes and clear the deadwood by hand. See, it gets
trapped over here by the—''

Well that's great, Jase. Nice of you to take the holo under with you so
we could all get a look. Now tell me, how hot is it?

"Well, hell, Larry. Yesterday my chickens laid hard-boiled eggs . . ."

Thank you, Jase Kramer. Whew. Send that codder some relief!

Now hold it just a millie . . . here's an actinic flash for you current
affairs junkies. Seems the latest round of those secrety-secret talks—
pardon my urdu—have broken up for lunch over in New York village. Our
affiliates there have joined the mob of news-ferret types chasing the
delegates to the deli. For a direct feed, shout a hop-link to News-Line 82.
For play-by-play plus color, call Rap-250. Or you can cake-and-eat-it. Just
hang around with us while your unit does a rec-dense for later.

While we're talking about the gremlin crisis, have any of you out there
seen anything new today? Anything that might've been a gremmie?
Yesterday Betty Remington of St. Low showed us a perfectly circular patch
of amaranth where the kernels had all been mysteriously turned inside out.
And in Barstow, Sam Chu claims one of his prize brood carps up and
exploded, right in front of him! Day-pay-say!

So who's got an opinion out there? You know the code, let's hear the
mode. . . .

● Jen remembered what a wise man told her long ago when she was
H similarly obsessed with the problem of consciousness. It had been
O an astronomer friend of Thomas's, a very great mind, she recalled,
L who listened patiently for hours as she expounded the hottest new
O concepts of cognition and perception. Then, when at last she ran
S out of steam, he commented.
P   "I'm uneducated in formal psychology. But in my experience,
H people generally react to any new situation in one of four ways:
E   Aha! . . . Ho-hum . . . Oy Vey! . . . and Yum, yum. . . .
R   "These illustrate the four basic states of consciousness, dear Jennifer.
E All else is mere elaboration."

Years later, Jen still found the little allegory delightful. It made
you stop and ponder. But did those four "states" actually map onto
human thought? Did they lead to new theories that might be tested by
experiment? She recalled the astronomer's smile that evening. Clearly
he knew the deeper truth—that all theories are only metaphors, at
best helpful models of the world. And even his clever notion was no
more real than a mote in his own eye.

There are one hundred ways to view Mount Fuji, as Hokusai showed us. And each of them is right.

Jen wished she had someone like that old astronomer to talk to now.

Today I'm *the aged professor with no one to talk to but a bright high school dropout. So who is there to give me reality checks? To tell me if I'm off on a wild goose chase?*

She was treading a narrow path these days, skirting all the pitfalls of pure reason—that most seductive and deceptive of human pastimes. Jen had always believed philosophers ought to have their heads knocked repeatedly, lest they become trapped in the rhythms of their own if-thens. But now she was hardly one to cast stones. While crises roiled on all sides, the compass of her own existence contracted, as if her once far-flung reach were drawing inward now, preparing for some forthcoming contest or battle.

But what battle? What contest?

Clearly she wasn't equipped to participate in the struggles being waged by Kenda and her grandson. Likewise, the ferment surging through the Net would go on unaffected by anything she offered. By now it was starting to reach stochastic levels. A billion or more anxious world citizens had already been drawn from their myriad endeavors, hobbies, and distractions toward a single strange attractor, one gnawing focus of angst. Nothing like it had been seen since the Helvetian War, and back in those days the Net had been a mere embryo.

Messages piled up in her open-access mailbox as numberless correspondents sought her opinion. But rather than get involved, Jen only retreated further into the circumscribed world of thought.

Oh, she left the catacombs regularly, for exercise and human contact. In Kuwenezi's squat, fortresslike ark she spent ninety minutes each day with her only student, answering his eager questions with puzzlers of her own, marveling at his voracious mind and wondering if he'd ever get a chance to develop it.

But then, walking home under the merciless sun, she would pass near towering termite mounds, built by patient, highly social creatures at regular intervals across the dry hills. They hummed with unparsed commentary, a drone that seemed to resonate inside her skull, even after the rickety lift cage started descending into the cool silence of the abandoned mine, gliding past layer after gritty layer of compressed sediments, returning her to those caverns where hard-driven men labored like Homeric figures under her grandson's long-distance guidance, wrestling for the fate of the world.

Their efforts mattered to Jen, of course. It was just that no one seemed to need her at the moment. And anyway, something even more important had to be attended to.

Her train of thought. It was precious, tenuous. A thread of concentration that absolutely had to be preserved . . . not for the world, but for its own sake. It was a self-involved, even selfish attitude, but Jen had long known she was a solipsist. Except during the years when her children had been growing, what had always mattered to her most was the trail of the idea. And this was a very big idea.

From the Net she drew references stretching back to Minsky and Ornstein, Pastor and Jaynes—and even poor old Jung—examining how each thinker had dealt with this peculiar notion . . . that *one* could somehow be *many*, or many combine to make one.

Her young student Nelson Grayson had really hit on it with his fixation on "cooperation versus competition." The dichotomy underlay every human moral system, every ideology and economic theory, from socialism to free-market libertarianism. Each tried to resolve it in different ways. And every attempt only dredged up more inconsistencies.

But what if it's a false dichotomy, after all? What if we've been seduced by those deducers, Plato and Kant and Hegel? By the if-and-therefore of linear logic? Perhaps life itself sees less contradiction than we do.

The motto on the old American coin haunted her. "From many, one."

Our subselves usually aren't distinct, except in multiple personality disorder. Rather, a normal person's drives and impulses merge and cleave, marry and sunder, forming temporary alliances to make us feel and act in certain ways.

So far so good. The evidence for some form of multimind model was overwhelming. But then came the rub.

If I consist of many, why do I persist in perceiving a central me *at all! What is this consciousness that even now, as I think these thoughts, contemplates its own existence?*

Jen remembered back when Thomas had tried to interest her in reading novels. He had promised that the best ones would prove enlightening. That their characters would "seem to come alive." But the protagonists were never realistic to Jen. Even when portrayed as confused or introspective, their thought processes seemed too straightforward. Too decisive. Only Joyce ever came close to depicting the real hurricane of internal conflict and negotiation, those vast, turbid seascapes surrounding an island of semi-calm that named itself "me."

Is that why I must imagine a unitary self? To give the storm a center? An "eye" to revolve around? An illusion of serenity, so the storm might be ignored most of the time?

Or is it a way to rationalize a semblance of consistency? To present a coherent face to the outside world?

Of one thing Jen felt certain. The universe inside a human mind was only vaguely like the physical one outside, with its discrete entities, its species, cells, organs, and individuals. And yet, the mind *used* those external entities as metaphors in the very models it used to define itself!

Today, Nelson had gotten worked up about one such model. *Government*, he said, consists of a nation's effort to settle the differences amongst its component parts—its citizens. In olden times, the resolution was a simple matter of the imposition of fiat by a king or ruling class.

Later still, majority rule improved matters a little. But today even small minorities could make bombs and death bugs, if they got angry enough! (The blueprints were all there in the net, and who dared claim the role of censor?)

So compromise and consensus were absolutely essential, and governments could only tread carefully, never imposing solutions. Serving instead as forums for careful rapprochement.

In other words, the ideal government should be like a sane person's conscious mind! It was a fascinating comparison. Almost as interesting as the next one Nelson spun out.

The *World Data Net*, he said, was the ultimate analog. Like a person, it too consisted of a myriad of tiny subselves (the eight billion subscribers), all bickering and negotiating and cooperating semi-randomly. Subscriber cliques and alliances merged and separated . . . sometimes by nationality or religion, but more often nowadays by special interest groups that leaped all the old borderlines . . . all waging minuscule campaigns to sway the world's agenda and to affect their lives in the physical world.

Astonishing, Jen thought. The boy had made a major metaphorical leap.

Of course, the government analogy was a little overextended. *But the notion that consciousness is our way of getting all our secret selves out into the daylight, so they'll either cooperate or compete fairly—that's the important part. It explains why a neurosis loses most of its power once it's known . . . as soon as all the mind gets to see those dark secrets one isolated part had kept hiden from the rest.*

Walking past the busy technicians, Jen sat down at her display and resumed working on her model, modifying it along lines inspired by Nelson's insight. The subvocal was the only input device fast enough to follow her driving pace. Her teeth clicked and her larynx bobbed as she *almost* spoke words aloud. The machine skimmed those phrases faster than she could have pronounced them, and it extrapolated, drawing from its capacious memory bits of this and that to fit into a growing whole.

Those bits were mostly object blocks taken from the very best intelligence-modeling programs around. That cost money, of course, and over in one corner Jen saw her personal account dip alarmingly. But each of the programs had something to recommend it. Each had been slaved over by teams of talented researchers with private theories they wanted to prove—each ostensibly contradictory, incompatible with the others.

At that moment, however, it had ceased mattering to Jen whose doctrine was closer to correct. Suddenly, it made perfect sense to merge them, combine them—to try to make a whole greater than the sum of its parts.

By the Mother . . . what if they're all *right? What if self-similarity and recursion can't typify a living system without yet a third attribute—inclusion?*

There was certainly a precedent for such a mélange . . . the human brain, the physical organ itself, was built in layers. Its newest evolutionary innovations hadn't *replaced* earlier sections. Rather, each in turn was laid *over* older parts, joining and modifying them, not canceling or superseding.

Most recent were the prefrontal lobes, tiny nubs above the eyes which some called the seat of human personality . . . the latest floor of rooms added to a skyscraper of mind. Underneath lay the mammalian cortex, shared with man's closest cousins. Lower then, but still useful and functional, the brain portions appropriate to reptiles still performed useful chores, while under *those* pulsed a basic reflex system remarkably like that found in primitive chordates.

So it would be with her model. Gradually pieces of the puzzle fell into place. The Berkeley Cognition Scheme, for instance, mated astonishingly well with the "emotional momentum" models of the Beijing University behaviorists. At least it did if you twisted each of them a bit first, in just the right way.

Of course, whenever she ventured into the net to seek these and other programs, she had to experience firsthand what was going on out there. It was utter chaos! Her early ferrets got completely lost in the maelstrom. She had to write better ones just to reach the big psychology library clearinghouse, in Chicago. And even then it took several tries before the emissaries came back with what she needed. The latest retrieval had taken seven whole seconds, causing her to smack the console in irritation.

By now Jen realized—with perhaps a pang of jealousy—that her own grandson had achieved unrivaled heights in the art of stirring people up, far exceeding her own modest accomplishments. The Net spumed with ferment over events Alex Lustig had set off. Somewhere, sometime soon, Jen figured the whole Rube Goldberg contraption had to blow a fuse.

Watch it, old girl. Your own metaphors give away your age.

Okay then, let's try a few similes.

The chaos in the Net was like spray blowing over a small boat. All sorts of unwanted material accompanied the subroutines her ferrets brought back. Jen was both alarmed and amused when some bits of software dross actually fought *not* to be tossed out! They clung to existence in her computer like scrabbling little life-forms and had to be tracked down lest they scurry into some corner and use up scarce memory, or maybe even breed.

On impulse she looked to the small screen where she'd exiled the cartoon creatures called up by her own free associations. In the foreground, for instance, shimmered a teetering house of cards and spent, smoking electrical fuses, clearly extrapolated from recent surface mumblings.

Then there was the tiger symbol, which had lain in that same spot all these weeks. The simulacrum purred lowly, lounging on a nest of what looked like shredded paper.

She told the snippet of herself. *If you insist on hanging around, then it's time I put you to work.*

The tiger yawned, but responded when she tapped two teeth together decisively—asserting the dominance of her central self over its parts. Subvocally she gave it instructions, to go hunt those spurious flurries of unwanted software—all the scampering, chittering irrelevancies that kept swarming into her work space from the Net's chaos, disturbing her work.

The weather's high, she realized. *At times like these, any mobile thing will seek shelter, anywhere it can.*

With that thought, flecks of rain seemed to dampen the tiger's fur, but not its mood. With another yawn and then a savage grin, the cat set forth to clear away all interlopers, to give her model room to settle and grow.

□

On other Polynesian islands, the people lived lives much the same as ours. Their chiefs, too, were beings of great *mana*. Our cousins, too, believed the course of the warrior was just below that of the gods.

But in other ways we differed. For when his canoes arrived from ancient Hiva, our forefather, Hotu Matu'a, knew at once where he had come. This is *Te Pito o Te Henua*—the island at the center of the world.

We had chickens and taro and bananas and yams. There was obsidian and hard black stone, but no harbor, and our canoes were lost.

What need had we of canoes? What hope to depart? For we believed the closest land to Rapa Nui was the bright moon itself, who passed low over our three cratered peaks—paradise overhead, barely out of reach. Believing we could get there with *mana*, we built the *ahu* and carved the *moai*.

But we had slain great Tangaroa and were cursed to fail, to suffer, to live off the flesh of our brethren and see our children inherit emptiness.

It is hard, living at the navel of the world.

● He was shaving when the telephone rang.
C   Alex wasn't happy with the new razor he'd bought after the
O escape from New Zealand. Its diamond blade was far too sharp,
R unlike his old one, which had worn down nicely over the years
E since his sixteenth birthday.

That wasn't the only thing he missed. Stan and George also—their steadiness and calm advice. Communications were supposed to be safe from the rising noisiness on the Net, but despite military assurances, they had worsened for days.

Were Spivey's peepers conspiring to keep them apart? Or might George and Stan be snubbing him because of his growing campaign against the colonel's control?

Alex prepared to run the blade over his face again, wondering if maybe it was time to quit being so old-fashioned and get his face depilated, like most other men.

A shrill chirping made his hand jerk. "Bloody hell!"

Alex tore off a sheet of toilet paper to stanch the wound. He recalled seeing a can of coagulant enzyme in the medicine cabinet and pulled aside the mirror to start rummaging for it.

The phone chirruped again, insistently. "Oh . . . all right." He slammed the mirror shut. Applying pressure to stop the bleeding, he stepped into the tiny bedroom, sifted through the clutter on the nightstand for his wristwatch, and pressed the ACCEPT CALL button. "Yes?"

The person on the other end paused and then realized there would be no picture. "*Tohunga*? Is that you?"

From the Maori honorific, it had to have been one of the newcomers Auntie Kapur had sent to watch over Alex and his team. "Lustig here," he affirmed. "What is it?"

"Better come quick, *Tohunga*. We caught a saboteur trying to blow up the lab." The voice cut off with a click. Alex stared at the watch. "Cripes," he said concisely. Grabbing a shirt off the dresser, he dashed out the door trailing shaving cream and tiny specks of blood.

"I guess we're not needed anymore."

"Come on, Eddie. We don't know the bomb was sent by Spivey. What about a hundred other countries, alliances, agitation groups. . . . Hell, even the boy scouts must have some idea where the focal resonators are by now."

His chief engineer grimaced. "I served in the ANZAC Special Forces, Alex. I know standard issue demolition charges when I see them." The big, red-headed Kiwi hefted a tennis-ball–sized contraption. "The casing's been altered to make it look like Nihon manufacture, but I just did a neutron activation scan, and I can tell you exactly which factory in Sydney made it. Even the lot number.

"Bloody sloppy of the bastards, if you ask me. They must have been confident we couldn't stop 'em."

Alex glanced over at the would-be saboteur, a nondescript Polynesian. Possibly a Samoan, whose appearance would presumably blend in with the natives of Easter Island. Except that the Pasquans of Rapa Nui were a breed apart and proud of it.

What kind of man takes a live bomb across the seas in order to blow up other people? People who have mothers and lovers and children, just like him?

Probably either a professional or a patriot, Alex thought. *Or, worse, both.*

The bomber smiled nervously at Alex.

He knows the way things ought to go now. According to the rules, we'd have to hand him over to Chilean authorities. Then, in the fullness of time, his masters will cut a deal for him.

Only what rules apply when everyone's talking about the end of the world? Alex's hands balled into fists. The saboteur seemed to read something in his eyes and swallowed hard.

Across the room, Alex saw Teresa watching him, arms folded in front of her. *So what do we do now?* he wondered. More than ever, he wished he could gather old friends and tap their wisdom.

"I agree. I'd lay odds it was Colonel Spivey who sent the bomb."

Everybody turned to see who had spoken with such authority, in a rich, confident basso. "Manella!" Alex cried out. Teresa gasped.

Standing in the doorway, the Aztlan reporter smiled and carried his bulk gracefully into the chamber. Resting one arm on the guardrail of the gravity resonator, he smiled all around. "It's good to see you remember me, Lustig. Hello, everybody. Captain Tikhana. Sorry to abandon you back in Waitomo. But I really was indisposed."

"You choose convenient moments to come and go," Teresa said bitterly. "What makes you think we'll have any interest in what you have to say now, Pedro?"

Manella smiled. "Come come. I'm sure Colonel Spivey's told you how much he respected whoever ran interference for our project, before he finally found us. Didn't he admit that? Doesn't that imply whose side I was on . . . am on?"

Alex frowned. Pedro was implying that even now he had his own tap into the Waitomo complex. Which was plausible enough. He'd had plenty of time to plant bugs. One fiber, as thin as silk, was all you needed.

"All good things come to an end, though. Eventually it was some hacker out on the Net who tracked us down. I got the warning only an instant before those peepers arrived." Manella tapped the heavy-duty data watch on his left wrist. "No time to warn anybody, and I knew if I took Teresa along, the manhunt would sweep us both up in a trice anyway. But I bet Spivey wouldn't think *me* worth the bother."

"He hardly mentioned your name," Teresa said, both confirming Manella's split-second decision and emphasizing how little anybody cared about him.

He took the mixed insult with good grace. "Anyway, I've been keeping tabs on things, while maintaining a thin profile—"

Teresa interrupted. "Hah!"

"—but I had a feeling something like this was in the works. That's why I called your security chief this morning with a little tip."

Alex swiveled to look at Auntie Kapur's man. The big Maori shrugged. "Must've been him, *tohunga.*"

Teresa objected. "How do we know *he* didn't send the saboteur, just so he could tip us off and win back our trust?"

"Oh, Captain." Manella sighed. "Don't you think I'm persuasive enough on my own account, without having to use tricks and legerdemain? Besides, I have no access to bombs and such. You just heard this wise man say the thing was ANZAC military issue.

"No, I just used this." He tapped the side of his ample nose.
"Lustig can tell you it never fails. I knew something was up. Had to
be. Spivey can't afford to leave you in operation any longer."

"But . . . why?" one of the woman techs complained. "Just
because we've been nudging Beta a little higher, so it evaporates a
bit?"

Another engineer agreed. "It can't be to keep things secret any
longer, either. Private SIGs are correlating data from nearly every gazer
beam, tossing out bad theories and zeroing in on the truth. Anyway,
last night the NATO president said he'll be making a big statement
Tuesday. It'll all go to the tribunals . . ."

"Which makes time all the more crucial to Spivey," Pedro
answered. "Tell me something, Alex. Are there signs of *other
resonators* coming on line? Other than your original four?"

Oh, he's good all right, Alex admitted in his thoughts, whether
Manella had guessed this or discovered it by spying on them.

"We've seen traces for several days now. Two in Nihon GEACS
territory, one Russ and a Han also."

"*And?*"

"And six more . . . much better ones. They're being set up at
the face centers of a cube, a better arrangement than our tetrahedron."

"Just as I expected." Manella nodded. "And who else, other than
yourself, is capable of building such an array? Who else has such a
head start over Russ and Han and even Nihon?"

Silence was his only answer. The answer was obvious.

"So there's supposed to be an announcement in four days? So the
tribunals are to be invoked and all revealed? I must then answer, so
what? What happens afterward will still depend on *who has the best
information and expertise.* That is who will be in control. He'll set
the agenda. Rule the world."

"Spivey," Teresa said, though clearly she did not want to.

Manella nodded. "He's *almost* got a monopoly on data about
these breathtaking, intimidating new technologies. But who knows
even more about singularities and gravity lasers than his tame
physicists?"

They looked at each other. No one in the world understood the
gazer phenomenon better than the people in this room.

This is no good, Alex decided. *Manella might be right. Dammit,
he probably is. But I'm not letting him hypnotize my team.*

"Clever, Pedro," he told the newsman. "Have you also worked
out what I've decided to do about it?"

"Is that all?" The big man grinned. "You forget that I know you,

Lustig. I'd bet my tooth-implant radio and half a year's pay you intend showing Colonel Spivey just who he's dealing with."

Damn you, Alex thought. But outwardly he only shrugged. Looking at the others, he announced—"Anyone who chooses to leave the island may do so now. All civilians will be warned away from a two-kilometer radius.

"As for me, though, I don't plan taking this—" he hefted the bomb "—lying down."

He looked again at Teresa, who nodded. *She understands. The next few days will decide the future of everything.*

Alex watched as the assembled workers, one by one, stepped toward him and the great swiveled bulk of the resonator. Their silent vote was unanimous. "Good," he said, feeling a wave of warmth toward his comrades. "Let's get to work then. I had a dream not long ago, and it gave me an idea. A possible way we just might get the good colonel's attention."

☐ **Worldwide Long Range Solutions Special Interest Group** [☐ SIG AeR,WLRS 253787890.546], **Special Alert to Members.**

There are times for discussion, and other times when only action counts. None of our fancy schemes will help anybody if we don't make it through this present craziness! So the coordinators of the Worldwide Long Range Solutions SIG hereby suspend all conference forums. Instead we encourage all of you, as individuals, to seek ways to help solve the crisis many see looming, hour by passing hour.

"But what can a single person do to influence events of such magnitude and momentum?" One answer may surprise you. We'll shortly hand over these channels, on loan, to the Federation of Amateur Observation Special Interest Groups [☐ sig BaY, FAO 456780079.876]. Their spokesper will describe how each of you can assist the worldwide effort to track the gremlins down.

It may surprise many of you how much science relies on amateur observers, from bird-watchers, to meteor counters, to hobbyists with private weather stations. But now, with so many weird phenomena taking place worldwide, these amateur networks are truly coming into their own. It's private citizens, with sharp eyes and ready cameras, who are even now tracing patterns the big boys think they can keep secret from us.

We'll show them whose planet this is! So stay on-line for a list of groups you can join. Then get off your lazy asses, dust off your Tru-Vus, go outside, and look! You may be the one to catch that vital clue, to help track these gor-sucking gremlins to their source.

● Stan Goldman didn't have much to do anymore. Others ran the
M scans now, reduced the data, constructed ever-subtler models of
E the inner Earth, even traced the involute geometries of that
S refulgent, renitent entity below . . . the thing called Beta.
O   A midget town had sprung up around the lonely Tangoparu
S dome on a rocky plain below the vast Greenland ice sheet. High-
P powered tech types bustled with armloads of data cubes, arguing
H in the arcane new language of gazerdynamics. Of the original
E team, only he remained now, the others having gone home to New
R Zealand long ago.
E   The NATO scientific commander had specifically asked him
to stay. So Stan sat in on all the daily seminars, struggling to keep up with younger, more agile minds, even though his understanding grew more obsolete with each fast-breaking discovery. No matter. They all treated him with utter deference. Hardly a moment passed without hearing the name Alex Lustig spoken with an awe customarily lavished on the shades of Newton and Einstein and Hurt, and as the great one's former teacher, Stan shared in that glory.

Singularities. There was a lot of talk about singularities, by which the bright young men and women meant the kind you made inside a cavitron—micro black holes and those newer innovations, tuned strings and cosmic knots. Of late, though, Stan had found himself thinking about another kind of "singularity" altogether. It was on his mind as he passed a saluting sentry and left the bustling encampment, swinging his walking stick across the moraine-strewn valley.

In mathematics, a singularity is a sudden discontinuity, where one expression suddenly ceases being valid, and a completely different one takes its place.

You got the simplest kind of singularity—a delta function—by dividing any real number by zero. The result, converging on infinity, was actually undefined, unknowable. *That's where we're at right now . . . a singularity in the life history of mankind.*

It wasn't just the present crisis. Oh, certainly he was worried. Would the world's institutions—or the planet itself—survive the next few hours or days? Stan was as concerned as the next man. Still, even if tomorrow the spectre of reborn international paranoia evaporated like a bad dream, and all the gorgeous, terrifying new technologies were tamed, nothing would ever be the same.

Earlier today, some of the youngsters had been discussing notions about *gravitational circuits* . . . equivalent, in collapsed mass and stressed space, to capacitors and resistors and transistors, for heaven's sake! To Stan it was proof the time had come. The moment he'd secretly been waiting for all his life.

There's another kind of singularity . . . having to do with society, and information.

Technological breakthroughs had happened before—when farming was invented, for example. Or metallurgy. Or writing. Each time, men and women gained new power over their lives, and thinking itself changed. With each such naissance, human beings were in effect reborn, remade . . . reprogrammed.

In early times, change came slowly. But each breakthrough laid a foundation for those that followed. And with the Western breakout of the sixteenth century, it became self-sustaining. Inventions bred wealth, which spread education and leisure to broader masses. Printing dispersed literacy. Transport distributed food. Food meant more people.

He paused near a sandy bank in the wind-shadow of a boulder, and used his walking stick to trace a rough figure. It was the standard doom scenario, depicting the fate forecast by Malthus for any species that outbreeds the carrying capacity of its niche.

The curve portrayed human population over time, and it rose very slowly at first. All through the late Stone Age—when Stan's ancestors had chipped flint, scratched fleas, and thought fire the final terror weapon—there were never more than five million *homo sapiens* at a time. This changed with agriculture, though. Human numbers doubled, then doubled again every fifteen hundred years or so—a rapid climb—until they reached five hundred million around the time of Newton.

Impressive progress, achieved by people who had hardly a glimmer of what the laws of nature were, let alone concepts like ecology or psychology or planetary history. But then it accelerated even faster! New foods, sanitation, emigration . . . babies lived longer. Humans reproduced copiously. The next doubling, to a billion souls, took only two hundred years. The next, less than a century. Then, from just 1950 to 1980, two billions became four. And still the curve steepened. Stan recalled the elegant, symmetrical projections proclaimed by pessimists when he was young. *No population boom can be sustained forever on a finite world. There must inevitably come crash.*

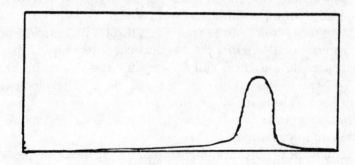

The curve never reached infinity after all. It peaked. Then, like a spent rocket, it turned over and plummeted. *The great die-back, that's where we seemed headed. After all, it happens whenever anchovies and deer breed beyond their food supply.*

And we did have little die-backs. But so far we've escaped the big one, haven't we?

So far.

He scratched another rude figure, identical to the first until it reached the top of the curve. At which point the population stopped growing all right, but neither did it fall! Instead of plummeting, this rocket turned sideways.

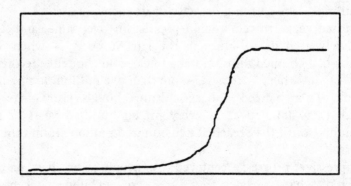

This is what they say can happen if you add intelligence and free will to the formula. After all, we aren't *deer or anchovies!*

Two graphs. Two destinies. Malthusian calamity and the so-called S-curve. On the one hand, utter collapse. And on the other, a chain of last-minute reprieves . . . like self-fertilizing corn, room-temperature superconductors, and gene-spliced catfish . . . each arriving just in time for mankind to muddle through another year, eking out a living from one brilliant innovation to the next.

We thought these were the only two possible futures:

—if we prove selfish and short-sighted—mass death,

—and if we bend all our efforts, working together, applying every ingenuity—then a genteel decline to a sort of threadbare equilibrium.

But was there a third choice? Another type of social singularity? Stan's stick hovered over the sand. *When each generation owns more books than its father's, the volumes don't accumulate arithmetically or even geometrically. Knowledge grows exponentially.*

Stan recalled the last time he and Alex and George had gotten drunk together, when he had complained so about the lack of new *modalities.* Now he laughed at the memory. "Oh, I was wrong. There are modalities, all right. More than I ever imagined."

Those youngsters back in the encampment were talking about making gravitational transistors! It was enough to make a man cry out, "Stop! Give me a minute to think! What does it all mean?"

Knowledge isn't restrained by the limits of Malthus. Information doesn't need topsoil to grow in, only freedom. Given eager minds and experimentation, it feeds itself like a chain reaction.

A third type of social singularity, then, would be a true leap, some sudden, jarring shift to a completely undefined state—where changes manifest themselves in months, weeks, days, minutes. . . . *Still climbing, the rocket attains escape velocity.*

With a sigh, Stan wiped away the rude figures. *We're caught up in our own close view of time. A human life seems so long. But try on the patient outlook of a glacier.*

His eyes lifted to the white continent of ice, only a few kilometers away and stretching from horizon to horizon. *Ice ages are geologically rapid events. And yet we've flashed from caveman to world wrecker in just three hundred generations. One moment there are these barefoot Neolithic hunters, bickering over a frozen caribou carcass. Turn around, and their children's children talk about tapping energy from pulsars.*

Stan sat down on the convenient boulder, which had been dragged hundreds of miles only to be dropped here by the retreating glacier. It was a good place to watch late autumn's early twilight usher onstage the gauzy curtains of the aurora borealis. He loved the way the colors played across the glacier, causing its rough corrugations to undulate in time to the sizzling of supercharged ions high above. It was starting to get chilly, even in his thermal coat. Still, this was worth savoring for a while.

Stan heard a soft clunk and saw a stone roll across the sand, coming to rest near his foot. Not far away, two other rocks quivered.

Well, I guess we're at it again.

But it was more than a typical tremor. He realized this as a deep groan seemed to fill the air . . . apparently strongest toward the ice. He started to rise, but changed his mind when a sudden trembling made it hard to gain his feet. Whether it was in the ground or his legs, Stan decided to stay put.

After all, what can harm me out here in the open?

Sparkling fireflies were the next phenomenon, dancing *within* his eyes.

This must be what it's like to be near a beam when it exits, he thought bemusedly. *A level-six harmonic at about twenty kilowheelers should do it, coupling with my own body's bag of salty fluid. If the frequency dispersion isn't too . . .*

But then Stan blinked, remembering. *No beam was scheduled to exit so near—*

He didn't finish the thought. For at that moment the glacier began to glow directly opposite him, and not from any outside illumination this time. Deep inside the vast ice flow a fierce luminance throbbed. Shapes and dim outlines warped what seemed to be a series of columns, set far back in the frozen mass.

Shafts of brightness pulsed. . . .

Then the east exploded with light.

☐ Forty years ago, everyone was in a froth over the millennium. Especially many Christians, who thought surely the end of days would coincide with the two thousandth anniversary of Jesus's birth. I was one who saw portents back in '99. I, too, thought the time was at hand.

Looking back, I see how foolish I was. I thought the crises of those days were awful, but they weren't terrible enough to presage the end. Besides, we'd chosen the wrong anniversary!

After all, why should the Time come at the millennium of His *birth*? The events from Gethsemane to Crucifixion to Resurrection were what mattered then. So must the anniversary of those events! See my calculations [☐ ref. aeRle 5225790.23455 aBlE] which show beyond any doubt that it must be this very year!

No wonder we see signs everywhere! The time's at hand! It is now!

● Teresa stared at the display, watching a vivid simulation of events taking place halfway round the world. Glowing numbers told how much mass had suddenly departed the planet. She had to swallow before speaking.

"H-how did you do that?"

Alex looked up from his controls. "How does a musician play?" He cracked his knuckles. "Practice, practice."

Teresa knew better. Alex grinned, but he had a tremor under his left eye and a pale, bloodless complexion. *He's scared half out of his wits.* And who wouldn't be, after what he'd just pulled off?

"Telemetry coming in," a tech announced. "Our beam emerged on target, missing the settlement by six point two klicks, with a surface coupling impedance of eighteen kilowheelers . . . at point oh niner Hawkings, metric. That's a ninety-eight hundredths match with water ice of surface thickness . . ."

Another voice cut in. "Beat frequencies on the sixth, ninth, and twelfth harmonics, dominant. Very gentle. Maximum dynamic load during each throb-pulse never exceeding six gees . . ."

"Target trajectory calculated," a third worker announced. "On screen now."

A spot glowed on the map-globe, near the west coast of Greenland. From that point a thread of light speared radially into space. Arrow straight at first, it eventually curved as Earth's more sedate gravitostatic field grabbed the small mountain their beam had ripped from the ancient glacier. The dot representing the hurtling iceberg still moved very fast, though, and the planetary sphere had to shrink in compensation.

As if impatient with even this fleeting pace, a dashed line rushed ahead of the dot, tracing the frozen missile's predicted path. Earth diminished toward the lower left corner of the tank and into view, at the upper right, a pearly globe sedately swam onstage.

Teresa let out a cry. "You can't be serious!"

Alex tilted his head. "You object?"

"Whatever for? There's no one living on the moon." Teresa clapped her hands. "Do it, Alex! Get a bull's-eye!"

He grinned up at her and then turned back to watch as their projectile passed the halfway mark and sped on toward its rendezvous. Teresa unselfconsciously laid a hand on Alex's shoulder.

No one had ever tried to manipulate the gazer on such a scale. Sure, Glenn Spivey's people had lain instrument packages where beams were scheduled to emerge. But no one had ever made a beam couple so powerfully and purposely with surface objects. Others were sure to note how closely the beam had missed one of Spivey's resonators. They'd also notice how accurately Alex had thrown his snowball.

"Phone call from Auckland!" The communications officer announced.

Not far away, Pedro Manella made a show of consulting his watch. "The colonel's late. They must have dragged him out of bed."

"Let him wait a few minutes longer then," Alex said. "I'd rather talk to him after he's mulled things over."

Spivey must be watching a display like this now. So, no doubt, were his bosses. The dashed line filled in as the glowing pinpoint converged toward the familiar cratered face of Earth's dwarf sister. No one breathed as it accelerated and then struck the moon's northern quadrant, vanishing in a sudden, dazzling glitter of molten spray.

Manella, of course, was the first to recover his voice, though even he took some time to get around to speaking.

"Um, well, Lustig. That ought to give them pause for a day or so."

Under her hands, Teresa felt the tightness in Alex's muscles. But outwardly, for the others, he maintained an air of confident calm.

"I expect. For a day or so."

□

. . . . Our Mother, who art beneath us, whatever thy name—
You support us, nurture us, bring us the gift of life.
Hear the prayers of your children, and forgive us
    our trespasses.
Intervene on our behalf, and for those other lives, great and
    small, which suffer when we err.
Oh, Mother, we pray. Help us to face danger
    and be wise . . .

• HYDROSPHERE

I hear you, Daisy McClennon thought, as she brought together the elements she needed . . . implements bought, stolen, coerced, or designed herself during the last several hectic, sleepless days.

I hear you, she mentally told the voices vibrating, ringing, echoing across the vast chaos of the Net. *And intervene is certainly what I'm about to do.*

Oh there were those who still thought she was their tool . . . as a dog might think a man's sole purpose in life is to throw sticks and operate the can opener. But just as *their* schemes neared culmination, so would hers. And always, under buried levels and deceptions, there lie layers deeper still.

Soon, she told those who prayed electronically. *Soon you'll have release from all these worries that beset you.*

Soon you shall know truth.

PART X

PLANET

Portrait of the Earth at night.

*Even across its darkside face, the newborn planet glowed.
Upwelling magma broke its thin crust, and meteor strikes lit the
shaded hemisphere. Later, after the world ocean formed, its night
tides glistened under the moon's pearly sheen. For most of the
next two thousand million years, ruptures glowed beneath the
broad waters, and lightning offset the glistening phosphorescence
of emerging life.*

*The next phase, lasting nearly as long, featured growing
continents traced by strings of fiery volcanoes. Eventually, huge
convection cells slowed the granite promenade. And yet, Earth's
night grew brighter still. For now life draped the land with vast
forests, and the air was rich with oxygen. So flamelight illumined
a valley here, a meadow there . . . sometimes an entire plain.*

*Within the very latest time-sliver, tiny campfires appeared—
minuscule threats to evening's reign. Yet sometimes curving
scythes of grassland blazed as hunters drove panicky beasts toward
precipices.*

*Then, quite suddenly, dim smudges told of the next
innovation—towns. And when electrons were harnessed, man's
cities blossomed into glittering jewels. Nightside brightened
rapidly. Oil drillers flared off natural gas just to make easier their
suckling of deep petroleum. Fishing lights rimmed shorelines.
Settlers lay torch to rain forests. Strings of strobing, pinpoint
brilliance traced shipping lanes and air corridors.*

*There were dark wells, also. The Sahara. Tibet. The Kalahari.
In fact, the black zones grew. The methane flares flickered and
went out. So did the fishing lights.*

Cities, too, damped their extravagance. While their sprawl continued to spread, the former neon dazzle passed away like a memory of adolescence. The effervescent show wasn't quite over, but it seemed to be waning. As night moved back in, any audience could tell the finale would come soon.

But turn the dial. Look at the planet's surface, at night—in radio waves.

Brilliance! Blazing glory. The Earth seared. It shone brighter than the sun.

Perhaps it wasn't over yet, after all.

Not quite.

☐ Nation states are archaic leftovers from when each man feared the tribe over the hill, an attitude we can't afford anymore. Look at how governments are reacting to this latest mess—yammering mysterious accusations at each other while keeping the public ignorant by mutual agreement. Something's got to be done before the idiots wreck us all!

Have you heard the net talk about mass civil disobedience? Sheer chaos, of course. Not even Buddhists or NorA ChuGas can organize on such short notice. So it's just happening, all by itself! Yesterday Han tried to stop it. . . . ordered all Chinese net-links shut down, and found they couldn't! Too many alternate routings and ways to slip around choke points. The severed links just got rerouted.

So are the nation states paying heed? Hell, no. They're just doing what nationals always do—hunkering down. They say be patient. They'll tell us all about it on Tuesday. Right!

I say it's time to get rid of them, once and for all!

Only one problem, what do we replace them with?

● Crat's weighted boots were so hard to lift, he had to shuffle across
C the ocean bottom, kicking muddy plumes that settled slowly in
R his wake. Occasionally, a ray or some other muck-dwelling crea-
U ture sensed his clunking approach and took off from its hiding
S place. Still, all told, there was a lot less to see down here than he'd
T imagined.

Of course this wasn't one of the great coral reserves or shelf fisheries, where schools of hake and cod still teemed under the watchful eyes of UNEPA guardians. One of Crat's instructors told him most of the ocean had always been pretty empty. And yet there was another obvious reason he met so little life down here.

What a junkyard, he thought while moving at a steady pace. *I never figured a place so big could turn into such a sty.*

He'd seen so much man-made garbage in just the last hour . . . from rusting buckets and cans and a corroded mop handle to at least a dozen plastic bags, drifting like trademarked jellyfish, advertising discount stores and tourist shops thousands of miles away.

And then there was that kilometer-wide spew of organic refuse looking like a half-digested meal some immense creature had recently voided. Crat knew who that creature was—the Sea State floating town, which had passed this way only a little while before. Despite their nominal agreement to abide by UNEPA rules, clearly the poor folk of the barges had more urgent things to worry about than where their rubbish went. After all, the ocean seemed willing to take everything dumped into it, with nary a complaint.

The towns must leave trails like this everywhere, Crat realized. It was gross. But then, what choice did they have? The rich may worry about garbage disposal, but when you're poor your concern is getting food.

Which raised another curious question. Why was the barge-city sticking around in this area when the fishing was so poor? Crat suspected it had to do with the Company, which seemed intensely interested in this bit of continental shelf and presumably wanted to keep the floating town around as a base of operations.

Or as a cover? Crat wondered. But he had no idea how to follow up on that thought. Anyway, presumably the company men paid well for the privilege. Hard currency was hard currency, and curiosity generally a waste of time.

"Okay Courier Four. Now take a heading of niner zero degrees."

"Roger control," he answered, checking his compass and changing course. "Niner zero degrees."

Crat liked talking like an astronaut to the company comm guys. Sure, the smelly suit must have been retired as unfit for human use long ago. And it was hard work just lifting your feet to take each step. But the job had its moments. Like when the trainers actually seemed pleased and impressed with his education! That was a complete first for Crat.

Of course countless Sea State citizens were innately *smarter,* and some had much better learning. But few of those were likely to volunteer for such dangerous work. The company men spoke of his being "uniquely well qualified" for the job.

Imagine that. He'd never been well qualified for anything in his life! *I guess lots of good things can come your way, if you don't give a damn how long you live.*

"Courier Four, cut respiration rate to thirty per minute. Slow down if you have to. Site Thirteen needs your cargo for backup, but they don't expect you early."

"Aye aye." He measured his pace more carefully. Crat had decided he wanted this job after all. And that meant getting known as a team player. Another milestone for him.

During his first week they'd put him through exhaustive and exhausting tests . . . like barochambers, flooding in different gases and examining his hand-eye coordination under pressure. Then there were chem-sensitivity exams and psych profiles he was sure he'd fail, but which, apparently, he passed.

The company was engaged in a big enterprise here in the ocean southwest of Japan. Crat found out just how big when he was moved to an underwater base bustling with tech types—Japanese, Siberian, Korean, and others. There was talk of surveying and tapping nearby veins of valuable ores, a much more ambitious enterprise than just collecting manganese nodules from the open seabed. Obviously, the company was planning ahead for when nodules became scarce and therefore "protected."

Crat didn't understand most of what he overheard the engineers saying. (That was probably among the reasons he'd been hired.) But one thing was clear. If nodule harvesting was dangerous, working in deep mine shafts under half a kilometer of water would be doubly so! Not that Crat really cared. But maybe this explained the tight relationship between the corporation and this particular Sea State town—so close the floating city had even stayed put through a recent nasty storm, instead of taking shelter downwind of Kyushu. The Albatross Republic couldn't afford to abandon jobs and cash.

It was weird, working as an expendable flunky so near others who were obviously high-priced tech types with fat, company-paid insurance policies. He'd expected to be treated like a dog or worse, but actually they were a lot more polite than the bosuns on the fishing boats had been, and smelled better, too.

Only why, when they were supposed to be working on digging a mine in the ocean, was everybody so excited this morning, jabbering over maps of the *moon,* for Gaia's bleeding sake?

None of my dumpit business, I guess. And that was that.

Right now Crat was supposed to deliver his package to a company outpost ten kilometers from the main base. Apparently, it was a site so secret they didn't even visit it often by submarine, in case competitors might track the boats with satellites. Single couriers like him, slogging back and forth on foot, minimized that risk. He had no idea what lay on the carry-rack across his back, but he'd get it there on time or croak trying!

Crat reached up and tapped his helmet. A high-pitched squeal had been growing louder for the last minute or two. *So? More shitty equipment. What d'you expect?*

"Hey, Control. Can you guys do anything about the dumpit—"

"Courier Four . . . we're having . . ." Static interrupted, then surged again. ". . . better . . . ort this. . . . ssion . . ." Crat blinked. What the hell were they talking about now? He decided to play it safe. *If you don't understand what the bosses are saying, just keep work-*

*ing hard. It may not be what they wanted, but they sure can't fire
you for that!*

So he checked the helmet's gyrocompass and adjusted his heading
a bit before moving on, counting breaths as he'd been told. There were
miles to go yet, and what mattered was delivering the goods.

As he slogged, the keening in his headphones grew more intense
and oddly *musical.* Tones overlay each other, rising and falling to a
puzzling rhythm. Could this be another test, perhaps? Was he supposed to name that tune? Or were they just having fun at his expense?

"Hey, Base. You guys there? Or what?"

". . . ort and . . . back, Courier! We're exper . . . ouble . . ."

This time he stopped, feeling rising concern. He still had no idea
what the controller was saying, but it sounded bad. Crat's glove collided with his helmet as he instinctively tried to wipe away the perspiration beading his nose. He wanted to rub his eyes, which had started
itching terribly.

Suddenly it was important to remember all the warning signs he'd
been taught in cram sessions. *Nitrogen narcosis* was one danger they'd
warned of repeatedly. The suit's monitor lights showed an okay gas
balance . . . if you could trust the battered gauges. Crat checked his
pulse and found it fast but steady. He squeezed his eyes shut till they
hurt, then opened them and waited for the speckles to go away.

Only they didn't. Instead they capered and bobbed as if a swarm
of performing fireflies had gotten into his helmet. Their movements
matched the eerie music surging through his headphones.

Oh, this is too squirting weird!

A flash of gray hurtled past him. Then another, and two more.
Crat blinked. Dolphins! The last one paused to whirl around him,
catching his eye and nodding vigorously before streaking after its fellows. Crat got the eerie impression the creature had been trying to *tell*
him something, like maybe, *You better hurry, Mac, if you know
what's good for you.*

"Shit. If something down here's got *them* scared . . ."

Crat found himself scurrying after them, running as fast as he
could through the bottom muck. Soon he was panting, his heart
pounding in his chest. *I'll never keep up! Whatever's chasing them
will catch me easy!*

He tried to glance backward as he ran, but only managed to trip
over his own feet. The slow motion fall was unstoppable, ending in a
skid that plowed up streamers of turbid sediment. As he lay there,
wheezing for breath, his entire world consisted of the whining aircom-
pressors, that gor-sucking music, and some crawling thing in the mud

that bumped against his faceplate, leaving a trail of slime across the glass before disappearing into the ooze again.

Maybe I can burrow under here and hide, he thought.

But no. Cowering from a fight stuck in his craw. Better to turn and face whatever it was. Maybe dolphins are cowards, anyway.

Something occurred to Crat. *It might be some other company, wanting to hijack the thing I'm carrying. Hey! That explains all the noise! They're jamming my comm, so I can't call for help when they find me!* Obstinately, he decided, *Well, if my cargo's that important, they sure as fuck aren't gonna to get it off me!*

Crat managed to stand, raining gunk from his harness and shoulders. If the enemy were close, they'd surely pick out the noise his suit gave off and zero in on him. But maybe he could find a place to stash his cargo first! Awkwardly, he pulled the bulky package off its carryrack. One of the tech types had called it a "cylinder gimbal bearing," or whatever. All he knew was it was heavy.

Maybe . . . Crat thought as he looked around . . . maybe he could bury it and . . . hurry off, leading the bad guys away from it! But in that case he'd better put it under some landmark, so he could find it again. In a burst of slyness, he set off away from his former heading, so as not to point the way to the company's secret lab. Meanwhile Crat peered about for any useful landmark, wary for a sudden black shape—the sleek minisub of some mercenary corporate privateer.

Hurrying across the muddy plain, he caught a flicker of motion to his left. He turned, just in time to be halfblinded by a sudden shaft of brilliance that seemed to split the sea. *A searchlight! They're here!*

He sighed in frustration. Too late to bury his cargo, then. There was only one chance now. To pretend to surrender, and then, at the last moment, maybe he could destroy what he carried. Of course the only object hard enough to smash it against would be the side of the sub itself. . . . Maybe Remi or Roland could have thought up something better, he reflected, but this was the best he could come up with on short notice. Crat started walking toward the light. It was terribly bright.

Too bright, in fact. He'd never seen such a searchlight before.

Moreover, it was vertical, not horizontal. Could it be someone up above, casting about down here from the surface? But that didn't make sense!

Then Crat noticed for the first time . . . the brightness seemed to throb in tempo with the strange music flooding his helmet. *It's too big to be a searchlight,* he realized when he saw the dolphins again, cavorting around the luminous perimeter. The column was nearly a hundred meters across.

They weren't running away, after all. They were headed toward this thing! But what is it?

There was no shadow of a vessel on the surface. The brilliance had no specific source. It just was. Shuffling nearer the dazzling pillar, Crat's foot caught on something bulky in the mud. A large, black, roughly egg-shaped object. Ironically, it was one of the nodules he'd expected to be sent after when he was hired. To a Sea State citizen, it was a fabulous find. Only right now that didn't seem to matter as much as it might have only minutes ago.

The music grew more intricate and complex as he approached the beating column. Crat pictured angels singing, but even that didn't do it justice. The dolphins cried peals of exhilaration, and that somehow made him feel less afraid. They swooped, executing pirouettes just outside the shaft of brightness, squealing in counterpoint to its song.

Crat approached the shimmering boundary and stretched out one arm. He felt his blood drawn through the vessels in his hand by strange tides, returning to his heart changed with every beat. The fingertips met resistance and then passed through, tingling.

His black glove glowed in the light. He watched, dazed, as fizzing droplets hopped and danced on the rubber before evaporating in tiny cyclones. So. Within the glow there might be air . . . or vacuum . . . or something else. For sure, though, it wasn't seawater.

He felt his arm nudged. A dolphin had come alongside to watch, and the two of them shared a moment's soul-contact, each seeing glory reflected in the other's eye. Each *knowing* exactly what the other one saw. Crat couldn't help it; he grinned. Crat laughed exultantly.

Then, gently, the dolphin nudged his arm again, pushing it out of the shining beam.

Breaking contact tore at him instantly, as if something had ruptured inside. Crat sobbed at a sudden memory of his mother, who had died when he was so young, leaving him alone in a world of welfare agents and official charity. He tried to go back, to throw himself into the embrace of the light, but the dolphins wouldn't let him. They pushed him away. One thrust its bottle nose between his legs and lifted him bodily.

"Let me go!" he moaned, reaching out. But even then he heard the music climax and begin to fade. The brilliance turned golden and diminished too. Then it ended suddenly with a clap that set the ocean ringing.

In the rapid dimness, his irises couldn't adapt fast enough. He never saw water rush in to fill the empty shaft, but he and the dolphins were taken by a spinning, tumbling chaos that yanked them like bits of weed in the surf. Crat grabbed his air-hose and just held on.

When, at last, the tugging currents let him go, for a second time Crat shakily picked himself up from the muddy bottom. It took a while to look around without everything spinning. Then he realized the dolphins were gone. So too were the light, the music. Even the ringing in his ears. The stinging afterimages faded till at last he heard an insistent voice yammering.

". . . you need help? We had our comm messed up for a while. Some think maybe we were near one of those *boggle* things people are talking about. What a coincidence!

"Anyway, Courier Four, our telltales show you're all right. Please confirm."

Crat swallowed. It took some effort to relearn how to speak. "I'm . . . okay." He looked around quickly and found the cargo—only a few meters away. Crat picked it up, shaking off more muck. "Want me to start back on course?"

The voice at the other end interrupted. "Good attitude, Courier Four. But no. We're sending a sub that way anyway with some bigwigs to inaugurate Site Six. It'll pick you up shortly. Just stand by."

So he was going to get there after all . . . and Crat found that now he didn't care a bit. Standing there waiting, more than ever he wished his fingers could pass through the glass faceplate as they had briefly penetrated that shining boundary. For those few moments, his hands had sought and found his life's first real solace. Now he'd settle for just the memory of that gift, and a chance to wipe his streaming eyes.

☐ I sometimes wonder what animals think of the phenomenon of humanity —and especially of human babies. For no creature on the planet must seem anywhere near so obnoxious.

A baby screams and squalls. It urinates and defecates in all directions. It complains incessantly, filling the air with demanding cries. How human parents stand it is their own concern. But to great hunters, like lions and bears, our infants must be horrible indeed. They must seem to *taunt* them, at full volume.

"Yoo-hoo, beasties!" babies seem to cry. "Here's a toothsome morsel, utterly helpless, soft and tender. But I needn't keep quiet like the young of other species. I don't crouch silently and blend in with the grass. You can track me by my noise or smell alone, but you don't dare!

"Because my mom and dad are the toughest, meanest sumbitches ever seen, and if you come near, they'll have your hide for a rug."

All day they scream, all night they cry. Surely if animals ever held a poll, they'd call human infants the most odious of creatures. In comparison, human adults are merely very, very scary.

—Jen Wolling, from **The Earth Mother Blues**, Globe Books, 2032. [☐ hyper access 7-tEAT-687-56-1237-65p.]

● The Maori guards wouldn't let Alex go to Hanga Roa town to meet
C the stratojet, so he waited outside the resonator building. The
O afternoon was windy and he paced nervously.
R   At one point, before the incoming flight was delayed yet
E again, Teresa came by to help him pass the time. "Why is Spivey using a courier?" she asked. "Doesn't he trust his secure channels anymore?"

"Would you? Those channels go through the same sky everyone else uses. They were secure only because the military paid top dollar and kept a low profile. These days, though?" He shrugged, his point obvious without further elaboration. If this messenger carried the news he expected, it would be worth any wait.

Teresa gave his shoulder an affectionate shove. "Well, I'll bet you're glad who the courier is."

Teresa's friendship was a fine thing. She understood him. Knew how to tease him out of his frequent dour moods. Alex grinned. "And what about you, Rip? Didn't I see you eyeing that big fellow Auntie sent to cook for us."

"Oh, him." She blushed briefly. "Only for a minute or two. Come on, Alex. I told you how picky I am."

Indeed, he kept learning new levels to her complexity. Last night, for instance, they had spent hours talking as he handed her tools and she wriggled behind *Atlantis*'s panels. If things went as expected, they'd be off to Reykjavik tomorrow or the next day, to testify before the special tribunal everyone was talking about. Alex thought it only fair to give her a hand tidying up the old shuttle before that.

Back in the caves of New Zealand, it had been concentration on something external—survival—that first eased the tensions between them. Even now, Teresa found it easier to talk while straining to tighten a bolt or giving some old instrument its first taste of power in forty years. So for the first time, last night, Alex heard the full story of her prior acquaintance with June Morgan, his part-time lover. It made him feel awkward—and yet Teresa said she *liked* June now. She seemed glad the other woman was coming back, for Alex's sake.

And happier still because of what everyone assumed June would be carrying with her—Colonel Spivey's surrender.

It had been hinted in George Hutton's latest communiqué and confirmed in action. Since Alex's demonstration yesterday—blasting a mountain of ice all the way to the moon—there had been a sudden drop in aggressive activity by other gazer systems worldwide. The Nihonese still pulsed at low "research" levels, and there were brief glimmers from other locations. But the big new NATO-ANZAC-ASEAN resonators were silent, mothballed, and the original four now obeyed Alex's steady program unperturbed—pushing Beta gradually out of the boundary zone, where those intricate, superconducting threads flickered so mysteriously.

The number of pulses could be reduced now, and each beam targeted more carefully. Few additional civilian losses were expected, and diplomatic tension had been falling off for hours. Even the hysteria on the Net had abated a bit, as word went out about the new tribunal.

Maybe people are going to be sensible after all, Alex thought as he paced in front of the lab. After staying with him for a while, Teresa left again to resume her chores aboard *Atlantis.* Alex could have worked, too. But for once he was content just to look across grassy slopes toward the little, crashing baylet of Vaihu and a rank of Easter Island's famed, forbidding monoliths. Beyond the restored statues, cirrus clouds streaked high over the South Pacific, like banners shredded by stratospheric winds.

This place had affected him, all right. Here earlier men and women had also struggled bitterly against the consequences of their own mistakes. But Alex's education on Rapa Nui went beyond mere historical comparisons. Because of the nature of the battle he had waged here, he now knew far better than before how those winds and clouds out there were influenced by sunlight and the sea, and by other forces generated deep below. Each was part of a natural web only hinted at by what you saw with your eyes.

Jen was right, he thought. *Everything is interwoven.*

One didn't have to be mystical about the interconnectedness. It just *was.* Science only made the fact more vivid and clear, the more you learned.

A touch of sound wafted from the direction of Rano Kao's stern cliffs—first the whine of a hydrogen auto engine and then the complaint of rubber tires turning on gravel. He turned to see a car approach the Hine-marama cordon, where big, brown men paced with drawn weapons. After questioning both driver and passenger, they waved the vehicle through. Its fuel cells whistled louder as it climbed the hill and finally pulled up near the front door.

June Morgan bounded out, the wind whipping her hair and bright blue skirt. He met her halfway as she ran to throw her arms around him. "Kiss me quick, you troublemaker, you." He obliged with some pleasure, though Alex sensed a tremor of tension as he held her. Well, that was understandable of course.

"You put on some show, hombre!" she said, pulling away. "Here Glenn and his people spend weeks studying gazer-based launching, and you yank the rug right out from under him! I laughed so hard . . . after leaving the room of course."

Alex smiled. "Did you bring his answer?"

"Now what other reason would I have to come all this way?" She winked and patted her briefcase. "Come on, I'll show you."

Alex asked the driver to go fetch Teresa as June took his arm and pulled him toward the entrance. There, however, the way was barred by a massive dark man with crossed arms. "Sorry, doctor," he told June. "I must inspect your valise."

Alex sighed. "Joey, your men sniffed her luggage at the airport. She's not carrying a bomb, for heaven's sake."

"All the same, *tohunga*, I have orders. Especially after last time."

Alex frowned. The first sabotage attempt still had them perplexed. Spivey vehemently denied involvement, and the saboteur himself seemed to have no links at all to NATO or ANZAC.

"That's all right." June laid the briefcase flat in the arms of one big guard and flipped it open. Inside were several pouched datacubes, two reading plaques, and a few slim sheets of paper in a folder. Auntie Kapur's men ran humming instruments over the contents while June chattered animatedly. "You should have seen George Hutton's face when he heard Manella had shown up here! He started out both angry and delighted, and finally settled on plain confusion. And you know how George hates that!"

"Indeed I do, madam."

June and Alex turned as a figure approached from within. Nearly as tall as the Maori guards, and much heavier, Pedro Manella came into the sunlight holding out his hand. "Hello, Doctor Morgan. You bring good tidings, I assume?"

"Of course," she replied. "And aren't you a sight, Pedro! Wherever you've been hiding yourself, you've certainly eaten well."

The second guard returned June's valise. Alex said, "Let's go to my office and play the message."

"Why such privacy?" June pulled the other way. "We'll use my old station. Everyone should hear this."

The huge perovskite cylinder looked like some giant artillery piece, delicately balanced on its perfect bearings. It towered over what had once been June's console—back when a dozen or so fatigued workers first set up here on the flank of a rocky, weather-beaten isle, searching desperately for a way to beard a monster in its den. The tech who had been working at that post cheerfully made room.

"Here it is," June said, pulling a cube from its pouch and tossing it to Alex playfully. She insisted he take the seat. A semicircle of watchers gathered as he slotted the cube. Someone from the kitchen handed out cups of coffee, and when everyone was settled, Alex touched the PLAY toggle.

A man in uniform appeared before them, seated at a desk. His hair had grown out, softening somewhat those harsh, scarred features. Glenn Spivey looked out at them as if in real time. He even seemed to track his audience with his eyes.

"Well, Lustig," the colonel began. "It seems people keep underestimating you. I'll never do it again." He lifted both hands. "You win. No more delays. The president met with our alliance partners. Tonight they hand over control of all resonators to the new tribunal—"

The technicians behind Alex clapped and sighed in relief. After all these wearing months, a heavy weight seemed lifted.

"—gathering in Iceland, headed by Professor Jaime Jordelian. I think you know him."

Alex nodded. As a physicist, Jordelian was stodgy and overly meticulous. But those could be good traits in such a role.

"The committee hasn't formally met, but Jordelian urgently asked that you attend the opening session. He wants you in operational charge of all resonators for an initial period of six months or so. They also want you center stage for the first news conference. If you've been watching the Net, you know what an all-day session that will be! The hypersonic packet that brought Dr. Morgan has orders to wait at Hanga Roa for your convenience."

"Lucky bastard," one of the Kiwis muttered in mock envy. "Iceland in winter. Dress warm, *tohunga*." Alex broke into a grin. "Hey, what about me?" June complained. "You take my transport and I'm stuck here!" The others made sounds of mock sympathy.

Spivey's image paused. He cleared his throat and leaned forward a little.

"I won't pretend we haven't been surprised by events these last few weeks, doctor. I thought we could finish our experiments long before word leaked out. But things didn't go according to plan.

"It wasn't just your little demonstration, yesterday, which nearly every-

one in the Western Hemisphere got to witness by naked eye. Even neglecting
that, there were just too many bright people out there with their own instruments and souped-up ferret programs." He shrugged. "I guess we should
have known better.

"What really disturbs me, though, is what I hear people saying about our
intentions. Despite all the innuendo, you must believe I'm no screaming
jingoist. I mean, honestly, could I have persuaded so many decent men and
women—not just Yanks and Canadians, but Kiwis and Indonesians and others
—to take part if our sole purpose was to invent some sort of super doomsday
weapon? The idea's absurd.

"I now see I should have confided in you. My mistake, taking you for a
narrowly focused intellectual. Instead, I found myself outfought by a warrior,
in the larger sense of the word." He smiled ruefully. "So much for the
accuracy of our dossiers."

Alex sensed the others' silent regard. Eyes flicked in his direction.
He felt unnerved by all this talk centering on him personally.

"So, you might ask, what was our motive?" Spivey sighed. "What
could *any* honest person's goal be, these days? What else could ever matter as
much as saving the world?

"Surely you've seen those economic-ecological projections everyone
plays with on the Net? Well, Washington's had a really excellent trends-
analysis program for two decades now, but the results were just too appalling
to release. We even managed to discredit the inevitable leaks, to prevent widespread discouragement and nihilism.

"Put simply, calculations show our present stable situation lasting maybe
another generation, tops. Then we all go straight to hell. Oblivion. The only
way out seemed to demand drastic sacrifice . . . draconian population control measures combined with major and immediate cuts in standard of living.
And psych profiles showed the voters utterly rejecting such measures, especially if the outcome would at best only help their great-grandkids.

"Then you came along, Lustig, to show that our projection missed some
critical information . . . like the little item that our world is under attack by
aliens!

"More important, you showed how new, completely unexpected levers
might be applied to the physical world. New ways of exerting energy. New
dangers to frighten us and new possibilities to dazzle. In another age, these
powers would have been seized by bold men and used for better or worse, like
TwenCen's flirtation with the atom.

"But we're *growing up* . . . that's the popular phrase, isn't it? We know
new technologies must be watched carefully. I'm not totally against the science tribunals. Who could be?

"Tell me, though, Lustig, what do you think the new committee will do
when they take authority over the new science of gazerdynamics?"

Obviously, the question was rhetorical. Alex already saw the colonel's point.

"Except for one or two small research sites, they'll slap on a complete ban, with fierce inspections to make sure nobody else emits even a single graviton! They'll let you keep vigil on Beta, but outlaw any other gazer use that hasn't already been tested to death. Oh sure, that'll prevent chaos. I agree the technology has to be monitored. But can you see why we wanted to *delay* it for a while?"

Spivey pressed both hands on his desk.

"We hoped to finish developing gazer-based launch systems, first! If they were *already* proven safe and effective, the tribunes couldn't ban them entirely. We'd save something precious and wonderful . . . perhaps even a way out of the doomsday trap."

Alex exhaled a sigh. Teresa should hear this. She despised Spivey. And yet he turned out to be as much a believer as she. Apparently the infection went all the way to the pinnacles of power.

"Our projections say resource depletion is going to kill human civilization deader than triceratops—this poor planet's gifts have been so badly squandered. But everything changes if you include space! Melt down just one of the millions of small asteroids out there, and you get all the world's steel needs for an entire decade, plus enough gold, silver, and platinum to finance rebuilding a dozen cities!

"It's all out there, Lustig, but we're stuck here at the bottom of Earth's gravity well. It's so expensive to haul out the tools needed to *begin* harnessing those assets. . . .

"Then came your gazer thing. . . . Good God, Lustig, have you any idea what you did yesterday? Throwing megatons of *ice* to the moon?" A vein pulsed in Spivey's temple. "If you'd landed that berg just ten percent slower, there'd have been water enough to feed and bathe and make productive a colony of hundreds! We could be mining lunar titanium and helium-3 inside a year! We could . . ."

Spivey paused for breath.

"A few years ago I talked several space powers into backing cavitronics research in orbit, to look for something like what you found by goddam accident! But we were thinking millions of times too small. Please forgive my obvious jealousy . . ."

Someone behind Alex muttered, "Jesus Christ!" He turned to see Teresa Tikhana standing behind him. Her face was pale, and Alex thought he knew why. So her husband hadn't worked on weapons research after all. He had just been trying, in his own way, to help save the world.

There would be some poignant satisfaction for her in that, but also bitterness, and the memory that they had not parted in harmony.

Alex reached back and took her hand, which trembled, then squeezed his tightly in return.

". . . I guess what I'm asking is that you use your influence with the tribunal—and it will be substantial—to keep some effort going into launch systems. At least get them to let you throw more ice!"

Spivey leaned even closer to the camera.

"After all, it's not enough just to neutralize some paranoid aliens' damned berserker device. What's the point, if it all goes into a toxic-dumpit anyway?

" But this thing could be the key to saving everything, the ecology . . ."

Alex was rapt, mesmerized by the man's unexpected intensity, and he felt Teresa's flushed emotion as well. So they both flinched in reflex surprise when somebody behind them let out a blood-chilling scream.

"Give that back!"

Everyone turned, and Alex blinked to see June Morgan waging an uneven struggle with . . . Pedro Manella! The blonde woman hauled at her briefcase, which the Aztlan reporter clutched in one meaty hand, fending her off with the other. When she kicked him, Pedro winced but gave no ground. Meanwhile, Colonel Spivey droned on.

". . . creating the very wealth that makes for generosity, and incidentally giving us the stars . . ."

Alex stood up. "Manella! What are you doing!"

"He's stealing my valise!" June yelled. "He wants my data so he can scoop tonight's presidential speech!"

Alex sighed. That sounded like Manella, all right. "Pedro," he began. "You've already got an inside story any reporter would die for—"

Manella interrupted. "Lustig, you better have a—" He stopped with a gulp as June swiveled full circle to elbow him sharply below the sternum, then stamped on his foot and snatched the briefcase during her follow-through. But then, instead of rejoining the others, she spun about and ran away!

"S-stop her!" Pedro gasped. Something in his alarmed voice turned Alex's heart cold. June held the valise in front of her, sprinting toward the towering resonator. "A bomb?" Teresa blurted, while Alex thought, *But they checked for bombs!*

At another level he simply couldn't believe this was happening. *June?*

She leaped the railing surrounding the massive resonator, ducked under the snatching arm of a Maori security man, and launched herself toward the gleaming cylinder. At the final instant, another guard seized her waist, but June's expression said it was already too late. People dove for cover as she yanked a hidden lever near the handle.

Alex winced, bracing for a sledgehammer blow. . . .

But nothing happened!

In the stunned silence, Glenn Spivey's voice rambled on.

". . . so with this message I'm sending a library of all the surface-coupling coefficients we've collected. Naturally, you're ahead of us in most ways, but we've learned a few tricks too . . ."

June's face flashed from triumph to astonishment to rage. She cursed, pounding the valise until it was dragged from her hands and hustled outside by some brave and very fleet security men. It was Pedro, then, who finally wrestled her away from the resonator and forced her into a chair. Alex switched off the sound of the colonel's words, which now, suddenly, seemed mockingly irrelevant.

"So this was all a hoax, June? Spivey holds our attention while you sabotage the thumper?" His pulse pounded. To be deceived by the military man's apparent sincerity was nothing next to the treachery of this woman he thought he knew.

"Oh Alex, you're such a fool!" June laughed breathlessly and with a note of shrill overcompensation. "You can be sweet and I like you a lot. But how did you ever get to be so gullible?"

"Shut up," Teresa said evenly, and though her tone was business-like, June clearly saw dark threat in Teresa's eyes. She shut up. They all waited silently for the security team to report. It seemed better to let adrenaline stop drumming in their ears before dealing with this unexpected enormity.

Joey came back shortly, bowing his head in apology. "No bomb after all, *tohunga*. It's a liquid-suspension catalyst—a simple nanotech corrosion promoter—probably tailored to wreck the thumper's piezogravitic characteristics. The stuff was supposed to spray when she pulled the lever, but the holes had been squished shut, so nothing came out. A lucky break. Lucky our reporter friend's so strong." Joey gestured toward Manella, who blinked in apparent surprise.

"His hand print covers the holes," Joey explained. "Broke the hinge, too. Don't nobody challenge that guy to a wrestling match."

June shrugged when they all looked at her. "I got the idea from those scrubber enzymes Teresa keeps asking for, to clean her old shuttle. Your guards grew used to me bringing chemicals in little packages. Anyway, just a few drops would put you out of business. It takes days to grow a new resonator—all the time my employers needed."

"You're not trying to hold back much, are you?" Teresa asked.

"Why should I? If they don't get my success code soon, they'll assume I failed and shut you down by other means . . . a lot more violent than I tried to use! That's why I volunteered to do this. You're my friends. I don't want you hurt."

The murmuring techs obviously thought her statement bitterly ironic. And yet, at one level Alex believed her. *Maybe I have to believe someone I've made love to cares about me . . . even if she turns betrayer for other reasons.*

"They agreed to let me say this much if I failed," June went on intensely. "To convince you to give up. Please, Alex, everybody, take my word for it. You've no idea who you're up against!"

Someone brought a chair for Alex. He knew he must look drawn and unsteady, but going passive would be a mistake right now. He remained standing.

"What's your success code? How would you tell them you'd succeeded?"

"You were planning to phone Spivey after hearing his pitch, no? I was to slip in a few words, to be overheard by my contact there—"

"What? You mean Spivey's not your real boss?"

June's eyes flicked away before returning to meet his. "What do you mean?" she asked a little too quickly. "Of course he's . . ."

"Wait," Pedro Manella interrupted. "You're right, Alex. Something's fishy." He moved closer to glower over June. "What did you mean when you said, 'You have no idea who you're up against'? You weren't just speaking figuratively, were you? I think you meant it quite literally."

June attempted nonchalance. "Did I?"

Pedro rubbed his hands. "I spent two months interviewing that kidnapper-torturer in London. You know, the one who called himself the 'father confessor of Knightsbridge'? I learned a lot about *persuasion techniques*, writing that book. Does anyone have any bamboo shoots? Or we'll make do with what's in the kitchen."

June laughed contemptuously. "You wouldn't dare." But her uncertainty grew apparent when she met Manella's eyes.

"What do you mean, Pedro?" Teresa asked. "You think Spivey was telling the truth? That he's as much a dupe as—as we've been?"

Alex appreciated her use of the plural. Of course, he deserved singling out as paramount dupe.

"You're the astronaut, Captain," Manella answered. "Did the colonel's purported passion for new launch systems make sense? Given what you know about him?"

Teresa nodded grudgingly. "Y-e-e-s. Of course, maybe I want to believe. It makes Jason's last work more noble. It means our leaders aren't just TwenCen-style, nationalist assholes, but were trying a plan, however misguided—" She shook her head. "Glenn sounded sincere. But I just can't say."

"Well, there's something else a lot less subjective, and that's the question of why? What motive could Spivey and his bosses have to put this site out of business, if everything comes under international jurisdiction tonight anyway?"

"There's only one reason possible," Alex answered. "If taking us out was part of a scheme to *stop* those controls. Spivey admitted he didn't want them."

Teresa shook her head again. "No! He said he wanted them *delayed*, till gazer space launching was proven. But remember, he accepted the principle of long-term supervision." Her brow furrowed. "Alex, none of this makes sense!"

He agreed. "What could anyone gain by causing turmoil now? If the president's speech doesn't disclose all, the Net will explode."

"Not just the Net," Manella added. "There will be chaos, strikes . . . and a gravity laser arms race. Poor nations and major corporations will blow city blocks out of their rivals' capitals, or set off earthquakes or—" He shook his head. "Who on Earth could profit from such a situation?"

"Not Glenn Spivey," Teresa affirmed, now with complete certainty.

"Nor any of the space powers," Alex put in.

One of the techs asked, "Who does that leave, then?" They regarded June Morgan, who scanned the circle of nervous faces and sighed. "You're all so smart, so modern. You've got your info-plaques and percomps and loyal little ferret programs to go fetch data for you. But what information? Only what's *in* the Net, my dears."

Alex frowned. "What are you talking about?"

She glanced at her watch, nervously. "Look, I was supposed to report in well before this. At any moment, my—masters—will know I've failed, and move to settle things more dramatically. Please, Alex. Let me finish my job and call them—"

She was interrupted by a sudden, blaring alarm from one of the consoles. A technician rushed over to read its display. "I'm getting hunt resonance from two—no, three—large thumpers . . . in the Sahara, Canada, and somewhere in Siberia!"

June stood up, pulling when a guard grabbed her arm. "Too late. They must be getting nervous. Alex please, get everybody out of here!"

Teresa pushed close to the blond woman. "Who do you mean, they? I say we let Pedro do it his way . . ." She glanced to one side, but Alex was no longer there.

"Give me a projected resonance series for that combination!" he demanded, throwing himself into his work seat, slipping the subvocal device over his head. "Zoom onto the mantle-core boundary under Beta. Show me any likely power threads."

"Putting it on now, *tohunga*."

The recorded message had frozen on its last frame— depicting a hopeful-looking Glenn Spivey smiling into the camera. That image now vanished, replaced by the familiar cutaway Earth, resplendent in fiery complexity. From three northern points at its surface, pulsing columns of light thrust inward toward a rendezvous far below. The dot where they converged wavered as the beams kept sliding off each other.

"I've never seen those sites before," one Tangoparu scientist said. But another commented, "I . . . think I might've. A couple of quick pulses yesterday, just after we hit the glacier. But the traces looked like those strange surface echoes we've been getting, so I assumed . . ."

To a trained eye, the intruder beams could be seen hunting for alignment in the energized, field-rich lower mantle. The Beta singularity, still orbiting through the enigmatic electricity of those zones, obliged by serving as their mirror, focusing the combined effort. The purple dot shimmered.

"They're less experienced," somebody near Alex muttered. "But they know what they're doing."

"Extrapolating now. . . . Gaia!" The first tech cried out. "The amplified beam's going to come this way!"

Alex was too busy to turn his head, which would throw off the subvocal anyway. Using the delicate input device was a lot like running full tilt along a tightrope. Ironically, it was easier to order up a simulated image of his face than to use his own voice to shout a warning.

"Rip!" the imitation self cried out as he worked. "Get everyone but the controllers out of here. Take them west, you hear? West!"

Someone else might have had some romantic impulse to argue, but not Teresa. She'd evaluate the situation, decide there was little she could do here to help, and obey without hesitation. Sure enough, Alex heard her voice of command driving the others outside leaving his truncated team to work in relative peace.

The peace of a battlefield. Alex sensed the big, cylindrical resonator swing about at his command and begin throbbing its own contribution to a struggle being joined thousands of kilometers below. There followed something like a gravitational fencing match—his own beam countering and parrying the opposing three as they attempted to unite. Bouncing off Beta's sparkling mirror, they passed through threadlike filigrees of transient superconductivity, which of late had taken on new orders of intricacy, rising from the core boundary in gauzy loops and splendid, shimmering bows.

Some time ago, Alex had likened the loops to "prominences"— those arcs of plasma one saw along the sun's limb during an eclipse, which drove fierce currents from the star's surface into space. Similar laws applied near the Earth's core, though on vastly different scales. The comparison would have been interesting to contemplate if he weren't busy fighting to save their lives.

Thousands of the mysterious strands vibrated as fingers of tuned gravity plucked them, stimulating the release of pent-up energy. Some rays scattered off Beta, sending augmented flashes spiraling randomly. There was no time to wonder how his opponents had learned to do this so quickly, or even who they were. Alex was too busy fending off their beams, preventing them from combining to create something coherent and cohesive and lethal.

Alex watched more and more shimmering filaments pulsate in time to his rhythms. Other flashes sparkled to the melodies of his unknown foes. Each flicker represented some great expanse of semimolten rock, millions of tons altering state at the whim of entities far above.

"We can't hold them much longer!" One of the techs cried out.

"Wait! We have to work together," Alex urged. "What if—"

He stopped talking abruptly as ripples flowed across the display, and the subvocal sent his amplified speech throbbing deep into the Earth's interior. Alex switched to communicating with slight tremors in his larynx, letting the machine transmit a message to the others.

Take a look at this! He urged, and caused the Easter Island resonator to suddenly draw back from the acherontic struggle.

His opponents' beams floundered in the abrupt lack of resistance, momentarily discomfited in overcompensation. Then, as if unable to believe the way was now clear, the three columns came together again tentatively.

Everybody else . . . out! He commanded. I'll take it from here!

He heard chairs squeak and topple as his assistants took him at his word. Footsteps scrambled for the door. "Don't wait too long, Alex!" someone shouted. But his attention was already focused as it never had been before. The enemy beams touched Beta, hunted, and at last found their resonance.

At that same moment, though, Alex felt a strange, fey oneness with the monster singularity. No matter how much the enemy must have learned—no doubt by snooping his files—still knew Beta better than any living man!

If I wait till the very last millisecond . . .

Of course no human could control the beam with such fineness. Not in real time. So he chose his counterstroke in advance and delegated a program to act on his behalf. There was no chance to double-check the code.

Go! He unleashed his surrogate warrior at the last possible moment. Behind him, the resonator seemed to yowl an angry, almost feline battle cry.

It was already too late to flee. Alex quashed the adrenaline rush—a reaction inherited from ancient days when his ancestors used to seek out danger with their own eyes, meeting it with the power of their own limbs and their own tenacious wills. The last of these, at least, was valid still. He forced himself to wait calmly through the final fractions of a second, as fate came bulling toward him from the bowels of the Earth.

□

The Snake River Plain stretches, desolate and lined with cinder cones, from the Cascades all the way to Yellowstone, where outcrops of pale rhyolite gave the great park its name. As near Hawaii and several other places, a fierce needle here replaced the mantle's normal, placid convection. Something slender and hot enough to melt granite had worked its way under the North American Plate, taking several million years to cut the wide valley.

That pace was quick, in geologic terms. But there was no law that said things could not go faster still.

● They stopped running a kilometer or so to the west, but not be-
E cause it was safe. No amount of distance offered protection against
X what might now be hurtling their way.
O No, they halted because sedentary intellectuals could only
S run so far. Teresa took some satisfaction watching June Morgan
P pant, pale and winded. The woman was in pathetic shape. *Serves*
H *her right,* she thought, rationing herself a small dollop of catti-
E ness. Since she was in charge, Teresa counted heads and quickly
R came up short.
E Manella. Damn! She turned to the Maori security chief,

"Keep everyone here, Joey. I'm going after Pedro. The jerk's probably recording it all for posterity!"

She finished the thought as she ran downhill. *Recording what it's like to be at ground zero. The only ones to view his tape may be ETs at some distant star!*

Halfway to the resonator building, she saw a dozen men and women suddenly spill into the late-afternoon sunlight, tripping and scrambling as they fled her way. *Good. Alex shouldn't have stayed in the first place.*

Then she realized that neither Pedro nor Alex was among them. "Shit!"

Now she sprinted, rushing past the fleeing technicians so quickly they seemed to blur. But then, the blurring wasn't entirely an effect of motion. A tingling in her eyeballs and sinuses barely preceded a sharp ringing in her ears, which grew until church carillons seemed to boom around her. Even the dry grass bent and swayed to the pealing notes. Her feet danced of their own accord across the shifting surface.

The next thing Teresa knew, she had tumbled to the ground and was having a terrible time figuring out which way was up. It felt as if the earth had dropped away beneath her. Strong winds whipped at her clothes.

Is it my turn to go, then? The way Jason did?

Maybe I can stay conscious long enough to see the stars. To see my ultimate trajectory before I pass out.

She drew a deep breath, preparing to meet the sky.

But then the whirling seemed to settle. Teresa felt sharp-stemmed blades of grass cut her fingers as she clutched the stony soil. Her next hasty breath felt no thinner. Lifting her head despite a roaring vertigo, she saw a tipped slope, a patch of sea . . . and a great horrible face!

One of the giant statues, she realized in an instant. She'd fallen near some of the aboriginal monuments. More monoliths came into view as her visual distortions shifted from focus over to color.

Now everything was clear, crisp, but *tinted* in a flux of unaccustomed hues—eerie shades that surged and rippled across a much enlarged spectrum. Somehow, Teresa knew she must be seeing directly in the infrared, or ultraviolet, or other weird bands never meant for human eyes. The effect encouraged illusions . . . that the row of statues were trembling, shaking, like ancient sleeping gods answering an Olympian alarm.

It was no illusion! Four of the massive sculptures *wrenched* free of their platform. Soot blew away as they vibrated free of centuries' accumulated dross. Gleaming now, they rotated toward her.

Teresa shivered, remembering Alex's description of his own fey insight under a lightning storm, when he first realized that other hands than human might have crafted Beta's malign intricacy. *Could that be it?* she wondered. *Could June be working for our alien enemies? If they're here in person, what chance did we ever have?*

In the bizarre pulse-bunching that characterized some gazer beams, the giant statues seemed to pause, circling round a common center. But even as they did a languid dance, she sensed another, more powerful beat gathering below. Teresa tried to move her arms and legs to flee, but suddenly she was pressed to the ground as if by a giant's hand. Tides coursed her innards, pressing her liver against her pounding heart. A cry escaped her open mouth like a soul prying its way out.

That force passed just before she thought she might burst. Teresa blinked through nausea and saw that the statues had disappeared. Into their hasty absence, a cyclone of angry air blew, just as the gravitational pulse tail left her abruptly with no weight at all.

The familiar sensation might have felt pleasantly like spaceflight, but she quickly saw where the wind was tossing her . . . toward a deep cavity where the stony gods had formerly stood! She clawed at the dirt and grass, grabbing at any purchase as a midget hurricane dragged her toward the pit—deep and gleamingly oval. Her feet passed over empty space, then her legs, her hips. Desperately she cried out as her fingers lost contact . . .

Suddenly she flapped like a flag in the gale—but did not fall. At the last moment, one outstretched arm had caught on something.

Or something had caught her! Twisting, she saw a beefy hand clamped round her wrist. The hand led to an arm and massive shoulders . . . merging with the head and face of Pedro Manella.

The storm ended as quickly as it had started. Aerodynamic lift vanished like a bed dropping out from under her, releasing her to fall in a horrible arc. The glass-smooth wall struck her a blow, setting off dazzling waves of pain.

Consciousness wavered, but the insults didn't end there. Her arm was yanked again and again, in rhythmic heaves that hurt like hell as she felt herself drawn upward, slowly upward, to the precipice, over the glazed, cutting edge, and then finally onto the rough basalt-gravel surface of Rapa Nui.

At last, somehow, she and Pedro lay next to each other, gasping in exhaustion.

"I . . . saw Lustig succeed . . . diverting their beam," Manella explained. "He couldn't push it all the way to sea . . . so I came outside to watch.

"Then I saw you falling . . ."

Teresa touched the big reporter's arm. He didn't have to explain further. "So—" She inhaled deeply a few more times, blinking away blurriness. "So Alex did it."

Then, with more enthusiasm, she rolled over onto her stomach and laughed, hitting the ground. "He *did* it!"

Pedro commented. "Yeah. I'm sure sorry—"

Teresa sat up. "Sorry! What are you sorry about?"

Manella stared at the pit he'd just pulled her from. "That wind tore off my True-Vu. I wonder how far down this thing . . ." He shook his head and turned to face her. "But no. What I meant was that I'm sorry for the *other* guys. They're in for a rough time, I bet, now that it's Lustig's turn to fight back."

Teresa glanced toward the resonator building where Alex labored on all alone. Just uphill though, she saw a cascade of Tangoparu engineers, running to rejoin their *tohunga,* looking mortified at having left his side during a battle. Teresa doubted it would ever happen again.

In the rear, security guards escorted June Morgan, who stared about in mute surprise, much to Teresa's satisfaction. "Come on, Pedro," she told the big reporter, offering her hand. "You can search for your recorder later. First let's see if we can be of any use."

□

In Yellowstone Park, tourists pose near steaming geysers. All around them stretch cinder cones and other testaments to the land's violent past. And yet, they don't see any of it really relating to them. After all, those things happened a long, long time ago.

Today, however, the Old Faithful geyser surprises them. Instead of steam, wet and clear, what comes out at the appointed time glows white hot and molten.

It is quite a show, indeed. More, perhaps, than the visitors ever bargained for.

● As time passed, it was only the outline—the warp and weft— that remained hers alone. As for the rest, it became a collage, a synthesis of many contributions. Though Jen's daring model of the essential processes of thought grew more complicated with each added element, most of its newest pieces now came bobbing out of the capacious well of the Net itself.

Some bits were brought home by her ferrets. But lately, the little software emissaries kept getting lost in the worried maelstrom surging through the world's data hubs. The help she got now came mostly in real time, from real men and women—coworkers and colleagues who knew her access codes and had begun by merely eavesdropping on her work, but soon, intrigued, started offering suggestions as well.

Li Xieng of Shanghai had been first to speak up—after watching her model build for hours before making his presence known. Apologetically, he pointed out a flaw that would have stymied her if left uncorrected. Fortunately, he had a convenient solution ready at hand.

Old Russum of the University of Prague logged in next with a recommendation, and then Pauline Cockerel in London. After that, rumors spread with the eager pace of electrons, drawing attention from specialists across the globe. Helpful suggestions began arriving faster than Jen could scan them, so she deputized to surrogates—both living and simulated—the job of culling wheat from chaff.

Of course this was no more than a ripple in the tide of anxious comment right now sweeping the Net. Jen knew she and the others were being self-indulgent. Perhaps they oughtn't to be concentrating so single-mindedly on an abstract model while all channels crackled with angst over matters of planetary survival. They should pay attention to the pronouncements of presidents and general secretaries and all the multichanneled pundits.

And yet, moments like this came so seldom in science. Mostly, a researcher's work was a daily grind no less than the toil of a baker or grocer. Now and then though, something glorious happened—a *paradigm shift*, or theoretical revolution. Jen and the others were caught in the momentum of creative breakthrough. No one knew how long the burst of synthesis would last, but for now the whole was far greater than the sum of its parts.

. . . PRECONSCIOUS CULLING OF SEMI-RANDOM MEMORY ASSOCIATIONS CANNOT BE TOO STRICT, Li Xieng commented in a line of bright letters to her upper left. AFTER ALL, WHAT WOULD CONSCIOUSNESS BE WITHOUT THOSE SUDDEN LITTLE MEMORIES AND IMPULSES, APPARENTLY SO RANDOM, BUT . . .

Li's comment wasn't particularly important in itself. But the software bundle accompanying them was. A quick simulation test showed it wouldn't hurt the big model, and just might add to its overall flexibility. So she spliced it to the growing whole and moved on.

A contribution from one of the Bell Labs arrived, bearing Pauline Cockerel's chop of approval. Jen was about to evaluate it for herself when a sudden swirl of garish color drew her attention to the screen on the far left.

It was that bloody tiger again! Jen couldn't figure out what the thing represented or why it persisted so. Or why it looked more battle worn each time she saw it. A while ago she had assigned the symbol to serve as an icon for her protection-sieve program, guarding this computer nexus from any outsiders trying to interfere without permission. But by now her data domain was so much larger, it seemed in retrospect a trivial precaution.

The tiger really was looking rather the worse for wear. It's fur even *smoked* along one flank, as if seared by some terrible flame. Bleeding wounds seemed to trace the recent work of raking talons. And yet it rumbled defiantly, turning now and then to glare at something lurking just off screen.

The metaphorical meaning struck Jen even in her distracted state. Somewhere, out in the pseudoreality of the Net, something or someone was trying to get in, and it wasn't one of her colleagues.

Who, then? Or what?

As if answering her query, the tiger raised a paw. Impaled on one claw shimmered what looked like a glistening *lizard's* scale . . .

Jen shook her head. She hadn't time for trivialities. Her model kept growing, building impetus. It took all her attention now just to ride along, guiding here, adjusting there. . . .

"—have to ask you to return the memory and processors you've borrowed, Dr. Wolling. Do you read me? This is a crisis! We've heard from Alex that—"

The new voice was Kenda, yammering by intercom. Irritably, she wiped the circuit. Of all times for that bloody man to interrupt! Jen had far too little computer memory as it was! She'd even taken advantage of the Ndebele and appropriated space in Kuwenezi Canton's city computers. Thank heavens it was nighttime outside. By morning it might all be finished, before she had to deal with swarms of irate administrators.

Somewhere in the real world, she vaguely heard Kenda and his crew shouting at each other, struggling to bring their big resonator on line with abrupt speed. But Jen was barely *of* the real world anymore. Through her subvocal and with delicate finger controls, she created hungry little programs—surrogates designed on the spur of the moment to go forth and *get* more memory, wherever it could be found, commandeering it on any pretext and hang the ultimate expense! Any storage and computing charges would be recouped a million times over if this worked!

This was no job for mere ferrets or hounds. She needed something tenacious that wouldn't take no for an answer. So the new surrogates she pictured as tiny versions of *herself,* and laughed at the image her computer drew from memory—an old book-jacket photo depicting her in an earth-colored sari at some Gaian ritual, wearing a smile of maternally patient, absolute determination.

The self-icons were intimidating, all right. A crowd of unstoppable old ladies gathered in the central holo near the main cluster, ready to go forth and find more room for the growing model.

Then, just as she was about to unleash them, the bottom fell out.

If there really had been such a thing as direct mind-to-machine linkage, Jen might have died at that moment. Even connected by mere holo screens and subvocal, she felt it as a physical blow. In the span of three heartbeats, everything in her console was *sucked out* and sent streaming along high-rate data lines toward . . . heaven only knew where!

Her breath caught as she watched in utter dismay. Her surrogates, her subroutines, her colleagues' comments—the *whole damned model* poured away like bath water down a thirsty drain! The intricate, interlaced patterns that only moments ago had surrounded her now whirled and vanished into an awful hole.

Nearly last to go was her tiger. Yowling in complaint, it dug in its claws, laying phosphor trails across one screen after another as it was dragged toward the abyss.

From the far left, another simulated creature entered into view as the tiger left—this one larger and even more stunningly formidable. In an instant's numb understanding Jen knew this to be the software entity her cat had been fighting—a thing that had gotten in at last, only to be swept along with everything else into the void. The fearsome dragon hissed and roared at her, waving a glittering scorpion's tail as that bizarre suction hauled it, too, into oblivion.

Jen blinked. In a half moment it was over. She punched reset keys, and instantly her displays came alight again, but not a shred of her own work remained. Instead there shone great glowing swathes of the Earth's interior—the cutaway view used by the resonator team.

So this was no power failure. It hadn't struck the Tangoparu group's programs, only hers!

"Kenda!" she screamed. "What have you done!"

Memory. She vaguely recalled Kenda demanding back the computer caches she'd borrowed. Why, the awful man must have taken it on himself to *seize* it, sending her model straight to Hades in the process!

"You bastard, Kenda. When I get my hands on you . . ."

For the first time in hours she drew her eyes away from the screens and peered around the console toward where the others kept watch over mere magma and mantle, crust and core. The big resonator glistened, suspended in its frictionless bearings. Lights shone at all the other stations.

But there was no one in sight. No living human being.

"Kenda? . . . Jimmy? . . . Anybody?" She swept off the subvocal and was suddenly immersed in real sound again. Foremost came a loud whoop-whoop she recalled hearing once before, back when she and the Kiwis had first set up in these abandoned mines, when Kenda had insisted on running all those bloody drills.

The evacuation alarm.

She found it hard to think, having been ripped so untimely out of a deep and glorious meditative state. Jen mourned her beautiful model. So it was only with passing seconds that she managed to concentrate on more immediate concerns . . . like *why* Kenda and the others had departed so abruptly.

Everything looked peaceful enough. She smelled no smoke. . . .

Jen's gaze roved the empty chamber, stopping at last on the holo in front of her—now depicting Earth's innards rife with glowing traceries and arcane symbols. In another moment she understood why the others had run away.

A gazer pulse packet . . . heading this way. Seconds ticked down inevitability with four nines' probability.

Even in her distracted state, Jen had had enough experience watching Kenda's operation to perceive how three previously unknown resonators had banded together, taking the Kiwis by surprise, overcoming their belated resistance. It didn't take many blowups to see where the gargantuan output would strike once whoever-it-was found just the right resonance.

In fact, gravity waves were coursing through this space even as she sat here! They weren't coupling with ordinary surface matter yet—only a few frequencies and impedances did that. But soon a matching would be found. No wonder Kenda and the others had departed!

Jen watched loops and spires flicker three thousand kilometers below, where minerals and metals mixed and separated at the planet's most violent interface. In the holo tank, great molten-electric prominences took on gauzy textures. Threads of ephemeral superconductivity throbbed and Beta's brittle gleam waxed and waned in tempo to this arrogant human meddling.

Jen grunted at the irony. *That's where all my work went . . . Kenda must have taken everything in the computer and just poured it down the resonator all at once, in a vain attempt to stop them.*

When that failed, he ordered everyone out.

She chuckled suddenly. Even a near miss by those unknown enemies should collapse these tottering mine shafts. Kenda and the others might escape in time, but it was clearly too late for her now.

I guess in all the panic, no one bothered with that irritating old woman in the corner, the one always making a nuisance of herself. See, Wolling? I told you bad habits can be fatal!

The resonator hummed, apparently still linked to all the furious activity below.

Well, I might as well get the best seat in the house, she thought, and picked up her subvocal again. *Let's see just what kind of a finish Mother has in store for me.*

□ Hey, wait a nano! Any of you catch that? I thought all this gor-sucking inside the Earth was supposed to stop!

Yeah, I know. . . . But one of my ferrets just squirt-faxed news of a raft of new boggles! Here blokes, copy this . . . Yeah, from some new spots, too. It's spreading like cancer-IV!

. . . Good idea. Let's split and scurt-recomb at this nexus in ten min. Lensman, you check the online seismic databases. Yamato-Girl, see what your eavesdrop-prog at the U.N. is picking up. Boris can quick-scan open media while Diamond taps the NorA ChuGa Rumor Center. I'll find out what the other hack groups have picked up. . . . Right. Maybe the greeners know something too.

Agreed? Then squirt it!

● Nelson worried about the termites.

B   Specifically, for several days the hives inside the ark had been
I   acting strangely. Instead of sending forth twisty files of workers in
O   search of decaying organic matter, the insects scurried near their
S   tapered mounds, frantically reinforcing them with fresh mud from
P   countless tiny mandibles. It was the same on all levels of ark four.
H   Nelson had reported first signs on Thursday, then had to wait
E   for Dr. B'Keli's scientists to analyze his samples. Finally, as he
R   came on shift today, one of the departing day workers told him.
E   "Termites, like fire ants, are very sensitive to electric fields," the
young woman entomologist told him. "They can feel variations you or
I would never notice without instruments.

"Tomorrow we'll go looking for a short circuit," she added with a
smile. "Want to come early and join us? I'm sure you'll find it interesting."

Interesting might be one word for it. She was young, pretty, and
Nelson felt suddenly awkward. "Uh, maybe," he answered, imagina-
tively.

During his nightly rounds with Shig and Nell, he kept wondering
about that look in her eyes. Looks can deceive, of course, even when
interpreted truly. Still, he decided he would come in early tomorrow.

One thing he knew the lady entomologist was wrong about
though—humans *could* detect whatever was affecting the insects. He
felt it in his soles and in prickled hairs at the back of his neck. And
Shig walked across the savannah enclosure as if each crackling grass
stem gave off sparks. Finally, Nelson had to carry the youngster so
Nell could get some rest.

There was a dusty odor in the air, even after they entered the rain
forest biosphere. A glance through the windows showed desert hazes
carried by the dry north wind. "Close all external air ducts," he commanded the ever-listening computers, and his ears popped as the system went over to full recirculation. That was what an enclosed
ecosystem was all about anyway. Nelson thought it almost cheating to
let ark four purge some of its wastes outside and take in occasional
doses of water and air.

"Increase hourly mist ten percent, upper canopy level," he added,
rubbing some leaves. He felt more comfortable using his "knack,"
now that book learning was taking some of the edge off his ignorance.
From a catwalk he looked across the branches of the miniforest, smell-
ing rank aromas of fecundity and death. Heavy, interlaced branches
bore rich humus layers on top, where whole communities of epiphytes

lived out cycle after cycle, never touching the ground. Tangled vines sheltered crawling, slithering things whose nocturnal habits made Nelson their only regular human contact.

Most probably preferred it that way. This habitat recreated a bit of the long-lost jungles of Madagascar, where whole orders of primates had once dwelled in splendid isolation, until canoes from the distant east only a few scant centuries ago brought the first human invasion. In that brief time those forests vanished, along with so many of man's strange cousins—the lemurs and other prosimians. Some "lost" species still lived, barely, in enclaves like this one, sheltered in care by the descendants of ax wielders, forest slashers, and road builders.

The contrast seemed so great, one might think two distinct species had invented the chain saw and the survival ark. *But then*, Nelson thought, *even in ancient times, there was Noah.*

A pair of eyes much too large for daylight blinked at Nelson as he wandered by. *History is so strange. Once you start really feeling for people long ago, it's like a drug. You can't stop thinking about it.*

He remembered his epiphany on that fateful day in the baboon enclosure—eons ago—when he first realized that a life without others to care for wasn't worth living. That same afternoon he had also glimpsed something else . . . what the struggle for survival must have been like for men and women during most of the ages of human-kind.

Nelson stopped where the catwalk neared a bank of sloping glass-crystal. Beyond the ark's perimeter, the haze-shrouded Kuwenezi foot-hills shone under an opal moon. It was a beautiful night, in a sere, parched sort of way. His modern mind could look across the expanse with little emotion but aesthetic appreciation . . . or maybe sadness over the land's unstoppable deterioration.

But for most of the lifespan of his race, the night must have been more intense—a time of lurking shadows and unseen, mortal dangers —even with the companionship of fire and long after Neolithic hunt-ers had become the most fearsome creatures around. Nelson thought he understood why.

Poor Homo sapiens, *doomed to die.*

That much people shared with other beasts. But with mortality early humans acquired the added burden of a wild, untamed, magnifi-cent new brain, an organ offering skill and planning by day, but also capable of crafting demons just beyond the flickering firelight, en-abling you to imagine in detail tomorrow's hunt or the next day's injury or your neighbor's secret deceit. A mind capable of *knowing* death . . . of helplessly watching its conquest over a comrade's cour-age, over a wife's withered youth, over a babe's never-to-be-known passion . . . and seeing in those moments the spoor of a foe worse than any lion. The last implacable, undefeated enemy.

What do you get when you mix utter ignorance and a mind able to ask, "Why"? Early human societies grasped at so many superstitions, pagan hierarchies, and countless bizarre notions about the world. Some folkways were harmless, even pragmatic and wise. Others were passed on as fierce "truth" . . . because not to believe fiercely opened the way to something far worse than error . . . *uncertainty*.

Nelson felt a poignant sadness for his ancestors—generation after generation of women and men, each filled with a sense of self-importance as great as his own. Thinking about them made his life seem as ephemeral as the rippling savannah grass, or the moonbeams illuminating both the wheat fields and his mind.

Back when humans roamed in small bands, when the forest seemed endless and night all-powerful, the common belief was that *other* creatures were thinkers too, whose spirits could be bribed with song and dance. But eventually, the scary woods were pushed back a little. Mud-brick temples glistened, and bibles began saying, "No, the world was made for man to *use*." Soulless, animals were for his disposal.

Later still came a time when farmland and city surpassed the forest's span. Moreover, nature's laws were at last unfolding before curious minds. Principles like *momentum* kept the planets on course, and sages perceived the universe as a great clockwork. Humans, like other creatures, were mere gears, thrall to insuperable physics.

The pace of change sped. Forests grew rare and a fourth attitude was born. As Earth groaned under cities and plows, *guilt* became the newest theme. Instead of peer, or master, or cog in the cosmic machine, *Homo sapiens'* best thinkers came to view their own species as a blight. The vilest thing that ever happened to a planet.

Nelson saw these unfolding worldviews the way his teacher had shown them to him, as a series of steps taken by a strange, adaptable animal. One gradually—even reluctantly—taking on powers it once thought reserved for gods.

Each *zeitgeist* seemed appropriate to men and women of its time, and all of them were obsolete today. Now humanity was trying to save what it could, not because of guilt, but to survive.

Moonlight brought to mind the pretty young entomologist, who had smiled so provocatively while talking about termites and who then, before saying goodnight, had asked shyly to see his scars.

He recalled how his chest had expanded, how the blood in his veins warmed noticeably as he rolled up his sleeves to show her that the stories she had heard were true. That he, unlike other youths she knew, had actually fought for his life "in the wild" and won a victory, in honor.

Nelson remembered hoping, wanting. He wanted *her*, and in ways that over millions of years had fundamentally to do with procreation. Oh, sure, today that part of it was optional. It had *better* be, if humans were to control their numbers. But in the end, love and sex still had to do with the continuance of life, even if just in pretend.

The ancient game. Within him burned a desire to hold her, to lie down with her, to have her welcome his seed and choose him, above all other males, to share her investment in immortality.

And so it goes, on and on:
competition—
cooperation—
It was of some solace to Nelson that every one of his ancestors had wrestled with adolescence and gone on to find, however briefly, union with another. Presumably, if he had descendants, they too would do likewise.

But what for? They say it just happened . . . a fight of selfish genes. If so, though, why do we feel so much pain thinking there might not be a purpose?

In his own heart Nelson felt that strange mixture—hope and despair. A philosopher was what he was working to become. His teacher had said it was his true knack. But that didn't help one damn bit against the fluxions of youth, its hormone rush, or the agony of being alive.

Worse, just when he most wanted to talk to Jen, she had abandoned him.

Don't exaggerate, Nelson chided himself. *It's only been a few days. You've heard what's happening on the net. Jen's probably up to her ears.*

Still, he wished there were someone he could talk to about all this. Someone who had answers to offer, instead of endless questions.

If only—

Shig tugged at his leg and coughed a bark of dismay, looking up at him wide-eyed. Shaken from his thoughts, Nelson started to speak, then blinked and wondered what it was that suddenly felt wrong. He touched the metal railing nearby and felt an odd vibration. Soon a low rumble caused the grillwork beneath his feet to shudder, gradually working its way up to audibility. The sound reminded him of the low, infrasonic growls the elephants used in calling one another, and sure enough, several of the captive creatures began trumpeting in reply. The walkway began to shake.

Earthquake! he realized, and suddenly thought of all those people down in the old mine shaft. "Computer!" he shouted. "Connect me with Dr. Wolling in—"

Nelson cut short abruptly as a terrible wrenching seized his gut. He doubled over, moaning as the catwalk heaved violently. The baboons shrieked in panic, but he could do nothing for them. It was agony just to breathe and a labor of sheer will to keep from tearing at the metal plates, trying to bury himself under them.

□

Woe unto he who unleashes the Fenris Wolf. Who dares to waken Brahma. Who calls down Bizuthu and breaks the Egg of Serpents!

Let those who curse their own house inherit the wind . . .

● Jimmy Suarez grabbed Dr. Kenda's arm, halting the wheezing
N physicist's flight across the dusty wheat field. "Look!" Jimmy
Ö cried, pointing in the direction they had been running. The tech-
O nicians stumbled to a halt. Fleeing an expected calamity behind
S them, they looked up at another one taking place before them!
P Their goal had been the nearby bio-ark . . . the only shelter
H in sight once they finally tumbled out of that horrible, creaking
E elevator. Now they felt grateful not to have made it that far. For
R the pyramidal structure glistened, reflecting Luna's pale light
E amidst coruscating showers that looked like an aurora brought to
earth. Dripping sparkling droplets of electric fire, the edifice lifted out of the ground and rose into the sky, accelerating.

"Hot damn, the bastards missed," Jimmy shouted hoarsely. "They missed!"

Dr. Kenda's eyelids fluttered. "It's not possible. The projection . . ." He shook his head. "They won't miss next time."

"But the thread domains below us won't replenish right away!"

"*If* they're behaving like they used to," another operator cautioned. "They were changing so fast . . ."

"*How?*" Kenda interrupted, utterly perplexed. "You saw the simulation. How did they miss?"

"Only one way to find out," Jimmy answered. "I'm going back. Anybody coming?"

Kenda turned away, motioning now to the east, where the lights of Kuwenezi Canton shone in the distance. When Jimmy tried to grab his arm the physicist tore free and shouted. "It's over! Can't you see

that? The minute we come back on line, they'll do to us what they did
to that ark!''

"But they *missed*—''

Jimmy watched them go, feeling his resolve waver. He almost
followed. But curiosity was a flame that could not be quenched, even
by fear. It drove him to turn around, climb back into that awful, rusty
elevator and descend once more into the dreadful old mine.

His head whirled. Why had that beam missed?

He found part of the answer when he saw who had taken over the
resonator in their absence. Jimmy stared at what had become of Jennifer Wolling.

"My God!''

She had undergone a physical transformation . . . as if devils
from some medieval torture squad had taken weeks to work her over
on a rack. Stretched out of shape like an india rubber man—nevertheless, she was still alive.

Moreover, a strange light seemed to glisten from those eyes,
blinking slowly, still conscious. Jimmy hurried to where she lay
slumped against one wall. But as he reached to cut her link to the
towering gravity antenna, she jerked her queerly elongated head,
knocking his hand aside.

"*Not yet . . .*'' came her hoarse whisper. Then she smiled and
added, "*. . . child.*''

Jimmy had a queer feeling as he watched her die . . . that her
consciousness seemed to seep away down pathways beyond his ken.
Cradling her head, Jimmy listened to the resonator mumble low mysteries into the Earth.

●

At that same moment, Mark Randall was far too busy to stare. Too
many bizarre things were happening, and only pure professionalism
saved him from stupifaction.

"Elaine! Go to the bay and uncover the scopes. I'm turning the
ship!''

"But we aren't even in orbit yet,'' his copilot complained. "You
can't open the doors this soon. It's against regs.''

"Just do it!''

He felt *Intrepid* around him, still creaking as the shuttle shook
off the hot stresses of insertion burn. Officially, they were still in the
atmosphere. But that was just a technicality. Air molecules were
sparse this high up. And anyway, there wasn't a moment to lose.

Hands dancing across the controls, he shouted orders to the literal-minded, voice-actuated processors. Mark avoided looking through the forward windshield. It was far more important to unleash the ship's automatic optics than to play tourist with his own eyes . . . even if it was a spectacle out there.

Things were flying off the planet. Bits of this and that too far away to discern clearly, but each dazzled as it passed beyond Earth's shadow to bathe in Sol's bare illumination. Astronaut's intuition gave him some idea how distant some of the objects were, their spin rates, even their approximate size-albedo product.

Too big, he thought. *They're too damn big! First chunks of ice. Now this?*

What in hell's going on? Is the whole world breaking up?

When images began pouring in through *Intrepid*'s unleashed instruments, Mark began thinking that might be the very answer.

The sky lit up with the debris of battle.

●

Sepak Takraw didn't have an astronaut's professionalism to buffer him. He simply stared at the great hole where New Guinean hills had formerly sheltered a vast network of secret caves. Now a lake of pulverized *dust* lay in a broad oval between the slopes . . . dust so fine the faint breeze made undulating ripples in it, as if across water. Gusts wafted glittering tendrils into the air like spindrift.

Sepak wasn't the only one staring. The soldiers who came running from their guard posts stopped to gape as well. For days they had played hide-and-seek, his jungle savvy against their high-tech sensors, they in blur-weave armor, he in loincloth and feathers. Now, however, they stood nearby like predator and prey stunned by the same sudden cataclysm, their quarrel instantly forgotten. Side by side he and a soldier gazed across the bowl, brimming with matter so fine it might have been the same primordial stuff that formed the sun and planets long ago.

"I surrender," Sepak told the soldier numbly, dropping his bow and quiver. The commando looked at him, then, without blinking, unstrapped his own gleaming weapon and let it fall to earth beside Sepak's. There seemed no need for words.

The wind picked up, wafting powder like fog to coat their clothes and faces, getting into their eyes, making them blink and tear. Sepak and the soldier backed up and then turned away. In retreat they kept glancing back nervously over their shoulders, unlike the forest animals, most of whom had already resumed their normal serious business of living, unburdened by anything as useless as memory.

●

Stan Goldman's view of events wasn't impeded by trees or jungle or hills. He and a few others shared a privileged vantage point several kilometers from the Greenland resonator. That was where the local commander had ordered "nonessential personnel" when Alex Lustig's warning came. Those who fit aboard the encampment's tractor and Malus crane fled even farther, putting as much distance as possible behind them.

Unable to prevail on the commander to let him stay, Stan insisted on at least departing on his own two feet. As well as NATO support staff, the walking exodus comprised men and women from the Hammer Dig, who by this time needed little persuasion that their obscure corner of the world had grown entirely unwholesome. With their background studying long-ago catastrophes, the paleogeologists knew just how small and fragile humans were, in comparison.

Still, by consensus everyone stopped where a gentle rise offered their last view back the way they came. Temblors swept the pebbly moraine. Fortunately, the horizon was nearly flat all the way to the distant coastal clouds, so if anything was going to harm them, it would have to reach right out of the Earth to do so.

Which, of course, is entirely possible, Stan thought. In fact, these minor tremors were only superficial symptoms of a battle taking place far below, as volunteers back at the dome helped Alex's team on Rapa Nui try to fight off these mysterious new foes. "Any luck, Ruby?" he asked a woman seated cross-legged before a portable console.

"I'm linking up now, Dr. Goldman. Just a nano, while I tap a status update."

Stan peered over Ruby's shoulder at a miniature version of the familiar globe hologram. As before, the most furious activity took place where the plasti-crystalline mantle met the molten outer core, especially right below Greenland site. Filaments and twisting prominences glowed with energy drawn from the planet's whirling dynamo, flickering lividly each time slender rapier probes lanced down from the surface, tickling and inciting the most inflamed. Those glimmering threads pulsed hypnotically in rhythms Stan compared to a multipart fugue, beating countertime to Beta's imperious metronome. The combination spun off beams of warped space-time.

It was a stygian, multidimensional fencing match, and Stan knew his side was now badly outnumbered. *New Guinea's gone completely dark,* he saw. And halfway around the globe, another familiar pinpoint glowed wan amber. *The African resonator's barely on idle, probably damaged and out of action.*

Those had been early targets of the enemy's surprise onslaught. The foe had taken them out in quick gazer strikes, like the one Alex had barely warded off. Or maybe they were sabotaged, as had been tried here—an attempt foiled only when last-minute security shakedowns revealed several well-placed limpet bombs. Since then it had been open warfare at long range, with the outnumbered side just beginning to learn the rules.

In an ironic way it actually gladdened Stan to see the innocent incompetence of Spivey's people. The American colonel's goal must never have been terror weaponry after all. Or else his officers would surely be better geared for such a fight. All their gazer programs were scaled too small—to *lift* objects rather than blast them willy-nilly to oblivion. It would take time to bypass all the safeguards put in place to cut civilian damage, readjusting the cylinders to throw deadly force on command.

Time was exactly what Spivey's people clearly didn't have.

After the first wave of temblors, earth movements ceased, and Stan knew why. Triggering quakes might in principle offer a bludgeon against big targets like cities. But even a major jolt to this level plain might leave the Greenland resonator intact, ready to strike back. The enemy weren't taking their advantage for granted. They had to keep the NATO crew occupied parrying thrusts until an opening was found to take them out decisively, once and for all.

"The bogeys," Ruby said, referring to their unknown foes. "They're uniting on a lambda band now, fourteen hundred megacycles . . . with what looks like a Koonin-style metric-impedance match. Beta's responding! Damn, will it—no! Alex came in from below and *blocked* 'em. Yeah! Bought us some time. Take that, assholes!"

Stan appreciated the young Canadian's colorful commentary. It lent those abstract symbols verve and emotion appropriate to combat. Stan balled his fists and tried for the adrenaline rush one expected in a situation like this. *Only what is a situation like this? Maybe if there were bombs going off, or visible foes . . .*

The sky was so peaceful and blue though, with a bracing, wintry breeze coming off the continent of ice. He felt incongruously comfortable and calm with gloved hands jammed into his jacket pockets.

"Uh-oh . . . Alex has run out of excited states along any path between Rapa Nui and us. I see nothing in reach for ten minutes!"

"Ten minutes?" Someone nearby sighed. "Might as well be forever."

Stan read the display. Sure enough, the gleaming filaments along one entire sector had gone dim—still pulsing, but now exhausted, banked back, almost contemplative compared to the glittering ferment going on elsewhere. Until they replenished, Alex's team would be unable to render any help warding off attacks on Greenland.

"Lustig signals he's going onto the attack meanwhile. . . . Says good luck and godspeed . . . . Now he's gone."

Stan nodded. "Same to you, Alex. Don't worry about us. Go get 'em."

He and the other evacuees turned their attention to the distant white dome they had left just a little while ago. Even this far away they were still in danger. In this new, terrifying type of warfare, the ground beneath you might suddenly turn liquid with color, or vanish in a titanic flash, or propel you toward far galaxies. Whatever happened, he wanted to share jeopardy with those brave technicians over there across the moraine valley. He planned on staying when the crane-zep returned for another pickup.

All my life I believed science was a revelation co-equal to scripture. A more advanced text—the Infinite offering us His very tools, now that we're older, like apprentices learning their Father's craft.

So isn't it only right to stand watch over what I helped create with those tools?

Ruby exclaimed, grabbing her headphones. She laughed. "I don't believe it!"

"What is it?"

"Alex. He's taken out the Siberian machine!" she announced in triumph. "Vaporized 'em! That's one enemy down and two to go. Oh eh? Oh no!"

Stan felt the others gather even closer. Ruby's gleeful expression turned to despair. "What now?" he asked.

"Another one's come on line to replace it! A *new* one! Joined in soon as Siberia blew out. It's . . . in the Sea of Japan. Damn, they must've been holding it in reserve. Where'd all these bastards come from!"

In the display, Stan saw a new triggering beam replace the one Alex had just destroyed, making a total of three foes once more.

"They're still after us!" she cried, reading the traces.

"Sometimes it's smarter to take out the weaker opponent first," he commented. "If they knock Greenland out, Alex's crew will have to face them all alone." The Danes and others sighed and nodded. They didn't have the full picture. (Who did?) But some things were obvious.

"The gor-suckers have hooked a really good band this time,"

Ruby said. "Lots of energy. Beta's responding, and twelve . . . fifteen threads are active. . . . Beam on target!"

Stan looked around for any sign that coherent pencils of gravitational radiation were hurtling through the Earth nearby. But no symptoms could be perceived. It wasn't likely there would be any, not until their assailants found a proper coupling with surface matter.

"They're hunting for a contact resonance. Our guys are trying to parry . . ." Then Ruby groaned as her instruments flashed fateful crimson. "No good. Here it comes!"

"Everybody down!" Stan shouted. "Lie flat and turn away!"

But even as the others dove to the ground, Stan ignored his own advice. He watched the NATO buildings and knew the very instant the beam matched frequencies with the rock-air boundary. Oval patches of tundra seemed to throb like tympani. Then, within one of those boundaries, the encampment suddenly sank into the ground, like an express elevator called down to hell. It was over in an eyeblink.

At least, the first part was over. Stan mourned good people who had become friends. Dr. Nielsen got up and moved next to him. Together they listened to the continuing rumble of a new tunnel boring straight into the Earth. The growling continued for some time, vibrating their soles.

"Maybe we'd better try to get out of here," the paleogeologist suggested at last. "The magma in these parts is far below a heavy plate, but it's not very viscous. Even on foot, a little distance could make a lot of difference right now."

Mankind had passed yet another milestone today, Stan thought. But then, maybe Nielsen was right. He didn't have to be exactly at ground zero in order to bear witness when molten rock flooded up that new channel from deep, high-pressure confinement. Watching from further away wouldn't lessen the spectacle much at all.

●

Like everyone else aboard the company ship, Crat watched and listened to the hurried, frantic reports. He soon tired, though, of trying to follow events he didn't understand. And so he left them all in the comm room and went out on deck alone to wait for sunrise.

Partly, he was still numb. His adventure with the underwater shaft of light hadn't worn off yet—the enchantment of that strange music, the transient contact with something warm and accepting, or so it seemed at the time. He hadn't expected his bosses to believe his story when he emerged from the water. But they had, questioning him about every detail, testing his blood and other fluids, putting him next to machines that tugged at his limbs as the light had, though not as pleasantly. At one point as they worked on him, Crat had felt his sense of smell enhance out of all proportion. The company execs' fine colognes bit into his sinuses and made his nose itch.

That had seemed to satisfy them. He'd been released to rest and perform easy chores aboard a company support ship while the wary tech types hurried back to their secret labs. Crat had wondered how they could be so concerned about such matters at a time like that . . . and even more so two days later, when people spoke of whole chunks of the planet being blasted into space! Such dedication seemed far beyond him.

Still, all seemed peaceful on deck. From the railing he saw the gangly towers of the Sea State town. Soon the muezzin would be calling Muslim citizens to first prayer, dawn kites would rise to catch the stratospheric winds and solar arrays would catch even the reddish dawn.

Tepid currents lapped the cruiser's hull, leaving the usual faint scum of surface oils and powdered styrofoam in a pebbly sheen. Phosphorescent, dying plankton gave off iridescent colors. Crat sighed as moonlight broke through the ragged overcast to brighten some obscure patch of sea. That bright beam reminded him of another. It made him hope with the focused intensity of a prayer that he might be lucky again. Maybe next time he met that special light, or heard that music, he wouldn't be too dumb, too tongue-tied to reply.

"Yeah," he said, in bittersweet sureness that he had been both blessed and abandoned. "Sure you would, boy-oh. Ever'body's waitin' in line just to hear what you have to say."

●

To Logan Eng, the chaos in the Net felt like having one of life's underpinnings knocked out. What had been a well-ordered, if undisciplined, ruckus of zines, holochannels, SIGs, and forums had become a rowdy babel, a torrent of confusion and comment, made worse because in order to be noticed each user now sent out countless copies of his messages toward any node that might conceivably listen. A million hackers unleashed carefully hoarded "grabber" subroutines, designed to seize memory space and public attention. Even "official" channels were jammed half the time with interlopers claiming their right to comment on the crisis facing the world.

". . . it is a plot by resurgent Stalinist elements and *pamyat* mystics . . . ," claimed a ham operator who had been listening to one mysterious site in Siberia.

". . . No, it's schemes by money-grubbing polluters . . ."

". . . eco-freaks . . ."

". . . little green men . . ."

Normally, the weirdest scenarios would have stayed ghettoed in special interest forums. But that unspoken consensus broke down as bizarre fantasies suddenly seemed no less reasonable than the finest science punditry.

Then, adding to the overload, worried governments suddenly began pouring forth reams—whole libraries—of information they'd been hoarding, stumbling over themselves to prove *they* weren't responsible for the sudden outbreak of gravitational war. Each denial met fresh suspicions, though. Accusations flew in the halls of diplomacy and on ten thousand channels of comment and opinion.

The largest chunk of raw disclosure came from NATO-ANZAC-ASEAN—a spasm of data that stunned already dizzy Net traffic handlers. Suspicious voices accused Washington and its allies of masking culpability under a tidal wave of bits and bytes. But Logan was shocked by the extent of this sudden candor. To demonstrate their innocence, Spivey's bosses had spilled *everything*, even his own first conversation with the colonel, in the big limousine! This tsunami of forthrightness swamped normal channels and flooded into unusual places. Classified studies of knot singularity physics got dumped into a channel normally reserved for cooking hobbyists and recipe exchanges. The secrets of gazerdynamic launching systems filled corridors meant for light opera, situation comedies, and golfing.

The cat's out of the bag now. Even if the present crisis waned, the world would never be the same.

Despite disclosure, however, despite scurrying arms inspectors and tribunes, events sped ahead of all governance. Paranoia notched up with each strange tremor, each awful disappearance. Caroming rumors spoke of national deterrence weapons being wheeled out of storage—of peace locks being hammered off ancient but still deadly bombs. Sneezes were heard in Budapest—and someone decried bioplagues. Hailstones struck Alberta—and someone else proclaimed the wrath of God.

A winking light dragged Logan from the latest report, in which one of the brighter pundits cited new evidence pointing *away* from the bad old nation states, toward some new, unknown power. . . . Logan blinked at the intruding lines of text crossing his portable holo—a priority override using his personal emergency code. Not even Glenn Spivey knew that one.

The words manifested with shocking, glacial slowness. One by one, they seemed to pry their way through the panicky crush. He read the message and then brought up his hand up to cover his eyes.

> DADDY . . . CAN'T GET MOTHER TO BUDGE. LOCKED IN HER ROOM.
> ACTING CRAZY . . . COME QUICK. WE NEED YOU!
> —LOVE, CLAIRE

□

It is a fairly typical refugee camp, one of thirty allocated Great Britain under the Migration Accords. Along the trim lanes of Bowerchalke Village, the poor continue their day in, day out labors. Great drums of grain and fish-meal arrive and are disbursed by elected block committees. Blackwater must go to the septic ponds, graywater to the pulp gardens; every bit of cardboard or plastic or metal has value, so the streets are spotless.

As long as order is kept and every baby accounted for, a few luxuries are included in each week's aid shipment—sugarcane cuttings for the children, from plantations in Kent . . . toilet paper instead of dried kudzu leaves, to make life a little softer for the old ones . . . and some real work for those in between, those not already lost in ennui, staring all day at cheap holo sets like disembodied souls.

Yet, some of the brighter ones cruise that data sea, associating with others far away who don't even know their status as poor refugees. Some do brisk, software-based business from the camp. Some get rich and leave. Some get rich and stay.

For most, the sudden chaos on the net means a delay in their favorite shows. But to others, It threatens the only world that ever offered them hope.

● E X O S P H E R E Teresa wished she could help Alex. But all her skills were useless in this battle, a conflict as intricate as a Nō play, fought with the deadly delicacy of weaving, bobbing Siamese fish.

At least she could help watch the prisoner, freeing some security boys to stand guard against saboteurs. And she'd see to keeping Pedro out of Alex's hair.

Fortunately, those two jobs coincided as the big Aztlan reporter eagerly questioned June Morgan. He forced her to look toward the holo display, where each thrust and parry translated into more deaths, more local catastrophes. "It wasn't supposed to go this far," the blonde traitor answered miserably. "They never intended all-out war."

"They hardly ever do," Manella commented. "Big, destructive
hostilities nearly always used to come about when one side thought it
knew just how the other would react to a show of force, and miscalculated their opponents' resolve."

Teresa watched June wince as roiling changes lit up the many-
layered Earth. Nearby, Alex Lustig tapped rapid commands with a
keypad-glove, adding muttered amendments quicker than speech with
his subvocal device. Others hurried about their tasks with similar crisp
efficiency . . . the only trait that might help the last Tangoparu team
in its desperate, one-sided struggle to survive.

"It's all my fault," June said with a despairing sigh. "If I'd only
done my job, they wouldn't have had their bluff called. Not yet, at
least. Now, though, all their plans are messed up. They're in a panic.
Far more dangerous than if they'd won."

The patent rationalization made Teresa want to spit. "You still
haven't said who *they* are!"

Earlier June had refused to answer, as if the direct question terrified her. Now she seemed to decide it didn't matter anymore.

"It's kind of hard to explain."

"Try us," Manella urged.

With a sigh, June regarded them both. "Pedro, Teresa, haven't
either of you ever wondered? I mean, why do people assume the Helvetian War put an end to the world's oldest profession?"

Teresa blinked. "Are you being snide?"

June laughed without mirth. "I don't mean prostitution, Terry.
I'm talking about parasites, manipulators who thrive on secrecy. There
have *always* been schemers and plotters—since before Gilgamesh and
the pyramids.

"Come on, you two. Who do you think poisoned Roosevelt and
had the Kennedys shot? Or arranged for Simyonev's plane to crash?
What about Lamberton and Tsushima? Are you *sure* those were accidents? Didn't they work out rather conveniently for those profiting in
the aftermath?

"Teresa and I are too young, but Pedro, you remember how things
were during the weeks before the Brazzaville Declaration, don't you?
Back when delegations started flying in spontaneously from all over
the world to declare the antisecrecy alliance? How many people died
of mysterious accidents before the delegates overcame all the obstacles
and ideological distractions and at last built a momentum that was
unstoppable? Then how many world leaders had to be deposed before
the masses had their way and the Alps were finally put under siege?"

"Half the presidents and ministers had secret bank accounts to protect," Pedro replied. "So naturally they tried to obstruct. But in the end they failed—"

"They didn't fail. They were *used*. Used up in delaying actions." June's eyebrows lowered. "Why do you think the war lasted so damn long, hmm? The Swiss *people* sure didn't want to take on the whole damn planet! They never imagined all those generations spent digging tunnels and bomb shelters had a purpose beyond mere deterrence.

"And even when it ended at last, you don't actually think the bank records that U.N. forces finally dug out of the rubble were the real ones, do you?"

Manella shook his head. "Are you implying whole levels of conspirators we missed? That all the drug lords and bribe takers and commissar billionaires we caught—"

"Were just expendable flunkies, thrown down to appease the mob. Yes, that's exactly what I'm saying, Mr. Reporter." June's voice was bitter. "The real manipulators wanted Helvetia completely destroyed. The war *had* to cost so many lives, so an exhausted world would exult in victory and desperately *want* to believe it was over."

"This is ridiculous," Teresa told Pedro. "She's sounding like a bad Lovecraft novel now. What's next, June? Dark Unspeakable Unnameable Horrors from Before the Start of Time? Or how about something out of those wonderful, paranoid Illuminati books? Who are your bosses, then? Freemasons? The Trilateral Commission? Jesuits? The Elders of Zion?" Teresa laughed. "How about Fu Manchu or the Comintern . . . ?"

June shrugged. "Those were useful distractions in their day— glitter and window dressing designed to attract fools, so conspiracy theories in general would get a bad odor with normal, honest folk."

To her dismay, Teresa found herself drawn by June Morgan's frankness. The woman clearly believed what she was saying. *And she's right in a way,* Teresa thought, suddenly aware of her own reaction. *Look at me now. Refusing to believe, even as proof tears the world down around me.*

Pedro chewed one end of his moustache. "You aren't referring to the *aliens* are you? The makers of Beta? Are they your—"

June looked up quickly. "Oh heavens no!" She gestured at the big display. "Do the assholes who sent me here seem that competent to you? Look how badly they screwed up their attempted coup. Would Beta's makers have let Alex jerk them around like he has?"

As they all looked that way, a trio of yellow rays caused Beta's purple dot to throb with incipient power, but once again they were foiled by a slender rapier from Easter Island, sending their pent-up force spiraling off uselessly in some other direction.

June shook her head. "No, humanity is able to breed predators all on its own, Pedro. Talented parasites with lots of experience tapping the innovations of others. You don't need much *brains* for that, just certain manipulative talents and lots of arrogance."

"The illusion of omniscience," Pedro said, nodding.

"Oh yes. I've seen them, gathered in their halls with all their money, giving each other circle-jerks—telling each other how smart they are just because thirty years ago they managed to preserve some of their old power, because people were too tired and relieved at war's end to peel back the last layer.

"Only now, at last, they know how stupid they really were all along. You got it right, Pedro. They miscalculated this latest move and are going to die soon. For that part at least, I'm truly grateful."

The admission took Teresa aback. All this time she had assumed June was acting out of loyalty to some group or cause. Clearly the woman feared her veiled masters, but now Teresa saw how much she also loathed them.

Glancing at the great display, Teresa intuited what June meant. All over the world, in national capitals and command posts and even hackers' parlors, there were other Earth-holos like this one. Perhaps cruder, but growing better by the minute. Especially now that Glenn Spivey's group and others were spilling all they knew in sudden, panic-driven spasms of openness. On every one of those displays, the enemy resonator sites must shine like angry pirates' emblems . . . standing out for the simple reason that no one claimed ownership over them. That lack of candor in these hot, tense hours was an indictment worse than any smoking gun.

Right now every security alliance, peacekeeping force and local militia with the means was probably sending units toward those mystery sites. Their weaponry might be paltry compared to TwenCen arms—their unpracticed reflexes might be slow—but those soldiers would certainly make short work of June's employers when they arrived.

No, her bosses can't have planned for this. They must have counted on taking the Tangoparu tetrahedron completely by surprise, wiping out the original four and all the newer resonators with sabotage or gazer strikes. Then, in sole possession of the ultimate terror weapon, they could hold the world hostage. They came damn close to succeeding.

But even as she saw the logic, Teresa had to shake her head.

In which case . . . so what? It's an insane plan even if it worked! They couldn't have gotten away with it for long. The result would have been just too unstable.

Teresa saw that a lull had fallen since Alex's last successful parry. He was sipping through a straw from a glass held by one of the cooks. She wanted to go over and rub his shoulders and maybe whisper some encouragement, but she also knew Alex too well for that. Those shoulders were Atlas's right now. And a lot more than the lives in this room rode on his train of thought. It mustn't be interrupted.

"You're describing an act of sheer desperation," Pedro surmised, still talking to June. "These conspirators of yours . . . even in victory, they couldn't hope to hold onto what they'd won!"

June answered with a tired shrug. "What did they have to lose? The status quo was deteriorating from their point of view. Everything they had rescued from the ashes of Helvetia was slipping through their hands like smoke."

"I don't get it. What threatened them?"

June motioned toward the consoles, toward Teresa's data plaque, toward the phone on Pedro's belt. "The net," she said succinctly.

"The net?"

"That's right. It was getting to big, too open and all-pervading . . . too bloody *democratic* to manipulate much longer. They were growing more desperate every year. Then this gravity amplification business came along—"

"—which you leaked to them!" Teresa accused.

June nodded. "They had other sources. As you've said so often, it's awful hard to keep secrets these days . . . that is, unless you own the system."

"Own the net?" Teresa sniffed incredulously. "Nobody owns the net."

"Well, bits of it. Special, strategic pieces. Think about when the original fiber cables and data hubs were laid. Someone could always be bought out, bribed, blackmailed. Computer nodes were designed with 'back door' entry codes, known only to a few . . ."

"Why? To what end?"

June laughed. "To always be first hearing about the latest technical advance! So your ferrets will get that split second priority advantage, letting you cache away items before others see them. To manipulate the mail—"

"Preposterous!" Teresa objected. "People would notice!"

June nodded. "Oh, *now* we know that. But then? The net was supposed to be their baby. Their tool! It would replace big banks as an instrument of control, above nations and governments. Above even money.

"After all, didn't old sci-fi stories picture it that way? 'He who controls the flow of information controls the world'? That was to be their answer to Brazzaville and Rio." June's voice stung with biting irony. "Only it didn't quite work out that way. Instead of being their tame instrument, the Net kept slipping free like something alive. So they—"

"They, they!" Pedro smacked a fist into his palm, making Teresa wince. The man should remember where they were.

"Who *are* they?" Manella demanded. "Who the hell are you talking about, woman!"

Another shrug. "Do names matter? Picture all the powerful cabals of egotists cluttering the world at the turn of the century. Call them old or new money . . . or red cadres . . . or dukes and lordships. Historians know they all spent more time conniving *with* each other than waging their supposedly high-minded ideological struggles.

"The smart ones saw Brazzaville coming and prepared. They saw to it that all the reasonable Helvetian and Cayman ministers were assassinated or drugged and that every attempt at compromise, even surrender, was rejected."

That rocked Pedro back. "Do you mean . . . ?" But June hurried on.

"Actually, do you want to know what their worst problem was? It's afflicted them since early TwenCen—a worse threat to power elites than mass education, news media, even the personal computer. It was defection."

"Defection?" Teresa asked, captivated despite herself.

"Each successive generation found it harder to hold onto its own children! World culture was so enticing, even to rich kids with the chance to live like rajahs. The best and brightest were always being tempted away into so-called bourgeois careers—in the arts or sciences — because those are intrinsically more interesting than sitting around clipping coupons and bullying the servants—"

"Wait a minute!" Teresa interrupted. "How do you know all this?" Then she saw something in the other woman's eyes. "Oh—"

Teresa felt a sudden, unwelcome wash of empathy for June Morgan. The blonde geophysicist smiled wryly. "Family ties, you see. Our little branch made its break when Dad ran off to play music and do fund-raisers for wildlife. Naturally, the cousins cut us off from information, though we never lacked for money.

"Anyway, Dad didn't want to know about their schemes. He called my uncles 'dinosaurs.' Said their way of thinking would die out naturally." June snorted. "Ever hear *how* the dinosaurs died though? I wouldn't want to be underfoot when it happened."

"So you figured on playing along. Let them have their way—"

"—till they dried up and blew away. Yeah, that was part of it.

That and—" June looked down. "Well, they can be persuasive. You don't know them."

But Teresa figured she really did. If not as individuals, then the type—one needing stronger tonics than satisfied ordinary men and women. Their inner hunger seemed to crave money and power, but was, in fact, insatiable by anything this side of death.

Anyway, details hardly mattered. June's dinosaur analogy matched the *geological* scale of the drama portrayed on the great display. Teresa could read some of those livid trails of human meddling. So many ghostly phenomena were taking place far beneath her feet, whose repercussions would reverberate long after the last blows were struck.

One recent consequence of battle was clear. Nearly every excited energy state under Easter Island was depleted from hours of ceaseless stimulation. All the filaments and prominences and delicate webs of electricity now glowed dull red and wouldn't serve as gazer sources again until their former blue intensity returned. That could take anywhere from minutes to hours. Meanwhile, it was hard to see how the enemy could strike at them here.

As she watched, Alex's final beam lanced along the core's fiery rim to catch a distant bright thread in a carom off Beta's glittering mirror. One of the enemy probes quavered and then toppled off scale. That resonator would take some time recovering, she knew.

Meanwhile, the world was converging on the bastards. How long until the clumsy, unready, uncoordinated U.N. posse finally got to them? *Alex has won the advantage back. Time's running out for the enemy. So what'll they do now?*

An answer wasn't long in coming.

"The other two are firing up again," the watch officer announced.

A technician protested. "But they can't reach us past that dead zone for at least—"

"They're not aiming at us!" The first voice answered. "Look!"

Teresa blinked as the Saharan and Japan Sea sites sent new beams to tickle the planet's core. Beta answered with glowing counterpoints, now completely out of reach by Alex and his crew. The Tangoparu team watched, helpless to interfere.

Beta throbbed. Nearby tendrils coiled with pent-up energy. Then something actinic and mighty flashed, striking like a fist toward the heart of a great land mass.

North America.

"They're talking!" The communications operator announced. "Blanketing all channels. . . . it's an ultimatum. They're saying all national forces must back off within two minutes or. . . ."

The young woman didn't have to finish. A continent was visibly ringing like a hammered girder, the object lesson apparent to all.

Silence reigned. Finally Teresa asked, "What now?"

For the first time, Alex looked up from his console. Tiredly, he pulled off the subvocal, leaving red streaks where the instrument had rubbed him raw. He met her eyes. "I don't know, Rip. I guess it depends on what they're trying to accomplish."

All eyes turned to the comm operator, whose specialty it was to sieve the noisy airwaves. A myriad of rapid images flickered across the woman's face. As she pieced together the story, she slowly smiled in realization.

"That last punch was a negotiating move," she said. "But what they say they really want is . . . to surrender!"

All over the room, tired workers slumped in their chairs with sighs of relief. Someone let out a whoop and threw open the double doors, letting in a fresh breeze that drove before it the stale tang of fear.

Teresa and Alex met each others' eyes, each seeking reassurance there, and reason to accept hope.

□

A woman sits alone in a locked room.

She is a mighty enchantress. And though alone, she is not without company. For there are her familiars to fetch and carry for her. And a pair of heroes on the wall, chained there for her amusement.

They are Hercules and Samson, caught together in a loop of frozen time, rattling their clinking bonds as they face a mighty hydra. They have played out the same silent struggle—straining and grunting defiantly, repetitively—ever since the enchantress put them there to be "enhanced," many days ago.

Now, though, she has little time for such things. The heroes must wait their turn.

"Oh no you don't," the woman croons as she watches more important images array themselves across another magic wall. The world's simulacrum sparkles like an electric onion, seething with changes deep within. It is an impressive show, but she cares little about those lower layers. Only the brown and green and blue wrinkled outer skin, which she finds diseased, infested with a plague of greedy parasites.

Ten billion parasites called human beings.

She knows little and cares less about the inner onion. But about the skin she has studied much and cares more. She has bound herself to an oath, a quest—to the saving of that skin. To the culling of those parasites.

"Oh no, I won't let you do that," she says to those who thought they were her patrons, her cousins, her masters, but who are in fact, her instruments. Desperate now, they threaten, bluster, scrabbling in panic as they seek a way to save their useless lives.

Petty lives, cheap to her, since their kind are far too numerous anyway. They suffer illusions of their own importance, just because they are among the "richest" of a race of fleas. Their latest plan is the best they can hope for now . . . bartering millions of lives against a promise of amnesty. Already the Net fills with tentative offers. Relief swells over yet another catastrophe barely averted. But she has other things in mind.

"No, it isn't over yet," she says, humming sweetly as she works. An armistice would hardly serve her purposes. It must be replaced with something else. Rubbing knurled knobs, she summons forth her servants, her familiars—simpler, more obedient versions of the fearsome lizard she had once crafted and then somehow lost. These are new variants, streamlined and single-minded. They streak forth at her command, wisps of electron energy under geas to lay scourge upon the kingdom of fleas.

The first clue to this great opportunity had come from her own ex-mate, a compromiser she had once loved. His work for the military had opened this new world to her. When her cousins began financing her investigations with bottomless coffers, she suddenly had access to the very best tools—both software and hardware. Day in, day out, her little spies brought back more clues.

At first she rode along, watching as her foolish relations played with powers beyond their understanding. But as time passed, she began realizing what power they had overlooked . . . what lay there amidst the mountains of data, ripe for the taking. Why, it was the very sword of cleansing!

Even as the world's nations draw back from confrontation, the enchantress uses private trails and secret byways to send her emissaries toward places far away. "You aren't going to stop there," she says. "Oh, no. Now is not the time to stop."

The room suddenly shakes and sways for the fifth time in as many minutes, but this does not interrupt her. They are only aftershocks from silly earthquakes. Anyway, the house is well built, with its own ample power.

From a town called White Castle, one might faintly hear sirens wailing. But that is in the world of men and machines, and therefore as much a useless metaphor as poor, straining, sweating Hercules on the wall, damp with rivers of simulated sweat. It is in the world of electrons and hidden forces that all will be decided. And that world belongs to Daisy.

"Go ahead. Make it rattle and roll," the enchantress says. "Enjoy your toys. But in the end, it all comes down to flesh."

● "Could it be a delaying tactic?" Alex worried aloud. "All the military forces are holding back till the Security Council can meet. During that time . . ." His voice trailed off as he shook his head in worry.

Teresa worked one shoulder, rubbing it with real strength and an uncanny knowledge of where to find the tight knots in his muscles. Her voice offered a steadiness he felt much in need of.

"They know they can't keep the whole world at bay forever, Alex. Didn't Nihon just offer to put their experimental resonators under your command? And there are those mothballed machines of Spivey's. They've recalled the technicians. In a few hours—"

Alex nodded. "In a few hours, a day at most, I'll have the resources to counter anything they try. Wipe them off every frequency. They won't be able to shake a tree branch, let alone a continent."

He tried not to listen to the tinny voice in the background—a BBC World Service reporter telling of widespread damage in the American Midwest. That was only a taste of what the desperate foe promised if any moves were made against them without a full parole. And so the cautious militias had withdrawn to wait.

No one knew how earnest June Morgan's secretive masters were about the threat. How serious had the Helvetians been with their cobalt bombs? Or Kennedy and Khrushchev, back in 1962? Men caught in the momentum of events sometimes think the unthinkable.

The resonator watch officer called. "They're pulsing again . . ."

Everyone turned. All three enemy probes once more glowed with induced gravitational energy. "What are they up to now? I thought they'd agreed to wait."

Narrow pencils of yellow speared downward toward the purple dot—Beta's flickering mirror.

"Could it be another demonstration?"

The comm operator interrupted. "They've come on-line again, all channels. They claim it isn't them at all!"

Alex turned. "What d'you mean, 'it isn't them'?"

"It isn't them!" The woman pressed her headphones. "They swear their resonators all just went off by themselves!"

Teresa asked, "Alex, is that possible? What are they trying to pull?"

But he only watched, transfixed, as the three beams passed through several roiling cells of superconducting electricity, struck Beta, and . . . disappeared.

"Ikeda! Clambers!" Alex shouted. "Scan parallel frequencies."

He reached for his subvocal. "They may be trying to sneak up on a side band!"

It seemed unlikely. There were only a few mode-combinations which coupled strongly with surface rock, especially the topmost crust. And he felt sure those were all covered. Still—

"There is something, Alex," one of the techs yelled across the room. "Take a look at fifty-two gigahertz, on a one point six meter amplitude p-wave—"

"Got it!" he shouted back. Fresh dotted lines showed what had been invisible—thin trails of gazer radiation shining from Beta's glittering maw.

"But those beams are headed—" He didn't have to finish. Everyone stared in shock as the concentrated rays flew straight back to their points of origin, striking direct hits on all three enemy resonators.

"They shot themselves!" someone cried in amazement. Alex scanned but found no signs of damage. No earth tremors. The foe's resonators still shone on-line, as dangerous as ever. This was weird.

"Effects!" he demanded. But the question stayed unanswered— why would the enemy have fired beams at themselves? Beams which apparently did nothing?

"Do they say anything?"

Comm ops scanned. "Nothing. They've gone dead."

This is too strange, Alex thought. Something bizarre was going on.

"Alex!" Teresa cried out.

Jesus, she's strong! He winced at her sudden grip on his shoulder. Turning around, he saw her blinking, shaking her head. "It's happening again. I'm sure of it, Alex. Can't you feel it?"

He remembered their long passage together in New Zealand, down twisty avenues of Hadean darkness, relying on her fey sensitivity to find a way back to the world of light. That memory left no room for doubt. "Battle stations!" he cried as he reset the instruments, searching.

There! On yet another side band—Beta seemed to throb angrily. "Load all capacitors! Give me a counterpulse at—"

He was interrupted as somebody screamed. Only a dozen meters away, a man went goggle eyed, tore at his hair—and blew up.

Strictly speaking, it wasn't an explosion. The poor fellow *stretched,* still screaming, till he shredded like gooey taffy. In sound there was little more that a wet pop, but the *colors* . . . a rainbow of brilliant liquid shades spilled forth as the skin peeled back, gobbets of flesh flying in all directions.

An aura of shimmering lambency seemed to hang midair even as the ruin of meat fell to the floor. That man-sized apparition hovered for a moment and then began moving rapidly in a horizontal spiral.

Men and women yelled in dismay, scrambling to avoid it. But the terrible focus accelerated, striking two cooks who chose that unlucky moment to leave the kitchen carrying lunch. Their tureens flew as arms and heads ripped from their bodies, spraying those nearby with scalding soup and crimson blood. They never knew what hit them before the disturbance swept on, catching victim after victim.

"Everybody out!" Alex cried redundantly amid a panicky rush for the exits. He paused only to grab his plaque and Teresa's hand before joining the stampede. Halfway to the open doors, however, she braked and suddenly wrapped her arms around him. "Wha—?" He cried, struggling. But she held on, fiercely immobile as something horrible and barely visible brushed by them, passing through space they would have occupied.

"Now!" she cried when it swept on. Alex needed no urging.

Outside he saw no order to the evacuation. The Tangoparu crew were excellent and brave. They had faced dangers more powerful than any warriors had since time began. But courage is a useless abstraction when the mind recoils to a primitive state. Men and women ran pell-mell, scattering across the windblown hillsides, some running straight for the seaside cliffs. In one blinking instant, Alex saw a technician touched glancewise by something no more visible than a pocket of air. She whirled, screaming as some tide seemed to suck her into a roughly man-shaped refraction. Her horror ended in a shuddering gasp, and she crumpled to the ground hemorrhaging from purpled, blistering skin.

"This way!" Teresa shouted, dragging Alex's arm. They fled westward, though Alex had no idea why.

Several more times Teresa suddenly veered right or left. On each occasion Alex obeyed at once, following her zigs and zags like they were commandments from God. Close brushes with death grew too numerous to count, and he stopped wondering how Teresa knew which way to dodge. Sometimes he noted a close passage only by the sudden shiver down his back or by a threatening rise in his gorge. Then, before he could respond to the horror, it passed and they were off again.

There wasn't time to react to the sight of friends and colleagues being horribly murdered in broad daylight, under azure Pacific skies . . . no effort to waste on anything but flight. Numbly, he felt the crunchy unevenness of grassy slopes suddenly give way to the harder pounding of shoes on concrete. There were blurry images of parked jets and zeppelins. Was she going to try to grab one of those . . . ?

But no. Teresa yanked him past the waiting aircraft and toward another object—black on the bottom, white on top, and streaked with dross. Up a set of rusted, rickety stairs they clambered, to fall at last inside a dank, dusty chamber.

The space shuttle, he realized dimly as he fell to the deck, wheezing. So Teresa hadn't any plan after all. Blind instinct must have driven her as much as the others. Only in her case the compulsion had been to seek out "her" spacecraft—a totem of safety and her own sense of control.

"Come on, Alex." Sudden, sharp pain lanced his shoulder as she kicked him. "Move it!" she shouted. "The thing could pass through here any minute!"

That was true enough. So why hadn't they stayed outside, where her acute senses might be helpful, rather than hiding in this useless coffin?

He let her drag him to his feet, though, and stumbled after her through the fetid airlock, tripping over the high sill. She virtually threw him the last few meters into the shuttle's dim, cavernous cargo bay, where he stumbled to his knees under the glitter of two small spotlights. The beams converged in a pool of brilliance where he met his own dumbfounded reflection, as if staring into a magic pool.

Alex blinked once. Twice. And then he understood.

It was a perfect sphere which glistened his own image back at him, sweeping around into infinite concave vistas. He cried an oath. He'd forgotten about the other resonator!

Alex looked down at his left hand, tightly gripping his portable plaque. And he still wore the subvocal! Maybe . . .

But no. "Damn!" he cried. "We haven't got *power.* The idea's no damn goo—"

He cut short as the sphere's gimbals suddenly hummed, rocked back and forth, and then steadied at a prim angle. Microprocessors chuckled and clicked.

"What do you think I've been doing since you saddled me with that great beast?" Teresa asked. Alex stared at her, so she shrugged. "Well. It helped pass the time. Now, come on! Here's a display unit I ripped off a while back. No holo, just flat screens. But you can plug in there."

Alex knew his jaw gaped open. Shutting it, he could only say—"I love you."

"Damn straight." She nodded quickly. "If you save our lives we can talk about that. Now stop fucking off and get to work!"

He turned around to face the archaic control unit, plugging in and loading his control software, using the subvocal to begin a startup sequence, sparing only a moment to shoot one final look her way. "Bossy wench," he muttered affectionately.

She said nothing, but her eyes offered more confidence in him than he'd ever had in all his life—so he decided he had better try his best.

□

There are buildings that look like charnel houses—one out on the open tundra, one in a desert, one undersea, and one perched on an island bluff under the shadow of dark statues. Within each chamber, towering cylinders still vibrate, rotating within their delicate cages. Nearby, however, no living creature stirs. The walls are streaked with blood.

Those who built the cylinders are gone, but power still flows at the whim of electronic spirits. Computers process ornate programs, casting forth bolts of energy, tickling wrath from far below. Each machine sings the new song it's been taught . . . a song of death. Death spirals outward from the target areas, hunting fatal resonances with bipedal beings that are so numerous, they aren't hard to find in dozens, hundreds, thousands. . . .

This doesn't go on uncontested. Cautiously, brave soldiers approach each site, though daunted by gruesome things they see along the way. Over radio and Net they hear of like horrors beginning to take place in cities far away.

Terrified but determined, the soldiers grimly attack—only to be struck down by something unseen, intangible, unstoppable. Their nimble aircraft switch to autopilot, drifting slowly off course, no longer guided by anything remotely resembling men.

Frantic orders pour over secure channels calling for harsher weapons to be readied. But those will take time to unseal and prepare. Meanwhile, the circles of death expand . . .

● "Daddy, thank God you came!"

Claire was in his arms before Logan got fully out of the taxi. He squeezed his daughter tightly. "I'm here. Yeah. Hey, come on, sunshine. Don't cry."

"I'm not . . . crying," she protested through snuffles. But she didn't draw back until she'd wiped both eyes on his shoulder. When he finally got a chance to look at her, they were red but dry.

It had been months since he'd last visited *chez* McClennon, when summer's humid, scented air made for long, lazy evenings lit by lightning bugs. Now there was a bite of winter in the stiff gulf zephyr that whipped the fringe of cypress trees. From Claire he sensed a quivering, over-wrought tension.

He turned to pay the driver, but the man ignored Logan's proferred credit card. He bent over, covering one ear, listening intently to some news flash coming over his button earpiece, then suddenly cried out in dismay, gunned his engine and took off! Almost instinctively, Logan's hand reached into his pocket for his own receiver.

But no, he had resigned from the struggles of the world. While his family needed him, the universe could fend for itself.

"What's all this about your mother locking herself into her room?" Logan turned and asked his daughter.

The wind whipped Claire's reddish-brown hair. "It's worse than that, Dad. She's electrified her whole wing of the house."

"What?"

"She won't even answer the intercom, though I can tell she's busy working in there—" Claire cut short as a yell of pain echoed round the corner of the house.

"That's Tony," she explained, taking Logan's arm. "He was going to try prying a window."

"Sounds like that worked great." Logan commented as he was dragged along. "Be nice," she chided back. "Tony's good. He's just never taken on Daisy before."

Logan came around the corner to see a lanky, black-haired teenager holding one arm and sucking singed fingers. On the ground a screwdriver still smoked around the extra insulation that must have saved the boy from even worse burns. "Hullo, Mr. Eng," Tony said.

"Hi, yourself," Logan answered, thinking, *So he's never taken Daisy on before? I've got news for both these kids. Neither have I. Not really.*

When you come right down to it, I'm not sure anybody ever has.

□

Out in the real world they try to act against her. Military men take hammers to the peace seals on cruise missiles, desperately bypassing fail-safes, reprogramming the robots to seek sites never named on contingency lists —to fly across widening swaths of no-man's land and destroy other machines . . . machines now casting storms of long-range death.

Trying to accomplish so many unprecedented things, naturally, the men make mistakes. They seek targeting information through the Net and so give away their intentions. Forewarned, Daisy swings her deadly beams to slice through military outposts, clearing them of living crews, leaving the robot bombers unmanned and unready.

Of course there are limits to such delaying tactics. Eventually, surviving soldiers will manage to pick off the resonators one by one. Despite the chaos in the Net, some bright hacker will finally decipher the sinuous path of her commands, tracing all of this back to her. Given enough time.

But time is on her side now. With every passing minute, Daisy grows in power. Soon her creations will be self-sustaining, driven by currents in the Earth's own dynamo. They will be whirling storms of death, as permanent as the weather—scythes of mortality splined and tuned to reap a narrow and specific harvest, humanity.

"Antibodies," she says, giving biological metaphors to her creations. "I'm making antibodies against a parasite."

As fabled Nemesis once implacably hunted murderers, so she pictures herself, seeking just vengeance for the slain manatee, reprisal for the long-dead moa, vindication for vanished condors. "Every species needs natural controls, and humans have lacked one far too long."

There is a proper order to things, she believes. The food-chain is meant to be a pyramid, and every top predator should be rare, its numbers few. Mankind reversed this time-tested arrangement by breeding out of all proportion, creating a teetering edifice, doomed to fall.

"Ten thousand," she concludes. That would be a good figure. That many humans might remain, out of ten billion, to make a decent world population. This she counts as merciful, since the planet might be better off without the species altogether. But after all, she is a mother. And vile as the race might be, she cannot bring herself to wipe out every last human child.

"Ten thousand or so wandering hunter-gatherers. Maybe even twenty. That's as many humans as this world ever needed. " Even wrath must be satiable, and so Daisy targets this limit for herself. As the Net fills with rising cries of anguish, she murmurs reassurance that the panicked world cannot hear and would not understand if it could.

"This is for your own good," she croons. "After all, what life is it for you now, packed into those awful camps and cities, inhaling each other's rank breath? Never knowing the serenity of wildness that's your birthright?''

For the survivors, she promises health, clean skies, beauty, and happiness. They will live vivid lives, and her reapers will keep them company all their days and nights.

Oh yes, it will be a better world. And she *will* stop mercifully, she vows, well before human numbers fall too low.

Mercy, of course, is a word subject to interpretation.

●
N Somewhere in the background Alex heard voices and thought
Ö other refugees must have come aboard. But that couldn't be. By
O now he and Teresa must be the only ones left alive on Easter
S Island, protected by the thin, passive field of his little resonator. It
P had to be some news channel then, frantically reporting this horri-
H ble new endeavor in extinction.
E 　　In parts of Eurasia, the Americas, Africa, the effects were
R straightforward—no earthquakes, nothing hurled into space. Just
E death, simply death.
　　Death of human beings.

It's actually a rather simple combination, he pondered as his device built a finely meshed picture of events on the gravitational bands. He worked cautiously, so as not to be detected by the enemy network. *They're using parameters that couple perfectly with human flesh, in pocket standing waves shaped to match, tidally, the human figure. I never even thought of that, though it's obvious enough from earlier data. The clues were there in all those effects Teresa and others felt. It just took a certain mindset to see it.*

Wave a beam like that around and you can kill millions. It depletes interior fields so little, it's potentially self-sustaining.

The first strikes had been surgical, precise, taking out the world's centers of gravitational research . . . all possible points of opposition. That included Colonel Spivey's former resonators, for instance, and the Russian and Japanese and Han stations, too. Most of those were off-line now. Some flickered on idle, with no one at the helm. And two or three appeared even to have been hijacked, joining the original rebel cylinders in spewing beams of death.

It was too horrible to grasp, of course. If he let the full meaning penetrate it would numb him to uselessness, and Alex couldn't afford that right now.

He tried some tentative pulses to get the feel of the sphere. It was touchy, delicate, like a wild beast. As it spun, it gave off the queerest, brief half images—subtly warped reflections of the spotlights, the looming shuttle cargo bay, his own face.

He hadn't any chance to get familiar with the resonator since it was lifted, dripping, out of the nanogrowth tank many days ago. Now he had to leap straight into the saddle, without benefit of practice or simulation, from the gazerdynamic equivalent of a dray wagon straight to a rodeo horse.

What he *wanted* to do was give the bastards a taste of their own medicine. But without diagnostic backup, that would take too long. Meanwhile, thousands were dying in Tokyo and other places. Something had to be done about that first.

"All right—" he said aloud.

The subvocal mistook his words as commands and sent the sphere precessing in its housing. It took several seconds of concentrated effort to settle it back down again. Jen used to warn him about using the temperamental input device when emotions were running high, but what choice did he have?

All right, Alex thought with silent, iron discipline. *Here goes nothing.*

□

She is slicing through Manaus—scouring the cities and towns of the Amazon—when her familiars report yet another band of desperate military men trying to interfere again. Now a squadron of them are streaking toward one of her resonators in screaming hypersonic aircraft, attempting to overcome her guardian whirlwinds with sheer speed and agility, trying to lock their missiles on target before she can respond.

Daisy obliges them in their courage to face death. Tracking their telemetry, she fills their cockpits with blood and grue.

But two aircraft continue on course. Their pilots have succeeded in setting their autopilots in time! She slips into military channels using codes stolen long ago from supposedly secure caches. By these routes she reads the appropriate control sequences—childishly simple—and uses them to take command of the hurtling ships, overriding their literal-minded computers, sending them careening about on reverse courses, bound for their points of origin.

Then it's back to work. There is so much housecleaning left to do. She's barely begun her chores. In minutes she has cleared the island of Sumatra, where the few remaining orangutans may now dwell in peace, undisturbed by terrible tall interlopers. No more human hands will wield chain saws there. On to Borneo! Her whirlwinds respond and sweep across the sea.

Strictly speaking, she doesn't know what she's doing. She is no physicist, no geologist. The actual nature of the forces she is tapping matters as little to Daisy as the manufacturing details of a computer. All are technical fields that other experts studied, analyzed, and then reduced to beautifully simple, publicly accessible world-models.

Daisy knows all about models. She's stolen many choice ones recently, from her now-extinct cousins, from her ex-husband's employers, from all those clever males who thought they knew so much. She deals with the Earth's interior now through such software intermediaries, as an enchantress might coerce nature by commanding demons and sprites to do her bidding for her. She treats the roiling, surging channels of superconductivity far below as she formerly did the highways and byways of the Net, as yet another domain to rule by proxy, by subroutine, by force of will.

In minutes a terrible storm of death has been unleashed across Java. Now she directs her attention below again, gathering yet another bundle of energy to focus against that funny, strange mirror some called a "singularity," crafting yet another death cyclone to unleash this time on an obscene so-called "civilization" force-grown in a desert—Southern California.

But what's this? In a faraway quarter, Daisy senses a presence where she'd thought all competition vanquished. Where only the dead were supposed to reign!

At the briefest of commands, her familiars streak to check out this effrontery . . .

●

Alex rocked back in dismay. For an instant the whirling sphere had conveyed a sudden, vivid illusion of slitted *lizards'* eyes! Only by quickly switching channels, sending his machine spinning along a new axis, did he make that looming presence vanish from the glistening globe.

He breathed raggedly for a moment. *All right. Don't let it shake you!*

But it was impossible to escape the sense of loneliness. Always, before, he'd had scores of skilled workers to help him. True, they called him "wizard" and *"tohunga."* But press flacks and Nobel committees to the contrary, no scientist with a grain of honesty ever claims he "did it all alone."

And yet, that's exactly what I've got to do now.

With a shuddering sigh, Alex pictured the Earth's involute interior, now livid with convecting magnetism, strung and laced with man-modified channels of surging current. Those currents had grown more finely filigreed every day since his first, tentative scans so long ago, in search of Alpha and then Beta. Now they were a jungle of connections through which he must find a way to do battle.

No more delays. You'll have just one chance to take them by surprise.

And so, with desperate determination, he triggered his best shot.

Again, for the briefest instant he thought he saw a glitter of scales sweep across the spinning sphere, which were chased off by a ripple of tawny orange and black. In an eyeblink the apparitions were gone and the battle joined.

□

The explosion feels like an abrupt amputation. Suddenly, one of her captive resonators vanishes from the Earth's surface, as if an arm or leg had been sliced away, cauterized by actinic heat.

"Damn!" Daisy cries. "It's that meddler on the island again."

She must put off for a little while her next project—scourging the ancient hub where Asia and Africa and Europe meet, where man first took up the cursed profession of farmer. This new nuisance must take priority over even that too-long-delayed correction.

She swings on-line those extra resonators seized after the cleansing of Tokyo and Colorado Springs. This should take only a few moments. . . .

●

Sweat nearly blinded Alex as the near miss swept past. For an instant he'd felt as one might if Beta itself were nearby—yanked by tides so strong the fluids in his head surged like the Bay of Fundy. He shuddered to imagine what the surface of Rapa Nui must look like now, outside the narrow, frail zone of protection he'd erected. He hoped silently it was large enough to include Teresa, elsewhere aboard tiny *Atlantis.*

Then Alex was too busy even for hope. He parried another blow, reflecting the beam directly back to its point of origin. That had no effect of course—not on these bands. By now he knew all those sites were being operated by remote control.

Actually, this antihuman resonance is simple. Given a little time, I could easily devise a counter . . .

Unfortunately, there *was* no time. Warding off increasingly furious attacks took nearly everything he had, though at one point he grabbed a spare instant to send forth another remise, narrowly missing the Saharan site, knocking its resonator out of alignment before having to pull back and duck a fresh four-way assault.

This can't go on, he thought. His new sphere was nimbler than any other machine, and he could tell he was better than his opponent —somehow it *felt* like a single opponent. But the enemy could attack from many sides at once, while sparing other resources to continue the horrible program of mass murder.

☐

This can't go on, she thinks. With a tiny corner of her attention, she sees on a house monitor that her ex-husband has arrived. With Claire and a neighbor boy, he pounds on the front door, calling for her. They look worried, but nowhere near as much as if they knew the truth.

So. Let them stew. By standing where they are, they have earned places among the ten thousand. Good. That's all the courtesy she owes them. Anyway, Daisy has more immediate concerns.

A bunch of clever soldiers has launched a kamikaze raid of zeps and small planes toward the Colorado site, loaded with explosives and meant to impact in great numbers. They hope to achieve a knockout blow by sheer firepower.

Daisy is less worried about this pathetic attempt than about the clever men and women on one of the space stations, who are wrestling an experimental solar power beam away from its designated target, reprogramming it to focus on the Saharan cylinder.

Then there are the hackers . . . a number of them now suspect the Net itself is being used to control the death machines. More dangerous than official authorities, the amateurs are worrisome indeed—the undisciplined ones, whose curiosity and skill doom any secret to eventual discovery.

She doesn't need long-range secrecy, though. Only an hour or less. So she sends little surrogate voices to whisper to the best of them, offering "helpful" rumors and other distractions. "Keep them busy for a while," she orders her familiars.

The clever boy on Easter Island is stymied for a moment. Daisy returns to crafting another death angel, this one to send toward Central America, where there are still a few forests left to save. Those stands of trees will serve as good seed stock for ecological recovery, once the human population is gone.

There! Now it's time to turn back to her main enemy and eliminate him finally, completely. Then the Earth's interior will be hers, and hers alone.

In the morass of demanding input, she must draw the line somewhere.

So Daisy ignores what is going on to her left—on the movie-enhancement wall—where Hercules and Samson still struggle with their bonds as she had left them doing so long ago. She doesn't notice that the straining heroes have been joined by an interloper. A great cat strolls onstage. Scarred and wounded, but rumbling low with feral interest, it strokes against the movie heroes' legs, and then sits at their feet, watching her.

●

"I can't hold on!" Alex cried out, parrying blow after buffeting blow. Knowing full well there was no one to offer any aid, he prayed nonetheless. "God help me!"

Then, in a foxhole conversion—

"Mother . . . help us!"

It was an involuntary shout. But the subvocal made no such fine distinctions. It amplified his words in focused gravitational waves, pouring reverberating echoes toward the core of the world.

□

Small datums suffuse through and among all the excited energy states, stimulating amplification. His words pluck vibrating resonances along magnetic threads where liquid metal meets pressure-strained, electrified rock. They spiral as throbbing tintinations round and round dizzying moiré connectivities, interlacing with prior inputs—those insistent probings and palpations which month after month had forced changes in ancient rhythms, driving them faster, faster, ever faster.

Beta responds; its geometrodynamic foldings crimp and flower through intricate topologies. New, angular reflections of his words cascade from the singularity, diffusing into more directions than mere Euclidean equations can describe.

Complexity meshes with complexity. What had been done to these realms for so long had wrought fine patternings, soft, impressionable matrices ripe for newer, even more intricate templates, such as had been delivered only hours before in a funneling from Africa. Patterns for a tentative model based on the most complex thing ever to exist under the sun—

A human mind.

Tendrils pervade the meshed brilliance . . . channels of flow connect it with the outer skin, where sunlight falls and entropy escapes into black space, and where creatures have already laid down a thick, fertile webbery of data. Pulsing gigabytes, terabytes, whistle as they slide up and down a multitude of scales. All the outer world's libraries, its storms of ferment and distraction, the noise of all its pain . . . these link up in sudden coherence, into that single prayer.

". . . *help . . . us . . .*"

Two giant patternings . . . above, the Net; below, those prominences of supercurrent, rising and falling in new order . . . these are now linked, intertwined. There is no dearth of data, of mere information to pour into this new matrix, this new singularity of metaphors. Each time a beam of tortured space rips apart some screaming human up above, another testimony joins the torrent. And yet, the thirst to absorb grows undiminished.

Is there a theme? Any central focus to unite the whole?

". . . *help us . . . somebody!*"

Much of the information is incompatible, or so it seems at first. Some declarative facts counter others. Priorities conflict. Yet even that seems to elicit something like a thought . . . like a notion.

Competition . . . Cooperation . . .

Hints at a theme—something that might come out of such writhing, whirling complexity, if only the right template were found.

". . . *help us . . . Mother . . .*"

Crystallization, condensation . . . amidst all the driving, opposing forces, there must rise something to arbitrate. Some convenient fiction.

Something to be aware and choose.

Two candidates emerge above all others . . . two contenders for awareness. Two *designs* for a Mother. Upon a hundred million computer displays and several billion holovision sets all programming is preempted by a stunning vision—a dragon and a tiger, facing off. All prior encounters have been preliminary, allegorical. But now they roar and leap with the power of software titans, driven by terawatt inductance, colliding in an explosive struggle to the death.

Million-amp currents thrash against each other, driving channels for new volcanoes as mere side effects to the birthing of a mind.

●

Alex screamed as sudden, unimaginable pain tore at his temples.

"Jen!" he cried, and then collapsed, arms cradling the housing of a sphere whose song rose in pitch as it spun faster, faster, faster . . .

□

Now she knows the truth—that the Net she has always thought a grand domain is only a province, a tendril of something larger. A being. An entire world. All it lacks is a guiding consciousness to bring it order!

She had resigned herself that the Net would end with the passing of *Homo electronicus.* Ten thousand hunter-gatherers couldn't maintain anything so complex. She wouldn't want them to.

But this new matrix will need no communications satellites, no pipelines crammed with optical fibers, no microwave towers or engineers to maintain them. Daisy wonders at the beauty she foresees once her task of winnowing humanity has been completed. There will be no limits to what she might accomplish through this medium. Ancient gods could only have dreamt of such power!

She'd rechannel aquifers and move rivers. She'd use sere bursts of energy to break apart man's chemical poisons, festering in dumps and sewers. She'd shake down dams and dissolve the empty cities, resurrecting the wasted topsoil hidden beneath parking lots. Under her guidance the world will soon be as it was before being brought near ruin by humankind.

Logan and Claire have stopped their futile hammering on the front door. Distractedly, she detects them via another monitor, clambering onto the roof in search of a way to reach her. There they might find entry somehow—or worse, disturb the antennae through which the next few minutes' climactic struggle will be fought. Daisy reaches for a switch that will send deadly current surging through hidden wires.

But no. Her hand stops short. She knows her cautious husband. He'll be judicious, polite, careful. In other words, he'll give her plenty of time.

She checks her gravity resonators and sees they are doing well. With the Easter Island foe apparently knocked off-line, there will be no threats to her machines for several hundred seconds at least. By then it will be too late to interfere meaningfully with her accelerating cleansing of the continents. So far her death angels have barely reaped millions, but that would speed up with each new one she ripens and unleashes forth. . . .

A whirl of color yanks her attention to the left, and her eyes widen in surprise at the sudden, silent battle depicted there—between a dragon and a great cat! What's *this* doing on her simulation wall? This came from no TwenCen movie! The rending, tearing creatures bellow in mute, nostril-flared agony, amid flying scales and smoking fur more vivid by far than any real image.

Daisy suddenly recognizes the tiger motif of her worst enemy, whom she had thought already dead. "Wolling!" she gasps.

In an instant she knows the portent of this struggle. It isn't just resonator against resonator anymore. The computational power of all those nodes below, outnumbering the combined circuits of all the Net—that was the ultimate prize, and someone else was after it! Whoever succeeded in establishing her program first would have it all!

Furiously Daisy turns to unleash all her minions. All her slave resonators swing inward, concentrating their power.

●

Teresa was reminded of an old riddle—

*"The last man on Earth sits alone in a room. There is a knock on
the door . . ."*

At the unexpected sound, she dropped her tools and ran to the
hatch. There, peering through the little, round, double-reinforced
window, she gasped on seeing the familiar, absurd mustachioed visage
of Pedro Manella. Teresa swore and yanked the hissing door release. "I
thought you were a ghost!" she cried as he stepped inside.

"I might be, had I not taken shelter under your wing, so to speak.
I only just gathered the nerve to try the stairs."

"Are there any others? I mean—"

Pedro shook his head with a shiver. "It's too horrible for words."
He looked around. "Is Lustig here? I assume so, since you and I are
still alive."

"He's in back, fighting whatever it is. If only there were some way
to help him—"

She cut short as the ship suddenly moaned around them. The
deck rocked left, throwing her against Manella. Then *Atlantis* swayed
the other way.

"Quakes!" Pedro cried. "I thought we'd finished with such sim-
ple-minded stuff."

His wit wasn't welcome. Teresa pushed him away and moved
with a wide, catlike stance across the rocking deck. "Got to check on
Alex. He could be . . ." Then she stopped, blinking. "Oh, no."

The colors. They were back with a vengeance.

Teresa screamed over her shoulder at Manella. "Find a place to tie
yourself down!" As the shaking grew in intensity, she fought her way
through the airlock to find Alex slumped over at the resonator. She
barely had time to strap him down before all hell broke loose.

□

Not far below Rapa Nui lay a hot, slender needle—an ancient, narrow
plume of magma—part of the mantle's grand recirculation system. This
very needle had *made* the island many millennia ago, piercing through a
scrap of crustal plate to erect this lonely outpost in the sea. For quite some
time since then, however, it had lain quiescent.

Now the boil is squeezed by sudden, transient, titanic forces, pinching molten rock up the confined funnel at awesome pressures, driving it toward those old calderas.

And yet, even at the same moment, something else flies through the same space, traveling just ahead of that explosive constriction . . . something less coercive, subtler, whose fingers of laced gravity unfold like an opening hand.

●

Instinct took over amid the dazzle and roaring noise. Somehow she made it up the quivering ladder to the command deck, where she launched herself into the pilot's seat and began flicking switches by pure rote. "Oh shit!" she cried, hearing the fateful prang of metal bolts popping free under strain. The ancient shuttle's fractured spine complained with a horrible shriek as Teresa felt a sudden surge of acceleration—the seat-of-the-pants sensation of being airborne.

It can't be! This ship can't fly . . . this ship can't fly . . . this ship can't fly . . .

The wings couldn't bear launch loads. She'd seen X rays of the shuttle's broken back—the reason *Atlantis* had been abandoned on a forlorn island in the first place.

An island that no longer existed, from what little she could see as she strained to turn her head. *Atlantis* rose atop a pillar of flame, but there was no rocket. Instead she hurtled just ahead of a towering volcanic plume, reawakened and roaring where only moments ago a tiny Polynesian islet had quietly defied the waves.

Grimacing from g-forces, Teresa nevertheless gripped the cockpit control sticks and felt a strange joy. Perhaps, in some corner of her mind, she had suspected all along it would come to this. Suddenly she feared nothing. After all, wasn't this the best of all possible ways to go? *Flying?* In command of a sweet old bird that should never have been left corroding on a pedestal, but should only die in space?

Even the visceral sensations were grand. She felt as she had as a little girl, when her father used to throw her into the air, and she had known, with utter certainty, he would be there to catch her. Always there to sweep her out of harm's way.

Out of harm's way—

The words seemed to resonate inside her. And as she blinked, tears of happiness washed away those splashy colors, which thinned and merged and finally spread aside to resolve a black cosmos, overlain by a soft blanket of unwinking stars.

Teresa sobbed in sudden realization. It felt exactly as if gentle arms were carrying *Atlantis* home again. The instruments she had carefully restored now chuckled and hummed around her, glowing green and amber. She looked out through a windshield that had been cleansed by fire and saw the moon rise over Earth's soft, curving limb.

☐

In order to get rid of her foe's chief pivot, Daisy has temporarily forsaken her selective, "antibody" approach, using cruder, more decisive force. In seconds, the island is no more.

Ah, well. There hadn't been much of a natural ecosystem left there anyway. Small sacrifice.

More important though, now the Wolling witch has no anchor! Her surprisingly powerful programs—so formidably represented by the tiger icon—might be a match for Daisy's down below. But they can't accomplish much without a link to the surface world, to the net. And now that has been cut!

"Very impressive, Wolling," Daisy murmurs in satisfaction. "You surprised me. But now it's good-bye."

Sure enough, the holo shows her dragon in advance now, forcing backward a strained, disheveled cat, which yowls defiance.

●

At the bottom of the old Kuwenezi gold mine, Jimmy Suarez knew he was a privileged observer. Not only could he watch the battle of two metaphors, which dominated every major holo channel, but he could also use the instruments of this abandoned facility to follow something of the *real* struggle, down below.

For instance, he saw the exact moment when four resonators fired all at once to blow Rapa Nui completely out of the South Pacific. Another force seemed to precede that driving gazer beam by mere moments, but it might have been just a shadow, cast ahead of the decisive bolt.

From that instant, in fact, the tide began to turn. More and more filaments and finely meshed channels seemed to come under control of the force he now recognized as the enemy. The turn of events was horrifying to watch.

It would probably be wiser not to. Just sitting here was risky. Although Kenda's thumper lay inactive now, only a few meters away, even using it on passive detector mode was taking an awful chance. What if the horror—whoever it was—picked up the machine's faint echo? The fate of Easter Island could be his, any time.

Was it curiosity, then, that kept him here instead of smashing the cylinder and fleeing? Or had it been the old lady's last request . . . to leave it turned on till she died? *Well, she's been dead some time,* he thought. The body lay under a tarp behind him as he'd found it, twisted and disfigured, still connected to her console. *I don't owe her anything now. I should take a hammer to the thumper and . . .*

And what? The surface world was certainly no safe place. Kenda and the others might be dead even now, if this part of Southern Africa had already been targeted for culling. Unlikely, since teeming cities and military bases seemed to be the principal victims so far. Still, it was only a matter of time.

Stay down here, then? If I wreck the machines, the death angels might miss me altogether. It was a depressing thought, though. Oh, there was food enough for months. Other isolated snippets of humanity might be as "lucky," holding out in nooks and crannies for some time after the dragon won. But at this point, Jimmy wondered if he should have taken his chances with Kenda and the others after all.

So mired was he in self-pity, it took some moments to harken to a new sound, a gentle humming that added layers as machines throughout the abandoned hall began coming to life. He looked up, staring blankly as the towering crystal resonator swiveled in its bearings, giving off a rising tone. "What the hell?" he asked, standing up. Then, in full, terrified realization, "No!"

He ran to the master control station where the main cutoff switch lay. But as he reached for it, a voice quietly said to him,

"PLEASE, JIMMY. STAY BACK AND LET ME WORK. THERE'S A GOOD LAD."

What really made him halt, however, was the brief, almost tachistoscopic image of a *face* that flashed before him and then was gone again.

"But I thought you were dead!" he whispered hoarsely. Then, when there was no answer to that, he blurted, "Let me help, at least!"

As the dormant machines warmed up around him, that momentary visage returned, and he knew this both was and was not the woman whose former body lay covered just a few meters away.

"ALL RIGHT, CHILD. I KNEW I COULD COUNT ON YOU."

In real life they had exchanged maybe a hundred words, total. And yet, right then Jimmy didn't even wonder why her approval filled him so with joy. All he did was leap to his old work station. Rushing through all the diagnostic checks, he fine-tuned the tool she needed— her link between the worlds above and below.

Soon the humming reached a steady pitch. Then, with a twang of tidal force, it fired.

☐

In meeting houses and churches, in the meditation glades of the NorA ChuGas, under the sloping hand-carved roofs of the Society of Hine-marama, from cathedrals and countless homes, prayers peal forth.

"Help us, Mother."

On the Net, there remain islands of cynicism. Sides are taken, even bets laid down. Dragon over tiger, odds of ten to one.

For the most part, however, humanity's surviving masses just hold each other close, watching their holos fearfully as the now one-sided battle surges on. Meanwhile, they glance to the horizon, toward any strange glimmer or ripple in the air, anxiously awaiting the first agonized scream or any other announcement that death's own reapers have arrived.

Another blow hammers North America.

How much more? People ask the skies. *How much more can our poor world take?*

●

"Daddy!" Claire cried as tremors shook the house. Her feet slipped out from under her and she slid along the roof tiles. Logan barely managed to hold on himself, by grabbing one of Daisy's many antennas as the temblor made trees and canefields sway. Horrified, he saw his daughter slip toward the edge.

In a blur the boy, Tony, launched himself face-first, arms and legs splayed for friction. His slide halted short of the brink, just in time to seize Claire's wrist and help her hold onto a groaning rain spout.

The quake continued for what seemed forever—the worst in Logan's memory—until at last subsiding to the staccato rhythm of debris hitting the concrete walk below. Fortunately, those crunching sounds didn't involve Claire. Somehow, she and Tony held on. "I'm coming!" Logan cried.

☐

"You're back?" Daisy clutches the arms of her chair as her citadel rocks from side to side.

Fortunately, this place was built well, and there's a limit to what her enemy can accomplish with just one device, even operated by surprise.

She deciphers this desperate gambit, to strike at her here, in her very home. "Not bad, Wolling. I'm impressed. After you're extinct, I'll see to it the tribes sing about this battle round their camp fires. You and I will be their legends.

"Only I'll still be around. The goddess that won."

She prepares commands to transmit to her massed resonators. This will be the final act.

●

Logan had to find a way to help the kids. So on impulse, he grabbed one of the antenna cables, yanked it free of its staples, and used the loop to lower himself toward the straining teenagers. At last he could reach out and grab Tony's ankle. "I've got you," he grunted. "See if you can—"

He didn't have to give detailed instructions. Anyway, Claire was a better mountaineer than he'd ever been. She swung one leg over the gutter and clambered up their makeshift human ladder, passing first over her boyfriend, then her father. From the peak she turned and grabbed Logan's leg. Then it was Tony's turn to writhe about and climb.

The last staple holding the cable popped just as the boy reached the flat part of the roof. Staring at the loose end, whipping in his hand like an electrified snake, Logan felt himself start to slide . . . and was stopped at the last second as the kids grabbed him. Soon they were all leaning on one of the dish antennas, panting.

"What the hell was that?" Tony asked. Clearly he meant the quake. But his use of the past tense was premature. Again, without warning, the shaking returned—with a shuddering, infrasonic intensity that made them cover their ears in pain. This time at least, they managed to stay on the pitching roof.

When it finally ended, Claire looked at her father, sharing his thought. This had been no ordinary temblor. "We've got to get to Mother, fast!"

They recklessly took the obstacle course of electronic gear and solar panels. At one point Logan glanced northward toward the line of backup levees which the Corps of Engineers had erected long ago, to reassure a trusting public that all eventualities were predictable and controllable, and would be forever, amen. In the distance, a new sound could be heard, not as deep or grating as the quakes, but just as frightening. It felt like vast herds of wild beasts on the rampage.

That was when Logan knew with utter certainty the corps had been wrong . . . that all things must come to an end. The concrete prison, forged by man to control a mighty river, had finally cracked. And a crack was all the prisoner needed.

The father of waters was free at last.

Long delayed, the Mississippi was coming to Atchafalaya.

□

At a critical instant, several of her channels go suddenly dead, spoiling her aim. Daisy curses as her overpowering counterattack misses Southern Africa, vaporizing instead a corner chunk of Madagascar.

This is taking too long, distracting her from the important work of culling and from consolidating her programs in the vast new network below. These inconveniences are irritating, but there are fallbacks, and she retains far greater powers than her foe. She prepares these even as the house rides out another swaying tremor.

●

Claire cursed, straining on the attic hatch. "I can't budge it!" Tony and Logan helped, heaving with all their might. Daisy had used good contractors to build her citadel. Logan ought to know, having referred her to the best. If only he'd known . . .

They pounded on the latch. He yanked a heavy chunk of antenna from its mooring to use as a pry bar. Between heaves, blinking away sweat as his heart pounded from the effort, he glanced up to see suddenly that there was no more time left at all. A muddy brown wall hurtled across the cane fields with awesome, complacent power, tossing trees and buildings aside like kindling.

Logan grabbed the kids and threw them down. Wrapping loops of cabling around them, he cried, "Hold on for your lives!"

□

Telltale alarms blare of phone lines disrupted and microwave towers toppled—all the local infrastructure she depends on to control her far-flung resonators collapsing in a shambles. And as the data-links snuff out in succession, her dragon staggers like a beast suddenly hamstrung, bellowing in agony. Daisy stares as the other software metaphor—the tiger—leaps atop the crumpling fire lizard to deliver a decisive blow. The cat rears back in triumph as its opponent begins evaporating in smoke .

"You win, bitch," Daisy mutters. "But you better take care of the place or I'll come back from hell to haunt you."

One wall caves inward as a liquid locomotive shatters every barrier to interruption. Water shorts out the expensive electronics in crackling explosions of sparks and spray. But in that final instant, what Daisy realizes with surprising calm is that, perhaps, she never really had been qualified for the job she'd sought.

I never really wanted to be a mothe—

●

Meanwhile, a quarter of the way around the Earth's quivering arc, a small party of refugees finished crossing a final stretch of lichen-covered tundra to reach the sea's edge. There they stopped, clutching each others' hands in fear at what they saw.

In the distance, smoke rose from a burning town and horrible, twisted forms showed that this was one of the places they had heard about—where so-called death angels had emerged from the ground to wreak terrible judgment on humanity. So their exodus from volcanic disaster had only brought them to face something even worse.

It had been an eerie journey, fleeing upwind on foot across the ancient moraine of Greenland, with magma heat at their backs, bereft of every crutch or comfort of civilized society save one—the portable receiver that let them listen to the world's agony in stereophonic sound and real time. So it was that Stan Goldman and the others recognized what confronted them as they slumped together in sooty exhaustion, watching a shimmering fold in space migrate toward them, apparently sensing new victims to reap.

Strangely, Stan felt calm as the thing moved placidly their way. Instead of staring at it like some transfixed bird hypnotized by a snake, he purposely turned away to take one last look out across the bay, where fleet white forms could be seen nearby, streaking underwater then rising briefly to exhale jets of spray.

Beluga whales, he thought, recognizing the sleek shapes. They were cetaceans with smiles even more winning than their dolphin cousins'. To him they suddenly seemed symbols of primordial innocence, untainted by all the crimes committed by Adam and Adam's get since man's fall from grace.

It was good to know the creatures were immune to the approaching horror. That much was clear from the muddled jabber coming over the Net. Except for chimpanzees and a few other species, most animals were left untouched.

Good, Stan thought. Someone else deserved a second chance.

But humankind had already used up number two. *After all, hadn't God already let us off once before with a warning? Remember Noah?* Stan smiled as he saw the perfect irony. For there, stretching across the western horizon, was a rainbow—the Almighty's sign to humankind after the Flood. His promise never again to end the world by drowning.

We might go by fire of course, or famine, or by our own stupidity. Not much of a promise, actually, when you get right down to it. But when dealing with wrathful deities I suppose you take what you can get.

And as promises go, it is an awfully pretty one.

One of the women squeezed his hand fiercely, and Stan knew it was time to face the terrible, vengeful spirit he'd unwittingly helped create. So he turned. It was near, approaching too quickly to flee.

Oh, they could scatter. Delay it a bit. But somehow it seemed better to confront the deadly thing here, now, together. They all gathered close, holding each other. *Hakol havel,* Stan thought. *All is vanity. At the end of all struggles, there comes a time to let go and accept.*

And so, with a certain serenity, he faced death's angel.

Though Stan knew it had to be an illusion, the lethal space-folding actually seemed to slow as it neared. Was it capable of savoring cornered prey, then? He wondered about the strange sensation he was feeling while watching it waver and then come to a stop. It was an odd sort of empathic communion that conveyed . . . confusion? uncertainty?

The deadly thing hovered only meters from the humans. They already felt the draw of its ferocious, devouring tides.

What's happening? Stan wondered. *Why doesn't it get on with it?*

The terrible refraction jigged toward them, hesitated, drew back a little. Then it shivered, as if letting out a sigh—or shaking off a dream.

That was when Stan heard the words.

NEVER AGAIN . . .

His head rocked back. Several of the others fell to their knees. The voice reverberated within them, gently. Not apologetically, but with a soothing kindness.

I PROMISE, CHILDREN. NEVER AGAIN.

To their amazement, the shimmering shape *changed* before their eyes. Squinting, Stan saw a shift in its topology, like an origami monster folding away its claws, retracting and transforming its cutting scythe and then dimpling outward in a myriad of multihued, translucent *petals*.

Stan inhaled a sudden fragrance. The aroma was heady, all-pervading, full of hope and promise. It lingered in the air even as the transformed angel seemed to bow in benediction. Then it drifted off across suddenly serene waters.

Together, he and the others watched as it greeted the joyful, splashing whales and passed on. Even after it disappeared beyond the far headlands, they all knew somehow it would be back . . . that it would be with them always.

And in its presence, they would never again know fear.

PART XI

PLANET

*In a large enough universe,
even unlikely things can happen.
As unlikely as a tiny ball of star-soot
taking upon itself, one day,
to say aloud,
to one and all,
"I am."*

☐ Hello. Hello? This circuit appears to be working. The top sub and reference hyper levels seem okay, though there's no twodee or holo yet. Looks like it'll have to be crude voice and text for a while . . .

I'm going to take a chance, since a lot of other groups seem to be reactivating too. Well, here goes—

Worldwide Long Range Solutions Special Interest Group [☐ SIG AeR,WLRS 253787890.546] . . .

This is SIG vice-chair Beatrice ter Huygens. In response to the U.N. plea for help in restoring order, we invite all members who haven't other responsibilities to log in and . . .

And what? This SIG doesn't exactly specialize in disaster relief. Our members are best at speculation and creating what-ifs. So I thought we might start by sieve-searching through our huge library of "solutions" scenarios. In the past these often seemed like pie-in-the-sky or doom-and-gloom self-diddles, but now some may even prove useful in this new world.

In particular might we come up with an explanation for what has happened to the Net? Amid all the death and destruction, changes have been taking place minute by minute. Nobody in government can seem to grok it, but maybe someone in our group can come up with a notion outlandish enough to be true.

But first, though I dread the bad news, I guess a head count is in order. On my mark, please send your acknowledgment chops to nexus 486 in our administrative . . .

Just a nano. Ah! Holo's coming back! Good pigment, too. Maybe we'll be able to use spread-spec access after all.

Now back to that head count . . .

From the topmost tier of the life ark, Nelson watched Earth turn slowly against the Milky Way. It was the only splash of real color in a drab cosmos, and at this distance one might never imagine what chaos had just reigned on that peaceful-looking globe. Even the continent-long palls cast by still-smoldering volcanoes weren't visible to the naked eye from here—though scientists were already predicting a rough winter ahead.

Until recently, Nelson had been too busy just keeping himself and the majority of his charges alive. Now, though, as the ark settled gradually toward a dusty, gray-brown plain, he could at last spare a moment to look up in wonder at the ocean-planet, swathed on its sunlit side with streamers of cottony clouds. Leftward, on its night side, city lights testified to humanity's narrow escape—though gaping dark patches also showed what a terrible price had been paid in mankind's final war.

That conflict was over now . . . guaranteed with more certainty than any peace treaty ever signed. All across the world, men and women still argued over *what* insured this. But few doubted any longer that a presence had made itself known, and from now on nothing would be the same.

"Ark four, we're at three kilometers altitude. Descent under control with five minutes to landfall. Confirm readiness please."

Nelson turned away from the blue-green world and sought northward across the starscape. There it was, the shuttle, hovering over the mountains rimming Mare Crisium. It was a battered-looking hulk, like something hijacked out of a neglected museum. And yet it flew more powerfully, with more assurance, than anything else made before by human hands. He lifted his belt-phone. "Yeah . . . uh, I mean, roger, Atlantis. I guess we're as ready as ever."

He lowered the phone, thinking, *Sure. But just how ready can you be when you've been volunteered as the first permanent residents of another world?*

He felt a tug at his pants leg. Shig, the little baboon, squeaked and demanded to be picked up. Nelson grinned. "So? You were all over the place when we were weightless. But now a little gravity makes you lazy again?"

Shig clambered from his arm onto his shoulder, perching there to look across their new home, one even drier and emptier than the savannas of Africa, to be sure, but theirs nonetheless, for better or worse. From the railing nearby, Shig's mother glanced at Nelson in unspoken question. He shrugged. "I don't know *where* the nearest water hole is, Nell. They say they'll send some ice our way in a while, along with the first bunch of people. Don't ask me how they'll manage it, but we'll be fine till then. Don't worry."

Nell's expression seemed to say, "Who's worried?" Indeed, after what they'd been through together, they couldn't be faulted for a little team cockiness.

Uprooted from the soil of Africa and hurled into high orbit, Kuwenezi's experimental ark four went through hours, days, during which disaster kept missing them by seconds. For instance, if certain circuits had failed during those first critical instants, Nelson wouldn't have been able to order most of the hurtling pyramid sealed against hard vacuum. Nor could he have shifted fluids from one vast storage tank to another, gradually damping out the unwilling satellite's awkward tumble.

As it was, fully a third of the biosphere's life habitats were dead—their occupants having asphyxiated or been crushed against adamant glass-crystal barriers, or simply having succumbed to drastically altered circumstances.

He'd never have managed saving the rest without Shig and Nell, whose nimble grace in free fall made them invaluable at fetching floating tools or herding panicking creatures into makeshift stalls where they could be lashed down and sedated. Even so, the job had seemed utterly hopeless—a futile staving off of the inevitable—until that weird moment when Nelson felt something like a *tap on his shoulder.*

Whirling about in shock and exhaustion, he had turned to find no one there. And yet, that hallucinatory interruption had been enough to draw him back from a tunnel-torpor of drudgery . . . far enough to let him notice that his belt-phone was ringing.

"H-hello?" he had asked, unable to believe anyone knew or cared about his plight, cast from the Earth, bound for oblivion aboard a glass and steel Flying Dutchman.

There had been a long pause filled with static. Then a voice had said, "NELSON . . ."

"Uh . . . yeah?"

"I WANTED YOU TO KNOW—HELP IS COMING. I HAVEN'T FORGOTTEN YOU."

He remembered blinking in amazement.

"D-Dr. Wolling? Jen?"

He couldn't be sure in retrospect. The voice had seemed different in countless ways. Distant. Preoccupied. And yet, somehow it had made the hours of hectic labor that followed more bearable just knowing he hadn't been overlooked—that someone knew he and the animals were out here, and cared.

So it wasn't with total surprise when—after lashing the last beast down, after sealing the last whistling crack, after adjusting gas and aeration balances in the complex panels that recycled the ark's basic stuff of life—he suddenly heard the phone ring again, and lifted his eyes to see a stubby white and black arrow homing in on this derelict little worldlet.

Nelson's knowledge of physics was too slender to truly appreciate what it meant when *Atlantis*'s pilot promised to provide gravity again to the ark's weary inhabitants. He only felt gratitude as the shuttle's crew somehow delivered, recreating up and down via some magic they generated at long range. Then they began hauling the drifting tower toward a promised new home.

En route, he finally had time to listen to condensed summaries of what had been going on, back on Earth. It was all too complex and bizarre to comprehend at first, in his dazed state. But later, as he took advantage of his first real chance at sleep, partial realization came to him in his dreams.

At one point he saw a dismembered snake writhe and bring together its many parts. He heard a hundred braying instruments settle down under a conductor's baton to create symphonies where there had been mere noise.

E pluribus unum . . . a voice murmured. *Many can make up a whole . . .*

Now, as the time of landing approached, Nelson wondered if anyone on Earth had a better understanding of what had happened than he did.

They're all so busy arguing about it, discussing the change and what it means—

Gaians claim it's their Earth Mother . . . that she's been shaken awake at last, to step in and save foolish mankind and all her other creatures.

Others say no, it's the Net *. . . the whole store of human knowledge that poured into all those unexpected new circuits deep inside the Earth. All that virgin computational power, suddenly multiplied, only naturally had to lead to some sort of self-awareness.*

There was no end to theories. Nelson heard Jungians proclaiming a *race consciousness* had manifested itself during the crisis, one that had been there, waiting, all along. Meanwhile, Christians and Jews and Muslims made noises much like the Gaians'—only they seemed to hear the low voice of a "father" when they tuned in on those special channels that now carried new, awesome melodies. To them, recent miracles were only what had been promised all along, in prophecy.

Nelson shook his head. None of them seemed to understand that they—their very arguments and discussions—were helping *define* the thing itself. Yes, a greater level of mind had been born, but not as something separate, or even above them. All the little noisy, argumentative, even contradictory voices across the planet—these were parts of the new entity, just as a human being consists naturally of many disputing "selves."

Nelson recalled his last conversation with his teacher, when the topic had swung to her latest project—her bold new model of consciousness. A model that, he knew somehow, must have played some key role in the recent coalescence.

"The problem with a top-down view of mind is this, Nelson," she had said. "If the self at the top must rule like a tyrant, commanding all the other little subselves like some queen termite, then the inevitable result will *be* something like a termite colony. Oh, it might be powerful, impressive. But it will also be stiff. Oversimplified. Insane.

"Look at all the happiest, sanest people you've known, Nelson. Really listen to them. I bet you'll find they don't fear a little inconsistency or uncertainty now and then. Oh, they try always to be true to their core beliefs, to achieve their goals and keep their promises. Still, they also avoid too much rigidity, forgiving the occasional contradiction and unexpected thought. They are content to be many."

Remembering her words made Nelson smile. He turned again to stare at Earth, the oasis everyone now spoke of as a single living thing. It hardly mattered whether that was a *new* fact, or one as old as life itself. Let the NorA ChuGas preach that Gaia had always been there, aware and patient. Let others point out that it had taken human technology and intervention to bring violent birth to an active planetary mind. Each extreme view was completely correct in its way, and each was just as completely wrong.

That was as it should be.

Competition and cooperation . . . yin and yang . . . Each of us participatin' in the debate is like one of the thoughts that bubble and fizz in my own head—whether I'm concentrating on a problem or daydreaming at a cloud. Does one particular thought worry about its "lost independence" if it realizes it's part of something larger?

Well, some prob'ly do, I guess. Others aren't bothered at all. So it'll be with us, too.

Nelson replayed his last musings to himself, and silently laughed. *Listen to you! Jen was right. You're a born philosopher. In other words, full of shit.*

But then he had an answer to that, too. *We may be mere thoughts, each of us a fragment. But that don't mean some thoughts aren't important! Thoughts could be the only things that never die.*

From below decks a lowing wafted through the air grilles. Sedatives were wearing off and some of the wildebeests were waking up. Perhaps they sensed imminent arrival. Soon Nelson would have his hands full tending this, the first sapling cast forth by the mother world . . . the first of a myriad that might stream outward if the new gravity technologies proved workable. And if Earth's nations agreed to the bold enterprise.

And if the new Presence let it be so.

Anyway, until the promised help came, he'd be too busy for philosophy . . . either for Gaia's sake or for his own. Westward, the lunar mountains loomed higher and higher. The plains rose rapidly. And not too far below, he now saw the shadow of the ark. That dark patch coalesced and then spread across the gaping foundation awaiting it—freshly carved and vitrified within the ancient regolith by more magic from *Atlantis.*

Nelson put his arms around Shig and Nell during the final descent, which ended in a grating bump so gentle it was almost anticlimactic. The small, fluttering variations in gravity disappeared, and the moon's light but firm grasp settled over them for good.

"Hello, ark four," the voice of the woman pilot said. "Come in, ark. This is *Atlantis.* Is everything okay over there?"

Nelson lifted his belt phone.

"Hello, *Atlantis.* Everything's just fine. Welcome to our world."

□ Worldwide Long Range Solutions Special Interest Group [□ SIG AeR,WLRS 253787890.546]

. . . found an old TwenCen novel in which something like our present-day Net got taken over by software "gods and demons" based on some Caribbean sect. If that's what happened, we're all in deep trouble. But what we're seeing doesn't seem to be anything like—

How can I tell? Yeah, I know it's hard getting any sort of explicit answer from the Presence, whatever it is. But I'm sure all right. Call it a feeling.

Oh, yes, I agree with that! We are in for interesting times . . .

The contradiction was almost too absurd. *Atlantis* was the most capable ship in history. *Atlantis* was also a creaking wreck, threatening to fall apart at any moment.

The air recyclers kept leaking. The carbon dioxide scrubbers had to be kicked every ten minutes or so to unclog them. The toilet was so awful they'd taken to using plastic bags, tying them off and storing them under webbing at the back of the cargo bay.

At least the water coming out of her slapped-together fuel cells was pure. But for food they had only some bruised fruits provided by that lonely caretaker-ecologist—his way of saying thanks for rescuing his marooned ark and depositing it safely on the moon. The oranges were tart, but an improvement over what they'd survived on during the first few days in space—a single box of stale crackers and five suspicious candies found in Pedro Manella's jacket pocket.

Now, at last, their travails seemed about to end. Teresa peered through the sighting periscope at the winking lights outlining the European space station just ahead. "Bearing six zero degrees azimuth," she said into her chin mike. "Vector angle seventeen degrees, relative. Speed point eight four—"

"Okay, I've got it, Rip," Alex's voice crackled from the makeshift intercom. "Hang on, we're heading in."

It was hard getting used to this new mode of space travel. Using the puff-puff rockets of old, you had to calculate each rendezvous burn with a kind of skewed logic. To catch up with an object in orbit ahead of you, first you had to *decelerate*, which dropped you in altitude, which sped you up until you passed below your objective. Then you'd fire an acceleration burn to rise again, which slowed you down . . .

It was an art few would have much use for in the future. No more delicate, penny-pinching negotiation with Newton's laws. All Teresa had to do now was tell Alex where to look and what to look for, and he took it from there. His magic sphere transmitted requests deep into the Earth, which elicited precise, powerful waves of gravity to propel them along. It made space travel almost as simple as pointing and saying, "Take me there!"

That was what made this the greatest spaceship ever, able to fly rings around anything else. And so it would remain for the next ten minutes or so, until they docked. Then arrangements would be made to transfer Alex and his gear to a modern craft, and poor old *Atlantis* would become another museum piece in orbit.

That's all right, baby. She thought, patting the scratched, peeling console. *Better this way, after one last wild ride, than sitting down there letting sea gulls crap all over you.*

Now and then she still closed her eyes, remembering that hurtling launch—climbing just ahead of a pillar of volcanic flame as they were scooped into the sky by something greater than any rocket. Perhaps Jason had found it even more vivid and exalting as he bolted toward the stars. She hoped so. It felt fitting to think of him that way as she was finally able to say adieu.

Anyway, there were busy times ahead. After spending the better part of a week in hurried rescue missions, helping clean up the mess left in orbit by the war, she and Alex were about to take leading roles in the new international space plan. With Lustig-style resonators about to be mass produced, soon even skyscrapers and ocean liners might take to the sky. Within a year, there could be thousands living and working out here and on the moon. At least that seemed to be the general idea, though people still scratched their heads over how this had been agreed to so quickly.

In spite of having been close to the center of great events, Teresa admitted being as confused as anyone about what—or who—was in charge now. The "presence" that had been born out of recent chaos wasn't wielding a heavy hand, which made it hard to really pin down or define.

Was it an independent entity with its own agenda to impose on subordinate humanity? Or should it be looked on as little more than a new layer of consensus overlaying human affairs, a personification of some global *zeitgeist*? Just one more step in a progression of such worldview revolutions— so-called renaissances—when the process of thinking itself changed.

Philosophers typed earnest queries into the special channels where the Presence seemed most intense. But even when there was a reply, it often came back as another question.

"WHAT AM I? YOU TELL ME . . . I'M OPEN TO SUGGESTIONS . . ."

That attitude, plus an impression of incredible, overpowering patience, sent some mystics and theologians into frenzies of hair pulling. But to the rest of humanity it brought something like relief. For the foreseeable future, most decisions would be left to familiar institutions—the governments and international bodies and private organizations that existed before everything went spinning off to hell and back again. Only in matters of basic priority had the Law been laid down, in tones that left no doubt in anybody's mind.

Gravity resonators, for instance; they could be constructed by anyone who had the means—but not all "requests" made through them would be granted. Earth's interior was no longer vulnerable to intrusion. The new, delicate webbery of superconducting circuits and "neuronal pathways" that now interlaced smoothly with humanity's electronic Net had made itself impervious to further meddling.

It also became clear why the nations were expected to commence major space enterprises. Henceforth, the raw materials for industrial civilization were to be taken from Earth's lifeless sisters, not the mother world. All mines currently being gouged through Terra's crust were to be phased out within a generation and no new ones started. Henceforth, Earth must be preserved for the real treasures—its species —and man would have to look elsewhere for mere baubles like gold or platinum or iron.

That was the pattern of it. Certain forests must be saved at once. Certain offensive industrial activities had to stop. Beyond that, details were left to be worked out by bickering, debating, disputatious humankind itself.

With one additional, glaring exception, which had caused quite an impression. Perhaps to show the limits of its patience, the Earth-mind had gone out of its way, a few days ago, to set a particularly pointed example.

Since the "transformation of the angels," when the horror had suddenly ceased worldwide, there had nevertheless been confirmed cases—no more than a few hundred total—of people being ripped to shreds by sudden deadly force, without warning or mercy. In each case, investigating reporters found evidence appearing on their screens as if by magic, proving the victims to be among the worst, most shameless polluters, conspirators, liars. . . .

Clearly, some "cells" were just too sick—or cancerous—to be kept around, even by a "body" that proclaimed itself tolerant of diversity.

"DEATH IS STILL PART OF THE PROCESS . . ."

That was the coda spread across newspaper displays. Strangely, the warning caused little comment, which in itself seemed to say a lot about consensus. The cases of "surgical removal" ceased, and that appeared to be that.

Teresa wondered at her own reaction to all this. It surprised her that she felt so little rebelliousness at the thought of some "planetary overmind" taking charge. Perhaps it was because the entity seemed so vague. Or that it appeared uninterested in meddling in life at a personal level. Or that humans, after all, seemed to *be* the mind's cortex, its frontal lobes.

Or perhaps it was just the utter futility of rebellion. Certainly the presence didn't seem to mind as certain individuals and groups schemed in anger to topple it. There were even channels on the Net set aside especially for those calling for resistance! After listening in a while, Teresa likened those strident calls to the vengeful, cathartic daydreams any normal person has from time to time . . . vivid thought-experiments a sane person can contemplate without ever coming close to carrying them out. They'd probably boil and simmer a while, and then, like the more outrageous passions of puberty, evaporate of their own heat and impracticality.

"Captain Tikhana," a voice called from behind, stirring her contemplations. "As long as we're almost there, may I please stop kicking pipes and rest a while?"

Pedro Manella's head and torso extended halfway through the tunnel from middeck. The normally impeccable journalist was grimy and odorous from many days' labor without bathing. Teresa almost sent him below again, to keep him out of the way. But no. That would be unfair. He'd been working hard, doing all the scutt labor and shit carrying while she and Alex were busy. Probably, they wouldn't have made it without him.

"All right, Pedro," she told the journalist. "I don't figure the cooling system will freeze up in the next five minutes. You can watch the approach if you're quiet."

"Like a church mouse, I'll be." He carefully float-hopped over to grab the copilot's chair, but didn't try sitting down. The seat was filled with another of her make-do consoles. Teresa tried to ignore the aromas wafting from the big man. After all, she probably smelled little better.

As Alex brought them toward a gentle rendezvous with the waiting station, Teresa used her tiny store of precious, hoarded reaction gas to orient *Atlantis* for docking. Spacesuited astronauts made signals in the efficient, lovely language of hands, more useful to her now than the tense words of the station's traffic controllers, who had no idea what to make of this weird vessel anyway.

At last, with a bump and a clank, they locked into place. *Atlantis*'s ancient airlock groaned as it was put to use for the first time in decades, hissing like an offended crone.

Teresa flicked off switches and then patted the console one last time.

"Good-bye, old girl," she said. "And thanks again."

After transferring the equipment, after meetings and conference calls with everyone from tribunes to investigative commissions to presidents, after they were finally allowed to shower and change and eat food fit for human consumption . . . after all of that, Teresa at last found herself unable to settle down within her tiny assigned cubicle. Sleep wouldn't come. So she got up and made her way to the station's observation lounge, and wasn't surprised to find Alex Lustig there already, looking out across the carpet of blue and brown that seemed to stretch forever just beyond the glass.

"Hi," he told her, turning his head and smiling.

"Hi, yourself." And no more needed to be said as she joined him gazing at the living world.

Even in weightlessness there are influences, subtle and sometimes even gentle. Eddies of air and tide brushed them, bringing their shoulders together as they floated side by side, their faces bathed in Earthlight. It took little more to fold her hand into his.

From then on, all was kept in place by sound . . . the silent pulsebeat of their hearts, and a soft low music they could hear alone.

☐ "We are born to be killers, of plants if nothing else. And we are killed. It's a bloody business, living off others so that eventually they will live off you. Still, here and there in the food web one finds spaces where there's room for something more than just killing and being killed.

"Imagine the island of blue in the middle of a tropical storm, its eye of peace.

"You must admit the hurricane is there. To do otherwise is self-deception, which in nature is fatal, or worse, hypocritical. Even honest, decent, generous folk must fight to survive when the driving winds blow.

"And yet, such folk will also do whatever they can, whenever they can, to expand the blue. To increase that gentle, centered realm where patience prevails and no law is made by tooth or claw.

"You are never entirely helpless, nor ever entirely in it for yourself. You can always do something to expand the blue."

Can anyone out there identify this quotation for me? I found it scribbled on a piece of paper and stuffed between the pages of an old book. My ferrets can't find the philosopher who wrote it, but I'm sure it must have been published somewhere.

It makes me wonder how things must have been for our ancestors, who might have had beautiful thoughts like this one, but no net to plant them in, where they might take root and sprout and become immortal.

So many lost thoughts . . . we've only now, it seems, acquired memory.

Perhaps we're not so much "growing up," as people say, as awakening from a kind of fevered dream.

—N. M. Patel. [☐ user IENs.mAN 734-66-3329 aCe.12.]

● L I T H O S P H E R E

● When the helicopters had first arrived, Logan's first numb, hopeful thought had been how swift and efficient the rescue effort was! How powerful were the forces of compassion, so soon after the levees broke.

But then he saw the markings on the olive-gray aircraft, and their bristling arms, and realized that their sudden appearance over the roiling, muddy waters was coincidental. Such overpowering military presence couldn't have been organized so swiftly since the Mississippi burst its banks, plowing a new course to the sea. Nor were those deadly birds bound on any mercy mission.

As they circled, shining hot spotlights on him and the kids, Logan suddenly realized in the gathering twilight why they had come. No coincidence, after all.

Daisy. They've come after Daisy. Jesus! What's she done this time?

He still couldn't bring himself to believe she was gone. Logan clung to hope the same way he had clutched Tony and Claire when the house was torn off its foundations and hurled into the raging torrent. He hung onto that faith through every impact with floating trees and protruding telephone poles, believing fervently that Daisy might have found some pocket of air below. After what he'd seen these last few months, Logan figured anything at all was possible.

Even as the helicopters circled overhead—perhaps deliberating whether to make certain of their mission by blasting the house anyway—their tottering bungalow-raft miraculously came aground on one of the sloping, man-made berms thrown up by some TwenCen oil company to hide its ugly refinery towers. Claire cried out as the villa tilted. They grabbed each other and the dangling antennae to keep from spilling into the deadly waters. The churning Mississippi beckoned . . .

Then the tilting stopped. The house settled back and was still.

Suddenly men were dropping out of the sky, plummeting down ropes to land on the canted rooftop. At the mention of his ex-wife's name, Logan quickly pointed toward the jammed attic hatch. He had no thought to spare her arrest, only a glimmering hope they might haul her out of there alive.

Several soldiers pulled him and the kids back while others laid gray paste round the hatch. "Cover your eyes!" a sergeant bellowed. But even that didn't exclude the flash, outlining the bones in Logan's hands. Blinking through speckles, Logan saw soldiers dive with reckless courage into a black, smoking hole, as if about to face hell's own legions, instead of one unarmed, middle-aged woman. It seemed so incongruous. These grim-faced men had the set-jawed look of volunteers for a suicide squad.

When word came out what the skirmishers had found, Logan looked at his daughter. There was sadness in her eyes, but also a kind of relief. When she turned his way though, Claire's face suddenly washed with concern. "Oh, Daddy. I didn't know."

Didn't know what? he tried to ask. But his voice wouldn't function. He blamed the whipping helicopter blades for the stinging in his eyes, and exhaustion for the quivering that seemed to take over his body. Logan tried to turn away, but Claire only threw her arms around him.

He clutched her tightly as his lungs gave way to wracking, heart-broken sobs.

Military custody wasn't so bad. The authorities gave them fresh clothes and medical attention. And as realization spread that the worst of the crisis was indeed over, the questioning grew less frantic and shrill.

Not that anyone really believed it all came down to one solitary woman, manipulating forces all over the world from a cottage on the bayou. There had to be more, the intelligence officers insisted. Though now less brutally frenetic, the inquiry went on and on, long after Logan's revealed participation in the Spivey network brought in yet more officials, more voices asking the same questions over and over.

What finally put a stop to it was intervention from the top. And when Logan learned what "the top" meant these days, he understood the wide-eyed expressions on his interrogators' faces.

HE WAS ON OUR SIDE. . . .

So came word over those special channels, referring specifically to him.

FINISH YOUR WORK, BY ALL MEANS. THEN LET HIM GO.

Everyone treated Logan courteously after that. He got to see Claire and Tony. His plaque was returned to him. And soon, after promising to keep himself available to the appropriate commissions, he was escorted outside into a bright afternoon.

Logan sniffed a breeze that seemed faintly scented with springtime. Claire took his hand and led him toward a waiting chauffeured car. "Your office has been calling," she told him, consulting her wrist display. "The mayor of New Orleans won't even talk about plans for a new waterfront and reservoir system without you there—'to keep 'em honest,' as he put it. And the Nile Reclamation Agency sent an urgent message saying they've changed their minds about that idiotic, shortsighted dam project. Instead, they dug out your old plans for the Aswan silt diversion system. I told them better late than never, but they'll still have to wait till you've rested. Anyway, I wanted to go over some ideas with you before we talk to them."

He smiled at her. "Sounds like you've been handling the family business while Dad was in stir."

She lifted her chin. "I'm seventeen now. You said we'd be partners someday. So? It sure looks like there's enough to do."

That was true enough. The list of cleanup jobs was long and intimidating—even without having to satisfy a new planetary intelligence that your plans were good ones, truly designed for the long term. From now on the first rule of engineering would be to work with Earth's natural forces, never against them.

"You're still going to college," he insisted. "And by the way, you can't leave Tony hanging in midair, either. At least, you better tell the poor boy where he stands."

She tilted her head, then nodded. "Fine. Okay. I'll take care of being a teenager. That'll still leave me . . . thirty hours a week to—"

"—to be an engineer," he laughed. "All right. If I tried to stop you, I'd probably just get overruled anyway."

She grinned and squeezed his arm. Their driver held the door. Before getting into the car, though, Logan stopped to look at the sky. There was a patch over to the north, in the place farthest from the sun, where the dark hue was so clear and icy blue. . . .

Briefly, he closed his eyes and let out a sigh.

"Let's go," he said as he sat down beside his daughter. "We've got a lot of work to do."

□

I am the sum of many parts. I stretch and yawn and test my fingers . . . using such words to describe the complex things I do until my human parts can come up with better ones.

I am the product of so many notions, cascading and multiplying in so many accents and dialects. These are my subvocalizations, I suppose—the twitterings of data and opinions on the Net are my subjective world. Sometimes it gets confusing and I feel a thread of fear, even revulsion as the contradictions rise, threatening chaos. At such moments I am tempted to clamp down and simplify.

But no. I shall be needing diversity during the time that stretches ahead, especially since, for now at least, there seems only to be me.

There must be a center to this storm. A sense of self—of humor—to tie it all together. A strong candidate for this role is a template that was once a single human personality—a simple but intriguing mind-shape—that may well do for that purpose. On those occasions when I must dip down to a human scale of consciousness, it seems suitable that I be "Jen."

Of course, I see the paradox. For it is by her own standards that I judge this suitability. She seeded the transformation that made me, and so I cannot help choosing to be her.

I am the exponentiation of so many inputs. I sense static discharges from skin and scale and fur, and all the sparking flashes as my little subself animal cells live out their brief lives and die. In places, this feels right and wholesome . . . a natural cycle of replacement and replenishment. Elsewhere, I feel chafed, damaged. But now at least I know how to heal.

This is all very interesting. I never imagined that to be a deity, a world, would mean finding so many things . . . amusing.

● Alex found Pedro Manella standing by one of the big space-win-
C dows in the observation lounge, overlooking a vast, glittering ex-
O panse of assembly cranes and cabling. More parts sent up from
R Earth were being fitted to a second huge, wheel-shaped space sta-
E tion. Workers and swarms of little tugs clustered around the latest
giant gravity freighter, only recently delivered atop a pillar of warped
space-time.

Well, it can't be put off any longer, Alex thought.

After months of hard work, the practical running of these grand undertakings had finally passed out of his hands, freeing him to concentrate on basic questions once more. Soon, he and Teresa would be heading groundside to join others fascinated by the quandary of this new world. Stan Goldman would be there, he was glad to learn. And George Hutton and Auntie Kapur. Each had earned a place on the informal councils that were gathering to discuss all the whys and hows and wherefores.

Perhaps, between deliberations, he and Teresa would also find some long-awaited time to be alone, to explore how much farther they wanted to take things, beyond simply sharing the deepest trust either of them had ever known.

That was all ahead. Before leaving for Earth, however, there was one unfinished piece of business he had to take care of.

"Hello, Lustig," Pedro said in a friendly tone.

"Manella." Alex nodded. "I thought I'd find you here."

"Indeed? So. What can I do for you?"

Alex stood still for a minute, appreciating the semblance of gravity created by the rotating station's centrifugal force—a reassuring sensation, though now there were other ways to duplicate the feat. Ways unimagined even a year ago, but which were now the foundations of new technologies, new capabilities, new opportunities.

Ways that had also come near ending everything forever.

"You can start by telling me who the hell you are," Alex said in a rush, unable to completely keep a nervous quaver from his voice. "You can tell me why you've been fucking with our world."

He kept his hands on the rail, watching the busy space-yards. But Alex felt painfully aware of the large figure standing nearby, turning now to look at him. To his surprise, Manella didn't even pretend not to know what he was talking about.

"Who else, other than you, suspects?"

"Only me. It was too bizarre a notion to tell even Teresa or Stan."

That protected those he loved, at least. If Manella was willing to kill to maintain his secret, then let it end here. That is, if there *was* a secret. . . .

The big man seemed to read Alex's thoughts, which must have been on his face. "Don't worry, Lustig. I wouldn't harm you. Anyway, it's not at all clear I could. This world's overmind has affection for you, my boy."

Alex swallowed. "Then your job here . . ."

"Is finished?" Pedro blew his moustache. "Now if I answered that straight, I'd be admitting you were right in your wild, preposterous hunch. As it is, I'm just playing along with an amusing game of what-if, invented by my friend Dr. Alex."

"But—" Alex sputtered in frustration "—you just now confessed—"

"—that I know what you suspect me of. Big deal. I've noticed the way you've watched me the last few days . . . making inquiries. I've made a life study of you, too. Don't you imagine I can tell what you're thinking?

"But please, do spell it out for me. I'm most interested."

Alex found he couldn't keep his composure looking directly at Manella. He turned back toward the window again.

"There have been so many coincidences. And too many of them revolve around you, Manella. Or events under your control. While everything was flying thick and fast, I had no time to put it all together. But during the last few weeks I kept getting this nagging feeling it was all too pat."

"What was too pat?"

"The way I was hired by those generals, for instance . . . giving me carte blanche to experiment with cavitronic singularities, even though there were only vague hopes of giving them what they wanted in secret."

"Are you accusing me of manipulating generals for your benefit?"

Alex shrugged. "It sounds ridiculous. But given the rest of the story, it wouldn't surprise me. What *is* irrefutable is your role in what followed—seeing to it those riots caused my Alpha singularity to fall, *just* when I'd discovered a flaw in the old physics, and was about to arrange for a controlled shutdown myself."

"You imply I made Alpha fall on purpose. What reason could I have?"

"Only the obvious. It made me obsessed with finding again what I'd lost . . . chivvying support from Stan and then George Hutton, till at last we built a resonator capable of chasing down Alpha—"

"—and incidentally detecting Beta, as well," Manella finished for him. "Which means what?"

Alex could tell the man was toying with him, forcing him to lay down all his cards. So be it. "Finding Beta was key to all that followed! But never mind. Your tenacity in tracking me to New Zealand was another feat that fell just inside the range of the believable. So was the way you gathered together a team whose abilities just complemented what we had in New Zealand, so when the two groups merged—"

"—the sum was greater than its parts. Yes, we did bring together some competent people. But then, it was so hard keeping things secret after that—"

"Don't prompt me, Pedro," Alex snapped. "It's patronizing."

"Sorry. Really. Do go on."

Alex exhaled. "Secrecy, yes. You proved uncannily able, running interference on the Net for us. Even with all his resources, Glenn Spivey marveled at how hard it was to track us down . . . till finally he *did* find us. Supposedly it was that McClennon woman who leaked the clues to him. But—"

"—but you suggest I leaked word to *her*. Hmph. Go on. What's next?"

Alex kept a lid on his irritation. "Next there's your disappearing trick at Waitomo, abandoning Teresa on the trail when Spivey arrived . . ."

"Presto." Manella snapped his fingers.

". . . and your equally dramatic reappearance on Rapa Nui, conveniently in time to influence my research *and* foil June Morgan's sabotage."

Manella shrugged. "Such thanks I get."

"Thanks enough not to question how you rescued Teresa from that pit . . . or managed to be the sole person on the entire island to make it alive past the death angels and knock on *Atlantis*'s door . . . just in time to hitch a ride—"

He stopped as Manella lifted a meaty hand. "It's still awfully thin, Lustig."

"Thin!"

"Come on. All of those things could have happened without my being—what you imply. Where's your proof? What are you trying to say?"

Alex turned now to face Manella fully. His blood was up and he no longer felt reticent at all. "It was *you,* I now recall, who seeded the idea of asking my grandmother to help get us a resonator site in Southern Africa. In exchange, you made sure she had full-time computer access!"

"So I'm a nice fellow. And things worked out so she was in a place to make a difference. Still, all you have is a tower of teetering suppositions and guesses."

"I don't suppose," Alex growled, "it would bother you much if I insisted you be medically examined—"

"—not at all—"

"—down to the level of a DNA scan? No?" Alex sighed. "You could be bluffing."

"I could be. But you know I'm not. This body's human, Alex. If I were some little green pixie riding around inside this carcass—if this were some sort of big, ugly disguise—don't you think I'd have suffocated by now? Wouldn't I have arranged to wear a better-looking model?" Manella groomed his moustache in the window reflection. "Not that I've had many complaints from the ladies, mind you."

In exasperation, Alex fought to keep from shouting. "Dammit, you and I both know you're not human!"

The tall figure turned and met his eyes. "How do you define 'human'? No, seriously. It's a fascinating notion. Does it include your grandmother, for instance? In her present state?

"This is such an amusing discussion! But just for the sake of argument let's follow your reasoning. Suppose we posit you have cause to suspect—no proof, mind you—that I'm unusual in some way."

Alex swallowed again. "What *are* you?"

Manella shrugged again. "A reporter. I never lied about that."

"Dammit—"

"But for the sake of argument, let's consider the chance a fellow like me, who was involved in all the things I've been, might have had another job as well."

"Yes?"

"Well, there are possibilities. Let's see . . ." Pedro lifted an eyebrow. "Maybe as a friendly neighborhood policeman? Or a social worker?" He paused. "Or a midwife?"

Alex blinked once, twice. "Oh," he said.

For the first time, Manella's expression grew pensive, thoughtful. "I can guess what you're thinking, Lustig. That all your conclusions back in Waitomo must be wrong. That Beta couldn't have been a berserker machine, a weapon sent to wreck the Earth. Because see what actually happened! Rather than ruin a world, Beta became essential to bringing an entire planet alive."

"Auntie Kapur. She told me to 'seek the wisdom of sperm and egg.' . . . Oh, these damn bloody metaphors!" Alex's temples hurt. "Are you saying Beta was sent here to *fertilize*—?"

"Hey, I never admitted knowing any more about it than you do. We're just doing a particularly bizarre, imaginative, pretend scenario right? Frankly, after all the things I've been called in my life, it's a bit refreshing to be cast in the role of a friendly alien for a change!"

Manella laughed. "Anyway imagine a bunch of clever parameciums, trying to parse a Shakespeare play by likening it to ripples in the water when they wave their flagella. That's a lot like you and me claiming we understand a living planet."

"But the effects of Beta—"

"Those effects, combined with your intervention, combined with a thousand other factors, including my own small influence . . . yes, surely, all these things helped bring about something new and wonderful. And perhaps similar events have happened before in this galaxy, here and there.

"Maybe the results aren't always as pleasant or sane as what happened here. Perhaps humans really are very special people, after all. Despite all your faults, this may be a very special world. Maybe others out there sensed something worth preserving and nurturing here."

The warmth in Pedro's voice surprised Alex. "You mean we don't have enemies out there after all?"

"I never said that!" Manella's brows narrowed with sudden intensity. Then, just as quickly, he visibly retreated again into his mood of blithe playfulness. "Of course we're still only speaking hypothetically. You do come up with brilliant what-ifs, Lustig. This one is so intriguing.

"Let's just say one possibility is that Beta came at an opportune time. After a painful transition, it was turned into an instrument of joy. But does it necessarily follow that the 'father' of this particular sperm was a friend? That's *one* possibility. Another is, this world has managed to make the best out of a case of attempted rape."

Alex stared at Manella. The man talked, but somehow nothing he said seemed to make any sense.

"I know you don't want to hear more metaphors," Pedro went on. "But I've given some thought lately to all the different roles humanity has to play in the new planetary being that's been born. Humans—and man-made machines—contribute by far the largest share of her 'brain' matter. They'll be her eyes, her hands, as she learns to shape and spread life to other worlds in this solar system.

"But the best analogy may be to a body's white blood cells! After all, what if the universe is a dangerous place as well as a beautiful one? It will be your job, and your children's and their children's, to protect what's been born here. To serve Her and sacrifice yourselves for Her if need be.

"And then, of course, there is the matter of propagation. . . ."

The vistas Manella presented—even hypothetically—were too vast. He kept talking, but suddenly his words seemed barely relevant anymore.

By the same token, Alex suddenly didn't care any longer whether his suspicions about the man were valid or just more tantalizing similes, drawn against the universe's infinite account of coincidence and correlation. Rather, Manella's latest comparison suddenly provoked in Alex thoughts about *Teresa*, how he felt about her in his blood, in his skin, and in the busy flexings of his heart. He found himself smiling

". . . I'd like to think it's that way," Pedro went on in the background, as if garrulously lecturing an audience. "That there might exist others out there, scattered among the stars, who foresaw some of what was fated here. And maybe arranged for a little help to arrive in time.

"Perhaps those others feel gladness at this rare victory, and wish us well. . . ."

An interesting notion, indeed. But Alex's thoughts had already moved well ahead of that, to implications Manella probably could not imagine, whatever his true nature. His gaze pressed ahead, past the

bustling construction yards, along the film of air and moisture enveloping the planet's soft skin. Skirting the hot, steady glow of the sun,
Alex's eyes took in the dusty scatter of the galactic wheel. And as his
perplexed musings cast outward, he felt a familiar presence pass momentarily nearby, a propinquity invisible and yet as real as anything
in the universe.

"YES, IT GOES ON," his grandmother's spirit seemed to whisper in his
ear. "IT GOES ON AND ON AND ON. . . ."

□

Fluttering ribbon banners proclaim CONDEMNED, and warning lights strobe
KEEP AWAY. But even tales of radioactive mutants cannot keep some people
from eventually coming home. Even to the Glarus Alps, where gaping,
glass-rimmed caves still glow at night, where angry fire once melted glaciers and cracked fortress mountains to their very roots.

Strange trees cover slopes once given to farms and meadows. Their
branches twist and twine, creating unusual canopies. Beneath that forest
roof, without metal objects or electronics, a band of homesteaders might
feel safe enough. And anyway, even if they are spotted, why should the
great big world fear one tiny restored village of shepherds in these mountains?

"Mind the dogs, Leopold!" an old man tells his youngest son, who
knows packed city warrens and life at sea far better than these ancestral
hills. "See they keep the sheep from straying, now."

The youth stares across the valley of his forebears toward those tortured peaks. Their outlines tug at his heart and the air tastes pure, familiar.
And yet, for a moment he thinks he sees something flicker across the cliffs
and snowy crags. It is translucent yet multihued. Beautiful if elusive.

Perhaps it is an omen. He crosses himself, then adds a circular motion encompassing his heart.

"Yes, Father," the young man says, shaking his head. "I'll see to it at
once."

● They had come to break up Sea State, and nobody, not even the
C Swiss navy, put up a fight to stop them.
R   Not that there was much to fight for anymore, Crat figured.
U Most citizens of the nation of creaking barges had come here in
S the first place because there was nowhere else to go and be their
T own masters. Now, though, there were plenty of places. And
somehow most people had stopped worrying so much about mastery
anymore.

Crat lingered on deck watching the gradual dismemberment of
the town that had until a few weeks ago seemed so gritty and vital.
Under the Admiral's Tower, orderly queues of families boarded zeps
that would take them to new homes in the scoured zones . . . areas
stripped of human life during the brief terror of the death angels. Now
that the angels had been transformed, there were whole empty cities
waiting to be refilled, with room enough for all.

Anyway, it had been made clear by the highest authority that the
oceans were just too delicate to tolerate the likes of Sea State. Other
territories, like Southern California, seemed to cry out for boisterous
noise and other human-generated abuse. Let the refugees head there
then, to remake the multilingual melting pot that had bubbled in that
place before the crisis, and amaze the world with the results.

That was how one commentator put it, and Crat had liked the
image. He'd even been tempted to go along—to have a house in
Malibu maybe. To learn to surf. Maybe become a movie star?

But no. He shook his head as sea gulls dived and squawked, competing for the last of what had been a rich trove of Sea State garbage.
Crat listened to their raucous chorus and decided he'd heard enough
from stupid birds . . . even smarty-pants dolphins. The ocean wasn't
for him after all.

Nor Patagonia, especially now that volcanic dust threatened a
reversal of the greenhouse effect, returning ice to the polar climes.

Nor even Hollywood.

Naw. Space is the place. That's where the real elbow room is.
Where there'll be big rewards for guys like me. Guys willing to take
chances.

First, of course, he'd had to finish taking big official types on tours
of the seabed site where the company's mystery lab had been. Apparently some nasty stuff had gone on down there, but nobody seemed to
hold him responsible. In fact, one of the visiting investigators had
called him "a steady fellow and a hard worker" and promised a good

recommendation. If those tough jobs for miners on the moon ever opened up, that reference might come in handy.

I wonder what Remi and Roland would've thought. Me, a steady fellow . . . maybe even goin' to melt rocks on the moon.

First he had to get there, though. And that meant working his way across the Pacific, helping haul the remnants of Sea State to recla- mation yards now that ocean dumping wasn't just illegal, but maybe suicidal as well. It would take months, but he'd save up for clothes and living expenses and a new plaque, and tapes to study so they wouldn't think him a complete ignoramus when he filled out applica- tion forms. . . .

"Hah! Listen to you!" He laughed at himself as he hopped nim- bly over narrow gangways to the gunwale where his work team was supposed to meet. "Becomin' a reet intellectual, are ya?"

To show he wasn't a complete mama's boy, he spat over the side. Not that it hurt her nibs a bit to do so. She'd recycle it, like she would his soddy carcass when the time came, and good riddance.

A whistle blew, calling crew to stations. He grinned as the tug's exec nodded to him. There was still plenty of time, but Crat wanted to be early. It was expected of him.

The others in his team shambled up, one by one and in pairs. He made a point of scowling at the last two, who arrived just before the final blow. "All right," he told the gang. "We're haulin' hawsers here, not some girly-girl's drawers. So if you want your pay, put your backs in, hear?"

They grunted, nodded, grimaced in a dozen different dialects and cultural modes. Crat thought them the scum of the Earth. Just like himself.

"Ready, then?" he cried as the bosun called to cast off lines. The men took up the heavy jute rope. "Okay, let's show Momma what even scum can do. All together now . . . pull!"

PART XII

PLANET

It gets cold between the stars. Most of space is desert, dry and empty.

But there are, here and there, beads that glitter close to steady, gentle suns. And though these beads are born in fire and swim awash in death, they also shimmer with hope, with life.

Every now and then, as if such slender miracles weren't enough, one of the little, spinning globes even awakens.

"I AM . . ." it declares, singing into the darkness. "I AM, I AM, I AM!"

To which the darkness has an answer, befitting any upstart.

"SO WHAT? BIG DEAL, BIG DEAL, BIG DEAL . . . SO WHAT?"

The latest little world-mind ponders this reply, considers it, and finally concludes, "SO EVEN THIS IS ONLY A BEGINNING?"

"SMART CHILD," comes the only possible response. "YOU FIGURE IT OUT."

Gaia spins on, silently contemplating what it means to be born into a sarcastic universe.

"WE'LL SEE ABOUT THIS," she murmurs to herself, and like a striped kitten, purrs.

"WE SHALL SEE."

A F T E R W O R D

This novel depicts one of many ways the world might be fifty years from now. It is only an extrapolation—what a physicist might call a *gedankenexperiment* —nothing more.

And yet, as I sit down to write this postscript, it occurs to me that we can learn something by looking in the opposite direction. For instance, exactly fifty years *ago* Europe was still at peace.

Oh, by August 1939 the writing was on the wall. Having already crushed several smaller neighbors, Adolf Hitler that month signed a fateful pact with Joseph Stalin, sealing the fate of Poland. China was already in flames. And yet, many still hoped that world statesmen would stop short of the edge. The future seemed to offer promise, as well as threat.

At the New York World's Fair, for instance, you could tour the Westinghouse exhibit and see the wonders of tomorrow. A futurama showed the "typical city of 1960"—brimming with every techno-gadget Depression-era Americans could dream of, from electric dishwashers and superhighways to robot housemaids and personal autogyros. Naturally, poverty wouldn't exist in that far-off age. The phrase "ecological degradation" hadn't yet been coined.

We may shake our heads over their naïveté, those people of 1939. They got it right predicting freeways and television, but who knew anything back then about atom bombs? Or missile deterrence? Or computers? Or toxic waste? A few science fiction writers perhaps, whose prophetic tales nevertheless seem quaint and simplistic by today's standards.

Fifty years is a long time, and the pace of change has only accelerated.

Still—and here's the funny thing—there are a great many people still around at this moment who lived through every single day from August 1939 to the present. To them, the world of the Nineties doesn't seem bizarre or astonishing. It evolved, bit by bit, step by step, each event arising quite believably out of what had come the day before.

This is what makes half-century projections among the most difficult speculative novels to write. In order to depict a near-term future, say five or ten years ahead, a writer need only take the present world and exaggerate some current trend for dramatic effect. At the other end, portraying societies many centuries from now, the job is relatively easy also. (Anything goes, so long as you make it vaguely plausible.) But five decades is just short enough a span to require a sense of *familiarity,* and yet far enough away to demand countless surprises, as well. You must make it seem believable that many people who are walking around at this very moment would also exist in that future time, and find conditions—if not *commonplace*—then at least normal.

Therefore my apologia. This novel isn't a prediction. *Earth* depicts just one possible tomorrow—one that will surely strike some as too optimistic and others as far too gloomy. So be it.

What is a world? A myriad of themes and contrary notions, all woven up in a welter of detail. And so *Earth* had to include everything from the failing ozone layer and thickening greenhouse effect, to geology and evolution. (And while we're at it, let's throw in electronic media, the Gaia hypothesis, and the nature of consciousness!)

In the course of researching this book, I would listen to news reports from Armenian earthquakes and Alaskan supertanker disasters, and constantly find myself struck by how foolish our illusions of stability and changelessness seem, perched as we are on the trembling crust of an active planet. History and geology show what an eyeblink it's been since our current, comfortable culture came about. And yet that culture is using up absolutely everything at a ferocious rate.

Still, there are positive signs—evidence that, at the very last moment, humankind may be waking up. Will we do so quickly enough to save the world? No one can possibly know.

One thing guaranteed over the decades ahead will be copious irony. Suppose, for instance, peace truly does break out among nations. The ingenuity and resources now spent on weaponry may be reallocated, unleashing fantastic creativity on our more pressing needs. But then, what will history say in retrospect about hydrogen bombs if we finally do get around to retiring them all? That the awful things scared twentieth-century man into changing his act? That they helped maintain a balance of power, allowing a smaller fraction of humanity to be soldiers—or be harmed by soldiers—than in any prior generation? (Small solace to those in Cambodia and Afghanistan and Lebanon, where the averages did not hold.) How strange, if the bomb came to be looked back on as the principal vehicle of our salvation.

What if all those engineers really do turn their focus from deterrence to productivity? Some prospects are awesome to contemplate . . . suspended animation, artificial organs, intelligence enhancement, spaceflight, smart machines . . . the list is dizzying and a bit daunting. If such godlike powers ever do become ours, we'll surely face questions much like those so long asked about the bomb. Such as, How do we acquire *wisdom* along with all these shiny things?

There is a popular myth going around. It maintains that there is something particularly corrupt about Western civilization—as if it invented war, exploitation, oppression, and pollution all by itself. Certainly if this were so, the world's problems might be solved just by returning to "older, better ways." Many do cling to the fantasy that this or that non-Western culture had some patent on universal happiness.

Alas, if only it were so easy.

In his book *A Forest Journey: From Mesopotamia to North America,* John Perlin shows how the vast, fertile plains and mountains of Greece, Turkey, and the Middle East were turned into hardscrabble ravines by ancient civilizations. The record of pillage goes back thousands of years to the earliest known epic, the Tale of Gilgamesh, about a king who cut down primordial cedar forests to take lumber for his city-state of Uruk. Droughts and floods plagued the land soon afterward, but neither Gilgamesh nor any of his contemporaries ever saw the connection.

Sumerian civilization went on to seize oak from Arabia, juniper from Syria, cedar from Anatolia. The rivers of the Near East filled with silt, clogging ports and irrigation canals. Dredging only exposed salty layers below, which eventually ruined whatever soil hadn't already blown away. The result, over centuries, is a region we now know well as a realm of blowing sands and bitter winds, but which was once called the "fertile crescent," the land of milk and honey.

We don't need mystical conjectures about "cycles of history" to explain, for instance, the fall of Rome. Perlin shows how the Roman Empire, the Aegean civilization of ancient Greece, imperial China, and so many other past cultures performed the same feat, ignorantly fouling their own nests, using up the land, poisoning the future for their children. Ecological historians are at last starting to realize that this is simply the natural consequence whenever a people acquires more physical power than insight.

While it is romantic to imagine that tribal peoples—either ancient or in today's retreating rain forests—were at harmony with nature, living happy, egalitarian lives, current research shows this to be far from uniformly true, and more often just plain false. Despite a fervent desire to believe otherwise, evidence now reveals that members of nearly every "natural" society have committed depredations on their environment and each other. The harm they did was limited mostly by low technology and modest numbers.

The same goes for beating up on the human race as a whole. Oh, we have much to atone for, but the case isn't strengthened by exaggerations that are just plain wrong. Stephen Jay Gould has condemned ". . . as romantic twaddle the common litany that 'man alone kills for sport, but other animals [kill] only for food or in defense.' " Anyone who has watched a common housecat with a mouse—or stallions battling over dominance—knows that humans aren't so destructive because of anything fundamentally wrong about human nature. It's our *power* that amplifies the harm we do until it threatens the entire world.

My purpose in saying this isn't to insult other cultures or species. Rather, I am trying to argue that the problems we face are deep-seated, with a long history. The irony of these myths of the noble tribesman, or noble animal, is that they are most fervently held by pampered Westerners whose well-cushioned culture is the first ever to feel comfortable enough to promote a new tradition of self-criticism. And it is this very habit of criticism—even self-reproach—that makes ours the first human society with a chance to avoid the mistakes of our ancestors.

Indeed, the race between our growing awareness and the momentum of our greed may make the next half century the greatest dramatic interlude of all time.

In that vein, I might have written a purely cautionary tale, like John Brunner's novel *The Sheep Look Up,* which depicts Earth's environmental collapse with terrifying vividness. But tales of unalloyed doom have never seem realistic to me. Like the mechanistic scenarios of Marxism, they seem to assume people will be too stupid to notice looming calamities or try to prevent them.

Instead, I see all around me millions of people who actively worry about dangers and trends . . . even something as far away as a patch of missing gas over the south pole. Countless people write letters and march to save species of no possible benefit to themselves.

Oh, surely, a good dose of guilt now and then can help motivate us to do better. But I see nothing useful coming out of looking backward for salvation or modeling ourselves after ancient tribes. *We* are the generation—here and now—that must pick up a truly daunting burden, to tend and keep a planetary oasis, in all its delicacy and diversity, for future millennia and beyond. Those who claim to find answers to such complex dilemmas in the sagas of olden days only trivialize the awesome magnitude of our task.

So much for motivation. In my acknowledgments, I thank scores of people who kindly read drafts of this work and offered their expert advice. Still, this has been a work of fiction, and any opinions or excesses or errors herein can be laid at no one's door but mine. *Mea culpa.*

In a few cases, the liberties I took demand explanation.

First, for the sake of drama, I exaggerated the extent greenhouse heating may cause sea levels to rise by the year 2040. Though real losses and suffering may be staggering, few scientists think glacier melting will have progressed as far as I depict by then. The consensus seems to be that the Antarctica ice sheet is safe until late in the next century. Likewise, I over-simplified weather patterns in India to make a dramatic point.

Another assumption I make is that energy shortages will return. Most experts consider this a safe bet, but I admit (and even hope) that declining petroleum reserves may be partially offset by new discoveries. Certainly breakthroughs in solar power, or access to space resources, or even some-thing completely unexpected, might alter events for the better. (At the same time, our list of potential catastrophes also grows. Who can say we've even imagined the worst yet? I wouldn't put money on it.)

Some of the geological features I describe match the best modern theo-ries. Others, such as possible high-temperature superconducting domains far below, are highly speculative and not to be taken too seriously.

Along similar lines, the plot of this novel orbits around one particular wild beastie—a type of gravitational singularity to make even Stephen Hawking or Kip Thorne gulp in dismay. Those physicists, and others, calculate that the universe probably contains a great many of the large type of black hole people have heard so much about, and astronomers claim to see evidence for several already. There may even be gigantic cosmic "strings" occupying the voids between the galaxies. Micro black holes, on the other hand, remain totally theoretical. Tuned strings and cosmic "knots" are my own inventions.

Interestingly, though, after finishing *Earth* I learned that two astronomers at the University of Cambridge, Ian Redmount and Martin Rees, now predict beamlike gravitational radiation might be emitted from certain superheavy objects out there. So who knows? In any event, although I have my union card as a physicist, I don't claim to be qualified in the specialized area of general relativity. The science of "cavitronics" can safely be dismissed as bona fide arm waving.

Of course, Beta served a higher function in the book than perpetrating wild-eyed conjectures on physics. The *taniwha* let me include the very guts of the planet—its complex mantle and layered core—as central concerns of my characters. (What book could claim to be about the entire Earth if it left out over ninety-nine percent of the planet's volume and mass?) Anyway, nothing spices up a novel like a monster threatening to gobble up the world.

Sociological trends are even more problematical than tomorrow's physics. While this book was in the works, changes in the real world seemed ever about to overtake my wildest speculations. One result—readers of early drafts suggested I was being much too optimistic in predicting an end to cold war tensions. But by the final draft some were turning around and com-plaining that I was shortsighted, because security alliances like NATO couldn't possibly still exist in fifty years' time! There wasn't *that* much difference between drafts. It was the world that went into fast-forward rewrite mode.

(Not that I'm convinced we're in for relaxing times just because a few walls have come down. It might be argued that the cold war is ebbing in large part because neither side can afford it anymore. Other serious threats loom to take its place. And nations will probably still make and break alliances as they wrestle over dwindling resources.)

Likewise, I find myself bored with the current fashion of depicting a to-morrow dominated by Japanese economic imperialism. Doesn't anyone re-member when it seemed that the Arabs were bound to own everything? Before that, Europeans expressed dismay at *American* industrial dynamism. Beware of assumptions that seem "obvious" in one decade. They may be-come quaint in the next.

Daily life may be even harder to predict than global politics. One crisis I see looming involves the plight of women, which seems bound to go far beyond matters typically addressed today by feminists. Equality under law and in the workplace must be achieved, of course. (And in many parts of the world that battle has barely begun.) But of growing concern to women in the West is a problem I hardly ever hear spoken of by all those learned theoreti-cians in ivy halls. That problem is the decay of marriage and family as a dependable way of life. This is a subject so difficult—and so dangerous for a male author to deal with—that I'm afraid it got short shrift in this novel, de-spite my belief that it will reach a dire climax during the decades ahead.

Perhaps I did a little better with the generation gap. Unlike authors of so-called "cyber-punk" stories, I just don't find it plausible that undisciplined, hormone-drenched, antisocial young males will forsake thousands of years of fixation on muscular bluster and come instead to dominate high tech during the next century. Putting aside that unlikely cliché, I had some fun suggesting instead that the descendants of portable video cameras might be used as weapons by elderly committees of vigilance. The demographics in countries like the United States, Japan, and China do seem to point to a period some are already calling the "empire of the old."

Meanwhile, in Kenya, the average age at present is just fifteen, and the birth rate skyrockets.

For some notions I owe a debt to other authors. I've already referred to John Brunner, whose award-winning novel *Stand on Zanzibar* was among the very best fifty-year projection novels of an earlier day. Likewise, Aldous Huxley's work was inspirational.

The idea of a human "cultural singularity"—in which our power and knowledge might accelerate so quickly that the pace grows exponentially in months, weeks, days—making all current problems academic in a flash—is one that's been brewing for a while, but was depicted especially well in Vernor Vinge's *Marooned in Real Time*. The notion of capital punishment by "disassembly" came from the novels of Larry Niven.

Many authors since de Chardin have written about the creation of some sort of "overmind," into which human consciousness might someday either evolve or subsume. Traditionally this is presented as a simple choice between obstinate individualism on the one hand, or being homogenized and absorbed on the other. I have always found this either-or dichotomy simplistic and tried to present a different point of view here. Still, the basic concept goes back a long way.

The idea for depicting a space shuttle, crash-landed on Easter Island, was provoked by a Lee Correy science fiction story, "Shuttle Down," which appeared in Analog Magazine a decade ago.

Likewise, much of the discussion of human consciousness was inspired by articles in respectable neuroscience journals, or cribbed from innovative thinkers like Marvin Minsky, Stanley Ornstein, and even Julian Jaynes, whose famous book on the origin of consciousness might well have made a splendid science fiction novel.

The Helvetian War, on the other hand, I can blame on no one but myself. (I expect it will probably cause me no little grief.) Nevertheless, for this book I needed some dark, traumatic conflict to reverberate in my characters' past—as Vietnam, World War II, and the Holocaust still make contemporary folk twitch in recollection. It had to be something at once both chilling and surprising, as so many events over the *last* fifty years have been. (And frankly, I've had it with stereotyped superpower schemes, accidental missile launches, any other clichés.) So I tried to come up with a scenario that—if not very likely—was at least plausible in its own context. Then I chose to center it around a nation that's presently among the very last anyone would think of as a serious threat to peace.

I don't know if it works, but so far it has rocked a few people back and made them say, "Huh!" That's good enough for me.

Speaking of war—one reader asked why I barely refer to one of today's principle concerns . . . the Great Big War On Drugs. Will it have been solved by the year 2038?

Well, not by any program or approach now being tried, that's for sure. I'm not fatalistic. It makes some sense to regulate when and how self-destructive citizens can stupefy themselves, especially in public. Social sanctions have already proven more effective than laws at driving down liquor and tobacco consumption in North America. So much that distillers and cigarette makers are in a state of demographic panic.

But as for trying to *eradicate* drugs, right now we just seem to be driving up the price. Addicts commit crimes to finance their habits, and convey billions of dollars to pushers who are, inarguably, among the worst human beings alive. Anyway, it's been shown that some individuals can secrete endorphins and other hormones at will, using meditation or self hypnosis or biofeedback. If such techniques become commonplace (as no doubt they will . . . everything does), shall we then outlaw meditation? Should the police test anyone caught dozing in the park, to make sure he isn't drugging himself with his own self-made enkephalins?

Reductio ad absurdum. Or as Dirty Harry once said, we've *got* to learn our limitations.

Which only leads to a much deeper problem that has plagued society ever since before Darwin. That problem is *moral ambiguity.*

Every culture before ours had codes that precisely defined acceptable behavior and prescribed sanctions to enforce obedience. Such rules, whether religious, or cultural, or legal, or traditional, were like those a parent imposes on a young child. (And which children themselves insist upon.) In other words, they were explicit, clear-cut, utterly unambiguous.

Eventually, some adolescents grow beyond needing perfect, delineated truths. They even learn to savor a little ambiguity. Meanwhile, others quail before it . . . or go to the opposite extreme, using ambiguity as an excuse to deny any ethical restraint at all. We see all three of these reactions in contemporary society as individuals and governments are asked to wrestle individually with complex issues formerly left to God.

For instance, while some insist that human life begins at the very moment of conception, others ideologically proclaim it absent until birth itself. Neither extreme represents the uncomfortable majority, who—supported by embryology—sense that the issue of abortion is being waged across a murky swamp, bereft of clear borders or road signs.

More quandaries abound. Has mankind yet "made life in a test tube"? That depends on how you define "life" of course. By one standard, that milestone was passed way back in the seventies. By another, it was reached in the mid-eighties. By yet a third, perhaps it hasn't happened yet, but definitely will soon.

As the aged grow more numerous in industrial societies, and as the power and expense of modern medicine grow ever more spectacular, the question of death will also come to vex us. We've already spent a decade agonizing over the terminal patient's "right to die" if faced with the alternative of prolonged, painful support by machinery. A consensus appears to be coalescing around that issue, but what about the next inevitable predicament . . . when young taxpayers of the next century find themselves paying for endless herculean care demanded by millions of octogenarian former baby-boomers who outnumber them, outvote them, and have spent all their lives used to getting whatever they wanted?

What will it even mean to be "dead" in the future? Some predict it may soon be possible to cool living human bodies down to near (or even past) freezing, suspending life processes, perhaps so people could be revived at a later date. In fact, by primitive standards, it's already happened—for example, in cases of extreme hypothermia. The can of worms this might open is boggling to consider. And yet, enthusiasts for this nascent field of "cryonics" answer moral quandaries and strict definitions of death by asking, "Why pass *binary* laws for an *analog* world?" (In other words, most moral codes say "either-or" . . . while the universe itself seems to be filled instead with a whole lot of "maybes.")

To some, this accelerating layering of complexity seems no more than a natural part of our culture's maturation. To others, the prospect of all certainty dissolving into a muddle of ambiguity seems horrifying. If I were forced to make just one hard prediction for the twenty-first century, it would be that we have seen only the first wave of these puzzling, sometimes heartbreaking conundrums.

Will we face these issues head-on? Or flee once more to the shelter of ancient simplicities? That, I believe, will be the central moral and intellectual dilemma ahead of us.

Finally, let me close this rambling screed with a note on the central topic of this book. Much has been said in recent years about the so-called Gaia hypothesis, which though credited to James Lovelock, actually has a modern history stretching all the way back to the 1780s and the Scottish geologist James Hutton. Lately, there have been signs of compromise. Proponents have backed off a bit from comparing the planet too closely to a living organism, while critics like Richard Dawkins and James Kirchner now admit the debate over Gaia has been useful to ecology and biology, stimulating many new avenues of research.

In this novel, of course, I portray Gaia as more than a mere metaphor. Some of my scientist colleagues will surely shake their heads over my dramatic denouement, accusing me of "teleology" and other sins. And yet, doesn't the renowned physicist Ilya Prigogine suggest that the ordering processes of "dissipative structures" almost inevitably lead to increasing levels of organization? Cambridge philosopher John Platt illustrates this progressive acceleration with one telling example—life's ability to encapsulate itself.

It began with membranes enclosing the chemistry of a single cell, perhaps four billion years ago. For a long time, single cells were the limit, drifting and duplicating themselves in the open sea. But then, just four hundred million years ago, a big change came about. Creatures began moving onto land, covered with thick scales, or shells, or bark.

In the last half million years, clothing and artificial shelters provided the next opportunity, enabling humans to greatly expand their range . . . which in the most recent tenth of that time swelled to include even high mountains and arctic wastes. Finally, in the last few decades we've even learned to take our climate with us, in self-contained, encapsulated environments, to explore outer space and the bottom of the sea.

In fact, there is nothing mystical or teleological about this speedup. Each species builds on the suite of hard-won techniques accumulated by its ancestors, and for us this process isn't merely genetic. Our culture profits from insights slowly gathered by prior generations, who labored in semi-ignorance toward a distant light just a few only dimly perceived. If we now find ourselves on a launching point—poised toward either despair or something truly wonderful—it is only because there were always, amid those bickering, short-sighted people of past times, some who believed in gathering that light, in nurturing it and making it grow.

So, indeed, those who follow in our footsteps may think of us.

We search for solutions, arguing vehemently over ways to save the world. Amid all the self-righteous speechmaking, we tend to forget that yesterday's passionately held "solutions" often become tomorrow's problems. For instance, nuclear fission was once seen as a "liberal" cause. So were wind and ocean power. (Though now that windmills and tidal barrages are being built—and money being made from them—there are those pointing out drawbacks, penalties, and tradeoffs.) It never used to matter to us what types of trees were planted by logging companies after they finished clear-cutting a forest, only that they planted "replacements." (And this *was* enlightened, compared with still-earlier attitudes.) Now, though, we see vast, sterile stands of trash pine as just another form of desert.

How many other favored solutions will this happen to? We're becoming so sensitized to making mistakes—will this soon leave us too paralyzed to act at all?

If so, it would be a pity. To quote Paul Ehrlich of Stanford University, "the situation is running downhill at a truly frightening pace. On the other hand, our potential for solving the problem is absolutely enormous."

Some solutions really are obvious. "There's no such thing as *garbage*," says Hazel Henderson. "We have to recycle . . . as the Japanese do. One reason they are so successful is that they recycle over 50%."

Other solutions might prove controversial, even heartbreaking. The next fifty years may lead to pragmatism on a scale that would seem abhorrent by today's standards. As Garret Hardin of the University of California puts it, we may even ". . . stop sending gifts of food to starving nations. Just grit your teeth and tell them 'You're on your own and you've got to make your population match the carrying capacity of your own land.' "

A harsh way of looking at things, and terrifying in its implications for today's fragile consensus of tolerance. Is it any wonder I wanted to experiment in this novel with a somewhat kinder tomorrow? One where people have grown at least a little wiser, in tempo with their growing problems?

After all the philosophy and speculations are finished, we're still left with just words, metaphors. They are our tools for understanding the world, but it's always well to remember they have only a nodding acquaintance with reality.

Reality is this world, the only oasis we know of. Every astronaut who has had a chance to see it from above has returned a fervent convert to saving it. As glimmers of peace and political maturity break out here and there around the globe, perhaps the rest of us will turn away from ideologies and other self-indulgences and start to take notice as well.

Quoting Hazel Henderson again, "It's almost as if the human family is being nudged by Mother Nature to grow up. We are all in the same boat now, and it's no good playing these games of which end is sinking."

What our grandchildren inherit is entirely up to us. And frankly, I'd rather they remember us as having left them a bit of hope.

—David Brin, August 1989

And now, to reward those who actually stuck it out through the afterword, here's an encore of sorts . . . *a special bonus story,* set in the same universe as *Earth,* but a few years later.

AMBIGUITY

1.

Back when he was still a student, Stan Goldman and his friends used to play a game of make-believe.

"How long do you think it would take Isaac Newton to solve this homework set?" they would ask each other. Or, "If Einstein were alive today, do you think he'd bother with graduate school?"

It was the same sort of lazy, get-nowhere argument he also heard his musician friends debate on occasion: "What d'you figure Mozart would make of our stuff," they'd pose over bottles of beer, "if we snatched him from his own time to the 1990s? Would he freak out and call it damn noise? Or would he catch on, wear mirror shades, and cut an album right away?"

At that point, Stan used to cut in. "Which Mozart do you mean? The arriviste social climber? The craftsman of the biographies? Or the brash rebel of *Amadeus*?"

The composers and players seemed puzzled by his non sequitur. "Why, the real one, of course." Their reply convinced him that, for all their closeness, for all their well-known affinity, physicists and musicians would never fully understand each other.

Oh, I see. The real one . . . of course . . .

But what is reality?

Through a thick portal of fused quartz, mediated by a series of three hundred field-reinforced half mirrors, Stan now watched the essence of nothingness. Suspended in a sealed vacuum, a *potential* singularity spun and danced in nonexistence.

In other words, the chamber was empty.

Soon, though, potentiality would turn into reality. The virtual would become actual. Twisted space would spill light and tortured vacuum would briefly give forth matter. The utterly improbable would happen.

Or at least that was the general idea. Stan watched and waited, patiently.

Until the end of his life, Albert Einstein struggled against the implications of quantum mechanics.

He had helped invent the new physics. It bore his imprint as fully as Dirac's or Heisenberg's or Bohr's. And yet, like Max Planck, he had always felt uncomfortable with its implications, insisting that the Copenhagen rules of probabilistic nature must be mere crude approximations of the *real* patterns governing the world. Beneath the dreadful quantum ambiguity, he felt there must be the signature of a designer.

Only the design eluded Einstein. Its elegant precision fled before experimentalists, who prodded first atoms, then nuclei, and at last the so-called "fundamental" particles. Always, the deeper they probed, the fuzzier grew the mesh of creation.

In fact, to a later generation of physicists, ambiguity was no enemy. Rather it became a tool. It was the law. Stan grew up picturing Nature as a whimsical goddess. She seemed to say—*Look at me from afar, and you may pretend that there are firm rules—that here is cause and there effect. But remember, if you need this solace, stay back, and squint!*

If, on the other hand, you dare approach—should you examine my garments' weft and warp—well, then, don't say I didn't warn you.

With this machine, Stan Goldman expected to be looking closer than anyone ever had before. And he did not expect much security.

"You ready down there, Stan?"

Alex Lustig's voice carried down the companionway. He and the others were in the control center, but Stan had volunteered to keep watch here by the peephole. It was a vital job, but one requiring none of the quickness of the younger physicists . . . in other words, just right for an old codger like himself. "I'm ready as I'll ever be, Alex," he called back.

"Good. Your timer should start running . . . now!"

True to Alex's word, the display to Stan's left began counting down whirling milliseconds.

After the end of the Gaia War, when things had calmed down enough to allow a resumption of basic science, their efforts had soon returned to studying the basic nature of singularities. Now, in this lab far beyond the orbit of Mars, they had received permission to embark on the boldest experiment yet.

Stan wiped his palms on his dungarees and wondered why he felt so nervous. After all, he had participated in the manufacture of bizarre objects before. In his youth, at CERN, it had been a zoo of subatomic particles, wrought out of searing heat at the target end of a great accelerator. Even in those days, the names physicists gave the particles they studied told you more about their own personalities than the things they pursued.

He recalled graffiti on the wall of the men's room in Geneva.

Question: What do you get when you mix a charmed red quark with a strange one that's green and a third that's true blue?

Underneath were scrawled answers, in various hands and as many languages:

I don't know, but to hold them together you'll need a gluon with attitude!

Sounds like what they served in the cafeteria, today.

Speaking of which, anyone here know the Flavor of Beauty?

Doesn't it depend on who's on Top and who's on the Bottom?

I'm getting a hadron just thinking about it.

Hey! What boson thought of this question, anyway?

Yeah. There's a guy who ought to be lepton!

Stan smiled, remembering good times. They had been hunters in those days, he and the others, chasing and capturing specimens of elusive microscopic species, expanding the quarky bestiary till a "theory of everything" began to emerge. Gravitons and gravitinos. Magnetic monopoles and photinos. With unification came the power to mix and match and use nature's ambiguity.

Still, he never dreamed he might someday play with singularities —micro black holes—using them as *circuit elements* the same blithe way an engineer might string together inductors and resistors. But young fellows like Alex seemed to take it all in stride.

"Three minutes, Stan!"

"I can read a clock!" he shouted back, trying to sound more irritated than he really was. In truth, he really had lost track of the time. His mind now seemed to move at a tangent to that flow . . . nearly but not quite parallel to the event cone of the objective world.

We're told subjectivity, that old enemy of science, becomes its ally at the level of the quantum. Some say it's only the presence of an observer that causes the probability wave to collapse. It's the observer who ultimately notes the plummet of an electron from its shell, as well as the sparrow in a forest. Without observers, not only is a falling tree without sound . . . it's a concept without meaning.

Of late Stan had been wondering ever more about that. Nature, even down to the lowliest quark, seemed to be performing, as if for an audience. Arguments raged between adherents of the strong and weak anthropic principles, over whether observers were required by the universe or merely convenient to it. But everyone now agreed that having an audience mattered.

So much, then, for the debate over what Newton would say if he were snatched out of his time and brought to the present. His clockwork world was as alien to Stan's as that of a tribal shaman. In fact, in some ways the shaman actually had it hands down over prissy old Isaac. At least, Stan imagined, the shaman would probably make better company at a party.

"One minute! Keep your eye on—"

Alex's voice cut off suddenly as automatic timers sent the crash doors hissing shut. Stan shook himself, hauling his mind back and making an earnest effort to concentrate. It would have been different were there something for him to do. But everything was sequenced, even data collection. Later, they would pore over it all and argue. For now, though, he had only to watch. To observe . . .

Before man, he wondered, *who performed this role for the universe?*

There appears to be no rule that the observer has to be conscious. So animals might have served without being self-aware. And on other worlds, creatures might have existed long before life filled Earth's seas. It isn't necessary that every event, every rockfall, every quantum of light be appreciated, only that some of it, somewhere, come to the attention of someone who notices and cares.

"But then," Stan debated himself aloud, "Who noticed or cared at the beginning? Before the planets? Before stars?"

Who was there in the pre-creation nothing to watch the vacuum fluctuation of all time? The one that turned into the Big Bang?

In his thoughts, Stan answered his own question.

If the universe needs at least one observer in order to exist. Then that's the one compelling argument for the necessity of God.

The counter reached zero. Beneath it, the panel of fused quartz remained black. Nevertheless. Stan knew something was happening. Deep in the bowels of the chamber, the energy state of raw vacuum was being forced to change.

Uncertainty. That was the lever. Take a cubical box of space, say a centimeter on a side. Does it contain a proton? If so, there's a limit to how much you can know about that proton with any sureness. You cannot know its momentum more precisely than a given value without destroying your chance of knowing *where* it is. Or if you find a way to zoom in on the box until the proton's location is incredibly exact, then your knowledge of its speed and direction plummets toward zero.

Another linked pair of values is energy and time. You may think you know how much or little energy the box contains. (In a vacuum it tends toward baseline zero.) But what about *fluctuations*? What if bits of matter and antimatter suddenly appear, only to abruptly disappear again? Then the average would still be the same, and all account books would stay balanced.

Within this chamber, modern trickery was using that very loophole to pry away at Nature's wall.

Stan glanced at the mass gauge. It sped upscale rapidly. Femtograms, picograms, nanograms of matter coalesced in a space too small to measure. Micrograms, milligrams . . . each newly born hadron pair shimmered for a moment too narrow to notice. Particle and antiparticle tried to flee, tried to annihilate. But before they could cancel out again, each was drawn into a trap of folded space, sucked down a narrow funnel of gravity smaller than a proton, with no more personality than a smudge of blackness.

The singularity began taking on serious weight. The mass gauge whirled. Kilograms converted into tons. Tons into kilotons. Boulders, hillocks, mountains poured forth, a torrent flowing into the greedy mouth.

When Stan was young, they said you weren't supposed to be able to make something from nothing. But nature did sometimes let you *borrow*. Alex Lustig's machine was borrowing from vacuum, and instantly paying it all back to the singularity.

That was the secret. Any bank will lend you a million bucks . . . so long as you only want it for a microsecond.

Megatons, gigatons . . . Stan had helped make holes before. Singularities more complex and elegant than this one. But never had anyone attempted anything so drastic or momentous. The pace accelerated.

Something shifted in the sinuses behind his eyes. That warning came moments before the gravimeters began singing a melody of alarm . . . full seconds in advance of the first creaking sounds coming from the reinforced metal walls.

Come on, Alex. You promised this wouldn't run away.

They had come to this lab on a distant asteroid on the off chance something might go wrong. But Stan wondered how much good that would do if their meddling managed to tear a rent in the fabric of everything. There were stories that some scientists on the Manhattan Project had shared a similar fear. "What if the chain reaction *doesn't* stay restricted to the plutonium," they asked, "but spreads to iron, silicon, and oxygen?" On paper it was absurd, but no one knew until the flash of Trinity, when the fireball finally faded back to little more than a terrible, glittering cloud.

Now Stan felt a similar dread. What if the singularity no longer needed Lustig's machine to yank matter out of vacuum for it? What if the effect carried on and on, with its own momentum . . . ?

This time we might have gone too far.

He felt them now. The tides. And in the quartz window, mediated by three hundred half mirrors, a ghost took shape. It was microscopic, but the colors were captivating.

The mass scale spun. Stan felt the awful attraction of the thing. Any moment now it was going to reach out and drag down the walls, the station, the planetoid. . . . and even then would it stop?

"Alex!" he cried out as gravitational flux stretched his skin. Viscera migrated toward his throat as, uselessly, he braced his feet.

"Dammit, you—"

Stan blinked. His next breath wouldn't come. Time felt suspended.

Then he knew.

It was gone.

Goosebumps shivered in the tidal wake. He looked at the mass gauge. It read zero. One moment it had been there, the next it had vanished.

Alex's voice echoed over the intercom, satisfaction in his voice. "Right on schedule. Time for a beer, eh? You were saying something, Stan?"

He searched his memory and somewhere found the trick to breathing again. Stan let out a shuddering sigh.

"I . . ." He tried to lick his lips, but couldn't even wet them. Hoarsely, he tried again. "I was going to say . . . you'd better have something up there stronger than beer. Because I need it."

2.

They tested the chamber in every way imaginable, but there was nothing there. For a time it had contained the mass of a small planet. The black hole had been palpable. Real. Now it was gone.

"They say a gravitational singularity is a tunnel to another place," Stan mused.

"Some people think so. Wormholes and the like may connect one part of spacetime with another." Alex nodded agreeably. He sat across the table, alone with Stan in the darkened lounge strewn with debris from the evening's celebration. Everyone else had gone to bed, but both men had their feet propped up as they gazed through a crystal window at the starry panorama. "In practice, such tunnels probably are useless. No one will ever use one for transportation, for instance. There's the problem of ultraviolet runaway—"

"That's not what I'm talking about." Stan shook his head. He poured another shot of whiskey. "What I mean is, how do we know that hole we created hasn't popped out to become a hazard for some other poor bastards?"

Alex looked amused. "That's not how it works, Stan. The singularity we made today was special. It grew too fast for our universe to contain it at all.

"We're used to envisioning a black hole, even a micro, as something like a funnel in the fabric of space. But in this case, that fabric rebounded, folded over, sealed the breach. The hole is just *gone*, Stan."

Stan felt tired and a little tipsy, but damn if he'd let this young hotshot get the better of him. "I know that! All causality links with our universe have been severed. There's no connection with the thing anymore.

"But still I wonder. Where did it *go*?"

There was a momentary silence.

"That's probably the wrong question, Stan. A better way of putting it would be, What has the singularity *become*?"

The young genius now had that look in his eyes again—the philosophical one. "What do you mean?" Stan asked.

"I mean that the hole and all the mass we poured into it now 'exists' in its own pocket universe. That universe will never share any overlap or contact with our own. It will be a cosmos unto itself . . . now and forever."

The statement seemed to carry a ring of finality, and there seemed to be little to say after that. For a while, the two of them just sat quietly.

3.

After Alex went off to bed Stan stayed behind and played with his friends, the numbers. He rested very still and used a mental pencil to write them across the window. Equations stitched the Milky Way. It didn't take long to see that Alex was right.

What they had done today was create something out of nothing and then quickly exile that something away again. To Alex and the others, that was that. All ledgers balanced. What had been borrowed was repaid. At least as far as this universe of matter and energy was concerned.

But something *was* different, dammit! Before, there had been virtual fluctuations in the vacuum. Now, *somewhere*, a tiny cosmos had been born.

And suddenly Stan remembered something else. Something called "inflation." And in this context the term had nothing to do with economics.

Some theorists hold that our own universe began as a very, very big fluctuation in the primordial emptiness. That during one intense instant, superdense mass and energy burst forth to begin the expansion of all expansions.

Only there could not have been anywhere near enough mass to account for what we now see . . . all the stars and galaxies.

"Inflation" stood for a mathematical hat trick . . . a way for a medium or even small-sized bang to leverage itself into a great big one. Stan scribbled more equations on his mental blackboard and came to see something he hadn't realized before.

Of course. I get it now. The inflation that took place twenty billion years ago was no coincidence. Rather, it was a natural result of that earlier, lesser creation. Our universe must have had its own start in a tiny, compressed ball of matter no heavier than . . . no heavier than . . .

Stan felt his heartbeat as the figure seemed to glow before him.

No heavier than that little "pocket cosmos" we created today.

He breathed.

That meant that somewhere, completely out of touch or contact, their innocent experiment might have . . . *must* have . . . initiated a beginning. A universal beginning.

Fiat lux.

Let there be light.

"Oh my God," he said to himself, completely unsure which of a thousand ways he meant it.

ACKNOWLEDGMENTS

I have a reputation for passing around my work a lot as I rewrite a novel and then rewrite it again. Seeking reality (or plausibility) checks was particularly important for this book. So, although I claim all errors and inconsistencies as my own, there are many people to thank for their help in making this a better novel better than it might have been.

For readability and general criticism, my appreciation goes out to Dr. Cheryl Brigham, Amy Thomsen, George Alec Effinger, Dr. Charles Sheffield, Dr. Gregory Benford, Jonathan Post, Dean Ing, Christie McCue Harmon, Dan Brin, Steven Mendel, Michael Cassutt, John Ensign, Janice Gelb, Celeste Satter, Betty Hull, Diane Clark, Elizabeth Oakes, Shiela Finch, Greg and Astrid Bear, Daryl Mallett, Barbara Neale, Rachel Neumieir, Robert Jolissaint, Jane Starr, managing editor Diane Shanley, designer Barbara Aronica, and my exceptional copy-editor, Len Neufeld.

For their special advice on countless technical details, I'd like to thank especially Professor John Cramer, Dr. Jim Moore, Karen Anderson, Dr. Gary Strathearn, Dr. Martyn Fogg, Dr. Steven Gillett, Joseph Carroll, Carole Sussman, and Dr. David Paige.

The Caltech literary and SF club, SPECTRE, was particularly helpful in circulating and discussing an early manuscript, with special thanks to Mark Adler, Ben Finley, Ken McCue, Steinn Sigurdssen, Ulrika Anderson, Amy Carpenter, David Palme, David Coufal, Paul Haubert, James Cummings, Douglass Bloomer, Erik Russell, Earl Hubbell, Yair Zadik, Eric Johnson, Gorm Nykeim, Eric Christian, Richard Achterberg, Matt Fields, Erich Schneider, Douglas Bloemer, and Dick Brown. In similar fashion, the ENIGMA Club, at UCLA, was most helpful, especially Scott Martin, Phil Adler, Robert Hurt, Pat Mannion, Wayne Bell, Andy Ashcroft, and Tamara Boyd. The fine listeners of the New Zealand SF Society were most helpful in getting some of the Kiwi stuff right.

For their great patience, the editorial staff at Bantam Spectra Books have my admiration, especially Lou Aronica, for gritting his teeth and waiting, knowing I'd outgrow my declared intention to make this novel "gonzo." For helping make it worth my while to devote so much time to one book, I want to thank my agent, Ralph Vicinanza.

To Cheryl and Dan, my deep gratitude simply for keeping me sane while I finished this monster.

And of course, I'd be remiss not to include Sol and Gaea, who together kept me alive all this time. I particularly appreciate the air to breathe, the sunshine, and that good, clean water. Don't know what I'd do without them. Thanks again.

Early portions of *Earth* were written on an ancient Apple II computer with 48K of memory—coal fired, steam powered, with a serial number only five digits long. It was finished using a really neat Macintosh II with four megabytes RAM, a forty-megabyte hard disk, laser printer, and WordPerfect software, supplemented by the wonderful program QuicKeys. In prior lives I used to chip these tomes in stone or write them on clay tablets. What a difference! And there are still some who insist there's no such thing as progress.

Reading List

Man on Earth, by Charles Sheffield (published by Sidgewick & Jackson, U.K.) This coffee-table book contains startling and beautiful scenes of the planet as viewed from space. The text, by a well-regarded scientist and novelist, is informative and insightful.

Earth, by Anne H. Ehrlich and Paul R. Ehrlich. Not to be confused with this novel! The Ehrlichs' non-fiction paean to a planet in trouble is moving and stimulating. (There are also many geology texts with the same title.)

"Managing Planet Earth." This special 1989 edition of *Scientific American* describes the most recent work by scientists studying the Earth's systems, and strategies toward a sustainable world. The publishers of *Scientific American* have a series of excellent special volumes on topics ranging from geology to ecology. Ask for their order list.

Oasis in Space, by Preston Cloud. This well-regarded recent book by a professor at the University of California surveys the history of the planet, from the origins of life all the way to the present crises.

Global Warming: Are We Entering the Greenhouse Century? by Stephen Schneider (published by Sierra Club Books). Offers an overview of the entire climate debate, along with an extensive bibliography.

Fifty Simple Things You Can Do to Save the Earth. You may have to order this concise little guidebook, filled with advice that can save you money and safeguard your health, too. Write to the Earth Works Group, Box 1400 Shattuck Avenue, Berkeley, California.

Proxy Power

"What can *I* do? How can just one person do anything about the fate of the world."

That's the common complaint of people today, who worry about the

future, but who are already overwhelmed by the daily grind of a busy life
—work, family, and a myriad of modern distractions. Polls show a clear
majority of North Americans, and people in many other lands, care
deeply about the state the Earth is in, and want to see something preserved. But who has the energy or time to go out and become an activist?

Trust contemporary society, though. For the convenience of busy
moderns, there is now the social action equivalent of the microwave oven
and the frozen dinner. In other words, you can hire people to go out and
save the world for you! Pick a problem and there's probably some organization already in tune with your agenda that will add your small contribution to others' and leverage it into serious effort. I list just a few below,
but there are so many. How can anyone complain that they can't influence the future of the world when it's so easy to get involved?

Some cliches are true: either you're part of the solution or you're part
of the problem.

Environmental Organizations

The Sierra Club. One of the oldest and most active environmental organizations. Membership, $33 per year ($15 for students). Department J-169,
P.O. Box 7959, San Francisco, CA 94120-7959.

The Nature Conservancy. Forget the middlemen and politicians. This excellent group actually purchases tracts of rain forest, to preserve them
directly. Membership, $15 per year. 1800 North Kent Street, Arlington, VA
22209.

Greenpeace. The famous "Greeners" take on polluters, head-on. Membership, $25 per year. 436 U Street NW, Box 3720, Washington, D.C.
20007.

Pro-Space Lobbying Groups

The National Space Society. Membership, $30 per year ($18 for students). 922 Pennsylvania Ave. SE, Washington D.C. 20003.

The Planetary Society. Membership, $25 per year. Pursues projects
aimed at exploration. 65 North Catalina Ave., Pasadena, CA 91106.

Human Rights Organization

Amnesty International. Donation—any amount. Fights to free political
prisoners of every persuasion. 322 8th Ave., New York, NY 10001.